UNITED CITIES OF SALLERIA

Burn Together

ANTONIO T SMITH JR

Trient Press
3375 S Rainbow Blvd
#81710, SMB 13135
Las Vegas,NV 89180

Ordering Information:
Quantity sales. Special discounts are available on quantity purchases by corporations, associations, and others. For details, contact the publisher at the address above.
Orders by U.S. trade bookstores and wholesalers. Please contact Trient Press: Tel: (775) 996-3844; or visit www.trientpress.com.

Printed in the United States of America

Publisher's Cataloging-in-Publication data
Ruscsak, M.L.
A title of a book :Working for Your Dreams: Making this year your best year
ISBN
Hard Cover
979-8-88990-056-6
Paper Back
979-8-88990-057-3
Ebook
979-8-88990-058-0

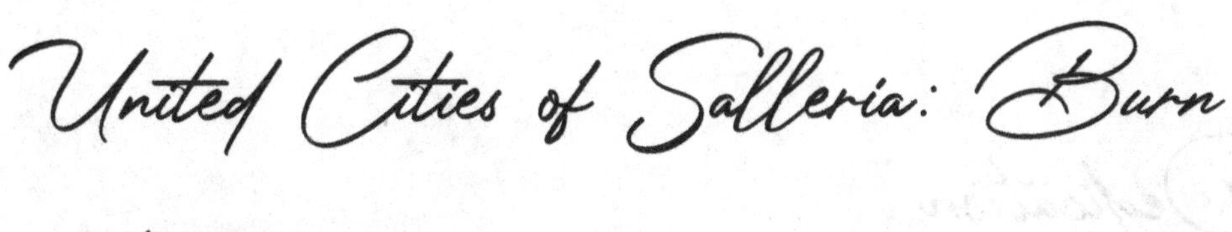

United Cities of Salleria: Burn Together

Thank you for buying this book. Sign up for Antonio's spam-free newsletter to learn more about future releases, special offers, and bonus content.

Subscribers will also receive access to exclusive giveaways.

Are you an Antonio T Smith Jr fan? Join him on social media. He would love to hear from you!

Official Facebook Page: https://www.facebook.com/theatsjr

Facebook Fan Club: https://www.facebook.com/groups/theofficialantoniotsmithjrfanclub

Author Website: AntonioTSmithJr.com

Catch Me On Tour: https://antoniotsmithjr.com/

Instagram: instagram.com/theatsjr

Email: books@antoniotsmithjr.com

Dedication

For Monique, Danni, Aiden, Ashton, and Erynn. I love you all, and you are my joyful responsibility- my assignments from Heaven.

For my mother, Linda Faye McCalister Smith, "Mama Linda." Thank you for coming back into my life near your end. You were the best gift I never knew I needed. I guess I will always be that six-year-old boy crying for his mother. Your grandkids love you. Erynn will go outside and play with her dolls forever.

For my father, Antonio Theodore Smith, "Papa Anthony." Thank you for spending over three hundred calendar hours on the phone with me to go over the entire book, scene for scene, with me. Your feedback truly changed this book. May you and my mother live forever in the United Cities of Salleria Universe.

Thank you, Deaunna, for spending about four hundred calendar hours on the phone with me. It was hard to keep you guessing each scene, but I managed to pull it off.

I leave you all in love and the light of the One Infinite Intelligence, the Creator. Go forth, then, rejoicing in the power and the peace of your dreams.

A Special Dedication

Thank you to all my fans. I still find it amazing that I have fans.

Tony

Every man must decide whether he will walk in the light of creative altruism or in the darkness of destructive selfishness.

Martin Luther King Jr.

Many people have a hand in the creation of this story. I'm grateful for all their help, criticism, and time. But I want to start with the people I wrote this book for—my fans. You are the very reason I spent years in secret working on my storytelling talent, and you were the personal strength I had to use to stretch my confidence to write fictional novels. I won't lie. It was not easy going from research-related, nonfiction, and self-help books to what you see today. But, this would not be possible without the consistent support of the fans who downloaded every podcast, watched every live stream, and consumed every written article. Your constant support of me gave me the strength to keep going and move forward. I am just a kid from Galveston, Texas. Kids from Galveston don't become best-selling authors and everything I have had the blessed pleasure of becoming today. Thank you.

For those of you waiting on my other books, I thank you for your patience and hope you enjoy *The United Cities of Salleria*. Before you dive in, here's a little background on how this story came to be.

Let's start at the beginning. It is a widely known fact that from five to fifteen, I was homeless and putting myself through public schools in the Galveston Independent School District. A lesser-known fact is that I failed the fifth and sixth grades. After all, I couldn't do homework during this period because I slept in a city dumpster. It was during this time of my life, after failing two grades in a row and watching all my peers go one and two grades ahead of me, that started me on my path today. Because of this terrible episode, I was forced to remember everything I read in books and every lecture my teachers gave during classes so I wouldn't fail any more grades. Homework implies that you *go home and read over what was just taught.* I didn't have that option, so I had to get everything the first time and remember every single thing I heard or read the first time, then do all my homework during class or right after while I still had access to electricity. When I returned to my city dumpster, it would be too dark to see, write, or read without the help of electricity.

It was here my mind would develop into near photographic memory, eventually leading me to score 76 on the Army ASVAB, Armed Services Vocational Aptitude Battery, with a GT Score of 139, or something like that. It was nearly maxed out. I don't even know what *GT* means, but the Army uses it like an IQ score. Supposedly, if you had 10 points to it, it is your IQ score. I am not sure how true that is, but the army loves it, and once my scores came back, I was immediately recommended for Military Intelligence and became an Intelligence Analyst. This was the beginning of my military career and my Top Secret Security Clearance with Sensitive Compartmentalized Access. From here, the army made me a machine.

I was exposed to Psychological Operations, where I excelled like a fish in water and numerous war tactics that I won't mention here. I was given the keys to the kingdom as an 18-year-old private in the United States Army, and my training was world-class. That training is poured out throughout the book, including declassified versions.

I participated in many combat situations and lost many friends along the way. This story is an accumulation of all that training and what was perceived as one of the greatest threats that could realistically bring the war to American soil. And that threat was a nuclear electromagnetic pulse (commonly abbreviated as nuclear EMP or NEMP), a burst of electromagnetic radiation created by a nuclear explosion. The rapidly varying electric and magnetic fields may couple with electrical and electronic systems to produce damaging current and voltage surges. EMPs, also called transient electromagnetic disturbances, are short bursts of electromagnetic energy. They are one of those things that many people think are fake, over-blown, or a conspiracy theorist's dream. But I can assure you, the US Government is an efficient entity that takes every threat to its citizens very seriously, and EMPs are at the top of the list. Therefore, an EMP Attack on US soil is a genuine possibility and danger.

A high-altitude nuclear detonation of an electromagnetic bomb can generate enough distraction that the potential to damage or destroy electronic devices over widespread areas. For example, a 1.4 Megaton bomb launched about 250 miles above Kansas would eliminate most of the electronics that were not protected in the entire Continental United States. During the brief return to atmospheric testing in 1962, a 1.4-megaton nuclear weapon was detonated over Johnston Island at an altitude of about 250 miles. The effects of EMP were observed in Hawaii, 800 miles east of the detonation. Streetlights and fuses failed on Oahu, and telephone service was disrupted on the Island of Kauai. Long story short, EMPs are very serious.

When I decided to write a series to entertain and educate people, I wanted to stay true to myself. I don't know many things well, but I am very good at warfare and anticipating the three most deadly attacks that could happen to American forces, and EMPs were always at the top of my list. Anticipating enemy threats and gathering the appropriate data to give to Command is at the heart of the role of an Intelligence Analyst.

Lastly, I wanted to write a book that I would read. I trusted myself, and I stood by my convictions. I wrote The United Cities of Salleria to begin a unique universe of characters and plot twists. I can tell you that the *Cities of Salleria Universe* contains five different book series with different characters and plot lines. These characters co-mingle with one another from time to mine, and I reserve the right to keep the lights off for all five of the book series, or I can cut them on in a clever way. And super-lastly, a special shout out to Deaunna and the real-life "Papa Anthony," who spent hundreds of hours with me reviewing the book scene by scene.

Let the *Cities of Salleria Universe* live on forever, and the character's within it.

Map of the United Cities of Salleria

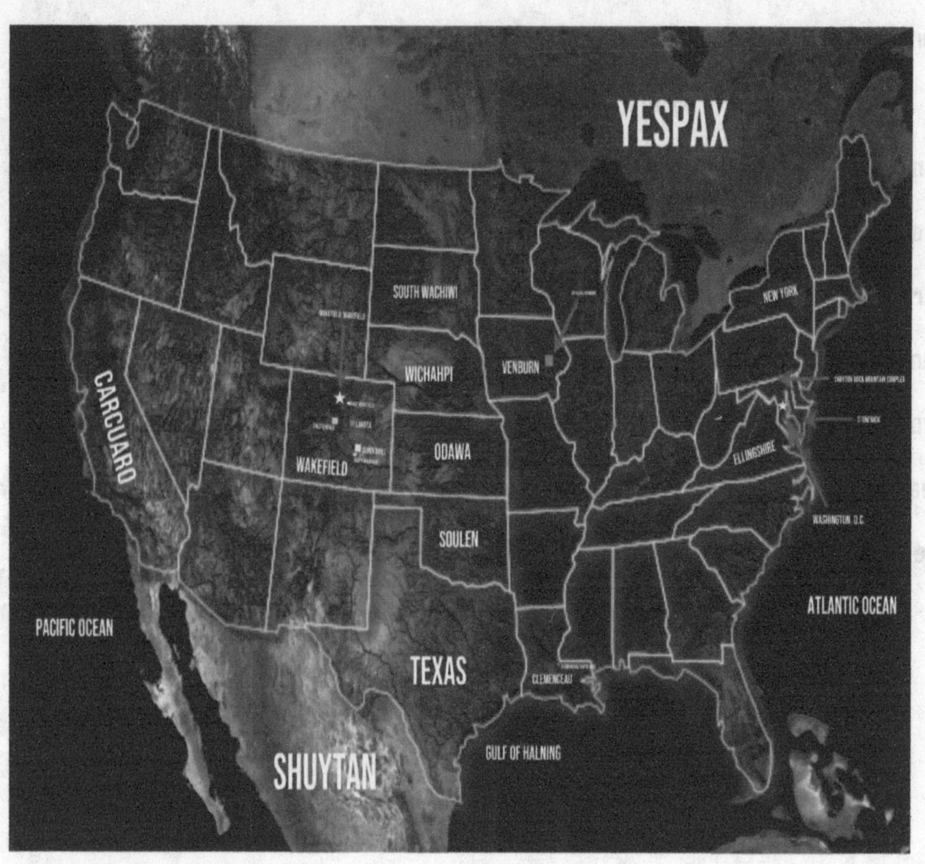

Country's Abroad

North Korea = North Kangavar
Soviets/ Russia = Kalinizran
India = Nacanne
Pakistan = Putralsland
Afghanistan = Bakghanistan

The SallerianVerse: A Treasure Hunt of Easter Eggs and Big Philosophical Concepts

I have a profound passion for exploring the theme of memory in my writing, and I take great care in leaving tantalizing plot twists and hidden clues for readers to discover in future installments of the SallerianVerse. The key to fully immersing oneself in this literary adventure is to remain vigilant to every detail, for even the smallest nuance may hold significant meaning. Each of my works is a gripping thriller that keeps readers on the edge of their seats, and I employ a masterful use of dialogue to drop subtle hints and cleverly connect the dots across the vast expanse of over 40 interconnected books in the SallerianVerse. If you relish a challenge and delight in exercising your intellect to keep pace with the writer, then you and I share a common passion.

I would like to express my intention to caution readers about what to anticipate in my writing, a passion that was supported by my father. My writing style is reminiscent of the films by renowned directors Christopher and Jonathan Nolan, in which I offer unadulterated responses through direct dialogue. My works frequently delve into profound philosophical ideas, wherein I challenge readers to confront complex concepts and encourage them to develop their own conclusions.

Additionally, I frequently explore big philosophical concepts and often leave the reader to struggle with these difficult ideas, fall in love with the struggle, and draw their own conclusions.

The exploration of human morality and decision-making is a subject that captivates me. I am particularly intrigued by how these facets of the human psyche can become corrupted and how our choices shape the reality we perceive. Furthermore, I am deeply fascinated by the concept of time and its impact on our morality and decision-making processes. Does time enhance or hinder our capacity for sound judgement? This is a question that I enjoy posing to my readers. In my SallerianVerse, I experiment with the notion of time as a non-linear construct, challenging the common perception of chronological progression. This intriguing concept is supported by the second law of thermodynamics, which posits that time is merely an illusion.

I derive pleasure from subverting the established norms of popular literary genres in order to challenge preconceived notions about books. My approach involves pushing the boundaries of traditional genres such as mystery, thriller, science fiction, superhero, and war in order to discover novel techniques and themes. I draw inspiration from notable filmmakers including Quentin Tarantino, Paul Thomas Anderson, the Wachowskis, Christopher and Jonathan Nolan, and the Coen brothers who have mastered the art of genre-bending and produced works that defy the limitations of conventional storytelling. By emulating their methods, I endeavor to create narratives that transcend genre classification and engage readers with a fresh perspective.

Challenging and subverting established literary genres has been a source of fascination and creative inspiration for me. I delight in exploring the boundaries of popular genres such as mysteries, thrillers, sci-fi, superheroes, and war, and experimenting with innovative storytelling techniques to push the limits of these established categories. This approach has been influenced by the groundbreaking work of visionary filmmakers like Quentin Tarantino, Paul Thomas Anderson, the Wachowskis, Christopher and Jonathan Nolan, and the Coen brothers, who have each demonstrated their own unique ability to reinvent and transcend traditional narrative forms.

My aim is to craft captivating and thought-provoking narratives in mainstream genres, while simultaneously expanding their horizons for the avid reader. My protagonists often hail from diverse ethnic backgrounds, without the requirement of explicit justification. By creating literature that caters to a broad audience, my intention is to foster a mutual appreciation and understanding of various cultural perspectives, irrespective of race or ethnicity.

My primary goal is to view books as an intricate art form and to prompt readers to question their preconceptions about literature. While a compelling narrative is undoubtedly crucial to the success of a book, I am particularly intrigued by exploring and, at times, altering the fundamental elements that constitute a book.

Anticipate my incorporation of the concept of interconnectedness, as I weave together ideas from the Law of One and various spiritual themes and motifs from diverse worldviews and philosophies. My aim is to offer my readers novel insights and provoke introspection that will foster a heightened collective consciousness and promote positive

change within their communities and beyond.

Finally, it is my aspiration that my books will stand the test of time and remain

relevant for generations to come. To that end, I am investing all of my passion, vitality, and

creativity into each work. I emphasize that these stories are not distinct and isolated but

rather interwoven and should be viewed as a single narrative.

Best,

Antonio, the guy messing with your head and forcing you to turn the page.

Preface

Before you start reading, you should know that *The United Cities of Salleria* takes place on Alternate Earth. It is everything you know our planet to be, but events and times have taken a different path and created changes through the ripple of time. I chose to make the world of this book in this manner because I wanted to write a four-book series that didn't focus on politics but on the *chaos* I believe will happen if the United States is attacked with a Nuclear EMP. Alternate Earth is more than just our *real Earth* reimagined. It could very well be the planet we become. *The United Cities of Salleria* is more than just a post-apocalyptic thriller about the aftermath of an attack on American soil. It's meant to be a mystery as much as a thriller. There are many EMP Thrillers out there, and I enjoy them all. I decided to write my story that included African and Creole folklore and Black American culture throughout the story. It was also important to me to weave *esoteric* lessons within the book so that when my children read it, I would secretly teach them essential life lessons, especially the difficult lessons that are so hard to teach. For example, killing people is wrong, but sometimes killing is necessary. How do you explain this to a child? Moreover, how do we explain to adults that good people die young and unfairly— and they die this way often? Or the idea that the people we judge the most often become the people we need the most during a crisis.

The United Cities of Salleria is more than a thriller. It is an esoteric treatise, filled with suspense, that sets out to answer a few simple questions:

> *This book,* Burn Together *sets out to answer only one question: Is America ready for an EMP attack?*

I have chosen to create four main heroes for the *United Cities of Salleria Saga.* Ashton— the born and raised assassin trying to be a good person, but life never seems to allow him to be one. Aiden, the honorable Police Chief who's only goal is to make his part of town as close to heaven on Earth as possible. Third, Erynn, the silent, sexy, and feminine counterpart to Ashton, is loyal to him and only wants to save Ashton from destroying himself. And, lastly, Monique. The fighter pilot-turned-politician top priority is to save and reunite with her son.

The United Cities of Salleria is a replica of the United States, but there are no states, just large territories known as cities. Each city is its government, and they all fall under a federal government, something with which you are already comfortable. Salleria has the same issues as America and the same political divides. Before the EMPs turned the entire country into a dark void, The United Cities were already divided by social media posts, for-profit news companies, and the growing movement of far-left and far-right groups clashing at every turn. There are very few issues that are *nonpartisan.* This book does not go into politics but focuses on the question: Are The United Cities of Salleria ready for a strategic Nuclear EMP attack? The time is the present day. All four books happen within six months.

While this four-part series is fiction, I am sad to relay that the events within have a strong likelihood of occurring in real life— on United States soil.

I hope these events never happen, especially the events in this saga. I am not ready to see what a post-apocalyptic nation looks like. I hope neither are you. However, to be fair to combat zones I have a personal relationship with, many once beautiful places now look like post-apocalyptic nations today.

With that said, I hope you enjoy the read. I took a Master Class with Dan Brown, author of *The Da Vinci Code* and he made this book more suspenseful than it was at first. As a result, if you get mad at me (and I hope I am good enough to upset you daily), blame Mr. Dan Brown. He is used to it. Feel free to reach out to me on social media or text me at 409-500-1546 if you have questions, comments, or anger you want to send my way.

Best,

Antonio T Smith Jr

—Start of Book 1—

Welcome to the saga of

The United Cities of Salleria: Burn Together

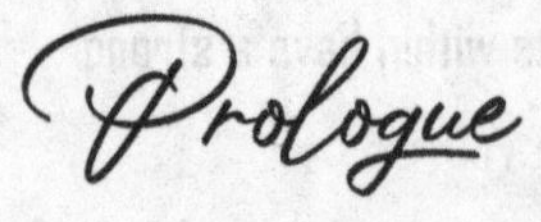

Prologue

Two Years Ago

Is this the mission that finally created World War III?

The Ghost had been asking himself this question for the last ninety minutes. His orders were simple. Do what you are told, and don't ask questions. Ashton, known to his six men as "The Ghost" boarded the top secret stealth helicopter holding all five of his closest friends in the belly of the bird. *The HeadHunters* was the very best of Army Special Forces. They did not exist, nor did this mission. None of their missions ever existed. The HeadHunters were the government's dirty little secret, and Ashton, The Ghost, was its number one killer. These days he wondered why the Army even called him a soldier.

The Ghost had killed a lot of people under the veil of secrecy. It wasn't his job to know much about his mission. The United Cities wanted someone dead, so they had to die. It was as simple as that. Lately, the job had been weighing heavy on Ashton's consciousness. Every day he would wake up and ask himself, *What do I want people to line up and thank me for when I am in my casket?* And the only answer he could ever come up with was, "Thank you for being the world's best assassin. It had been this way since Ashton was a kid. He was born into this life and raised as a weapon.

"This is what evil people like me deserve," Ashton said as he boarded the chopper, giving a respectful nod to his brothers-in-arms. But, day in and day out, The Ghost began to wonder, *Will I ever live a life that I don't have to hurt people?* Probably not. Ashton was an agent of death; it had been like that for thirty-one years.

The top secret bird looked like a heavily modified Sikorsky EH-60 variant. Statistically, The Ghost was one of the best Special Forces operatives to serve in the United Cities Army. His kill count ranked in the top one percent, and his IQ was one hundred and fifty-seven, but each night he suffered. His kills were beginning to haunt him, and his dreams were getting heavier and heavier to hold.

Looking up at his brothers-in-arms was always a surefire way to not think about the burden of his missions. These men were his family, and each would die for the other. With each assignment, it was usually too early to tell the correct time. In most missions, Ashton would sit in the belly of the bird and mentally go through his training to keep himself sharp and his mind off his painful dreams. But this mission was different. It came directly from the President of the United Cities of Salleria, which was very unusual.

The chopper swooped low over flat fields on the approach to North Kangavar. The pilot was a pro. Tensions between Kangavar and The United Cities of Salleria were at an all-time high. Both countries were always on the brink of war, but this year was different. Everyone thought the two countries would go to war. Neither country liked one another. The Sallerians saw the North Kangavarians as a violently suppressive regime crushing the rights of its people. Sallerian-Kangavarian relations were steadily declining, with the Thomas Conrad Administration adopting a much harder stance on the North Kangavar nuclear program from 2000-2008. Simultaneously, Kim Yang Su-Il was fiercely critical of

Salleria's war against the Republic of Avrinyth and doubled down on his atomic efforts, announcing a successful test in 2006 - a claim backed up by a South Kangavar seismic monitoring center in 2006.

Little did anyone know, but The Ghost was hanging up his boots in just a few weeks. He didn't intend to reenlist. He was done killing. The thing he wanted most in life was to be a good person. So Ashton figured he would buy a house with all the money he had saved, and it was plenty, and hide away so violence would never find him again.

Lately, Ashton found himself going to sleep tired and waking up the same way. He couldn't seem to get his life together; as usual, his life was in shambles. Ashton was never really good at anything but killing people and getting into trouble. The problem was he needed to improve at getting out of trouble. He was probably the world's best assassin— at least the powers that be thought so. Unfortunately, no one outside of the military liked him much. His best friend, Erynn, was the closest person in his life; and he only met Erynn because he was sent to kill her when he was twelve— she was eleven. After Erynn, he only had two other people he loved: His sister and his niece. Erynn was also a governmental assassin, just like The Ghost. She grew up with Ashton and was raised as an assassin, too.

Combat was the only time Ashton never got into trouble. He was good at being The Ghost, but what kind of life after the military could being a trained killer provide him? Living a simpler life and starting a business in Wakefield would be a good idea. After being in combat for over three decades, he figured someone else could fight. It wasn't hard to think about a war-free life when he was always staring at six-man teams armed with automatic machine guns, grenades, and silenced pistols.

Fantasy life was good, but it was hard to maintain those happy thoughts while he was conducting a final weapons check and twisting a silencer onto his government-issue pistol. He was beginning to question if his fantasy life in Wakefield would ever happen now.

The pilot swooped low over the demilitarized zone, snapping the Ghost out of his fantasy and back onto his mission. It wasn't hard to see why North Kangavar and South Kangavar border was known as the most dangerous border in the world. To the north of the border, North Kangavar was one of the most oppressive and violent regimes on the planet. The border included heavily armed guards surrounded by barbed wire, landmines, and every imaginable defensive weapon known to man. In addition, he could see surface-to-air missile launchers and handheld RPGs readily accessible to the enemy at a moment's notice.

There were troops stationed on both sides of the border, so close they could practically smell the gun oil on the enemy's weapons. The North and South Kangavarian border was a gasoline booby trap waiting for a spark. But, unfortunately, the HeadHunters, the name of Ashton's Special Forces team, were being dropped right into the middle of it. "Shit was about to get very real," The Ghost said out loud to himself, under his breath.

The Head Hunters specialized in deep reconnaissance missions. Trained in search, seizure, and raid activities, the team, was escorting a North Kangavarian double agent into enemy territory with as little information as possible. The details were never Ashton's luxury, and risking his life on a need-to-know basis always bothered him. And, at this present moment, he was very uneasy about the entire raid. Something didn't feel right. He didn't consider himself a clairvoyant, to where he could see beyond the range of ordinary perception, but The Ghost was usually right when he felt uneasy about things. Right now, the thin Kangavarian man dressed in black, wearing stealth battle gear, sitting across the troop hold gave him an odd vibe. He didn't trust him, and he had never seen an outside asset in all his years in covert operations, given this much internal access. But maybe the thin man wasn't as *outside* as he thought? Or was it The Ghost who was actually on the outside?

The thin Kangavarian man's wary eyes met his gaze for a moment before The Ghost looked away from his team members. The men were all dressed in the preferred black stealth uniforms. When not in war, the black BDUs are the preferred choice of Special Units personnel who want to stand out from their fellow service members in other units and push psychological warfare to the limit. Each man wore black-clad armor, fatigues, and helmets mounted with "four eyes" night vision optics. They all carried suppressed M4s as well as suppressed M9s. Most of their missions were stealth recon or extraction missions. If you knew the HeadHuters were there, they didn't do their job right.

Choosing his silenced pistol Mk 22, The Ghost was ready for close combat and narrow fields of vision, if needed. The Mk 22 is a modified Smith & Wesson M39 pistol with a silencer. Most Operators called it the "Hush Puppy."

Sergeant First Class Norman Bass, the middle-aged team lead, took his usual position, standing in front of the men in a position of authority. He began briefing the team on the final details of the top-secret mission they were about to undertake as the rotors silently thumped overhead. Bass was a no-nonsense leader. As he met each man's eyes with the stare that only a battled-tested Sergeant First Class could give, he began to talk, "None of you assholes have my permission to die tonight. We all come back together. Don't do anything stupid; expect resistance at every level of this mission. There will be blood. Remember your training." The Ghost wasn't sure if he liked Bass much, but he damn sure respected him. "In and out. That is the plan," Bass interjected between Ashton's private thoughts.

Bass valued rules and respect over anything else. SFC Bass continued, "All right. Listen up, my favorite assholes," everyone cracked a battle-hardened smile. "Because we don't have much time," Bass said in a firm, authoritative voice. "Our orders come directly from the top, from the Commander in Chief himself. President Andrew Shelton wants this done as cleanly and as quickly as possible. No witnesses because this mission does not exist. If you see someone, terminate them, so don't see anyone." Bass reached into his vest and pulled out two pictures. The first showed a beautiful young woman looking like she didn't have a care in the world. She was probably some PictoGram Influencer.

This is Adeline Romani, or Lima 1," Bass said. He passed the photo around to the men. As the picture circulated, Bass held up the other image of a dark-haired wearing a shirt with a skateboard on it. "This is Caitlin Wheeler, or Lima 2. Caitlin was beautiful and seemed like the lawyer type. But, the bottom line is this. These girls fucked up and are now in a North Kangavrian prison. And, we," Bass paused for a long time and stared into the eyes of each of the six men. Ashton paid attention to every detail and watched Bass' every move. But something wasn't right; something was very off about this mission.

"Are about to drop you into that very prison. Our intel says they do not expect us coming, but you know how those intel boys get shit wrong all the time. To make the matter even more fucked up, we don't know anything about the area, and there are no maps to help us. These North Kangavarians don't use the internet the way the rest of the world does. So since we have no intel for you to get around this shit hole prison, this is why our friend," Bass pointed to the thin Kangavarian man who met The Ghost's eyes a few moments before. "Mr. Rang Kyung-Gu is here. He is our guide and defected from this very same prison."

The photos reached The Ghost, and he studied the faces of the young women. They looked nice and sweet. He couldn't help but wonder how two girls who looked like WeTube vloggers who made a living asking people to like, share, and subscribe ended up in a North Kangavar prison. Eventually, The Ghost passed the pictures to the next person, but only after looking at Rang Kyung-Gu again. Why was he here, and what was he promised? This was a suicide mission, and The Ghost knew it, so what would make Rang Kyung-Gu volunteer for it?

Bass pointed at the thin Kangavarian man across from The Ghost. "Kyung-Gu here used to work at the prison before he defected to South Kangavar." Every battle-ready eye turned to Kyung-Gu. Ashton wasn't one to judge; his past wasn't exemplary, he was raised by a secret society as an orphan and was one of the world's best assassins by the time he was ten, so he had no right to judge. But there was something about having a double agent in their midst that didn't sit right with him, and he wondered what the other team members were thinking.

"What's so special about these girls?" asked Staff Sergeant Peter Jacobs. "They're Sallerian citizens and college students who went to Takistan for spring break and got kidnapped sometime during. They are our problem now, and this mission is political: boys, a word of advice to all of you. Always get on the right side of a political mission. As important as we are, we are *"expendable" important.* If anything goes wrong, we are on our own and will become the scapegoats."

"Hang on just a sec, Sarge," Jacobs said. "Romani? Are the girls related to John Romani, as in Senator John Romani?" Bass didn't answer, which was louder than the actual answer would have been, but the Sergeant First Class continued speaking. "Now that you understand the shit we are in, one of these ladies may or may not be the daughter of one of the most powerful Senators in our Congress." Ashton could guess how the rest of the story went. First, Romani pulled strings, and blah blah blah, and now they were sneaking into the country. And, his favorite part. If caught, none of them, or this mission, ever existed. They would be on their own.

"This is not the time to argue about favor and the abuse of politics. We are the HeadHunters, and this is what the fuck we do!" Bass said with fierce authority. The Ghost found his tone to be a bit inspirational. "We follow orders, and we follow our chain of command. We do not ask questions. We do not complain. We must extract our targets and bring them safely back to post." Bass said his following three words in a call-and-response cadence. "Do you copy?" The Head Hunters answered in unison, "Yes, Sarge!" Bass picked up where he left off. "We have intel that Lima 1 and 2 are both being held here," he said with 100% confidence. "There are twelve buildings in the compound, but our intel points right here." "If those Intelligence know-it-alls are wrong, the Senator's daughter is dead, and so is her friend. If we do not execute our orders perfectly, they are both dead, and the President has a shitty day in the press in less than four hours."

"Kyung-Gu has given us a rundown of the defenses. Intelligence says there are at least thirty men armed to the teeth, and they are not shy about pulling the trigger. We'll first remove the guard towers with the M240 to clear a path. Then we split up and head in." Bass pointed at The Ghost. "Staff Sergeants Jace and Malone, you're with me on Alpha Team. Kyung-Gu will guide us. Everyone else, you're on Bravo Team with Staff Sergeant Jacobs as the lead." The Ghost caught Malone's nervous gaze and tried to give him a reassuring smile. The kid had been on many missions with the Head Hunters, but nothing like this. Hell, none of them had ever done something this crazy. Maybe I should have stayed in the cult, Ashton thought. At least when you were raised to be an assassin in a cult, you knew who your enemies were.

Bass interrupted Ashton's private thoughts again, "North Kangavar leadership has no idea they have kidnapped a person of importance yet. Otherwise, they would be dead or bait for some ungodly request on Fox News. The HeadHunters have never failed a mission or lost a man. Don't start new habits now. President Drake wants this right now and is not hearing no for an answer, which means speed is more important than stealth. Understood?"

Everyone nodded their heads in understanding. "They will kill us all if we get caught," Kyung-Gu said in broken English. Bass jumped back in the conversation, "The plan is to get the girls and get out as quickly as possible. Bravo team has the C4, and Jacobs will plant it."

"Sarge," Malone said, "just curious, but what happens when the Supreme Leader finds out the United Cities was responsible for this raid?" "He won't because there is no raid. We are not here. And when people see us here, we will make sure they *can no longer see us here*", Bass said while shutting down the conversation and letting everyone know the Rules of Engagement are to kill onsite if seen. "Prepare for radio silence," one of the pilots said over the comms. "We're approaching the landing zone."

"Any questions?" Bass asked. The Ghost listened to his heart thump in his chest, barely noticing the low whoosh of the stealth rotors that flew him into immediate danger as he flipped his optics into position. Hid raised his black skull bandana— something he and Erynn did before each mission. The bandana was black and had an even darker skull on it. The Ghost was an agent of darkness. If you saw him coming, you were lying.

A green-hued view of the North Kangavar countryside stretched across Ashton's field of vision. In the distance, clustered at the base of the mountains, was their target. A small North Kangavar facility indicated the Kangavarians had no idea who they were holding hostage. Ashton hoped that meant fewer armed guards.

There was no backup coming to help them. It was just the Head Hunters against a small army of North Kangavarians that could call in close air support at any moment. Those odds seemed fair, he thought to himself. However, the North Kangavarians may need a few more resources to stand against the six-man team, he thought to himself. They should call the Avengers. That would make even the odds.

Bacardi Superior Rum would hit the spot right now, The Ghost thought to himself. *The Ghost,* he thought about his call sign and nickname. It had been given to him because of his battlefield persona. *No one ever saw him coming, and no one ever lived to talk about it.* The Ghost was a ruthless soldier of fortune because his country trained him to be one and consistently asked for it. No, Salleria demanded; Salleria never asked. If he wanted to make it out of this mission alive, he had to continue to be one of the most efficient Special Forces Operators in recent history.

One of the most common mistakes the media makes daily is confusing the terms Special Operations Forces (SOF) and Special Forces (SF) and making them interchangeable. The Ghost started as an Intelligence Analyst, attached to a Special Operations Unit, but he proved himself. Things changed, and the right people noticed him. Special Operations, sometimes referred more accurately to as Special Operations Forces, include any unit that falls under the United Cites Special Operations Command (SOCOM). Naval Special Warfare, Air Force Special Operations Command, Army Special Operations Command, and Marine Special Operations Command are all under this umbrella.

Special Forces is not a generic term in the UCS military and refers to a specific unit. For example, the 1st Special Forces Regiment falls under the command of the Army Special Operations Command and includes the 1st, 3rd, 5th, 7th, 10th, 19th, and 20th Special Forces

Groups. Ashton was in one of these, but his clearance is Top Secret, and his unit has never existed. So, the world will never know, and he can never discuss anything about his service.

Bass gave the order with a quick flash of his hand; 7.62 mm rounds sang in unison through the troop hold. Tracer rounds lanced into the cinder blocks as the pilots circled. Everything turned into rubble, and stealth was no longer an option. Speed was the agenda, and speed was likely to kill them. "Fuck!" The Ghost said to himself. "This is now a suicide mission. Do they even want us to come back alive?" It was a serious thought in his mind, and he made a mental note to be ready if someone tried to shoot him in the face. But, for now, he had to stay alive until it got to the point.

All Chaos had erupted, and a North Kangavarian soldier was shot in the throat before he could raise his weapon. He tumbled over the side and plummeted to the ground. "Clear!" Bass said. Ashton and his unit brothers were lined up and ready to jump within seconds. As he scanned the terrain, a single hostile came out of the middle of a nearby building. Staff Sergeant Jacobs, the first Operator out of the stealth chopper, took a knee and fired a shot. The soldier was down.

A North Kangavarian flag waved on a flag pole nearby. Ashton moved to the next section of the grid. To his right was trouble. Armor-piercing rounds forced him to take cover. He was surprised he wasn't dead yet. "Contacts!" Malone said. Ashton took a knee ahead of them and fired on two North Kangavarian guards running out of the front door of the first building. Both soldiers dropped to the ground without further resistance. The crack of automatic gunfire sounded from the left. With a spinning move, The Ghost hit the dirt, steadied his rifle, held his breath for the best trigger squeeze possible, and the soldier shooting at his head exploded in a dark red mist. There would be no open casket for that guy. Gunfire was coming at all six men from all directions. Securing himself behind a large boulder for cover, The Ghost let off six rounds of gunfire. Each round entered the heads of six North Kangavarian soldiers. Each man fell to the ground without trying to break their falls. Ashton was not a mathematician, but more than thirty men were guarding this small prison.

Retirement was just a few weeks away, and he didn't want to blow it by being stupid, arrogant, and sloppy. He waited a few moments for the gunfire to stop while Alpha and Bravo teams did their jobs and advanced. The stealth chopper was circling, giving them air support and letting everyone soldier in all twelve buildings they saw earlier know their exact location. Rolling away from the boulder that was saving his life, The Ghost lifted his NVGs to get a clear picture of who was trying to kill him, but he couldn't find the shooters. Bullets erupted from behind him and tore through the ground behind him. The sound of suppressed fire answered. "Hostiles down," Bass said in his comms. "Thanks, Sarge," The Ghost responded. "Just saving my favorite asshole. Nothing special about it," Bass said with his usual rough persona.

An armor-piercing round almost took off Ashton's head. The shooter was somewhere in front of him. With a quick decision, The Ghost rolled to the left as more shots pecked at the ground. He scanned the area where he had seen the muzzle flashes. He squeezed off a quick three-round burst, followed by another, trying to force his enemy to fire again so that he could get a good lock on his location. One of the soldiers yelled in Kangavarian, and another replied with a shout. The butt of his Special Forces Combat Assault Rifle, better known as the SCAR, tucked perfectly in the left soft meat of his chest and shoulder, the Ghost fired one round. A green cloud of mist exploded in the NVGs. *Crack!* He fired another round. A second green midst jumped moments after the first. "Targets down," he said into his comms. Combat was always emotionless for Ashton. He was a machine trained to take down enemy targets and complete his mission.

Looking over one of his team member's shoulders at a two-story building, he saw a flicker of motion in a window on the second floor. Down below, a North Kangavarian guard missing an arm crawled out, still screaming. Now on Ashton's right shoulder, Jacobs took out two more tangos with perfect marksmanship. Unfortunately, everything was turning into a shit show. Advancing, a shot that narrowly missed Ashton's right ear hit Jacobs through his throat. Hot blood splattered over Ashton's face. More rounds rocked Jacobs' body before he even hit the dirt. He was dead before he hit the ground. The Ghost felt a round whizz by his helmet as he crawled back to the rock for cover. "Jacobs!" He shouted at his friend, but there was no response. A fire raged through Ashton's veins, and his killer instincts activated. He was going to kill everyone shooting. Grabbing his SCAR, he popped his helmet up to look for the bastard that had killed his friend. A muzzle flash came from the window, and a split-second later, a round slammed into the rock, forcing The Ghost to hide his head again. "Jace, what the hell is happening back there?" Bass said over the channel.

"They got Jacobs Sarge. He is dead, and I'm pinned down! There's a sniper at—" Another shot pushed him to the dirt. He lay on his back, staring at the sky, angry and waiting for his moment to attack. The Ghost, diagnosed as a highly functioning Sociopath, had only a limited range of emotions. Doubt and dread were not one of these emotions, but anger and revenge were. The green tracer rounds dancing in the sky came from the sniper that had him pinned down.

There was a strange calm that settled over The Ghost. He was patiently waiting for his moment to get revenge for Jacobs. "I'm heading in," Bass said over the comms. He ordered Bravo to follow him into the building. Still pinned down, Ashton recognized there was no response to Jacobs being down, and Bass was entering the building instead of shooting the sniper. He was right about being expendable. The mission was to extract two high-value targets. It didn't matter who would make it out alive.

Jumping to his feet, he shot a round of fire toward the sniper and then sprinted toward a larger boulder for cover and a better vantage. The Ghost was fast, but not fast enough. Someone shot The Ghost square in his chest. The jolt of the round threw his weapon from his hands and caused his vision to go blurry. Barely able to see, he reached for his gun, but the sniper fired off a round meant for his head. His vest had taken the brunt of the impact, and he was glad whoever shot him was not using armor-piercing rounds.

Gasping for any breath that would go into his lungs, The Ghost looked back at Jacob's ruined body. A shot pinged off the top of the boulder. Pulling his suppressed M9, he took a long breath and then pushed himself up, squeezing off two shots at the North Kangavarian sniper. There was a shout over the comms about an RPG, but The Ghost continued firing. Six rounds later, he found his target with vengeful satisfaction. It wasn't his usual one-round-one-kill habit, but it got the job done. The Ghost watched the sniper's body slump and fall into a green NVG-hue of gore and midst.

Crash! The nearby building exploded into pieces as an RPG projectile did its job to perfection. The shockwave from the blast hit The Ghost so hard he felt it inside of his body. The shockwave tossed Ashton like a rag doll and sent him into an awkward backflip. He crashed-landed on something brutal and unforgiving. Intense pain rushed through his body, and stars filled his vision. Old gospel hymns he used to sing in his grandmother's church echoed in his ears. The song lyrics, "I don't want no trouble at the river," danced over the old pipe organ and timed slowed down instantly. He could feel the rush of blood screaming in his ears. Everything hurt.

"Ghost! Where the hell are you? Ghost," someone was calling over the comms, but The Ghost couldn't make out the voice. Head pounding, he knew he had to move beyond the pain. *Crash!* Another explosion hit the prison compound, far enough away to where he only fell, rumbling through the ground. Several odd-shaped figures made their way toward him. The rest of the team had the high-value targets hiding behind them, both bruised but recognizable. It was time to get the hell out of harm's way.

The stealth bird was hovering a few hundred feet away while Bass remained behind. He pointed at Jacobs's body and yelled orders for his body to be retrieved. The Ghost was glad to see that he was wrong about everyone being expendable. A shout came from behind them. "Wait!" Kyung-Gu shouted. "My brother!" He ran over and grabbed Bass' arm, tugging it and trying to drag him back to the prison block. Without warning, Sergeant First Class Bass pulled his weapon and put a round between Kyung-Gu's eyes. He turned toward The Ghost. Knowing he was about to get shot just like the double agent, The Ghost closed his eyes and accepted his fate. Bass already had the drop on him.

"Come on, Ghost. Let's get our brother's body back to safety. I am sorry we couldn't save him," Bass said over the comms for everyone to hear. Relieved, he opened his eyes and ran towards the bird. Looking back at the fallen double agent, he asked Brass, "He was never going to make it out here alive?" Bass, running in stride with The Ghost, responded without taking his eyes off the bird, "The government doesn't want any witnesses. We have never been here. This mission never happened. Someone had to take the blame for this, and it couldn't be Uncle Sam. We were never here."

The Ghost looked at his four remaining brothers. His heart sank to his stomach. He looked at the mangled body of his friend, Jacobs, and leaned close enough to Jacob's body to say something that only he could hear. "I hope heaven lets you hear me, my brother. I am sorry I got you killed. Everything I do hurts people. You will be the last one ever."

Chapter One

Present Day

The back of young Jared's head throbbed, and a gnawing pain ate at his neck. He couldn't move. His vision was failing, and his neck was on fire. Young Jared kept trying to move, but it felt like he was trapped under a building. His left hand was free, but he was too weak to move. It was as if his life force was leaving his body. Is this a bad dream, he thought to himself. Why can't I wake up? The pain was so intense. Suddenly the pain became so sharp that it felt like one thousand ants were biting into the right side of his neck at the same time. "I... can't...," Jared was in the middle of saying something, but it was pointless now. Young Jared died before he could finish his sentence.

Police Chief Aiden Jahmar was investigating a missing person's case. He was praying to God to let him save his good friend, Truth Parker's, six-year-old son Jared. Wakefield Police Department's Chief Aiden Jahmar is a formidable figure, his muscular frame honed by years of rigorous training and experience on the force. He stands tall at six feet, commanding attention with his commanding presence. His dark black shoulder-length locs, with their striking blonde tips, are swept back with a single, effortless gesture, revealing a handsome face with chiseled features and a square jaw. He is a man of contrasts, his masculine exterior belies a pair of feminine eyes that seem to take in the world with a knowing gaze.

His midnight black police jacket is zipped up to his chin, emphasizing the sharp lines of his shoulders and the breadth of his chest. The blue shirt he wears underneath adds a touch of color to the otherwise somber ensemble, hinting at the depth of character beneath the uniform. He is a man of action, who embodies the spirit of the Wakefield Mountains that rise up behind him, snow-capped and statuesque. With a beautiful smile and a determined glint in his eye, Aiden Jahmar is a force to be reckoned with.

Forcing his eyes away from the beautiful view, Aiden willed himself to face his ugly situation— six-year-old Jared was probably dead.

The Police Chief had been doing the job long enough to know the first forty-eight hours of a missing person's case was the most important. The kid had been missing for three days now. The clock was ticking, and Aiden had to make a miracle happen now. His investigators have the best chance of following up on leads before people's memories fade. Missing persons who authorities believe may be vulnerable— such as children and those with a mental illness— are expedited because time is of the essence to get the word out to the public to look for them. There's a certain point after about a week or two where you have to think about the potential that the missing person is dead, and now it's a matter of trying to find their body and bring closure to the family and determine if you now have a homicide investigation. Every passing hour was killing Aiden inside. He had to keep everyone safe in his town. It was his job. After serving in the military, he became a police officer— he had seen too many lives taken in war. He wanted to be an agent of change and create peace.

His good friends, Truth and Jenny Parker, were missing their little boy. Aiden hated himself for recognizing that Jared wasn't old or tall enough to learn how to drive. But he was more than old enough to be kidnapped. The killer never asked for a ransom or set any demands, which terrified Aiden. He had never seen a kidnapping where the killer didn't want anything. Aiden felt the killer didn't want anything because his only plan was to kill Jared.

In science, the theory is essentially worthless if there's no way to test a hypothesis and prove it wrong. Aiden's father always taught him that when our minds remain closed or we keep opposing arguments out, our theories, misinformation, and lies always run into the prevailing evidence. Aiden's father would lecture him daily about how our tribal echo chambers get louder and louder with the sounds of the same misleading voices. And if we aren't willing to be proven wrong, injustice and mistruths will always prevail as the winner. Aiden tried to remember his father's teachings and pulled out all the stops to find Jared. He didn't want to be correct. He wanted to test his hypothesis no matter what. Jared deserved that much. Truth and Jenny counted on him to be diligent, not right.

Remembering these lessons, Aiden was ready to cross any depth to ensure he gave Jared his best effort. He knew within his heart that if he didn't hurry to find the boy, Wakefield would become a little bit darker with his death.

A crimson sunset illuminated the interior of the gray clouds drifting over the mountains. It was a Friday in early October, and the temperature was dropping. It had constantly been raining in the past few days, which was a clear sign of a cold winter on its way. Aiden had lived in Wakefield his entire life. His dad was a Military Intelligence officer for the UCS Army and drilled into Aiden's integrity, leadership, and the Law of Attraction. So he was used to Wakefield's hot, mucky weather and the cold, rigid snow.

With each passing second, the likelihood of Jared's death increased significantly. Jared was last seen walking inside Frank's market, a small grocery store in town. Frank's store was a common midway stop for the after-school crowd as they walked home from school. Every available citizen of Wakefield was combing Cherry Hill, looking for signs of life— or death. Then, Aiden's cell phone vibrated in his pocket. It had been ringing all night. He was expecting to see a call from Mayor Julia Harris, but it was his wife, Dawn. She was waiting at home with their sixteen-year-old daughter, Lillian. "Hey, honey," Aiden swiped the screen as he brought the phone to his ear. "Have you eaten, Aiden," Dawn asked. "Not yet, baby, but I will," pleaded Aiden. "You need to eat, baby, and you can't find anyone when you don't have enough energy to pay attention. I hid some power bars and energy drinks in your glove compartment. Go and get them, "she said with the loving tone that only a wife could pull off during such a stressful time. "Thank you, baby!" Aiden said. "I am walking to the car now."

"Where are you, Aiden?" Dawn asked. "I'm at the Harmony Park trail waiting for Ashton and Erynn, and the weather is starting to look pretty bad. How are you? And, how is Lillian?" "I'm fine. Lillian is good, but she keeps asking when you will find Jared. Lillian was Aiden's sixteen-year-old daughter. Her first job was babysitting Jared, so she was fully invested in Jared's safety. "When will you be home?" Dawn asked her husband. "It could be a while. Ashton is an hour late; you know how inconsistent he can be. I don't even know what condition he will be in when he gets here. Who knows?"

There was a long and uncomfortable pause, and Aiden knew precisely what it meant. His wife pieces things together. Dawn was one of the most intuitive women he knew. Every full moon, she practiced moonlight rituals and had an altar in their house for Ancestor offerings, and she was an active listener. In addition to all her gifts and spiritual practices, she knew Aiden like the back of her hand. After sixteen years of marriage, Aiden could read his wife like a book. "Go ahead and ask your uncomfortable question, baby?" Aiden playfully asked his wife. It was good for him to get his mind off the case for a moment. "Do you trust Ashton and Erynn, Hunny? You keep having to arrest Ashton, who is not your biggest fan." "He is a selfish troublemaker who only thinks about himself. He seems to have the worst luck on the planet and is a magnet for trouble. So, no. I don't trust him— or Erynn. However, and this is a big *however*, he was vital to me finding Jeanette Copeland earlier this year. But this case feels different. Something is very off, and I need both of them. Whatever they taught them in Special Forces cannot be duplicated. They are the only Special Forces-trained people Wakefield has ever seen. So we need them, baby— for Jared's sake." Aiden sighed after he finished what he was saying. "Very true, baby.", she said with a supportive tone. "I just want you to be safe, and I hope you both get along this time," she said. "We will, baby. I promise. Well, as long as he has a damn good excuse for being an hour late for a missing person's case", he grumbled. "Relax, baby," his wife supported. "It will all be perfect, and Aiden is not that selfish to be an hour late on a missing person's case." Thanks, baby." Aiden responded to his loving wife.

I got a tip that brought me Cherry Hill tonight, but that's all I can say." "People forget how dangerous Wakefield can be." "Ain't that the truth? Dawn said.

Mr. Smith had already killed Jared and was close enough to Ashton and Erynn to kill them, too. No one knew he was in town except his little brother Jacob. Smith's real targets were the Jace family, especially these two assholes he was following right now. Erynn wasn't technically family, but she was close enough. Close enough to die right along with the lot of them.

The Ghost and Erynn were speeding down some dirt road in this shit-hole, God-forsaken town. He wasn't worried about Ashton driving too fast for him to keep up because he had already attached a GPS tracker under the right passenger side wheel. These idiots had no idea they were being followed. "I ought to kill both of you right now," Smith said grudgingly. "I could have killed you two hours ago. Your face was in my crosshairs, you two sons of a bitches," Smith said while tailing the two love birds, or whatever they were. He let Ashton live two hours ago because Erynn couldn't be contained. She wouldn't let her guard down. It was like she knew someone was watching them. Mr. Smith knew deep down that Erynn was too much of a force to leave unchecked. She was gorgeous, and that is what made her so deadly. Everyone underestimated how much of an assassin Erynn was. She was ex-Recon Special Forces, and one of the world's deadliest killers by the time she was ten years old. She was also the only person on the planet that could kill the great Ashton *The Ghost* Jace.

Smith was going to prove everyone wrong. He was going to kill The Ghost, and he was going to make sure the entire world knew who was the best. While his car was thrashing the dirt road ahead, Smith thought about using his sniper rifle right now and blowing Ashton's head into pieces with one shot. It would be an impressive shot, too. Two moving cars drove faster than recommended on a twisting and winding road. Smith was about thirty car lengths behind them. He figured he would give it a shot. Grabbing his weapon from the passenger seat by the barrel, Smith lifted the butt of the rifle off the passenger side floor and attempted to take one hell of an impressive shot. He would be long gone before Erynn could even react. He aimed his rifle and squeezed the trigger.

Aiden's mind drifted to a heavy snow day in Wakefield when his daughter Lillian was six-years-old. Aiden, Dawn, and Lillian played in the snow until they couldn't feel their fingers. It was a day of snowball fights and laughter. Then, just as Aiden was getting lost in one of his favorite memories, Jared's investigation violently brought him back to reality. "Baby, I have to go and find this kid. I will talk to you later, sexy," Aiden said softly to his wife. "Okay, baby. I will see you when you get home," Dawn finished. Aiden hung up the phone and put it back into his pocket.

Aiden promised Truth he would bring Jared home, but after two tours in Bakghanistan and four years of service as Police Chief, he knew things didn't always end up as they did in the movies. Sometimes things never got better. Aiden was not an overly religious man, but he respected God. He didn't have a problem with religion, either. At this point, he hoped every religion would help him find Jared.

Pushing his locs across his head, Aiden swallowed a hard swallow. He didn't want to admit to his wife he had called Ashton and Erynn out of desperation. The Ghost had developed bad habits and made deplorable choices since coming home from the Army, but he and Erynn were the best. If anyone were to help Aiden find Jared, it would be them. He wasn't willing to lose the boy because of his pride. They were Aiden's last hope to find Jared.

Over the endless mountain horizon, the sky changed colors as the sun set and became a purple and pinkish background, as if a master painter was drawing in the sky for all to see. The clouds swallowed the final rays of light, the wind crashed against the trees like a symphony of magical symbols, and the birds sang their favorite nighttime songs of bliss. The wind gusted through the blanket buildings without a care in the world. The trees danced at its mercy. Tonight would have been one of the most beautiful autumn nights of the year. But, instead, it was a night of panic. Jared was running out of time. Only three people in the world can help find him now. One was Aiden, Chief of Police. The other two were an hour late. Aiden let out a big sigh and continued to wait impatiently.

The rocks screamed under Ashton's moving tires as his 1989 Dodge Ram grew larger in Aiden's vision. He was an hour late, and he didn't try to be. Erynn was convinced someone was watching them. Besides, he didn't like Aiden, so he didn't care to explain anything. He was here, and Aiden should be happy. Ashton wasn't trying to cause any trouble with Aiden, but he would be damned if he rolled over and took any of his bullshit today. There was a kid to save, and Aiden had better remember that.

The Dodge Ram raced up the path, and a trail of dust and exhaust kicked into the air. Aiden looked like he wasn't amused, but Ashton didn't care. He had good reason to be late. His life was possibly in danger. He figured if the Chief started his bullshit, he would do his best not to make a big deal out of it— at least not yet.

It was almost six o'clock, and a nasty storm was rolling in from the west. Ashton knew Aiden would be in a big hurry because the rain would wash away any evidence they may find. He wanted to find Jared, too, and as quickly as the Chief. But he didn't feel like being bullied because Aiden would be in a bad mood.

He cursed their luck and opened and reached into the glove compartment of the Dodge and grabbed two ponchos nicely rolled into six-inch bundles. He took one for himself and handed the other to the passenger side seat, where Erynn held hers. It was going to be a long, cold, wet night. Pulling into the lot in front of Aiden, the Jeep was over thirty years old, but Ashton took good care of it. There wasn't a scratch on it. The engine was in top condition. The truck was fitted with oversized tires that could handle just about anything, a front grill guard, and a winch. Ashton had turned a 1989 Dodge Ram into a makeshift armored personnel carrier.

"Chief," Ashton said, opening his door and stepping onto the asphalt. Erynn opened the passenger door and let herself out. Erynn never talked. She took a vow of silence many years ago, so she did most of her talking with her facial expressions, and it was one of the most beautiful faces God had ever made. Her skin was copper-brown, like a windfall autumn leaf. She had dazzling, champagne-brown eyes and half-moon cheekbones. Her hair was coral-black and crashed over her shoulders in waves. She had puffy, pouting lips, and they were blossom soft, and when she smiled, she revealed sparkling, wizard-white teeth that enhanced her succubus-like smile. She was as curvaceous as an Olympic Track And Field sprinter and had a runway model-shaped waist. Everyone assumed Ashton and Erynn were lovers because of their chemistry and loyalty to one another, but Ashton never took any steps to make anything happen. Aiden was an honest man, faithful to his wife, but Ashton caught him sneaking a peek, running his eyes over her body, just like everyone else who saw her. Erynn was a rare beauty— and she was one of the deadliest humans alive. Man or woman.

Ashton and Erynn were a perfect fit for each other. Both were extremely attractive, and both were Recon Special Forces. They were inseparable. Erynn was the second female Army Green Beret ever, and her kill count was nearly as high as Ashton's. They did not get to serve in the same unit but grew up together back in Clemenceau. They grew up around the swamps. Erynn had known Ashton and his sister since they were kids, and they were all thick as thieves since then. Ashton and Erynn were the Special Forces version of Bonnie And Clyde, except Erynn never got into trouble. She was always helping Ashton get out of it. That was her life. Ashton would get into trouble, and she was always there to ease his fall. She never complained and never wanted anything in return but for Ashton to grow into the good person he always wanted to be.

Erynn had taken a vow of silence because one day long ago, Erynn was, "Nice Truck," Aiden said, making an effort to sound friendly, interrupting Ashton's thoughts of Erynn's past. The Ghost grinned and patted the hood. "A ram-headed truck for a ram-headed man," said Ashton. Erynn facepalmed. "Thought you were working on being bull-headed," Aiden said with a laugh. "I'm ram-headed now. So I'm making progress Chief, asked Erynn," Aiden didn't respond. That was enough small talk.

Mr. Smith was watching all three of them in his binoculars. They were meeting to find Jared, but Jared was dead. About twenty minutes before, Smith did take a shot from his sniper rifle at The Ghost while he was driving, but he missed. The bullet went wide left because in the nick of time, the road turned right and saved Ashton's life. The duo didn't even hear the shot over the sound of the off-road vehicle driving over a dirt road.

For now, Smith figured he would have some fun and study his prey. He wanted to learn their movements and check for any weaknesses. Smith didn't know much about the cop, which excited him even more. He would study his future victims for as long as they were out here and then meet up with his brother Jacob, where they stashed Jared's body.

"Rain is coming." Ashton's ears instantly became irritated at Aiden telling him something he could see for himself. "I hope you both brought your Green Beret skills with you," Aiden said to them both. However, Ashton kept his original comment to himself and went with the milder, "We never leave home without them, Chief."

Erynn nodded her head up and down. Aiden swung a pack around his shoulders. "You do realize why I called you out here, right?" Rummaging in the back of the Dodge, looking for more gear, Ashton snorted without turning around to address the Chief. "Jared is missing, Chief. I don't need to be reminded. I want to find the kid, too." Aiden barely mustered up enough patience to ignore Ashton's evident frustration. "I only say what I see," Aiden responded. Ashton wanted to punch him in the nose right there. For whatever reason, Aiden was always picking on Ashton and arresting him. The Ghost was already tired of being around Aiden, and they hadn't even started looking for Jared yet.

The Ghost and Erynn tightened their backpacks over their shoulders almost in unison. The Ghost was a force to be reckoned with, his impressive physique honed through countless hours of training and discipline. His dark, chocolate brown skin was like a work of art, stretched taut over his Spartan-like muscles, and his crew cut framing his sharp features. But it was his eyes that truly revealed the depth of his character - fierce and intelligent, always scanning his surroundings for potential threats.

Despite his intimidating presence, there was something undeniably captivating about The Ghost. His disarming smile, with its perfect white teeth and dimpled chin, was like a beacon in the darkness, drawing people in with its charm and warmth. He moved with the grace and power of a lion, his walk more of a prowl as he surveyed the room, and his voice commanded attention like the roll of thunder.

His mustache and well-groomed beard were the perfect complement to his striking features, and his opal-like eyes revealed the depths of his soul and his truest emotions. He exuded a devil-may-care attitude, his charismatic voice commanding attention like bottled thunder. At thirty-three, he appeared nearly a decade younger, a testament to both his physical perfection and his unwavering spirit.

Lighting his cigar and taking a long pull from it, Ashton directed his voice towards Aiden, "I had to cancel a date with a sweet little tourist to be here, Chief. So let's find this bastard and rescue Jared." "Sorry about your date. I am sure you have another behind her," Aiden said. Ashton could tell the Chief assumed he would have groves of women, but that wasn't a weakness Ashton had. Besides, he didn't trust people enough to let them close. So he decided to ignore Aiden's assumption and let him keep talking. "Jared was last seen at Franks, and no one has seen him again. The only witnesses were a dozen kids, but no one can remember anything," Aiden briefed Ashton and Erynn.

"Okay. I guess we better get moving before that storm hits us," Ashton suggested. Together, Ashton and Erynn began to walk in sync. "When you finish that cigar, we'll get moving," Aiden firmly interrupted. Ashton slowly came to a stop. His adrenaline spiked. He knew the Chief would start some of his bullshit, and he was happy to end it. "Is this where you try to arrest me, Chief? Because you only arrest me because I fucking let you. I wouldn't underestimate me if I were you," Ashton said in reply to Aiden's cigar comment. "I don't need to arrest you, Ashton. The cigar tells our killer we are coming and can be smelled miles away. I thought you learned that in the military?" Aiden quickly matched Ashton's wits. Ashton was about to respond when Erynn stepped between the two men, looked them both in the eye, and started looking for Jared, sending a clear signal to both men.

Realizing that he and Erynn weren't the only deadly people with tracking skills tonight, Ashton eased up on the Chief. Aiden was very efficient and highly military-trained, as well. Finally, he relented and gave up his fight for power. "I was going to put it out. Stop worrying, Chief." The Ghost returned to his truck, threw the cigar to the ground, and pulled his Duane Dieter's Master of Defense CQD knives, his HK416, his suppressed Glock-19, and his AN/PVS-21 NVGs. Erynn already had all of her weapons equipped. She had the same weapons payload as Ashton.

Ashton loved his close-quarter combat knives, and he constantly carried two. Their custom blades are manufactured with a strap cutter, glass-break prong, friction tape, and a custom seal containing a serial number on the blade's edge. The company made small and large versions of the knives. Both Ashton and Erynn preferred the larger edition.

During his career, Ashton mastered Krav Maga. It was his favorite form of defense fighting, and he spent much of his military career in close-quarter combat situations that tested those Krav Maga skills. Krav Maga is known as the world's most influential, dangerous, and deadly form of martial arts in the world. This combat style didn't care for rules, which is why you often didn't see it in sports arenas. It had one mission: kill who was trying to kill you. Erynn was Leonardo Da Vinci of hand-to-hand combat, and you never wanted to get into hand-to-hand combat with her. Ashton was the Albert Einstein of close combat knife combat. He was the most competent man to ever live with knives. No one ever lived to tell a different story if they met in battle. Ashton never went anywhere without his knives, and Erynn never lost a close-quarters fight. Together, they were the *gods of close-quarters death*.

Aston and Erynn used the same weapons as interchangeable battle pieces on the battlefield. However, Ashton and Erynn updated their weapons of choice after their military careers. They got rid of their Army-issued pistols and transitioned to the Glock 19s with a threaded barrel, M-6 laser light, high-capacity magazines, and a sound/flash suppressor. It shoots surgically and is nearly unmatched in close combat situations.

They each used the M-6 Tactical Laser illuminator, a gun-mounted tactical light integrated laser/white light combo that offers uniquely integrated, high-power, visible Flashlights combined with a high-intensity, white light in a military-proven design. It is lightweight and only adds 3.7 oz to a weapon. It is built to military specifications and features technology currently used by U.S. special operations. The M-6 Illuminator could light up a dark room and have it as bright as a midday summer pool party.

Their HK416 assault rifles were Erynn's favorites. She was a faster shot than Ashton, but their accuracy was the same. The piston operating system on this assault rifle significantly reduced malfunctions while increasing the life of parts. They kept their rifles tucked away in a Pelican impact-resistant cases full of 30-round magazines, modded with an EOTech optic, EXPS2-0 mounted holographic site, a sound/flash suppressor, and an AN/PEQ-2 (infrared beam used for illuminating targets visible only by night vision goggles). The EXPS2-0 holographic site was much easier to take on and off while maintaining zero; able to easily accept a magnifier because the buttons are on the side and comes with the fast standard reticle. The AN/PEQ-2 Infrared Target Pointer/ Illuminator/ Aiming Laser (ITPIAL) has built a reputation for service and reliability among U.S. Warfighters. The AN/PEQ2A incorporates lessons learned with aiming lights in Desert Storm, other combat operations, extensive field evaluation, and production experience with over 50,000 US Military standard aiming lights. The result is a dual beam multi-function laser, which combines the utility and operational effectiveness of aiming lights and illuminator/ pointers in a single device.

Their NVGs, the AN/PVS-21, could be used in any aggressive special operations situation and all environments. Unlike other NVGs, these provided a smooth transition from dark to light. If someone flicks on the lights, the green image fades, and you see as if you were looking through clear goggles. The transparent lenses also provide the most depth perception of head-mounted night-vision goggles.

Aiden shook his head in amazement as he looked at Ashton and Erynn. Ashton figured he saw what they looked like in full battle gear. Ashton and Erynn wore a dual knife leather holster that hid their knives behind their backs but kept them ready to be thrown at any time. Ashton figured whatever the Chief was thinking when he was looking at them, *let's save this kid had to be somewhere in it.*

Ashton nodded to Erynn, "Erynn, you track, and I take the middle. Chief, if you can stay with me in a rear or flanking position to watch our six, that would be great. Oh, and keep up! Erynn has superhuman lungs," Ashton said to the Chief, but Erynn had already begun to do her tracker thing. Ashton chose Erynn to lead the hunt because she could run about fifty miles before stopping. For Erynn and Ashton, a path lit up, just like it always did for as long as they could remember. They were both excellent at tracking from when they were kids. Hunting food in the swamps of Clemenceau wasn't easy. Trails would get lost, plus they had to pay attention to signs of crocodiles with every step. Nevertheless, Erynn and Ashton could always see what others had missed, especially Erynn. They were raised as assassins and often used the darkness to their advantage.

Ashton could tell Erynn had picked up on some tire tracks. She must have thought they were out of place in this area. Maybe they belonged to a vehicle with smaller tires, which wasn't typical for being this deep in the woods. Whatever the case was, Erynn took off with confidence, and she led the three-person rescue team as Ashton and Aiden crouched down behind her and followed her every moment. The hunt was on!

Erynn pointed towards Harmony Park. Aiden confidently took over and began to explain the plan. First, he wanted the team to head up to Harmony Park trail to Sunset Lake, where the campers had reported seeing an F-150 truck acting mysteriously and then speeding off. "Do you think this truck is still there?" Ashton asked. "We are about to find out," Aiden responded. "All right then, Chief," Ashton said with a cocky grin. "Let's get to work."

Major Ernest Maddox felt a smile coming on as the gates to United Cities of Salleria Airforce Special Operations Command (Airborne and Psychological Operations) (UCSSOC) opened. An MP saluted as Ernest drove out onto the open road. "Finally," he said. He cracked open one of his carbonated waters and took a long swig as he sped away. After months of training and working six days a week, he was utterly exhausted. No, exhausted was an understatement. He would need an excellent audiobook to keep him awake during the drive to Chesterfolk. Ernest loved crime, mystery, and thriller novels and listened to audiobooks the most. It felt like he was watching a movie, but a movie he got to create with his mind as he listened. His favorite books always included covert operations or post-apocalyptic settings and plots. He enjoyed reading these kinds of books because they kept his skills sharp. The Covert operative military life was all he knew.

His nephew, Chase, was at a basketball camp in Chesterfolk, and Ernest had planned a surprise trip to visit the kid. As soon as Ernest pulled onto the highway, he clicked the phone symbol on his steering wheel. "Call Monique Maddox," he said. The ringtone chimed from the speakers. Ernest downed the rest of his carbonated water while waiting for his sister to pick it up. In a few hours, he would be looking at the beautiful mountains of Chesterfolk, listening to his nephew's stories about basketball camp. There was indeed no place like it on earth. Even the tornados that happened way too much were a beautiful sight to behold. He couldn't think of a better way to enjoy his few precious days off than spending time with his only nephew, who was getting taller by the day. Chase had a natural talent and had a legitimate shot at making it to the National Basketball Association. He also wanted to be a spy when he got older. Ernest had never known a kid who wanted to be a spy.

A firm yet feminine voice emerged from the speakers. "Good evening, Major." Ernest smiled. "Good evening, Madam Vice President. How's D.C.?" "A political pissing match, per usual. How's my favorite big brother?" "I'm your only big brother," Ernest said, chuckling at their familiar sibling banter. "And I'm looking forward to spending some time with Chase. Thought I would call and ask if you had any special requests before I pick up Chase." Her voice grew serious. "Just one, Ernest. Don't rush him into becoming a spy like you did last time. He has plenty of time to do dangerous things and risk his life for his country. But, for right now, he is my little boy, and I want him to enjoy this time while he can. You and I know you only get to be a kid once, and adulthood is a big trap." Ernest nodded his head in submission as if she was sitting in the passenger seat next to see him. "I promise. I promise. And for the record, you have a very persuasive son. He convinces me to rush him into being a spy, not the other way around. He is just as stubborn as his mother and equally as crafty as her with words. I think he could get elected to Vice President, just like his mom, if someone were to give him a microphone." Monique laughed. "He's going to be so surprised when he sees you," she said joyfully.

It had been a long time since Ernest had heard his sister laugh. He was grateful because her husband was now a star on the wall in the CIA. He had been a star for a few years now. Monique's fallen husband was a good man. She worked hard not to let him only be a painful memory. There was another pause, longer than the first. "Things are getting bad in the world, big brother," she said. All trace of laughter had left her voice. "And, things aren't good here in D.C., Ernest. We've got major domestic problems, but my biggest fear is with North Kangavar. We have intercepted intel that they are planning to attack us on a large scale, and all reports point to a nuclear attack. President Shelton is tired of playing politics and has taken an aggressive stance against Kim Yang Su-Il," Monique shared with her big brother. "I've heard the same thing, little sister. We are on high alert at UCSSOC. But a nuclear attack Sis? That doesn't make sense. That would effectively destroy half the world and kill nearly a billion people. Yang Su-Il has to know we would retaliate and wipe North Kangavar off the map," Ernest offered.

"There is a lot of tension at the demilitarized zone, especially after news about a top-secret raid leaked." "Raid? I haven't heard anything." "Yep. About two years ago, and that's why they call it 'top secret, silly," she said quietly. He knew better than to ask questions. "We are only telling key personnel, and you happen to be on the shortlist," Monique said. "I have a few buddies stationed at the border. They have all been ready for an attack and are on high alert," Ernest said with real concern. A loud sigh came from Monique's end of the line. She responded after her sigh, "If Kim Yang Su-Il decides to invade the south, it will be sheer devastation and a South Kangavarian blood bath. No, as a massacre. The North Kangavarian Army is strong, fierce, and over a million strong."

The sound of rustling came from Monique's line. "Hold on a second," she said. Ernest twisted open another bottle of his favorite carbonated water as he waited. Before he could get the bottle to his lips, Monique returned to the phone. "I'm sorry, Ernest, but I have to cut this short. Everyone here is acting more panicked than usual, so I need to see what is happening. If it is as bad as they are making it seem, you will get a call within a few minutes. I'll connect with you tomorrow, okay?" "Roger that. Love you, Sis." "Love you, too, and thanks again for doing this. Means a lot to Chase and me." "You bet. Stay safe, and talk to you soon."

He hung up and began going through his smartphone for the next audiobook he would devour for the long drive. It was good to chat with his sister, something that seemed to happen less and less now since she had been elected Vice President and he had been promoted to Major. The radio interrupted his search for an audiobook. "Tonight, we bring you a new report from the Kangavarian peninsula. Kim Yang Su-Il has released a statement that he will retaliate against the United Cities of Salleria for their open quote:

Actions of betrayal and murder they hid for two years.

End quote," "Jesus," Ernest said. Monique was right; things were crazy over in Kangavar. And what did he mean by retaliating? What the hell have we done? He had a Top Secret Security Clearance, and he didn't know, which made him worry about how bad this was. Whatever it was, it had to be so top secret that it was causing a North Kangavarian *retaliation*. He wondered exactly how far Kim Yang Su-Il was willing to go. North Kangavar always threatened to hit the United Cities with a nuke, but there was no proof they had the capability.

Ernest told himself this was another one of Kim Yang Su-Il's scare tactics. He went to switch the station when his Bluetooth buzzed. His blood began to pump as if he was in combat when he saw it was Colonel McKay. His sister just told him *"If it is as bad as they are making it seem, you will be getting a call within a few minutes."* Clicking the call button, he prepared for bad news as he said, "This is Major Maddox, Sir." The Colonel didn't offer any small talk. "Major, wherever you are, I need you to turn back around as quickly as possible. We have a top-secret mission, and I need your Airborne, Air Assault, and fighter pilot skills asap! This mission will be dangerous, son. Do you copy?" "Roger that, Colonel! I have a *good copy*, and I will be at your office in fifteen mikes, sir." "Out-damn-standing, Major. See you then!" The call disconnected without delay, and Ernest hoped this was all just a precaution and not the real thing. Either way, his weekend getaway with Chase was ruined, and now all he could do was think about taking a leak before he was stuck thousands of feet in the air the combat, pilot gear in a bird with no toilets.

Chapter Two

Ashton liked Aiden about as much as he enjoyed stubbing his pinky toe against his bed frame. He would rather deal with the deathly pain of a nearly broken pinky toe than spend time with Aiden. Unfortunately, his so-called integrity also made him prejudiced against anyone who challenged the rules. While Ashton wanted to prove to everyone that he could be more than just a government killer and a deadly assassin, he also had no intentions of being disrespected or run over. There had to be a line between the two, and he was determined to figure it out. Ashton knew beating people up was not a good option. He would have to learn how to solve problems without close-quarters combat.

Erynn was bolting up the trail ahead while thinking about all these things. She was doing their superhero tracking thing. There weren't too many people alive that good out tracks them or hides from them. A video monitor appeared in Ashton's mind as he ran behind Erynn. Kim Yang Su-Il was giving a speech to the leaders he thought was private. Ashton was watching it on a nine-inch tablet each of his team members had on that infamous mission from two years before in North Kangavar. Kim Yang Su-Il is in a throne room. And he's angry. Bodyguards and a translator are hovering nervously around him. Yang Su-Il is speaking in Kangavarian. Someone from Army intelligence has added English subtitles in the lower third of the tablet screen. Each man watched intensely before Sergeant First Class Norman Bass gave them their mission brief about the two kidnapped young women.

No, No, No -- the time is not correct. The United Cities are too strong. We will wait for this, you understand? This is my law. Anyone who disagrees will be shot on sight. Let Salleria think that my powers have become so weak that they can play with me as they wish. You will see — I will strike a fatal blow when the evidence is clear. Then you will relish our story. The entire Salleria will fall. Mark my words. I will not fail.

The video went black, and Bass stood and gave the men the orders that would end in explosions, murder, and a cover-up. Ashton was jerked from his memory of Yang Su-Il planning to start a war with the United Cities of Salleria when his pain-in-the-ass running mate, Aiden, nearly ran into him as they were trekking through the forest, following Ashton. He genuinely had no respect for the guy, mostly because he could tell the Chief had no respect for him. He didn't like people who automatically assumed he was the wrong person. It wasn't his fault the military made him do bad things, and it wasn't his fault his father beat the crap out of him as a kid. And it wasn't his fault he was born into a secret society assassin cult. Ashton was trying to be a better man, and no one would let him.

Ashton had a problem with most people in authority because they never did the right things with it. Just about everyone he met, who had power over others, used it for their selfish gain and not for the greater good. So Ashton never took advantage of his authority. Fighting for the little people was a sense of honor for him. So he should have taken advantage of his leadership positions.

Ashton, born and assassin, tried hard not to be evil. But he was failing. The Army used him and turned him into a killing machine. His sister Alison always tried to see the good in him, but whenever he wanted to help her, she would get hurt. After his last mission, everyone he ever killed on duty kept haunting him in his dreams. The more time passed, the more he realized that *following orders* was precisely what the people shooting at him were doing. Ashton couldn't tell right from wrong anymore. Was he a murderer? Killing for his government was legal. But how much does legality have to do with morality, he wondered. His nightmares were paralyzing. Ashton only feared falling asleep— so he drank more alcohol than he should. And, right now, he was paying for it running through the forest. His head was pounding.

The quick movements of Erynn's athleticism pulled Ashton back into the moment once again. They were following a western trail leading them towards a water rush. To the west was the Lareto River, which originated at Witry Lake. From there, it flowed through Sunset Lake and down the valley to where it met Harptown River. Unfortunately, the storm caught up with them twenty minutes before, and it was pouring. The loose dirt and rocks were already slippery, and their boots offered limited traction. One misstep, and it was an early grave for all of them.

Aiden trekked ahead with his Colt M4 Carbine lowered toward the ground. Tonight, he was more friendly to Ashton than usual. Maybe it was the miles they had already run without taking a break. Unfortunately, Ashton didn't buy into the buddy-buddy act and was waiting on whatever crazy favor Aiden would ask him tonight. Save the kid and collect your check—

Ashton mentally repeated to himself. Whoever took Jared, Ashton had a bullet with the bastard's name on it.

The grumble of thunder broke in the distance. A dozen people died from lightning strikes here every year, and the rain rapidly killed the trail Erynn was following. She motioned for the team to follow her. "Storm's getting worse," Aiden said in between labored exhales. Lightning moved like dancing lightbulbs across the night sky and over the mountains of Wakefield. The thunder boomed like a chorus of arguments within the clouds. The radio on Aiden's hip crackled, and he plucked it off his belt. "Aiden here. Go ahead." "Chief, it's Vincent reporting in, Chief. Trail's cold out here." Aiden glanced at Ashton before replying, "We've got something out here. Erynn is onto something. You havin' any luck on Harmony Park?" Vincent came in over the crackle of the radio, "Maybe, Chief. I'll report back later." "Copy that. Good luck." Aiden finished.

Sheets of rain hit the three-person search team with unforgiving power. Most of the rain seemed to be blowing in sideways. Aiden attached the radio back to his belt. "You want to turn back," Ashton asked. Aiden frowned and then said, "No. I can't look Truth Parker in the eye if I didn't do everything I could to find his son. But, unfortunately, the clock is ticking, and we are running out of time."

Erynn took off, running deeper into the woods. She was swift and agile. She had the fitness of a track star with the flexibility of a gymnast. She wasn't just running through the trees; she was gracefully flipping through branches without breaking a stride. Even in the rain, Erynn showed the complete confidence of someone who knew what they were doing.

Together, the crew believed tonight would be the night of closure— or rescue. One way or another, Ashton was ready to finish this investigation and stop working with the Chief. Aiden would get his piece tonight and report to whomever he needed. But his job would be complete, and he could leave.

They continued along the path for another thirty minutes, jogging to reserve whatever energy they had left. All three of them hadn't stopped for more than a few moments, and that was just for Erynn to adjust and pick back up her trail. Aiden didn't say much while running, and Ashton was fine. He was lost in his thoughts and didn't need any extra conversations. He'd grown up in a household that was almost entirely silent. Ashton was an introvert, and the idea of human interaction always drained him. His father beat him practically every day. There was always some made-up reason why it was time to get punched repeatedly. All the beatings his father gave him in the narrow hallways of his childhood home were the reason he mastered Krav Maga. He vowed never to be so weak in a fight. Since small spaces were his form of torture as a child, he wanted them to be his strength as an adult. So close-quarters combat became his sanctuary, and all sinners who dared to enter must be sacrificed.

Erynn slowed from a jog to a near power walk. Aiden ruined Ashton's silence. "What have you been up to lately, Ashton? Staying out of trouble." Ashton hated this type of question. Ashton replied, "Why must I avoid trouble all the time? Am I the only person in Wakefield with the first half of their story? Am I the only one with a past, "Ashton smugly said out loud. "Taking it easy, man. I'm just trying to make the hunt a bit easier. No disrespect intended," Aiden replied. Ashton didn't respond, and Erynn started running again. She jumped over a fallen log. When Ashton angled his flashlight into the trees, Erynn was already picking up the pace. Aiden was right behind them both. Ashton was impressed with how the Chief had been keeping up with them. Maybe they could work together more often if he didn't arrest him so much. There was no real reason for Aiden to stay in peak physical condition. He was the Police Chief in a quiet tourist town. But the Chief was both brave and fit enough to be on Special Forces with him and Erynn. "Not too bad, Chief," Ashton said out loud. Aiden responded kindly.

They all hurried over the terrain, careful not to slip on the wet bed of pine needles or loose dirt. The rain continued to come at them sideways— fast and heavy. But neither of them slowed down. They all knew what was at stake. Ashton and Erynn's pants, boots, and ponchos were waterproof. Ashton wasn't sure if Aiden had taken such precautions, but he figured he was just as bright and prepared as them.

Putting every worry out of his mind, Ashton focused on finding the boy. They were still a good three miles from Sunset Lake. The forest became a two-dimensional canvas, and The Ghost divided the terrain horizontally into thirds as the Army taught him. He scanned the tree line from left to right, right to the left, looking for any movement. They ran and then ran some more. The ground constantly reached up and tried to trip each of them. Branches reached out, grabbing their necks and shoulders like screaming fans who didn't respect boundaries. The rain came down so hard it was as if the sky was falling, but Erynn kept moving them forward. All three of their flashlights danced over the trees and the narrow path. The clock was ticking. Neither of them wanted to stop running. Finally, Erynn turned her head quickly and bolted into a different section of the woods. The sound of Ashton's HK416 dangling from the strap on his chest was beginning to scratch at his ears. No matter how hard he tried to shake the feeling, the more he ran, the more he felt they were sprinting into bad news.

Ashton was conscious about keeping his flashlight beam low to the ground. He didn't want whoever they were chasing to know they were coming. But, he would be damned if the boy lost his life because of him. He had enough guilt on his shoulders already. Ashton didn't need the death of a kid added to it. He ran until his lungs felt like they would pop, so he negotiated with his mind to tell his body to shut the hell up. And that is what his body did. When he caught up with Erynn, he saw she was in a battle position and no longer running. Something was up. He moved into place and looked into the tree lines— Aiden did the same. A couple of tense seconds passed, and then Erynn took off running and zigzagging to avoid branches that wanted to pull at their exposed skin. As quickly as she started running, she stopped. They all did. Aiden shouldered his rifle and approached cautiously while Erynn raked her light over the ground. She held the light on what looked like a footprint. She quickly raised a hand, and both men leaned down to get a closer look at the partially filled track with water. It was male, about a size twelve or thirteen. This was too far off the trail to be the random track of a camper, and if Erynn had picked up a footprint here, they couldn't be far from their Jared. They were close. But something rustled in the distance, and each of them instantly knew they were being watched. Someone was nearby—waiting, watching. All three of them raised their rifles to fire.

A voice came over the channel. "Jumper 3, this is Miracle. You have traffic at nine o'clock. Avrinythian Airbus A220, 100 miles, angles 35, heading 120 toward Chesterfolk. Check." Ernest wasn't in his car anymore. The last thing he expected tonight was a sign of any actual activity. He was on his way to a short vacation. Now, it looked like he was on his way to air combat. It didn't make any sense. He checked the radar for an Avrinythian commercial airliner heading east at thirty-five thousand feet. "Copy that, Miracle. Jumper 3 is radar contact." Ernest watched the radar blips for Jumper 3 and 4 change direction to intercept the Avrinythian plane. It was shaping up to be one hell of a night.

Everyone was going crazy tonight, he thought. And, now, he had to miss a weekend getaway with his nephew. The Avrinythian plane was flying into the United Cities of Saleria airspace. He glanced at Park's jet and opened a private line. "Park, keep sharp. Something's off. Something is very fucking off, brother." Another message came over the channel. "Jumper 3, Miracle. That Airbus A220 is now angle 38, heading 135. Pilots are unresponsive." "Copy that, Miracle. We're on it. I'll let you know when we have visual," Morse replied.

Ernest made every excuse book for the Avrinythian plane to be non-responsive, but all of his training told him this was now a live mission, and there was about to be a shootout miles in the sky. Could there be a technical problem aboard the Avrinythian craft?, he wondered. If so, why were they going faster, changing direction, and soaring higher?

Nothing about this seemed innocent, and Ernest had a horrible feeling in his stomach. They kept growing louder and louder the more he tried to make excuses for the Avrinythian aircraft. He knew if he were flying in enemy airspace and didn't have comms, he would do everything possible not to get shot down and start by descending and showing himself friendly. That would be first on his agenda.

Why in the hell did they change course? If they kept this heading, they would be above Chesterfolk and all its mountains within thirty minutes. "Frosty, I got a bad feeling about this," Park said. "Agreed. Stay on me." Ernest wanted so badly for there to be a rational explanation for this. It had to be. He couldn't imagine what an Airbus A220 could be doing at this altitude and what they were planning to do with it.

The A220 has become the clear favorite of passengers in the 100 to 150-seat aircraft category, with rave reviews for its roomy cabin, large windows, spacious overhead bins, intelligent in-flight entertainment systems, and Wi-Fi. This plane was not a fighter jet, so what the fuck was going on. Ernest was wracking his brain trying to make sense of the situation, but no matter how hard he tried, his gut kept telling him this was some act of war. But that didn't make sense. *Where are all the warplanes?* Where are the fighter jets? This didn't make any sense. A commercial airliner is no real threat.

Maybe they were about to drop poisonous gas over a metropolitan area and hundreds of thousands of people. This was too much. Ernest hated not knowing things. Sometimes pilots lost contact with the ground and changed course due to technical issues. Could this be what is happening? Is this all a big misunderstanding, and are the pilots trying to reach out? He would never forgive himself if he shot down one hundred fifty people, plus the staff because he made a panicked decision. Maybe this wasn't a bullshit mission.

Ernest opened a line to Jumper 3. "Robin, Frosty. Do you have a visual?" "Negative, Frosty." Ernest studied the radar. The air traffic controller came back online, but his voice panicked this time. "Jumper 3, Avrinythian Airbus A220, is still unresponsive. Angles are now 46." That update forced Ernest to stop making excuses for the Avrinythian aircraft and take offensive maneuvers. He prepared himself for the mental anguish he would face from himself, his superior officers, and the Sallerian public. The F-16s had a max ceiling of fifty thousand feet. Short and Morse wouldn't be able to pursue much past that, and this aircraft threatened to go much higher. "What the fuck!" Ernest screamed to himself. "Frosty, This is Robin. I have a limited visual," Morse said. There was a pause, and then, "You said that was an Airbus A220, right?" "Copy that, Robin." "Stand by for confirmation," Morse said. Ernest's F-16 rattled as he shot through a pocket of turbulence. He held steady and waited for Morse to relay a visual.

The sound of his fighter jet was going to freak out a lot of civilians, Major Ernest Maddox thought to himself. He earned his call sign, "Frosty," for never cracking under pressure despite all the close calls he faced in his F-16 fighter jet. His younger sister left the skies to settle down with a family and a career in Washington, and now she was the Vice President of The United Cities. She was also a fighter pilot. Ernest had never married or had children. He used to think he wasn't much of a family man, but when his sister had her son, it worried him. Suddenly, the family seemed like a reasonable possibility. He proved to be a loving uncle. He was surprised at how much he enjoyed being one. Ernest wanted to be a role model for Chase.

1st Lieutenant Johnny "Robin" Morse returned over the comms, "Frosty, this is Robin. This craft is not an Airbus A220. I'm looking at what appears to be a Kangavarian-built," Static broke over the line. "Robin, Come again. I didn't get your last." Ernest breathed as his brain brought a horrific thought to the front of his mind. "We are under attack!" Ernest swallowed hard as he said to himself. That couldn't be right. The latest intel they had on any North Kangavarian bird was supposed to have a max service ceiling of around forty thousand feet, but this bird was going way past that.

We can't even follow a bird that high in a fighter jet. "Weapons hot, Park," Ernest said. "This is not a drill. On me! We have to take this fucking plane down right now before we can't follow it." So Major Ernest Maddox and 1st Lieutenant Warren "Park" Pace came together in a fighting formation and ripped south over Chesterfolk Mountains, punching toward Mach 3 as the North Kangavarian bird continued ascending. The plane was now at fifty thousand feet.

Questions ping-ponged in Ernest's mind, but one kept coming to the surface: How could the North Kangavarians have made it into UCS airspace disguised as an Avrinythian Airbus A220? Is this an inside job, or were they much more competent than we ever gave them credit?

"Miracle, this is Frosty. I am weapons hot. Do I have permission to engage?" "Copy that, Frosty. Take that plane down and—" The transmission suddenly cut out in a wave of static, the connection severed. Ernest dipped his helmet to check the radar, but the enemy airplane was gone. "The transmission just ended," Park said. "What the hell happened!" Ernest said and rechecked the radar, but it was too late. An instant later, a brilliant flash lit the sky to the south. "Evasive maneuvers!" he yelled. "Get out of there, Park!" But it was for nothing.

Everything was dead. All the lights on the Major's dashboard were gone. There was no response from Park. His bird wasn't making any noises. He couldn't even hear the roar of the engine anymore. It was dark, and his bird slowed down its ascent and seemed to stall in place for a long time.

There was no radio static. Ernest felt his stomach lurch. He was no longer ascending but falling out of the sky without the engine's resistance. Something was very wrong, and he was scared shitless. He dropped out of the sky like a bowling ball tossed from the highest mountain. He lost complete control of his bird. All he could do was pray. He was going to die. His only choice was to eject. He knew if he was ejected from his F-16, if he survived, he would be bruised and battered and possibly fracture a few bones and tear a few ligaments. The rest was up to God and gravity. He wasn't sure which *"G"* word had more power at fifty thousand feet in the air. He was close enough to God but was God going to prove to be stronger than the pull of gravity?

No pilot ever wants to eject. Losing the aircraft is often coupled with the sting of severe physical injury. But compared to the alternative, his choice is clear. Major Ernest Maddox closed his eyes and ejected.

Chapter Three

Ashton, Erynn, and Aiden had their weapons shouldered. A deer broke a few tree branches and gave away his position. He thought about choking it to death with his bare hands. However, even the deer didn't see Mr. Smith. Smith was disguised flawlessly within the tree line in an elevated position of a sturdy tree branch. He had all three of his enemies in his sites, but he was wise enough to detach his NX8 4-32x50 FI sniper scope because he didn't want the moonlight to hit the lens area of his scope and have the reflection reveal his position. His surveillance was a stealth operation. Unfortunately, the deer did not get the memo.

Smith had been following the rescue team at every step. He timed his steps and spaced his strides so they would not be able to tell the sound of his feet crashing against the ground from their own. Step after step, Mr. Smith traveled their entire journey. He found it laughable that the rescue team was looking for him when all they had to do was turn around. Amateurs, Mr. Smith, thought to himself. He could have killed all of them hours ago, but he was enjoying the game he set up for them. They had no idea about the big surprise they would find in a few moments once they found Jared.

The forest was smothered with rain blankets, making it easier for him to hide in plain sight. He was impressed by the team's stamina, but he was most impressed by Erynn. She didn't miss a beat. She didn't fall for any of his tricks. He had fake tracks and misdirection all over the place, but she didn't fall for them. He told himself he would remember how good she was at tracking and her into a trap the next time she tracked him. He would make sure it would be their very last hunt.

He could see the team using their hand signals to maintain stealth and the element of surprise. He wasn't worried. They would be looking at the ground and at eye level. He was more than twenty feet in the air and out of site. Even if they did manage to look up to the sky, the heavy rain would gouge their eyes out before they would find him. Still, he wanted to see how they worked together under pressure. The rescue team didn't like each other, so Smith expectations were not high.

The cop's radio crackled: "Come in, Chief. This is..." The Police Chief turned down his radio as Erynn and Ashton looked at the blundering fool with disgust. Strangely enough, the crew worked surprisingly well together. They took flanking positions while Erynn stayed in the middle, heading the pack. *She's ballsy,* he thought to himself. He would remember that, too. She liked to take the risk and keep herself out front while others did the flanking. Mr. Smith also noticed The Ghost took a right flanking position while the cop took the left one. They moved as if they had done this before. Their actions seemed more of a result of muscle memory than present orders.

Mr. Smith logged this into his mind for later. He had their movements down. He had a first-hand experience with their combat readiness and endurance. They would be a most formidable foe. He relished the thought of sharing this information with his younger brother. Smith also decided that his final plan was not good enough. He would have to condense their movements somehow. They were too free to flank in open spaces. He would fix this little matter, too.

They were close to him now. Erynn stepped into the tree line, and the others and Ashton closed the gap. He noticed The Ghost grab two knives while Erynn kept her rifle ready. *Very interesting.* Smith thought to himself. They are so in sync that they instinctively know who would cover close combat and handle the long threat. The Chief seemed to sweep the mid-range areas for any threats. Then, at once, the deer ran from the tree line directly at The Ghost. He did not panic, and he didn't attack. Within a split second, probably less, The Ghost could assess the threat and recognize it was not one. Erynn turned with such quickness, saw it was a deer, trusted Ashton would handle the situation, and within a moment, her rifle was back on any possible long-range threats. Mr. Smith knew then he would have to separate The Ghost and Erynn from the calvary whenever the time would come. They were his most significant threats.

Before he could make any more assessments, a blinding light filled the sky. It was almost as bright as day for a few seconds. Everyone was blinded. Amazed at how bright the lightning could get this high in the mountains, all Smith could do now was wait for his pupils to adjust to the dark again.

Side-stepping a terrified dear and sheathing his knives, Ashton looked into the sky after his bones rattled from the rumble of thunder. Never had he ever experienced such a roar from the clouds. It sounded like a bomb going off, and the trees were still shaking from the blast of the thunder. "What the hell was that," Aiden asked. He was as rattled as Ashton. "The loudest thunder I've ever heard," Ashton responded. Erynn nodded in agreement. The entire rescue party had apparent reactions to the lightning strike. The skyline lit up, and for a split second, the night became day, and the bright flash of the lightning lingered for longer than usual.

Darkness swallowed them, and the hunt became that much harder. Ashton's eyes took about ten seconds to adjust to the darkness. Clouds blocked the moon, and the rain felt more like it was coming from the ground than from the sky. He was cold but also hot and sweaty. He was muddy, and his thighs were heavy from all the running they had done so far. They waited several minutes, searching for any threats, and then retreated out of the heavy tree line. Lightning webbed across the sky.

Ashton finally gained the courage to say something he had been feeling since Erynn was acting jumpy hours before it started raining. "I think someone's out here, Chief," he whispered. Aiden nodded in agreement. "Erynn felt like someone was watching us earlier, as well." Erynn walked over to Ashton and pointed up to the sky. She looked back into Ashton's gaze and shook her head. "Chief, Erynn says something is wrong with the sky." It *was* too dark and *way too* quiet. It felt creepy. Something felt very wrong.

Aiden didn't pay much attention to what Ashton and Erynn were saying. His air left his lungs. Ashton imagined his world slowing down and nothing seeming to matter. Instead, Aiden was staring at young Jared's lifeless and mutilated body. He was curled into a fetal position, still dressed in his last clothes. His body was gray, a very unusual and unhealthy gray.

Alison Jace sat patiently in her Honda Civic, trying to get her car started, but nothing would work. It was working fine earlier, but now it wouldn't start. Her scrubs were neatly pressed and fresh from the washing machine, but if she couldn't get the car started soon, she'd be late for her shift at the medical center. She didn't know the first thing about cars.

It was too cold outside to walk to work, and it was raining, and working in wet scrubs for an entire 12-hour shift was not in her plans— and never would be. She could practically feel her wet socks irritating her feet every minute of her shift. Yet, it seemed like she might not have a choice. She had to get to work. She was a nurse, and she saved lives for a living. Fifteen minutes earlier, the car had lost power, coasting to the side of the highway about three miles from town after the brightest lightning strike she had ever seen.

As she began to calm down and pay better attention to her surroundings, she realized all the cars around her looked like they didn't work. "This would explain why traffic was so heavy," she roared. Tourists had been returning from the Wakefield Mountain attractions, their vacations spoiled by the storm. Alison looked as far as her eyes could see. There were hundreds of cars stranded. It seemed the whole city was dark.

One moment she had been thinking about her nightly routine at the hospital—wondering what the staffing ratio would be and if Doctor Kerry would be ready for another busy Friday night. She didn't understand why people enjoyed coming to the ER sick or with some unnecessary injury on Fridays. The next moment jets were falling from the sky and crashing into bright orange flames. What was going on?

She reached for her phone to call her brother. Her brother and his best friend Erynn were with Police Chief Aiden looking for a missing kid. She hoped they were okay. She was beginning to worry. What could make planes fall from the sky? It was like someone had flipped a switch, and everything lost power at the same time. But that was ridiculous, and nothing could do that. This isn't a movie. Even in the rain, the fires from those downed planes burnt bright in the distance.

Alison had been under a lot of stress lately. Both at work and home. Yet, what was bothering her the most was a strange text that came to her phone earlier that day. It left her feeling violated. It was so disturbing it ruined her appetite. She jumped in her car about an hour earlier than usual because she wanted to listen to music and clear her mind. She was not having a good week. At least Paige was safe, she thought to herself. Her daughter, Paige, was staying with her father, Nathan, at his new home in East Wakefield. Alison had a child with Nathan after she left her incredibly sadistic ex-husband. She was vulnerable and had too many glasses of wine; the next thing she knew, she was pregnant. She had just started dating the guy. It turns out Nathan was also physically abusive. He wasn't nearly anything as crazy as her ex-husband, but she had finally had enough abuse and chose to walk away.

Paige was only eight and wanted to see her father. Alison didn't know how to tell her daughter that her father had no real goals for himself and was wasting his life away. Instead, she reluctantly agreed to overnight visits once a week. Sometime during the last week or so, Alison started getting terrifying messages on her phone. Sometimes they came with images. Sometimes they were wrong text-only messages. Whenever she tried to call the number to see who it was, the automated system would say *We're sorry. The number you have dialed has been disconnected or is no longer in service.* Whenever she would block the number so it couldn't text her anymore, she would receive even worse messages from different numbers.

Alison didn't want to tell Ashton because he was already in enough trouble and trying to turn his life around. Some stranger having her number and sending sick messages to her phone made her paranoid about letting Paige out of her sight. Nathan had laughed off her worries, telling her she was overreacting as usual and that it was just some kids playing on her phones. For all Alison knew, Nathan was behind the text messages. She had no proof, but she would never put it past him.

Now that her car wasn't working, planes were falling from the sky, and everything she could see was pitch black— she felt helpless. She felt like she was a world away from Paige. Paige was about thirty-five miles away by car, but her car wasn't working. No one was.

Alison picked up her phone to call Ashton, but nothing happened. Her cellphone was utterly non-responsive. Whatever was happening affected the phones as well. "Hey!" someone shouted at her. She flinched and dropped her phone on the driver's side floor. A man dressed in jeans, cowboy boots, and a sweatshirt slowly made his way to her car. She cracked her door open to listen, trying not to let in any rain.

"Does anyone know what's going on," he asked as he passed other cars. "Nothing is working, and all the power is out. Does anyone know what's happening?" He yelled to everyone in earshot, hoping to get an answer. Alison was right. All the power *was* out. What could do such a thing? The man was wet and looked exhausted, like he had been up for twenty-four hours, but he didn't seem to notice. Alison had never seen him around town and instantly labeled the man a tourist. He took off his baseball cap as he approached her car. If he didn't know what was going on with the vehicles, she certainly didn't. Alison didn't know the first thing about fixing a car and never wanted to learn. As the man approached, she immediately saw something was off. His eyes darted from side to side, his hands shook, and he seemed paranoid.

As a nurse and a victim of abuse, she picked up on the signs immediately—the signs that she'd ignored in Nathan for far too long. Nathan would hit her every time he was using drugs, and he kept a crazed look in his eyes when he was high. She would never forget that look. It was a look she should have known. The same one her mother had every night she got drunk. It was the same look as her ex-boyfriend Joshua before he became abusive. Alison had finally come to grips with the fact that she only picked men who abused her. She hated bullies. Every day, her father would come home and beat Ashton for no reason. It happened so much that Ashton stopped crying and took the punches and the kicks. The more he hit Ashton; the more Ashton would take it without crying. It was a miracle Ashton survived childhood.

Her entire life, she had ignored the signs. But she would be damned if she ignored them now. She made a vow to herself never to allow Paige to see her broken and abused again. Alison turned her head straight so as not to look at the man anymore. She closed her door as discreetly as possible and locked it. The rain began to let up. It went from a torrential downpour to single, inconsistent drops tapping her windshield. Alison closed her eyes and wished the man away. She hoped that he would go to someone else's car. The knuckles rapping on the window dashed her hopeful dreams of avoiding an awkward interaction with the man. She looked up to see the man flash a nervous, non-threatening smile, coupled with polite mannerisms, as he bent down toward her door. She instantly felt guilty. He isn't strung out. He is just afraid. *Not every man is an abusive asshole Alison. Don't become that woman.*

"Ma'am. Excuse me, Ma'am. Do you have any idea what's going on?" The man said with the most polite tone, making Alison feel even more guilty. She unlocked the door and cracked it slowly enough to avoid hitting the man. "I'm not sure," she said. "I was hoping that you would know. You look like a man who knows your way around a car— at least, I was hoping you were." The man raised his eyebrows. "No, ma'am. I only know how to drive them."

Enough time passed, and a large crowd gathered at the edge of the road to stare at the fires dotting the mountains. The man pointed at them. "It doesn't make any sense. How could all the planes have fallen out of the sky like that? How is that even possible?" Panic was rising in his voice. Shaking her head, Alison said, "I have no idea."

Alison had already made her decision. *No one was coming to save them.* Bending down to grab her fallen phone, she opened the door, grabbed what she needed to get to work, and politely said goodbye to the panicked man. She grabbed her jacket from the passenger seat and prepared herself for the long walk into town.

Ashton had insisted she keep a gun in the glove compartment. She was glad she finally relented; this was most certainly a time to have one. With her weapon tucked in the small of her back, and locked her car door manually when the automatic lock button didn't work. She figured once she reached the hospital, she would find out what was happening and return for her car after her shift.

Before anyone could give her orders, she would call Nathan first to see if the same thing was happening on their side of town. But, for now, she needed to get to the hospital and get some answers. So, throwing her backpack over her shoulders, she began walking past stranded motorists and into town. One thing at a time, Alison, she thought. Get to the hospital and check on Paige. Find out what the hell was going on. This was her plan. "You can do this," she said to herself.

Alison was in top shape and ran every day. After a quarter mile of walking, she started into a trot. Her tennis shoes crashed against the wet concrete. She ran around cars and panicked people. At this pace, she could be in the hospital in thirty minutes. There was supposed to be a distant glow of Wakefield reflected in the sky by city lights. But there was no glow— only darkness.

"Where are you going?" A woman shouted after her. "To get help," Alison replied. And, without saying another word, she kept running. She ran at a steady pace. She smelled the fresh air scent, remembering why she loved running so much. Running always helped take her mind off the burdens of life. There wasn't much room to worry about bills and work promotions when your lungs were laboring for oxygen. She ran more than a few times while her ribs were bruised from punches. She'd run as hard as she could to forget that pain.

Growing up in the swap areas of Clemenceau, life was suffocating. Out here in Wakefield, the mountains were so beautiful they breathed life back into her. But Alison always felt like she was running away from life and not towards it. She had been running for ten minutes. Her thighs were beginning to burn. Her lungs were tired and had developed a healthy cadence. She looked at the beautiful terrain and did a double-take when she saw something hanging from a tree across the river. Curious. She picked up her speed, half expecting it to be a kite.

As she got closer, she couldn't believe for one second what she was seeing. She didn't want to jump to conclusions, but she was pretty sure she was looking at a parachute. No way! She thought to herself. She was beyond curious now. She worked her way carefully down to the water's edge. She couldn't believe it. It was a damn parachute. Could this day get any weirder? But where was the *parachuter*? No longer running, Alison slowly walked closer to the parachute. She heard a noise from behind her. Someone was coming towards her. In one motion, as her brother taught her, she pulled her gun from the small of her back, found her target's face, and squeezed the trigger.

"I was hoping Jared would be alive. I knew the odds were against it, but I was hoping," Aiden said to the group. He said it with such pain that even Ashton felt sorry for him. "Look at his body! How am I supposed to tell Truth And Jenny," Aiden's words trailed into silence. He gathered himself, swallowing the tears in his throat. And in a low voice that broke his heart, he finished, "How am I supposed to tell Truth And Jenny, their son was tortured and mutilated." No one said anything. What could they say? Jared's body lay on the ground, twisted, and it looked like he was completely drained of all his blood. It just didn't make any sense. Where was all the blood?

"I'm sorry, Chief," Ashton said, but Aiden couldn't reply. He was too heartbroken. He slowly rolled Jared onto his back, exposing large holes in Jared's neck. "Are these teeth marks? These can't be teeth marks," Aiden asked in bewilderment. "They look more like fang marks," Ashton said in agreement. Erynn and Ashton stole a look at one another. Aiden shook his head in disbelief but forced himself to keep looking. He wanted to remember every single detail. He tried to remember how his investigation took too long to save a little kid. He wanted to feel all the pain to remind him never to let it happen again.

Aiden blamed himself. It was his job to keep Wakefield safe. Looking at Jared's mangled body was the punishment he deserved for failing his city. Aiden looked at the entire crime scene. He couldn't find any blood on the ground. "Where is all the blood?" Aiden asked. "Maybe the rain washed it all way, Chief," Ashton offered. It came off more as a question than a statement. "Maybe. Something doesn't feel right," Aiden countered. "We can agree on that, Chief."

Aiden took his eyes off Jared and looked towards the trees. "I think someone is toying with us. I'm starting to agree with you two. It feels like we are being watched," Aiden admitted. Erynn raised her rifle to the tree line. She must have felt it, too; Someone was playing games with them. "Well, whoever is watching us, if they wanted us dead, we'd all be dead by now," Aiden said to the group. Both Ashton and Erynn nodded in agreement. They were standing in a perfect ambush spot. At any second, they all could be lying next to Jared. "Stay alert. If we are being watched, they could attack us at any time," Aiden said as quietly as he could.

"Jesus," Aiden muttered. He bent down and brushed the leaves and dirt off Jared's thighs. Two large holes were in Jared's thighs, too. The holes in Jared's legs were more prominent than the holes in his neck. "These are fang marks. But the marks on his legs aren't the same size as those on his neck. Maybe we have more than one killer," Aiden said to the team. Ashton and Erynn both thought it over. Finally, Ashton spoke for both of them.

"Okay, let's go with more than one killer. That doubles the chances of having blood on the ground. But I can't find any traces of blood, not even in any of the pockets of water." "Good point. I don't know what to think right now," Aiden responded. Aiden's mind was running in circles.

Aiden pulled his radio from his belt, turned the volume back up, and spoke, "Blake, you copy? Over." Thunder rolled in the distance. The storm was loud and moving throughout the sky towards the west, but the rumble drowned out the crackle of static from the radio in Aiden's hand. Blake came online a moment later. "Roger that, sir. I just arrived at the station. You on your way back, Chief?" With a calm voice, Aiden said, "We found Jared." He paused, sucked in a breath, and exhaled. "He's gone. Call the medical examiner and get them to the Harmony and Sunset Lake trailhead ASAP."

Then, white noise broke over the channel. The growl of thunder sounded again. Aiden glanced at the sky. Odd, he thought. He heard thunder, but where was the lightning? The weather in the Wakefield Mountains could be strange, and often the weather in the mountains could be unpredictable, but this was a bit unusual.

"Blake, did you get my last over?" Aiden said. Aiden looked down at the radio; the screen was black and unresponsive. "Did the batteries just die," Ashton asked? "That's impossible. They were fully charged," Aiden replied. Aiden turned the knob again. And, again. Yet, nothing happened. "Shit," Aiden said, smacking the side of the radio. "The batteries were fine when I checked this morning." Aiden defended himself. "Maybe the radio just messed up, Chief," Ashton offered support. Ashton went back to staring at the sky. Aiden looked at him, wondering what he was thinking. Finally, he began to look at the sky himself. He was looking for the lightning causing all of this thunder, but there was none. The rain had nearly stopped. There were a few drizzles here and there, but the thunder kept rolling in. It just didn't make any sense.

"What are you looking at?" Aiden asked. "I—I'm not sure." Just then, a pair of F-16s raced over the sky. All three of the rescue team lowered their weapons and lifted their gazes. The pair of jets suddenly broke away from one another, peeling off in different directions and climbing the sky. All at once, both jets seemed to be going backward. Then, as if Ashton was reading his mind, he asked, "Chief, did that jet just go in reverse?" "Something's not right. Jet's don't go in reverse." Aiden said.

Aiden was looking at Erynn; she was trying to tell him something. Her body language suggests she knew what was happening. Moments later, one of the jets appeared to fly in a weird pattern. A pattern no pilot would ever fly. "These planes aren't going in reverse, Chief. They are falling from the sky!" Ashton said to Aiden in an octave much higher than he usually spoke. Seconds later, the jet crashed violently into one of the mountains. A fiery explosion licked the night. Each member shielded their eyes from the bright blast. Before they could recover, the second fighter jet exploded a few seconds later. The mountainside was covered in explosions. Flames licked the rocks and touched the sky. "My God," Aiden said quietly. He stood over Jared's body and then looked towards the fallen jets. "What the fu—," Aiden didn't get to finish before Ashton asked in a panic, "Did you see anyone eject?" Aiden and Erynn both shook their heads and stood there in silence.

Mr. Smith gaped at the smoking mountainside. This night was turning out to be one he would remember forever. With his sniper scope still in his pocket, Smith looked down the thin metal barrel of his rifle at the three do-gooders. He thought about firing fifteen quick shots as The Ghost coughed and shifted. But, instead, Smith aimed the barrel at him first. He was such an easy target at this angle. Next, Smith pivoted the barrel Erynn's way. He was having too much fun. Smith imagined a thin scarlet line of a laser sight fixed to its barrel passing six inches over the exploded Police Chief's head. He could do it. He could do it right now, he thought to himself.

Planes were falling from the sky. Smith took it as a good omen. His brother Jacob was close by, awaiting his orders to kill, but Smith was pleased with how things were going. Then, they found the boy's body. He died pitifully. They are making kids so soft these days.

He killed Jared with great pleasure. Then, he would kill each of them with even more fun. And the best prize of it all, they had no idea what he would do next. But he did. He would see them back in Wakefield for a particular party he was throwing. And they were *all* invited.

Aiden shook his head in disbelief. "What the hell were fighter jets doing out here in Wakefield?" Aiden asked while bending down to pick up Jared's body. Ashton and Erynn crouched to help. "I've got him," Aiden said defiantly. Ashton just stared at him. Aiden took this one personally and didn't need their help carrying his mistakes. He was the reason Jared was dead, and he would bear its full impact. He wondered how he would tell his wife, Dawn, that he let Truth and Jenny down. He asked how he would tell his daughter, Lillian. She was sixteen, and babysitting Jared was her first job a few years back. She, too, would be heartbroken.

Police protocol called for Aiden to leave Jared's body, but with the rain washing away all the evidence and planes falling from the sky, he decided to be a father and bring the kid back to his father. He would have wanted the same done for him. Thoroughly defeated, the rescue team turned towards Wakefield and started walking. There was no reason to run now. The clock on Jared's life had ticked down to zero.

Aiden noticed the town was in complete darkness. He couldn't see the light bouncing off the horizon like normal. The only lights that were out tonight were the two crashed planes, still exploding upon themselves. Their flames are still licking the sky.

"Whoa! Ma'am! I'm one of the good guys," the man who snuck behind Alison said. "I'm glad you forgot to take off your safety. I would be dead by now if you didn't. Nice spin move, by the way," the strange man said to Alison. He was wearing a flight suit and holding a helmet. He was limping and holding his right shoulder. Alison realized the man was wearing an Air Force flight suit. She lowered her weapon. "What do you mean, one of the good guys," Alison asked. She noticed he structured his sentence as if he was expecting *bad guys.*

The Air Force man held up his free hand. "Ma'am. I'm not going to hurt you. I am Air Force Special Warfare. My name is Major Ernest Maddox, and I just ejected from fifty thousand feet in the air. I can't even begin to tell you how painful that experience was." Alison put her gun in the small of her back. "Safety was on, you say? That's probably a good thing, considering you are out here scaring women half to death," Alison said. Major Maddox smiled and offered a pleasant energy in her direction, calming her down.

The moonlight revealed the Major's handsome, chiseled face. He was in his mid-thirties with a full head of black hair and beautiful brown eyes. "I injured my shoulder pretty bad and need to get to the nearest town as quickly as possible," he said. "Can you point me in the right direction?" Alison gave him the elevator eyes treatment. His navy blue flight suit was soaked up to his waist, and his boots were covered in mud. He limped a step closer, but with caution as he did not want to frighten her.

Alison saw he wasn't trying to scare her and appreciated his gentleness. He was severely hurt but still thinking for her. He grimaced as he looked at her. "I'm a nurse," Alison said without thinking. The pilot's eyes smiled at hers in the moonlight. "Then I'd be grateful if you quickly looked at my right shoulder." Alison hesitated, then pulled off her backpack and set it on the ground.

As an abuse victim, who was also a nurse, she carried a medical kit with her everywhere. "Come here, let me see. You will have to unzip your flight suit and take off your shirt," Alison said. She could have sworn that she saw the Special Warfare man blush. Alison reviewed his shoulder for about twenty seconds. "You have a forward dislocation to your right shoulder. I am going to have to pop it back into place. I am going to count to," *Pop*. You could hear the Major's bone go back into its proper position. Ernest let out a controlled grunt. He was powerful, Alison thought to herself. "What happened to you counting?" Ernest said while gritting his teeth. "I guess public school never taught me how to count," Alison threw his zinger right back at him. They both laughed.

"Thanks," he said while rotating his shoulder in circles. "My name's Ernest, by the way. Major Ernest Maddox." She smiled thinly at him. "You said that already major, right after I shot you in the face. I'm Alison. Nice to meet you." "Oh, yeah," Ernest responded. "I guess you lose your memory when people shoot you in the face." He rotated his shoulder in the air a few more times and went back into business mode. "How far are we from the nearest town? Did you see the other pilot eject?" Alison opened her med kit, talking as she worked. "Two miles or so from Wakefield, maybe less. I didn't see anyone else but you. Can't you call them on your radio?" When Ernest didn't reply, Alison grew suspicious and asked, "What happened to your plane?"

Before he could answer, *Pop*, she snapped his ankle back in place with one motion. "You are fortunate, Major. Ankle dislocations are very rare and usually come with a fractured bone. I don't have the right machinery in the middle of nowhere, but I don't think you suffer much with this ankle. Your shoulder was much worse," Alison briefly told the Major. She noticed he barely showed any pain as his body flinched accordingly. She was impressed. He was as strong as her ex but lovely as a college professor. "I guess you forgot to count again?" Ernest said with a smirk on his face. "Public school didn't teach me, remember?"

He reminded her of her brother, Ashton. He was also as powerful, and they came and nice to her. "What happened to your plane, Major?" "I'm not authorized to say, ma'am, but I am very grateful for your help." He craned his neck at the road. "Please hurry. I need to get to that town immediately." Alison ensured he had no other significant injuries to any other part of his body. She figured he would be okay because he just took these injuries. "The rest of your body seems okay, Major, but you didn't answer my question. Your plane?" Alison said. Ernest didn't respond, but his eyes told her he was not trying to be rude.

"Major, I may be just a nurse, but I know fighter jets don't drop out of the sky like that. My brother just retired from Army Special Forces and lives in the closest town. You may need him." Ernest stared at Alison, but she wasn't finished. "I popped your ankle and shoulder back in place, and you didn't flinch. This tells me you aren't just Air Force Special Warfare but have anti-torture training. So, from what I gather so far, you are a Major trained for Special Warfare; in addition to being a fighter pilot, you are an anti-torture trained, which means you make your living behind enemy lines, and about an hour ago, right when all the cars stopped working, you were forced to eject at fifty-thousand feet." I understand that no pilot wants to eject because they know it will likely cause serious injuries, as you had. You quickly asked me about the ejection status of another pilot, which means you were not flying alone, which also explains the other crashed plane. You are scared he didn't get to eject in time. And now, despite being seriously injured, you are trying to get to the closest town. A town you have never been to, which tells me you aren't from around here, and you can't use your million-dollar radio the military gave you. So are you going to stop treating me like I am a regular civilian and tell me what the fuck is going on, or am I going to have to kill you with my sarcasm and bad jokes?"

Ernest smiled. He was irritated by her persistence, grateful for her health care, and impressed by her ability to piece things together quickly. He cleared his throat as if he was considering his following words carefully. Finally, he looked at Alison directly and said, "The United Cities of Salleria has just been attacked."

Chapter Four

At the time of his formal sentencing in Clemenceau for eleven known murders, the former Special Forces Captain, and pattern killer Finley Smith, known simply as Mr. Smith, was lectured and condescended to by United Cities of Salleria District Judge Elsie Fisher. At least, that's how he took the judicial scolding, and he took it personally. He was going to kill everyone involved — starting with the lying whore that turned him in. He trusted her. This was Mr. Smith's only mistake.

"Mr. Smith, by any criteria I know, you are the evilest human being who has ever come before me in this courtroom. You may very well be the evilest human being to have ever been born of a woman's womb, and some despicable characters have come, "Smith interrupted. "Thank you very much, Judge Fisher. I am honored by your kind words, and I am sure you were very pleased to hear yourself talk. Women like you usually are. As for me? Well, thank you for noticing that I am the best. Who wouldn't want to be noticed as the best?

Do continue, your honor. This is truly music to my ears." Smith had a way of singing his words as he talked. It was his carefree way of viewing life and very irritating to others. He irritated them for his mere amusement.

Judge Fisher nodded calmly, then went on as if Smith had not spoken a word. "In reparation for these unspeakable murders and repeated acts of torture, you are hereby sentenced to death. Until such a sentence is passed, you will spend the remainder of your life in a super maximum-security prison. Once there, you will have no human contact, as most of us know. You will never see the sun again. May you suffer every day of whatever little life you have left!"

"You have a flare for the dramatic," Mr. Smith called to Judge Fisher as he was escorted from the courtroom, "But it's not going to happen that way. You've just given yourself a death sentence. I am smarter than you. I am smarter than all of you. I will see the sun again. I will drink the blood of your children. I will kill you, Judge. You have my word on it, my solemn promise before all these witnesses, cameramen, and reporters who honor me with your presence. And you can guarantee I will kill that bitch," as soon as they were out of view of the cameras, an officer struck Smith in the back of the head with a police baton with such force it concussed him, knocking him unconscious before he could finish the threat against the woman who turned him into the FBI.

In the audience, amongst the cameras and reporters, was the love of his life. She listened to her former lover's empty threats. And yet she couldn't help hoping Clemenceau Super Max Correctional Facility was as secure as it was supposed to be.

Aiden carefully carried Jared's body down the trail that led back into town. The rain let up, but his heart was still broken. Things had changed when those jets crashed. He had to get back into town and figure out exactly what was happening. His arms burned as he carried Jared over the slick terrain, but he needed to feel the pain. He deserved it. He let his friends down. Besides, the burn in his arms would not hurt worse than Truth's And

Jenny's aching hearts. No parent deserves to outlive their children or to have their child murdered.

"You sure you don't want me to carry him?" Ashton asked. "No, I'm fine. Just keep making sure we don't get ambushed." A million doomsday scenarios ran through his mind as he stared at the fires in the distance. He couldn't think of a solution for either one. He wondered how long the fires would burn and how much forest they would consume. "Chief, what do you think is going on? Have you come up with any theories?" Ashton asked. He stood at the side of the trail with his arms crossed over his stomach. He held his Glock 19 across his chest, and Erynn stood to his left, her HK416 at the ready. Both were soaked and muddied from the rain.

"I have a few theories. But, unfortunately, neither one of them is good. I am sure you have a few thoughts yourself." Aiden said. "I do. But none I should mention now because if any of them is true, the world's end began about an hour ago." Ashton responded grimly. Whatever is going on, Chief, it is not good, and we need to be a full strength to handle it. Why don't you let me carry the boy for a while?" "I said I'm fine," Aiden glared at Ashton. Ashton muttered something that sounded a lot like *asshole* and turned away, clearly not a fan of Aiden.

Aiden was angry. Jared was dead, a killer was on the loose, fighter jets were falling from the sky, the radio was down, and he was cold and wet. He was wrestling with the idea that the jets fell from the sky when his radio stopped working. As a cop, Aiden didn't believe in coincidences. He had to get back to town to get some better answers.

The trio continued down the path. The rain began to pour again, soaking their clothes again. Aiden was doing his best to keep it together, but tonight was one of the worst days of his life, and it was getting worse by the second. Aiden could feel Ashton's eyes on him, and it was getting under his skin. "What?" Aiden asked forcefully. "You got something else to say?" "Nope," Ashton said. Aiden hoisted Jared's body against his chest, and pain lanced up his arm and neck. He gritted his teeth and pushed forward.

Aiden did his very best always to be a man who did the right thing for others— even if it meant being tough on some. He was hard on Ashton because he was wasting his potential. He was determined to get Ashton to stop slowly killing himself. But Aiden was lost in his thoughts. His heart broke, and his mind followed. He wanted to walk in silence back to town, but Ashton had other plans. "Want me to carry him for a while now, Chief?" "Goddammit, Ashton, I told you to watch our backs." Ashton stopped mid-stride, "You trusted me enough to help you look after the kid, but you don't trust me enough to help you carry him?" "You're right. I don't trust you," Aiden said. Ashton halted. Ashton reached the end of his patience. "Fuck you, Chief. Let's get one thing clear, goddammit. I don't fucking need you. You need me. You may not like me, and I damn sure don't like you. So, you can keep your critical observations of me to yourself and kiss my ass if you want to arrest me, fine! But one day, you will have trouble when I don't feel like being arrested. I will show you an entirely new meaning of resisting. I'm tired of you pushing me around, and if you keep thinking I am a bad person, I will fucking show you what a bad person can look like."

Aiden narrowed his eyes as if he was about to say something, but he decided against it. Arguing with Ashton was surprisingly helpful because it stopped Aiden from arguing with himself. Impressed with Ashton for telling the truth *this time* and not being so wishy-washy with his motives, he still didn't like Ashton or trust him, but at least now he knew for sure which side of the fence he stood on. "I am not afraid of you or Erynn. You are not the only highly trained combat soldier on this team, and it would take a whole army with you to kill me, Ashton. You cause another problem in Wakefield, you and I will have that war you are itching for, and I will be more than happy to show you how battle ready I am." Aiden responded calmly but with the bravado of Muhammed Ali.

Both men held their grounds. They stared at each other, neither man blinking or showing weakness. Finally, Erynn decided not to intervene. Maybe she knew Aiden and Ashton would get to this point sooner or later. Or, perhaps she was taking a flanking position to get the better of Aiden. It didn't matter. He didn't care what she was doing. There was no way he would let Ashton think that he would ever back down from a fight. Especially not one with him.

Ashton looked down at Jared, then up at the Chief. Then, with a deep growl, he said the last words, "And they say I'm the asshole." Ashton turned around and started walking towards Wakefield. Aiden let out a frustrated breath and began walking. The veins in his muscular forearms bulged as he tightened his grip around the dead boy. How would he tell his Lillian that she wouldn't be babysitting Jared anymore because he failed to save his life?

The wind whistled through the treetops, and the smell of fresh mountain water filled his nose. A small tear trickled down Aiden's face. It had been long since he cried, and he was too busy staring through the canopy of trees to wipe it away. Ashton turned around and noticed the Chief was crying silently to himself. Aiden could only assume he felt like an ass for trying to fight him. Aiden couldn't help but wonder how there was no time or space for disharmony. Jared was dead, and they didn't know why fighter jets were falling from the sky.

Overhead, a thundercloud rolled across the horizon, leaving behind a battered black and grey sky. "You're not going to tell me a theory about what happened to those jets?" Ashton asked. When Aiden only grunted in response, he continued, "I have a few, and all of them begin with *this end of the world.*" "End of the world?" Aiden asked. "See, that's the path I don't want to go down right now." Ashton interrupted Aiden's interruption and kept talking. "Listen for a change Chief. Here are the facts: As you said, all three of us are high, combat-trained veterans. We all saw the sky light up and heard the thunder roll for much longer than it should have. After that, we kept hearing thunder without lightning. Before we figured it out, Erynn pointed to the sky and said something was off. Two fighter jets fell from the sky, and we haven't even asked what they were doing up there." "Go on," Aiden said, starting to see Ashton had been putting a lot of thought into it. Erynn nodded in approval. "The radios don't work. Our cell phones don't work. And, there is not a single light shining in Wakefield. Not a single fucking light. At first, I thought of a major power outage, but it wouldn't explain one, the fighter jets being on a mission, or two, them falling to destruction. This will sound crazy, but I think we may have been victims of a nuclear electromagnetic pulse." Ashton finished. "Okay," Aiden said. "Let's say for a second I agree with you. You make a lot of sense now, but why would anyone do a nuclear strike on Wakefield? There is nothing here but mountains and tourists." "Exactly," replied Ashton. "That is exactly why." We are in the center of Salleria, and some mountains are three miles above the ground. If you want an EMP to do maximum damage, you have to get it far higher than the mountains, or it wouldn't have the range you wanted. Think of it as a cell phone signal that can get over the other side of the mountains. But if you were on top of the mountains, you could get a signal on both sides. If I were to wipe out all the power in Salleria, I would use more than one EMP. One for the west coast, one for the middle, and one for the east coast. That would send us to the Stone Age and our neighboring countries."

Aiden started to take Ashton seriously. Erynn seemed to be agreeing. If the jets falling from the sky were an act of war, Jared was only a big problem in the middle of a thousand more significant issues. "Okay, Ashton. Let's say you are correct. For an EMP to work, it would have to be high enough to affect the entire Cities of Salleria. "Correct!" Ashton said. "It works like this, Chief. An EMP would arrive in three phases—a near-instantaneous, powerful pulse known as E1. That would explain that bright flash we initially took for lightning. A subsequent high-amplitude pulse known as E2, and a slower and lower-amplitude, but still very damaging, waveform known as E3. That would explain why we kept hearing thunder without seeing lightning." Shocked at seeing this side of Ashton, Aiden asked, "How the fuck do you know this?" Erynn smiled and motioned to Ashton to tell him. "Erynn and I weren't just Special Forces Chief. We were part of a top-secret company that did the Army's dirty work. The more our six-man teams did, the more we didn't need wars or battles. Let's say we did these kinds of things on much smaller scales with drones." Aiden looked at Ashton and Erynn and said, "We have to hurry and get back into town. Now!

October 27, 2018,

Six years to the day later, Mr. Smith was still being held in Clemenceau Super Max Correctional Facility. He hadn't seen the sun in all that time. He was completely cut off from most human interaction and was as angry as he'd ever been. It had been six whole years. Fantasizing daily about how he would kill everyone involved in his capture, on every level, regardless of how much they had to do with his case. If the janitor took out the trash in the DNA laboratory, he would have to die painfully, too. No one was exempt. Especially his beautiful lover, who turned him in. The bitch dared to testify against him. She was going to die the worst.

His fellow inmates included a man who killed one hundred sixty-eight people in a downtown office. He blew up the entire building — Wyatt Douglas, an Al Qaeda terrorist, Fateen al-Alam, and a man who murdered and ate the brains and hearts of six people in a small rural town— Emerson Cote. They didn't get to go outside and play in the rain, either.

Each was locked away in soundproof, seven-by-twelve concrete cells for twenty-three hours a day, completely isolated from one another and all the guards. They could only interact with their lawyers and the high-security guards. Living in Clemenceau Super Max was compared to dying every single day. There was no other hope than death by capital punishment.

Even Mr. Smith admitted that escaping from Clemenceau Super Max was the most daunting challenge he had ever faced. With an IQ of 170 and a grandiose sense of self-importance, failure to conform to social norms, and lack of remorse, Finley Smith was already serving a prison sentence for murdering eleven people while employed as an Army Special Forces Captain. They only caught him for eleven, but he murdered more than seventy. Breaking free from this prison proved to be an extraordinary task. No one had ever escaped. Not one. Not ever.

Still half asleep, Vice President Monique Maddox scanned a dark room and tried to remember where she was. It was much darker than usual, but that was normal. She slept in the pitch black. Her husband died a few years back, and Chase was thirteen now. He husband was now a star on the wall in the CIA building. No one would ever know he died saving the world. He was a hero amongst heroes. Chase wanted to be just like him. But, for now, he was in Chesterfolk at a basketball camp with a coaching staff that believed he could make it to the NBA.

Before her career in politics, Monique was one of the first female pilots to fly combat missions from the cockpit of an F-16N. She served honorably in The United Cities of Salleria

Navy. By every standard imaginable, Monique was both a legend in the air and a legend on the campaign trail.

She was a fearless woman— a superstar amongst women and a champion for the underserved. She was a black woman with a majority of non-black following. The public share in the loss of her husband and was now sharing in the hopeful journey of her son becoming an NBA player. His backup plan was to become a spy, just like his father.

Her room was cold. Too cold. She rubbed her eyes and scanned the bedroom of her Washington, D.C., apartment. It was only a few blocks from Capitol Hill. She could not hear the air conditioning running nor the hustle and bustle of traffic outside. Washington, D.C., was far too quiet. Silence filled her ears.

The bedside alarm wasn't working. The red LED light that usually lit under her flatscreen tv was gone. She reached for her cell phone only to discover— it was non-responsive. She tried it a second time— nothing. Did the building lose power? But that wouldn't explain her cell phone not working. It was charging all night.

She crossed the room to the window and pulled back the curtain. Rain slid down the glass. Past the blur of water, she gazed out over the Sallerian capital. Everything was shrouded in darkness, not just the city but everything. An arc of lightning webbed across the skyline, providing a momentary glimpse of the town. The outlines of the United Cities of Salleria Capitol, the White House, and the Congressional Mall emerged before the light receded. Eight stories below, she could see the silhouettes of cars on the street, but none were moving. Monique couldn't believe it. Of all places in the world, Washington, D.C., didn't have a single car driving in the streets. There were no stoplights or porch lights. There wasn't a single establishment open for business.

She was almost sure she could see a fire in the streets. But how? Who would be lighting fires in barrels on the road in this part of town? *Knock, knock, knock.* Someone was aggressively knocking at Monique's door. She jumped at the sound of the knocks. Then, another knock sounded on the apartment door before she could begin to make sense of things. The knocks were louder this time. "Hold on," Monique said as she threw on slacks and a t-shirt. She opened the door to see the trusted face of her Chief of staff, Brayden Barber. The thirty-five-year-old staffer was drenched to the bone. He was panting and trying his hardest to catch his breath. "Brayden! Are you okay? Why are you out of breath?" Monique stepped to the side and gestured for Brayden to come in. "I ran here, Madam Vice President," Brayden said between each labored breath. Finally, he took another long drag and added, "From the Capitol." "From the Capitol?" Monique said in utter disbelief. "Sit down and get a hold of yourself." "And why did you run from the Capitol, Brayden." "Ma'am, there's a situation," Brayden said, causing Monique's adrenaline to spike.

Jacob Smith was a stone-cold killer who had only two goals in life. Kill as many people as possible, and make his older brother happy. He was looking over the dark city in Wakefield— something had happened to the lights. *So this is how the rich and famous life. Quietly and stupidly, and very arrogantly, for sure*

Jacob began his checklist of possibilities for getting to his target. The building was secure, but the rich were always arrogant. His brother, Mr. Smith, had one target in mind, but he planned to kill as many as possible to hide their actual target. Tonight's target had been pre-selected.

She lived at 255 St Paul Street in Lakota, about eighty-three miles southeast of Wakefield's capital. Neither the residents nor its loyal employees rarely used the service entrance at the back of the super-luxury apartment. The underground parking garage was treated like a stepchild. People only entertained when it needed attention. It was the building's most vulnerable entry point.

A single reinforced door shows off no external hardware. The frame was wired on all sides. Jacob thought about brute force entry, but that idea would trigger multiple alarm systems at the St. Paul Collection main office and with the Lakota police department. On the ceilings, professional box cameras bolstering crystal clear video surveillance and reliable performance monitored all deliveries and foot traffic during the day. Use of the entrance was forbidden after seven p.m. when motion detectors were also engaged.

No, bother. Jacob was a professional. Mr. Smith had taught him everything he knew, and Jacob was a natural talent. All of these security features would prove to be an advantage to him. Jacob had been an Army Ranger for twelve years. He had a sixth sense about such things. He could detect the flaw in every secure security system because the more secure something is, the more confident its designer feels. And confidence birthed arrogance. A security designer's biggest flaw is their dependency on technology. It made them complacent and blind to the danger he posed.

The best way into St. Paul's Luxury Apartments was also his easiest way. Trash. Trash collection was the answer. Jacob knew it was carried out every Monday, Wednesday, and Friday afternoon, without fail. Unfortunately, St Paul's loved to spoil its residents, and its superior customer service was another of the luxury building's vulnerabilities. *Superior customer service was also Serial murder service.*

"There's always a situation, Brayden." "Of course, ma'am, but this may be the last situation you will ever face," Brayden said as he pulled off his coat and waited for a few seconds until he could control his breathing. Brayden was one of Monique's most loyal. He proved one of her most trusted allies and never expected anything in return. Brayden was practical and a realist. He had Monique's full attention because this was unusual behavior. He rose to ranks as of the highest-ranking Capitol police at only thirty-five years old. "Is this some sort of wide-scale power failure?" "Not exactly, Madam Vice President," Brayden said. He allowed himself another breath and put his hands on his chin, which was attached to a beautiful egg-white face. Her mind was racing, and her adrenaline spiked like it did when she flew an F-16N into battle for a living. "Brayden, catch your breath and then tell me what the hell is going on. Be straight with me and give me the worst of it first." "I got a call from General Phillip Hartman a couple hours ago. He tried calling you first, but you didn't pick up." "My phone's dead," Monique said.

General Phillip Hartman was an old friend now serving as Chief of Staff of the United Cities of Salleria Air Force. They were friends way before the fame and always treated each other with the utmost respect and admiration. However, this was the first time he had called her at night. "I'm supposed to meet with him tomorrow at the Pentagon" "This wasn't about your meeting, Monique. He had new intel on the situation in North Kangavar." Monique narrowed her brown eyes. The last time Brayden had called her by her first name was thirteen years ago, the night Chase was born. "What kind of intel?" "He wouldn't say ma'am; he just told me to tell you to call him. Could the power outage be from an attack on the grid?" Monique asked Brayden.

She moved into the other room to look out the window again. The tensions were at an all-time high between The UCS and North Kangavar. They couldn't prove the Sallerians had been behind the raid that had saved Senator John Romani's granddaughter twenty-four months prior, but between the raid and President Shelton's aggressive stance on North Kangavar, the UCS has been on edge. "Ma'am, all hell has broken loose. There is pandemonium in the streets, and the entire city has no power. Not even the White House. It is not safe outside. You are not safe." Brayden said with a matter-of-fact tone. Monique took notice. "Every car I saw is dead. Every house is in the dark, and every sensible-minded person is panicking".

Monique's mind reeled. She clung to one urgent thought, "I have to get to my son, Brayden. Is your phone working?" Chase is at basketball camp Chesterfolk." "I don't have a signal," Brayden said, holding up his phone. He slipped it back into his pocket. "I'll find someone that does and have Chase picked up immediately. This is my highest priority, ma'am." "Thank you, Brayden. "But how will you ensure he is okay if all the power is out,"

Monique asked. "The power can't be out everywhere, right?" Monique shook her head, uncertain. "The White House has backup power.", Brayden answered.

A horrible suspicion entered her mind as she studied the darkened city. She was beginning to think this was a terrorist attack. She was putting pieces together and didn't like the way the pieces were fitting. She'd been briefed about the possibility of a coordinated electromagnetic pulse attack, but it was the fifth most likely axis of advance, and no one took it seriously—not even her. It was only mentioned for less than a minute.

"Ma'am, I need your orders," Brayden declared. Half of Monique's focus was in Chesterfolk. She prayed to God Ernest was already in Chesterfolk. He would never let anything happen to Chase. "Brayden, we need to get to the Capitol Police. If the power is out, the city is no longer safe. People will begin to panic and become violent," Monique said while reaching under her pillow and grabbing her Glock 30. She went to the closet, reached the top shelf, and grabbed three ammo boxes. "Go get my car keys from the kitchen table, just in case," she told Brayden. A few minutes later, he returned and handed her the key ring.

"Do you trust me, Brayden?" she asked. There wasn't a single second of hesitation in his voice. "Yes, Madam Vice President." "Good, because I feel that whatever has happened may have changed the world, and The United Cities of Salleria has fallen."

Chapter Five

"What do you mean the country has been attacked," Alison asked the wounded pilot. "It's pretty much what I said, ma'am. I didn't just fall out of the air. My bird lost all power, and if I didn't eject. Well, you can use your imagination. I can't tell you anything more than that because I don't know." Ernest limped down the dirt path, rotating his injured right shoulder, wincing with each twist. His ankle was killing him. But his shoulder was more than questionable.

"So you can tell me we've been attacked, but not by who, why, or," Ernest interrupted Alison. "That's what I'm saying. I'm a pilot. I take orders. I give orders. The questions you are asking come from politicians, not Majors. But I'm sure you've heard the news." "North Kangavar?" Alison asked. Ernest didn't reply. Ignoring the searing pain in his ankle, Ernest began to walk so fast it was hard for Alison to keep up. He was moving more at a slow jog. "Listen, I'm not going to tell anyone, but I am sure you were ejected with a weapon," Alison said. "Yes. I did, ma'am." "Stop calling me that. My name is Alison Jace, and I am not an old lady." "I'm sorry, Alison. The whole country is in danger, and right now, I am the only person with information that can help us, and I need to get to a radio ASAP." Ernest halted and turned around so fast she almost ran into him. They were close enough that she could smell his cologne; it was a wonderful scent. He was a handsome man. Get it together, Alison. This is far from the right time. Besides, she was a bit uncomfortable with him being so close. She hadn't been this close to a man in a few years.

"Ms. Jace," "Call me Alison. Ms. Jace still makes me feel old." "Fair enough, Alison. We need to get to town as fast now." Alison started jogging to keep up with the pilot. They were making their way down the road that led them into Wakefield. "Keep low," Ernest said, watching the cars and stranded motorists on the road above as if he wanted to avoid civilians. "The last thing we want to do is be seen while I am in uniform. It is the reason I was hiding when you found me. People are likely panicking and looking for anyone in authority to give them answers, and I don't have any for them." "Okay, that makes sense," Alison said. "They will also be looking for someone to blame as well. So it will not be good for you to be seen with me in uniform," Ernest warned her. Alison considered what he was saying. She had the same idea of avoiding other people. But, deep down, Alison knew he was right because she was blaming him, too. That's why she kept asking him so many questions.

The United Cities of Salleria had been at war for as long as she could remember. Congress was always sending troops to fight some battle that had nothing to do with Salleria. Then, something suddenly hit Alison like a ton of bricks. She paused in her tracks, her heart beating so hard she could feel it throbbing in her neck. "Major, should I be worried about my daughter's safety?" Ernest had opened his mouth to reply when a shout echoed from the road.

"Hey! Hey, you! Hey Army boy! Down there!" Alison and Ernest looked up to the road. A crowd of stranded citizens on the shoulder of the highway were in their pickup trucks. On the back of one of the pickup trucks stood an oversized Sallerian flag. There were four men in the truck, and each wore a red *Make Salleria Great Again* hat. In the front of the group stood a barrel-chested man wearing a tight flannel shirt and gestured for Alison And Ernest to come his way. He wedged a chewed-up cigar between his lips and spoke with a twang. "You one of them pilots, Mister," the barrel-chested man asked, expecting an immediate answer.

Alison and Ernest both took a step back when they saw the man had an assault rifle in his hands. "Stay by your vehicles. Help is coming," Ernest yelled back. The man fired one round into the air and tipped him *Make Salleria Great Again* hat. He hawked spit over the railing, and with a menacing tone, he said, "Like hell, you fucking Libtard. I want to know what killed our cars, Army boy." Ernest wanted to say, *I'm in the Air Force, dumbass* but he thought better of it. The man continued, "Maybe you killed our cars, Army boy."

"Keep walking, Alison," Ernest whispered. "Follow my lead, and I sure hope that gun you pulled on me earlier was loaded." "Hey! You goddamn commie bastard. I'm talking to you." the man yelled. "I asked you a goddamn question, Feminazi? Don't you turn your back on me, you fucking Baby-Killer." Ernest stopped and pivoted back to the road. "I don't know what happened, sir, but help is on the way. Just stay where you are or walk into town." The other people muttered and began to disperse, but not the man with the assault rifle. He was angry, motivated, and armed. "Get back here and tell me what the hell is going on, Snowflake. This is our country, and we deserve some goddamn answers, you son of a bitch. We pay your salary, asshole." "Is this guy serious?" Alison muttered. Ernest turned his back on the irate man and started running, but not before uttering, "We don't have time for this." Alison eyed the assault rifle one more time, then took off running after Ernest.

After running a short while, Ernest turned to his companion and said, "Alison, take the lead." That was nice, she thought. He must have seen he was too far ahead of me. It had only been an hour since the planes fell from the sky. In Alison's opinion, fear is the most powerful emotion in the world. Fear had trapped her in abusive relationships. And, now, it seemed the entire city of Wakefield was falling into a state of fear. Things would get much worse if the lights didn't come back on. She wondered how long it would take before average; law-abiding citizens became panicked mobs.

Just as she was wondering how long it would take for civilization to crumble, Alison flinched at the crack of a gunshot nearby. The guy with the *Make Salleria Great Again* hat was fucking shooting at them! And he was shooting to kill.

Sure enough, just as Jacob expected, the door to the service entrance opened from the inside. Even with the power out, the apartment staff was still working to keep the residents feeling *upscale*. A tall white janitor in stained green coveralls and silver hair latched a chain from the inside door to hook on the outside wall. Unfortunately, his extra large, rolling dolly, loaded with bulging plastic bags reeked of fast-food and surgery drinks, was too wide to negotiate the opening.

The man worked harder than he desired to take the trash to the pair of commercial dumpsters at the far end of the covered loading dock. Jacob found this level of superior customer service to be pathetic. There were no lights, and none of the vehicles worked. Who was coming to get the trash? Jacob grew disgusted with every step the lackey took toward the commercial dumpsters. Now, he wanted to kill the rich woman even more. She was the problem with Salleria. She was a *have*, and he was a *have not*, and with no power anywhere in the city, she was still keeping this guy in a subservient role. No one was in charge anymore. There were no more social classes. God, how much he loathed rich people who didn't care enough for the people who made their lives better. The little people, like the janitors of the world, truly made a difference in life.

Jacob kept staring at the lackey, struggling to empty the trash. *This man is still a slave to the elite. Look at him— he was pathetic.* Jacob thought about killing him, too, but decided this would be his lucky day. Instead, he turned his eyes off the enslaved person and counted. Twelve paces away from the door, thirteen seconds to throw the garbage bags in, then back again. On the man's third trip, Jacob slipped by him unnoticed. He, too, was wearing stained green coveralls. It was the perfect disguise in high society. No one paid attention to the help. Not even the people who could be watching the camera feed in the main security building. He'd be long gone when anyone came to investigate the security breach. His target would be dead.

He quickly found the poorly lit service stairs and took the first flight of stairs cautiously. He didn't want any surprises. He turned his head upwards to the next floor, seeing clear coast. He sprinted up the stairs. The running released pent-up adrenaline, which helped me get under control. Exiting on the fourth floor, Jacob found an unused utility closet, where he stashed the garment bag he had carried in. Eight more floors to go.

Less than three and a half minutes later, he was standing in apartment 1207. With his finger hovering over the peephole in the door, he rang the doorbell in his mind. But he went no further than that. This was just a test run, and it went fairly well. Turning on his heels, he left the way he had come in and hid in the utility closet on the fourth floor. He didn't plan to murder her for another hour. He had his reasons and always followed his plans to the letter. Comfortably seated between what he assumed to be a mop and an industrial floor buffer, a smile broke across his face as he realized with the power out, no one could watch him over the cameras. The odds were stacked in his favor, and he was ready to finish his mission.

He was invisible in the St Paul luxury apartments. No one even looked his way. He had no feelings about his mission one way or the other. If Mr. Smith wanted him to cancel it, he would. Then, when the time came, Jacob would be ready to accomplish his mission. He would kill his target without regret, and Salleria would fall, one murder at a time.

UC

"Did you hear that?" Ashton asked while helping Aiden lay Jared's limp body in the Chief's F-150. "Sounded like a gunshot." "I didn't hear anything, but considering you know a gunshot when you hear it, let's go check it out," Aiden said. "Maybe I'm just hearing things." "Maybe," Aiden responded.

"You heading back into town?" You can follow me to the station, and I'll have Janice cut you a check." Erynn looked at Ashton for a long few seconds that seemed to say, *this one is one the house.* "Not this time Chief. This one is personal. Donate our checks to Jared's parents." Aiden nodded respectfully.

Aiden climbed into the driver's seat and inserted the key into the ignition, saying, "So, if it was an EMP, this truck won't...." His words trailed off as if nothing had happened. "What the hell?" Aiden muttered. He cranked the key again, but still, there was nothing. There was no click. No whining sound. Nothing. Glancing up, he checked the overhead lights, then turned to look in the back seat. "Won't turn on? I have a pair of cables," Ashton said. He stepped closer to the truck, eyeing the dark tail lights. There is no way the EMP theory was true. Right? Ashton was thinking to himself. Somehow he knew he was right, but he didn't want to be correct. With shock in his tone, Aiden looked toward Ashton and said, "I hate to say it, but your EMP theory is starting to look like a real possibility."

Aiden stepped back out onto the parking lot, rocks crunching under the weight of his boots. "I have a theory, Ashton. We will prove your EMP theory to be one hundred percent true if I'm right." Ashton watched warily as the Chief began eyeing his Dodge. Aiden held out his hand. "Give me your keys." Ashton was in the middle of lighting a cigar. He took a long pull from it and threw Aiden his keys. Then, exhaling a cloud of smoke, he asked, "What are you thinking?" Aiden slid behind the wheel of Ashton's Dodge and cranked it. The engine rumbled to life. He turned it off again and looked at Ashton. "How old is your Dodge?" "1989. This baby's just two years younger than me." "Shit," Aiden muttered. "This is not good, Ashton." "You want to tell Erynn and me what the hell is going on, Chief? "You want to know my theory? Well, here it goes, Ashton. I think you are one hundred percent right," Aiden said with disgust and amazement. Ashton shook his head and responded," You've got to be fucking kidding me. I wasn't supposed to be correct." Erynn looked at both men with an I-told-you-so look.

"Haven't you been listening to the news, man?" Aiden said, "The situation with North Kangavar is horrible. There's a rumor that a senator's kid got caught on the wrong side of the border, and we killed many people to get her back. They said we blew up an entire prison or something like that," Aiden finished. Ashton's stomach plummeted. His heart sank. *Am I responsible for all of this,* he thought to himself? He thought about confessing to the Chief about his part in his last mission two years ago that freed the Senator's daughter and her friend. He tried not to think about his final mission too often, but it always weighed heavy on him. And if it was the reason the world was going to end, he didn't want to think about it.

In the two years since leaving the Army, Ashton tried to drown those memories in a bottle. He developed a drinking habit. He wasn't a bad person. He wasn't even a troublemaker. He was a killer designed by the Army. A soldier forged through battle. "Following orders" ruined his life, and now it looked like it would ruin the world. In the end, none of the drinking worked. Every night, he would see Jacobs' face shattered by a high-velocity round. That image would fade into the shock and horror permanently painted on the thin Kangavarian man's face before Bass blew his brains out. Bass, too, was just *following orders.*

Ashton felt like everything he ever touched would burn, and this time, he touched the country. For now, he knew Aiden didn't have proof the North Kangavarians were behind the

EMP attack, and there was no way he could know Ashton had been part of the team that rescued Romani's daughter. "I do not doubt that the flash we saw in the sky was an EMP. Our first two objectives should be to protect our resources and get more intel," Aiden said, interrupting Ashton's conscience.

"Hold on, Chief," Ashton said, holding up his hands. "If this is true, then we need to assume every house, car, and electrical device in the region would be dead, which explains your car, the radio, and our cellphones. It's also the reason we can't see the Wakefield lights because everyone has lost power. So, how are we supposed to get more intel? And why is my car still working?" "Aiden jerked his chin toward the fires in the distance. "Your Dodge was built before these fancy computers were installed in cars. You also don't have any electronic parts. So you didn't have anything for the EMP to kill. As far as how are we going to get more intel? I have no idea. Hopefully, our radios work," Aiden answered.

"Must have been a powerful EMP to drop those jets out of the air," Aiden continued. "My guess is, all of this area is without power." "Looks like we are all carpooling then," Aiden finished while still sitting in Ashton's car seat. "I guess we are riding in the back of our own car Erynn," Ashton offered as a response. "Okay, but hurry it up. I need to pee." Aiden said. "Yeah. I need to check on my sister." Ashton replied. Once everyone moved towards the Dodge, Aiden walked somberly towards his truck and lifted Jared's body. He overlooked Erynn and Ashton following behind him, but this time, Aiden let them both help. It was a silent communication of respect.

They carried his little body out of the F-150 and into the back of the Dodge. Erynn sat in the front seat, Ashton was in the back, and Aiden was driving. The blanket covering Jared's face slipped as Ashton carefully set him inside. Then, reaching over the back seats, he used deliberate care and pulled it back up to cover his face. Aiden took notice and made one more trip back to his F-150 and retrieved a heavy duffel bag, a shotgun, and his Colt M4 Carbine. He stacked them neatly in the back of the Ashton's Dodge. Aiden got into the driver's seat and put the keys into the ignition and his foot on the break. Before he could switch gears, he screamed, causing Ashton and Erynn to panic. "Oh my God," he shouted. "What!" Ashton asked. "I just realized something." An uncomfortable silence filled the truck. "Nuclear Fallout," Aiden said quietly. "If that was a nuke, the radiation could kill us all." Erynn shook her head and put her face in the palm of her hand.

Chapter Six

Fifty-nine minutes after his flawless rehearsal, Jacob Smith returned to the twelfth floor. He stood in front of apartment 1207, mission ready. The power was still out, and the floor was dark. His cover, should anyone ask, was being called up to the room to take out the trash or do whatever the janitors did. He figured he would make it up to fit whoever had the nerve to get into his business.

His target was one of Wakefield's wealthy and careless Sallerian tenants. This time was for real, and someone would die soon. His stomach was queasy. Today was a big day for him and his cause. Anna Dean was his target, and her death was essential.

Knock. Knock. Knock. Jacob didn't bother with the doorbell. The power was out. He had been dreaming of this moment for such a long time. The three knocks he tapped on the door were ten years in the making. "Yes?" "Hi, ma'am. As one of our VIP tenets, your apartment has been scheduled for scheduled butler service every six hours during the power outage." Jacob had practiced this line a hundred times in his head for months. He added the bit bout the power outage while he was sitting in the fourth-floor utility closet. "I am here to take out your trash and do anything else that is unworthy of someone with your prestige, ma'am." He made this lineup on the spot. He thought it was an excellent touch to stroke her ego before he killed her for his cause.

There was no doubt he would look like any other black-skinned maintenance worker to this woman — someone who was *supposed* to notice details in her line of work. First, she was a well-known journalist with her television show on CNN. Second, she had the third-highest ratings and viewers, right after Anderson Cooper, first, and Don Lemon, second. Third, there was Anna Dean. She covered the "Mr. Smith" trial in 2012, and she was *not truthful.* She smeared his older brother, and now it was time for him to smear her all over the walls of her apartment.

"I'm not dressed right now, and no one called," she said. "I don't know anything about it, but I would be grateful if you come back later." "I was supposed to clock out ten minutes ago, ma'am, and no one else returns for two days. But that is okay. I will leave you to it, and I think they will find someone for you tomorrow." Anna sighed with the unconcealed exasperation of a person with too little time for regular people. "Oh, for God's sake," she said. "Come in, then. Hurry it up. You have the worse timing. I'm not dressed. And what the hell is going on with the lights?"

At the click of the deadbolt, Jacob readied himself. As soon as she cracked the door and he saw her nose, he charged forward like a rhino. And he was as one. He didn't need extreme force, he didn't necessarily like her attitude, and he wanted her to regret being disrespectful. Anna fell back several steps and then crashed down hard on her behind. The towel she was wrapped in came loose. She had a nice bottom and perfect breasts. She must have been taking a shower. He wondered if the water was still running. She came out of her flip-flops and exposed beautiful toes polished with pink toenails. He had to admit to himself; she was gorgeous. She had beautiful pink nipples with medium-sized areoles and six-pack abs. Her blond hair covered part of her chest as she fell, but not enough for him to notice how she hit the genetic lottery.

Before her shock gave way to a scream, Jacob pressed against her chest with his total body weight. "Before you scream, Anna, I am not a rapist. You will not be violated sexually. The circle spindle of silver duct tape he had taped to his back quickly transferred to the woman's mouth. He made sure the tape was on hard. He didn't want her to have any hope. She was not going to live to see the next hour. "You are going to die. If you resist, I will kill you, no questions asked. No warning. You will not get a second chance." She must have believed him because she did not resist. "If you don't resist, I will let you live," he said, one of his many lies.

He flipped her onto her stomach, exposing her naked body from the doggy-style position. Then, he strapped a Bible to her stomach with duct tape. He wasn't religious, but the Bible would play its part soon enough. It was a *clue,* and just the first that he would leave here for the police to discover. Anna was about forty. She was a natural blonde and physically fit. He brought his knife because he was going to cut off her clothes and strip her naked, but his plan worked so well. She did all the hard work for him.

Leaning forward, he laid on top of her, fully clothed; of course, he would not insert her today. He wanted her to feel that he could if he wanted. With a cold voice, he whispered, "Get up, you whore. You thought it was okay to kill my brother with your words publicly. Now, you will die in front of your darling public. You claimed to be reporting the *naked truth*. Now, you will be naked to see our truth.

He startled her when she tried to rise with a sharp grab to her throat. He had her naked and on her stomach and grabbed her throat. He imagined this would be something she would enjoy under different circumstances, but not tonight. And not by some peasant. No! She only gave herself to the rich and famous. A janitor could never see her like this.

It was time for her to die. The clue was secure, and his actress was ready. In her living room was a wall filled with books; a few were Anna's. Just ahead was a glass sliding door. It led to a terrace filled with fancy garden furniture and a shiny black grill. "Don't move. I need to set the stage for your beautiful death," Jacob said with no emotion. He quickly set up the living room just the way he wanted. Then, he returned to his naked victim, who hadn't moved. She was a suitable victim. He liked that.

"I must say, Anna, looking at you now. You are much prettier in person. Your tv show doesn't do your body the justice it deserves. You are prettier in real life. Sexier without clothes." He paused for a few seconds. He wanted the moment to wash over her. She needed to feel violated by his words, just as she did his brother ten years before. "Now, get up. I want you to go to those sliding doors, climb over the railing, and jump to your death. You are going to be even more famous, Anna. I promise. Your fans are waiting for you." As Anna heard these words, she sobbed through her duct tape. Tears fell from her eyes. She pleaded for her life, but Jacob didn't listen. She was going to die. Finally, he leaned towards her left ear in the middle of her sobs and said seven words that got her attention, "Jump. Or I will slit your throat."

Alison's lungs felt like they were about to explode as she ran through the woods. The Major was on her right, keeping her pace. He didn't seem to be struggling, but he also hadn't run as far as she had. She was a runner, but Ernest seemed to be the Greek God of running. It looked like he was just getting started. Her thighs were on fire. Today was turning out to be a horrible day, she thought. She twisted her ankle on a large rock. "Keep moving," Ernest whispered.

Moonlight and adrenaline guided them deeper into the forest and closer to Wakefield. She was worried about Ernest's shoulder. There was no way that the jolt and friction of running were not tearing him apart. His pain tolerance must have been incredible. He never complained once. *Crack!* Another shot from the asshole chasing them nearly took off her head. Frustrated, Ernest told her to stop running and to take cover. She knelt next to him with her Glock 30 in her hand. Alison remembered Ernest asking earlier if she knew how to shoot her weapon. There was no time to answer, but she would get to Paige, no matter what. Although Ashton had taught her well, it didn't matter if she knew how to use it. She understood for the first time and was willing to use it.

Alison's breaths came out in foggy visuals. She was wet, cold, and bleeding a bit from a few scratches from tree branches due to running away from the asshole shooting at them. "Do you see him," Ernest asked after a few moments of silence." No, maybe he gave up," she responded? "How far are we from town?" Ernest asked, "Maybe ten minutes if we keep up this pace." Ernest looked over Alison's shoulder, squinting as if he was trying to focus. She turned and froze. Alison's heart was punching her ribs when she saw a colossal silhouette moving through the trees. As the figure moved toward them, she realized it wasn't the asshole shooting at them. It was something much worse. It was a bear. A real bear! And it looked hungry.

After a few intense moments of an empty stare down, the bear roared, and a smaller silhouette moved into the light. It was a bear cub. "She's just protecting her child," Ernest said to Alison. "Back away slowly and let her have that path." They both slowly backed. When Alison thought running was safe, she took off at nearly full speed. The mother bear did not give chase; she only wanted her child's safety. Alison could relate. She would kill anyone to protect Paige.

She had difficulty seeing anything, with only the moon's glimmer guiding them. She couldn't tell if they were being followed, but she knew the bear didn't give chase. Where was *Captain Asshole?* She hoped the bear scared him off, too. She had to get Ernest into town to get answers and get to Paige. Her daughter would be in bed by now, so Alison figured she had at least eight hours to find a ride to East Wakefield to get her daughter. She needed to trust Nathan more to make good decisions in the case of an emergency. And if Ernest was telling the truth, Salleria was in one big crisis.

Finally, they reached the road leading into town. "Do you know where we are?" Ernest asked. "We are at the city limits. The police station is right over..." her sentence was caught off by an unwanted welcomed company. "There you are!" The man with the assault rifle stumbled out of the bushes. "Dammit," Ernest growled. He held up a hand. "Listen, sir. We don't want any trouble. I'm just trying to get to town." "Should we run?" she whispered. Ernest shook his head from side to side. He was tired of running. "I told you to wait up," the man said. He pointed his assault rifle at them both.

"Is this some terrorist attack? "The only terrorist I see, sir, is you," Ernest said in defiance. "Bullshit libtard. This is our country." Ernest had reached his limit with this guy. Rules of Engagement or not, before this man shot another round, he was going to kill him right where he stood. "I need to know. I need to prepare," the barrel-chested man said, still holding his assault rifle at Ernest and Alison. Ernest refused to reply. Alison was growing angry. The man didn't know both of them were armed. He was lucky they didn't return fire, but that luck was running out. She had to get to Paige, and this asshole was in the way.

Still pointing the assault rifle, the man continued to walk toward them. "You hard of hearing or what?" Again, Ernest purposely didn't respond. Ernest must have been planning to attack. Alison decided she would attack him. She understood that the time was now or never. Alison had to get to her daughter, and Ernest had to get a message to someone important. She had no idea how this fat-muscular asshole kept up with them. Maybe he knew they were coming to this trial, and he took a shortcut. But Alison decided to shoot him as soon as she could see his trigger finger. It was too dark, and she needed him just a bit closer. She didn't know what Ernest would do, but she was sure he was getting ready for a battle.

The man took a few more steps closer. Keep coming, Alison said inside her head. Just three more steps, you asshole. Almost there. Three more steps, and you are dead. Two more. One more.

Out of nowhere, headlight beams swept across the road and steadied on the man with the assault rifle. "Well, I'll be damned. It looks like the cars are back on," Mr. Assault Rifle shouted. Ernest grabbed Alison by the wrist, moved her behind him, and acted as a human shield. She barely knew Ernest, but the more he protected her, the more she admired him. "Hey, bitch, who said you could move? Goddammit!" The man shouldered his assault rifle and pointed it directly at Alison. With a cold tone, Ernest pushed her behind his body and responded, "If you point that weapon at her again, I will kill you." He reached for his gun for the first time." Ernest was angry and didn't plan on being held up for another minute.

The source of the headlights was an old 1989 Dodge Ram. Alison smiled for the first time since her car had died. "That's my brother," she whispered into Ernest's ear. Ernest didn't move and kept his eyes on the man in the red hat. The Dodge stopped directly behind Alison and Ernest but kept its headlights on the man pointing the assault rifle. Two men and a beautiful woman stepped onto the road. It was her brother, Erynn, and the Chief.

"Evenin', Chief," the man in the red MSGA hat said. He was still pointing his assault rifle at them. Aiden got out of the Dodge driver's seat, holding his rifle. From what Alison could see, he didn't like what he saw. A man in a military uniform shielded Ashton's sister from a man pointing an assault rifle at them. He was the only person with a weapon drawn. For now, Aiden kept the muzzle of his rifle towards the ground. "Colten," Aiden replied coldly. "Want to tell me why you are pointing that assault rifle at two people?" Ashton and Erynn took opposite flanking positions, Erynn to the left and Ashton to the right. Unlike Aiden, they had their HK416 assault rifles pointed at Colten, the armed suspect.

"Reckon, we're under attack, Chief. Just trying to get some answers," Colten replied. "These people aren't a threat to you. They aren't the ones attacking us," Aiden said. "Why don't you lower your gun? I don't think this fight ends too well for you. You do see who I have with me, don't you?" Colten looked at the two people pointing their guns at him. He didn't recognize either one of them. "I don't know either one of them, Chief. Maybe they are the people attacking us, Colten answered defiantly. "Ghost, why don't you introduce you and your friend to Mr. Colten Browning here? I think he might benefit from knowing you two," Aiden said without taking his eyes off Colten.

"I'm your huckleberry," Ashton said with all the Creole twang he could muster. "This is just my game," he finished. Alison chuckled. She got the reference. Ashton quoted his favorite character from a scene from the 1993 historical action film *Tombstone*. Ashton wasn't done yet, however. "Alison, why don't you come next to me before our good friend Mr. Ringo finishes his conversation with Wyatt Earp," Ashton said with extreme sarcasm. "Don't worry. If he moves a muscle, Erynn will show Mr. Ringo what the waiting room in heaven looks like."

Alison ran towards her brother while whispering something in the Major's ear that no one could hear but him. Ashton reached out and gave his sister a cold, wet hug. Ashton couldn't resist himself. He just had to say, "Why, Johnny Ringo, you look like someone just walked over your grave." Erynn made a big show of shouldering her rifle, even though it was already pointed at Colten. She wanted him to see her do it again. Alison knew Ashton was quoting Doc Holiday. With a .45 single action revolver, history says Doc Holiday could shoot a target and replace the gun in his holster in .0175 seconds, and over his lifetime, he won more than 3500 trophies, 800 championship titles, and bagged 18 world records in speed-shooting. Rumor was, Erynn was faster. The asshole that had been shooting at them for the past twenty mins was dead if he tried anything.

However, Alison was more focused on her brother. She knew that look he had in his eye. It was a strange calmness under pressure. She didn't understand how he did it. Alison snuck a look at Erynn. She had a grin that looked much like Ashton's. Erynn and Ashton would be the perfect couple. She couldn't understand why he didn't just settle down with her. They were the only two people on earth who ever understood each other. Ashton once told Alison, Erynn was surgical with a weapon. She hadn't seen it before, but if this guy pointing a gun at them didn't calm down, Alison feared she was about to see first hand. Ashton told her Erynn never missed. Never. He said she was the *god of death*.

"What the hell are you doing out here, Alison?" Ashton whispered. "It's a long story, but your training kept me alive more than once," she told him. Aiden walked closer to Colten, with his muzzle still towards the ground and his pistol holstered on his right hip. His left hand held his rifle towards the ground. "I'm not going to tell you again to lower that rifle, Colten." "I want answers, goddammit," Colten said as he shifted focus from Ernest and pointed the barrel of his rifle toward Aiden. This was a big mistake. With one synchronized motion, Erynn and Ashton took three steps forward, and we're now in point-blank range of Colten. Erynn aimed between Colten's eyes. Ashton aimed at Colten's heart. There was no way he was going to survive this encounter. She was amazed at how Erynn and Ashton knew where to aim and what each other would do before they did it.

"You are completely outgunned, Colten. Don't die at the hands of friendly's. Save your bullets for the real enemy," Ashton said to Colten. Alison remembered hearing that Chief Aiden was charismatic and handled most of his problems with words, not arrests. Except when it came to her brother. He was always picking on her brother. "I'm just protecting myself, Chief," Colten said. "From what, Colten? Have these two done anything to you? Did they make the power go out?" "No," Colten replied. "Then how about you put the gun down before my friends here start protecting me like I am Wyatt Earp. I like the movie *Tombstone*." Alison was impressed that Aiden got the reference from a few moments ago. "They probably like that movie a little too much. Think you can be Doc Holiday later, Ghost." Aiden said. "Nope. Say when Ringo. Say when," Ashton's tone implied he was done with the back-and-forth banter. "Colten. I'd listen carefully, and I don't think my friends are giving us more time to negotiate." Colten looked at all five of his targets. Three of them had guns he could see, and he had no idea what the bitch and the Army boy were carrying.

Major Ernest said in a firm voice. "This police officer asked you to drop your gun. It seems to me that would be the easiest option here, sir." Colten's nostrils flared, and his eyes widened as he focused on the Chief. "Drop the gun," Aiden repeated in a low voice. "This is your final warning, Colten." "I'm a Sallerian, dammit. Not a fucking terrorist," Colten said. "You're going to have to pry my gun out my dead cold..." before Colten could finish his sentence, with one quick motion, Aiden moved his Colt M4 Carbine to Colten's forehead and pressed the cold steel against it. "I do not have time for this right now, Colten. Mr. Ghost? Ms. Erynn? could one of you, please take *Johnny Ringo's* weapon away for him before he gets shot in the head.

Ashton didn't hesitate. He pried the gun away from Colten. "You're going to regret that, Nigger," Colten said to Ashton. Major Ernest punched Colten in the jaw, knocking him down. "Don't say that word around me, sir. And be glad I kept my weapon holstered." Colten looked up from the ground. Then, anger in his eyes, he responded angrily, "You are a white man taking up for these darkies?" Before anyone could react, Ernest kicked dirt in his mouth, causing him to choke, "Don't say that word, either, sir." Alison wanted to scowl at the downed man, but she was more impressed with Ernest. "My sister is black, my mother is black, and my nephew is black, sir," Ernest snarled. This comment drew curious eyes from everyone, none more than Alison. She vowed to ask him about this as soon as she could.

Ernest backed away, never drawing his sidearm, respecting the military's rules of engagement, even in the face of certain death. "Sir," Ernest directed his politeness to the Wakefield Police Chief, Aiden Jahmar. "My name is Major Ernest Maddox, Sallerian Airforce, Special Operations Command. I am on a Top Secret assignment and could use a ride into town. Will that be a problem?" "Nope, I've got much better movies than *Tombstone* back in my office at the Police Station. How about we leave here and watch one together, Major?" Aiden said as he took Colten's gun from Ashton and slung it over his back.

Ashton was still glaring at Colten. "This guy is not getting in my Dodge Chief unless I'm his Huckleberry first," Colten spat on the ground. "I wouldn't dream of it nig... Colten thought twice about repeating the word." Aiden took Colten's weapon off his back, walked over to him, and gave it back. "I'm giving this back to you, fully loaded. Please don't make me regret this, Colten. I feel we will need your gun for the enemy very soon. Remember who the enemy is next time," Aiden said kindly. Alison saw he indeed did have a way with people. The rumors were accurate; Aiden had a way with people. He was like a wizard. Colten seemed to be calming down.

When the rescue team, plus the Major and Alison, got to the Dodge, Aiden offered his hand to Ernest. "Chief of Police Aiden Jahmar." "Major Ernest Maddox." They shook hands, and everyone got in the truck. It was a tight fit with all of them in the Dodge, but it was better than having a racist aiming a gun at them. "What happened up there, Major?" Aiden asked politely. Ernest politely bypassed the question. "You didn't see my wingman eject, did you?" "Afraid not, but I didn't see you eject either so that he could have made it out." Aiden looked toward the back of the Dodge. "We're transporting the body of a young boy back to town. "Oh, My God. You all found Jared," Alison asked. Jared and Paige were about the same age, which only lit a fire under her to get to East Wakefield faster. Her mind went to the worse scenario. What if Paige is dead, too?

Candles burned on a centrally-located wooden table, and the glow dancing off the walls could be seen everywhere. Vice President Monique Maddox had one of the most recognizable faces in the United Cities. She did her very best to avoid the gazes of everyone lined in the streets and took comfort in candlelit houses. But, unfortunately, Alison didn't have any answers for anyone. She didn't know anything, so she needed to get to the command as quickly as possible.

An older woman with a cane shuffled over towards Monique. "Vice President, do you," Brayden met her halfway and redirected the question to himself. "Do you know why the lights are out, sir? It's cold in my apartment. When are they going to turn the heat back on?" Monique always had a heart for the people of Salleria. She patted Brayden on the shoulder and whispered something in the woman's ear that made her smile. After that, the older woman left without further issues. "How do you do that, Madam Vice President," Brayden asked. "The same way you calm me down, Brayden, when you see I am not okay. You remind me that I am more important than the situation," Monique answered with a smile.

Without waiting for a response from Brayden, she heaved her backpack over her shoulders and motioned for Brayden to lead the way. It had to be after midnight now, but she needed to be more sure. She wasn't sure how long she was asleep.

The streets were filled with people looking for answers. Finally, the double glass doors swung open, and Weston Levy rushed inside wearing his usual navy blue suit, his combat dress shoes, and his Secret Service body armor that fit neatly under his suit and over his very muscular frame. Upon entering the apartment lobby, he cleared the room with the beam of a heavy flashlight, stopping when he saw Monique. "Damn, it's good to see you, Wes," Monique said. Her eyes flitted to his shoes. "How are you so well dressed right now? No one can even find their bearings, yet you and you managed to find a full suit and concealed combat gear," Monique said jokingly. Weston wiped his forehead. "You know me, ma'am. Always ready to protect you and go to war, if needed." "Is your family okay?" Monique asked. "My wife Tracy is taking our daughters Sasha And Tera to her mom's house first thing in the morning. It's about a day's walk out of the city. My brother Thomas is going with them." "That's probably a good idea," Monique said. She reached up to put a hand on Weston's shoulder. "I appreciate you sticking with me, like always, Big Wes. I know you'd rather be with them." "Not abandoning you now, ma'am." His Texas drawl was strong and reassuring.

Monique was glad to have him by her side. Weston was her right-hand man and her protector. No one made her feel safer, and no one was more loyal to her than Weston. Between Weston and Brayden, she had all seeded to survive. All she needed now was the answers to what the hell was going on. But she figured answers would come later. For now, surviving the night was her highest priority. The six-foot-eight former basketball player had been on her security detail for five years, and he'd seen her through some hard times. She valued Weston more than anyone because he protected her with his life and was far more kind to her than he was protective. She was grateful more than he could ever know.

"Let's head out," Weston commanded. "We need to get you to the White House, ma'am." "Are you sure that's a good idea? Maybe we should stay put for now," Brayden responded. "We trained for this, sir. We will ensure you and the Vice President are safely escorted to The White House." Brayden didn't put up a fight. He nodded kindly. "We're not going to fix anything by staying here," Monique said. "Let's go." Weston opened the door and waved them onto the sidewalk. Weston kept out in front, walking slowly. One hand inside his suit jacket, the other directing a flashlight on every civilian. Until he got Monique to safety, everyone was a threat.

Darkness swallowed the city. "Stay close, ma'am." Monique did as Weston said and walked directly behind him, leaving little room for an ambush. Weston was efficient. He centered his flashlight on the sidewalk, pointing out hazards for Brayden and Monique to avoid. Monique looked around at all the candles flickering in the windows of apartment buildings. Some people were already panicking, while others played board games under candlelight to make the time pass. Finally, everyone asked the same question: "Why are the lights off?"

Monique saw the subtle movement from Weston. He motioned Monique and Brayden to cross the street as they approached a local grocery store. It was being looted. Broken glass covered the sidewalk, and Weston quickly decided to ignore it. "Keep moving. This is not our fight," he said while escorting them.

Monique feared there would be more looting or riots if the power didn't come back soon. She thought about her brother Ernest and prayed he could make it to Chase. *Please let my son be okay, God. Please.* She tried to keep herself calm because falling apart wouldn't help Chase or Ernest. The country needed her. Her son needed her.

"My car won't turn on," Monique heard a young woman yelling at a local police officer who was failing to keep the crowd under control. "Someone needs to tell the city to get their shit together and fix the power," a man yelled. "Idiot," snapped another woman. "Haven't you been listening to the news? North Kangavar probably attacked us." "Please, people, calm down," the officer said. But, unfortunately, there was another officer with him.

Without power, any communications and emergency services would be hard to come by. Civilization would fall apart quickly. Even a short-term failure of the banks and financial system would be enough to trip supply chains to a halt. Monique knew if people couldn't get the medicines they needed for their loved ones, all hell would break loose. She had to get to the White House and figure out what was happening.

She went over scenarios in her mind. But the more she thought about it, the more it didn't make sense. Why would North Kangavar launch a preemptive EMP attack? Surely, they knew mutually assured destruction would come next. Both Salleria and North Kangavar would be annihilated. She thought about how long it would take for both countries' allies to get involved. Fearing the entire world was about to go to war, she wondered what would be the benefit of billions of people losing their lives. It just didn't make any sense. Who could benefit from worldwide, mutually assured destruction?

"Wouldn't go that way if I were you," a teenage boy shouted at Monique and her crew. He was walking with four other kids his age. "Somebody got shot in the head as soon as the lights went off. You can see his brains all over the ground." The teenagers were standing on the corner of the sidewalk now. They pointed toward an ambulance halfway down the street. Oddly, it was in the area when the shots were fired. Several people were lingering around the paramedics. "Go home," Weston ordered. "Already on the way!" the teenager responded for his group.

Monique could see the wheels turning in Weston's mind. With a wave of his flashlight, he directed them onward. They kept to the side of the street opposite the paramedics. She could tell Weston was preparing for an attack from them. Maybe he thought they were hitmen dressed as paramedics, and they set this entire scenario up. She wondered about the odds of an ambulance being around the corner when someone was murdered.

She stared intently at the medics. Why were they working on someone who received a headshot wound? She knew Weston was not the type of man who would leave anything to chance. As they walked closer, one of the paramedics looked their way. The other, a woman, lifted herself from the body. Monique's adrenaline spiked! Weston removed his hand from the inside of his jacket. With it was his Glock 19 MOS Gen5 Pistol, the new sidearm issued to Secret Service Officers. Weston stopped halfway before extending his right arm in their direction. "Call it," the female paramedic said as she stood and pulled off bloody gloves. They were not assassins, just everyday heroes doing their jobs. Weston returned his weapon to his shoulder harness. "Let's keep moving, Ma'am," he said to Monique. Everyone was on edge.

Monique was still focused on the bloody gloves and didn't notice the blur of motion coming around the corner until it was too late. Someone threw a brick into a liquor store and smashed the windows. "Grab the hard shit," someone shouted as two men rushed into the liquor store. "Get back," Weston said, waving Monique and Brayden behind him. A woman screamed as the two hooded men used bricks to punch away the jagged glass. They dropped the bricks, climbed inside, and filled their arms with what they could carry. Bystanders jumped in and began to take bottles as well. Weston held out a tree trunk of an arm and ushered her away from the broken windows.

"Ma'am, let's go." More people were watching now, and the crowd was now growing bigger. "Ma'am!" Weston repeated when Monique didn't move. He turned to look at her, his eyes widening as he saw the gun in her hands. She could see the shock in his eyes. Yet, he remained calm and respectful when asked, "Carrying your sidearm tonight, Madam Vice President?" He was staring at her Glock 30. Pulling her weapon after seeing the bloody gloves and hearing the loud crash of the brick behind her was a reflex. She was trained to protect herself, Vice President or not. The smooth handle of the gun felt reassuring in her hands. She was determined to make it to The White House. She had to get to her son.

"Hey, you!" Shouted a voice from a distance. Two figures were approaching. They were police officers with shotguns shouldered. "Agent Levy, Secret Service," Weston called back. He held out his badge, but both officers were already directing their guns toward the looters. "Hands on your head!" one of them shouted. Both of the men stepped forward, glass crunching under their shoes. The bigger of the pair dropped all his liquor bottles to the ground with a dramatic crash ending in liquid splashing everywhere. "Don't move!" The other officer yelled. The looters took off in separate directions, and dozens of other looters ran out of the liquor store simultaneously. Good try, officers, Monique thought to herself, but law and order are pointless until we fix the power and give the public some good answers. The officers gave chase, and Monique finally lowered her gun. She stuck it back into her waistband as the police vanished around the next corner. "Ma'am," Weston began to say. "I know. Let's go," Monique interrupted Big Wes, expecting him to reprimand her. "I'm glad you have your Glock tonight, ma'am. I have a feeling things are going to get much worse. We could use the extra gun." Weston said while moving them away from the liquor store.

The paramedics retreated to their ambulance, and the crowd moved on. People began looting the liquor store until the last bottle was gone. The chatter of the shocked citizens echoed down the streets. Weston kept his gun out as he crossed onto Pennsylvania Avenue. The dome of the Capitol looked eerie in the moonlight. It was strangely beautiful. It also depressed Monique because it was too far away.

They turned down 12th street. At a walking pace, it would take about fourteen minutes if they took Pennsylvania Avenue NW to get to the White House. There would be some restricted streets with unique access, and she figured Weston planned to use them since all three had clearance. They walked around the dead vehicles, some still guarded by their owners. Every driver was waiting to be rescued or told what to do. They peppered

Monique with dozens of questions as soon as they recognized who she was. She didn't have any answers for any of them.

She couldn't help but think how they were defensively trekking down Pennsylvania Avenue in total darkness, armed, and defending themselves from Sallerian citizens. Getting answers was slowly becoming her second problem. Stopping the fall of civilization had just pushed itself to the top spot. The United Cities did not seem ready for a country-wide catastrophe. People had only been without their cell phones and take-out dinners for an hour and a half. What would happen if this lasted for a week? Monique thought about what was happening to everyone who was on life support. She thought about all the people in the middle of surgery when the power went out. What happened to them? How many people were dying on surgery tables as she was hiding from citizens on Pennsylvania Avenue?

She was lost in her thoughts when suddenly, *Pop, pop, pop.* Gunshots sounded nearby, and Monique's hand instinctively went for her gun. West took a combat position. Monique pushed Brayden behind Weston and took her combat position in the rear. All three of them scanned the area for immediate threats. There was no way to know if officers were firing on the dangers or if the threats were firing on officers. After a few long, tense moments, Weston waved them forward with the beam of his flashlight. "Come on, ma'am. We're almost there." The familiar shapes of Pershing Park emerged in the darkness.

Monique kept pace with Weston stride-for-stride. They had made it to The United Cities Department of Treasury when another sound seemed to shake the earth beneath them. It started as a low rumbling sound. A roaring sound followed them. And morphed into a loud whooshing a few moments later. Shortly after and loud and deep double *Boom* exploded in the air like a thousand car crashes simultaneously.

Monique, Weston, and Brayden halted in the middle of the empty street. Far beyond the edges of the dark city, something had risen into the sky above the ocean, leaving a trail of fiery exhaust. Their eyes followed the path upwards. To her surprise, Monique instantly recognized the nuclear-tipped ballistic missiles. *Mutually assured destruction,* she thought before letting out a deep sigh.

Intellectually, she had already accepted that this could be the world's end. But seeing so many nukes leaving Sallerian air space while protecting herself from Sallerian civilians made this moment surreal. She would never forget tonight. No one would. It would be far more destructive than what hit Salleria. There were so many missiles streaking into the clouds. She imagined them curving away from a Sallerian submarine lurking somewhere under the chilly surface of the Atlantic Ocean.

There was no doubt they were headed to North Kangavar. "My God," Brayden said. "Not God," Monique whispered, "Humans." She was losing hope of ever seeing her son again. Weston lowered his gun and flashlight like a soldier surrendering to the enemy. "Were those nukes, ma'am?" Monique nodded, "Yes. Yes, they were," She said to her most trusted friend. The Vice President watched the final missile disappear into the sky. And then she took off running towards the White House.

Jacob Smith smacked Anna on her naked butt as she struggled to her feet. The Bible clue was tapped firmly to her flat stomach. She was such a beautiful specimen, and Jacob's excitement grew with her every step. She trembled as she backed onto the opened sliding doors until the iron railing caught the small of her back.

She looked him in the eyes. She was pleading for her life. Twelve stories below, there was no foot traffic. That was about the change. The loud thump of her body and the screams of the first witnesses would bring everyone outside to witness his glorious stage play.

Jacob tore the tape from her mouth. Then, finally, it was time for her to perform. He wanted her to be as loud as she was ten years ago when she was smearing his brother's name. So, in a low voice that resembled a growl, Jacob said to her, "Scream, Anna. Scream like you mean it. Scream, or I will slit your throat right now."

"Please., Please don't kill me. I will give you anything you want," Anna pleaded with Jacob quietly. She was not a good stage partner, and he stared at her angrily. He figured he would play along for now. After all, *Vengeance was his.* She continued, "Please, I have a lot of money. You can have anything you want. There is a safe in my room. It has hundreds of thousands in it." "What I want, Anna, is for you to pay for your sins. You have a new God now, and his wrath is upon you." Before Jacob finished his sentence, he cut the left side of her neck. The cut was deep enough to draw blood but not deep enough to kill her. She would fall to her death tonight. Exactly how she made his brother's legacy fall.

Anna screamed in both pain and horror. "There you go." Again, he cut her right shoulder. This time the cut was deep. She would need stitches. It was such a shame to ruin her perfect body. Anna screamed even louder. "Yes! Now, you are being a good girl. Scream again." Anna screamed so loud people began to poke their heads out of their windows and patio doors. A small crowd started to gather on the terrace below.

Jacob leaned in closer and pressed the knife deep into her right shoulder. The screams poured in. With a quick movement, he grabbed Anna by her legs, and with a powerful hoist, he had her over the railing, hanging upside down. She screamed, and she screamed. Once people could see in the darkness that someone was holding her over the railing, other screams joined hers. He was so delighted. It sounded like a symphony of screams.

His audience would not believe what they were about to see. Finally, Jacob released his hold of Anna and gravity took over. She screamed down each floor, and her body exploded on the pavement. Her bones shattered, and her blood collided with everyone on the terrace. Even the grill wasn't spared. It received its fair share of blood. Backing away talking to himself, Jacob said coldly, *"Vengeance is his."*

Chapter Seven

Hundreds of people were staring at Ashton's truck. It was the only known car working.

Ashton was still attempting to process everything that had happened in the past four hours, and Major Maddox wasn't helping. "This is all confidential," Ernest was saying. "Understood," Aiden said. "First Lieutenant Pace and I were sent on a combat air patrol earlier this evening at the governor's request. It seemed like a routine CAP. Thirty minutes in, the air traffic control from Spindle Air Force Base in Soumen contacted the two other pilots from the 19th to check out an Avrinyth commercial airliner heading toward Odawa over the Wakefield Mountains. A few minutes after that, the Avrinyth pilots became unresponsive. The airliner changed course toward Lakota and started climbing." "Avrinyth?"

Ashton asked. "So this wasn't North Kangavar?" "Let the major finish," Aiden said. "I'm guessing there's more to the story." Ernest nodded. "It wasn't an Avrinyth plane; it was a North Kangavarian Ilyushin Il-28 carrying a nuclear weapon. The best way I can figure it out is the North Kangavarians used fake transponder codes to look like an Avrinyth plane. Everyone knows the Kangavarians are some of the world's best hackers. Pace and I turned around for support when the plane went off the radar. By the time we saw the blast, it was too late. The EMP fried our systems, and I was falling out of the sky." Ashton felt his soul leave his body. He felt this was all his fault. His jaw clenched as if he was trying to eat the confession of his last mission in North Kangavar twenty-four months earlier.

Alison caught his gaze in the rearview mirror. "I have to find a working radio to contact Command," Ernest said. "Do you have any ham radios at the station?" Aiden shook his head. "Sorry, Major. We are all digital. A big mistake now." "My nephew is in Chesterfolk. If I can't find a radio here, my next priority is to reach him. How far is it from here?" "It's about ninety miles south of here. That's two hours by car and at least twenty-five hours on foot," Ashton answered. "And that doesn't include," Aiden jerked the Dodge around an abandoned car, barely missing it. "Hey! Watch my car, Chief." Aiden ignored the sly remark from Ashton and asked Ernest, "Major, what about the nuke? How much of the grid would it have knocked out?" "Hard to say. Depends on how power-ful the nuke was." "Guess," Ashton said.

Ernest rubbed his head to help him think. "From what I know about nuclear attacks, experts say about three or four simultaneously detonated nukes over the right parts of Salleria would take out the entire country. Especially if each of the warheads were detonated high enough." "How far up was that plane?" Ashton asked. "Over fifty thousand feet," Ernest replied. "It is possible all of Salleria is in the dark." Alison gasped from the back seat. "The entire country?" "What about radiation?" Aiden asked. "Should we be worried?" Ernest focused his brown eyes on Aiden. "It depends on the wind, but either way, eventually, the nuclear fallout will turn Salleria into a post-apocalyptic video game with mutated creatures or whatever happens with Nuclear fallout." "I'll ask my officers to find the battery-operated Geiger counters as soon as we get back to the station," Aiden replied.

A stiff silence filled the vehicle. Ashton wished some tunes would play on the radio to lighten the mood, but no regular channels were broadcasting. The idea of locking himself in a room and forgetting everything crossed his mind, but what would that help? The last two years wouldn't just disappear because he did.

Aiden eased off the gas as they approached a group of people waving in the center of the road just outside of town. "Keep driving," Ashton ordered. "We probably have the only working vehicle in the country." No one spoke for several moments. Finally, Alison broke the silence with a whimper. She cupped her head with her hands. "This day keeps getting worse. First, that text, then," "What text?" Ashton asked. Alison looked up and shook her head. "It's nothing. I need to get to Paige." "Don't worry, Sis. We'll get her after we get to the station."

Jacob pretended to panic with the rest of the onlookers. He stood between two poorly dressed women, fake sobbing into his hands. No police cars were arriving. Anna's body lay mangled on the terrace floor, and no one could be notified of the emergency. He loved it. All of them were admiring his handiwork. The brilliant journalist, Anna Dean, was no more. She was gone but not forgotten. Anna played her role brilliantly, and the audience was held spellbound from the moment she started screaming. Many of the onlookers were still in awe.

Some were already spreading rumors as they pretended to be a reliable sources of information. He could hear their inaccuracies in their hushed whispers.

What a fitting encore this was. Jacob thought his stage looked even better from the first floor. Of course, being on the twelfth floor had advantages, but being with his audience, rubbing shoulders with them, was exhilarating. New admirers arrived every few minutes. Jacob thought this was better than going viral on social media or being covered on Fox News.

A woman nudged a man's elbow two feet in front of him. "Do you see what I see?" The man craned his neck, looking left, then right. "Where? There's so much going on. What do you see?" The woman pointed to Anna's stomach. "There is something taped to her stomach," she said. "Oh my God. You are right?"

Jacob stood back and admired his work. This was undoubtedly turning out to be a fine day, and it was only the first of my many shows. The show is a hit!

Monique was flying through the air in her fighter jet, dropping bombs on the North Kangavar. She was angry and deadly. But those were just thoughts. One day, she would teach them a lesson they would never forget. For now, she was still shocked rockets were on their way to Yeonsu-Daejeon, the capitol of North Kangavar, and key cities of the country. Most of North

Kangavar's government leaders and their families would already be underground. For the past forty years, the North Kangavarians built underground bunkers. Recent intel even showed evidence of underground cities.

Monique thought about the twenty-eight thousand Sallerian troops stationed on the border who were now in harm's way. She prayed they got to safety before it was too late. As far as the North Kangavarians, hundreds of millions of innocent civilians would die. She couldn't imagine how they could survive as many nukes as she saw disappear in the night sky. It takes seventy-two hours to evacuate a city. At best, North Kangavar had thirty minutes until each nuke would level the country. Some nukes would explode just above the city skyline for maximum damage, while others would act as bunker busters and detonate on impact, destroying anything underground.

"You okay, ma'am?" Brayden asked. Monique lied to her Chief of Staff with a nod and continued down Pennsylvania NW on her way to the White House. The soothing trickle of rain, and the breeze that followed, whispered through the branches. At first glance, The White House was clear of debris, which was a surprise. Monique expected a full-scale attack from the North Kangavarians. She thought that if she were the one attacking, she would not have spared the White House. However, Monique was grateful for Kim Yang Su's ignorance. She was almost to safety.

Looking at the White House in total darkness as a refugee was weird. Nothing stirred in the shadows. "Ma'am," Weston said, keeping his voice low. He pointed at a restricted route only for top personnel to access. Monique ran to catch up. Brayden labored for breath a few paces behind her. "I told you to quit smoking," Monique said. Brayden forced a smile between breaths. "Welp, as you can see, ma'am. Working for you is stressful. "Start ordering hookers and develop a gambling habit or keep my smoking habit." Monique laughed. It felt good to laugh right now, but it was short-lived.

Weston clicked off his flashlight when they reached the restricted corridor and halted. A cloud swallowed the moon, and blinding darkness spread across. "Why are we stopping?" Brayden whispered. Monique strained to see through the wall of darkness. It swallowed everything. Fear rose throughout her body. She wondered what had Weston so shaken. Were they about to die?

"Stay back," Weston said. "Madam Vice President, Brayden, get behind me and do everything I do." Monique made out shapes moving across the corridor. She wondered if her eyes were playing tricks on her. Had they just walked into a trap? She had to get to her son. Was she about to die before she could save him? She reached for her Glock 30, "Do not touch your weapon, ma'am. Do not move." Weston's tone was severe and threatening. He was afraid for her life.

"Big Wes, can we get some light back here?" Brayden asked. Weston didn't reply, and Monique slowly pulled out her Glock 30. Weston saw her, but he didn't offer a correction. She was a fighter. If she were going to die, it would be with no rounds in her magazine. Something had the big guy spooked. The sound of footfalls on the concrete sent a spike of adrenaline through her veins, the tingle prickling up her arms. Footsteps closed in from every direction. They sounded like they were surrounded, but the corridor was so narrow.

How could that be? Monique hadn't seen anyone behind them. "Ma'am, Brayden, put your hands above your heads right now," Weston said, his voice calm but firm. A sliver of the moon suddenly emerged, and its glow fell over two dozen very armed Secret Service Agents surrounding them. They came from all directions, submachine guns, and sniper rifles shouldered. Most of them were dressed in SWAT gear. She noticed another group of men and women. They were known as the best and only wore black suits and ties. The leader of this surprise assault team, a middle-aged man with a crew cut and solid jawline, shouldered an FN P90 Submachine Gun. "Drop your weapons!" he shouted.

When they reached the town, the Chief turned onto the main street. A stretch of restaurants, jewelry and t-shirt shops, ice cream parlors, and hiking stores that was usually alive with tourists now stood vacant. In the streets, dozens of people were looking for resources and answers. One of them pointed at Ashton's Dodge, and Aiden hit the gas. Aiden pulled into the lot, put the Dodge in the parking spot, and tossed Ashton back his keys. Ashton tucked an unlit cigar between his lips. If the world were ending, he'd need to ration his sticks. "I'll help you with Jared, and then we're out of here. My sister needs to get her daughter." Ashton said. "You don't want to stick around to see the radiation levels," Aiden asked. "That's all the more reason to hurry and get Paige. So she can be with us." "Understood," Aiden said. Aiden got out of the truck and threw the strap of his Colt M4 Carbine over his back. Aiden checked with Alison, but she shook her head. "I have to get to Paige, Chief," Aiden said, seeming to satisfy her with his response.

"Thanks for setting my shoulder back in place, Alison," Ernest said, holding his hand to her in a romantic gesture. Ashton hated the way the Major looked at his sister. He had his thoughts, for now. Paige was more important. "Best of luck getting to your daughter." Ernest glanced at Ashton next. "Be careful out there. The roads are going to get dangerous. You drive to East Wakefield as fast as you can and don't stop for anything until you get there. That goes double for the trip back." "Yes, sir," Ashton replied, barely keeping the sarcasm from his voice.

Between Aiden and this guy, he felt he was back in the Army again, being ordered around by a couple of people who liked the sound of their voices. Ernest looked at Alison one more time and smiled, then walked towards town hall— his limp was barely noticeable. Alison climbed into the front seat, and Erynn held the door open for her. The look of determination on Erynn's face was palpable. She knew it was time to get Paige and was willing to do whatever it took. Ashton knew he wasn't going to get Paige alone. Erynn would be right by his side. He always knew she would protect him at all costs. He would do the same for her. They did everything together.

Ashton knew Alison always wanted what her brother and Erynn had. They loved each other without conditions. She had never seen them argue, although they didn't always agree on everything. They were as thick as thieves and loyal to one another as soulmates. Erynn was fearless and unapologetically pure feminine power. She was everything every woman wanted to be. Erynn was the best woman he knew.

Aston saw Aiden drop his gear outside the front doors of the town hall building. He propped the door open with one of his bags and then returned for Jared's body. With Ashton's assistance, they lifted the kid respectfully from the Dodge. "Thanks for what you did up there. When you get back from East Wakefield, stop by the station. I'll make sure you get paid, plus a bonus for the extra trouble," Aiden said. Ashton had forgotten entirely about the check, which was very unlike him. "Thanks, Chief."

Ashton turned to walk away and then paused and then added, "I'm sorry we couldn't save him." Aiden picked Jared up in both arms and carried the dead boy's body into the building. "See you later, Ashton. Take care of Erynn like she takes care of you." "Will do, Chief," Ashton said with mutual respect. Several officers came to help. One of them was Ewan Hawkins, who gave Ashton a stern look. If it were up to the patrol sergeant, Ashton would be sitting behind bars in the Wakefield County Jail. Instead, Ashton used his middle finger to wave hello to him and walked away.

"You know where those Geiger counters are, Ewan?" Aiden asked. Ashton didn't stick around to listen to the conversation. Instead, he shut the lift gate after retrieving his weapons. Jumping into the truck, he wondered if Alison was carrying her gun. She pulled it from her waist and showed it to him. "Good because you're riding shotgun tonight, little sister. Let's go get Paige."

Jacob had already moved to his second victim. He was going to make this death more spectacular than the last one. *He was so excited. His plan was working so well. The police had to be at least fifteen steps behind him.*

He was a completely different character now. He was no longer a janitor. No, that wouldn't fit for this kill. He had to be in high society. Jacob knew this would be the performance of his life, and he had to deliver, or all was lost. He was General Cain Palmer. *What killer wouldn't kill to be a General of the Army? It was a perfect role for tonight.*

The sidewalk in front of The Ogden Theatre was littered with a few people. Some asked questions about the power, but most ticket holders stayed inside to enjoy the show— even in the dark. *The show much go on,* Jacob thought to himself. The event staff lit the stage with battery-powered flashlights. Everyone in attendance assumed that there was a power outage, and no one wanted the abandon the show.

It looked to be a sellout audience. Jacob loved a crowd, and tonight would be a night they would never forget. There was no need for a rehearsal. Jacob— who wasn't a star himself— assumed his role as General Cain Palmer. The double doors were open as General Cain Palmer entered the theater from the sidewalk. Then four intentional doors led farther into the theater's carpeted lobby. He noticed everything and wouldn't forget a single detail.

Almost believing that he was General Cain Palmer now, getting more deeply into the role, Jacob moved casually. There was a small crowd walking in the shrouded darkness. They seemed to be either trying to get cellphone reception, answers, or coming from the toilets. Jacob intentionally walked no more quickly or slowly than the toilet crowd. Finally, they seemed to be headed back inside the main theatre.

Thick-tinted glasses, a grey beard, and a Class-A Army dress uniform with the appropriate chest medals helped to keep him undetected. He was a prestigious General, and everyone paid him the proper respect. He bore two stars for the Lieutenant General rank on both shoulders.

He was just another theater over, he was thinking. Yet, he couldn't help having the slightest doubt about not rehearsing. *What if he blew it? What if someone recognized him? What if he made a mistake?* His eyes took in the scene, and he pushed forward. The play was

Ryan Poole

In

We Were Soldiers

The hot-shot Hollywood actor Ryan Pool was spending a year doing stage plays. Everyone loved him. Mr. Smith did not. The pool had to die. He did a poor job representing his brother on film. He made his brother seem confused and even made people believe he had a mental breakdown. Never! His brother would never have a mental breakdown, and he had to die for his gross misrepresentation.

However, Ryan Poole was such a big draw. He was the sole reason for the sold-out performance tonight. Poole was one of Hollywood's best. And here he was, performing live in Lakota. Women especially loved Ryan Pool. He was indeed a heartthrob.

Inside the auditorium, the actors did a fantastic job without microphones projecting their voices. General Cain Palmer quickly found his seat, IA. He was front and left-centered. Jacob was getting into the part—good stuff and very well played. He was highly impressed by how they kept acting with no power. They did such a good job no one inside the theatre knew the entire city was without power. He was positioned only steps from one of the four illuminated fire exits.

This murder would be spectacular, and as good as these seats were, he needed to be on stage. Ryan Poole's murder needed to happen right where he was standing. General Cain Palmer had seen all that he needed to see for now. He rose from his seat and knew what he needed to do. He had to get on stage. It was all *for his vengeance, of course.*

Weston quickly placed his weapon on the ground and identified himself as "Weston Levy, Deputy Assistant Special Agent in Charge." An officer in SWAT gear kicked the pistol away from Weston and put his hands behind his back. "Hands above your heads!" someone shouted at Monique and Brayden. They both did as ordered. "I'm Vice President Monique Montgomery, and I'm trying to get to my office," Monique said. The leader lowered his assault rifle as the SWAT officers patted Monique and Brayden down. One of the men yanked Monique's Glock 30 away. A flashlight shone on her face. She squinted at the bright light but didn't raise a hand to shield her eyes. The man with the assault rifle kept the flashlight on Monique.

"I'm Special Agent Tobias Whitfield with the Secret Service. What's your security number, Vice President?" "1999ThereIsNoSpoonNeo," Monique quickly replied. Agent Whitfield directed the light to a pad and then glanced back up. "My apologies, ma'am, but we've moved to DEFCON 1, so I have to check everyone. After that, my team will escort you into the White House." Monique wanted to ask a hundred questions, but there was just one that mattered right now. "How widespread is the power outage?" Whitfield was looking over his shoulder, distracted. "Agent?" "Sorry, Madam Vice President, as our initial intel suggests, ma'am, the entire country is dark. There is no power anywhere. Things are chaotic, and communications are slow," Whitfield said.

"We need to keep moving. You will receive a full briefing once you get to safety. COOP has been implemented. We will be evacuating somewhere safe as soon as we have transportation. The White House is no longer safe, Madam Vice President." "COOP, as in the Continuity of Operations Plan?" Brayden asked, glancing at Monique. "Correct," Whitfield said. "So that means," Brayden began to speak. Monique finished his thought. "We're being moved out of D.C."

At this point, nothing surprised Monique anymore. She just watched the country go dark, twenty-something nukes left Sallerian airspace, and she had to be escorted from her apartment to get here. Things would never be the same again, she thought. The world was forever changed. She began to wonder. If all the power was out, how long would supplies last? How would people get food?

"My gun, please," she said and reached for her Glock 30. The officer who had taken the weapon handed it to her. "Sorry, ma'am." "No worries. I would have done the same thing to you." Monique replied with her patent charm that always made people feel better. She was indeed a politician. There were other checkpoints already set up to the west and east. Everyone was armed and ready for anything that would come next. Whitfield motioned for three of his team members, and they fanned out across the restricted area of the White House.

Weston dipped his chin, signaling it was okay for Monique and Brayden to follow. They continued down the street after Whitfield and his men. Dozens of Secret Service officers and Capitol Police with assault rifles patrolled the grounds as if they were preparing for an imminent attack.

∞

A few thousand dedicated souls were cheering the actors on in a cloud of darkness. It was indeed a beautiful spectacle. A crew of thirty-seven worked behind the scenes here. Impressive. Expensive, too. It was a star-studded cast led by Mr. Ryan Poole himself. Jacob wondered how much each actor was getting paid to be so amazing.

General Cain Palmer was the only lone figure awaiting his director debut. Or, maybe it was his *act-tutorial* debut. He wondered to himself. Is that even a word? It didn't matter. It was his big moment, and he was ready for fame. At nine fifty-seven at night, he would come in through the stage door. A whiteboard and a few phrases about the enemy attacking in flanking positions. In his pocket were a few props.

> *A brown dry-erase marker.*
>> *knife, just in case things got out of hand.*
>> *Butane torch.*
>
> *Supply of ethanol.*

At precisely nine fifty-seven p.m., Ryan Poole was well into a scene in which he talked about how unfair life was and how he demanded more respect. Mr. Poole was a fantastic actor. Jacob almost forgot he was General Cain Palmer, and it was time for Ryan to die. Everyone was shocked when the trapdoor on the stage floor, usually used only in the third act, flew open.

"What the—. "Ladies and Gentlemen, I am so sorry for the interruption," said General Cain Palmer in a loud, clear, commanding voice that could be heard way up in the cheap seats. "But I need your undivided attention. Someone is about to die, and you can do nothing to save him."

Chapter Eight

Nothing ever starts where we think it does. So, of course, this doesn't begin with the cowardly murder of Anna Dean. FBI Special Agent Connor Mason only believed that it did— and Connor was very wrong.

It had been four hours since the power went off. Connor slept through the first three and a half hours until his best friend, Brentley Miller, knocked on his door as if the world was ending. It turns out it *was*. Brentley was saved by the world's end because Connor's mother, Linda Faye Mason, was a sixty-six-year-old feisty warrior. She became addicted to opioids when Connor was six years old and had no chance to come back into his life until he was thirty-seven. As fate would have it, Connor reunited with his parents when he was thirty-seven, and they all loved each other as if time was never lost. Without a doubt, the Masons were a family full of love. One thing was for sure; Mama Linda was the unofficial head of the household.

Connor's father, Anthony Theodore Mason, was a pastor. Even though Daddy Mason spent some time in prison, he was paroled around the same time his wife Linda Faye kicked her drug habit. Papa Anthony was the nurturer of the family; he was the heart of the house and the elder statesman of 758 Fillmore Street, Lakota. And Linda Faye was the outspoken muscle. Despite having a rough childhood, Connor did well for himself, and his family got to lay their head in a two-million dollar house nightly. His two kids, eight-year-old son Riley Mason and his ten-year-old daughter, Sophia Mason. Life was fantastic.

Connor's path to the Bureau was undoubtedly a unique one. His nickname at the Bureau is "Dr. Quantum" because Connor spent the first half of his life as a theoretical physicist. He was first in his physics class and graduated summa cum laude from Harvard University in 2004. Then, in Berkeley, at the University of Carcuaro, Mason received his Ph.D. in Physics in 2012. In that same year, he began lecturing at Princeton University.

Dr. Quantum then moved on to research quantum mechanics at The City University of New York (CUNY), and he held the Henry Semat Chair and Professorship in theoretical physics at the CUNY, where he taught for over five years.

"Mama? Can you get that?" I called from my bedroom. "It's for you. You might as well get it yourself," his feisty mother called back. "It's Brentley, and it looks like someone took a dump in his breakfast cereal." "It's too early for breakfast cereal, Mama Linda," Brentley said through the fancy screen door, especially for Lakota winters. "Come in, baby, and don't talk back to me. It's never too early for breakfast," Mama Linda said with a matter-of-fact tone.

Connor could feel his stomach rolling. This wasn't the way he wanted to start his morning. But wait, was it morning yet? "Shit. Fuck me," Connor said out loud when he realized the sun wasn't close to coming up. Mama Linda looked up from her early morning pint of chocolate ice cream habit and shot Connor a mean look. It was one of those, *you may pay all the bills, but this is my house* looks. "Watch your language, Connor," Mama Linda said. "The only person getting away with cussing around here will be me."

Connor immediately saw the grim look on Brentley's face. Connor and Brentley became best friends when Connor was nine, and they have been inseparable since. They could read each other like a book. "What's wrong big guy," Connor said to Bentley, who stood six feet and eight inches and weighed about two hundred and seventy pounds. Connor was a bit shorter than Brentley, coming in at six feet and four inches. "There's been a bad murder just around the corner at an apartment building," Bentley said solemnly. "Are we in for a long night, bro?" "A lot longer than you expect, man." "Did we call the medical examiner," Connor asked while grabbing his jacket, gun, and badge. "We can't. All the power is out all over Lakota."

"What! For how long?" Connor asked. "For about four hours, which is not the worst. The murder was at St. Paul's Collection. It was Anna. Someone threw her off her twelfth floor patio, and," Brentley's voice trailed off. He knew his following words would crush Connor no matter what he said. "She's dead, Connor. In an evil way. And, she was tortured before she died." Connor nearly fell to the floor and cried in front of Mamma Linda and Poppa Mason. Anna Dean was his fiancé.

Aiden loudly cleared his throat and waited for the chatter to stop. There were bad nights on the job, and then there were terrible nights. This one was the worse in Aiden's years of law enforcement. He thought about how long Wakefield's supplies would last. "I am activating our Emergency Operations Center," Aiden said to his officers, including his best friend and right-hand man, Captain Derrick Mercer. "I'm on it, Chief," Derrick responded. "I already have the EOC ready to go. I was awaiting your orders." Aiden appreciated Derrick. Their friendship spanned decades. Aiden always thought Derrick could be the police chief. He was well respected and far more competent than him. Derrick never seems to want the job, however.

Derrick stood next to Aiden. His burly form and toned, chiseled jawline made him appear too big for the small conference room. "Hold all your questions and stay calm, and let us do our jobs so you can get some answers you need," Derrick said in his authoritative voice. He rolled up his sleeves like he was preparing for a fistfight, revealing several biker-like tattoos—his way of telling everyone to shut up.

Years ago, Derrick and Aiden became friends when both of Derrick's parent's died in a tragic car accident. Aiden's mom took Derrick in, and the rest is history. They were both born in Wakefield and joined the UCS Army on the "buddy system." Aiden, black, and Derrick, white, grew up as brothers. They had a blast growing up together.

After their time in the Army, they decided to come back home to Wakefield and become police officers. After a few short years, Aiden rose to Chief and appointed Derrick as his Deputy Chief. Between his size, his tattoos, and his booming voice, around the station, Derrick was called "Eivor,"; the famed Assassin's Creed protagonist in the Assassin's Creed Valhalla version of the game released in late 2020.

Officers Charles Walker and Peyton Michael filed into the conference room. Both officers were young, but Officer Michael and his wife delivered their first child last week. Officer Michael had dozens of questions about the lights and power and heat. He was worried about his newborn freezing to death. Aiden didn't know how to answer most of his questions.

After being pelted with a dozen rapid-fire questions from Officer Michael, Aiden gestured for them both officers to take a seat next to Janice, the station's administrative assistant and dispatcher. For now, Aiden was more worried about surviving nuclear fallout. He hoped the battery-powered Geiger counters would help them all from dying of radiation poisoning.

Once Aiden figured out how many different threats they were dealing with, he could devise a solid plan for everyone. Unfortunately for Aiden, the end of the world didn't stop politicians from acting like politicians. He was expecting a power struggle with Wakefield's Mayor and all of her staff. However, a small portion of his mind ran through scenarios that would keep her both happy and out of his way, just in case she hindered rescue efforts with bureaucracy.

He hoped it wouldn't come to a power struggle. He didn't care who was in charge. Aiden wanted people to stay alive. He had enough death for a while. *But when did people not struggle for power?* Aiden thought to himself. He made a silent promise to himself that no matter what happened tonight, he wouldn't complicate things with his ego.

Aiden was lamenting the conversation he had to have with his friend, Truth. He didn't know how to tell someone their child was brutally murdered and suffered a painful death. After that, Aiden would have to tell Dawn and Lillian. He figured he would say to them both simultaneously when he got home.

30

It took Connor and Brentley fifteen minutes to make it to 255 ST. Paul Street, traveling on foot. Neither of their cars worked. Poppa Anthony's didn't work either. Finally, they arrived in the middle of the night. The Lakota Police and EMS were already there. "Special Agents Miller and Mason, we've been assigned to the case," Brentley said to the officer keeping civilians behind the yellow tape. Connor and Brentley flashed their credentials and ducked under the police tape. Connor took a deep breath and strolled over to Anna's naked body. He was reeling. Brentley acknowledged a tall blonde Lakota Police Officer he knew. Connor could see the officer was disturbed by what he saw.

The grill was covered in blood, brain matter, and chunks of exploded human flesh. Connor forced himself to keep walking. He needed to see Anna. He instantly regretted his decision to see his fiancé. Her face was swollen, broken, and unrecognizable. It was battered and blue. Most of her teeth were broken from the impact. She fell back first into the pavement, and the back of her skull was completely missing. The parts of her face that weren't swollen sank into her head. She was naked for all to see. Connor wanted to cover her so badly. He hated this, but he knew he could not. "Let's go to her apartment, Connor. We need to find out exactly what happened to catch this son of a bitch."

36

"Has anyone been able to get ahold of Mayor Harris?" Aiden asked. "You don't want her here right now, sir?" Detective Skylar Schwartz answered from across the table. Aiden had recruited the feisty brunette from Lakota as the newest member of his team, but sometimes he wondered if he'd made a mistake. Skylar's hair was midnight-black, and it flowed over her shoulders.

Aiden acted like he didn't hear Skylar, but she was right. He didn't have time for the mayor's power struggle habits during a possible worldwide crisis. Mayor Julia Harris was a micromanager, and she didn't know how or want to know how to stay out of police business. Aiden didn't care about politics and didn't want to be anyone's mayor. His goal was to save lives.

"All right, everyone, listen up. It's going to be a very long night, probably one of the longest nights of your life. Here's the situation. The Ghost, Erynn, and I found Jared Parker about four hours ago in Harmony Park in Parkland. He didn't make it. His death was brutal, and he died under extremely suspicious circumstances. While we were up there, a pair of fighter jets fell from the sky after a nuclear electromagnetic pulse weapon was detonated at fifty-two thousand feet."

The gathered officers gasped, and Skylar shouted, "Bullshit!" "Skylar, this is the part where you listen so you can catch up." Aiden had no choice but to control the flow of the room. He needed all of his officers with him. He continued before anyone else questioned or commented. "Major Ernest Maddox," Aiden pointed to his right, and everyone stared at the Air Force man, still in uniform, "was able to eject from his fighter jet before it crashed. He won't answer any questions because he has to use his skills to fix one of our radios, contact his base and chain command, and give them the intel I just gave you. What I just told you is highly classified. The EMP knocked out every electronic in the city, and we don't know how far the damage goes. We need to find out how much of Salleria is in the dark. The one thing we do know is Wakefield is in the dark, and no one is coming to help us. What you see in this room are our reinforcements. The help we need."

Detective Dylan Graham ran a hand through his blonde hair. "A nuke? Are you sure?" "My wife and I heard something loud a few hours ago," Walker said. "It sounded like a massive explosion, but we thought it was the storm." Skylar was still shaking her head. "You're sure, Chief?" "Hold your questions until I'm done. But, yes, Dylan and Skylar, I am very sure." Skylar folded her arms and listened to Chief intently.

At first, the only noticeable stir in the audience was riffling pages as dozens of people looked at their programs to see who this actor was on stage.

The Hollywood hotshot, Ryan Poole, turned his back to the audience and spoke in an angry whisper. "Who do you think you are, dumbass. Get off the stage now before I kick your," before Ryan Poole could finish his empty threat, General Cain Palmer sliced off his left ear. Blood gushed from the side of his head, and Ryan screamed so loudly everyone immediately got the picture they were no longer watching the play as advertised. This play was now a Jacob Smith production. Oh, how he wanted to be a star for all to see.

Poole, still screaming, "Please, please. Please don't kill me. I will do whatever you want. Just calm down, please." "Call nine-one-one," someone yelled out in the front row. "Hello, everyone. My name is General Cain Palmer, and I am your villain tonight. I will be killing Mr. Ryan Poole before your eyes," Jacob said to the crowd.

He turned to the bleeding actor and cut off his other ear. The crowd screamed. "I have placed bombs at every exit. The entire theatre will explode if anyone tries to leave, and we will die together." General Cain. He wanted them to stay for his execution of Ryan Poole.

General Palmer leaned closer, "This is almost as much fun as watching you sleep, Ryan." Then, holding his knife on the actor in one hand, Palmer began to pour ethanol on every inch of the actor's body. "The smell was so intense that Ryan gagged and vomited. "Please. No. What are you doing? Please don't hurt me," Ryan Poole cried out.

The audience was gasping as well. There wasn't a single person in the theatre who was not on their feet. Shouts came from the balcony. "Stop him! Somebody get security!"

General Cain Palmer used his theatre voice to get the audience's attention. "Anyone who comes to the stage will be shot dead," He pulled a hidden pistol from the small of his back. "I am not finished with this scene. So pay attention and witness something you will never forget." General Palmer turned to face Ryan Poole once more. Both of his hands were covering holes where his ears once were.

The General placed the pistol back in the small of his back and sparked a butane torch in his hand. He pointed the torch at Ryan's face, and the ethanol exploded into flame and consumed Ryan Poole's entire body. He screamed and flapped his arms around until he fell off the stage and seemed to burst into more flames. The firing was crisping his skin, and the smell of burnt flesh filled the air.

"He burned my brother's reputation with his terrible performance in his movie. Now, he must burn himself. Delicate things are not as easy to break as you may think," General Palmer said to a dying Ryan Poole. Then, turning to the audience, he said, "Hold your applause! Please, hold your applause," he called to the audience, *his* audience now. "Thank you so much! Thank you! You all deserve to live, for now. But I will be watching you!" He did a half bow, then disappeared off the stage. Next, he jumped down a flight of stairs with minimal effort and bolted out of an emergency exit.

Once he reached the street, General Palmer took a left and escaped into an alleyway. He poured ethanol into a led barrel he had placed there five days ago, took off his complete disguise, including his clothes, and set everything on fire. After that, General Cain Palmer was no more.

His mission was complete, and he played his role to perfection. He walked ten feet away from the burning barrel and moved a crate that contained civilian clothes for his getaway. Jacob prepared for everything. *My God, I am getting better at this,* he thought to himself. The world will remember me forever. And, it was all for Mr. Smith. *Vengeance is his because he is Lord.*

"Most of you were here for the 2016 tornados," Aiden continued. "We were cut off then, and it looks like we're cut off now. It took us two weeks to get supplies, and much of the town was destroyed. Many of us still have not fully recovered. However, this is different. We may be at risk from nuclear fallout, and there's a murderer on the loose draining all the blood out of children."

Aiden scanned his officers. Several of the men and women in this room were rookies. Most of his officers chose this part of Wakefield because it was quiet and full of tourists, unlike the major crimes that happened in towns like Lakota. Wakefield is a small town in the city of Wakefield. Early settlers thought the town was so beautiful they wanted it to be named after the city itself. The last murder in Wakefield was years ago.

But these were all excellent officers, and he had to trust them. There was no one else left to count. The entire city was dark, and the cavalry wasn't coming because the cavalry didn't have any power. "I've put Derrick in charge of the Emergency Operations Center, but things will work differently than last time. For one, we probably don't have access to the Red Cross, National Guard, or other agencies. We will have to plant our foods, and everyone in the city will have to empty their refrigerators before their food goes bad. Then, we will have to convince the town folk to pool all our resources to feed everyone. I'm hoping we can contact Police Chief Archie Jordan in Everett, but he will have his hands full, just like us. They are about sixty-one miles northeast of here, which would make that about a sixteen-hour walk— assuming conditions stay the same."

The officers began muttering anxiously again, and Derrick stepped in to settle them down. "We are lucky to be alive. It could have been a different nuclear attack, so calm down. Plus, it is our off-season. There are probably only around ten thousand people in town tonight. But if we don't get a good grip on the situation, that will become a ten thousand-member mob coming straight for us." Aiden nodded. "Derrick, I want you to work with Skylar and Janice on an inventory of every resource in town. We need everything from can goods to ketchup packets. And let's get an accurate count of all the vehicles that still work. We will also need the full name of everyone here and their current skillsets, gifts and talents, and handicaps. Speaking of handicaps, have Janice work on an allergy list as well. We don't need people dying on us because they carried a bag of peanuts."

Aiden was in a zone. His mind was connecting dots faster than his mouth could move. He wanted to give as many orders as possible to get a grip on the situation and show his officers he was not panicking.

"We will also need to figure out how to get some running water so we can flush toilets around here, or the town will smell like something none of us can bare. If it could be useful, I want it on the list," Aiden said with a commanding voice. "Roger that, sir. I'll start first thing in the morning." Aiden shook his head. "Not in the morning. Right after this meeting. We can all be dead by morning." "Do we have a single working vehicle?" Skylar asked. No one replied. Aiden told everyone that Ashton had a working vehicle but went to East Wakefield to get his niece. Before anyone could question if Ashton would return to help out, Aiden assured everyone that he would and that he had been accommodating these past few days.

A considerable part of Aiden's wish was that he should have commandeered the Dodge when he had the chance. "How about that guy on McAuthor Avenue with the old cars for sale?" Graham asked. "I bet those will work. Maybe our military-grade hummer will start, too." "Someone check it out after this," Aiden said. "I haven't started up my 1971 Dodge pickup in a while," Derrick said. "I'll try it when I get home." "Sounds good. Ashton's Dodge pickup was eighty-something, so that should work fine if you can get it started. Let's see if we can determine how many people in town know how to work on cars, take parts out of dead cars, and put them to use differently around town. We need to get as creative as possible, people. And can someone check on Major Maddox's progress with the radio? The faster we can reach someone who knows more than us, the better,"

Aiden demanded.

"I'll go," Janice said. "What about refugees?" Derrick asked. "If there's going to be fallout, people will start leaving the bigger cities and make their way to resource-heavy cities like ours." Aiden shared a deep sigh and thought for a moment, then looked directly into Derrick's eyes. "We're going to have to set up shelters," Aiden said, but we need to be careful who we let into town. There is no need to be mean about it, but we need people with skills we can use. Everyone must pull their weight because everything will always return to feeding people. We can only afford to feed them if they prove themselves useful. The world has changed. And, we all must remember, we are probably housing a murderer as we speak.

No one said anything. Everyone seemed to process there was a murderer on the loose, and he could be hiding amongst them now. "What about the Embassy Suites?" Officer Charles Walker asked. Aiden paused and thought about the questions for a moment. "Good question. I'll talk to Thomas," Aiden said. Thomas was the owner of the Embassy Suites, and he and Aiden had been friends for a long time. The place had become a popular tourist hotel with enough room and auxiliary buildings to house thousands. It was a start.

"Refugees and stranded tourists aren't our only concern," Aiden added to the conversation. "Once people figure out what's going on, they will raid every supermarket, pharmacy, and hardware store. Most of the perishable stuff is going to be spoiled in a day. We must find a way to cook it all before it goes bad. Let's gather as many barbecue pits as possible and find other ways to cook things. Maybe if we cook a lot of the meat and stuff, we can find a way to preserve it a little longer," Aiden finished said.

His mind was racing with ideas and things to do, but there was one thing he knew he had to do first, but Aiden was sure it would cause a power struggle with the mayor, which he didn't want. But what choice did he have? It was now or never. Without regret, Aiden's words would change Wakefield for days and weeks. "The first thing I'm officially doing as Chief of Police is declaring a state of emergency. I want an armed officer stationed at every building we deem a critical facility, starting with food, water, and medicine." The order drew a few uncertain gazes, but he continued giving orders. "We are in a unique situation, folks. Do you want to die? Do you want your children to starve? What we do next can save the entire town or doom it. We have a constant water supply from the mountains, and we have a decent stock of food. We also need to keep an eye on everyone who owns weapons. We also can't let everyone go out, killing all the wild animals in the woods. We will run out of food supply. We need cooks, people who can skin livestock, and people who know how to be creative with the scraps that don't get used. We cannot afford to waste anything. If that nuke knocked out power to more than Wakefield, we can't expect help soon."

Several voices broke out around the table. "What do you mean? Do you think there was more than one nuke?" Skylar asked. "Could there be more attacks?" Walker asked. "Chief, my wife and I have a baby at home," Michael said. "If there's a killer on the loose," Aiden sighed. "Everyone, please calm down." The questions kept coming until Derrick finally walked in front of the Chief, folded his arms, and narrowed his eyes. "Chief Aiden said to calm down!" he boomed. The room quieted as an angry parent suddenly walked in.

Aiden looked at each of his officers and chose his following words wisely. "I give you all my word. I will not let you down. I don't know how I will make everything work, but I can assure each of you that I will not give up. As long as I am breathing, Officer Michael, I will ensure you and your wife can raise your child. Skylar, we don't know if there was more than one nuke. That is why Major Maddox is trying to get to a working radio. I will make this work, but I will need your help. We must survive whatever is happening in Wakefield."

The lobby of the luxury apartment building was relatively quiet and completely dark. However, Connor recognized a couple of uniformed officers holding battery power flashlights. The officers were checking credentials and using their lights to illuminate walking paths.

The elevator wasn't an option, so Connor and Brentley took the stairs. When they arrived at apartment 1207, Connor felt an unpleasant chill. At the apartment's front door, a petite Hispanic woman Connor recognized as a Lakota PD techie was dusting for prints. There was no blood in the apartment and few signs of a struggle. Connor feared that whatever happened to Anna happened so fast that she didn't have any time to put up a fight. He wondered if that meant she knew her attacker or did it mean her attacker ambushed her. Connor needed more evidence to make a better assessment of the crime scene.

The living room looked undisturbed. There were built-in bookshelves on every wall. "What are you thinking?" Brentley finally spoke. He was letting Connor get his thoughts together. He forgot there were about a dozen people in Anna's living room. He was so focused on analyzing the crime scene that he was alone in his mind going through all the details.

"Looks like he came in through the front door. There is no sign of forced entry. From how Anna died, I would save he managed to get her to open the door disguised as something she would have seen as non-threatening," Connor relayed to Brentley. "Maybe he dressed as a waiter or room service," Brentley offered. "Fair points. Either of those would have worked. The power was off so that the killer would have blended in flawlessly as any service-related job," Connor explained.

Upon his arrival, Connor was now the Special Agent in Charge. This was his crime scene. "Anything missing?" Brentley asked one of the agents on the scene who secured the crime scene before they arrived. It was the natural question to ask. The agent shook his head. "Nothing real obvious. As of now, it doesn't look like this was a robbery, Agent Miller." Connor took in the details of the conversation between Brentley and the agent. He was making conclusions and using data to eliminate every incorrect possibility. He wanted the truth. Everything else was in the way.

"Agent, downstairs on the terrace, I noticed tape around Anna's midsection. Can you tell me more about that?" Connor asked the agent Brentley had been talking to moments before. "It seemed to be a Bible. It was open to a page, but everything was blacked out. The only thing that wasn't was the word *Psalm*." "I don't follow," Connor said. "That's just it, sir," the agent responded to Connor. Every word in the Bible was completely blacked out except one: the word, *Psalm*. The killer wanted us to see this. It was as if he was leaving a clue," the agent told Connor and Brentley.

Connor didn't respond for a few seconds. The silence was thick, but Brentley knew this was how his friend worked. Connor used his experience as a quantum physicist to organize all the facts of the crime scene and separate them from assumptions and habits. He was taking his time to reconstruct the crime scene in his head. He saw the killer rush into the door and overpower Anna, and he concluded the killer disguised himself in a service uniform of some sort. Connor assumed the killer was clever, even brilliant. He would have also been attractive, but not his looks made people feel comfortable. His disguise must have made him look forgettable because no one knew anything. Connor knew he was dealing with a very resourceful person.

After a long silence, Connor spoke. "So, he's got every opportunity to kill her in private, but he marches her to those sliding doors and throws her off the balcony instead?" Connor paused in between sentences. He didn't let his emotions get the best of him and stayed in the mind of a scientist. During the silence, Brentley, the agent, and the other ten people in the living room processing the crime scene all looked towards the sliding doors that led to the patio. Connor continued speaking once they caught up with his thinking. 'The killer leaves a clue on the body, and I am willing to believe he left a clue here, too. It would be fair to assume the killer understood we would examine the body and come to her apartment afterward. My guess is the clue on her body is the first clue, and whatever we find up here will lead to a bigger part of the story he is orchestrating for us. And, make no mistakes about it, ladies and gentlemen, our killer is directing a movie scene that he wants us to all watch simultaneously. I don't think the killer knew our victim personally, but this murder was very personal to him. He wanted to execute her publicly. I do not know yet for what reason, but I believe the killer's clues will tell us. Our clues also prove the killer expects us to be as smart as him, which also tells us that our killer is brilliant."

Connor paused for another long moment, but Brentley interrupted the silence. "Keep going." Brentley said. "This was a public execution from the start, and our killer is telling us a story and punishing his victim. Since the entire Bible was blacked out, save one word. And we haven't found any clues yet, which leads me to believe our killer will have multiple crime scenes across the city, and he has been planning these killings for quite some time. He doesn't leave anything to chance. He prepares for every possible outcome and loves an audience. I would say he has no intentions of killing anyone without an audience. This was a performance. The killer came here to put on a show. We are his audience and will stay ten steps behind him until he wants us to catch up."

Everyone looked at Connor. He was brilliant and always made people feel more intelligent than him. Connor knew they understood what he was saying, but there was something he didn't say out loud. He kept it to himself for now because if he were wrong, he would cause unnecessary panic. Connor didn't mention that the killer likely had more than one killing schedule for the night, and things were about to get much worse for all of them. He couldn't prove it, but he was sure they were looking at the first kill of a brilliant serial killer. Anna was simply victim number one.

Icy mountains arced over the highway as Ashton, Alison, and Erynn sped to East Wakefield. It was about a forty-five-minute drive headed east on Highway 34. The moon lit the sky and created just enough light to see abandoned cars and debris on the road. Luckily, the headlights on the Dodge worked even better than the moonlight. Finally, they were headed to Paige. Alison felt like an idiot for letting the news about the strange texts she was receiving slip out as she panicked about getting to Paige. She hoped Ashton and Erynn forgot that she mentioned it.

Ashton drove carefully and kept an eye out for stranded tourists or worse. He also looked out for wildlife, attempting to cross the road safely. Ashton said hitting a deer or an elk would end his Dodge—likely all three of their lives. Alison was glad he was thinking of things that she was not. She had to get to Paige.

Erynn sat quietly in the back seat, inspecting her weapons. She knew Erynn didn't like Nathan. Alison didn't know what to expect when all three showed up to get Paige.

Alison stared blankly out the passenger window. Finally, she decided to tell Erynn and Ashton about the cryptic text messages she had received and why they had her so worried about Paige. After five minutes of debating in her mind and going over all the details, Alison spent the next fifteen minutes telling Ashton and Erynn about all the text messages and how each time Alison blocked the number, the messages continued from another number. She didn't leave out any details. She gave them both one hundred percent of the truth. Ashton asked many questions, and the conversation ended with her promising to tell him if anything else happened.

Before he could say anything else, Ashton twisted the steering wheel to avoid a minivan partially stuck in his lane. The headlights captured a man putting gas into a Honda Civic with a red canister. He looked toward the Dodge, shielding his eyes with one hand. Ashton glanced at the fuel gauge; the Dodge was less than half a tank. "Damn! We will have to do something about gas sooner or later." Half a tank left would get to East Wakefield, but only some of the way back home. "Ashton, do you think Paige is safe?" Alison asked her big brother. "Of course, Sis. We'll get Paige and me, and Erynn won't let anything happen to either of you. Besides, Nathan doesn't have a history of hurting Paige. The coward likes to hurt you when I am out of the country."

Ashton pulled the cigar from his top pocket and put it between his lips, but it was wet and breaking from all night's events. He told himself he would save it for later because throwing a cigar away during the end of the world didn't feel right. Alison hated it when he smoked around her and never let him smoke around Paige, but she was sure he needed to take all this stress off his mind. To her surprise, Ashton decided against smoking and put the cigar up.

It was already ten p.m., and it would take another forty-five minutes to get to East Wakefield, driving at this speed. Unfortunately, Ashton had to go slower than expected on the winding roads, and there was no way to reach the speed limit because the streets were filled with abandoned cars.

That would put him back in Wakefield around one a.m., as long as everything went smoothly. But, of course, nothing tonight went smoothly. "Think Nathan is going to let her go willingly?" Ashton asked. Alison's shoulders tensed, but she didn't reply immediately. "It's okay," Ashton repeated. The tires thumped over the road as they approached a bridge. They were silent for the next ten minutes, which worked out for Alison. Whenever she saw a stranded vehicle, she wondered where the drivers were. Finally, she asked if they were safe.

Alison wondered if someone would shoot at the windows of the Dodge and try to take it from them, but that never happened. There was a family on the side of the road begging for help, but Ashton didn't stop. She knew he couldn't, but the pain of leaving them on the side of the road lingered longer than she wanted. A man and his wife were holding the hands of their two kids as they made their way toward East Wakefield. They were guided only by a tiny flashlight. There was no room in Ashton's truck.

Alison knew that Ashton's Dodge would be a prime target once people figured out what was happening. They had to pick up Paige before the shit hit the fan. She was curious to know if Ashton and Erynn would go back and help Aiden. The more she thought about it, the more it didn't seem like it would be their best option. No matter what, Alison knew she had to get back to the hospital.

They were almost in East Wakefield. Ashton kept his foot on the gas as they climbed a steep incline. The crimson glow of fire rose over the foothills. Everyone in the Dodge saw it at the same time. Alison leaned forward and asked, "What is that?" "I have no idea," Ashton said while gently pressing the gas pedal. They drove for several minutes in silence. Each looked out the windows for a better view of what was causing the fires. "That looks close to the city," Alison said. "Don't worry. It's on the outskirts. So far from where Nathan lives," Ashton responded.

The fire increased in size as they approached until it was a massive, flaming ball. They were looking at the wreckage of a commercial airplane. It looked like a Boeing 757 passenger airplane. It was completely wrecked, and everything was on fire. Alison searched the wreckage with her eyes but couldn't find a single sign of life. Ashton broke the silence. "The EMP must have knocked all the planes out of the sky. Anyone in the air is probably dead now." "So many innocent people," Alison said so low it was almost a whisper. "Sis, I believe we will have many," "Watch out!" Alison screamed as loud as she could. Ashton swerved just in time to avoid an 18-wheeler abandoned in the middle of the lane. He jerked the wheel to the left so hard that Erynn's head smashed the window with such force Alison heard the thump in the front seat.

"I'm sorry," Ashton said. His body was reeling from the shot of adrenaline. "I didn't see it." He checked his sister with a glance and then looked at Erynn through the rearview mirror. Erynn stared back with an unaffected smirk on her face. Alison gripped her chest as if he had a heart attack.

They were closer to the wreckage of the plane. It was just off the highway. It looks like the pilots appeared to have attempted an emergency landing on the road but missed it and crashed into a field instead. If anyone was alive, they had already walked away. One thing was certainly evident. There were no first responders who would arrive on the scene. Odds are, no one was called about this plane crash. "My God!" Alison said, shaking while shaking her head in shock.

Alison's tears quickly turned into anger. She wanted someone to pay for what they did to these innocent people. As they passed the wreck, Alison saw Ashton force his gaze back to the road. There still needed to be a single working vehicle in sight. "I should get back to the medical center as soon as possible, Ashton," Alison said. "They are going to need me. You save lives through war. I save them through science." Ashton nodded. He agreed, and he wasn't going to stand in her way.

"Are you ready for everything that is coming, Sis? If planes fall from the sky, the hospitals are also in the dark. Think about all the life-support people who died because the power went out. Make sure you strengthen your heart to face that. You will be going into a war zone, Sis." Alison's hand fell from her chest, and she sank into her seat. "London," she whispered. "Who's London?" "A five-year boy who lost his right arm to Necrotizing Fasciitis." "Necrotizing what now?" "Flesh-eating bacteria." Ashton bit the inside of his lip. "He's on a ventilator," Alison said. "How about I take Paige back to my place while you go to the hospital? I'll come to get you after your shift." "Are you going back to help the Chief?" Ashton seemed to give it some serious thought. Ashton had a good heart. But, unfortunately, sometimes, his decisions would get in the way.

It was almost midnight when Ashton drove through the city limits of East Wakefield. Everyone seemed to be wide awake. The plane crash on the edge of town had half the population standing outside their homes, looking trying to get a better view. Many more people were out on the sidewalks and standing in the streets. Some pointed or waved at Ashton's Dodge, but most seemed preoccupied with the fire. "I can't believe how many people are outside," Ashton muttered.

Alison made sure her gun was still in the small of her waist. "Let me do the talking when we get to Nathan's," she said. She wasn't sure what made Ashton smile and her comment, but it was a gentle smile. Alison was a healer at heart, but she was also a fighter, and when it came to Paige, she was as fierce as two Erynn. At least, she hoped to be. But, unfortunately, Alison went from one wrong man to another. She couldn't figure out why, but she kept dating people who eventually hurt her.

The Dodge rolled slowly past the rundown liquor store around the corner to close Nathan's, and Ashton turned onto his street. "Which house is his?" "The white one on the corner," Alison responded. Alison grew nervous with each passing moment. She knew Paige was coming with her. What Alison didn't know was if Nathan would survive the night. Neither Ashton nor Erynn liked him, and she knew Nathan would do something stupid.

The last time Ashton was here, he threw Nathan against a few walls because Nathan would not respect the healthy boundaries Alison established for herself. "That's the one," Alison said. She pointed at a large ranch-style house at the next intersection. "Remember, Ashton, let me do all the talking. We're going to get Paige and haul ass back to the car.

Okay?" Ashton nodded, cut the ignition to the Dodge, and stuffed the key in his pocket. He took his Glock 19 off his hip and twisted the suppressor. Erynn got out of the car and did the same. Alison hoped Nathan wouldn't start any trouble. From the looks of it, Ashton and Erynn were not in the mood.

Alison figured it would be best to leave her fun under the passenger seat. She was sure her two companions would not hide their weapons from Nathan. Alison walked casually to the front door. Erynn was on her left, and Ashton was on her right. Both had that gun visible but in non-aiming positions. Alison knocked on the door, and after a few moments, it creaked open. A silhouette of a large man appeared. Nathan stepped into the moonlight, his blue eyes flitting from Alison to Ashton to Erynn. "What the hell are you three doing here?" Nathan asked with a hint of a drunken slur. Alison faced him, catching a whiff of what smelled like whiskey on his breath. She didn't offer her observations. "Evening, Erynn," Erynn responded to Nathan's greeting with a polite head nod.

"We're here to pick up Paige. I know it's late, but." Nathan cut Alison off with a grunt. "Like hell. I have rights, you know. This is my night with her." He stepped closer to Alison. Neither Erynn nor Ashton moved. Instead, they held their positions in a non-threatening manner. As usual, the two of them were on the same page. Alison, her hands at her sides. Nathan was a coward who preferred pushing women around but was too afraid to fight a man. "You want to keep those rights?" Alison asked. "Because I can smell liquor on your breath. You reek of it. You said you were sober, Nathan. You promised you were sober." "I am sober." He ran a hand over his thinning hairline. "I haven't had a drink since," He looked at the fire on the horizon, squinting like he hadn't noticed it before.

"Mommy?" A voice whispered. Alison pulled the screen door open. "Paige! Come here, sweetheart." Nathan blocked his daughter from touching Alison and spoke to his ex-girlfriend in a raised voice. In unison, Erynn and Ashton's right hands lifted just enough to catch Nathan's attention. Nathan immediately lowered his volume. "Like hell, you're taking her in the middle of the night. She's supposed to be in bed right now. And you," he shook a finger at Ashton, "No way I'm letting you in my house after what you did last time. I haven't forgotten." Ashton ignored him and smiled at his niece. Alison was shocked Ashton hadn't said a single word yet. Maybe he was growing.

"Hey, baby. Do you want to go home?" Paige nodded and clutched her stuffed elephant closer to her chest. "I want to go with Mommy. It's dark here. The lights are all out." "Just a power outage. Now go back up to your room." Alison was getting frustrated with Nathan. "No, Nathan, all the lights are off in the city. People say The United Cities is under attack, and you are too drunk even to notice." Alison snorted at him. Nathan looked toward the horizon, his eyes unfocused in his drunken haze. "Is something on fire?" "You know what. That is an entire plane that fell from the sky, and everyone on it is dead, and you slept through it. We are not doing this tonight," Alison said to Nathan. "No one is taking away my daughter." Nathan turned his back on Alison and began closing the door. "Come back tomorrow. Without your brother and his sexy bodyguard."

Before the door could close, Alison stuck her foot, put a shoulder into it, and pushed her way inside. Nathan sprawled backward to the floor, letting out a muffled cry. Alison reached for Paige's hand and said, "Time to go, baby." Paige jumped into her mother's arms. Nathan was already getting to his feet. "Some bitches never learn." He said on his way, getting up. "Close your eyes, baby," Alison said. "You're trespassing, you stupid whore," Alison dropped Nathan a second time with a punch straight to the nose. She refused to be afraid of him ever again. A thump followed the crack of breaking cartilage as Nathan crashed back to the floor. "Be glad my brother and his sexy bodyguard stayed outside. You could have much worse than a broken nose," Alison said while rubbing her knuckles and grinning at Erynn and Ashton.

UC

Ewan Hawkins stepped into the room, holding a large plastic crate. With the biggest smile, he announced, "I found them!" Skylar scooted over to make room. "What are those for?" "They detect radiation," Aiden said. "Great work Hawkins. Let's hope we don't ever need these." Aiden pulled out one of the Geiger counters and held up the probe. It was bright yellow. Aiden found the audio switch. A clicking sound came from the device as he walked into the hallway and out of the building. Everyone followed behind him. Several flashlights flicked on, spreading beams over the parking lot.

Outside, it was eerily quiet. Soft drizzles fell from the sky. As Aiden held the probe of the Geiger counter to the sky, he watched the needle. Then, the machine started hissing and making a lot of noise as Aiden waved the counter back and forth. "That doesn't sound good," Derrick said. Ewan leaned closer. "What's the reading?" After making another pass, Aiden rechecked the screen and turned around to face everyone.

"Looks like about .04 milliards per hour right now, which is normal. But the fallout might not have hit us yet. There is no way to tell if it is coming and from which direction. For now, let's not underestimate anything. Nuclear fallout could take a day or more to reach us, depending on the winds." As soon as Aiden said this, the front doors swung open, and Ernest walked out. He eyed the Geiger counter and raised an eyebrow. "Are you detecting any radiation?" the pilot asked. "Not yet," Aiden said. Ernest looked to the sky. "I'm not an expert, but a radioactive cloud might still be headed our way," Ernest said. "I'm unsure because I have no form of communication to confirm anything. Everything digital is fried. What I need is a battery-powered analog radio. Doesn't anybody have a ham radio in this town? That's my best shot of contacting Command." "Rory Cooper is a ham radio operator," Derrick said. "He used to be a technician for the power company, way back in the day, as well." "That's if he isn't wearing his tin foil hat today. He is the biggest conspiracy theorist in the world, and last I heard, he is waiting for the aliens to come back and make us all supreme beings. Or something like that." Skylar added her two cents to the conversation. "Yeah, he's not a big fan of the government, police officers, politicians, or anyone who isn't an alien, so he definitely won't help us willingly if we ask for assistance," Derrick said. Aiden lowered the probe and shut off the Geiger counter. You need to head that way, Derrick, and use your intimidation factor so that when you ask for his help, it doesn't come off as a question. Get the EOC up and running, head straight to Rory, and get him to fix every available radio in the city. We'll need his help whether he likes it or not." "On it, Chief."

"I'll ride with Derrick," Ernest said. "If that's okay with you, Chief? No disrespect intended." Aiden nodded at the pilot. "None was taken, Major. Whatever you need, Major. The rest of you head back inside for your assignments." Aiden lingered outside, looking up at the moon, and admiring the stars. The sky looked peaceful enough, but Aiden wasn't so sure. He had a sinking feeling in his gut and still felt like he was being watched. As he looked over the horizon, trying to see if a green cloud of Nuclear Fallout was coming their way, he would take care of ten thousand people plus refugees in times like this. Aiden needed to figure out what to do next for the first time in his career.

A uniformed cop called from across the room. "Excuse me, Agent?" Connor and Brentley both turned. "Uh, *Dr. Quantum?* There's a question for you from CSI in the back room."

Connor and Brentley followed the uniform down a narrow hallway into the den. It was lined with more books, plaques, and awards. Anna's apartment seemed to have quality furnishings everywhere. Everything was highly polished, oiled, or fluffed. A cardboard liquor box delivered from a high-end winery was sitting by the door. *Was the killer the delivery guy? Was that how he got in here?*

A love seat was arranged in the corner, along with a television on a console. The cabinet doors were open, but something unusual was in front of the television.

Connor noticed a sticky note on a shelf. There was something written on it. "Somebody should maybe bag this sticky note," Connor said. "It seems out of place." A young woman at a crime scene, Windbreaker, was waiting for Connor and Brentley by the cabinet with the TV. "Over here, Agents."

"What are we looking at?" Brentley asked. "Maybe nothing... but this handheld radio is blocking the television. There are no other radios in the house. Also, it is the only thing in the house with power." Connor's eyes went wide. "Do you want me to press the call button and see if anyone will answer?" The CSI techie was *green* but Connor respected that she knew to honor the crime scene.

"Latent prints all done in here?" Connor asked courteously. "Yes, sir." "Were the cabinet doors open or closed, to begin with?" Connor asked. "They were found open, just like you see them now. "Everyone out," Connor said. "Now." A handful of other cops had gathered at the door to see what was up in the den. "Dr. Quantum," one of them said, "I'm the lead Detective for Lakota on this case. I know you have the lead, but I should be here. With all due respect." "I agree. Me telling everyone to leave is not a display of power but an execution of an information vacuum. I want you to talk to everyone who was just in here. Make sure this stays tight." Connor shut the door to the den. "What's your name, by the way,

Detective?" "Detective Kayla Lowe," the lead for the Lakota Police department said. She said it confidently but not boastfully. She was an attractive woman and seemed to have a lot of experience and walked with an heir of respect and honor. "Pleasure to meet you, Detective Lowe. My large friend here is Special Agent Brentley Miller, and I am Special Agent Connor Mason."

Now that the pleasantries were over. Connor gave Brentley a looked. Then, after a moment of intense silence, Brentley pressed the button on the side of the radio to make contact with whoever was on the other side. At first, there was just static. Then came a series of beeps. And then everyone's heart stopped.

United Cities of Salleria District Judge Elsie Fisher and her boyfriend, Levi Ware, the CEO of the Pinewood Springs Mental Health Hospital, moved quickly as the midnight fog began to roll in like a blanket meant to obscure one's vision. Mr. Smith took it as a good sign. He was in the Pinewood Springs area of Wakefield, about a four-hour hike from where he murdered Jared. He trusted his younger brother Jacob was doing his part in Lakota.

The couple looked sleek, even beautiful, in the shimmer of the moonlight. It was fitting these two would die together. Mr. Smith could still hear the arrogant judges' last words to him.

"Mr. Smith, by any criteria I know, you are the evilest human being who has ever come before me in this courtroom. You may very well be the evilest human being to have ever been born of a woman's womb, and some despicable characters have come. In reparation for these unspeakable murders and repeated acts of torture, you are hereby sentenced to death. Until such a sentence is passed, you will spend the remainder of your life in a super maximum-security prison. Once there, you will have no human contact, as most of us know. You will never see the sun again. May you suffer every day of whatever little life you have left!"

No, bitch. May you and your boyfriend suffer for whatever few seconds you have left. Judge Fisher heard the first low growl and thought it must have been in her mind. Smith thought it was amusing the pair were keeping up with their fitness routine, even while all the power was off around the city.

After a few more minutes of running, Levi heard the low growl. Mr. Smith decided he was going to die first. After all, Levi's expert testimony during the Mr. Smith trial killed Smith's public persona significantly. Judge Fisher was more physically fit than her boyfriend. So much for men being better than women. Fisher was out, running him with ease. She made sure not to embarrass him, but he couldn't keep up with her stamina.

"There aren't any cats in this park, right?" Levi asked. "I mean, like panthers or lions or something." "Of course not, Hunny. Don't be silly. We are in the middle of Wakefield. "Let's get out of these woods, baby. I just heard a growl. Maybe it was a bear," Levi said to Judge Fisher. He did his best to sound brave.

There was another loud growl— this time, it was very close, and both heard it simultaneously. It sounded as if it was right on both of their heels and coming straight for them. "Come one, Levi. Let's get out here, now!" Judge Fisher said in a panic to her boyfriend. But it was already too late. Another eerie growl pierced the fog, practically on top of them.

Judge Fisher had picked up her pace, and the distance between her and her boyfriend widened considerably. "Come on, Levi. Keep up. We have to get out of here!" The judge called over her shoulder. Heavy footsteps accompanied the sound of the next growl. Judge Fisher could hear leaves crushing and heavy breathing. It was a large animal.

"I can't keep up, baby! Go get help," Levi shouted to his girlfriend. "Run! Run! It's right behind us." Adrenaline filled Judge Fisher's body, and she ran as fast and hard as if competing in the Olympics. But then, she heard male screams behind her. It sounded like Levi.

She pushed it into a gear she didn't even know she had. Judge Fisher rationalized that she had to run until she found help, and then she could have them come back and save Levi. Her boyfriend's screams were ringing in her ears, and she was in total panic.

She ran to a Ranger station, where there was a Jeep with bright headlights. She ran as fast as possible towards the Jeep, screaming, "Help! Help! There is something after us, and it got my boyfriend." The two men in the Jeep started driving toward her. She knew they would help and everything would be okay. "Help me, please. Judge Fisher said as she finally got close enough to the two men. They both hopped in the Jeep. One man was carrying a crowbar and swung it so hard at her that it broke her left arm. She felt excruciating pain rip through her body.

Everything went from bad to worse. The judge went down hard. The other man took his right hand and punched her so hard he broke one of her teeth. Judge Fisher, reeling in pain, looked up at her attackers and immediately wished she didn't. Instead, she saw two open mouths with sharpened teeth. She felt one of the men bite into her neck and the other bite into her inner thigh. What was happening, she thought?

Judge Fisher screamed until her throat was raw. She fought with all of her might, but it was pointless. She would be dead within a matter of minutes. Her eyes were fading to black, but before, she passed over until whatever was waiting on the other side. Then, a familiar face slowly appeared in her vision.

"I told you I was smarter than you, Judge Fisher. I told you I would see the sun again. It was a beautiful day today. Wouldn't you say, Elsie? Before you die, I want you to know I killed your sister watching your daughter, and I made your daughter watch. And then I drank all of your daughter's blood. I always keep my promises," Mr. Smith said as a tear fell from Judge Fisher's eye. She passed over unto the other side.

Chapter Nine

The White House was in complete disarray. Monique followed Brayden and Weston through hallways lit by emergency lamps. She was happy to see lights somewhere. Monique wasn't sure if these were battery-powered, gas-powered, or something else. But she didn't care. She wasn't in the dark anymore, and she was grateful.

She still couldn't do her popular Vice President TikTok dance videos, but she was okay with that. Agent Whitfield led the way. Everyone was asking a thousand questions. It turned out that he only knew a little more than anyone else. Secret Service Agents, Capitol Police, and metro police officers wearing SWAT uniforms stood every ten feet, cradling automatic rifles across heavy body armor, and makeshift command centers were set up every thirty feet.

The sight of all that firepower did little to relieve Monique's anxiety. While most of the country was outside looking for answers or thinking about how they would keep their perishable food items fresh, WWIII was well underway, and she had a front-row seat. Monique thought of Chase. Suddenly, reality hit her. He couldn't possibly be safe right now. There was no power anywhere. He is probably terrified and praying that his mommy comes and saves him. The NBA was the last thing on his mind.

Monique promised herself that no matter what happened, she would rescue her son.

Please, God, let Chase be safe with Ernest right now. He is all I have left in this world.

Monique prayed within her mind. She didn't want to show everyone how rattled she was, but everything happening would make anyone break.

Monique's new entourage continued through the busy halls. She realized they were only a few doors down from her office. "Can I make a stop?" she asked. "I just need to grab something." Whitfield turned to one of his men to have him escort the Vice President to her office. Without missing a beat, Whitfield asked one of his men, "Do we have an update on vehicles?" "ETA about fifteen minutes, sir. "One of his men responded. "You got five minutes, Madam Vice President Whitfield responded and gestured for one of his men to keep her safe.

Weston opened the door to the reception area and holstered his pistol. "Ma'am, I'll be right outside if you need me." "Thanks, Big Wes. You did a fine job getting us here." Brayden entered, sweeping his flashlight over the space as Monique walked to her private office. The Vice President of the United Cities of Salleria has two office spaces: a nondescript room in the West Wing of the White House and an ornate ceremonial office in the Eisenhower Executive Office Building next door. Monique still needed to decorate her West Wing office, but she added photos of Chase and her late husband, Author. On the top shelf was a model of a fighter jet just like the one she used to fly.

Monique sat down at her desk and took a deep breath. Her office smelled of leather and books, and the familiar surroundings comforted her. She'd spent countless hours in her West Wing Office because she wanted to be the best. She knew she wasn't the most talented person for the job, but she committed to working the hardest at it.

Letting her eyes close, Monique pretended this was just a typical day, like any other. "We really should hurry, Ma'am," Brayden reminded her. And, just like that, Brayden's interruption tumbled her world. Taking a deep breath, *The Vice President of The Crumbling Salleria* responded, "Okay, I'm all set." Brayden joined her at the door.

Whitfield gave her five mins, and Monique only took three. Then, finally, they returned to the hallway to find Senator John Romani waiting for them. He was an old-school politician who had held his seat for three decades. He is also the grandfather of one of the kidnapped girls taken prisoner in the North Kangavar catastrophe twenty-four months ago. "Please tell me this shit isn't true," Romani said in his heavy Texas accent. "We don't know anything more than you do, Senator. But all the intel suggests this is retaliation from the North Kangavar incident." Monique replied with kindness. She thought she would be angry with the Senator from Houston, but now that Chase was missing, she understood him.

"This was an attack by the North Kangavarians," came a voice intruding into the conversation. It belonged to Senator Dean Byers, one of the oldest members of Congress, who was walking down the hallway with several staffers. Even during the end of the world, he managed to be both smug and important. Despite the hour, the old Southern Republican looked like he'd just come from the Senate floor. "My staff just confirmed it," Byers said. Romani' didn't bother replying for now. "Those were nukes we launched, weren't they? And they were heading toward North Kangavar, right?" Monique just stared at the Byers. There was no reason to say anything right now. It wouldn't get the country out of the dark. She let him finish talking. "I sure hope they kill every one of those fucking bastards. It's time to show the world," Brayden interrupted, "Good evening, fine gentleman." Both Senators ignored the Chief of Staff. "We're at war," Byers said, stroking his long mustache. "Power is out all along the East Coast, not just here. I'm," "Where else?" Monique interrupted the well-dressed Senator. Byers shook his head. "Everywhere, Madam Vice President. Every goddamn where." Byers replied.

Monique gasped. Everywhere? How were they going to run the country with no power? Finally, Monique said the obvious statement everyone was thinking. "Virtually every aspect of Sallerian society depends on power. Without it, our cities will become chaotic, and civilization will crumble." The hallway quickly filled with more Congressmen and their support staff. Political party lines were a thing of the past as they scrambled for every scrap of news. In the dark, it seemed all politicians were equal, and partisanship was preferred. No one wanted to be out of the information loop, and everyone *needed* information.

"It's time to move, Vice President Maddox," Weston said. He had his gun drawn again. A dozen Secret Service Agents and police officers rushed down the hallway, armed with automatic rifles or shotguns. Flashlight beams pin-balled across every available hard and soft surface like strobe lights. Halfway down the passage, Special Agent Whitfield talked to Senator Bayleigh Guerra. For whatever reason, the Senator decided at the end of the world that she would wear heels. She sported a designer purse in one hand and an expensive briefcase in the other. Her dark navy-blue suit was accented with tasteful gold jewelry. Leave it to her to get dressed for the end of the world.

"Everyone, please come with us," Whitfield said. "We're evacuating. Now." "And going where?" Romani grunted. Monique interrupted, "Not now, John. "Please follow me, sir," Whitfield said, avoiding the question. Then, passing through the darkness, Special Agent Whitfield led a large group of Senators, their teams, Presidential Cabinet members, and their teams away from the White House. Both the Capitol Building and White House members were being ushered to safety.

Monique couldn't help but wonder if this were the last time she would ever see this place. Two heavily armed men were standing guard at the back exit. They wore earpieces that hung uselessly from their ears. The man on the left propped the door open, allowing Whitfield to advance with his assault rifle shouldered. Monique half expected to hear the whoosh of a Black Hawk as they left the building, but as soon as they were outside, the night's stillness was the only thing there.

Monique hurried after the group. She was doing her best not to fear the worst, but the worse was already happening. Whitfield waved the group toward a half dozen black Suburbans. Even more, officers waited around the vehicles. "Vice President Maddox and Senator Romani, with me," Whitfield said. He moved to the sixth truck and opened the rear passenger-side door. Brayden and Weston tried to follow, but Whitfield shook his head. "I'm sorry, gentlemen, but this is a priority transport." Monique halted and asked, "What do you mean?" Romani elbowed passed her and climbed in, sliding his bulk over the seats. "We don't have room to evacuate everyone right now," Whitfield said solemnly.

Monique could tell he didn't like this part of his job, and Whitfield was following orders. "We will come back for the others." Monique watched other ranking senators pile into the vehicles ahead, but when she turned, Guerra and Byers were still standing with a small group behind the SUVs. "We need to hurry, ma'am," Whitfield said. There was an urgency to his words that scared Monique. She felt something was off. Secret Service Agents rarely lost their nerve. The threat, whatever it is, must be imminent. "It's okay," Brayden said. "You go." "No," Monique replied. "I'm not leaving them. There's room for everyone if we squeeze in." Whitfield cursed under his breath. To her surprise, Monique didn't have to say another word. Whitfield had a heart much bigger than she thought. He jerked his chin at the vehicle. Brayden and Weston hurried into the car.

"Thank you," Monique said. "Why are we not being evacuated?" Guerra asked. "I want to go with them. I don't want to wait here to die!" She rushed past Whitfield, but the convoy was already moving. Several staffers ran after her, and Monique's heart broke as she watched. She forced herself to look for a few more agonizing seconds before she looked away. Monique didn't want to feel special, but the country had protocols.

"Hold on," the driver of her vehicle said. "We're going to be moving pretty fast in a minute." "Where are we going?" Romani asked. The driver, a Secret Service Agent, cautiously drove through the restricted access road until he turned the wheel to the right and pulled out onto H St NW, providing Monique with the answer. She knew what building was in that direction. Brayden leaned closer to Monique and said, "I thought we would be leaving D.C." "I did, too, but there must not be a way to get us out in time," she whispered back. "I think we are under attack." The convoy picked up speed as they moved east down H St NW, weaving around stalled cars, tires squealing. Monique didn't bother asking how the Secret Service had procured available vehicles. They could have been underground, or perhaps they were hardened against EMPs. Either way, she was one step closer to finding her son.

Stranded motorists got out of their cars and waved from the side of the road, but the driver didn't slow down. Within minutes, their headlights shot across The Cheesecake Factory by the Milken Institute, capturing Secret Service and Marines running to set up positions.

Behind them was Marine One, the aircraft carrying the President of The United Cities of Salleria. The trucks rolled to a halt alongside the Starbucks on H St NW, a few blocks after passing The Cheesecake Factory, and then made a complete circle and returned to the White House. Weston jumped out and opened the back door, holding out a hand for Monique. She grabbed her backpack, climbed out of the Suburban, and followed the group toward an unnamed dark building. Her first instinct was to jump in Marine One and take it to Chesterfolk and get her son, but she decided against it.

"This way, Madam Vice President," Weston said. He directed her toward the heavily guarded back entrance. She figured the convoy was driving full speed to confuse any enemy threats in the vicinity. The goal would have been to disguise their motives and the identities of those in each vehicle. This may be why Special Agent Whitfield didn't want to bring everyone. Or perhaps they were spooked by intel they received while they were driving. She didn't know what was happening anymore, but she could tell they were in a different section of The White House. A very familiar part— The West Wing. They were back where they started. What the hell is going on?:

There was a series of beeps, and it sounded like someone pushed play on an audio player. Was it the killer? Connor wondered. Who else would it be? He'd left a working radio, hadn't he? So how in the hell did he get a working radio? He wanted us to see it, and he wanted us to use it. There was no doubt in Connor's mind that the killer had them all in an elaborate game.

Initially, there was only static. Followed by hissing sounds, and then a voice began to speak. There was a strong southern accent. It sounded like a Creole accent— definitely from the Deep South. Now, this was stranger than strange. It took Connor's breath away. Listening to the sounds coming over the short-wave hand receiver was like listening to the radio back in the 1950s.

Connor's gut tightened another notch. Were we about to learn about the killer? Whatever we knew, it could not have been anything good. At least not good for us.

"It is time for the people of the Wakefield and Lakota to listen for a change," the man said in heavily southern-accented English. "Each of you is going to die very soon. I have ensured each of you would be standing in the room right where you are. You turned your back on our Lord. He is the *Captain* of your fate and has determined that you must die since I have your attention now. The occupant of this apartment defamed our Lord. She blasphemed him named, and she now has suffered his vengeance. By the time you have heard this recording, your Captain would have judged at least three more souls. They were all wicked and unjust."

This was our guy. The one who'd thrown Anna twelve stories to her death? And before that, he made her scream to get everyone's attention.

"You tried to blot out the sun. Now we will make sure you live in eternal darkness. "And now, you will pay with your lives. Each one of you will pay. You took away his freedom. We will take away your families, your friends, and your lives. You all will die gloriously, and the world will remember your embarrassment forever. None of you are safe."

The audio played some more, but there were no more spoken words. The audio ended strangely. Like a phone operator, an automated voice said, "You have one minute left." And after precisely one minute, the computerized voice returned only to say, "Goodbye."

"Holy shit!" Brentley said into the maddening silence. "What the hell was that? Who the hell is this maniac?" Detective Kayla Lowe uttered.

The white noise and static returned just as everyone thought everything was over.

Alison studied the building as Ashton pulled up to the Wakefield Medical Center around one in the morning. "You see any lights?" she asked. Ashton shook his head. "The generators must not be working." Alison continued running her hand through Paige's hair. She was sleeping peacefully, and Alison hated to wake her, but it was time for her to get to work.

"Wake up, baby girl," Alison whispered in Paige's ear. It was amazing how dark it was, even with the moon high in the sky. Alison could hardly see Paige's face as she blinked groggily. "You can go back to sleep in a little bit, baby," Alison told her. "Mommy has to work for a while. People need my help." "I want to come with you, Mommy." "You get to stay with me for a bit, Niece." Ashton interrupted playfully to keep his sister from hurting Paige's feelings. Ashton grinned, his teeth so white they seemed to glow in the faint moonlight. "Come on. Let's go to your crazy uncle's house and do things mommy doesn't want us to do." "Yay," Paige screamed with excitement. "She'll be safe with Erynn and me," Ashton said. "What time should we come back to get you?" "What time is it right now?" Ashton looked at his analog watch. "A quarter after one," he said with a yawn. "That thing works?" He shrugged. "Looks like it." "Stop back around one then." "On it."

Alison handed Paige to Erynn, and Erynn held Paige as if she was her own. It amazed Alison how feminine Erynn was but with all the moxie of an alpha male. "I wish you'd get a car seat, Ashton," Alison said to her brother. "Sis, how can I pick up the ladies with a car seat." he huffed. "Women love a man who can care for children, dummy!" "Hmm. Great point. Besides, she's fine, and I'm tired. I promise I'll drive safe." Alison leaned forward and kissed Paige on the forehead. "I love you, baby. Be good to Uncle Ashton." "Okay, Mommy." Alison locked eyes with Ashton one more time, and he offered a reassuring nod. Then, holding in tears, she walked toward the emergency room.

Where there should have been flashing red and blue lights accompanied by an alarming siren in the distance, coupled with never-staying-closed double doors of the emergency room, there was a dark, EMP version of the emergency room. Several nurses, doctors, other medical staff, and a lone hospital stretcher with a bloody, wounded patient resting. When Alison arrived, everyone welcomed her into chaotic emergency room drama.

There was a lantern in the small lobby. Several people were sleeping in chairs with blankets draped over their bodies. "Alison, thank God you're here." A voluptuous woman with a beautiful, thick British accent said as she hurried out from behind the receptionist's desk. It was the nursing supervisor, Zara Ryan. She repositioned a candle on the counter and motioned for Alison to come to the small office. "I'm so sorry," Alison whispered, keeping her voice low, so she didn't wake the sleepers in the lobby. "I was in the park when," Alison caught herself from revealing what she knew about the EMP attack. "When my car died. My brother picked me up and took me to East Wakefield to get Paige."

After the two exchanged sincere niceties, Zara explained to Alison how the generators were not working, how all the power was out, and how there were only two doctors in the ER, one in the skilled nursing facility, and only four of their usual ten nurses had shown up for work. "It is pure hell, Alison. We lost two patients on life support," Zara finished, looking at the floor. Alison turned toward the doors leading to the ICU and ER. She was afraid to open the doors. Three patients were connected to life support, and London was one of them.

"None of the key cards work, Alison. You'll have to use this," Zara said. She grabbed an extra key from a ring on the wall and handed it to Alison.

"Alison, about time you showed up," Doctor Kerry said. There was frustration in his tone, but Alison couldn't blame him for that. He was sitting beside London's bedside, carefully pumping air by Ambu bag, a handheld tool used to deliver positive pressure ventilation to any subject with insufficient or ineffective breaths. It consists of a self-inflating bag, a one-way valve, a mask, and an oxygen reservoir to pump by hand. It had been hours since the lights had gone out, and there was no telling how long Doctor Kerry had manually pumped air into London's lungs. Alison's heart warmed at the site. Only so many doctors would have assigned themselves such a painful task. Manually pumping air into London's lungs was a job for a nurse, but Doctor Kerry didn't see it that way.

London, the only surviving life support patient, was also the youngest. He was just a little boy in a chemically-induced coma. The flesh-eating disease had infected so much of his arm the hospital had to cut it off at the elbow. Alison was shocked to see London still alive, but the odds of his survival were grim. No one could manually push air into a patience lunges forever. Alison feared the worst— everyone in the hospital was going to die.

The white noise cracked across the radio speaker, and Connor, Brentley, and Detective Kayla Lowe were frozen in place. At first, there was only white noise, and you could hear someone breathing. Then, three knocks wrapped on a door, and Connor's heart dropped to his stomach. It was Anna. The trio was listening to Anna respond to someone knocking at her door. "Oh my God, did the killer record our murder scene?" Kayla asked, but no one answered.

Moments later, someone claiming to be a VIP serviceman for the luxury apartment was asking to remove the trash. After a bit of back and forth, Anna opened the door, and you could hear her body crash to the ground with extreme force. She never stood a chance. "Son of a bitch!" Brentley said. "The sick fuck recording everything so we can hear." Connor was still holding his breath. He didn't know what to say. He wanted to say something but the shock of losing his fiancé and getting to hear her last moments had his words in a chokehold.

He had recorded everything, playing to an audience the whole time he was here. The feeling in the den went from bad to a lot worse. Connor's; the brain was working overtime analyzing the facts and dissecting the killer's psychological profile. Every single detail was recorded, including her screams as he cut her. The killer wanted an audience and as many people to see Anna's death as possible. Anna's murder was both calculated and personal. But strangely enough, Connor didn't feel it was personal to the killer. He seemed detached from the murder and attached at the same time. It was odd.

The trio could hear the killer hoist Anna upside over the balcony railing. He didn't toy with her anymore. His breathing was calm and unlabored— at it was clear, too. The killer's sound quality led Connor to believe the killer was wearing a lapel mic. But how? There was no power? And how would the killer know to use audio instead of video? Did the killer know the power would be out? Or was he smart enough to have every contingency planned?

All three heard Anna's body hitting the ground with destructive force. It was terrible. How could anyone murder someone in cold blood and want to be seen doing it? Connor felt rage racing through his body. He wanted to kill this bastard, but there was no time to dwell on the feeling because the shock and awe antics weren't over just as the situation couldn't get any worse. As if on Que, the killer showed us he was in complete control and twenty steps ahead of us. The killer spoke. His voice was soft and evil. "I hope you are listening to this recording Detective Lowe. I am sure they will assign you this case. Did you find my radio? I know so much more about you than you know of me. If you stay out of my way, I won't kill you. Now, be a good girl and move two steps to your right. I want to see Dr. Quantum." Everyone in the room gasped in horror. What did he mean by *see* Dr. Quantum, and how did he know I was here? Was there a camera on this radio? And if so, how was it working when all the power was out?

And then, the killer spoke into the microphone as if he was only talking to Connor. "You can try to capture me," he said, "but who will watch Mama Linda and Papa Anthony? Or what about Sophia and little Riley?" Connor and Kayla were speechless, and all Brentley could manage was, "Holy shit, Connor. This bastard is targeting you."

Ready or not, Connor was one of the main characters in a game he didn't sign up to play. The white noise stopped as soon as Connor caught his breath, and the killer's voice came through as clear as pure water. "Keep this radio with you, Dr. Quantum. Your *Lord* will contact you very soon. After all, *Vengeance is his.*"

Flanked by Weston and Brayden, Monique rushed after the politicians and staffers on the list to be evacuated first. She tried not to think of Senator Guerra running after the convoy in high heels and throwing her designer purse to the side. It had no more value to her since she thought she would die. But Monique was sure Senator Guerra thought she would die— maybe she was right.

Monique was directed through several vault doors. A Secret Service Agent instructed them to wait as he punched biometric access codes into the control systems and swiped his card. The final door opened to an elevator. The agent gestured toward Monique, and she quickly stepped into the elevator and hugged the left wall. "Why is this elevator working when the lights aren't?" Senator Romani asked. No one replied to his question. Monique figured everyone was too stuck in their minds to answer. Somehow the engineers of the White House had prepared for such an attack on the United Cities. Monique began to think about the fake evacuation that had happened. Was it all for a show? If so, a show for whom?

Who was watching? Did North Kangvar have working Satellites? Were they on Sallerian soil? She didn't know.

From what she knew about North Kangavar's Hwasong-14 and Hwasong-15 missile systems, with the 15s thought to have a maximum range of about 8,100 miles, puts North Kangavar missiles within reach of more or less all of the United Cities of Salleria cities. Monique was so confused with all the possible death scenarios running through her mind. It would take a land-based missile about 30 minutes to fly between Kalinizran and the United Cities; a submarine-based missile could strike in as little as 10 to 15 minutes after launch. She wondered how many more attacks were coming.

Still in the elevator, in her mind's eye, Monique pictured them moving down six stories to the Presidential Emergency Operations Center. It hardly seemed deep enough to survive a direct hit from a nuclear bomb, but that was what it had been designed to withstand. So she was shocked when she saw the doors of the elevator open. The White House was EMP fortified after all, or at least the grid connecting to the PEOC had been spared. Either way, this was the first time in what seemed like an eternity she saw *actual* electricity. *There was light underground.* Monique almost passed out from excitement.

Footfalls echoed down the tile floor as the group continued toward the East Wing. With every step, Monique felt a seed of hope blooming inside of her. Her odds of finally getting the information she needed to discover what was happening to the world and she was finally a step closer to finding Chase.

Monique was grateful the government was more prepared for an EMP attack than she thought. She couldn't wait to see President Andrew Shelton. He was her good friend; if anyone knew how to escape this disaster, it would be him. Shelton wasn't only a respected war hero but a leader who brought people together from both sides of the aisle. He was the most popular President of all time, and his approval ratings had been in the nineties for the past three years. by the entire United Cities.

The double doors parted, revealing a room she'd only seen in pictures. The walls were lined with large monitors and data scrolling across the screens. There was video footage playing on other monitors, and at the center of the room was a long table that seated at least thirty people. They were officially below the East Wing of the White House in the President's Emergency Operations Center. The PEOC exists to handle nuclear contingencies and is different from the White House Situation Room, which is located in the basement of the West Wing of the White House. In 2010 the elevator Monique just rode and many secret corridors leading to the POC were built in secrecy. A separate, underground electric grid was created for the PEOC, and EMP defenses were built.

The blast doors clanked shut behind Monique. She walked toward the table with Romani and Brayden. A dozen people were seated, including Secretary of State Hallie Barrera and Secretary of Defense Evie Baxter. "Welcome to the PEOC," Senator Ryan Anderson said in the crisp voice that typically made Monique shudder. Senator Ryan Anderson was the only sitting Senator that outwardly attempted to make Monique's life hell. He hated her; she never intended to kiss his ass or change his mind. Monique had no desire to set women back 400 years by appealing to his little fragile male ego. As far as she was concerned, he was a little man in a prominent position.

However, It was the end of the world, and the country's most influential people were hiding underground. So Monique decided to let her hair down. She spoke to Senator Anderson without hostility, then let her hair down by it out of a ponytail. Monique let her hair flow over her copper-brown skin, the same color as an autumn leaf. She had smoldering, doe-brown eyes and a queenly figure. Her hair was velvet-black, caressing her pinched-in cheekbones and swooping in coils over her swan's neck. She had puffy, pouting lips, and they were blossom soft and sparkling, wizard-white teeth matching an angelic smile that made everyone fall in love with her within seconds of meeting her. She represented every bit of the male fantasy and carried herself with supreme confidence. She was highly sexualized by others, but she never let any man have access to her, which only made her more desirable. Monique oozed both danger and prosperity and was physically undeniable.

She ran her sleeve across her wet forehead and asked, "Where's President Shelton and Secretary of Defense Baxter?" Anderson lowered his head, and for a moment, everyone in the room stopped what they were doing. The non-response was the only answer Monique needed. She slowly took a seat in the closest chair, her brief feeling of hope deflating like air from a punctured tire. "Air Force One went down a few hours ago somewhere over Wichahpi. It was taking President Shelton to a secure location after a public event in South Wachiwi," Anderson said. "Secretary of Defense Baxter's plane took her to Chayton Rock Mountain Complex when it disappeared from radar."

A dozen other conversations were going on in the background after Senator Anderson gave her the report, but Monique blocked them all out. If the EMP had knocked Air Force One out of the sky above Wichahpi, it would have also hit Chestorfolk. Wichahpi and Chestorfolk were neighboring cities.

"How?" Senator Romani asked. "How were these EMPs set off?" "We're still trying to piece together the evidence, but it appears the North Kangavarians used fake transponder codes to get several aircraft into our airspace," Anderson said. "We managed to take out two of them, but the other three were able to detonate nukes at altitudes ranging from fifty-two thousand to sixty-five thousand feet at strategic points over the United Cities." "The North Kangavarians set off multiple nukes?" Monique asked. "Yes, Madam Vice President Maddox." "There is one more thing, Ma'am. Effectively immediately, you are no longer our first African Sallerian Vice President. You are now the first female African Sallerian President. You are in command of this PEOC, ma'am. First, we need to get you sworn in, and then we are all awaiting your orders."

All eyes centered on Monique. She almost passed out from shock. *What a fucking night,* she thought.

The air was thin. Erynn took a deep breath and sucked it deep into her lungs. It wasn't enough. She tried again, her open mouth taking in more blood than air. She was dying.

Her heart began to race, her mind quickly following suit. Another long breath, and again it was not enough to satisfy her hungry lungs. This was it; Erynn Aliza Justice was minutes away from dying. It happened so fast.

She heard the quiet bubbling of blood exiting her chest. The bubbling grew, her mind transforming it into a deafening roar. How on earth did she get shot? Ashton was driving, and Paige was sleeping in her arms. How could anyone get the best of them? It didn't make any sense because they were always careful. But there was no time for questions. She had to do something and do it now. Before her, she drowned in her blood.

Her heart beat faster inside its protective cage of bone. It was pounding as it if was the lead drummer in a marching band. She surveyed the area, searching for anything about Ashton, the Dodge, the enemy. But the brown dirt of Wakefield stared back at her, soaking up her blood. She dreamed of a life without war for so long.

She sucked in another long breath, her mind ignoring the deafening roar of blood leaving her body. She wanted air— air meant life. And Ashton still needed her. Her blood was draining out of her body, taking her life force with it. Soon her mind would slow to a crawl, and she would slip into unconsciousness and go into whatever world awaited her. She doubted it would be Heaven. But she wasn't a bad person. She had a lousy job.

In the distance, there was another deafening roar. At first, Erynn thought her mind was playing tricks on her, but lying on her back, she saw a helicopter approaching from the distance. But who had working helicopters? The noise increased, and she blinked, straining her eyes. Something was making its way toward her.

With everyone once of her remaining strength, she tried to focus her fading eyes so she could see in the distance, but her body was losing blood too fast. The helicopter cruised the skyline and momentarily crossed in front of the moon, giving her enough time to identify the helicopter as a North Kangavarian bird. Suddenly everything came back to her. While everyone was worried about the EMP and nuclear fallout, the North Kangavarians had invaded key areas in secrecy. The high-powered machine guns ripped through the Dodge from the air, and neither she nor Ashton ever saw it coming.

As the chopper came into focus, she saw the North Kangavarian flag. Its circled star burned bright red in the night sky. She figured they saw a moving car and opened fire. The growl of the helicopter's rotors drowned out the sound of blood escaping her body. For a moment, fear replaced her desire for oxygen. She quickly stifled her fear and decided she would die on her feet. They would have to shoot her off her feet because she was not going down without a fight.

With her breath labored and weak and her head pounding as stars crept across her vision, the sound of the chopper grew closer. An involuntary tear fell from her face as the helicopter hovered above her. She grabbed her rifle and stood to her feet. It took a herculean effort, and nearly 98% of her energy was left. But these losers would shoot her off her feet. She refused to turn her face from them in fear.

Dozens of stars danced across her vision, mixed with a tint of red. Her brain was shutting down. She had only seconds of consciousness left. But she couldn't die yet; she had to return fire. She never missed these bastards who didn't give her a fair chance to fight back. With all her might, she shouldered her rifle. It felt like it weighed ninety pounds. She looked to where she thought the pilot would be, waiting for the right time to take him with her.

Coughing, she lurched forward, nearly falling to the ground. She blinked, hoping her eyes would come into focus, but life was already leaving her. It was too late. Her vision was fading. Then, in the blink of an eye, it was gone. Her body collapsed to the ground, and she could feel the tears flowing freely down her face. She was about to die in seconds. With one last desperate breath, before her mind shut down, Erynn raised her hand to the sound of the helicopter and shot the middle finger at the pilot. If she couldn't get off a round, shooting the finger would have to suffice. Before her hand fell back to her side, Erynn Aliza Justice was dead.

Less than two hours later, Connor and Detective Kayla Lowe were inside the morgue at Pinewood Springs. Brentley volunteered to stay back in Lakota and finish processing the crime scene in the St. Paul luxury apartments. Brentley was thorough and investigated crime scenes with the very best of them. As a result, he is more than able to get any remaining details.

They were joined by the chief medical examiner, Zak Atkinson, and the dental expert, Dr. Brendon Steele. Dr. Brendon Steele took his time examining both bodies before he said anything to us. He had already studied photographs of the bite areas at the crime scene. He was a funny-looking man. He was overweight, balding, and had three or four strands of hair looped across his big oval head. He looked like Homer Simpson. However, he was a pleasant man and very thorough with his work. He left no stone unturned.

"Okay, okay. I'm ready to talk about the nature of the bites now." After a lengthy examination, he turned to Connor and Detective Kayla Lowe. The man was brilliant. There were so many big words in his explanation. Kayla was sure Connor thought he traveled back when he was a Ph.D. candidate. She understood the jest of what the Homer Simpson-looking man was saying. She admired Connor for not attempting to *mansplain* anything to her. Homer Simpson guy was so excited he had a nerdgasm talking to the medical examiner because he wasn't briefing the two law enforcement representatives in the cold and dark room.

Kayla ran through her mind what she understood from the talk. On both victims, there were multiple bite marks. The male was bitten severely, and he was sure the bites came from both a man and a wolf. He said the same thing about the female, too. But he said the women seemed to the medical examiner said the woman would have died from blunt trauma to the head even if she wasn't bitten. The ME explained how she took a significant beating before the wolf and people bit into her. Kayla asked how Homer Simpson could tell the difference between the wolf and the people, and he went on to explain humans and heterodonts, and blah blah blah— oh, and something about the different functions of teeth and how some animals have evolved to have the same type of teeth.

From his experience, he believed the attacking animal was a rather large Northwestern Wolf. But the real shocker was Homer Simpson man didn't want to call the attacks an animal attack. He said the animal was following the instructions of a man, and when the man told him to stop, the animal did. He classified this as a powerful group of men hunting with a wolf. And both victims were drained of their blood. He then said the humans drank the blood, not the wolves, because wolves don't drink blood, they eat flesh with blood on it.

The medical examiner then looked at Kayla and Connor and said, "Whoever you two are looking for is unlike that which you have ever seen. You can't train for a man who leads wolves into battle." Kayla and Connor were both left speechless.

Chapter Ten

Aiden froze like there was a gun pointed at his head. His heart dropped to his stomach, and his adrenaline spiked. Truth and Jenny Parker were standing outside, and Aiden didn't talk to them yet. But he knew it was time to tell them. If the shoe was reversed, Aiden knew he would want to know— no matter how much the truth hurt.

Aiden stood slowly and grabbed the lantern off his desk. The darkness felt heavy, oppressive, and almost supernatural. Aiden felt like he was swallowed up in nothingness. He was so nervous about telling his friend how he failed to save his son that he couldn't see Truth's And Jenny's faces for a brief moment. He took a deep breath and waited for his friends' faces to reappear. Aiden's eyes slowly came back into focus as his heart rate slowed, saving his heart from bursting within his chest.

Exhausted and unprepared to talk with the Parkers, he walked out of his office like a soldier heading home after losing his friends in battle. Derrick walked with him, his head bowed. Derrick always had a sixth sense when it came to Aiden, and Aiden needed his superhero-looking friend now— more than ever. Derrick didn't offer any words. He knew there were no words that would work right now. So instead, he provided his big, hulking presence as a shield against the disappointment of failure.

With each step, Aiden's anxiety built with every step he took through the station. Finally, he knew it was time to break the bad news. Unlocking the door to the lobby beyond his office, Aiden and Derrick walked what felt like a thousand steps. Truth stood just beyond the door, holding his wife, Jenny. She trembled in his arms. Behind them, outside the glass doors, people gathered in the streets and Triangle Garden. They all waited for answers. Aiden wasn't any more ready for them than he was prepared for Truth And Jenny.

"Truth, Jenny," Aiden said, slowly walking toward them. "I'm so sorry. We did everything we could, but we were too late." Jenny burst into tears, burying her face against her husband's swelling chest. Aiden didn't want to stretch out there waiting, so he decided to tell them about their son within seconds of seeing them. "Where is he, Aiden?" Truth asked. His voice was surprisingly solid and gentle towards the Chief. "He's here at the station. I broke protocol and brought him here because I knew it's what you would do for me." "Thank you, Aiden. Jenny and I are grateful for you." Aiden swallowed, tears forming in his throat. "You are a better friend than what I deserve, Truth. I am so sorry." When Aiden said this, he could no longer hold in tears. He broke into tears.

"Follow us," Derrick stepped in and gently said to Truth and Jenny. "Let's go say goodbye to your son." Side by side, the two officers led Truth and Jenny into the office. Aiden stopped outside the door to the empty room where they stored Jared's body. Derrick inserted the key and opened the door. The glow from the lantern spread through the room, washing over the blanket covering little Jared's body.

Truth and Jenny slowly walked into the room. Halfway across, Jenny collapsed to her knees. Her screams tore through the office walls like the screams of a thousand mothers. Truth put his hands under her and helped her stand, and they continued to the table. "My

God," Jenny cried out. "Why is he grey?" She looked over her shoulder, eyes pleading with Aiden.

Aiden put a hand on Truth's shoulder. "I hate telling you this, but I know you want to know, even though it will haunt you forever. Jared was drained of all his blood. There are two fang-like holes in his thigh and two in his neck. It is as if someone sucked the blood out of him. Truth pulled from Aiden's grip. "What the hell do you mean, Aiden? What the hell happened to our baby?" Aiden set the lantern down on the floor. "Your son was murdered, Truth. I don't know who did it or why, but I promise you I will do everything I can to find that person." Aiden was as gentle as he had ever been.

Truth pulled the blanket away from Jared's neck and down to his chest. His expression twisted into a mask of horror in the dim light, and there was a moment of silence before the big man broke into tears. His screams were louder than Jenny's.

"Erynn, wake up!" a voice screamed. Two strong hands gripped her, shaking her violently. "Erynn!" the voice yelled again. The dense fog hovering over Erynn's eyes slowly began to clear, and a face emerged. It was Ashton. "You were having a nightmare," he said. Erynn sat up, clawing at her tired eyes. She used sign language to tell Ashton she had a bad dream about North Kangavar. The conversation included all the details of her dream, how she died and couldn't find him or Paige anywhere. She ended by telling Ashton how she believed the night was just getting started and how she felt North Kangavarian troops were on the ground and they needed to be extra careful.

Ashton sat next to Erynn and wrapped his arms around her shoulders. She laid her head on his chest and regained her composure. After a few minutes, Erynn raised her head. She finally realized she was in the safety of Ashton's house, and neither of them was dead.

Erynn laid her head back down on the small pillow. She knew she didn't need to tell Ashton anything else because he knew Erynn had great intuition. He knew it would come true if she said they would have to worry about ground troops. She was rarely wrong about anything and always seemed to know things before anyone else knew them.

Ashton knew her better than anyone else. "Go back to sleep, Erynn. I won't let anything happen to you." Darkness flooded the room. She closed her eyes and found the image of the North Kangavarian flag entering her thoughts. She would be ready for them next time. No one was allowed to kill her and get away with it— not even in her dreams.

Connor and Kayla were on their way back to Lakota. Finally, they didn't have to travel the two-hour drive on foot, which would have made it a fifteen-hour walk. Kayla had an old 1970 Chevrolet Chevelle SS 454. Connor loved every bit of it. It was all black with chrome trimming, and from what he knew about old-school muscle cars, this was the apex of them all. The more time Connor spent with Kayla, the more he realized she was as bright as beautiful. She was humble, too. But she was a ferocious investigator— one of the best he had ever seen.

They talked for the entire drive back about the facts of the case. Kayla began the conversation by telling Connor everything she had established before and after he arrived at the crime scene. She didn't miss a beat and connected dots he hadn't seen himself. She was impressive. After she ran down all of what she was thinking, she asked, "So what is in that big mind of yours, Connor?" "Our guy is smart— probably smarter than both of us combined, but I can't shake the feeling he is taking orders from someone much smarter than our killer. I also think we have multiple killers on our hands because unless there are a thousand working cars driving the streets, this killing seemed to happen about the same time Anna died."

Connor noticed Kayla's eyebrows lift as he mentioned Anna by her first name. It was a mistake of his, but Kayla didn't push. She let the moment pass, and Connor was grateful for her tact. "I am confused about one thing in particular," Connor admitted. "It feels like our killer, *or killers,* aren't from around here, but sometimes it feels they know the city well. They don't seem to have issues coordinating large distances and synchronized kills." Kayla didn't say anything. She seemed to be letting it all sink in. Connor kept going. "As I am sure you have guessed, I have been working high-profile cases in the Wakefield and Lakota areas for years. So I guess you are no stranger to high-profile cases, too." Kayla nodded her approval. Was she impressed by Connor noticing her expertise? He wasn't sure. "One thing is pretty clear," Connor continued. "Our killers will kill again and probably already have. We are too many steps behind them. There is a recognizable pattern to these killings. They are very violent and public— not to mention this new wrinkle of the blood drained from the victims. And I don't even know how to process killers who hunt with wolves. What's that about?"

Kayla finally said something. "Can you clarify that, Agent Mason?" "Sure, but call me Connor. All my friends do." "So, we are friends now?" Kayla tossed in his direction jokingly. "Well, it seems we headed in that direction." "Okay, Connor, go into more details for me." Connor looked into Kayla's big brown eyes and started." "Our St. Paul killer opened with a loud boom. I think he may be warming up to something much bigger. But to what, I don't know." Kayla jumped into the conversation and said what Connor didn't want to see. "I guess we must wait until he kills again to get the next piece of the puzzle?" "Exactly." They both sat in silence for a few short seconds. Neither of them wants the killer to kill again, but both know he would have to for them to track him better.

"I think our killer will stick to killing one person at a time," Connor said. "Really? Why is that?" "That's a fair question, but I believe he wants these killings to be about him. If he kills too many people at once, the media, and I am not even sure if they can publish anything with the power being out, will make the killings about the victims. He doesn't want that. He wants to be the star. No! He needs to be the star." "That is what bothers me the most, Connor," Kayla said with grave concern. She kept talking. "If the killer wants this murder to be all about him, and I agree with you, how did he know you and your friend... what's his name?" "Brentley." "Yes. Brentley. How did he know all three of us would be at the crime scene? It is as if he knew more about our respective departments than us. He knew all three of us would work *Ms. Anna's* case." Kayla said Anna's name with empathy. Connor wanted to kick himself. She made the connection that Connor knew her. But again, she didn't push. "I think he wants so much attention that caused the biggest scene possible and put enough pieces in motion to where all three high-profile investigators in the area would be on the case." Connor thought about this for a moment. She was right. The killer did play the system to his advantage. He would certainly get all the attention he wanted now.

"I think you are right, Detective Lowe." "Please, call me Kayla. Since we are becoming friends and all." Her big brown eyes shone brightly in the dark. "Kayla. I think you are right, Kayla." The two smiled at each other and rode in silence for the remaining fifteen-minute trip back into Lakota.

"Do you have news from the outside?" Dr. Aaron Brooks asked Alison. He supervised another patient with two nurses across the room in an area cordoned off by curtains. "We heard Chief Aiden found Jared, and there's talk of an attack." "Are we really at war?" Dr. Kerry asked the second consecutive question at Alison. The whole truth almost rolled off

Alison's tongue, but she stopped herself. *The truth*, she feared, would only encourage hospital staff to abandon the patients and go home to their families. She asked God for forgiveness and said, "I don't know much of anything, but I hope they fixed whatever is going on."

Everyone needed to focus on saving lives and not spreading gossip. Alison looked at Dr. Kerry and gently said to him, "Let me take over." Dr. Kerry and Alison changed hands, and she began squeezing the bag in a slow, steady rhythm. Dr. Kerry closed his eyes for a brief moment. Alison wondered if he was silently praying for the people they'd already lost.

"We can't keep this up for long," Kerry said. "London needs more than air. He needs medicine that requires refrigeration, and everything we have on ice right will melt soon without power." Alison looked up and met Dr. Kerry's gaze. "What are we going to do?" He heaved a defeated sigh. "Honestly, I have no idea. But I'm afraid we'll lose London if the power doesn't come back soon." Alison's heart broke.

The large dark brown Northwestern wolf was growling, and his teeth were showing. He moved in for the kill. The growling sound was nearly demon-like. Every animal in the vicinity took flight in one way or another. Birds flew, insects crawled, and anything that could run.

The wolf was ten feet long, muscular, and weighed just over two hundred and fifty pounds. Ordinarily, the wolf would eat deer, bison, elk, and moose. But not this wolf; he preferred human flesh. Unfortunately, there were a lot of humans in Wakefield and Lakota.

The wolf pounced quickly, his powerful body moving effortlessly. Its prey, a muscular black man, didn't even try to resist. He was a dead man. The Northwestern wolf opened his massive jaws, flexing his 2,500 pounds per square inch bite pressure, then clamped down onto the man's head. His jaws were strong enough to crush the man's skull like an empty eggshell. It was over before it ever started.

The tall, muscular black man screamed, "Stop! Stop! *Stop!* And that is what the wolf did— he stopped. It was a sight to behold. The wolf stopped on verbal command. "You win." The black man said to the overgrown wolf and then patted him on his head.

But it wasn't over. The man twisted his body and backflipped with fantastic agility, and his moves were almost as quick and effortless as the wolf's. It was time for the wolf to die now. With quick steps, the man took flight, kicking the wolf on its side and then putting it in a choke hold to snap his neck. "Got you back, killer," the black man said to the wolf. "You are still my little buddy, aren't you."

Jacob Smith stood at a distance, watching his older brother wrestle with his wolf and win. They told Finley he would never see the sun again. Now, he was Lord of all— even wolves. Finley was a beautiful man. He had the body of a greek god and the mind of Einstein. And, the best thing of all, no one knew he escaped prison, nor did they know he had waged war on both Wakefield and Lakota. Everyone was going to die. He already executed the

Judge who sentenced him to rot in the Clemenceau Super Max Correctional Facility. As a bonus, he killed her boyfriend, too. Mr. Levi Ware should have kept his fucking mouth shut, but he wanted to testify at his brother's trial. That didn't work out too well for him.

Jacob awaited orders from his *Master*. He especially loved how his brother let him execute his orders his way. Jacob was a star, and Finley understood that.

As Jacob stared at his Lord being a master over creation, he marveled at how much his big brother had taught him everything he knew. Including his power of wolves. After all, they were one with wolves. The two of them were evolution. Wolves wanted to be them. Each day he grew grateful for the master plan unfolding and about shedding all the baggage of his old life. Soon he would have no false morals or religion. He was a master of his body and inhibitions, and the world was his playground. No. The world was his *Master's* playground. He was his Master's General.

Jacob was getting closer to the truth. As close to the ultimate truth, just like his Lord Finley. They had been killing for years together, and then that bitch got his brother caught. But that was okay. His Master hated her, but he hated one person above all. And his name was The Ghost. All of these killings were to draw him out. He revered the day The Ghost would die at his brother's hand. *Vengeance was his, and he is Lord.*

"We have a couple who needs to be taught a lesson," Jacob said to Harrison, Jacob's trusted right-hand man. Harrison Roy was an attractive man with a sculpted body and sharpened teeth, just like the rest of the Bitterfang Wolf Pack. Harrison stood around six-four and was solid muscle. The Master was the Alpha, and Jacob was the pack's Beta, next in line to lead the pack whenever the Master decided to step down.

Jacob was thrilled being number two. He loved The Master, who happened to be his big brother. There was no power struggle. Whatever his Master wanted, Jacob would see it through. His loyalty is why Jacob liked Harrison so much. Harrison was to Jacob what Jacob was to The Master.

"That's excellent," Harrison said, and he smiled, revealing his perfectly sharpened fangs. "What are my orders, sir?" Jacob shrugged. "We will play this one by ear and make sure they die gloriously. I want Lakota to gossip for weeks about our kill," Jacob said to Harrison without emotion. It was all business for him. "Who are they, sir?" Jacob shrugged again. "Just people we will teach to stay in their place." "Harrison's face saddened. "I hope one day you will tell me all of what you know, sir. I promise not to let you down." "The Master did not give me details. He wants them dead," Jacob explained.

Harrison asked no further questions. His obedience to The Master was absolute. *If Mr. Smith told you what to think, you thought of nothing else. If he told you what to say, you said what you were told. The Master knew all and was above all. Through The Master, they were saved.* Everyone in the Bitterfang Wolfpack despised this world. They hated its rules and social classes. They wanted to see it all burn to the ground.

Jacob and Harrison arrived at their target's house within fifteen minutes. The walk was pleasant, and neither of them said a word during their short journey. Upon arriving at the large house, Jacob could immediately tell the coupled who lived there were rich. There were more than two dozen windows, and the driveway was large enough to lead into a museum. The more Jacob looked at the house, the more he began to think it had to be a museum.

Jacob and Harrison walked in harmony. The strides were silent and purposeful. Harrison looked to his left to catch Jacob's eye. He did. There was a brief moment of silent communication between the two, and Jacob permitted Harrison to take the lead.

Harrison walked right in the front door, and Jacob followed. The foyer was beautiful, and the ceiling had to be thirty feet high. These people were wealthy. None of the furniture in the house looked common. It all seemed to be handcrafted and imported from somewhere most Sallerians could not afford.

They found the couple in the bedroom, naked. The woman was lying on the man's chest. There were three candles lit around the room. Maybe they knew the power was out. Or, maybe they had a romantic night that ended in lovemaking. It didn't matter to Jacob. They were as good as dead.

"Did he give you an orgasm, ma'am?" Harrison asked through a mischievous smile. Jacob laughed to himself. What a great way to announce there are strangers in the house, he thought to himself.

"Whoa!" The unsuspecting man said outlaid as he rose to his feet. The woman screamed something Jacob couldn't make out. They were both standing naked. Their perfect bodies are worthy enough for him and Harrison to feed. Jacob taught the pack to be careful about who they drank. After all, *you are what you eat.*

The male was close to six-five, and the woman was around five-eleven. They both had track sprinters' bodies, and Jacob couldn't help but notice how goofy the man looked with his hands in the air. "You can put your hands down, Mister," Jacob said nicely to the surprised man while staring at his wife's nicely tanned breasts. Then, Jacob turned back towards the man to make eye contact and said, "We are unarmed."

"What the hell do you guys think you are doing? Get out of my house right now." "There is no need to be hostile, sir," Harrison said in a playful voice. "Don't tell me what to do! I am a cop! Get out now, and we can forget this whole thing happened." Harrison couldn't help himself. His response let Jacob know he was having a lot of fun and was very relaxed. "Where's your gun, sir? It looks like the pretty lady already drained the gun. We can see now." Harrison was staring at the man's genitals. "Did you drain him, ma'am? Do you drain him more than once a week? An attractive man like this deserves to be drained at least twice daily."

Before she could reply, Harrison answered for her. "Yeah. Look at how beautiful you are. I bet you love jumping on him and draining him every chance. Ten points for Gryffindor!" Harrison yelled in the naked woman's direction, giving him best Albus Dumbledore impression. Harrison waited for her to reply with her last name, but she didn't respond. The woman began to sob softly. "It's okay, Hunny. We are going to be okay," the husband said to his wife. Jacob and Harrison looked at each other and shared an evil laugh. "He must love you, ma'am?" Jacob butted in. "You are both about to die a horrible death, and he wants to make sure you have hope as you die." "Aww. That's so sweet," Harrison responded to Jacob's taunt.

"You two are trespassing, and I can make life bad for you both. Why don't you turn around and leave, and we will forget this whole thing happened," the husband said domineeringly. "Get out, you two! Right now!" The man kept shouting. Jacob and Harrison stood there smiling. "Hey, you assholes, can you hear me?"

It was like a switch flipped for Jacob. He roared into the air, and when his roar was over, in a flash, Jacob jumped into the man's chest. They fell to the floor with a loud crash, and Jacob sank his teeth into the left side of his neck. Before his wife could scream, Harrison was on top of her naked body, drinking from her carotid artery.

Both the husband and wife kicked and squirmed until their bodies went limp, and the screams took on silence. Then, finally, Jacob looked into the man's dying eyes and said in a menacing voice," We are not assholes, sir. We are Rougarou."

Ernest sat in the operations room of the Wakefield police station, staring at the radio equipment in extreme frustration. Everything was destroyed. Never in his life had he felt this defeated.

His wingman and friend were dead, his nephew was close to a nuclear blast zone, he had no idea what was happening to his sister, and there was no real way to contact her. Ernest ran his fingers up and down his scalp and bowed his head, trying to think. He needed a plan, but what could he do without a radio or a vehicle?

"Sir?" came a soft voice interrupting his pity party. Ernest turned to see the female detective with freckles and red hair from the meeting earlier. She held out an ancient-looking radio in a wooden box. "This is a vintage tube radio I got from my grandfather before he died. I had the six vacuum tubes replaced a few years ago. The batteries were museum pieces and cost me a small fortune, but I think it will work." The freckled detective pushed the ancient box toward Ernest. On its left side, in tiny writing, it read, *1937 Zenith 6S157 Zephyr Console Tube Radio.* Ernest didn't know what that meant, but it had to work if it was from 1937. "Go ahead and try it out, Major."

Ernest tried to remember her name. "Thank you, Detective...?" "Schwartz. Skylar Schwartz," she said with a smile. "Here, let me show you how it works.

Skylar set the battery-operated tube radio on the table in front of the oil lantern and leaned over to work the dials. Then, after a few minutes of instructions, Aiden joined them. The police chief's shoulders sagged slightly with defeat and despair. Ernest had heard the scream the screams a little while earlier, and he could guess Aiden had just told the parents their worst nightmare had come true.

Ernest placed the radio down for a moment. "I've been there more than once after we returned home from battle Chief. I am sorry I can't tell you anything to take your pain away." Aiden smiled slightly. "Any updates on the equipment?" Aiden asked. To keep from crying, Ernest figured asking that question was the best the Chief could do. "Nothing good so far. I can't get anything to work, but Detective Schwartz brought this old tube radio five minutes ago. It seems to work. We can't contact anyone with it, but we can listen and see if we can get any news."

Skylar leaned over the table and continued to scroll through the stations. White noise crackled from the old speakers. She moved the dials with deliberate care until there was a beeping sound. As if it was a reflex, Aiden stepped in closer, hovering behind her.

Turning the radio dial much slower now, Skylar twisted until a voice came over the speaker. *"This message is transmitted at the request of the Federal Emergency Management Agency. At 8:21 p.m. Pacific Standard Time, NORAD detected multiple foreign threats in Sallerian airspace moving east over the country. It is believed that these aircraft were carrying weapons of mass destruction."* The message ended and, after a pause, began again. "Multiple threats?" Skylar asked. "All of Salleria is in the dark, just as I feared," Ernest Responded. Aiden cursed under his breath. Skylar finally believed everything The Chief was saying an hour ago.

Connor continued to be impressed with Kayla. Her intellect was sharp, and her investigative skills were next to none. Yet, she was a force of a woman. Connor couldn't help but notice how tenacious and professional she was. She was a *detective's* detective, and from what he learned from their two-hour drive back to Lakota, Kayla was the only female lead detective in the big metropolitan city.

The Lakota Police Department is the primary law enforcement apparatus for the city of Lakota. Officially formed in 1859 as a small group of marshals, today's Lakota Police Department consists of more than 1,500 officers in sixteen units active in a metropolitan city of more than 620,000 residents. Of all these highly trained professionals, Kayla was the very best. And she was modest, too. Connor liked that. He noticed every good thing about her as they dissected the case. He also noticed how beautiful she was, too.

And Kayla was drop-dead gorgeous. Her mouth bowed forward, her brow sloped back, and her skull shone a dark chocolate haze of hair, which hovered about her head like the remembered shape of an altered thing. She was as thick as thunderstorm clouds with a flat stomach and track runner thighs. Her breasts grew from her chest like two tamed mountains. So Connor imagined when she put on an old dress. Her bosom hugged the fabric tight like a second skin. She had beautiful brown eyes that pierced into his soul as she talked, and she stood six-one. She was a brick house.

Kayla was a force, and she was confusing Connor. His fiancé was dead, but he couldn't stop getting distracted by Kayla. Connor was a one-woman man who didn't often date because he had two little children. His wife died shortly after giving birth to Riley eight years ago. He was a widower and a single father. He got lucky when he found Anna, and in the beginning, they had a great relationship, but this last year was rough. She had been unfaithful to Connor, and he had difficulty trusting her again.

Connor lost track of time as Kayla pulled left into Connor's driveway. He'd forgotten he had given her his address: 758 Fillmore Street, Lakota, Wakefield. Kayla was smiling in his direction. "Here you are, friend," Kayla said softly to Connor. "I will pick you up in a few hours." "I feel you aren't asking me but telling me, *friend.*" "I guess you are smart, Dr. Quantum." Kayla wore her long black leather jacket, and even after a little past three in the morning, she looked ready to go out on a date. *Maybe she did have a date,* Connor thought to himself. A breakfast date. "I will see you in a few hours, Connor said. They smiled warmly at one another, and Kayla slowly backed out of the driveway.

Connor saw her smile, and she backed away. She never took her eyes off him, and he returned the favor. After she was gone, Connor stood in the driveway, leaning against the brick steps leading toward his house's entrance. He sighed, shook his head, and felt a familiar weariness settling in his heart. He was alone again. His wife died eight years ago. His fiancé died less than eight hours ago, and for some strange reason, he felt oddly connected to Kayla. It was like he had always known her and always will. He wondered why he didn't offer her to come inside and rest. He wondered why he didn't stay with her and kept working on the case. He wondered if she was thinking about him the way he was thinking about her.

But deep down, Connor knew the reason. It wasn't too complicated. The last two women he cared about had died. They were no longer here. He felt like if he got close to anyone, they would die, too. His wife and his fiancé were both women he loved. They both were dead.

Anna's killer was still out there, and Lakota had killers on the loose hunting with wolves. Connor accepted his fate for today. He knew it was going to be one violent day.

It was a lucky break. Mr. Smith happened to be headed to the St. Paul Luxury apartment to check on the great work Jacob had done hours ago, and he saw a car. He was shocked. There was a working car. He thought about robbing the driver, which was his original plan until he followed the driver to 758 Fillmore Street. He recognized both occupants immediately. He even knew their names. Connor Mason, FBI. A supposed genius from quantum physics is now working in the FBI. And Kayla Lowe. A big case detective from the Lakota Police Department. She was, by reputation, the best.

My, how his luck was working out in his favor. He got to shadow his nemesis, Ashton Jace, for most of the day, and now, he could shadow the people investigating the other cases in his master plan. Mr. Smith beamed with joy. His plan *was* working perfectly, and now he knew where Connor lived. This was too easy, he thought to himself.

They were looking for the rougarou, but the rougarou found them first. Soon, Smith would have all members of the Bifferfang Wolfpack following Ashton, his crew, and Connor and his. Life was good.

The Ghost was the most dangerous of all of them, however. She was as strong as any of Mr. Smith's rougarou and as brilliant as himself. Smith hated The Ghost with every fiber of his being. He was going to kill him slowly and with his bare hands. But he would kill Connor and his newest partner first.

He knew this to be the truth, but it sounded too much like a rule and Smith fucking hated rules. The enemy's numbers were growing too quickly, he admitted. The Ghost has at least eight to nine more people he would have to deal with now that The Ghost is buddy-buddy with the police chief. Connor would have access to at least six people due to his FBI role, and Kayla could draw another eight from her squad. That equals twenty more people who were not in his original plan.

It didn't matter. Smith had a solution. There was a place in Lakota called *The Order of the Blind Phoenix*, and it was for those who wanted to become Rougarous. It was an old warehouse someone had renovated. It was filled with the fifteenth and sixteenth-century furniture and displayed the most exotic decorations. There would be hundreds of people he could choose from there. Of course, he knew quite a few people who frequented, but that was ten years ago. A lot has changed in ten years.

Nevertheless, he would stop by The Order of the Blind Phoenix and make himself known again. Mr. Smith snickered to himself, rolling his eyes in laughter. No one had any idea he was coming, nor did they know how going to prison for ten years only made him more powerful. His followers worshipped him now. He was a God among men.

Mr. Smith watched Kayla drive out of Connor's driveway and stared at Connor leaning against the wall in his driveway, seemingly lost in his thoughts. Mr. Smith wondered what Connor was thinking and if he should kill him now— right where he stood.

A shadow whizzed crossed the damp soil of the trail at breakneck speed. For a moment, panic raced through Erynn's mind, but it was only a moment. She was no stranger to combat. Erynn let off a round and hit a tango between the eyes.

The enemy numbers were about eleven. *They should have brought more,* Erynn thought to herself. Using her Glock 19, the silencer was not attached; Erynn shot another man in the forehead. Turning to her left, Erynn grabbed the next tango's right wrist as he held his pistol. She forced both his hands upwards into the air with her left hand. While holding the man's hands, she put a round into the face of another tango standing to his left. Now that there were no more immediate threats, she shot the man she was holding by the wrist three times. The first round went into his left thigh, the second into his abdomen. As the force of the second bullet bent the man forward, she put a third round into his head, and his body fell to the ground. That was three men down so far. Spinning quickly to her right,

Erynn grabbed her Glock 19 with both hands and, with her elbows tucked close to her body, extended her arms outward into a standing firing position and fired one round into the fourth man's head. *That's four men down and six rounds fired.*

It took her four total seconds to fire all six rounds. She moved her head on a swivel to the right. A tango shot three rounds at her upper body that nearly hit her. The house was comprised.

These men thought everyone in the house was sleeping— they thought wrong. Erynn was waiting for them. She couldn't get back to sleep after her horrible dream and heard light footfalls on the gravel. Ashton purposely kept his driveway gravel and all the surrounding area of the house. He thought of it as his silent house alarm. It didn't matter how trained you were. No one can silently walk on loose gravel.

Three more rounds flew by her head. Erynn jumped out of the way of the bullets and leaped over the medal railing leading to the second floor. She landed on both feet and fired another round into an unsuspecting tango. He went down after his head exploded into a red mist. Everyone was silent now, but she could have sworn she heard someone speaking quiet orders in Kangavarian. The last man she shot fell to the floor in Ashton's kitchen; Erynn shot him in the head again for good measure.

She moved her head to the left, her arms still in a combat firing position facing the right. Standing still, she heard footsteps from her left, so she pivoted her Glock 19 in that direction. A man with a light attached to his head took a round to the face. He's dead. Erynn turned her head back to the right and entered the kitchen, where she doubled-tapped a tango for good measure. Then, sensing she had time and not wanting to take any chances, Erynn leaned her back against the kitchen side wall closest to the stairs and moved her pistol to her right hand. She went into her left pocket and performed a combat reload.

The house is pitch black, but little lights are bobbing around at eye level, easily marking her tangos. Erynn can hear someone breathing on the other side of the wall. Without thinking, she launched forward with both hands holding her Glock 19, chopping the tango's firing hand. He uses only one hand to secure his weapon— a rookie mistake. As his gun falls to the floor, Erynn spins left towards him and used her pistol to hit him in his esophagus. After hearing a satisfying crunch, she threw the man in the kitchen, along the right wall. With her gun still in her right hand, she knees the man with her left leg in the midsection and then performs a Judo hip toss. With her gun still in her right hand, Erynn drags the man by his left arm and crouches to shoot an advancing tango in the throat. Once she sees the advancing man falling to the ground clutching his throat, Erynn turns to the man she is holding and shoots him in the back of the head.

Silence fills the house. In the mirror, Erynn catches the reflection of two men moving toward her position. As soon as the man on the right gets close enough, Erynn jumps on him, wrapping her legs around his waist, and uses her breasts to complicate his breathing. Before his partner can get off round, Erynn switches to her left hand to put a round into his forehead, then spins the man she has mounted onto the ground and shoots him between the eyes.

Erynn loses track of how many men she has killed, but she estimates she has about eight more rounds left in her magazine. Finally, the house looks to be clear. Panting and angry, Erynn turns towards the stairs to see Ashton sitting down and eating an apple. He has a smirk on his face. Erynn returns Ashton's look with a deadly glare. "What! I shot this guy," Ashton responded in defense. She looks to find a body at Ashton's feet. She must have missed one of them. "Now, what would you have done if I didn't come and help you?" Erynn looked at him without changing her death stare. But she eventually smiles, and Ashton begins to laugh.

Using sign language, Erynn tells Ashton, "See, I told you my dream was true." "And I told you that I believed you, silly." Ashton was the only person on the planet that knew Erynn used sign language to communicate. She kept true to her vow of silence, but once Erynn realized her dreams would tell her things that would happen in the future, she learned sign language to tell Ashton all about them. He learned sign language, as well, because that is how much he loved Erynn. If she wanted to do something, he would go to the ends of the earth to give it to her. "How many men came into the house beside the one I got?" Ashton asked. Erynn shrugged her shoulders. She honestly lost count in the chaos. "By my count, that was nine men and thirteen shots. Your double taps were a bit overkill. But, of course, who am I to judge?" Erynn shrugged her shoulders again.

"I see you still haven't missed a shot yet." Then, using sign language, Erynn told Ashton, "I will never miss a shot."

Erynn and Ashton looked around the house at all the chaos. "Damn, Erynn. These look like North Kangavarian special forces. They must be on the ground going house to house." Erynn looked at Ashton and signed one more time. "Alison is going to kill us. We told her Paige would be safe over here." "Man. I guess it's time to get her back to her mom. The hospital will be safer than the rest of the city."

"Connor, come look at this. You will never believe what it is. Hell, I can't believe what it is. You coming or what?" Kayla was holding up something in a clear plastic evidence bag. She was standing next to Brentley and all of his six-eight glory. Kayla held her own next to Connor's gigantic best friend. She stood six-one and seemed larger than life. Especially right now with that familiar gleam in her eyes.

Kayla and Brentley were standing center stage at the Ogden Theatre. When Connor made it off the balcony floor, Kayla and Brentley were both busting his balls for being a slow poke. "Did you hurt your knee walking, Sweetie?" Brentley teased Connor too much more of Kayla's amusement than he'd expected. "It's good to see my oldest friend and my newest friend in life are getting along just fine. At my expense," Connor jabbed back at these two ball busters. "Aw, you must be one of those sensitive Cancers," Kayla asked. She wasn't finished either. "That tough outer crab shell hiding your busy inside?" She kept going.

Connor joined in the laughter now. "I shall have you know, Ms. Smarty Pants. Give up your career as a psychic. I am an Aquarius, thank you very much. January 24, 1984, if you must know." Connor replied in a snobby voice that made all three of them laugh.

"But seriously, what did you find?" "Show him the Bible page, Kayla," Brentley said. "Found it next to the victim's body. It had been exactly two hours since Kayla left Connor's driveway. She returned two hours earlier when the Lakota Police Dispatch told her on a short-wave radio there was another murder at the Ogden Theatre. Connor suspected it was the same killer from the St. Paul Collection due to the public execution-style murder and the presence of another large crowd.

Kayla gave Connor the Bible page, and everything was blacked out except one verse: *Psalm 59:13.* "What the heck does Psalms fifty-nine and thirteen say? I need to brush up on my theology skills." Brentley asked Connor. "I am a quantum physicist, not a theologian," Connor shrugged. "I know more about gravity, space-time, and quantum entanglement than the Bible," Connor snorted. "Fellas, I can fix this easily. There is a Bible in my car. Let me go grab it," Kayla said. A few moments later returned with a smirk on her face. "Wait until you read this. Holy Shit!" "Are you supposed to curse while holding the Bible?" Connor teased her. "Fair point. Sorry God," she said as she handed Connor the Bible. Brentley inched closer as Connor read the verse out loud.

" Destroy them in wrath, destroy them that they may be no more;

That men may know that God rules in Jacob

To the ends of the earth."

"Holy Shit!" Connor and Brentley said at the same time. "Now, who's cursing with the Bible in their hands." Brentley looked at Connor, "Papa Anthony will be disappointed with you. Did you know his dad was a Pastor, Kayla?" "I certainly did not. And does your dad know you don't know much about the Bible, Dr. Quantum?" Connor rolled his eyes at both of his abusers. "Let's make sure he doesn't know we are cussing sinners," Connor responded.

Before anyone could speak again, Brentley broke into the conversation. "When you two left the crime scene, a tech from the terrace level pulled another Bible page from Anna's body. It was the entire Bible. It was strapped to her stomach with duct tape." Connor saw that Kayla retook notice that both he and Brentley called the victim by her first name. She *was* a smart one.

"What page was it on?" Kayla asked. "Every word in the book was blacked out except for one verse," Brentley paused before finishing. "It was Micah 7:8." As if that was his cue, Connor flipped Kayla's Bible to the end of the Old Testament and found Micah 7:8. All those early years of his grandmother forcing him to be on the church drill team when he was little were paying off. Everyone on the team had to remember the sixty-six books of the Bible in order. Connor had no problem finding the book of Micah.

This time, Kayla inched in close to Conner. She was so close he could smell her perfume. Connor read out loud,

240

" Do not gloat over me, my enemy! Though I have fallen, I will rise. Though I sit in darkness, the LORD will be my light."

"Holy," Kayla and Brentley looked at Connor before he could finish. "Moly," Connor clumsily replaced his original word. "Our killer is leaving clues. But what do they mean?" Kayla asked. "I don't know. I don't even think we can know unless," Brentley finished Connor's sentence. "Unless our killer kills more people and leaves us more clues." An intense silence lingered between the three of them for longer than desired. "Goddammit," Brentley broke the silence. He was holding the Bible with Connor, but neither he nor Kayla said anything. They felt the same frustration as Brentley. They were too many steps behind the killer, and getting clues after people died is not how you solve murder cases.

Moreover, they were publicly embarrassed. It was a blessing the power was out, Connor thought. The media would be abusing the three of them right now and plastering their failures on every channel and paper. The embarrassment would last for weeks. Maybe even months.

"This guy was supposedly a General— an older white man or something," Kayla said. "No, it's the same killer. He changes his appearance with each kill. Our killer is clever and has access to makeup and aesthetics. He can look like anyone, and he can sneak anywhere. First, he was a janitor. Now he is a general. He is a mastermind." Neither Kayla nor Brentley seemed to like what they were hearing. They were being outsmarted, and neither appreciated losing so publicly.

Retired Staff Sergeant Ashton *The Ghost* Jace twirled a razor-sharp Duane Dieter's close combat knife between his fingers. He owned two of them; the other was still on his left hip. The Ghost was pissed. An elite North Kangavarian team tried to kill him, his niece, and the only woman outside of his sister he ever loved, Erynn. She made quick work of the bastards. He mostly sat back and watched because no one can be Erynn in close-quarters combat. No one! She was the best he'd ever seen, outside of himself. Ashton was the only person who could beat Erynn in close-quarters combat, and Erynn was the only person alive who could shoot better than The Ghost. They were perfect.

Since leaving their house, all hell had broken loose. And to make matters worse, Paige was still with them, and he and Erynn picked up two of Chief's men along the way. Still twirling his knife in his fingers, The Ghost was remarkably fast despite being retired for two years. A tribal tattoo followed the bulge of his veins from the bottom of his right bicep upward and disappeared under his rolled-up sleeve. He was dressed in black stealth camouflage, and so was Erynn.

Erynn and Ashton were studying the wall of monitors and screens, trying to piece together what was happening. But no matter what Ashton tried, he couldn't make sense of anything. The one thing he knew for sure was that thousands of enemy forces were on the ground.

Just moments before, Erynn and Ashton heard gunfire and investigated. Two Wakefield officers took cover and returned fire on North Kangavarian troops. After hiding Paige in a secure area, The Ghost and Erynn helped the two officers take out about forty infantry soldiers. After checking each fallen soldier for identification and belongings, they stumbled on the area of a Mobile Tactical Operation Command Center. Together, The Ghost and Erynn took out the four soldiers with their silenced pistols, then killed the two technicians who opened fire on them when they opened the doors to the trailer attached to a Sallerian-made semi-truck. There were monitors on every trailer wall and analog radios bursting with chatter. The North Kangavarians were spying on Sallerian communications, what little there was, and no one was the wiser.

Behind Erynn, Officer Samuel Willis fidgeted with his Wakefield Police Department-issued Glock 23, aiming at invisible targets in the command center and practicing his quick draw technique. Finally, he placed the weapon and ran his hands through his blond hair. He couldn't have been older than twenty-three. He was one of Chief Aiden's fresh rookie officers.

To Ashton's eyes, the young officer was nothing more than a boy in his way, but he was fighting the good fight, so as long as he did what The Ghost said, he would stay alive. Studying the young officer's face, Ashton decided he make sure he got back to the Chief safely. Erynn rolled back her chair to one of the monitors. She stared intently. An assortment of data crawled across the screen from all the Sallerian Department of Defense facilities. Most of the information was in Kangavarian. Ashton and Erynn spoke multiple languages, but neither spoke Kangavrian.

The computers receiving all the information ran on an ancient analog system, which surprised Ashton. It also told him that whatever was outside was bad enough to have the North Kangavarians riding around in semi-truck-pulled trailers operating ancient analog computers. Ashton sighed. He looked at Erynn. She returned the look with a shoulder shrug, saying she didn't know what was going on either.

Behind the rookie cop stood Police Corporal Benjamin Hunter. Ashton liked him, and he liked Ashton. Ashton spun to address the corporal, who stood with his lean and muscular frame. "Did you get the generator working, Hunter?" Ashton asked with authority. He was in charge now, and everyone followed his lead. "It was already fixed. I think one of the Kangavarian soldiers flipped the on/off/ switch to off when they heard all the shooting outside. I think they were trying to hide. So I flipped it back on." Hunter responded. "Excellent work, Hunter. It only took you two days to get it done," Ashton replied sarcastically.

Ashton had no idea how many enemy troops stood in their way between here and getting Paige to safety. The hospital was also close to the police station, which would add more reinforcements. The Chief needed to know the enemy was on the ground and we were at war. It had been about 4 hours since Ashton and Erynn dropped off Alison at the hospital for her shift. Ashton decided it would be best to leave the Dodge at the house when they heard all the gunshots because they didn't want to alert the enemy. But taking this trailer back to his house was not an option. They would have to get out of here soon, but they needed to get all the intel they could first.

Ashton popped in an earbud and strained his hearing, hoping he would hear something in a language he knew. The first few changes were foggy, sounded distant, and were only in Kangavarian. But he kept scanning through them until one voice stood out. It was almost crystal clear, and it was in English. From the sounds of it, it sounded like someone from the Sallerian military.

"Have you found anything yet, sir?" The rookie cop asked. Ashton didn't even bother to turn in his direction. "Wait one second. I am trying to make sense of what I'm hearing," Ashton responded without moving his head. *"Recorded at 02 a.m. The White House reported the sky changing colors into bright white, and then all power was lost. The entire North Salleria is without power, including Yespax to the North and Shuytan to the South. It is believed the entire North Sallerian continent is without power."*

"Erynn, come listen to this, now!" Ashton gave Erynn his seat, and he watched as her face twisted into an expression of shock. One by one, he let the rookie and the corporal listen to the looped recording, and then he ended with Paige listening lastly. Finally, the mobile command center fell into complete silence. Ashton knew he had to do something. "Listen up, everybody," Ashton spoke in a calm voice filled with the fire of war. "I won't like to you. Whatever the worse thing you could have guessed, this is much worse. But I do not plan to die tonight. My best guess is there are about three thousand enemy troops between us and safety. We need to get out of this command center, back to my house to get my Dodge, which may be the only working vehicle we will ever see again, and then we have to get to the hospital to get my niece to safety and lastly, to the police station to get to back up. I don't have time for a power struggle. I don't have time for you to question my orders."

Ashton stood and walked over to another monitor. He hoped everyone was looking at him and wanted them only to see The Ghost. "Anyone who was not willing to follow will be left. Is this clear?" Both men and Paige nodded their heads. Good. None of us will die. Erynn and I are the best. "We know, sir. We know all about you both. The Chief makes us keep an eye out for you every time you cause trouble around the city," the rookie cop, Samuel Willis, responded. Corporal Benjamin Hunter gave the rookie a look that suggested he shut the fuck up. "Indeed, your Chief and I don't care for one another, but I will get you back to him," Erynn cleared her throat. "Correction, *we* will get you back to him. Just follow my orders. Erynn, you take the rear position and shoot everything moving. Hunter, you are upfront with me, and rookie, you are in the middle with my niece. You keep my niece safe. Hunter and I will clear the path, and Erynn will keep all of us safe. She never misses a shot. I doubt she plans to start now." Erynn huffed. "See, she doesn't plan on missing."

Ashton was about to say something else when everyone turned to one of the monitors at the same time. Ashton turned to see. Erynn did something on the mousepad, and the screen zoomed in. A Humvee was racing down the adjacent road in the middle of the screen. It was zipping in and out of camera view and swerving around abandoned cars. "Who the hell is controlling the camera?" The rookie screamed. It was a damn good question, yet,

Ashton hadn't thought about that. "There must be one central location feeding this command center, which tells me there are more mobile TOCs like this, and one big brain center feeding them all this same information. That means everyone in the immediate area knows about this Humvee, and we will have to leave this TOC immediately because none of us know Kangavarian, and the sounds coming out of the radios are probably radio checks or orders to stop this vehicle. If we stay silent for much longer, hundreds of troops will come and check on us."

"What are your orders, Staff Sergeant Ghost? You have my gun. Get us out of here, please," Corporal Hunter said. Hunter's dedication to Ashton also seemed to straighten the rookie's resolve. Ashton thought for a moment before speaking. There were hundreds of red and yellow heat signatures following the Humvee. His next words rang like gunfire in a small closet throughout the Mobile TOC. "You two, grab a pair of these NVGs lying around here. You will need them. Restock your ammo and get ready to fire your weapons. Erynn, download a map from that mainframe and any other intel you can get. We are busting out of this death trap in two minutes. We will save whoever is driving that fucking Humvee, kill the enemies, and then we will have two working vehicles."

The rookie cop grinned, stood up, and yelled, "Yes, sir!" Two minutes later, Ashton's feet were the first to hit the ground. His weapon was at the ready.

Connor, Brentley, and Kayla were miles away from the Ogden Theatre. They were in an antique bookstore, but from the looks of the place, it didn't matter if the power was off; any customers who came here liked it dark. There wasn't a light switch in the entire building. At least not one Connor could see. He looked towards the ceiling. There were no light fixtures either. Candles lit all four corners of the bookstore, but they were so far spaced apart they didn't help add any light.

The three of them were following a lead. There was an address on the back side of the trap door, written in small print. Kayla is the one who noticed it. After further inspection, the address seemed out of place. It was just written there, and the ink looked fresh. They had no idea who they would meet, but all roads led to 290 Filmore Street, Lakota.

It was a heavy feeling being so far behind a killer. Connor was not accustomed to being so clueless in a case. He felt helpless. So helpless, he followed an address written on a trap door at a crime scene with no evidence he was doing the right thing.

"You three are very out of place here," a voice came from a very tall and slender man who seemed to be in charge. "We are no strangers to being out of place. We like it that way," Brentley said to the equally tall man. Brentley had about a hundred and fifty pounds over him, however. Connor took the lead. "I am Special Agent Connor Mason. These are my partners, Special Agent Brentley Miller and Detective Kayla Lowe." Connor flashed his badge, not knowing if he made any difference in the poorly candlelit bookstore.

"I am at your service," the slender, tall man responded. "We are here because," "Not to be rude, Special Agent," Reid said while cutting Conner off mid-sentence. "But I know why you are here. I've been expecting you." "Oh? Well, do impress me, kind sir," Connor shot back. "Very well. You are here because you can't find a killer and found the right clues to lead you here." Kayla's mouth opened wide. Brentley put his hand over his pistol, and Connor was utterly flabbergasted. "Before you try to arrest me. No, I am not your killer or working with your killer. It seems I have been drug into your game, too." Reid slid Connor an envelope. "I can assure you the envelope is safe, and nothing can harm you." "I am not afraid, but thank you for your kindness. I will remember it and repay you in kind," Connor responded. Looking into the envelope, Connor was so shocked he dropped it. His breath left his body. "It seems you know more than we do, Mr. Reid." "It seems I do, Agent Mason."

"What the hell is going on, Connor?" Brentley asked. His hand was still on his pistol. "Agent Miller, I believe your partner said. You won't need your gun in here. It won't help you in here, anyway." "Is that a threat?" Brentley responded to the weirdo. "No, sir. It is a simple fact. You are in a place where firearms have little effect on who you pursue." Finally, Kayla couldn't take it anymore. She dropped her guard, bent over, picked up the envelope, and saw what scared Connor. "Brentley, you may want to look at this envelope," Kayla said while handing the envelope to Brentley. "Relax, Brent. I don't think this is a combat situation," Connor said to his best friend. Connor knew calling Brentley *Brent* got his attention. He only called Brentley that when his wife died eight years ago. Something was wrong, and he wanted his best friend to know it. They were outmatched and in a losing position. They needed to do what the envelope said.

There were eight things inside the envelope.

3 newspaper clippings. Each with all three of their names on them.

1 picture of a wolf with blood-red eyes and large sharp teeth. But the wolf looked like more man than a wolf.

3 passport pictures. One of Brentley. One of Kayla. And One of Connor.

1 typed message on a square piece of paper that read, " Talk to them when they come, or die after I kill your wife and daughter."

October 27, 2022. One Week Before The EMP Events Recorded In Ch 2

During the ten years Finley Smith was in Clemenceau Super Max Facility, he only ever had one visitor — a journalist. Finley sold the television rights to his life to a journalist, Kasen Burt. Kasen had struck a Hollywood deal to shoot a Netflix Series about the life of Finley Smith. The Special Forces Captain killed more than eighty people but could only be tried for eleven of those murders. It was widely thought Mr. Smith killed more than one hundred people, and Smith promised to tell everything in his television series. As a result, the only person who could ever visit was Kasen.

Every Saturday at eight a.m., Kasen would arrive thirty minutes early, go through all the security checkpoints, and finally be allowed in the room with Mr. Smith. Every Saturday, Kasen would walk into the security gate and wait for the tower guard to pop the lock on the first security gate. Every Saturday, Kasen would look up at the facial recognition camera and smile a big smile. He made sure to comply with every rule and always made sure they got a perfect camera shot of his first. Upon his exit, he would look towards the sky and flash his big smile towards the same camera. Always making sure he complied with their every rule. Kasen didn't want any trouble.

Every Saturday, Kasen wore the same thing. A blue jacket with big red letters on the back that read *NETFLIX* in all capital letters. His long black dreadlocks would always cover half of the letters as if they flowed down his back. He wore a big brown belt with a shiny gold belt buckle featuring a large Stag on the front. And stone-washed blue jeans that fit well, as if they were tailored to his lower body. To top off his outfit, he wore shiny black dress shoes that would reflect his face when he gazed downward. The shiny shoes knocked loudly against the tile prison floor. With each step, you could hear the three hundred and thirteen steps it took to get to the visiting room they held, Mr. Smith. Smith knew it was precisely three hundred and thirteen because every Saturday, he counted Kasen's steps for fun.

Kasen never missed a step, and he never wore anything else. Every week they would sit for the two-hour contact visit in silence, and every twelve minutes, Kasen would ask the same ten questions until the time expired. Kasen, the journalist, would ask Mr. Smith one question, Stand up and walk around for twelve minutes, then sit back down and ask the following question. After Mr. Smith gave a prompt answer, Kasen would stand back up, pace back and forth for another twelve minutes, and then sit back down and ask another question.

Each week, without fail, Kasen would ask the same questions, and Mr. Smith would always give the same answers.

Are you sorry for anything you have done?

No.

How many people did you kill?

147.

Will you kill again?

Yes.

But how when you will never see the light again?

I am the light. He who does not block my light will be saved.

Why did you kill your victims?

There are no victims. Only creators.

Where are your victims?

None of them are victims. They are where they lay.

Where did you bury the bodies?

All could not be buried.

How will you break out of prison?

I am the way, the truth, and the light.

Do you believe in God?

You believe in the Father. Believe also in me.

How do we know you have killed 147 people?

Blessed are those who believe and have not seen.

After their visit was over, the two men would rise together. Mr. Smith would walk around the left side of the table, Kasen would turn his back towards the door, and the two men would embrace for a long hug. This happened every week.

This week differed just a bit. Kasen gave Mr. Smith a warm embrace, as usual. But this time, instead of hugging Kasen, Mr. Smith put both hands in Kasen's pants, reached into his underwear, and pulled out two realistic face masks with the same quality as the Hollywood studios. One mask was the replica of Kasen Burt. The other is Finley Smith. While still being hugged, Mr. Smith put on Kasen's face. It was like looking into a mirror. And then Mr. Smith put on Kasen's face. Both men stripped naked, and within two minutes, they swapped clothes.

Smith was now Kasen. Kasen was now dressed like Smith and walked around the left side of the table, as Smith always did, and returned to his seat. Smith, who was now Kasen, knocked twice on the door, as always, and walked the three hundred and thirteen steps. The shoes were as loud as they had been for the last ten years.

As usual, Mr. Smith was allowed to leave once Kasen had completely exited both security gates and submitted his face to the facial recognition camera. When Mr. Smith closed the first gate, he looked towards the sky as Kasen did every week for the last ten years and smiled a big smile. The tower guard popped the second gate, and Smith strolled out of the gate and let the sunshine on his face. He was a free man. He reached into what used to be Kasen's right pocket and grabbed the car keys. Smith hit the lock button on the keyless entry device until a horn showed him where the car was parked. Mr. Smith got into the car, turned on the radio, and drove away.

Meanwhile, after Smith passed through the second gate and facial recognition camera, the guard entered the visitation room and told Smith, now Kasen, to stand. Kasen was six-two, the same height as Mr. Smith. He spent the last ten years toning his body to be the same muscle mass as Smith. They both had the same color eyes and were dark brown in skin color. Kasen had never had dreadlocks. When not visiting the Clemenceau Super Max Correction Facility, he wore his hair short. But for the last ten years, he would wear the locs just like Smith. When they changed closed, there was no need to make any hair adjustments because Smith and Kasen already had the same hairstyle. It had been that way for ten years. *This was all for you, my Lord. May every knew bow to your glory. Vengeance is yours,* Kasen thought to himself. The guard never noticed the two men had switched bodies. He locked Kasen in his super max cell and closed the slit that let any hallway light inside the small room.

When the guard came back to make his rounds and slide Finley Smith his food through the small slit in the door, he couldn't believe what he saw. He immediately pushed the panic button on his belt. Then he waited for help to come running. Still, the guard couldn't take his eyes away from the jail cell. Finley Smith had hung himself!

Chapter Eleven

November 2, 2022. Twenty-Four Hours Before The EMP Events Recorded In Ch 2

"Will that be all for you, sir," said the clerk at the gas station? "Yes, Ma'am, that will be all." The clerk pushed a few keys on the point of sales system before she began small talk that triggered Mr. Smith in the evilest ways. The door swung open at once. Finley Smith was miles away from the Clemenceau Super Max Correctional Facility, 1292 miles away, to be exact. He had a very stern face, and his 's first thought after entering Wakefield city limits was the arrogant judge who told him he would never see the light of day again and had to die a horrible death. "How has your day been so far?" The gas station clerk asked politely. "Why does it matter to you?" Smith responded, staring at her coldly. A long uncomfortable silence choked the space between them. Smith twists open the top of his Coco-Cola he hasn't purchased yet, never breaking eye contact with the gas station clerk. She swallows a hard lump in her throat.

"I asked you a question. Why does it matter to you?" "I didn't mean any harm, sir. Just passing the time." "Did I say it was you who caused me harm? That's your second assumption about me, and I've only known you for one minute." The gas station clerk blinked unconsciously. She wasn't sure what to say. It was four in the morning, and she was tired a few seconds ago, but now she was sweating under her armpits. She was incredibly uncomfortable. The large, well-built man stood before her, looking through her. "Two assumptions, sir?" The gas station attendant asked, her heart beating so hard in her throat she could taste her blood dancing on the back of her tongue.

The gas station was empty and quiet. She was all alone. Blood rushed to her ears, and the annoying hum of the soft drink machine on the left wall filled the empty spaces. She hoped to God someone would walk in and save her from this weirdo in front of her. But, instead, Smith, still staring at her with murderous energy, responded. "Your first assumption was thinking I was open to conversation. Your second was assuming that you could cause me any harm." "I didn't mean nothing by it, Mister." "But you did mean something by it. But you did," Smith said coldly." "I don't—," the gas stationed attendant struggled to speak. Words raced through her mind faster than the speed of light. Her mouth couldn't catch any of them to relay how sorry she was and how much she didn't want any trouble. "What's the problem? Do you think your silence will get you out of this situation? Do you think your silence will convince me not to do what I am thinking?"

The attendant didn't know what to say. She was having trouble breathing, and her hands were shaking so severely that she had to hold the open register to keep them still. "Are you nervous?" The gas station attendant moved her head up and down, still unable to catch any words flying through her mind.

Smith took a long swig of his Coco-Cola, his eyes never leaving the small woman in front of him. He stared at her like the devil. Maybe he was the devil. Placing the drink on the counter, Smith opened his mouth just enough for the gas station attendant to see his large, sharp fangs. "This soda is not quenching my thirst. I usually drink something a bit thicker."

Before she knew was she was saying, the words left her mouth without her permission. "What do you normally drink, sir?" Smith stared menacingly at the bulging vein on the side of her neck.

"Let's play a game. If you lose, you will learn what I drink." "What do I get if I win?" The gas station attendant's words came out again without her permission. "Today." Smith coldly responded. "I don't understand." "You don't need to understand if you win. You will, however, understand if you lose." "That doesn't make any sense." "It doesn't need to make sense. Do you agree to play a game with me?" What if I say no, sir." "Then you lose." "But how can I lose a game I am not playing." "You entered the game as soon as you spoke to me." "But how can I enter a game I don't know is being played." "You ask many questions, don't you?" Smith said. A slight irritation rose in his voice. "Only when I don't understand," the gas station attendant replied.

Smith, completely ignoring the gas station attendant's last remark, stepped closer to the counter. His robust frame filled the space, taking all of her breath away. The last movie he watched before going into prison was Quentin Tarintno's *No Country For Old Men*. Inspired by the iconic *Coin Toss Scene* Smith gave his demand to the young lady. "Pick a number one through ten," Smith said. His eyes lingered on the gas station attendant's small and thin frame. She nervously tried to flatten her hair. "What?" She said. "What is not a number? Pick a number one through ten." "I don't want to play your game, sir." "You are already playing. Pick a number or lose. Pick the wrong number, and you lose. And if you don't pick a number in the next few seconds, you automatically lose."

The gas station attendant's heart gave a horrible jolt. A game? What had she gotten herself into so early in the morning? She didn't know what number to pick— what on earth was she going to do? She looked around anxiously and saw Mr. Smith staring at her. His face was completely blank of any emotion she could read. Why had no one else come into the store? She tried her hardest not to listen to the screams in her mind. She had never been more nervous in her life. Finally, her eyes darted to the door. Maybe she could make a run for it?

Then something happened that made her jump about a foot in the air. She screamed so loud she thought it was something else screaming. She nearly threw up all over the register. The gas station attendant could not believe what she was seeing. The man removed his face. It peeled off his body like glue. But how could this be? "Pick a number now," Smith said in a sharp voice. "Nine!" The gas station attendant blurted out in an instant. She knew she was going to die. Why did she say nine? She wasn't even thinking of any number.

"Give me your license." Smith told the gas station attendant. "My license?" "Don't make me repeat it." The young woman reached under the counter, grabbed her purse from where she was storing it, pulled out her license, and gave it to the man with a new face. "167 E Elkhorn Ave. Do you live alone?" "No," the gas station attendant answered. "Well, you won the game. You picked the right number." A warm surge of relief washed over the gas station attendant like a hot shower after a long day. "From now on, nine is your lucky number. I'm going to keep your license. If anyone knows about our conversation or game, I will kill everyone inside 167 E Elkhorn Ave, no matter their age. Is this understood?" The gas station attendant moved her head up and down.

Smith paid for his Coco-Cola and gave the gas station attendant a nine-dollar tip. "Nine is your lucky number. Don't ever forget it. Nine is your lucky number." Mr. Smith turned to his left and walked out of the gas station. When he drove away, the young attendant ran to the doors, locked them, and cried uncontrollably. She clocked out at six a.m. and vowed never to mention what just happened to anyone. Ever. She had a newborn baby and a husband sleeping peacefully at 167 E Elkhorn Ave.

Reid Porter didn't say a word. He let the shock of the moment be over his three unsuspecting guests. They were more in the dark than he was. Finally, after many curse words and passing of questions that weren't, Reid spoke.

"As you can see, we are all here by someone's design. As for me, my family is being held captive until I give you the information you need. And from the looks of it, those three pictures are your actual passport pictures. So someone snuck into all three of your houses and cut the pictures out of your passports or got your pictures in some other way more clever than I thought." Reid paused, hoping his words would sink in quickly. Then, after seeing the three of them listening, he continued.

"As I said before, I am Reid Porter, descended from Jean-Claude Fouquet," Reid could tell his visitors had no idea of the importance or fame nor the death toll of Jean-Claude Fouquet. Reid smiled at the ignorance, showing his sharpened fangs.

The one who seemed to be in charge spoke first. "Do you know why we are here, Mr. Reid, and why did you say our guns won't work here?" Connor asked. "Yes. I believe I do know why you are here. And, if I am correct, you are up for the fight of your lives." "Why do you say that?" Connor responded. "Because only five people could spike this much fear and coordination, and our world is very organized." "Our world?" The leader of the group responded by showing his ignorance. "What did you say your name was again, Agent?" "Special Agent Connor Mason, but you can call me Connor. On the account that it seems we are all trapped in the same mouse trap." "I agree. We are all in the same mouse trap, Connor. And to answer your question. You have entered the world of the *Rougarou.* "The Rouga-what?" The taller Special Agent said. "The Rougarou. It would probably make more sense if I said werewolf. Maybe you would understand it that way," Reid offered politely. The six-nine special agent chuckled. "Yeah, fucking right. Werewolves don't exist," the tallest Special Agent continued defiantly. "And, could you repeat your name for me, Agent?" "Special Agent Brentley Miller, and you can call me unamused." "Reid smiled. He wasn't offended. A wolf doesn't argue with its prey. "That picture of a wolf that looks like a man in that envelope, that's a Rougarou. And, my guess is, you are tracking one or more of them, and you have been sent here to learn about our world." Reid said. His tone was a matter of factly.

The pretty woman with them spoke up. "Could you tell us all about your world, Reid?" "For a woman as beautiful as you, of course," Reid responded. "The Rougarou make their headquarters in Clemenceau. You must know cajun folklore to know the basics, but I will catch you up quickly. The Rougarou is a man as quick as a wolf. Some of us can shape-shift and look like anyone we desire. We all have superhuman strength, which is why your gun won't work here. None of your guns will. At lease not on real Rougarou. Some of us are simply, pretending. Other's of us were not born in Clemenceau. The most powerful Rougarou's come from where it all began."

Reid noticed the doubt on all their faces. But they were cops. He didn't expect someone as simple as blue color workers to get it. But he continued anyway. "We drink blood," when Reid said this, all three of them changed their hardened expressions. "By your reactions, I can only guess you are finding bodies drained of their blood." Connor looked at Reid. He looked as if he was trying to make his mind grab hold of this new world Reid was describing. "Think of a Rougarou as a cross between a werewolf and a vampire. We have the strength of a wolf but the quickness and agility of the undead. There are only three ways to kill a Rougarou: fire, decapitation, or severe destruction of the body. We eat bullets for breakfast to bring the conversation back to your guns."

"Are there any Rougarou's in Wakefield and Lakota," Connor asked? "Most certainly," Reid said. "There are more than quite a few, I should say." Special Agent Brentley Miller butted in the conversation again. "Bullshit. Enough bullets will stop anything." "I am sure you believe so, sir. I am sure of it," Reid responded. "Mr. Connor, you and the lady seem to be taking this new information better than your friend. Am I to assume that you both believe me?" Reid asked, looking towards Connor and the beautiful lady cop. "Belief is a much stronger word than I would use," Conner said, "but I've seen some crazy things tonight." "What kind of crazy things did you see tonight?" Connor looked like he started not to answer the question due to the nature of discussing open cases, but he decided against it. He needed answers, and this pasty, slender man seemed to have them. "I've seen the blood drained from multiple people and a manhunt with a large wolf and commanded it."

A look of terror flashed across Reid's face. He somehow became pastier than his already pasty complexion. They were all in big trouble if they were chasing a man who hunted with a wolf, including himself. "Everyone listen up," Reid said with authority. "It doesn't matter if you believe me. I will tell you everything because if what you are saying is true, we are all already dead. All he has to do is decide, and it is done." "What do you mean by that," the pretty officer said. "I promise to answer your questions, pretty lady," Reid was politely interrupted. "Please, call me Kayla. Pretty lady is my mother's name." Reid smiled, revealing his fangs again. "As you wish, Kayla."

"If what you say is true, about a man hunting with a wolf," Reid picked up where he left off, "We are all in big trouble. They call that one *The Master* and he is the strongest and smartest. He has his following, and he runs this world. If he gives the order for us to be dead, there is nothing we can do about it. But, if he truly has my wife and daughter, they are as good as dead if I don't do what he asked. *The Master* has no mercy and never leaves a promise unfulfilled."

"According to the cajun folklore, a Rougarou is a human placed under a spell. Those under the spell can change back to a human after 101 days, but only by transferring the curse to a willing victim. Others are permanently cursed, shapeshifting into their beast form at night and changing back to their human form by sunrise. But don't think of this change like a Hollywood movie. Most of us look like humans because we are. And do not dismiss this as fake and folklore. The one you are hunting may have dozens of Rougarou at his disposal, and he will be smarter and stronger than all."

"You're right. I'm very skeptical," Connor admitted. Connor told Reid everything the three of them had investigated over the past few hours, and he even told Reid everything he was thinking and piecing together. Connor was a brilliant man. After a long conversation of back-and-forth information swapping, Connor and the team learned there are thousands of Rougarou spread across the United Cities, and while many of them are posers, a real Rougarou is cursed with an extraordinary gift. They can absorb, channel, transform, and manipulate the life force of whoever they drink. And the more they feed, the stronger they become. Reid revealed to the team that blood is the source of *the life force*, and Rougarou highly coveted it.

Connor, Brentley, and Kayla learned so much new information that they finally felt they weren't far behind the killer anymore. They learned there were clans of Rougarou, and the most powerful of them led their clans. Sometimes the clan could have hundreds of Rougarous, while the minor clans would have packs of eight. There was an exciting bit of information that the team discovered. Of all the United Cities, there were only three significant clans, and everyone else fell under them. The one they called *The Master* was the leader of the most prominent clan, which was also the strongest. The Master was also the strongest Rougarou in The United Cities, and everyone feared him.

After the conversation was over, there was a long and intense silence. Reid opened the silence and said moment. "Let me tell you something, Connor. I have told you everything I know, and everything I have told you is true. If you and your team plan on living past tomorrow, do not underestimate anything I have told you. My guess is you are already being watched, and you were followed here. You are completely outnumbered, and it doesn't seem like you or your friends here are The Master's primary targets. You may even be able to walk away, should you choose. But, I know neither of you is the walking away type," Reid finished talking. It was more like a plea for them to walk away. "One more thing," Reid offered to the group. "I am not from Clemenceau, so I can't tell you everything. But if you ever find someone from the city. They will be able to tell you much more than I have about the curse. You will need this information more than you know." Reid was done now.

Connor shrugged. "I guess we are the Three Stooges, my friend. Because we aren't walking away." Before Reid could respond to what Connor had just said, a scream burst through the building from the front door, "Daddy!" A woman and a girl walked into the front doors. The woman was gagged, and her hands were tied in front of her body. The little girl was not gagged, and her hands were not tied. Reid ran to the front door and grabbed his wife and daughter. They were safe.

After the little girl hugged her father and all the tears were shed, she walked towards Connor and said, "The bad man told me to give this to you." It was another envelope. A thick silence filled the room as Connor opened the envelope. It was a picture of Papa Anthony sitting in the dark under an oil lamp. He looked like he was sleeping peacefully. Behind the picture was a note that read, "Blessed is that servant whose master finds him doing so when he returns. Don't worry. Everyone is still alive. See you soon, Connor."

The Master signed the letter.

The Master's Wrath. That's what Jacob called their murderous tour. He and Harrison were on a roll now. They killed a man driving an old van. No other vehicles were working, so the old man died for a good cause. The Master's Wrath had to continue. The couple they killed in their own house was assigned to them by the Master. The husband was one of the detectives who worked on his case, so he had to die. The woman was just food, and she was tasty.

There was nothing that could stop them. They were on their way to Wakefield, a small town inside Wakefield itself. It was a quiet mountain town that was about to get much louder. The Master had more people connected to his trial that needed to die.

Like so many other young males, Jacob and Harrison felt invincible, and they were. They were super-humans. Everyone else was food. Young Harrison never took anything seriously, and Jacob liked that about him. Then, finally, the sun started to show itself. It had to be around five a.m. or so. "Is this part of the plan, sir?" Harrison asked as Jacob approached their next destination.

It was another wealthy couple's house. "The Master says this couple didn't become rich and famous until after his trial. They used his murder case to profit as they slandered his good name," Jacob said to Harrison. "Then they must die painfully, sir." "Indeed, they must, Harrison."

The couple was attorneys, and they prosecuted The Master's case. After their victory, they began their practice and started charging a high dollar to defend the elite. Without The Master's case, they would still be a short time.

"How should we proceed, sir?" Harrison asked his leader. He was a faithful soldier. "Our intel says the couple leads a secret life. They like group sex with strangers," Jacob said. He told Harrison the plan, and they exited the van. The game was on. This was going to be so good, so delicious.

Monique wanted to scream and run for the blast doors. But there was no way she was The President of the United Cities of Salleria, the leader of the most powerful nation in the world. Yet, instead of running, she forced herself to remain seated at the conference table. The only outward sign of her distress was tapping her foot on the floor, which she hoped no one could see. She had to keep believing that Chase was alive, but her mind kept telling her if President Andrew Shelton didn't make it, what chance would Chase have?

Senator Gill and Secretary of State Barrera sat down at the table next to her. More staff filed in behind them. Marshall Tate, one of the leading experts on North Kangavar at the CIA, wedged between Barrera and Monique. The last time she had seen Tate, he was at an Armed Services Committee hearing, confidently convincing the nation's leaders about the current North Kangavarian nuclear capabilities. He told a room full of the most influential people in Salleria that the North Kangavarians were decades away from developing weapons that could threaten the continental United Cities. Boy was he wrong, she thought to herself. But Monique didn't take any pleasure in it. They were screwed either way, and what was done could not be changed. The world had been changed forever.

Secretary of State Hallie Barrera shut the door and walked to the wall-mounted monitor. "Good morning to all of you. If you are wondering, the time is seven-thirty a.m. EST. As I'm sure you're all aware, I gave commands to launch a nuclear attack against Yeonsu-Daejeon, the Capitol City of North Kangavar, approximately two hours ago," Barrera said, her voice strong and steady. "The duty fell on me when we couldn't contact President Shelton, Vice President Maddox, or Speaker Scott. The twenty warheads I authorized were plenty to turn their targets into radioactive craters." Monique was shocked by the Secretary's demeanor and confidence. She always knew Barrera was a powerhouse but seeing her take control at the end of the world was a sight to behold. Monique secretly hoped she would be able to lead so fiercely.

The Secretary of Defense continued talking. "The Presidential duties are no longer mine and are forfeited immediately and passed back to their rightful holder, the forty-seventh President of the United Cities of Salleria, Madam Monique Maddox." Leaning forward in her chair, Monique focused on the screen and smiled graciously at everyone in the room. Monique was aware that she was taking a legend's place. President Andrew Shelton was loved on both sides of the aisle. She stared at the monitors streaming a feed from an aircraft. Unfortunately, clouds blocked the view, and although digital telemetry scrolled across the bottom, she couldn't make out the data.

Secretary of State Hallie Barrera continued her briefing. "I will update everyone of everything that has occurred in all the confusion and then be seated and take my new orders from our new President." Barrera pointed to the screen. "This is the live video from one of our drones over North Kangavar. You're about to see what's left of Yeonsu-Daejeon." The clouds peeled away to reveal a glimpse of hell. "My God," Senator Bayleigh Guerra said, her face ashen. Monique didn't blame her. The destruction on the screen was incredible. It was post-apocalyptic. Monique had flown her share of bombing runs over Bakghanistan, and knowing she'd killed civilians and militant insurgents weighed heavily on her conscience. Monique knew all too well what damage her payload had done to the cities she bombed, but to see the destruction of a capital city, filled with millions of innocent civilians who more than likely never received a warning to evacuate, was heartbreaking. Even if they did get a warning, you can't evacuate millions of people in twenty-five minutes.

Monique looked at Barrera in both shock and admiration— but mostly shock. She couldn't imagine how Barrera could order the death of millions of people and then do a mission briefing as calmly as she was doing now. But Monique also wondered if she should be as fearless as Barrera and make the same call if the time came. Did she have what it took to order a nuclear strike that would kill millions more to protect Salleria? And who decided millions of Sallerian lives were worth much more than millions of North Kangavarian lives?

Monique kept looking at the screen, but it was hard to determine what she saw beyond the muddied video feed. The clouds were too thick—no, not clouds, Monique realized. The drone passed through smoke, ash, and the atomized remains of over two point five million people. What on earth happened to nearly three million souls, Monique wondered to herself. And how was Barrera's soul holding up? She just killed over two million people.

Secretary of State Hallie Barrera moved away from the monitor and sat at the table. "I'm showing you this footage, so you understand the gravity of our situation. World War Three is well underway and has arrived on our very soil. As a result, we nuked most of North Kangavar. As a result, no one will be able to live in that country for a century. So please take everything very seriously, people. Word War Three has begun," Barrera said one more time.

Jacob and Harrison were already in the house. To their great pleasure, the couple was already going at it. They had to walk upstairs to the main bedroom because the pair could hear the pleasure moans downstairs. They didn't bother being subtle.

"Can we join?" The couple didn't even hear Jacob and Harrison. So, they both stripped naked. They were used to nudity. The Bitterfang Wolf Pack often hunted together in the nude. Jacob and Harrison were beautiful and perfect bodies and impossibly flat stomachs. They were both naked now, both hard and both well endowed. "Excuse us, can we join you two?" The woman screamed but looked Jacob in the eye. It was too late for her now. She wanted him. Why wouldn't she? He was perfect. The husband looked Harrison in the eyes, and it became too late for him. They both wanted Jacob and Harrison to join.

They stood by the door, letting the couple look at their perfect bodies. Their members were hard and standing at attention. Jacob could see the man licking his lips. "We have lots of fun toys," the woman finally broke the silence. "You won't need them tonight, beautiful. We will be your toys," Harrison responded. Jacob wanted to kill the woman for bringing up toys, but she could live for now. She was beautiful, and so was her husband.

Jacob glanced around the room and was surprised he didn't hate it. "Don't you two remember us?" Jacob asked the couple, who had never met them before. Full of hot passion, the man lied to Jacob and Harrison, "Yes. I think we do remember you two, right, Hunny?" The woman agreed instantly. She was caught in Jacob's web. He could tell she wanted to be the only woman in a room with three well-built, attractive men. She was in heaven. She would have agreed to remember a leprechaun if her husband had asked.

Jacob smiled at the couple. The man gestured they get into bed with them. "Good choice," Jacob said. "We won't disappoint you. "Oh my, my, my," the woman whispered. I am about to have so much fun.

There was no more reason to keep the suspense going any longer. As if their movements were coordinated, Jacob and Harrison mounted the couple, this time, Harrison took the man, and they both sank their teeth in their throats. The man struggled so hard to escape Harrison that he dislocated his hip. The woman succumbed to the pain so quickly that she collapsed into Jacob's arms. She died almost as if she enjoyed the way she did. Jacob and Harrison drank the couple entirely until they were empty. Their Lord had vengeance again.

The Humvee tore down the gravel road, a cloud of dust exploding from under the massive off-road tires. Ashton was driving, his hands gripping the steering wheel as if his life depended on it. He steered hard to the right to avoid an empty minivan parked in the middle of the road and roared past it. Ashton never intended to be driving the van. But, unfortunately, his plan didn't work out the way he wanted. Ashton, Erynn, Officer Samuel Willis, Corporal Benjamin Hunter, and Paige fought through forty men to get to the Humvee. The North Kangavarians had infantry soldiers on the ground, and they looked to be clearing buildings and killing Sallerians in cold blood. The man driving the Humvee was nearly killed. The team arrived just before a North Kangivar drone blew it off the road with its explosive payload.

"Where are we headed?" Hunter asked. "Haven't figured that out yet exactly," Ashton said. "I'm not sure if we should go back to my place or take this Humvee back to Hasly Mountain," Ashton finished. "Hasly Mountain? The Top Secret Facility that houses NORAD in South Wakefield?" Officer Willis asked. "Yeah, " Ashton said, screaming over the roaring engine sound. Erynn, watch everything on the right. This is a military Humvee, so I can't see much of anything over there." Erynn nodded her head, taking Ashton's orders. Ashton pulled into the woods and pushed down hard on the brakes. It was time to get some answers. He put the Humvee in park, left the engine running, and turned to the extra passenger in the back seat.

"Who the hell are you, and what are you doing out here?" Ashton asked. The scared thirty-something-year-old man looked up defiantly. He looked more like a school teacher than someone brave enough to drive through the heart of the enemy. He wasn't a soldier, Ashton thought to himself. "My name is Kian Price. And I'm nobody special. I was with some military guys, and they got shot, so I took the Humvee and started driving like crazy." Erynn and Ashton exchanged a look. Ashton didn't trust him, and he already didn't like him. "Do as I say, and you live, you got that," Ashton demanded. "Yeah, I got it. You're the dictator-king," Kian snorted. "I'm part of the crew that just saved your ass. Let's go, everybody. We are going back to my place to get the other vehicle and restock on weapons and ammo," Ashton said to everyone. He looked towards Paige and softened his tone. "Keep your head out of site, Paige. Uncle Ashton and Aunty Erynn will keep you safe."

"Ashton, we have to go right now. Hundreds of drones are headed this way," Corporal Hunter said quickly. Then, without responding, Ashton put the Humvee in reverse, turned towards the side of Wakefield, and smashed on the gas. "I'm not ready to die," the Rookie cop said aloud. No one could blame him. They were all thinking the same thing. "Staying alive is our first objective," Ashton responded. "No one is dying in front of my niece."

Ashton took a left and slid out onto the highway that led back to the small town of Wakefield inside of Wakefield, kicking up another cloud of dust. "Everyone, keep your eyes peeled. The enemy is everywhere, and those fucking drones aren't regular drones. Something is very different about them. They seem to be very advanced in technology," Ashton barked.

The truck zipped over the street, its headlights illuminating the empty vehicles on all sides. The sun was rising. It was almost seven a.m. MST. There were so many cars abandoned on the road. It was a miracle that Ashton could keep his fast pace and not crash into anything that would kill them all.

The emptiness of the streets was eerie. Ashton hardly had time to think about getting everyone back to safety. He knew Erynn could care for herself, but everyone else needed maximum protection. Well, maybe not Hunter. He seemed to handle himself well. But now everything was beginning to eat at Ashton, and as the battlefield they just left faded into small unrecognizable dots in the rearview mirror, he felt a sense of uneasiness crawling through her.

Ashton tore himself from the mirror and stole a look into Erynn's eyes. She was always right there, no matter what. She smiled at Ashton, and the world became a safe place just that fast. Ashton smiled back and then turned his head back to the road ahead. The rising sun was a welcomed friend, making it easier for Ashton to navigate this maze of destruction.

Erynn pointed to something ahead. "Watch out!" The Rookie shouted. Ashton slammed on the brakes, narrowly missing a drone that seemed to be malfunctioning in the middle of the road. The drones were amazing. It was almost as if the North Kangavarians spent all the country's money developing unmanned aerial vehicles. The technology was so advanced it was almost alien. Ashton was almost positive that some drones were shooting electronic, magnetic pulse energy rays at the Humvee before they rescued the irritating nerd in the back seat.

"Ashton, we need to stop and go back and check out that drone so we can know what we are dealing with," Hunter said. As much as Ashton hated to stop, Hunter was right. They were fighting an enemy they had underestimated, and Ashton was becoming more convinced by the second North Kangavar didn't care anything about the ground troops they had already defeated, but these drones were special.

Ashton came to a comfortable stop and put the Humvee in reverse. Kian objected the entire time. "Shut the fuck up, Kian, before Erynn makes you," Ashton said. When Kian looked at Erynn's beautiful face, he seemed to get the picture. While Erynn was gorgeous, she was a killer, and somehow people knew when they were on the wrong side of her. Kian got the picture.

When Ashton backed up to the malfunctioning drone, Hunter didn't even wait until the Humvee stopped. He jumped out to get a closer look. Erynn did the same. They both wanted to know what they were up against. "Mr. Dick-tator, sir," Ashton couldn't help but notice Kian stressed the *Dic* in dictator. "What do you want, Kian?" "I'm a computer engineer. I may be able to give us a better idea about the drones than anyone else." "Get your ass out, Kian, and be helpful." Kian got out of the Humvee, saying something under his breath that sounded like *fucking asshole.*

The drone was flowing in mid-air, but something was wrong with it. It had some jet propulsion that allowed it to hover like a spacecraft you see in the movies, but it was man-made. The drone had the North Kangavarian flag on its topside. There were four cameras mounted to it to capture video on all sides. There was also an antenna that relayed communications or received communications.

"Shit," Ashton said, putting the truck in park. "Come with me, baby," Ashton said to his niece. Stay right behind your uncle at all times. He went to twist the key to the Humvee but opted to leave it running. If things got dicey, he wanted to make a fast escape. And Ashton was sure things were about to get dicey.

"Come look at this, Ashton," Hunter called in his direction. Kian was standing next to Corporal Hunter. "I recognize a lot of this tech, but there are things on this drone that I have never seen before. And I haven't even looked inside it yet," Kian said. The drone hovered about two feet above the ground, but it was something wrong with it.

"This is fascinating. The drone appears to be highly advanced, and I don't think anyone is piloting the drone. I am sure someone can, but if you ask me, the North Kangavarians have secretly developed their artificial intelligence capabilities more than anyone else. From the looks of it, I would say this tech is ten to fifteen years, maybe even twenty into the future. I believe this drone sufficiently operates as an independent part of one central brain. It can think for itself and relays all of its information back to the main hive, so to speak, in real-time," Kian said with excitement. He was impressed with the drone and was in nerd heaven. Ashton was glad he didn't have to punch Kian in the face since he was making himself a valuable part of the team. "It is quite possible, since these drones are mass-produced, that this particular one had some manufacturing error that ruined it. But I won't know until I take it and examine it," Kian said. "There is no way we are taking this drone to where we will examine what you can and find another when we have a far more secure location. I can't take the chance of it having some GPS tracking on it, and we are going back to my house. Which, right now, despite what happened earlier, is the safest place we can be," Ashton said. "What happened earlier?" The Rookie asked. It's a long story, and we will tell you on the way.

"Don't get too close to that thing," The Rookie warned. "He's right, guys," Ashton said. "We don't know if it has a self-destruct or anything." 'Relax." Kian said. I know what I'm doing *Dick-tator*." Kian was forced to eat those words when a few seconds later, a ripple ripped through the drone, and loud, high-pitched noise screamed from the drone, and it crashed to the ground in a violent but controlled explosion. Everyone looked in awe.

"Everybody back in the Humvee, now!" Ashton screamed. "That was a self-destruct from some sort of command center." "Chill out *Dick-tator*. I told you there was no reason to worry. I checked for any camera activity and didn't find any," Kian said arrogantly. "Well, did you check for any thermal sensors on the drone?" Ashton asked. "You aren't the only smart one here, Kian."

Before Kian could respond, a popping sound broke through the silence from a distance, and it sounded like something was flying toward them. "Get in the truck now!" Ashton ordered. This time he didn't debate. Instead, he grabbed Paige, ran back to the Humvee, and put her in the backseat. By the time he made his way towards the driver's seat, everyone had gotten the picture and was loading into the military truck.

"Get us out of here!" The Rooked yelled. Ashton had no intention of debating their next move or gathering more research. He saw all he needed to see for now. They were grossly outnumbered, and the enemy had more tech and firepower than them. He smashed on the gas, and the tires made a loud noise as they screeched across the highway asphalt. The

Humvee engine protested as Ashton navigated the vehicle at top speeds and around debris and abandoned vehicles.

They were getting pretty close to the exit that would take them back to Ashton's house when they all heard it— the same high-pitched sonic engine noise that tore threw the sky when the drone they were inspecting self-destructed. But this time, the noise was much closer.

"What is that?" Kian asked. "What you told me couldn't happen. It's another drone on our ass trying to take us out," Ashton responded. A flash of heat rushed through Ashton's body. He couldn't let Paige or Erynn die this way. His eyes darted to the rearview mirror, where he could see the shape of the craft tailing them. He stole another look at Erynn. She nodded at him as if to tell him *You Got This!*

"Well, I'm allowed to be wrong now and then," Kian said in defense. Ashton didn't bother to respond, instead punching the gas harder. If this were real, he wouldn't go down without a fight. The truck ripped onto the gravel road, fishtailing and sending a cloud of dust into the sky. Ashton thought it best to get off the highway and take this fight to a more evenly matched battlefield. He wanted to be back in the tree line again. He didn't want to return to the house until they killed this drone.

Ashton pushed down harder on the pedal, the vibration from the potent engine mixing with the adrenaline pumping in his veins. A little further and he would have enough tree cover to launch an attack and plan what could be their last defense. But the drone was fast and caught up with the truck in seconds, hovering over it. Ashton hit the brakes, threw the Humvee into the park, and jumped out into the grass with his weapon at the ready.

Ashton fired a burst of rounds into what he thought was controlling the drone's navigation. He noticed earlier that most of the drown would be hard to take down with ballistic ammo unless they targeted the components attached to the drone. All of those specialized components would be its weak points. "Erynn, shoot at all the cameras and attachments on the drone. All the components are its weak areas," Ashton screamed to his best friend.

One by one, each component was getting weaker, but the weapon system of the drown activated. There was a blue glow of something that looked to be electric energy. Ashton didn't know if it was EMP related or a missile or some sort. He took a deep breath, spitting chunks of dirt out his mouth. Before he could see what type of weapon was about to be fired from the drone, it exploded like fireworks on the Fourth of July. Ashton didn't know what the hell had happened. He got off his knees, stood up to look around, and there was Corporal Hunter. He was standing with a rocket launcher hoisted on his right shoulder. The barrel was smoking.

Hunter caught eye contact with Ashton and said, "It was in the back of the Humvee, so I used it. Ashton never thought one time to check the back for any cargo. He was too busy killing the enemy and keeping everyone safe. He was glad he was right about Hunter, though. He *could* take care of himself and save all of their lives.

As he had done so many times before, probably a dozen times by now, The Master watched The Ghost and all of his heroics without him knowing. Sure, he could have helped Ashton fight off the North Kangavarians on his way to saving the lesser man driving the Humvee, but he figured if they could kill his most hated person on the planet for him, he would let them. Of course, all the North Kangavarian soldiers failed, and once again, The Ghost walked away with everyone thinking he was a hero. God, he hated Ashton so much. The Ghost was his number one reason for breaking out of prison. Of course, killing everyone who put him there was high on his list, but no one was more responsible for putting Mr. Smith in prison than The Ghost. And no one, absolutely no one, was more responsible for the pain The Master had to deal with every single day than The Ghost. Ashton would die, and Mr. Smith would do it in hand-to-hand combat. He wanted to feel the life drain from his body with his own hands.

The Ghost had to die, he thought. What an incredible story that was unfolding. If anyone had cared enough to study Mr. Smith's past carefully, they would have discovered all the keys to everything that had happened. But people were so lazy these days— and arrogant. Everyone always figured they knew everything they were supposed to know, which would be all they needed.

Smith was a killer's killer. He was well-organized and lacked empathy. It didn't matter how often the shrinks would try to figure him out. They never would. He was an evolved human. They needed to figure out if they wanted to catch up to Smith's thinking.

The Master hated everything about Ashton, and he would kill everyone who loved him. Even the little bitch he was protecting. She couldn't have been more than six or seven years old. He was going to make sure she died a horrible death and forced The Ghost to watch it. Not that he was capable of feeling bad, but if he was, The Ghost deserved all of his family to die, especially after what he did to Mr. Smith. No one had ever defied Smith and lived to tell about it. No one, except Ashton *The Fucking* Ghost.

UC

Benjy Shkolnik addressed the girl now, and he had to speak loudly over the gargling sounds of her dying brother. He was drowning in his blood, and the girl was screaming as loud as she could. She begged for help, and all Benjy did was let her scream. He wanted as much attention as possible. "Keep screaming, lady. You aren't loud enough," Benjy taunted her.

The girl's boot heels scraped the concrete as she tried to get further away from him. Benjy didn't care. He wanted the attention. It didn't matter if it was the North Kangavarians or the Wakefield Police. The sun was in the sky now. All his other killings were at night. He was glad these two would die in broad daylight, even if it were the early crack of the morning.

One block ahead, there was a low-income apartment complex, and Benjy needed all of them to wake up so his plan could work perfectly. The young lady was pretty, but she wasn't screaming loud enough. He didn't like that, but he planned to get her much louder. Without warning, Benjy finished her dying brother by shooting him in the forehead. The crack of the gunshot was loud, just as Benjy wanted. People began to poke their heads out of their doors now to see what was causing the ruckus. The kid would die anyway; Benjy had already slit his throat. So he did the kid a favor and put him out of his misery.

The girl was seventeen, the boy was fourteen, and they both deserved to die. It was very personal. Benjy Shkolnik looked over the railing again to check the apartment complex scene. There was a crowd gathering now. He decided to let the girl go. "There is help for you in that apartment complex. Tell them what I did and avenge your brother," Benjy said to the girl.

He let her go, and just as he suspected, she screamed for help for the entire two-block run to the apartment. The killer's *third* story had begun, involving children. He liked that. Jacob was now Benjy Shkolnik, and he dressed the part. He was now a disgruntled Jewish accountant, playing his part well. He wore a cheap, plastic President Barack Obama mask. He figured the President Obama mask would stand out and be noticeable since he was in a black neighborhood and front of a predominately black apartment complex. *He was right.* The crowd was building now, and the girl was one block away from the apartment complex.

Her screams garnered so much attention, and she was bloodied from the beating Jacob had given her. It was his orders. The Master wanted Harrison to trail the next target while Jacob dispatched these two. The two kids were the children of the Editor and Chief of the Wakefield News company, and he had so much to say, The Master. Unfortunately, the Editor And Chief died while the Master was in prison, so it was decided that his two children had to die in his place.

The crowd was now in considerable numbers. Benjy Shkolnik had a hard time believing anyone was left inside. As soon as someone grabbed the girl, he used his sniper rifle and blew the back of her head into pieces. The bullet traveled through the girl and smoked the window of one of the parked cars. Benjy Shkolnik stood in the middle of the street and took a bow as the crowd ran as screamed. *"I'm baaa-acck!"* he announced. *"Did you miss me? Of course, you did."*

Benjy Shkolnik calmly walked around the corner and burned everything Benjy had in a designated spot he had pre-picked. He put on a new pair of clothes, and Benjy Shkolnik was burned in the fire, never to be seen or heard from again. *This was all for his Master. Vengeance was his.*

Kian ripped a hangnail off his index finger as he huffed and puffed in annoying anger. "I'd like to know what the hell is going on." "Are you blind, Kian? Salleria is under attack, and the North Kangavarians have soldiers on the ground and drones in the air." Corporal Hunter responded. Ashton didn't bother addressing Kian. They were back in the safety of his house, they had two working vehicles now, and Kian was just an asshole that would never shut up.

During his military career, Ashton lost his ability to deal with men like Kian, and his *follow your orders and do what you are told* days were over. Kian was a good representation of someone who just wanted to bark orders and have people do whatever he said. "Hey, I'm talking to you, *Dick-tator,*" Kian persisted while sitting in Ashton's and Erynn's house. Ashton gave him a quick "shut your mouth before I shut it for you" look. It worked. Kian rolled his eyes to the top of his head and asked, "What's to eat in this dump?"

"Do you believe that guy," The Rookie stared. "He doesn't even care. Ashton saved his life; we are now guests in his house." "Sounds like a nut job to me." Hunter said. Ashton didn't say much. Instead, he twirled his combat knives in his hands until the next steps of his plan unfolded in his mind. He knew they couldn't stay at his house forever, and at some point, he would have to brief Aiden on everything happening. Ashton honestly didn't believe there was anything living that knew there were North Kangavarian troops on the ground and drones in the air. The Kangavirans seemed to be on a shoot-to-kill order.

"How's the girl, Ashton," Hunter asked. This question seems to snap Ashton out of his mind. "She is tough. She hasn't cried a bit and had to see at least one hundred people die within the last 4 hours. I think she knows Erynn and I are going to bring her to her mom safely, so she isn't worried too much." "Speaking of Erynn, are you two," Ashton cut Hunter off before he could finish. He knew what he was thinking. Everyone thought it. "Erynn and I are soulmates, that is for sure. We live together and own this house together. We have dedicated our entire lives in service to one another, but no, we are not together," Ashton responded. "If you don't mind me saying, Ashton. You two are together. You are a good guy who doesn't want to mess up the one perfect thing in your life, so you never cross the line. But one day, that line may decide to cross you, or one of you will die before it ever has the chance. Just think about it, bro. That's all I'm saying."

Hunter knocked Ashton off his guard. Ordinarily, he would ignore or correct the person who said something like that about him and Erynn but something about what Hunter felt was right. Before he could respond, Erynn was walking back downstairs. She let Erynn know all the guns and ammo they would need were ready and could go back into the Dodge.

Kian laughed. "Ha! The man can't lead himself into a healthy relationship but wants to lead us into battle." Ashton took a deep breath, calming himself before knocking a few teeth out of Kian's mouth. But they had more significant problems right now. They needed to finish regrouping, account for the enemy, and then make it to the hospital to drop off Paige. She would be much safer with her mom.

Ashton was growing tired of Kian, but he didn't make much of it for now. The day had gone from bad to worst, and he was the team leader, even though he didn't choose to be. Getting these people back home safe to their families was not up for question. It was his job, but it weighed on him.

"Listen up, everyone. I don't know everything that is happening outside, but we are outnumbered, and all of you want to get back to whoever you love safely." Ashton shook his head and sucked deep, straightening his back. "All I know is we have to move forward, and until further notice, every one of you is now a soldier. So grab a weapon," Ashton pointed to Erynn, placing spare rifles, machine guns, and pistols on a couch, "And get ready for war. Because rather you like it or not, we are in one." Ashton started walking toward every person in the room and looked at each of them directly. "I know you have had an impossible night and are exhausted. But, unfortunately, your impossible night has now become morning. With respect, anyone can say anything at any time, but as long as bullets are flying over our heads or about to fly, you take your orders from Erynn and me. Understood?" Everyone in the room nodded in affirmation except Kian, but Ashton wasn't surprised or disturbed by his disrespect.

A knock rapped on the door, and General Asher Valentine stepped inside carrying a laptop. "Madam President, we have a situation," he said. "We just got a report from the Washington Navy Yard of a container ship on the Potomac River. I had a Marine unit call it in." Valentine set his laptop on the table and flipped it open. "I ordered several joint forces and special ops units, the best of the best, to keep an eye on the river. This feed is being broadcast from one of those special units." "How are their cameras working?" Barrera asked. "Several of our units in D.C. had equipment designed to survive an EMP attack, Madam Secretary," Valentine replied. "You are looking at the camera feed of one of those units. We also have several F-22s that survived the EMP blast in the area that are on standby. They have been notified and are en route." "All of this is good news," Monique said. She was possibly giving out her first compliment as President of the United Cities. She hoped it wouldn't be her last.

The camera was positioned on a bridge over the Potomac. The joint Army and Marine forces shouldered their M4s at a container ship downstream. Several Humvees with mounted M240s rolled onto the bridge and set up position. Valentine looked up from his laptop. "We just got confirmation that the ship was outside the blast zone of the EMP. I say again. This ship we are tracking was not in the blast zone. It was spotted sailing in from the Atlantic a few hours ago, and now it is on the Potomac, Madam President. Madam President, I do not believe in coincidence, so I sent the farm to it. Convenient timing. The country of origin appears to be the People's Republic of Avrinyth, and whoever is at the helm seems to be ignoring our forces. Our intel from the crafts that detonated the EMPs is similar to this— our intel says it was People's Republic of Avrinyth crafts that became unresponsive when detected."

Everyone in the room fell silent but Tate. He rose from his seat, breathing heavily. "This could be a second attack. We already know the North Kangavarians spoofed the transponder codes. They could have hijacked an Avrinyth container ship much more easily." "As the new President of the UCS, Monique gave her first orders to General Valentine, "You discovered this General. You give the order to end it." Immediately Valentine settled into his element and barked, "Colonel, order the troops to board the ships." Valentine nodded as he gave the order.

Several minutes passed before a video feed was transferred to the primary monitor that showed a Zodiac carrying a small fire team of six Marines launch from the shore. A few moments later, audio crackled from the wall-mounted speakers in the room. "Eagle's Nest, this is Rabbit 1, preparing to board the bogey." Rabbit 1 directed his helmet-mounted night vision camera at the container ship. Another soldier tossed a rope up to the deck. One by one, the team climbed up. Monique watched the rattling green-hued image as Rabbit 1 stormed past the containers and toward the superstructure. "No sign of contacts," Rabbit 1 reported. "We're heading to the—." the sound of gunfire cracked from the speakers. A marine was down, resting on his face. Another Marine took a knee beside the fallen man and fired at a contact out of sight. Monique felt helpless as she watched the battle unfold. She hated this, which is not how the first hour of being President should go. She laced her fingers together to keep from tapping on the table. On-screen, Rabbit 1 continued climbing and followed the other men across the platform in stealth movements until he arrived at the fallen Marine. "Rabbit 3 is KIA," Rabbit 1 said. "Proceeding to the bridge." The team shouldered their weapons and approached the next corner cautiously. As the point man cautiously turned the corner, a gunshot tore through his helmet and dropped him instantly. There was no reason to wonder if the Marine had lived as he dropped to the platform without trying to break his fall. His body fell with a loud thump and folded into an awkward position that no living person would voluntarily endure. Two of the four remaining men pulled him back to safety, but Monique knew it was already too late for the man. She thought about how brave these men were to see two of their friends die and still march toward active and well-aimed gunfire.

The sound of gunfire cracked from the speakers again. But this time more violently than the first two times— another Marine took a round to the chest and crashed into a railing. This time what came from the speakers was not the sound of violent gunfire but the sound of all hell breaking loose. The feed bobbed up and down while Rabbit 1 moved from position to position. He stopped to fire at contacts Monique still couldn't see and then continued. His team was gunned down one by one in front of him until only two Marines remained.

She gripped the side of the table as Valentine looked up from his laptop, unable to hide his alarmed expression. Rabbit 1's helmet caught three North Kangavarian soldiers on the platform. They, too, now rested in unnatural body positions. She was glad they were dead and hoped they felt every bullet that tore through their bodies. Rabbit 1 put a bullet into the skull of one of the men trying to crawl away. Then he put a hand on the back of the other Marine and prepared to storm the bridge. Valentine ordered the F-22s to provide fire, hoping the remaining two marines could escape harm. "F-22s are thirty seconds out, sir," someone reported to Valentine over the laptop's speakers. Monique bit down on her lip hard enough to register the iron taste of blood. Rabbit 1 and his teammate burst inside the room and were immediately fired upon by a contact inside. The Marine next to Rabbit 1 took several rounds and crashed to the deck. Rabbit 1 took the North Kangavarian soldier down with a three-round burst to his chest. "Eagle's Nest, the bridge is clear. Rabbit 2, 3, 4, 5, and 6 are all KIA," he said heavily.

Valentine responded, "Good job Rabbit 1. Your men fought bravely, and their losses will haunt us for the rest of our lives. Let us pray we both get the revenge we deserve." "Roger that, Sir.", Rabbit 1 said, with redemption in his voice. General Valentine looked up from his laptop and over to President Monique Maddox. They both knew Rabbit 1 was seconds away from joining the rest of his team. The Marine quickly ran over to the dead North Kangavarian man and pulled a small device from his hand. He held it up toward the camera. The rumble of F-22s sounded like fiery blasts sent containers cartwheeling into the sky. Monique breathed as a blinding explosion bloomed out of the ship's center, instantly killing the feed. "Did we take it out?" Monique asked. Valentine nodded solemnly. "Target destroyed." There were several seconds of silence, every head in the room bowed to contemplate the loss of the brave Marines. Then, a deep and raucous roar shattered the quiet. Monique knew right away the sound wasn't from the F-22s. That was the sound of a nuclear bomb. She instantly realized the timer one of the losers had in their hands was a countdown to a nuclear strike. She immediately stood from her chair and announced to everyone in the room, "I know where that bomb is going. It is coming straight for the White House. That is exactly what I would do."

But, she was too late— far too late. Before she could take her seat and finish another sentence, the room shook violently. The walls, floor, and ceiling were buckling in one motion and all at the same time. And then it happened. Everything exploded around everyone in the

PEOC. There was not an inch of the PEOC spared. Monique was lifted from the ground and crashed into the ceiling, or maybe the ceiling crashed into her. She couldn't tell anymore. Her body felt weightless. Her lungs burned with hot air, and she suffocated on ash and smoke that used to be solid walls. Dust rained down from the ceiling, and the Presidential Seal affixed to the wall rattled and fell to the ground. The main screen went next, shattering. All around her, the top officials of the UCS government were screaming and crawling under the table. As she lay motionless, President Monique Maddox was lying on the ground, debris around her. General Valentine grabbed the President before the entire building crashed around him and pulled her to the best possible safety he could achieve.

Shockwaves pounded the room. There was a cracking sound and then a terrible groan as the steel beams that were supposed to hold the bunker together gave way, bending and ultimately snapping like bones. In General Valentine's arms, in the swirl of emergency lights, Valentine saw what was left of the CIA advisor. He was dead. A large metal beam split his body in half from top to bottom. A storm of smoke and dust swirled through the operations room. Valentine covered his mouth, coughing and trying to move. The President's body was lying limp in his arms. From every direction came the cries of his colleagues. The grinding of rock against concrete and steel did little to drown out the screams. Finally, he saw a figure run for the door, only to vanish into a gaping hole in the floor. The shifting walls and ceiling swallowed the horrified scream. Darkness flooded the room. With one final effort, Valentine put his body over President Maddox to shield her from further harm— then the room went completely black.

They weren't going to know what hit them this time! Jacob had arrived at Stanley Park in Wakefield. He double-checked his address. *1400 Manford Ave.* He was in the right spot. It was the baseball championship game, and the Wakefield Bobcats were favored to win. Jacob grabbed a soda and a hot dog, then smiled politely at people walking in front of him.

He was having a good time blending in. He felt normal for a few short moments, but now he had a strong urge to stand out. It was time for his fourth story to unfold. Out of the corner of his eye, he could see some baseball players warming up. Players were hitting balls into nets, perfecting their swings, and pitchers were loosening their arms. And the very best part of it all was a sell-out crowd.

The game wouldn't start for another four hours, but Jacob wanted to take advantage of the early worker crowd and turn them into his crowd. He wanted to be responsible for turning this buzzing baseball field into a parking lot full of screams and gossip.

Some particularly high-spirited fans were excited and talking loudly, while others wore the Wakefield Bobcats emblems on their clothes. There were about four hundred people in attendance, with tens of thousands expected later this afternoon. Jacob was Nigerian for his fourth story. His name was Adejoke Adeboyejo, the financial consultant for Agu Oby, the richest Igbo man in Nigeria. Agu Oby is the wealthiest businessman in Nigeria.

He is also a prince. His net worth is US$5.8 billion, and he created Nigerian Petroleum International Limited. His business was oil, and he wanted to buy a Sallerian baseball team, and this was his first stop. Agu was too busy to travel, so he sent his most trusted business advisor Adejoke Adeboyejo. Jacob was completely into his role, and his southern accent was gone. His accent was authentically Nigerian.

Adeboyejo wanted to go where all could see his face and hear his accent. He worked so hard to be Nigerian. It was only fitting that people hear him speak. Logically, he needed to get to the stadium's control booth, and if he could control the scoreboard, that would be a bonus.

Adejoke Adeboyejo knocked on the metal door. He was expected. Adejoke made phone calls last week, setting his fourth story in motion. The door opened. In a robust Nigerian accent, Adejoke spoke, "Hi, I'm Adejoke Adeboyejo. I am so happy to be in Salleria." Jacob knew the thick accent and the even thicker humility would win anyone over. He was counting on it. Before the two men in the control room could respond, Adejoke Adeboyejo shot them both in the head. His pistol was suppressed, and the sound of the rounds leaving his gun was drowned by the thousand other noises happening in the stadium.

Adejoke Adeboyejo pushed both bodies to the floor, sat at their logged-in computers, and controlled the scoreboard.

I KILLED THE TWO PEOPLE IN THE BOOTH. I KILLED A THIRD PERSON ABOUT AN HOUR AGO, AS WELL. HE WAS MY REAL TARGET. THE TWO MEN UP HERE WERE JUST

Mr. Smith took a break from watching The Ghost and his merry band of idiots and was about a mile up the road and The Ghost's therapist's house, Ra. The old man was a legend around these parts, and Smith figured it was time to start taking things from the same way Ashton took from him.

He arrived at the old man's house at about eight a.m. MST. When the old man saw who was knocking on his door, hell fainted like someone hit his "off" switch. Smith managed to catch the old man before he fell on his head and seriously hurt himself. He wasn't going to hurt the old man. Smith was here for his money. Smith knew the old man didn't trust the banks and kept a few million dollars in small bills tucked away in a few safes in his house.

Moments later, he was reviving the old man in his living room and smiling over his face. "It's been a long time, old man," Smith said. Mr. Smith thought he would faint again, but he kept his consciousness. "Finley," the old man groaned. "When did they let you out?" "They

294

didn't exactly let me out," Finley responded. "I took my freedom into my own hands. And you are the only person outside my brother who knows I am a free man." The old man, Ra, took a hard swallow and strained to push out a few words, "So you came here to kill me then?" "Oh no," Finely gave an honest answer. I'm here for your money."

I won't be here for more than an hour. I have to get back to Ashton. He doesn't know I am a mile from his house. The old man stared up at Finley now. He managed to pick himself up and sit in his favorite chair in the living room. As defiant as ever, the old man offered his opinion to Finley, "Even if Ashton doesn't know you are watching him, he will find out. He always does. And how do you expect to get past Erynn? She will see you coming from a mile away?" "She hasn't seen me yet, old man," Finley responded harshly to the old man. "Before we have a verbal pissing match, give me the codes to all the safes, and I will be on my way.

The old man did as he was told, and a few minutes later, Finley Smith was a few million dollars richer. When he returned to the living room to say goodbye to the old man, he intended to let him live. And then he thought about what The Ghost had taken from him, and there was no way he could let the old man live now. He wanted The Ghost to feel all the pain he felt.

He didn't even try to sneak up on the old man. Mr. Smith was pretty sure the old man had already accepted his fate. "I'm going to kill you quickly. It won't hurt much," Finley said with coldness. He didn't care how much it would hurt the old man, but he genuinely didn't come to his house to kill him. But the universe had already decided his fate.

"Close your eyes, "I am going to count to three and make this painless." The old man closed his eyes, and Finley shot him in the head without counting. His body flew back into his favorite, and his brains painted the walls behind him. Smith didn't care. The Ghost deserved it, so he leaned close to the old man's dead body and took a deep breath. He wanted to see his lifeless body collapse into a deformed position. This was fun. Speaking of fun, Smith wondered if the old man had any board games lying around the house. He got bored watching Ashton sometimes and figured he would roll some dice and win some fake money.

After looking around the house for any board games, Smith grew angry. He couldn't find any and shot the old man right between the eyes once more and then three more times. When his anger subsided, the old man no longer had a head. He looked more like a body with an enormous rotten tomato oozing out of the place his neck should be. Smith erupted in spontaneous laughter and sat next to the old man's bullet-riddled body, kicked his feet on his lap, and started counting his money. He figured he would catch up with The Ghost in about an hour. Unfortunately, the morning was still young.

Holding his Glock in one hand, Aiden pulled back the curtain covering the window to his bedroom while his wife and daughter slept in the bed behind him. It was finally another day. The longest night of his life was over, but the joy did not come in the morning. His wife Dawn sat up, her braided hair falling over her Wakefield Police Department t-shirt. "What time is it, Aiden?" "Little after six." His daughter Lillian stirred and rolled from her side onto her back. Aiden tucked the comforter around his daughter and studied her in the faint light of dawn—the brown braids that matched her mother's and the dark brown eyes.

Aiden didn't have much appetite, and neither he nor Dawn figured out how to tell Lillian that her friend was dead. But she was sixteen, so it would be best to tell her sooner than later. Aiden figured he would rip the bandage off. "Hey, Lillian." His daughter peaked open her eyes and began to sit up. "Why is it so cold, dad?" "There's a killer on the loose, the country's been attacked, and the power wasn't going to come back on anytime soon," Aiden said heavily. "I don't know where to start, Lillian, so here goes." After explaining everything to Lillian and watching her go through all the emotions he had at least nine hours to go through, she did much better than he did, and it only took her thirty minutes of denial and finally reaching acceptance a few minutes afterward. "The whole town is looking to me for answers, but all I have is bad news." Dawn grabbed his hand. "You start by going to town hall and doing what you always do. You lead, Aiden." "It's going to be a hard winter, love. We need to conserve everything and plan for the long haul. That means rationing food and water." Dawn told Aiden.

Aiden did the math in his head. He ran down a list of supplies they would need to survive the winter and told his wife, "I need to get to town hall and meet with Mayor Harris." "Knowing Julia, she's probably already there." "She's going to be mad." "Because you declared a state of emergency?" "No, because I didn't consult with her first." Dawn came up behind Aiden and put a hand on his shoulder. She always knew how to calm Aiden down and brought the best out of him.

Aiden knew it was time for him to upgrade his weapons. He entered his weapons closet and grabbed his Barrett M82 rifle with a scope. This high-powered sniper rifle was designed to destroy sensitive enemy equipment, like parked aircraft, radar units, trucks, and other vital assets at long range. In addition, it is used for the remote destruction of explosive ordnance. After admiring his Barrett M82, Aiden grabbed his Sig Sauer P22. The Sig is known for its accuracy due to its X-Ray Day/Night front sight. The easy-to-see green front sight allows the user to acquire targets in daylight. Tritium insert aids night shooting in the fiber optic ring. Ergonomics are improved by the evenly distributed weight of the pistol. It's tough enough to have a history of use by Navy SEALs. It's also in use by the UCS Secret Service. Police can choose different calibers, such as the 9x19mm Parabellum, .40 Smith & Wesson, or .357 SIG. Lastly, Aiden grabbed Gerber 06 Auto Knife. The Gerber 06 Auto Knife is fully automatic and ready to deploy instantly. This particular Gerber pocket knife is crafted with premium stainless steel, S30V. This knife also has some unique and valuable features, like its oversized release button, which is for the times you wear gloves while working. Its aluminum handle has comfortable contours for a reliable grip and a convenient lanyard hold.

Aiden holstered the pistol and then grabbed the Barrett M82. When he turned to leave, Dawn was standing at the door. "Be careful, Aiden. Please, by God, be careful out there." "Do you have your Glock?" he asked. She lifted her shirt and turned, cocking a hip. The black grip of the pistol was sticking out of her waistband. "Good girl," Aiden said with a grin. Just then, a loud horn honked, catching both of their attention. Aiden hurried to the living room and looked through the window. In their driveway was Derrick Mercer's red 1971 Dodge pickup. Aiden grabbed his backpack with a smile on his face.

Aiden looked over the vintage truck. The windshield had a significant crack and smelled like mothballs, but it worked. The chrome grill was off, and only two tires had hubcaps, but the tires were perfect, and the lights shined bright. Derrick put his hands on his hips and turned to look at Aiden. "She may be old, but she runs," he said. "Rebuilt the engine with my own hands." "I didn't say anything," Aiden said, laughing. "I think we're looking at our new squad car." Derrick patted the hood fondly. "You're beautiful, baby. Don't let anyone tell you differently." "We better get going.

Mayor Harris is probably on her way to the town hall." "She's already there. I dropped her off before coming to get you. She isn't happy, and she wants to talk to you." Dawn laughed. "Told you, Aiden." Aiden kissed his wife on the cheek. "See you tonight." Then waved goodbye to his teenage daughter, Lillian. "I love you. Be good while I'm gone." "Love you too, Dad." He grabbed his new gear and weapons and forced himself to walk away. He didn't like leaving them during this time. Leaving them suddenly felt wrong, but he had a duty to his town. Everyone would be counting on him, and with threats coming from all sides, he had to get to work.

Aiden climbed into the truck's passenger seat, and Derrick wedged his bulk behind the steering wheel and turned the key. The engine coughed to life. "Got any updates for me?"

Aiden asked. "Detective Schwartz has been checking the Geiger counters every hour. Looks okay so far. Still trying to contact all the reps for the EOC. The lights are still off. No one has started rioting, but questions are flying around, which is to be expected. Oh, and we still don't have any leads on the killer, but other than that, all is well. Or, at least, as well as you left it. We've got officers stationed at all critical facilities, including the YMCA." "The YMCA?" "I read a book about an EMP strike years ago, and they used the pool as an additional water source." "Good call. Must have been a great book." Aiden said. "But that won't last very long. We need to think long-term here." "I know. Once I drop you off, I'm heading to Bill Catcher's with Major Maddox. Maybe he can get some answers from his base. He's certified crazy, but he is smart."

Aiden pointed at the dashboard of the truck. "Have you tried this radio yet?" "Yeah, but I didn't get anything but static." "You mind?" Aiden asked, reaching for the tuning knob. "Knock yourself out." Aiden spun the dial as they pulled out of the driveway. "We're going to need to hold a town hall meeting," Derrick said. "Tell people what's going on." "The mayor is probably spinning this as my fault and planting negative seeds against me for her purposes so that town hall can wait a little longer ."

Derrick took one hand off the steering wheel to scratch his mustache. "You've never been a man of many words." "There's a killer out there, and I—" Aiden paused as the sound of a garbled transmission came over the radio. He slowly twisted the knob back to the left. "Stop the car," Aiden said with excitement in his voice. Derrick drove onto the shoulder, kicking up a storm of dust. He shifted into neutral and waited. White noise broke from the old speakers. "I don't hear nothing—" Derrick began to say. A robotic voice from the radio cut him off.

"Sometime before 5 a.m., a second attack...." "Second attack?" Derrick asked. Aiden raised a finger and waited for the message to continue, but there was only the hiss of static. "Dammit," Aiden said. With everything in him, he wanted to hear the rest of this message to know what he was up against. He wanted to know everything he could to plan a defense for what was to come. Adrenaline pumping and turning the radio knob ever so slightly to the left, a beeping sound came through the crackling storm and, finally, a barely audible voice. "This is a national emergency. Important instructions will follow...." The beeping returned for several agonizing moments. Aiden stared at the knob. "Come on, goddammit, come on."

"The following message is transmitted at the request of the United Cities government. This is not a test. At approximately 7:21 p.m. Pacific Standard Time, three North Kangavarn planes detonated nuclear warheads above Venburn, Ellingshire, and Wakefield. The subsequent electromagnetic pulse knocked out power across the entire United Cities. At 5:45 a.m. Eastern Standard Time, a second attack took place. A nuclear bomb was detonated from the Potomac River just outside Washington, D.C." "Holy shit," Derrick muttered. Aiden stared at the radio in disbelief. "D.C. is gone?" "All residents within a four-hundred-mile radius of the attack should seek a fallout shelter. Fallout is a product of a nuclear attack. Prolonged exposure will result in certain death. If there is a nearby fallout shelter, go there now. Otherwise, seek shelter in the interior of a building on the lowest floor. Do not leave the shelter until an all-clear has been issued." The annoying beeping began again. Derrick was shocked and released a slew of curse words. "This is an emergency action notification. All networks and cable systems shall transmit this action message." Aiden couldn't believe what he'd just heard. Even though Major Maddox told them what was happening, he couldn't wrap his mind around just how bad it was and the idea of nuclear fallout. He was secretly hoping that he was overreacting about using the Geiger counters, but now the government was confirming that the nuclear fallout was a genuine threat. No, not just real, but inevitable. This was Armageddon. How could it have happened? And why had the North Kangavarians followed up their devastating EMP attack with a direct nuclear strike on Washington? What the hell was going on? Who was in charge because they had failed? And how many people *who were* in charge were still alive. How on earth could the United Cities be outsmarted like this?

Derrick pounded the steering wheel and then grabbed it with both hands, squeezing until his knuckles and fingertips burned from the friction. The tattooed image of a coiled rattlesnake and the words "Surely goodness and mercy shall follow me all the days of my life." showed on his forearm. It was part of the last verse of Psalm twenty-three. Derrick was a religious man. He always tried to make sure he did right by God and never reached the comfort of being both a cop and a Christian. Something about merging the two was always a struggle for him. "That's it." Aiden said as he noticed the scripture was lost in a mass of Reece's Peanut Butter-colored scar tissue from an old shrapnel wound. "The protection of the government followed all the Cities of Salleria day-in-and-day-out. The government couldn't show its grace and mercy on its United Cities." Derrick's eyebrows drew together in a single, heavy line. "What the hell, man?"

"D.C. was God, and our grace and mercy died with him in the nuclear attack. We are on our own. With the seat of our government gone, we will have a hell of a time managing any recovery efforts." "So what you're saying is that help ain't coming," Derrick said. "Shit, Aiden, I could have told you that. We handled our problems back in the flood of '2016, and we'll take care of ourselves again now." Derrick was always a good friend and someone Aiden could count on consistently. He pulled back onto the road and punched the accelerator. The metal bones of the old truck groaned. Gritting his teeth, Aiden looked at the mountains in the distance. Derrick swallowed hard as he thought about the fight that was to come. How was he going to protect his city? How was he going to protect his best friend, Aiden? He had always felt isolated up here, away from society. It could be a lonely feeling, but maybe now that isolation wasn't such a bad thing.

As they drove through Wakefield, Derrick saw a crowd gathering outside the town hall. At the front, facing the others, was Major Maddox. He had his hands up like he was fending off questions. "Shit," Aiden said. "Should have told him to lay low. Now they're going to want to know why a jet pilot is wandering around town." Derrick waved at the major and pointed to the parking lot. Ernest nodded, said something else to the crowd, and then walked casually to the truck. When Ernest took a seat, Derrick said, "Play that message for Major Maddox. Shit just got real."

It wasn't that Ashton was afraid to die. On the contrary, he didn't want to right now. He had things he wanted to accomplish and still had much more beer-drinking left.

As a soldier, he knew the possibility of life after death was slim to none. He believed in bullets and bombs because they showed up in his life to destroy it. He'd never believed in the devil. So he couldn't understand why such a powerful God would owe one of his creations so much that he would have to kill his son.

Ashton didn't have a problem with religion. His real problem was seeing the true wickedness of man in combat zones didn't leave much room for believing in a benevolent God who saved people. He'd seen innocent civilians die. After all, their patriarchs poured poison down their throats because they converted to another religion. He'd seen six-year-old girls trained as semi-automatic insurgents protecting borders that wouldn't allow them to drive once she became of age. Ashton didn't have a single problem with God or religion. His problem was with men. It was men who invaded countries, not God. Men raped women and pillaged communities, not God.

Erynn was driving now. About fifteen minutes before, Ashton decided not to take more than one vehicle because he couldn't trust Kian to behave while Corporal Hunter drove the Humvee, and he certainly didn't want Kian riding with him, Erynn, and Paige in the Dodge. So, Ashton left Paige back at the house with Corporal Hunter, The Rookie, and Kian. He knew Hunter would protect the house and everyone in it if anything happened.

Erynn and Ashton were in the Dodge, checking for any survivors. Ashton also figured while they were out, they would do a little reconnaissance, too. Ashton stared out the window of the ancient Dodge and was lost in his thoughts. It was only when Erynn ran over a tree branch was he snapped back into the present.

It was about ten a.m. MST and the sun shone brighter than ever. Erynn and Ashton could see for miles, and both of their eyes surveyed the air and ground, looking for potential threats. There were no signs of survivors or signs of enemies. Maybe everyone is in a shelter, Ashton thought to himself.

The dark blacktop was littered with empty vehicles, sending a chill down Ashton's spine. Wakefield was really in bad shape. It was much easier at night to deal with all the chaos because it wasn't so easy to see. But with the sun shining brightly, Ashton began to realize how bad things were. *Keep your head in the game Ashton. Erynn and Paige need you to stay alive and take care of them.*

Erynn jerked the wheel to the left, steering the Dodge around another pair of sedans and up a hill. The truck moaned and whined, the muffler spit trails of black smoke into the air as it crept down the highway, but the Dodge stayed true. Then, a shadow shot across the road ahead, causing Ashton's adrenaline to spike. It was a single bird flying through the air. Ashton wondered if something had spooked the bird. Was it one of those advanced drones they saw earlier?

Ashton kept his hands on his rifle, ready for anything that may happen. He could feel his heart thumping, faster and faster, as Erynn drove slowly, waiting for a drone to show its ugly face. But nothing came. For a second, Ashton regretted wanting to see if there were survivors, but he quickly disregarded the feeling and sucked in a deep breath. He was a good person, no matter how much life forced him to do bad things. Finding survivors when he and Erynn were capable was the right thing to do.

"Everything looks clear," Ashton said, crossing the passenger seat towards Erynn, who was gripping the steering with both hands, ready to make any evasive maneuvers necessary. Erynn hit the gas. They kept looking for civilians who would be in trouble or alive.

They drove for a few more miles until they saw a drone flying low. It must have been looking for something, but what? They watched the drone inch across the asphalt, leaving a faint heat vapor in its wake. The drone had no eyes or face, but it looked like a menacing monster, even from this distance. Once they were convinced the drone didn't spot them and wasn't on a constantly rotating path, they inched slowly. "Pull over into the trees, Erynn. We've taken the Dodge as far as we can get it without being detected."

Erynn pulled over, and they both grabbed their weapons and got out on foot. They both knew it wasn't worth risking a trip down the highway with drones flying so close. Ashton craned his head to look in Erynn's direction, "You good, Erynn?" She nodded her head and slowly inched forward.

Just as Ashton was getting ready to tell Erynn to turn around and get back into the Dodge, he saw Erynn using her binoculars. He could tell by looking at her face she was using the range fining function and zooming in on something that got her attention. So Ashton put on his binoculars and did the same.

"Fuck," Ashton said, dropping his head toward the grass. It was just what he had been afraid of— finding a kid in the middle. Somehow kids always find a way to get themselves into the worst messes. Ashton let out a big sigh. "You are looking at the kid, aren't you, Erynn?" He didn't need her to do so, but she nodded in confirmation. Of course, it didn't help matters any when Ashton saw the kid walking towards enemy ground troops looking like he was about to ask the North Kangavarians for directions to the arcade.

Erynn gave Ashton a look that seemed to say, "Which one of us is being the hero, and which one of us is going back to the Dodge to rescue the hero when bullets start flying?" Ashton sighed again. "Grab the car, and you better save me before I did, or I'm going to come back and haunt you forever," Ashton said to Erynn. She smiled and took off back to the Dodge. "Now, let's see if I'm as fast as I used to be," Ashton said to himself under his breath.

Chapter Twelve

As Derrick steered up the twisty roads around Cherry Hill, he wondered what Ernest was thinking. He hoped Ernest was wrong about nuclear fallout heading towards Wakefield. After all, it was an EMP. But, on the other hand, Derrick wasn't even sure if the blast from an EMP would work like a regular nuclear bomb and create nuclear fallout.

Out the window, Ernest held his Geiger counter and watched the needle while the words of the emergency broadcast repeated inside his head. During the earlier part of the drive, Ernest shared with Derrick his pain about the friends lost. They were more like his brothers, who were flying jets with him when the EMP was detonated. Their planes fell from the sky as bricks fell out of wheel barrels. But, from what Derrick understood, the only thing keeping him going now was the thought of his rescuing his nephew. He was in Chesterfolk, but Ernest had no idea if his nephew was alive. And, if he was, how much longer would he be?

Derrick could see Ernest was still lost in a maze of his thoughts. "What's the Geiger counter say?" Derrick asked, hoping to snap Ernest out of whatever death scenario he was running through his mind. "We're good for now," Ernest replied. Derrick drummed his fingers on the steering wheel before she said, "it's been a crazy twenty-four hours. And that is putting it lightly, not to mention you have been on the ass-end of it just about all of it. But you landed in one of the best towns in Salleria. There is nothing that Aiden or I won't do to help you. Aiden is a great man. If there is anything that he can do for your nephew, he will get it done. Man has always done right by people, no matter what. So you're welcome to stay if we cannot get you a radio. You are welcome to come back after you find your nephew, too." Derrick stopped talking for a moment.

He let his words sink in as he drove around abandoned cars. "Trust me. We need a good man like you." "Thanks, but I have to get to Chesterfolk to find my nephew after I reach Command," Ernest said. "I understand, Major. Your nephew needs you, and I know you will not quit until you find him. If my girls weren't safe home in Wakefield with their mom, I'd be trying to get to them, too." Derrick took a swig of bottled water and offered it to Ernest. "No thanks." "Major, take a drink. You can't get to your nephew dead or dehydrated." Ernest nodded his head and mumbled something under his breath that sounded something like *I guess you're right*, he relented and took a swig of the water bottle. He usually wouldn't drink behind another person, but it was the apocalypse.

"Rory Cooper lives off the grid up here. He's a paranoid bastard and doesn't care much for law enforcement, the military," Derrick rattled off about eight more law enforcement and government sounded job positions. His goal was to ensure Ernest knew how much of a nutcase Rory was— it worked. "Oh, he doesn't like any other living human being either. I think he is waiting for the aliens to come and take him away from here." Derrick grinned, and the two men laughed. Derrick wasn't making fun of Rory. Instead, he was trying to give Ernest a heads-up because they were walking into the Lion's Den. Except, there were no lions, just one man with a tinfoil hat and a laundry list of conspiracy theories.

"Well, you should probably do the talking," Ernest said with a smirk. He got the picture Derrick was painting. "That's what I was thinking. If I don't end up with a gun pointed at my head as soon as we get on his property. So I figured it would be good to offer Rory some diesel in return for his help. I think he will be okay with a favor-for-a-favor swap." Derrick said.

They say if you are genuinely crazy, you will be the last person to know that you are. Rory was one of those people. He either doesn't know he is crazy or has no idea what crazy looks like. He was always going on about the end of the world and how the judgment was coming. Derrick used to laugh at the thought, but maybe Rory was right. Maybe he knew about this EMP, and maybe everyone else was crazy but Rory. That's a scary thought. Derrick was ready for any possibility when they got to Rory's place. Rory wasn't the type to fear anything, and the threat of jail or consequences didn't phase him. This made popping up unannounced at Rory's house a risky move.

Derrick thought about this and decided to park on the side of the road and kill the engine. He didn't want to sneak to Rory's property, but he didn't want Rory to see a car coming up his driveway after an EMP blast and alarm him. Ernest, who was no longer limping and didn't seem to be suffering from any apparent injuries, jumped out of the car and immediately walked alongside Derrick. He did it without asking any questions and without needing to be coerced. Derrick was both impressed and grateful. The backup made him feel better. "Damn, we could use a man like Ernest," Derrick thought.

The mid-morning sun rays were beaming over the open terrain as Ashton put away his binoculars, his irritation meter getting higher by the second. All he wanted to do was get his niece back to her mother. Saving kids in the middle of war zones was not on his agenda. He wasn't even sure if he liked kids. He turned out to be a great uncle, but Ashton didn't like kids outside his niece. The little crumb snatchers were too demanding and too needy. *Damn.* Ashton thought to himself. *When will I ever get to live a normal life?*

He was going to have to use his HK416 for this mission. Reaching into his gear strapped on his body, Ashton slowly grabbed his suppressor and twisted it on the barrel. He didn't want to attract any attention. Ashton scanned the shoulder of the highway and jumped behind a rock formation. Using his EXPS2-0 mounted holographic site, he marked each tango, including drones between him and the kid. "That's seven tangos," Ashton muttered under his breath.

To his left was another mobile TOC center. There was no way to tell how many tangos were inside. His guess was four, but no one was guarding it. To his right was an old Ranch House in which Ashton counted seven tangos using at a base or something. And to the middle was an open field he labeled the death zone. No matter what, Ashton didn't want to get trapped in the middle because it was flat, visibility was at one hundred percent, and anyone with a gun could get an easy shot on him. Stealth was vital, but how many men could he take out before an android or footsteps gave away his position? If he were spotted too soon, he would be dead. *Fucking kids!*

Ashton rechecked the safety and shouldered his firearm to survey the building, the TOC, and the area ahead. A small red dot in the corner of his EXPS2-O site showed about a quarter klick between him and the parking lot. The little Ankle Biter was walking directly toward the enemy and would be spotted any second. He knew that wasn't the kid's name, but Ankle Biter would do just fine for now.

An enemy in the middle of the field, between the TOC and the house first. Ashton pulled his trigger slightly, a round left his suppressed barrel, and the unsuspecting man's nose exploded into a bloody mess. He was dead on impact. His partner heard the body in the ground, and before he could make sense of what was happening, Ashton put a suppressed round into his right ear, making the last thing the man ever heard was the sound of his death. The Ghost was now two for two.

From what he could tell, four more men were in the open area, and six were in the house. The four men left were now alert and screaming orders in North Kangavarian. Ashton, still lying in the prone position, his weapon shouldered to his left, was making quick decisions on what to do with these four tangos before all hell broke loose. It would be easier to fight the other seven-plus men if these four were eating dirt.

Ashton held his breath and squeezed a round into the head of the tango to the far left. He didn't understand how but one of the two drones became alert. *Who the fuck was watching in the camera feed?* He paused and studied the remains with his scope before a career of training took over, and he took off running down the shoulder of the road. There was no time to hesitate, no time to ask questions, no time to do anything but trust his training. Stealth—and hesitation—was no longer an option if he was going to save this Ankle Biter.

Ashton used abandoned cars to cover and shield them from bullets coming. The enemy was looking for him, but they couldn't find him yet. There had to be at least ten tangos left, and he still didn't know how many were in the TOC. Then, a few feet ahead, the highway turned off and connected with a frontage road. There was a small shopping plaza behind that, and several adjoining parking lots filled North Kangavarian Tangos. He was fucked. He skidded to a halt when he saw it. A new threat was whizzing towards him at breakneck speeds. The ominous roar of a drone was coming his way. And as Ashton got a better look, he saw hundreds of dead bodies in its bloody wake. Ashton was standing in the middle of a North Kangavarian kill zone. His stomach lurched again, and blood began to pound in his ears. *Trust your training. You've seen worse.* It wasn't a lie—but it wasn't exactly the truth, either. He'd never seen anything quite like what he was seeing now. This wasn't a war. This was a massacre.

Erynn knew well enough to stay back and out of sight until he took out more tangos. They had done this together more than a few times to trust each other with their lives. If Erynn thought The Ghost was in real trouble, she would fire off a round and kill something in his line of sight. She was the better shot. That would signal to him that she deemed him no longer in a situation he could handle alone.

Ashton shouldered his weapon, and with a well-aimed three-round burst of armor-piercing rounds Erynn put in his magazine before they left the house, Ashton shot the drone until it exploded and crashed to the hard ground with a loud thud. Stealth was definitely out of the picture now. There was no way no one didn't hear that. Ashton had no idea if the drone's cameras saw him, but he didn't have time to think about it. He had to save this little Ankle Biter and get out of there because they all ended up dead.

Ashton shuddered as the sound broke through the silence and alerted everyone in a one-hundred-foot radius. Ashton felt it sounded like a dozen footsteps were headed in his direction, and each step was coming from all directions. "What the fuck," he said under his breath. He attempted to still his racing heartbeat, taking a deep breath to calm his nerves. But that shit didn't work. He was trapped and outnumbered. Another deep breath—a glance around the bumper—a glance behind him—another deep breath. Nothing. His heart raced. The sounds came closer.

Ashton spun around and raised his rifle, and shot the next tango in the head. Anyone in the TOC and the Ranch House was coming towards him in the parking. From what Ashton could see, ten tangos were headed in his direction.

Ashton shot a tango in the forehead and then shot the one next to him in the upper chest. He lost count of how many bad guys were left, so he would shoot anything moving. Ashton shot another tango in the head as he was running toward the parking lot. With a reflexive reaction, the tango did Ashton a favor and shot his running mate in the back. As soon as the tango hit the ground from Friendly Fire, Ashton put him out of his memory by taking off the top of his head.

Ashton stood behind an abandoned truck and watched as two North Kangavarian soldiers pulled their fallen comrade to safety. Ashton didn't shoot those two. He respected the gesture.

With a grunt, he suppressed his fear and pulled himself from behind the vehicle. He had no intention of dying this morning. In less than a second, he was running toward the enemy. One of them almost fainted when they saw The Ghost running toward them with no cover whatsoever. There were at least a dozen. His first assessment wasn't even close. Each man looked ready to kill, and all had weapons aimed in his direction. Ashton fired three rounds before each of them could fire, and all three men fell to the ground, never to rise again.

Ashton took cover behind another abandoned vehicle and waited for the onslaught of rounds to end. He took out another four tangos and saw there were only five left. Just ahead, he saw the little Ankle Biter hiding behind a wall covering his ears. As Ashton ran past a tango holding his throat where a round had entered it, he realized he would have to kill five more tangos before he could rescue this kid and get out of there. He neared the end of the parking, still attracting the most attention. But this time, it worked in his favor. Each time the five tangos shot, he knew where they were and how well they could shoot. Ashton was closing in on the kid's location and took out another tango. There were now four left. Ashton dug deeper and pushed his legs. The muscles strained and pulled but held firm as he maneuvered between the empty vehicles, trying to hug their frames for cover. His lunges felt like they were going to explode.

He neared the end of the parking lot without getting shot. The four tangos were now far ahead and closing in on the kid's location. Somewhere in the firefight, they must have recognized who The Ghost was after and decided the little Ankle Biter was a target they could use as leverage to draw him out. The kid screamed as Ashton swung his head around an abandoned vehicle to get a better look. One of the tangos was closing in on the Ankle Biter. He only had moments to create a plan. Ashton scanned the terrain and decided he would hit the first tango while he was running and take out the other three however the randomness of war would allow.

Seconds later, Ashton squeezed the trigger and shot the first of the remaining four tangos in the right side of the head. Blood exploded all over the Ankle Biter's face. The kid screamed louder! Ashton didn't hesitate when he saw the other three tangos were busy looking for him instead of capturing the Ankle Breaker. Ashton followed his training and shot the three men in the head. It wasn't easy, though. After she shot one of the three tangos, a red cloud of blood jumped from the top of his head.

Ashton attempted to fire another volley of shots at the remaining tangos but was met with a terrifying *Click.* His magazine was empty. He wasn't counting his round. What a rookie mistake. He knew better than that. Just a few hours earlier, Ashton watched playfully as Erynn dismantled a crew of men, and he watched as she combated loaded each time she thought she was running low on rounds. He should have been more mindful like her. But Erynn wasn't fighting drones and ground troops in open terrain, in broad daylight, either.

Ashton thought to himself. He knew she was somewhere behind him watching and couldn't wait to tease him about running out of rounds in the middle of a gunfight.

Ashton's heart pounded in his chest, a steady flow of adrenaline pumping through his arteries. He remembered his training. Focus on your target, control your trigger squeeze and watch your breathing.

Ashton couldn't believe what he saw in the middle of combat loading. *But it couldn't be. That was impossible.* Before he could make sense of what was happening, one of the three lunged towards Ashton and hit him with such force it was like being hit by a mountain. Stars flew across Ashton's vision, and he winced in pain before bringing the butt of his rifle down onto the tango's head. Only it wasn't a tango. At least not a human tango. This was a machine.

From a distance, these last three tangos looked normal, but as Ashton struggled to his feet, he saw the brilliant red glow of machinery. It all made sense now. These three tangos never fired a round, nor did they carry firearms. They weren't even human. *What the hell did North Kangavar send to Salleria?* First unmanned drones flying throughout the air now advance, nonorganic soldiers.

Ashton gritted his teeth and shot the lunging Android directly in its bright, red eyes. The brilliant color seemed to fade from its body as the chunk of metal fell to the ground with a metallic thud. "At least these things are easy to kill," Ashton said to himself. There was no time to lift his rifle and shoot the next attacking Android. Ashton grabbed his knives from his waist, and when the Android attacked him, he dodged an overhand right cross, took the

Duane Dieter's knife in his right hand, and slashed left, slitting its throat. Hot, electrical red fluid gushed from its neck area, but it kept moving. Ashton parried to the back towards his right and then slashed his knife in his left hand upwards from the neck to the chin, opening up the entire bottom half of the Android's facial structure. With his right hand, Ashton reached into the Android's neck and pulled everything he could grab out of its neck. The second Android fell to the ground, dead. Or whatever you would call a machine that can no longer move.

There was no time to celebrate. Ashton was too late to guard himself. The remaining Android had jumped high in the sky and was coming down on Ashton's head. There was nothing he could do but brace himself for impact. Ashton closed his eyes and was nearly crushed by the falling Android. Hot gooey fluid spilled into Ashton's mouth. The Android was dead. Erynn had shot it on the way down. She saved Ashton's life, but the damage was already done. Whatever the Android was holding had stabbed Ashton and stabbed him deeply. Ashton pushed the Android off him only to see the Ankle Biter running toward him and Erynn. *Fucking kids!*

"You want to know my name?" Mr. Smith asked a blond lady flirting with him. He was in a breakfast diner pretending to eat as he watched The Ghost fight for his life. "My name is

Ashton. Ashton Jace," Smith lied to the lady. Smith laughed to himself. His brother was an actor. He wondered if he could pull off being The Ghost. He didn't care how well he pulled off his character. Jacob was the actual actor. Masterminding came naturally for Smith. And, right now, he had already planned that he was going to kill this woman.

He could tell she wanted to get into his pants, and she probably wouldn't remember his name anyhow. She was looking for a good time, and all the power was out. For all he knew, she was bored and horny. He was going to *slay* her since she wanted it. But when would she figure out his idea of slaying her was very different from hers?

It was strange, Smith thought to himself. The power was still out, and no one had any answers, but people were still creatures of habit. Two employees still came to work at the small breakfast diner, but only one would live to stay an employee. The employee flirting with him, the one who *wouldn't* live to clock in tomorrow, was an attractive, chesty blonde woman. After a bit of small talk, she began to flirt with Smith. He flirted back. He was in such a good mood. Winning always puts him in a good mood.

Once the waitress discovered the owner was sending everyone home until the power came back on, the chesty woman touched Smith gently on the hand and said, "Want to come back to my place? It's right around the corner." Smith knew he had better things to do, but The Ghost wouldn't make it back to his house before Smith would. He was in a vehicle now, just like The Ghost. He decided to take the attractive woman home. He tried to think of her name but realized she never told him, and she wasn't wearing a name badge either. Good, he thought. She would die without a name. The more he thought about it. She was going to die without a real reason. He could decline and let her live, but he let the gas station attendant lived yesterday. Someone had to die for talking to him. He hated small talk. "*There it is!*" Smith accidentally said to himself out loud. His chesty date overheard him. "Oh, nothing, sexy. I found something I was looking for in my pocket." He didn't like the pretty woman, but he didn't tell the complete truth either.

When he said, "There it is," he responded to his internal conversation with himself. He didn't know why he was going to kill her, and it suddenly struck him. She had small-talked him to death. She didn't know she was dead. He told the gas station attendant he didn't like small talk, and now this waitress would pay. Smith wondered if he would go and visit the gas station attendant later. He had her address. Maybe, he thought to himself.

Mr. Smith was telling the chesty woman the truth. However, he did find something in his pocket — his knife. She was going to find it, too, in about fifteen minutes.

Connor was in bad shape. He couldn't think. His mind was racing, and all he could think about was Papa Anthony and how the sick son of a bitch was standing over him, watching him sleep. His head was pounding.

Connor didn't even hear Brentley talking to him. He was sure his best friend of more than three decades was trying to tell him, "Everything is going to be alright, Connor." "I won't let anything happen to Mama Linda, Papa Anthony, and the kids." But Connor couldn't hear anything. He didn't even notice how fast Kayla was driving or how many laws she was breaking to get them to his house. Connor was in full panic.

"The asshole was at my house!" Connor said with so much anger he was sure it scared Kayla. He didn't care right now. All he cared about was getting back home and killing anyone in the house who didn't belong. "And who the fuck is walking around with a polaroid camera, dammit," Connor said somewhere in between a string of curse words that seemed to have no end.

It felt like an eternity before Kayla's Chevrolet Chevelle screeched to a halt in Connor's drive. It was morning now. It had to be about eleven a.m. MST and the screeching car were so unexpected everyone in the house came outside. Mama Linda hit the porch first. "I know you don't want to get cut," Mama Linda screamed at Kayla. Sophia was screaming, "What's going on?" And Riley was hiding behind his big sister, peaking his head around her. Before Connor could ask if everyone was okay? He saw Papa Anthony strolling out of the house without a care. He was standing with his grey hair and his six-one frame. He was getting old now, but he was still sharper than ever. "You alright there, son?" Papa Anthony asked Connor.

Connor didn't know what to say. He didn't know if he should cry, get angry, or laugh that Mama Linda was still trying to cut Kayla with her knife. Finally, Brentley stepped in and told everyone what was going on. He didn't hide a single detail. He knew Connor would want everyone to know, even his kids. Brentley also introduced everyone to Kayla. Mama Linda was too funny. First, she was ready to stab Kayla, and then she offered her some cookies instantly. Next, she bragged about how her deceased daughter-in-law, Monae, cooked Connor the thickest pancakes and gave Kayla the rundown. "If you are going to be flirting with my son, young lady, you got to be as good as these kid's mother. Can you even cook pancakes?" Mama Linda laid into Kayla and read her rights on the spot. "Baby," Papa Anthony said calmly, trying to get Mama Linda from saying way too much.

"Because Monae was a good child, and I always told Connor that he better not ever leave her cause that was a good child," Mama Linda continued. She was relentless when she got started. Although, now that Conner thought about it, she never *not* started. "And watch how you come up to this driveway next time. And I will not be power washing your tire marks off the driveway. Shol' not!" "Baby! That's enough," Papa Anthony used his big voice that time. That was the only thing that could get Mama Linda to be quiet. "The boy just said we almost died, baby," Papa Anthony said, talking some sense into Mama Linda and finally getting her back into the conversation everyone was having. "Aint nobody coming up in my house and killing nobody," Mama Linda said with all the breath in her chest. "If they touch anybody in my family, it will be the last thing they ever do! Thank I'm lying," Mama Linda continued for another three or four minutes before she felt she was done.

Kayla walked over to Connor. She looked to be struggling from holding in a thousand giggles. Connor knew that as soon as they got back into the car, Brentley and Kayla would give him the hardest of times— all the jokes would be on him. Finally Connor. "Go ahead and say it, Kayla. You look like you will pee on yourself from holding in all those laughs." Kayla didn't let out a thousand giggles, but Connor was sure about fifteen escaped her mouth. On second thought. Maybe it was twenty giggles. "I think your mom was going to stab me," Kayla said while laughing. "Don't laugh too much. She is good with a knife and was going to stab you. She never jokes about that." Kayla's eyes widened, and then Brentley laughed his thousand giggles, not holding a single laugh back. Then the whole family laughed.

"Have you eaten, Ashton?" The chesty woman was still calling Mr. Smith by his character name. He had almost forgotten he pulled a page out of his younger brother Jacob's book. Smith and the woman were in her house now. It was impressive for a waitress. It was spotless and spacious. The small apartment was decorated with modern furniture, and she had her kitchen counter set up like an open bar. He was not the first man she brought home.

"How about we skip the meal, and you come and give me a hug?" Mr. Smith told the chesty woman because he wanted to feel her breasts. They were big and perky. She smiled and seductively walked towards Smith, and he could smell her perfume. He hated it. She hugged and kissed him on the lips, and he kissed her back. Smith had forgotten what a woman felt like. It had been ten years, and he honestly was so consumed with his master plan he didn't think about sex. But when she kissed him, his body responded. Fire ran through his lower regions. She had soft breasts, and her body was softer.

Very friendly, he thought to himself. Maybe I won't kill her. Or maybe I will. Let's see how this goes. "Take off your clothes. I want to see your chest," Smith demanded of her. She did as she was told, and she was submissive. He liked that. When her top dropped to the floor, Smith stared at her perfect breasts. Her nipples were erect. She had smooth, olive-colored skin. As soon as he felt his body respond, Smith knew exactly what he wanted from the chesty woman.

Not wishing to waste any more time, Mr. Smith removed his knife from his left pocket and thrust the blade deep into her chest between her perfect breasts. He didn't want to ruin them. She screamed as the life left her eyes. As she was dying, he kissed her lips softly as her eyes rolled into her forehead. Then she was no more, submitting to his waiting arms.

"You are a beautiful woman, chesty girl. Let's make love, shall we?" The woman was dead. I told you I was going to *slay* you. Mr. Smith had his way with her and then kissed her lips softly one more time. Afterward, he returned to the car and drove back to Ashton's place. On his way back, he saw Erynn bandaging the wound Ashton suffered. But, once again, they didn't see him. No one ever saw Mr. Smith until it was too late.

Derrick and Ernest approached Rory's house slowly with their hands by their sides. Both did their best to show the crazy man they were unarmed. Ernest was following Derrick's lead.

He didn't have time to die in the front yard of some weirdo. He had to get to his nephew and reach Command. So far, everything Derrick said about Rory was proving to be true. Ernest hadn't met Rory yet, but his place was just weird. To the east stood a small barn that looked like it had been made from salvaged wood. Surveying the area, Ernest looked to his west and saw a water well. He hoped Rory didn't dump dead bodies in because fresh water was about to become essential.

There were solar panels on Rory's roof. Ernest liked this idea. If you were going to live off the grid, it made sense not to have a light bill. That also meant Rory's house more than likely had power. Solar panels would have faired well after an EMP. Ernest was sure Rory was entirely off the grid and that his solar panels wouldn't be grid-connected by he would have an off-grid capable solar array with battery storage. "Derrick," Ernest said in a low voice. "Rory's house should have power. Solar panels don't have electronics in them. They consist of silicon solar cells, wiring, and a junction box with diodes. There are no circuit boards with delicate electronics," Ernest informed Derrick. "Well, I'll be damned. Rory was right all this time. Who would have known," Derrick responded.

Ernest noticed Rory had a garden and his pigs and cows. Rory wasn't just off the grid. He was one hundred percent self-sufficient, and Ernest was impressed. Maybe Rory was a genius that no one understood. It sure seemed that way from his point of view. Also, there were tarps and rain barrels stored on the front porch. Ernest figured they were there to catch rainwater for storage. Ernest was sure Derrick probably wished he had his own house set up this way and that the town should have listened to Rory more. The house was ugly, but it was efficiently built and carefully maintained.

"You see anything?" Derrick asked. Ernest shook his head. "Looks like no one is home. But I've got a bad feeling about this." "Rory!" Derrick said in a loud but non-threatening voice. "It's Derrick Mercer and my buddy Ernest. We are here as friends." They stood about a hundred feet from the porch, a breeze gusting against them. But there was no answer at all. "Rory is always home," Derrick said under his breath to Ernest. "Something isn't right. There is no way Rory would leave his home when all the power in the city is out. There is just no way."

"Rory, you home?" Derrick asked louder. The answering silence was unsettling.

Ernest didn't like the feeling he was getting in his stomach. "Maybe he walked into town," Ernest said. "Doubtful. Rory doesn't like anyone and has no real reason to go into town. Get your weapon ready, Major. I don't like this." Derrick said to Ernest as he jerked his head toward the porch. "You stay out front. I'm going to see if he's around back." Derrick walked around the side of the house, leaving Ernest alone. Ernest didn't know what Rory looked like, so he was nervous about shooting. Ernest wasn't sure who to protect or what to do if someone came outside the front door. He kicked himself for not asking Derrick for Rory's description. Maybe a man in a tin foil hat will come out. That would make it easier to know who was who, Derrick thought.

The major was an excellent shot with any weapon; pistols, rifles, grenade launchers. It didn't matter, but he didn't know who to shoot. This made him vulnerable, and he didn't like it. A sweat dripped down Ernest's forehead, and the hair was on the back of his neck.

He couldn't take it anymore. Just standing by the porch made him a sitting target, so Ernest decided to take matters into his own hands. He kept his weapon holstered, walked to the front door, and knocked as loud as he could— not too aggressive, but loud enough to be seen and heard. His knock was between a police officer serving a felony warrant and a delivery man leaving boxes at the front door. But his knocks went unanswered. Finally, Ernest touched the door knob to the front door and turned it. It was unlocked at gave way. He politely walked through the unlocked door, announcing himself. A shadow moved in the corner of the room, and Ernest pulled his gun and almost shot a cat right between the eyes. "Stupid cat," Ernest said to himself after he cursed a few times.

"Major, get over here!" Derrick shouted. Ernest looked around one last time and went to the sound of Derrick's voice. He was in the backyard, and his face was pale. What could make a man as big as Derrick pale? Derrick thought to himself.

"You're going to want to see this," Derrick said. His voice was severe. Ernest couldn't see something had the big man spooked. Ernest walked closer and saw what made the big cop pale. A dead body swayed slowly in the wind. "Is this Rory, Derrick?" "It sure is, Major. What's left of him." Rory's body had been drained of his blood, just like Jared's. There were two holes in his neck that Ernest could have sworn looked like fanged teeth marks. Butt that didn't make any sense.

Rory's skin wasn't the right color. He was a white man, but he looked more grey than anything. His body was swinging from a rope, and unless he killed himself and then hung himself to a tree, Rory was murdered, Ernest figured. Whoever killed Rory strung him up and drained him of all his blood, but no blood gathered underneath Rory. "What kind of sick bastard did this?" Ernest asked. Derrick shook his head. "I don't know, but I returned to the station to tell Aiden. Whoever killed Jared didn't stop with the kid."

Ashton winced as Erynn massaged some green and white chemical gel into his open wound. Ashton looked at Erynn as if she was torturing him. "That hurts, dammit!" She laughed and pressed her finger into the wound showing him who was the real boss of their relationship. Ashton screamed in anger, his face breaking into a sweat as he felt the veins in his neck pulse. When he told her it hurt, he was lying. It didn't hurt much. Her gel took away most of the pain, but Ashton pressed his luck too far, and Erynn taught him a lesson. She always knew when he was lying. He guessed she wanted to tell him she knew it, too.

Ashton gritted his teeth and waited for the pain racing down his arm to stop. But, above all three of their heads, Erynn, Ashton, and the Ankle Bitter, drones were zigzagging over the empty streets, scanning for life and looking for violence. Scanning for them. Ashton knew they were scanning for them because it was precisely what he would do if he were in charge.

Erynn and Ashton spent their entire military careers in recon and ranked up often. She ended her military career as a Master Sergeant while Ashton, on the other hand, turned his promotions down. He didn't care about money or rank. Ashton didn't have kids and was constantly deployed, so his money piled up, collecting dust in the bank. When he retired from the army, he retired with a lot of money and bought a lovely house in Wakefield.

His passion was for the fight. Ashton loved the heat of the battle, the scent of gun oil, and the fear that only battle and gunfire could cause. It was what he lived for until things began to change. Until then, Ashton lived for the hunt, but now he was hunted. A familiar knot grew in his stomach as the gel finally cauterized his wound through an invisible chemical reaction. Ashton was ready for battle again. But, this time, the enemy would pay.

"Erynn, we need to get back to the Dodge and drive off the road under cover of trees. There is crazy shit going on, and get that damn kid." Ashton jerked his head to the little boy. He was probably six, maybe seven. Ashton didn't have time to figure it out or ask why the little Ankle Biter was out here. He needed to get them all back to the safety of his house until he could come up with another plan. "See if any of them *things* have radios on them, Erynn. Check the people too. We need to know what the enemy is saying if we can," he ordered.

Erynn did as she was told, and Ashton began to explain all the events while she was away. First, he told her about the human soldiers, drones, and now the *Artificials*. He didn't know what else to call them.

Within a few moments, all three were in the Dodge and into the tree-lined hills. It was getting closer to noon, so the sun was nearly directly over them, which wasn't doing much to cover their movements or the dirt trail they were causing as they drove into the distance. But what else was there to do? They had to get back to safety and fast.

For an hour, Erynn did her best to conceal the Dodge's wake as it ripped through the terrain. The ride felt like it took forever. *That may be the last time we look for survivors.* Ashton didn't want to admit it, but the North Kangavarian's surprised EMP attack and, subsequently, military invasion caught Salleria by surprise. North Kangavar had unleashed a full technological assault on the United Cities that catapulted the country back into the Stone Age. To make matters worse, North Kangavar also used some version of super-tech soldiers that Ashton didn't understand. But there was one thing he did grasp that made Ashton feel more comfortable about the invasion. The Artificials could be killed.

There was something else that bothered Ashton. It was the complete silence of the day. It was almost noon, and the only way he could describe the noise around him was *nothingness.* It was creepy. No tires were dragging across the pavement. He never realized how loud the world was until the power was gone. The only thing he could hear was the sound of the Dodge's tires ripping through the grass, the strain of the engine, and the sniffles of the Ankle Biter in the backseat. However, the kid kept his mouth shut, which was a good thing. The Dodge was already loud enough and created more noise than he desired.

A boom tore through the silence, and Erynn and Ashton flinched in their seats. They each glanced over their shoulders to see one of the flying drones sip across the sunny horizon. It was looking for them, but they weren't spotted. Erynn smashed the brake pedal, and the ground protested. Erynn and Ashton gave each other a look and decided going more than five miles per hour would be a death trap. Staying alive was the most important thing they could do for now. The mission to look for survivors was over. The new mission began: *Stay alive as survivors.*

A combination of Kian's complaining and The Rookie's corrections of those complaints caused Corporal Benjamin Hunter to need a strong drink. Paige was sitting next to Hunter in the living room corner, holding a teddy bear in her lap. She was doing well for a kid surviving the end of the world. Hunter wondered why she acted more maturely than Kian, a grown man.

Nearby, Kian paced back and forth like a caged animal, his complaints growing by the number every passing minute. Hunter decided to ignore him, but it wasn't helping much. He was at his wit's end with Kian and couldn't take much more of his complaining.

Hunter was a calm man. He didn't want much in fly, but he didn't want too little either. And right now, she wanted Kian to shut the fuck up. He was still having difficulty processing that his world, the world, had changed overnight. Forty-eight hours ago, he was thinking about going on vacation, and now he was thinking about getting to fresh water and keeping everyone safe.

Kian's voice interrupted Hunter's thoughts. "How long have they been gone? It's been too long; something must have happened. Are either one of you going to do anything to save us?" When Kian asked his last question, his voice was high-pitched and panicked. He was no longer pacing back and forth. Instead, he graduated to finger-pointing and exaggerated hand movements. His words were a random assortment of questions and comment Hunter found very difficult to process.

Hunter paced over to Kian and eyed him angrily, "Are you intentionally trying to let the enemy know we are held up in this house?" Although Hunter was doing his best to keep his composure, he felt like a bottle of soda someone had shaken vigorously and was waiting for someone to open the top so the bottle could explode. "You are so loud you are giving away our fucking location? Is that what you want? You want to get us all killed?" Hunter's face twisted into an expression that suggested Kian should quiet down immediately or else. Kian got the picture.

Paige started crying, "I want my uncle," she choked, tears streaking down her face. Before Hunter could say anything, The Rookie opened his mouth and said, "There's a North Kangavarian Humvee coming this way." Everyone ducked down, and Hunter gestured to

Paige to keep quiet. "Just for a little bit, Hunny, your uncle will be back soon, but it's some bad guys outside. Can you keep quiet for me while I check things out?" Paige nodded her head in approval.

"I don't see anything," Kian said in a whisper. Slide me that pair of binoculars," Hunter said to Kian. He pointed to the table between them that held a pair of high-tech binoculars. By the time Hunter got the binoculars, he didn't need to use them. The North Kangavarians were so close to the house that his regular eyes worked fine.

"There," Kian pointed outside towards the front of the house. Hunter felt a tug on his pants from behind him, and he turned to see Paige staring at him. "Can I see?" In the second it took for Hunter to consider Paige's requests, he watched Kian nearly die from fear. His face went completely white. Hunter turned around and saw what put the fear of God into Kian so quickly. It wasn't human; It was a machine. But that didn't make any sense. The machine had a man's body, but a complicated version of a face sat where there should have been a face. It was as if someone had an idea of what a face should look like and built a robotic version. Instead of white eyeballs, the machine had a radiant red glow where the eyes should have been. It didn't walk entirely like a man, but it also didn't walk like a machine, either. Hunter was looking at some advanced tech that could come right out of the *Terminator* movie. Was that what this was? Had machines come back in time to kill Sarah Connor?

Hunter forced himself to look away from the advanced tech walking towards the house. He wasn't sure if it was using cameras for eyes or the machine was using thermal heat signature technology. Either way, hunter grabbed his pistol and took one of the rifles off the couch Erynn put on the couch. He ensured his M4 carbine was loaded with a forty-round magazine, and The Rookie did the same. Timothy didn't grab anything. Instead, he ran into the kitchen and hid somewhere out of site. "Coward," The Rookie said loud enough for everyone to hear him.

Hunter turned towards Paige and pointed upstairs. "Paige, can you do me a favor and keep being strong for me and run and hide upstairs and lock the door behind you." Hunter wasn't trying to scare the kid, but he needed her out of the way right now. He didn't want anything to happen to her, and Ashton left him in charge, and he had no intentions of messing up. "Pick any room, okay, Sweetie, and lock the door behind you. Can you do that for us?" Paige looked up at Hunter, her wide eyes showing a hint of fear. "Yes, I can." She ran out of sight, and Hunter racked a round into the chamber of his M4. He left his pistol on his hip.

Erynn slipped into the brightly lit house she and Ashton had worked so hard to buy and keep a home. They saw the North Kangavarians go into the house about five mins ago, but there was nothing she could do but smash the gas and get here as fast as possible. Ashton told the little boy to say in the Dodge and hide in the back seat on the floor until they came back.

Erynn and Ashton both entered the house at the same time. Two human soldiers were down on the ground. Both were bleeding on the front porch. When Erynn entered, she saw one of the Artificials twitching on the living room floor. The hungry red glow of light that came from their eyes was gone. It was dead. Or whatever you call a machine that was shot in the head. Someone had taken it out before Erynn and Ashton got there.

Gunfire erupted in the kitchen, and Erynn saw The Rookie shooting one of the Artificials standing over him. It must have gotten the best of The Rookie, but he let off a barrage of rounds into its chest and neck area before it could finish him off.

From where Erynn was standing, she could see three more Artificials. Each of them had glowing red veins outside its body. It was like looking at a black leather robot with red hieroglyphics on the outside of its body, with each marking glowing a blinding red glow. Erynn shot one of the robots in the back of the head while Ashton took the head off one with his knives. Hunter killed the last of the Artificials. He shot it in the head, and it fell to the floor crushing Ashton's and Erynn's fine glass living room table. The house was clear. "Good shot Hunter. Where's my niece?" Erynn cleared her throat loudly and glared at Ashton. "Sorry. Thanks, Hunter, for keeping everyone safe as you promised." Ashton glared back at Erynn and shrugged his shoulders. He said something so low and so quick Erynn couldn't hear it, but it sounded a lot like, "Are you happy now, Mom?" Ashton turned back towards Hunter, and before he could repeat his obvious question about his niece, Hunter beat him to it. "She's upstairs, my friend. She's safe and unharmed."

Kian ran out of the kitchen, and with a loud and irritating voice, he complained, "See what happens when we don't stick together!" Erynn, Ashton, and Hunter all glared in Kian's direction. He didn't say another word for a few long minutes.

Kayla and Connor were standing outside talking to one another. They were in the backyard. Connor's house was impressive and not a house you can get on a cop's salary or an FBI agent's. No, this house resulted from the Dr. Quantum side of Connor. Together, they both leaned against the second house on the property. It was located at the end of the driveway and should have been a garage, but it wasn't a bit more.

The garage was converted into a living area. It's where Connor preferred to do his studies and write his books. Kayla was impressed. The more she talked to Connor, the more she realized he was anything but ordinary. He wasn't just brilliant. He was compassionate and forgiving. It took some prying, but Kayla learned Connor was the author of eleven best-selling books on Quantum Physics. It explained his three-million-dollar house and converted garage that looked more like an upscale coffee shop with living room and office furniture.

They spent a good hour talking about his first book, *Beyond Einstein: The Cosmic Quest for Bending The Fabric of Time And Space.* The way his face happily twisted into excitement as he taught her the key concepts in her book made her feel the warmth she had never felt.

336

Kayla couldn't explain it, but she understood then, and there Connor was her *Teacher*, and he would be her last. She wasn't trying to fall for Connor.

Kayla made a reputation in the Lakota Police Department for being unachievable. As a result, she never dated anyone at the job and never would. It was a vow she made to herself, and she would always keep it. But without effort, Connor walked right through her vow and captured her attention. And he didn't even know he did it.

Papa Anthony came out a few times to check on Kayla. Mama Linda had him busy lifting heavy things around the house. Kayla did her best to hide the twinkle forming in her eye about Connor, but she was sure Papa Anthony saw it. But he didn't say anything. Instead, Papa Anthony occasionally walked back and ensured she wasn't thirsty. She got a feeling he was welcoming her to the family. He seemed like a man who knew much more than he ever said.

During their conversation, Kayla finally asked Connor about Anna, the woman who was thrown over her balcony. She didn't want to pry too much, but to her surprise, Connor was kind and upfront. He told her about their whole story, how they dated, but he never brought her around the house, and how she never met his children, although they dated for almost three years. When she asked him about it, he told her the timing was never right and how he always had a check on her spirit. Connor never said anything terrible about Anna. And when he told her about Anna's infidelity, he did it in the kindest way possible. He even blamed himself for consistently working and not opening up to her the way she wanted. Her heart broke for Connor, and she had no idea how he made it out of her crime scene without falling apart.

Kayla told Conner about what made her want to be a cop and eventually a detective. He was a good listener and never interrupted her. Their conversation was natural and unforced. The way he looked at her made her melt.

Every time the twinkle in her eye grew brighter, there was Papa Anthony, coming to see if she needed anything. How did he know? He couldn't have been watching them. From where they were leaning against the wall and talking, she could see clear through the house to where he stood each time he went back inside.

The back of Connor's house was mostly grey with white trim. There were two large windows on the left side of the house and three smaller windows on the right side of the house. Between all five windows were two beautiful glass doors that led into the house. Papa Anthony was three rooms away from those glass doors. She could see all the way through to where he stood when he went back inside. So how did he know when to come and make her feel comfortable and welcomed? Papa Anthony was an intuitive man. Far intuitive than she would ever understand. Kayla told herself not to fall for this man, but the more she tried not to, the more it seemed their fates were intertwined. Oh, only if life were that simple, Kayla thought to herself.

Kayla asked Connor about his favorite movies, but the list wasn't long. Connor was a deep thinker, and he thought in multiple dimensions. The movies he named were all mind-benders. The one that stood out to her the most was a complex movie to understand, and the book was equally as hard to get, too. *Cloud Atlas.* Connor quoted a line from the book. *Power, time, gravity, love. The forces that kick ass are all invisible.* This man was excellent, and his mind belonged in a museum. She couldn't believe Connor walked around with all this intelligence and confidence yet never assumed a position of arrogance. He was quite the opposite.

Kayla and Connor talked for another hour, and the air felt lighter. The sun was brighter, and Kayla completely forgot about the murder cases they were investigating and all the power being out. Neither Mama Linda nor Papa Anthony pressured Kayla to leave, and Kayla wasn't in a hurry. From what she could tell, neither was Connor. He seemed to need their conversation as much as she did.

Connor was interesting to Kayla for many reasons, but the main one was that she wanted him to be her *Teacher.* This was a role she held in close regard. She didn't let anyone teach her— anything. And all she wanted to do was sit under this man and let him guide her through life. She was an alpha woman, but she wanted someone to let her be a *woman.*

"You okay," Connor asked. Kayla's eyes must have communicated concern. Kayla was usually good at keeping a wall up, disguising her genuine emotions, but Connor saw through all of her practiced behaviors. "Sorry, Connor. I just went away for a minute." Kayla said. She was embarrassed she got caught drifting into a future timeline when she and Connor were happily ever after. Kayla didn't know how to handle all of her emotions. It had been so long since she was in love. She didn't want to go down that road again, but Connor took her breath away. He made her nervous and happy. He made her horny.

"And where did you go, If I may ask," Connor said to Kayla while looking into her with his beautiful brown eyes. Kayla couldn't help but think, what the hell am I doing falling for this white man? But he was a damn good-looking white man, she admitted to herself. If he keeps this up, he will get him a lifetime of chocolate. Kayla giggled at her thoughts. "Now, you are giggling. Did you go somewhere again?" Connor asked. "Oh my God. I'm so sorry. Yes. But I am back now, for real this time," Kayla said. Her body responded to the arousal hormones her brain was sending to it.

"Actually, Connor, I was thinking about us," Kayla said the words before she knew she was saying them. "So was I," Connor responded before she could take her last statement back. "What the heck is going to become of us, Connor?" Kayla asked, staring deep into Connor's eyes.

"Well, we will catch a few murderers and make our city safe. But before that, we will have to walk in front of Mama Linda and see if she has anything to say about me and you being back here for so long. And if I know her, she has something to say." Kayla laughed. "Are we going to make all the same mistakes we made before we met each other," Kayla asked.

Connor looked into Kayla's eyes. He didn't say anything. "That's what I figured, Connor, Kayla said. "We are doomed." When she finished her sentence, Connor leaned forward and kissed Kayla. It was the kind of kiss that came from The French. *Doomed* never felt so good.

36

Mr. Smith watched The Ghost leave the Dodge and save the day again. He hated that about him. Smith hated everything about The Ghost. He wondered if he and Erynn were ever going to hook up. They loved each other, and it was apparent Erynn was saving herself for him. He thought about killing them both, but he was having too much fun watching the North Kangavarians get so close with their advanced tech.

The fragrance of honeysuckle, jasmine, and gardenias was heavy in the air. He sucked in a breath. So pleasant. Mr. Smith knew more things than most people, and right now, he knew two things. The house the little Rescue Crew was hiding in was now compromised, and Ashton would be coming up with a plan to leave his house behind and go back into the populated part of Wakefield. He would take one car because he could protect everyone better than way. God, The Ghost was so predictable.

He stared at Erynn through his rifle scope. She really *was* a gorgeous woman. The Ghost didn't deserve her. Maybe he would spend some time with her as he did with the waitress. Warmth flowed through the lower regions of Mr. Smith's body. The idea of spending time with Erynn like that turned him on for many reasons. The highest reason of them all, he would kill The Ghost. He loved the idea of hurting Ashton by violating Erynn.

Smith turned his scope to see Ashton looking like he was giving commands. He knew they wouldn't leave yet but would be on their way very soon unless something stopped them. He thought about shooting The Ghost, but he decided to spare him.

The reason he spared The Ghost: A long-distance kill wouldn't let him see the life leave his eyes when he died.

"We're at war," Aiden said. He knew this information would not go over well, and he hated talking to politicians, and he was currently in a room with six of them. Aiden would rather be in combat than in this room. No, he would rather each chocolate and then put his mouth over an ant pile than be in this room.

Aiden always thought politicians had an agenda for more power. He could understand the idea and the temptation for more power. He was human. He understood what power felt like and the desire to get more. He just never understood the desire to get more because he feared you were going to lose the power you had. That was how cowards thought, and Aiden wasn't a man who feared much. He rarely became angry and refused to stay in fear of anyone. So the idea of getting more power because you are afraid to lose the power you had, made it hard for him to have decent conversations with politicians.

Across the table from him was Mayor Julia Harris, a sixty-year-old woman with winter-white hair that she wore short and swooped. She was well kept like Meryl Streep's character from *The Devil Wears Prada*. When she wasn't trying to micromanage every aspect of the town, including police affairs, she ran a local grocery store. It was the kind of store that catered to customers who didn't want to go to the big brands like Walmart, and her store was the most successful in Wakefield. She knew how to run a business. People wanted her to open a chain of stores, but she always said she preferred to be good at just one location.

To her right was the town administrator, Christian Barrett, an older man who lived down the street from City Hall and is a reclusive character. He only talked when he was rude, and being rude to Police Chief Aiden Jahmar was his favorite pastime. Technically, he was Aiden's supervisor. Aiden laughed internally at the irony of the town administrator's name: *Christian* because he acted more like the devil. Even though Christian was in his 60s, he was physically fit. He bore a very muscular physique and took excellent care of himself. Aiden was sure Christian could run five to six miles nonstop. In addition, he was an attractive man who kind of resembled Burt Reynolds, the famous actor. Because of this, all the women in Wakefield crushed on Christian as much as they possibly could.

Aiden didn't like the Burt Reynolds look-a-like much. But on the other hand, he was a sneaky leader who always wanted more power and took credit for other people's actions. Christian was officially Aiden's supervisor, but most of the time, he worked directly with Julia.

The rest of the room, including the city's engineer, the town clerk, and several officers from Aiden's staff, all of whom were trying to talk at once. "What do we do?" "Who's in charge?" "What do you mean, war?" "The government is gone?" "The power can't be out everywhere, can it?" "Who is coming to help us? "Who is in charge right now? "How are we going to get paid?" What about the murderer? If we're stranded here, then so is he." Aiden calmly raised his hand, and everyone stopped talking with a commanding voice. He said, "Listen up, everyone. What we discuss stays in this room for now." He reported everything he knew about the attack for the next several minutes. It was like a thief stole the air from the room because it seemed as if no one was breathing, and then all at once, panic and chaos took over. Barrett's voice was the loudest of them all. "What are we going to do?" he kept repeating. "Calm down, everyone. We will get through this, and everything will certainly be under control," Aiden said.

Julia glared at Aiden. She didn't like Aiden getting too much attention and people looking to him as the *Leader of Wakefield.* That was her job, and she was elected to lead the city. Aiden didn't bother looking in her direction. He already knew what she was thinking.

Aiden was not the type of man who would fold under pressure, and this was not the first disaster the people wanted him to lead the city out of— he was their savior each time disaster struck. Aiden got the distinct impression Julia wanted to see Aiden fall on his face and publicly. It was well known she wanted to show the town she was Wakefield's undisputed Leader, and this situation was the perfect opportunity. It was *her* perfect opportunity.

Aiden didn't care about any power struggle. He just wanted to help people and do his job. "I've already put my people to work," Aiden said as he restored calm back into the leading officials of Wakefield. "I've declared a state of emergency and activated the EOC. We still haven't been able to reach anybody from the sheriff's office, but we're working on it.

Now, what I need you to do is—" Major Julia Harris cleared her throat. "Aiden, you know I respect you, but I'm not going to let you take over the town. You are not in charge, and I am the highest-ranking official. If you give out all the orders, we will live in a dictatorship, and that is the last thing any of us want in the middle of a war, as you put it. So there have to be checks and balances." Julia said to Aiden. Aiden could tell she was talking to all the leaders in the room. He had to admit Julia strategically placed every word into the atmosphere and knew the division it would cause. He knew he had to act fast and strategically to keep division out of anyone's mind. He didn't care about her trying to embarrass him, but the division was the last thing he wanted to be involved in during this time.

"Yes, ma'am Madam Mayor, you are one hundred percent correct, and I don't mean to be a dictator. You are wise and most beloved. And, it goes without saying you are the highest ranking person in the room and the city." Aiden paused for a few long seconds. He knew the time to turn things around in the town's favor was now. "Please accept my apologies, Mayor, if I have stepped outside of my boundaries as the highest-ranking law enforcement agent in the city. I certainly don't want to go *unchecked and unbalanced*. This is why I need you, law-making folks, to step up. I'll take care of the policing and securing our borders, but I'll need you and Christian," Aiden had them right where he wanted them now. He was going to take Mayor Harris' outburst and use it as an opportunity to give orders to each of the politicians and pass them off as pleas for help. He wouldn't have to resort to war games if they would stop fighting for power. But they were here now, and he didn't have any intention of losing the crowd or this moment to turn things around in the town's favor.

"Christian, if you don't mind, we could use your expertise and authority to work with Derrick on the administrative and recovery stuff. If we all work together, no one has to starve to death and go without resources, especially with a brutal winter coming. If necessary, I have developed a solid plan to feed us for the next six to nine months. If anyone has a better plan than the one I came up with, I am happy to submit and assist in their plan." Aiden finished his talk with the sly tongue of a politician. He paused for a long moment to ensure everyone knew he was the only one who thought of a plan to feed the city. "Excellent, everyone," Aiden jumped back in to finish the talk he had started. "Since there are no other plans to feed and secure the city, we will go with the plan in place and work together as one unit. For example, I will be the first to submit to any level of the chain of command to make things run smoothly."

Aiden said a few more intelligent things to a room full of hungry, influential people. But he had an advantage over all of them. They were scared. He was prepared. He didn't like politicians, but he knew how to speak their language to get them off his back. "What about the fallout?" Barrett asked. "How are you going to protect us from that?" "I don't know, but the plan is currently being worked out. I can safely report we are currently using Geiger counters and have not seen any spike in radiation as of yet." Aiden replied.

"So far, we plan to evacuate people to our three emergency shelters. During the panic," Aiden made sure to say this so everyone could know his team was not panicking, "We have taken the time to ensure the shelters are stocked with supplies for at least three days. We are working on more as we speak. That is all we can do for now besides keeping everyone calm. As you all know, people do violent things when there is no food to pass around. We can't let them know what's happening until we're prepared." Aiden was winning the power struggle, but he didn't want it. He wanted Major Julia to feel well respected and revered. She would be safe in a shelter and get all the credit for protecting everyone. He didn't care about anything of that.

A knock pounded on the door, and Derrick pushed it open without waiting for a response. His muscular frame entered everyone's view as he looked at the Chief. "Sir, I need to talk to you," Derrick said firmly. Before Aiden could respond, he noticed the look in Derrick's eye and the blood on his uniform. "If you'll all excuse me, I'll be right back," Aiden said without waiting for a response. Barrett stood and waved a finger at him. "Whatever news Captain Derrick Mercer has, we all deserve to know." "Christian is right," Julia said. Aiden scanned the frightened faces in the room and then looked back at Derrick. Ernest was standing in the hallway, his arms folded across his chest. With a reluctant nod, Aiden gave Derrick the okay to speak.

"It's Rory Cooper, Chief." Derrick let out a breath as he didn't want to say what he was about to say in front of civilians. "He was murdered. Looks like the same person that killed Jared." The room erupted into panicked and angry shouting again. Aiden cursed under his breath. He had just had the damn room calm, and now this shit happens.

"What are you going to do, Aiden?" Julia glared at him for the second time in just ten minutes. "And what do you expect us to do? The town needs to know what's going on. We can't keep people in the dark," Julia said to Aiden with venom. "I think we should hold a town meeting," Barrett said. The other city officials began nodding and muttering their agreement. "Fine," Aiden said. "I'll be there, but I have something to do first." As he turned to leave the room, Julia called after him. "Where are you going? We haven't adjourned yet!" "Sorry, Julia," he said. "'Unless you want to be murdered next, or anyone in this room, I've got a killer to track down. Should I stop a murderer, or would you like me to wait until I am dismissed?" Julia didn't respond. She couldn't. "Thank you, ma'am. I will be back with a report, and I will be at the town meeting."

Although he hated the thought of owing the man a favor, Aiden knew he couldn't do this alone. He would have to convince "The Ghost" to help him again. Aiden hoped Erynn would help convince him to help.

Chapter Thirteen

"I want my Mommy," the little Ankle Biter screamed. "What the fuck. We have two kids with us now," Kian, the most irritating person in the known world, shouted. Hunter was reaching his breaking point with Kian. All Kian did was complain, and it wasn't helpful. "For God's sake, Kian, please shut up!" Hunter said.

"Kian, shut up before I break your nose," Ashton demanded. His adrenaline was racing through his veins, and he knew more tangos were close. He needed to think of a plan and fast. But what? The house was compromised, and there was little time to set up a defense, and Kian was right. There were two kids now. Ashton stole a look at Erynn. Whatever answers he was looking for in her face weren't there. There were no answers.

"Contacts!" The Rookie was looking out one of the windows to the house facing the driveway. "How many?" Hunter asked. Ashton didn't need to ask. He knew it would be a small squad, mixed with human contacts and Artificials. *No,* Ashton thought to himself. They wouldn't send humans this time. If it were him, he would send two squads of Artificials to get the job done, maybe even three.

Ashton was still unclear about the North Kangavarian tech. He had so many questions in his head. He figured the drones were piloted by humans somewhere far away. But the black and red ground troops, were they piloted like a video game? Or were they completely autonomous? Answers didn't matter right now. Ashton knew what he needed to do. They couldn't move. Although the house was compromised, it was easily defendable.

"We have to move," Ashton ordered. "There's nowhere to go," Kian replied in a panic.

We aren't moving from here, but we are moving *in* here. "Erynn, I need you in multiple sniping positions. Start picking them off in the driveway if you can, and then keep shooting over our shoulders. You must be snipe for me, Hunter, and the Rookie." Ashton had it all figured out now. The house was big, and if he kept Erynn shooting, she wouldn't miss a shot.

Hunter had proved himself to be a worthy fighter, and to his surprise, The Rookie was brave and dependable. All he had to do was spread all four of them out and keep the enemy funneled in key positions so they could kill anyone who came into the house. That left Paige, the Ankle Biter, and Kian to deal with. Ashton figured he probably needed to learn the kid's name soon, but he would attempt when bullets stopped flying around him.

"Kian, you and the kids go upstairs. Hunter, there is only one way upstairs. Take cover any way you can buy those stairs and kill anything moving," Ashton finished giving out his plan. It wasn't the best plan, but a bad plan was better than not having any plan.

"Paige, come here, baby," Ashton beckoned his niece. The most precious thing to his sister in the world. "I'm going to get you back to Mommy, but I need you to take this," he handed Paige a small pistol. Her eyes widened. You hide somewhere, and if it's not a good guy coming to get you, pull the trigger until Uncle gets there. Okay, baby?" Paige nodded to Ashton and took off running upstairs.

Ashton knew his sister would kill him, but what other choice did he have? It is not like he was being his usual irresponsible self. None of the things happening was his fault.

Technically, they were, but how was he supposed to know his last mission would cause World War III?

The house was well-lit. It was about two p.m. MST time, and the sign was coming through the kitchen area doors. Ashton and Erynn's house was secluded in the woods of Wakefield, but the kitchen was modern and pretty much all glass. There were double doors leading to the kitchen outside the house, and they were glass, too. So from outside the kitchen area of the house, you could see directly into the first part of the living room. The part of the living room that was by the door.

Ashton knew he couldn't put Erynn there because the sun's glare would mess with her vision. So that is where he would do most of his damage. However, Erynn could handle herself and would probably take over eight firing positions. Which meant he had to put The Rookie in the living room.

"Hey, Rookie," Ashton didn't wait for him to respond. Your area of defense will be the living room. It won't be safe, but unless they break through walls, there is only one way into it. Kill as many in the doorway as possible. Erynn will cover you." "Yes, sir! I won't let you down, Ghost." "Good, kid. I promise to get you back to Aiden as soon as we kill these bastards." The Rookie nodded his head, and his face morphed into a hardened battle face.

Erynn looked Ashton in the eyes. Ashton wasn't sure, but he could swear Erynn was afraid. He smiled at her. She returned the smile, and her face seemed to suggest she wanted him to make it out of this alive.

Thump. Crash. Thump. Crash.

The familiar sound filled the silent space, sending a chill down Ashton's back. He remembered that sound. *Thump. Crash. Thump. Crash.* That's what the Artificials sounded like when they walked. Ashton took a deep sigh. He was right. They didn't send any humans this time. He could see at least eight Artificials so far— which was just on his side of the house. He had no idea what was coming in the front door. He was too busy watching the double glass doors that led outside.

There was nothing Ashton could do for anyone at this point. He had already given his instructions. It was a terrible plan, but it had to work. If not, they were all going to die. He was convinced of it. Ashton swallowed and watched the black and red silhouettes walk into focus in his vision. He heard the front door to the house open, but he couldn't turn around to see what was happening because six feet in front of him were three Artificials.

Thump. Crash. Thump. Crash.

His heart skipped a beat. Within seconds he would be in the fight of his life. The thought of him losing Erynn and Paige was too much to bear. He had to make it out of this alive and keep them safe. Gunfire erupted behind Ashton, and he knew all hell was breaking loose in the living room. But the strangest thing happened. The three Artificials stopped right at the doors to lead into the kitchen and only looked at Ashton. Their bright red eyes glowed like hell's fire in mechanical eye sockets. Then, all at once, the three Artificials slowly turned their heads to the living room as if they were programmed to have synchronized head movements.

Ashton turned to see what the Artificials were looking at. Ashton's stomach lurched when he saw what had their attention. He coughed bile into his mouth but forced it down. Unfortunately, there was no time to shed tears because four Artificials had breached the living room. Unfortunately, it looks like the team took out one of them. Its black and red mechanical body was twisted on the ground in an awkward position. The last thing Ashton saw before the three Artificials breached through the kitchen's double doors was one of the Artificials ripping off the left arm at the shoulder of Officer Samuel Willis, *The Rookie*. His arm fell off his body with such ease Ashton thought it looked more like a scene out of a low-budget Sci-Fi.

Mr. Smith watched as The Ghost and Erynn faced what he could only call certain death. They were outnumbered three to one, and he was sure they didn't know. Smith also knew something else they didn't know, but they were about to find out in the next few minutes; if they survived that long. Smith was shocked himself. He had never seen anything like it. What was about to happen to the beautiful house he was looking at was something the world had never seen.

He almost felt bad for The Ghost. It was unfair. There was no way they could win this battle. The North Kangavarians were playing dirty. He thought about warning them, but

Smith didn't know why. Why would he want to warn his mortal enemy? Finley remembered what The Ghost did to his life. He was the reason Smith came up with his master plan. If it weren't for Ashton, maybe Smith would let everyone live. But he couldn't. They all deserved to die.

He had important things to do, not the least of which was carrying out a most exciting plan for revenge against everyone who had hurt him in the past. Everyone! It was usually about revenge for Smith, the idea of hurting—sometimes torturing— the people who offended him, and that certainly hadn't changed. But he still couldn't figure out why he wanted to warn The Ghost.

And then it hit him all of a sudden. He knew that in about five minutes, The Ghost and all the people he was trying to protect would die. There was no way they could beat what was coming next, and that bothered him. The Ghost was his kill. He didn't mind The Ghost dying to some mere mortal. He would consider it as a gift from the Universe. But *this!* Watching The Ghost die this way was just wrong. He hated Ashton, but he was a formidable opponent, and North Kangavar was wrong for cheating like this. Even Smith wouldn't stoop to their level.

After a few long seconds of deliberation, Smith decided this was fate. On the other hand, maybe it was The Ghost's karma catching up with him. He let his disappointment leave his body and became perfectly fine with what would happen next. Goodbye Ghost. There is no way you can win now. No one could.

Ashton pulled the handle of his Duane Dieter's CQC knife out of the neck of an Artificial. The hot red liquid that glowed throughout their bodies sprayed all over his face. It tasted metallic, like sucking on a hand full of pennies or licking a double battery. But there was no time to celebrate. Ashton leaped to the second Artificial and used his left knife to stab it in the right eye, then drug his right knife across its throat. His hands were slimy, red, and warm with the crimson metallic liquid that poured from the Artificial's body.

The last Artificial kicked Ashton so hard in the ribs he was sure one of them cracked. Ashton sucked in the air, but nothing came. *Thump. Crash. Thump. Crash.* The Artificial was nearly on top of him, and his knives were still in the body of the last Artificial he killed. His Glock 19 was still on his hip, and his HK416 was strapped on his back.

The Artificial threw a mechanical right jab that missed Ashton by inches. His shoulder screamed in pain, and he still couldn't breathe. Next, the Artificial kicked Ashton in the ribs. Someone had to be controlling these things. That was a Judo Front Kick. *How the fuck did these Artificials know boxing and Judo?* That's mixed martial arts.

Ashton was pissed. He still couldn't breathe, his left ribs were tinder, and his shoulder pain was screaming, but he lifted his pistol and shot the Artificial in both its eyes. When the body hit the ground, Ashton stood off its head and shot it two more times for kicking him. "Fucking asshole!" Ashton grabbed his favorite knives out of the mechanical remains of the fallen Artificial. Ashton ran towards the living room.

Connor was feeling lonely and edgy. He was all messed up. He had a fantastic time with Kayla, but about an hour ago, she left to work on the case and promised she would stop by Connor's house in a couple of hours. Unfortunately, the phones didn't work, and she had one of the only working vehicles in Lakota— maybe even all of Wakefield, too— so drop by the house was the only real plan they could execute.

Connor didn't try to do it. He didn't even know he started waking, but somewhere about forty-five minutes after Kayla left his house, Connor found himself standing outside Anna's luxury apartment. It was now two p.m. MST, and Connor had no idea why he was there. Was it guilt for kissing Kayla? He couldn't even remember who made the first move, but he could remember that their kiss felt like heaven.

Anna's crime scene had been thoroughly investigated, and all the evidence was bagged and tagged. So why was Connor here? He honestly had no idea. He didn't even realize he was at her apartment door until it was time for him to put his key in the doorknob.

No, Connor was in the main bedroom. The apartment was still dark, as the power was still out. So why in the hell did Connor come back? Connor began searching the closet for new details, knowing he wouldn't find anything new. No one had been in here. It was restricted by yellow police tape.

Connor was just about to leave when he turned his head and saw something that caught his eye. He was sure he hadn't been there before. Connor was tempted to run outside the apartment so he wouldn't be alone in the dark. But he resisted the urge to run. *But there it was.* Right on her dresser drawer was a Bible. Connor couldn't help but think it was strange. All the Bibles were collected and sent to the station since Anna died with a Bible taped to her body. But this one is on the dresser. As if it was waiting for him to find it.

Connor had a small flashlight he started keeping in his pocket since all the power went out. It all happened so fast when he pulled it out of his pocket. Connor was hit twice. The second blow hit Connor so hard that he almost lost consciousness. He tried to whip his head around to see who hit him, but another attacker kicked him in the knees forcing him to fall. Connor went down hard.

His knees were throbbing, and his vision was blurred, but Connor was big. He was six-three, two-hundred and twenty-five pounds, and he fell on top of one of his attackers. Connor heard a loud crack. He hoped he had broken one of the killers' bones. A scream echoed throughout the apartment. It was one of the attacker's screams. Whoever it was, let Connor go and grabbed whatever part of their body Connor cracked with his weight.

Connor got up and put his boxing skills to the test. The fight was over so fast Connor didn't even break a sweat. These couldn't be the killers. Connor put his flash in their faces; they couldn't have been older than twenty-five. Connor touched his head, surprised to see there was no blood. *Why the fuck were they in Anna's apartment, and why did they attack him?*

Connor was furious and wanted answers. "You both are under arrest," Connor yelled at both men. They growled at Connor, nothing revealing fangs. Were they Rougarou? Things were starting to make sense.

A single bead of sweat crawled down The Rookie's forehead. His left arm, however, was gushing blood. He was a dead man, and he knew it. From what he saw in movies, he had about another ten minutes to live before he bled out, and he would make it the most important ten minutes of his life.

All the Artificials were dead now, and his body was going into shock. The power being out didn't help make things easier. The air was hot and sticky, even though it was late October. Wakefield had a funny way of being hot in the day and very cold at night during the winter. Unless it was snowing, if that was the case, it was cold as balls no matter what time of day it was.

Ashton and Erynn were trying to save his life, but after some considerable back and forth, The Rookie convinced them to let him die like the man he wanted to be. Ashton was the first to agree. He hated The Rookie and wasn't going to see Aiden again, but there was a look in Ashton's eye that seemed to understand The Rookie wanted to go out on his terms. He wasn't trying to be a hero. Instead, he was trying to be free. Free from fear and the guilt of dying in front of his teammates.

Several long minutes passed before the sound of the Artificials returned. *Thump. Crash. Thump. Crash.* Erynn took out two more with her long-distance shooting, and Ashton took out another two, shooting from the house's kitchen area. The Rookie blinked rapidly. He would kill as many of them as he could before he died. He still had one arm left. That was good enough for him. He was losing blood quickly, so he had to make all these rounds counts. After that, long-distance shots wouldn't work. He could carefully keep himself standing, and with the loss of his left arm, he felt off balance— or maybe that was the rapid loss of blood he was experiencing.

The Rookie walked to the door and started shooting anything with glowing red blood. Panic gripped him, and he suddenly felt woozy. But he didn't care. They killed him, so he was going to kill them all. A few of his rounds went wide, but necessary rounds connected, and one of the Artificials went down. The neon red glow in its eyes faded away. Screaming like a madman, he let off rounds and killed another two Artificials until his weapon *clicked.* He was out of rounds. He couldn't reload. His vision was blurry— no, it was fading quickly. He wanted to kill one more of the artificial demons before he died.

The Rookie walked out the front door, and the ground shook. His heart dropped to his stomach and lurched in his chest. Maybe it was the blood loss because what he saw was impossible. The other Artificials had a small but bright red glow about them. But what he was looking at was new.

Crash. Crash. There was no thump. This Artificial was too big to make a thump. Instead, with each step it took, its foot crashed into the ground violently. The red glow grew brighter and brighter with every passing second, and the sound amplified. *Crash. Crash.* The piercing sound forced The Rookie to stand there paralyzed. He would have panicked more, but he was losing too much blood. He fell to his knees, but it wouldn't have mattered. The Artificial coming towards him was like nothing anyone had ever seen. It had the body of a man, not a Greek God. He wanted to pull his eyes away, but he couldn't. The Artificial legs were gigantic and seemed reinforced with some hard metal or something. Its chest had a few moving parts, and its eyes shined the same red color, but its eyes looked more serpent-like.

In his final thoughts, The Rookie figured the Artificials they had been fighting were just the lower tier of troops the North Kangavarian military had at their disposal. A wave of helplessness washed over The Rookie. He used the last of his strength to ensure he wasn't losing his mind. Towering in front of him was a thirteen-foot-tall monstrosity. The Rookie scanned the Artificial in shock. *Crash. Crash.* It took the last two steps towards him that it would need to take, and the very last thing The Rookie saw was his legs on the ground and guts dangling nearly fifteen feet off the ground. His vision went black, and all his pain went away.

This Artificial was fast. It grabbed The Rookie and ripped his torso from his body, and then while holding his upper body in the air, the Artificial used its other hand to crush The Rookie's head like a grape. Everyone watched in horror and disbelief as The Rookie's blood sprayed through the air in every direction.

Rougarous? "Is that what you crazy idiots are?" Connor asked the two people who nearly fatally surprised attack him. Their names were Elie Lort and Arnaud Prejean, both Cajun with strong Cajun accents. They arrived in the Lakota-Wakefield area last week to honor *The*

Master. Connor asked a barrage of questions that were all answered in a few minutes. He discovered The Master had only been in Wakefield for a week and was causing all of this trouble.

Brentley miraculously showed up after Connor subdued his attackers. How did he get here? *How did he know Connor was there?* Maybe we were watching his old friend and wanted to ensure Connor was okay. Elie and Arnaud talked like singing birds, but it wasn't because they were afraid or had loose lips. No, Connor got the impression they were ordered to talk and tell everything they knew. While they gave plenty of information, very little of it was new. The tall pasty man in that weird coffee shop, an art place that visited a few hours before, had already given them most of this information.

Was this a backup plan? Had The Master been watching Connor the entire time? Or was all of this a coincidence? Connor was lost in his thoughts as Brentley took over the questioning of the suspects. Just then, Brentley's radio roared to life. "Where did you get a working radio? And where's mine," Connor asked curiously. "I will tell you about it later, and I am working on getting you one now. I have my connections."

As brilliant as Connor was, it was Brentley who was more competent. Brentley was both kind and ruthless. He had the best instincts of all the FBI agents of Salleria, and he was up for promotion. Brentley is the Special Agent in Charge and runs all the sub-offices between Mid-West and West Salleria. People believed he would run the FBI one day. He certainly is the best man for the job. Connor was also a Special Agent In Charge, but not technically. Sometimes he would introduce himself that way as a running inside joke between him and Brentley to see who was really in charge. But it was always Brentley, and it always would be. Brentley was just better at the politics of the Bureau. Connor didn't care much for them. Connor is officially the Assistant Special Agent in Charge, meaning Brentley should be getting a radio pronto.

Brentley's radio continued to roar in the quiet and dark room. "Go ahead," Brentley said into the radio's microphone. Then, finally, the white noise disappeared, and the voice broke through. "There's been another murder," someone on the other end of the radio said. "The victim doesn't have any more blood, sir. In the small town of Wakefield. And it looks like it's been more than one." Wakefield was a large city, but there was a place so beautiful inside of the city the founders decided to name the town Wakefield, Wakefield.

Elie and Arnaud laughed and mocked Brentley and Connor. "The Master is ending, you all, you stupid fuckers. All of you are going to die." Brentley walked over to Arnaud and accidentally slammed his head onto the table until he was handcuffed. "Ouch, man. You almost broke my nose," the young Rougarou yelled to Brentley. Brentley never even looked back to address Arnaud. He went back to talking on his radio instead.

Ashton's lungs were about to explode. He put seventeen to eighteen rounds into that thirteen-foot monstrosity from this count. He could see more rounds hitting the huge

Artificial as well. Ashton concentrated all his fire between the right side of the black and red demon's neck and its right eye. He made every bullet count.

Paige ran downstairs against Ashton's wishes. She aimed the pistol Ashton gave her earlier and shot rounds well after everyone stopped. *Click. Click. Click.* "It's empty, baby. Here, let me show you how to reload. Ashton went into one of the bags that held all the ammo Erynn brought down to the living room and walked Paige through the reloading process. "Your mom is going to kill me. Let's make sure we don't lead with the story of you killing an Artificial when we see her again," Ashton said softly to his favorite niece. His only niece. "Maybe we can start with you telling her how much fun you had with your Uncle," Ashton finished with a smile. He was always soft with Paige but never tried to hide anything from her. He never wanted her to grow up too fast, but after everything her mother went through with men and everything he had seen during the war, he wanted Paige to be strong enough to recognize bad people when she saw them.

"Do you think Mommy is okay, Uncle Ashton," Paige asked. The question broke Ashton's heart into a thousand little pieces. "I know she is, baby," Ashton kissed Paige on the cheek. "I don't think the Artificials made it to where Mommy is yet, which means we have to get to her before they do." Paige nodded her head in agreement. She was a tough kid. Tough, just like her father. Nathan Gibson, the dimwitted and womanizing drunk Paige was with about thirteen hours ago, wasn't Paige's birth father. Her birth father, Ashton and Erynn were once very close. They were all best friends and young soldiers of fortune in one of Salleria's oldest secret societies.

As Ashton's relationship grew strained with his blood relatives, he gained lifelong friendships with Erynn Justice and Finley Smith. Ashton's father beat him senseless every day, and his mother let it happen. His little sister Alison would always tend to his bruises and wounds daily. As a child, Finley wanted to make friends and be around people. And Ashton became his first friend, Erynn became his second. Ashton, Erynn, And Finley were born into a world that expected them to be ruthless. Finley was groomed to take over his father's position, The Chair of the High Council of The Order of the Corrupted Leaf. Some many years later, Finley's father, Declan Ward, ordered Ashton to kill his only son, Finley. Ashton was the only person Finley ever loved. After the failed assassination attempt, Finley internalized everyone's hatred for him and Ashton's betrayal, and in his teenage years, Finley began to hate everyone. *Finely was Paige's father.*

In the distance, a scream broke through the silence. And Ashton and Erynn instantly shoulder their rifles. Hunter followed. "What the hell was that?" Hunter whispered. "That was the Ankle Biter and the irritating guy. The Artificials must have found a way to get into the house from upstairs," Ashton said. Ashton was moving before he finished his sentence, racing through the front door and back into the shelving room. He wasn't about to let the little Ankle Biter and Kian die today. One dead team member was enough. Over his shoulder, he screamed to Erynn, "Erynn, get the Dodge packed and kill anything coming to our house. We leave as soon as we kill everything trying to kill us."

Pain swept over Monique's skin like burning acid. The pain was so unbearable that she thought it would be better to die. Monique felt like her skin was melted, and her muscles were sliding away from her bones. She tried screaming, but her throat didn't work. When she tried again, she opened her mouth wider and pushed out a scream with all her might, but all the earth's sand and dirt fell into it. At least, that is what it felt like to Monique.

Still struggling to live, Monique tried to move, but she couldn't muster the strength, and her limbs didn't work— just blinking her eyelids required a monumental effort. Where am I? What happened? Why does everything hurt? Am I dead? Her pain was louder than her prayers. Monique drew in a breath of hot, steamy air that filled her nostrils with the unmistakable scent of burned flesh and hair. She forced her arms to move, willing them to touch her face. Finally, after a long battle with gravity, she touched her face. It felt wrong. Blisters popped as her nails grazed her cheeks. Every inch of her exposed skin was burned.

Her first moments as President were all wrong. Everything was so very wrong. She hadn't been President for two hours, and the White House was destroyed. "Hello," she choked, her voice a low rasp. "Hello?" There was no reply. There was only the sound of the crumbling infrastructure and things being consumed by fire.

The bunker! Monique remembered now. She was in the PEOC, deep beneath the White House, along with what remained of the federal government. As her memory came flooding back, she realized her son was still missing, and she would die before she found him. She tried to cry, but even that hurt. All she could think about right now was how much dying hurt. And it hurt.

Monique refused to believe Chase was dead and doubly refused to die before she got to him. Chase was okay, and he was more than likely scared and lonely. The pain and the terror faded, replaced by determination. Get up, Monique, she thought to herself. Chase needs you. Get up right now, dammit, and stop being a baby. Get up!

Digging her fingernails into the debris-strewn carpet, she dragged herself across the room, stopping when she bumped into a body. She groped blindly and felt an arm, then a chest, and as she reached for a face, there was nothing but a wet pool of something warm and sticky. Realizing it was blood, a bloody mess of whoever laid here, this person no longer had a head. She threw up all over the ground, splashing the headless body and herself. Now frantic, she used all her strength, dragging herself around, looking for another survivor. She couldn't be the only person alive. Could she? Brayden and Weston were in the adjacent room. Monique considered calling out to them, but she already knew if they'd survived, her loyal team would be helping anyone they could while searching for her.

Monique also thought twice about revealing her location. North Kangavar just nuked the White House, and they would undoubtedly send ground troops to verify the kills. Proof of death. That is what she was to the North Kangavarians— just *proof of death*. If Brayden and Weston were still alive, they were on their own. And so was she. Rescuing herself was her only option.

Monique lay there for a long moment, gathering her energy and plotting her next move. She was a fighter pilot, and she was not going to die without a fight. "Help!" Someone was yelling out to her. "God, it hurts. Please, someone, help me." Monique recognized the voice.

It was Senator Ryan Anderson. She never thought she would be so happy to hear his voice since they were sworn, political enemies. But she was overjoyed to hear him. She wasn't the only one alive.

"Senator, hang on. I'm coming," Monique said franticly. She fumbled across the floor on all fours like a soldier going through a timed obstacle course, pulling herself over debris. "Trapped," Anderson groaned. "Please, I can't move." The Senator said each word as if they had sharp talons attached to them cutting his throat. He was struggling to breathe and talk. "I'm coming," Monique said with all her might. As Monique fought to rescue the Senator, she wondered what was coming next. They were trapped down here, deep underground; if the building didn't cave in and kill them, they would most certainly die horrible deaths from radiation poison. She did everything she could to get to the Senator but was it all for nothing?

Each body she crashed into or stumbled over, she checked for signs of life, but no one responded to her poking and prodding. As far as Monique could tell, Senator Anderson and herself were alive. She knew she had to get to her feet. Grunting in excruciating pain, Monique pushed herself to her feet, bumping her head on something hanging from the partially collapsed ceiling. A jolt of pain rushed down her back. She must have scraped her head on a massive chunk of cement. The pain from smashing her head against the hard cement was unforgiving and sent shockwaves to the rest of her skull. It felt like fire and ice were crawling through her scalp.

"Sir, where are you?" Monique screamed as loud as she could. "This is Maddox." She didn't feel comfortable calling herself President yet. Especially now since she had failed so badly in her first few moments as President. "Over here." The Senator said, seeming to struggle at the attempt. "Stuck." He could still only get one strained out at a time. The Senator sounded horrible. Monique wondered if she would get to him in time. Finally, she turned in the direction of his voice. Monique prayed Anderson didn't die before she got to him. She could tell his breathing was getting worse.

The room shook like the walls in the subway as the train whizzed by at top speed. There was no way they could stay underground much longer. The PEOC was about to cave in at any second. The PEOC walls were built to withstand a direct hit from a nuclear weapon, yet they were falling around her. What the hell kind of nuclear bomb hit this place? And how many hit us, she wondered?

Monique carefully waded through the darkness, risking her life, limbs, and health, desperate to save a man she didn't even like but needed to save him. She needed to save him because something had to go right today— someone had to live. The last twenty-four hours were hell, and she needed at least one victory. A few minutes ago, she watched a team of Army and Marine troops raid a cargo ship under the four p.m. EST sunshine. Monique waded in total darkness only a few minutes later, crawling over headless colleagues. If she couldn't save Chase, she could at least save Anderson. Maybe fate would smile down on her and extend Chase's life because she went out of her way to save Anderson.

"Hang on, sir. I'm almost there," Monique said. She froze as something began pounding against the walls or ceiling—she couldn't tell where it was coming from, but whatever was causing the noise sounded deliberate. It sounded like someone was trying to break through the walls. Was this the *proof of death* she feared? Were the North Kangavarians coming to verify their assassination attempt? She needed to get to Anderson quickly and find some way to arm herself and defend whatever little chance of living they both had left. She wasn't going to let the bastards take her alive.

She heard voices in the other room, faint but unmistakable. Those were voices. Monique didn't dare breathe as she listened. "Over there!" "This one's gone." It was a group of men. Their voices sounded foreign. She didn't have a weapon and was too far away to save Anderson. Monique hated today. It was indeed the worse day of her life. Nothing went right, and she couldn't save a man forty feet away from her. So what made her think she could save Chase? He was a thousand miles away.

She couldn't save Anderson, and now they were both going to die because she was too weak to come to the rescue and set up a defense for the trained killers getting ready to snuff out their lives. So, she thought to herself. Maybe if I play dead, I can jump on one of the intruders and kill at least one before I die.

The operation room door crashed to the ground, and light beams penetrated the inky darkness. This was it. This was her time to die. Monique held a hand up to shield her sensitive eyes. She decided she was not going to play dead. She was a fighter pilot and would die on her feet fighting for her country. She would kill at least one of the enemies. It would be a fight to the death.

"There," one of them said, pointing in Monique's direction. His voice still sounded strangely muffled and foreign, and Monique wasn't sure if it was from her damaged hearing or the breathing apparatus inside the man's suit. "Madam President, it's going to be all right. Help is coming." Monique's legs began to shake, and her eyes grew dark. She spent the last of her energy getting ready to die on her feet like the warrior she was. But these men were friendlies. Before she passed out, Monique pointed toward where she'd heard Anderson's voice. "Help the Senator," she said before taking her last breath.

Twenty-One Years Ago — Mr. Smith's Story.

Mr. Smith was the oldest son of Declan Ward, leader of the secret Rougarou Society, The Order of the Corrupted Leaf. He was made the Chairman of The Order of the Corrupted Leaf after he killed his father and the other sitting Council Members in cold blood, causing the Rougarous of Clemenceau to spread across Salleria and establish clans. All Rougarous fear him as a monster amongst monsters. With nobody to connect to when he was younger, Mr. Smith grew up hating the world and looking only for himself, giving his life meaning by killing anyone he came across— until he met Ashton and Erynn when he was twelve.

Because of heavy cuts to The Order of the Corrupted Leaf's budget by Declan Ward, Mr. Smith's father, Declan hated his son's so much that he didn't even give them his last name, choosing to give them the generic last of Smith. Before his boys could read, Declan forced his oldest son Finley and his brother Jacob to serve as weapons for the mega city Serpent's Stead in Clemenceau. By age five, Mr. Smith had become one of the most deadly Rougarou Assassins employed by The Order of the Corrupted Leaf. His deadly reputation made him hated by everyone, and none of the parents in Serpent's Stead would allow their children to associate with Finley.

Mr. Smith was raised in isolation during his early life, taught a Western form of Ninjutsu by his father, and cared for by his maternal uncle, Nico Lancaster. When he was allowed to roam around the big city, Mr. Smith would try to connect with the citizens, being kind to them and offering them any assistance. However, being a lead assassin frightened the citizens of Mr. Smith; adults avoided him, and when they couldn't treat him delicately while children ran from him on sight. Mr. Smith would try to assure them he meant no harm, but he was never good with people and, in the process, would scare them with his awkward people skills. Mr. Smith did not understand the pain he caused others when he only wanted to be accepted. When he was six years old, Mr. Smith asked his uncle Nico Lancaster to explain his pain. From Nico's explanation, Mr. Smith believed he knew pain because he walked around with an unbearable agony in his heart. After all, no one liked him— and no one wanted to talk to him.

Nico elaborated that physical pain, what causes one to bleed, could be cured with medicine and time, whereas the pain of the heart, like Mr. Smith experienced, could only be cured with love. Mr. Smith's mother died giving birth to him, and his father was brutally punished and beat both of his boys. With each unsuccessful interaction with others, Mr. Smith was dismayed and wanted to understand why he was treated like a monster when he was only following his father's orders. One day when Smith was eight, he sat alone trying to figure out this answer. Mr. Smith was attacked by one of the high-ranking Generals in The Order of the Corrupted Leaf. Smith quickly defended his attacker and mortally wounded him. When he unmasked the General, Mr. Smith discovered it was the only person who ever loved him, his uncle Nico Lancaster.

Mr. Smith was devastated by Nico's assassination attempt because his uncle was the only person ever to love him. Before Nico took his last breath, Smith asked demanded an explanation. His uncle confided in him that he didn't want to kill him, but it was a mission given to him by Declan, Mr. Smith's father. The Order of the Corrupted Leaf decided Smith was too dangerous and would be a threat to them all when he got older. In truth, Mr. Smith never wanted any power. He wanted friends he could play with. Upon discovering the council wanted him dead, Smith killed the twelve-man council, including his father. Smith tried to find solace in that his uncle Nico was ordered to kill him, but Nico insisted, lying to Mr. Smith to protect the council members, that he volunteered and that he'd always hated secretly hated Smith for being better than him. Traumatized by this false explanation, Smith vowed never to love or trust anyone again except his brother Jacob.

After losing everything that tied him to this world, Smith decided he would, from that point forward, live up to his reputation and be the horrible monster everyone thought him to be. Overwhelmed with grief, Smith killed dozens more people for simply looking at him or speaking to him. With all the council members dead, When Smith was twelve, he took the vacant throne and assumed power over all the Rougarou clans in Salleria— no one dared to oppose him. Soon after taking the throne, Mr. Smith meets Ashton and Erynn, and all three of their lives would change forever.

When Connor got back to 758 Fillmore Street, he was tired. His brain was moving at a thousand miles per hour, and the case weighed on him. "That girl came by for you, Connor," Mama Linda said. Her tone was hard to read. Connor couldn't tell if it had a hint of sarcasm or love. "Which girl?" Connor asked. Although he already knew the answer. Maybe he asked because he wanted to get a rise out of Mama Linda? Or, maybe he wanted to see what she was thinking. Either way, he didn't get an answer. "Fix yourself a plate" was all that left her mouth. "Yes, Ma'am." Connor knew not to say anything else.

Somehow there was a meal on the table. The power was still off, but there were green beans, corn, and hotdogs on the table. Upon further investigation, which only involved Connor looking around the counters for can goods and the trashcan for evidence, Connor saw Mama Linda go into the cabinets and prepare a cold meal of all the nonperishables. *The show must go on.*

Connor fixed himself a plate as instructed and sat in the living room, where everyone was gathered. Mama and Papa Anthony and Sophia and Riley were all eating together. "Oh, so it only took the city going dark for all of us to sit in one room and eat together?" Connor poked at everyone. After a few minutes of back-and-forth banter, Papa Anthony told Connor that Kayla had driven by a few mins before Connor came back and said she had a break in the case and was going to Wakefield to check a lead and she would be back later tonight. It was around 2:30 p.m. MST, and Connor figured she would make it to Wakefield by 4:40 p.m.

But why would she go alone? Connor supposed that all cops, from the FBI down to local police, had an independent streak. That's what made them so good at their jobs. Connor knew he would have gone alone, too, if a lead needed his immediate attention. More than a few times, he had run off and got himself into a few situations he didn't need to during his career because he chased a lead without having someone with him. But Connor figured Kayla would be fine. She was a Major Crimes Detective and probably had a contact in Wakefield she would be working with on the case.

"What exactly did she say, Dad?" Connor asked Papa Anthony. Papa Anthony recalled putting a cold hotdog into his mouth and talking between chews, "She said there had been Rougarou killings in Wakefield that matched your cases, and she knew a cop in the Wakefield Police Department that would have some information for her. She said his name was Hawkins or something like that." Papa Anthony paused to swallow his food, washed it with a canned soda, and continued. "She said Wakefield is where everything is going down, and it's supposedly where The Master is." "Where? Why didn't you tell her to wait for me, Dad? She shouldn't go chasing The Master by herself," Connor said. "So you want your deal, old dad, to understand women now?" "Fair point," Connor said to the immediate protest of Mama Linda. She went on and on about how women don't need men to understand them, and men need to learn to listen more. Sophia and Riley snuck in a few giggles at the grownups' expense.

"Oh, and by the way, son," Papa said as Connor got lost in his thoughts. "I fixed that old Honda Civic back there." Connor rose to excitement. "Did you?" "I sure did. I figured you wouldn't want your new girlfriend driving you around everywhere, so I opened the hood and changed some stuff around." Papa Anthony was a genius with his hands. He was an electrical engineer by trade but a carpenter by gift. "I don't know what's going on with all the cars or the power, but I have a few thoughts," Connor said to his dad. Everyone was eavesdropping now. Connor didn't share his theories for now, but he was grateful to have his old 1995 Honda Civic up and running again. He loved that car. He had it during high school.

Connor joined in a few more conversations, but he couldn't shake the ominous feeling that came over him. He spent time with his family for a few more minutes, devoured his cold nonperishable meal, and then went out back into his office. He had almost forgotten that he and Kayla had shared their first kiss until he walked past the spot to open the door. So much

happened after they shared their kiss. His mind was everywhere. Connor sat down to work on the case and cleared his mind, and nodded off within a few minutes. He was exhausted.

Kayla was thinking about something Connor had said earlier that day. One of his favorite movies was *Cloud Atlas*, and he read the book, too. She didn't make a big deal of it, but it was also one of her favorite books. The book and movie were classics. Kayla thought about one of her favorite lines from Cloud Atlas.

> *Travel far enough, you meet yourself.*

Is that what she was doing now? Was she found herself in Wakefield? Was she running from Connor or running toward him? Why was she in the car alone, and why didn't she wait for him? The truth was a bit more complicated than that, as it usually is.

Kayla stopped by to grab Connor to tell him about the breakthrough she made in the case, but when he wasn't home, she asked Papa Anthony if he knew where Connor went. He told her Connor went walking, and Kayla figured she would give Connor some time. But, unfortunately, only two things she could think would make a man she had just kissed after his fiancé died less than twenty-four hours ago, and both things returned to Anna. She didn't feel bad for liking Connor but felt terrible about their circumstances. So, she decided to head to Wakefield to check on the lead, and she would talk to Connor later tonight to see what they would do next.

She was about thirty minutes from Wakefield and was going to look for her friend Officer Ewan Hawkins. He worked closely with Police Chief Aiden Jahmar, and he would have some details on the case. Ewan was a complicated relationship, however. They dated before she joined the force, and she never got too close to him. Something always stopped her, but she never figured out what. Either way, they had remained friends and had a decent enough relationship to swap intel.

She was alone, but she was heavily armed, and she wasn't a pushover. Anyone who was going to bother her was going to earn their ass whooping, for sure, Kayla thought to herself. She wasn't going to roll over for anyone. She'd been down this road before and always came out fine. Besides, someone was out here killing people, and they needed to be stopped. And stopping murderers was her job. Kayla figured as long as she was on the road by seven, which was a little more than four hours from now, she could get back to Connor in time and maybe get another kiss if he wanted one. Time will tell. For now, there were murderers to catch.

Kayla was in Wakefield now. She stopped by the Wakefield Police department and looked for Officer Hawkins, but he was out securing supplies. She asked for Police Chief Aiden Jahmar but was told he was out headed to someone who was a hard ass or a badass. She couldn't remember which one because it honestly sounded like the person. Her name was Detective Skylar Schwartz, she was saying the man was both a badass and a hard ass, she wasn't sure. He had a funny name, *The Ghost*.

She had been in Wakefield for fifteen minutes, and everything she wanted to do was a bust. She jumped into her car and started driving away from the Police Department for another fifteen minutes. She was familiar with the area and wanted to check out a hunch. An old farm used to keep wild animals— the exotic kind. Kayla hoped to ask someone in the area if they had seen anyone with a wolf.

She had just gotten out of the car when two men appeared. They were next to her in a matter of moments. Both men were beautiful and wore no shirts. Their bodies were chiseled. They both had beautiful dark skin, and she could tell the men had no problem getting dates. "Can I help you, fellas?" "That depends," the taller of the men asked. He was a Herculean man who was perfect every day and oozed confidence. "Depends on what?" Kayla asked. "Well, Kayla," at the sound of her name. Kayla had two immediate reactions. Her first was a wide-eyed shock as she wondered how these strangers knew her name. And the second was to reach for her Glock. "That depends on how quickly you will die when she drinks all of your blood. You can help us by staying alive as long as possible while we feed you to The Master." The Herculean man said this as if he were reading a newspaper statistic. He had no emotion.

He didn't care either way. He said it was as if it was a fact that would happen. Kayla had found her killers. Both of them cornered her.

Jacob and Harrison had been following Kayla for hours now. She didn't even know it. And now, she was all theirs. Jacob loved seeing the shock in her eyes, and the best part about it. He didn't even have to play a character. He could have her as himself. Jacob reveled in this opportunity.

Detective Kayla Lowe was indeed a perfect specimen. Her dark chocolate skin made her look like a voluptuous chocolate playmate. She had a full figure— a figure he would explore at every inch. Jacob wanted to take her right there. He wanted to bite into her neck and take her to the middle of the street for everyone to see. Kayla would be one of his finest trophies. Today had been a long day. He killed multiple people for The Master, and it was time for a reward. Was Kayla this reward? He sure hoped so.

She made a move for her pistol, but Harrison was too fast. He subdued and disarmed her quickly. Kayla was no match for the Rougarou, but she would be a great meal. Jacob didn't feel the need to move. Harrison was well able to handle her. So Jacob just watched. He looked at her plump breasts bounce up and down as she struggled to break free. "Don't scream, or my friend here will snap your neck, Kayla," Jacob said to her coldly. His tone reflected no remorse and no emotion. But throughout, he remained seductive, and he wanted her.

Before Kayla could resist, Harrison got right in her face and showed Kayla his fangs. Jacob finally showed some emotion— it was laughter. The Great Detective Kayla Lowe had lost. She belonged to The Master now.

Chapter Fourteen

Every time Ashton had ever thought he was incapable of completing a mission, his training would alway kick in and he would get the job done. After serving his entire adult life in the military, quitting was not an option— neither was failure. Muscle memory, that's what was currently happening to Ashton. His senses were no longer his own.

Someone's life was in danger and he knew he had to do everything he could to save them. The loss of The Rookie was weighing heavy on him, but he couldn't think about that now. His number one priority right now was to let his training, experience, and survival instincts kick in and take over. And, that is what he did.

Ashton had no idea what he was walking into to, but for now, the living room was clear. Turning to his right, he could see the kitchen was clear as well. Ashton knew Erynn would keep any North Kangavarians out of the house, or die trying. He didn't think about how he was going to get up the nineteen stairs that led to his second floor without getting shot in the head, nor did he think about shouldering his rifle tight against his body, or the pain that it caused his injured shoulder. Whatever was upstairs was going to kill him or he was going to kill it. Whatever it was, he would deal with it. He was a goddamned Special Forces Operator.

Reaching the top of the stairs, Ashton seen a human soldier pointing a gun at the back on Kian's head; they were straight ahead about 20 feet. Without thinking, Ashton removed the knife on his right hip, it went directly in the enemies throat. He fell to the ground clutching his throat, while his weapon fell to the ground. Still not completely up the stairs yet shot two rounds into an Artificial. The first round went into the eye of the Artificial and the second went somewhere into its chest area. Clearing the stairs and now running and full speed, Ashton shot a three round burst into the chest of the last Aritificial tango. As it fell to the ground, Ashton stood over its head, fired a shot into the recently fallen Artificial and then fired two rounds into the head of the previously fallen Artificial, because it was still moving.

"Where's the kid?" Ashton said to Kian quickly while retrieving his knife from the throat of the man choking on his blood. Ashton shot him in the head. It was a mercy kill. Even though he was the enemy, no one deserved to drown in their own blood. Still waiting for Kian to answer the question about the kid, Ashton looked over his shoulder and called down the stairs, "All clear." Ashton was yelling out towards Erynn. "Kian. Where is the kid," Ashton asked again, now frustrated. "What about me man? You almost stabbed me with your stupid little knife and you almost shot me dammit." Kian complained.

The kid came out the upstairs bathroom holding his ears and stood by Ashton. Ashton was so angry with the complaining Kian and the sound of his voice made him cringe. With one swift move, Ashton punched Kian in the nose and felt a satisfying crunch. He didn't hit him with all of his might but he didn't pull his punch either. Falling to his knees, Kian groaned in pain holding his nose. It was bleeding to Ashton's satisfaction. "Now, get your ass up and go down stairs and do whatever the fuck Erynn tells you to do, or I am going to kick your ass. Do you understand me?" With a nasally response that had to flow through his cuffed hands,

Kian responded. "Fine! Dick-Tator." Picking the kid up in his right harm, Ashton followed his broken nose nuisance down the stairs.

Kayla instantly realized she didn't have the only working car in Salleria when her shoulder crashed hard against the rear seat of the truck the two men were driving. Her kidnapers moved with calmness like kidnapping was a daily exercise for them. She expected the truck to start up and take off with a jolt. Instead, the kidnappers eased into a comfortable cruising speed.

Kayla tried to concentrate on everything about the trip. She remember smells, the sounds of the different roads— concentrating on the difference between asphalt and gravel. She tried to remember her never best which directions the truck turned. Since there was no traffic, it was a little easier to pay attention to everything, but she wasn't sure if she was getting everything right.

Soon, the truck traveled on a dirt road. She could tell from the rocks kicking the underside of the truck. Wherever the kidnappers were taking her, it only took ten to fifteen minutes to get there. The man who took her gun picked her up with ease. He was incredibly strong. He flashed his fangs at Kayla and packed her into an old farm house. Kayla realized this *was* her lead. This is the place she heard about that housed exotic animals. There were at least a dozen other people on the property. Each of them laughed at her and she could see all of their fangs. *What the hell have you gotten yourself into Kayla?*

The taller of the men, she thought she heard someone call him Jacob, leaned in and told her, "The Master has been watching you. And, now, you will learn what happens to those who seek The Master." His voice was menacing and he spoke in a matter-of-fact tone. Oddly, she didn't know why, but he seemed familiar. Kayla dismissed the thought, telling herself she didn't know anything Rougarous. Everyone she knew were fangless.

Something the man made Kayla feel like she was going to die. He had a way about him that she couldn't explain. He was both seductive and psychotic. She had a feeling he would kill her without any hesitation. He kept looking at her. His look was a mixture of arousal and hatred. Kayla knew whatever was waiting for her was going to end in her death.

"I don't know anything about The Master," Kayla lied. She would say anything for the chance to get back in her car and leave Wakefield. How could a town so beautiful have this many Rougarous in it. What was happening in Wakefield and how didn't anyone know? "Honestly, this is all a big mistake. I was just driving and stopped to look for my dog. He got out the gate last night," Kayla said, knowing these men didn't know much about her. She was trying to be as believable as possible. She had to get out of here now. "Now, Kayla," The man called Jacob said to her. "We like liars, they taste better." Kayla couldn't believe it. He said that with a straight face. Do all of these fanged weirdos eat people? She had a thousand questions racing through her mind. Jacob continued talking. "You don't have a dog and you live alone in Lakota. And, Special Agent Connor Mason is your knew boy toy. Good for you, for being able to see past racial barriers."

Kayla's heart stopped. How did he know so much? How was The Master always watching them? She remembered at Anna's house the voice over the radio knew everyone who was in the room and even told her to move two steps to the left, or some direction. Her mind memory was getting jumbled between fear and the threat of dying a painful death. Is Jacob The Master, Kayla thought to herself.

The man who took her gun was now staring at her. He, too, was seductive and she could see how him being so attractive made it easier for him to kill people. "If you know all of that, then you know I am a cop." Kayla said to her kidnappers. She found the urge to be defiant. She wanted to put fear into them. "You boys don't want a war with the police. If anything happens to me, the police and the FBI would never stop hovering over this place. They won't stop until everyone is arrested." Both men only laughed. Kayla was about to die and there was nothing she could do about it. She still hadn't lived a full life yet. She didn't have any children. She had never married, and when she died she would not have anything to show for it because she always put her career before her life.

Kayla felt an overwhelming sadness grip her. The sadness was so strong, it replaced the fear. Kayla accepted the fact that she was going to die and there was nothing she could do about it.

Connor lifted his head. Two hours had passed and Kayla was in Wakefield by now, but he couldn't shake the bad feeling he had. Leaning back in his chair, Connor tried to concentrate on the details of the case. He was missing something and it was right in front of him, but he couldn't figure it out. The more Connor tried to think, the more his mind wouldn't let him— it only wanted him to focus on Kayla.

Connor told himself to be patient and everything was going to work out find, but the feeling in his stomach wouldn't leave. Looking around his office, it was getting dark again, and Connor told himself he would have to find a way to get electricity back in his office. From the looks of the sun setting, Connor figured it was about six thirty p.m. MST and it would be dark in a matter of minutes.

Just as Connor was in the middle of a panic, he heard a horn blow politely right outside his office door. It had to be Kayla. Connor jumped up and ran to the door, and his heart sank. It was Papa Anthony. He was in the driver side seat of the Honda Civic he fixed earlier. Connor knew is dad wanted to talk when Papa Anthony motioned him to get into the car.

"What's up, Dad?" "Switch seats with me, Son." Confused, Connor didn't know what to say, but he did as Papa Anthony instructed. They both got out the car and switched seats. Connor was now in the driver's seat. "Son," Papa Anthony began to talk. He had this way about him that always suggested he had searched through thousands of words to say and had just decided the words he was about to tell you were the ones you needed to get his message. Papa Anthony handed Connor the keys to the Honda. "Go inside Son, and get your gun, a backup gun, and don't wear a suit. Listen to me very closely. Put on dark jeans and your baseball cleats you haven't warn in a while. Make sure you wear your belt, you are going to need it. When you came home earlier, you had a radio in your hand."

Connor interrupted his dad. "That's not my radio dad, It's a long story." "Keep listening son," Papa Anthony said calmly. "Take the radio with you. And make sure you bring extra ammo. Your pistol and your back up pistol, some jeans you can move well in, and your belt, is all you will need. Don't forget your belt." Connor didn't know what to say to his dad. Papa Anthony was weird and always talking cryptically. "Dad, what are you talking about. Everything is fine." Papa Anthony looked at his Son. Connor could tell he was decided how he was going to say what he was going to say next. "Tonight Son, you will make a new friend, re-meet an old enemy, be swallowed by the darkness, and save my daughter in law. But the one who will cause you the most harm will be there with you, but you won't meet until four more."

Connor gave his father a confused look. But Papa Anthony didn't saying anything else but, "Do what I said, Son. Trust your father," and then opened the passenger door and walked around the driver side door and made sure Connor went back inside and did what he said.

It was the longest two hour drive of Connor's life— he was only one hour into it. Wakefield was a nice sized city. And to the very north of it, was a small town named after the city itself— Wakefield. It had its own lake and was covered by the most beautiful mountains.

Connor's mind was running through the worst of scenarios and to make matters worse, he tried to get into with his best friend and partner Brentley but with the power being out, it wasn't possible. On the way out of town, he drove by Brentley's house but there wasn't an answer. Connor went through all his notes and figured Kayla would be headed to either the Police Department or an old farm that housed wild animals. He figured he'd try the farm house, first.

Connor's thoughts were getting worse. At one point, he saw Kayla being raped and tortured. At another point, he saw her being burnt alive. *Think Connor. Think.* What is the most likely result to happen? Connor searched and searched his mind. He went through every possible scenario and kept coming back to one result. Kayla walked into an ambush. It all made sense. It seemed like every second of this case, they were being watched and always twenty-five moves behind. Connor was willing to bet he was being watch, right now. He looked into his rearview mirrors but didn't see any headlights. It was too dark now to drive without them.

An hour later, it was eight thirty p.m. MST. Connor couldn't believe what happened next. The radio from Anna's crime scene start crackling out white noise. There was a series of beeps and then a voice came and ruined Connor's entire night.

Welcome to Wakefield Connor. Kayla is alive— for now. She is a feisty one isn't she. You know, I really didn't have a problem with you but you are just so fun to me now. Do you think I am a man with a plan, Connor? If you do, you are right about me. I plan for every possible scenario. Remember, I told you to keep this radio hours ago. I planned for this very moment. I planned for Kayla's capture. I planned for you to meet me with way, Connor. But Connor, I am not The Master, but I am the one who killed that bitch Anna for you. She deserved to die. She gave herself away to someone else while you were with her, didn't she? Do you think Kayla will give herself to me? I hope she doesn't. I hope she forces me to take her against her will.

Connor was furious. He pulled over to the side of the road and grab the radio and began to yell in it. "You son of a bitch. I am going to get you. And, if you hurt one hair on her head, I swear I will kill you goddammit! You sick son of a bitch." Connor's rage exploded.

The warm glow that had flared inside him at the thought of his mind exaggerating things and that Kayla wasn't even in Wakefield was extinguished as something icy flooded the pit of his stomach. All of a sudden— after yearning to get any information on Kayla — he felt he would rather been better off not nothing anything at all. And, how on earth did his father know to send him out here, and to bring the radio with him. There was a strained silence in which Connor longed for the white noise of the radio to crackle again. "Hello! Answer me you bastard." Connor's stomach fell onto the floor of the car. Did he ruin his chance to get information to Kayla's whereabouts? Just as he had given up hope, the radio came to life again.

Language Connor. I thought you were a man of distinction— a distinguished gentleman.

Connor's mind reeled and race. What was the damn range on this radio? This wasn't a recording. The voice on the other side of the radio could hear Connor in real time.

Yes, I know what you are thinking. No, this is not a recording. You are actually talking to the one he killed your fiancé, and all those other people. My name is Jacob. Did you get my clue? Psalm 59:13. Destroy them in wrath, destroy them that they may be no more; That men may know that God rules in Jacob, to the ends of the earth. That's right Connor. I am Jacob, the hand of God's Vengeance. You have been found guilty. It is by my hand, you and your very sexy lady friend here, must die.

Connor wanted to say something so bad. He wanted to scream into the radio how he was going to kill Jacob, but he needed information. He needed to know where Kayla was, so he stored his anger.

The Master has plans. I have plans. You know what I am, Connor? I am the thoughts of The Lord. That's me. I know what The Master thinks as he thinks it, because I am those thoughts. So when I say killing you and Kayla is nothing

personal to me, you know I am telling the truth. I am just a manifestation of The

Master. He think, therefore, I am.

Look you son of a bitch. Tell me where Kayla is right now. You want to kill me, tell me where she is and you will have your chance. That's if you are man enough to kill me. The white noise of the radio crackled.

Get back on the road and keep driving. You have two friends waiting for you just

ahead. They will show you where I am. They don't know I have been watching

them, too. Believe me that I am in The Master and The Master is in me, or else

believe on account of the works themselves. Chow. Connor. Drink your blood,

soon.

What the fuck had just happened? Connor tried at the radio a few more times, but nothing happened. How did Jacob know Connor was pulled over? And who was waiting for him? Was he driving into an ambush?

Connor drove a few more miles and saw Kayla's car on the side of the road. The keys were missing. Connor knew where Kayla was now. She *did* go to the farm house. But was she kidnapped?

When Connor arrived at the farm house property, he was hit with his biggest surprise yet, Brentley. Brentley was standing outside with a muscular black police officer Connor

391

recognized immediately. He didn't personally know the man, but he knew him by reputation—

and his reputation was impeccable. The officer was dressed in a midnight black police jacket,

zipped to his chin, and sky blue shirt. Connor got out his car and approached both men.

"Good to see you, Connor. This is Police Chief Aiden Jahmar. He is actually the police

chief of all of Wakefield, including Lakota," Brentley said conversationally. Still confused by

Brentley's presence in Wakefield, Connor shook Police Chief Jahmar's hand. "Pleasure to

meet you, sir. Your reputation proceeds you." "As does your, Dr. Quantum. Me and Brentley

go back a few years," Aiden added to the conversation. Connor honestly didn't know

Brentley knew Aiden, but it made sense. He was the highest ranking FBI agent around, so

knowing police chiefs in each territory would be part of his job functions. Brentley was also

good at keeping secrets, too. Even from Connor.

"Brent," Connor only called Brentley that when something was very wrong or very

good. The former was accurate in this case. "I know Connor," Brentley stopped Connor

before he could finish. "Let me catch you up real quick so we can all be on the same page,"

Connor said to Brentley. "Papa Anthony came to me when you started walking earlier today

and told me to check on you at Anna's house and as soon as I was done, get in touch with

Chief Aiden here, because he had reason to belief an officer was in danger." If Connor's first

look was a confused one, this second look he had stole the cake, for sure.

Connor interjected, "But how could he have known Kayla was in trouble two hours

before she even left Lakota?" Connor asked. "That's your dad," Brentley kept going. "You

know how weird he is. Anyway, The Chief was on his way to meet another person in this city you need to meet, his name is Ashton. He is may be the most dangerous man in all of Salleria, but he is on the Chief's side. He's an ex Special Forces Operator. I got a hold of the chief via radio, about two hours ago and he made a little detour to help us save Kayla. When we finish, he will finish his other mission. Chief Aiden is responsible for securing Wakefield during this EMP Strike," Brentley dropped the bombshell on Connor.

"EMP Strike?" Connor asked. "As in a nuclear attack? "Chief, you want to take it from here?" Brentley asked Aiden. Aiden proceeded to run down the last twenty four hours to Connor. He told him about meeting Ernest and how Ernest was on his way to try to reach out to Command or anyone in charge. He told Connor about North Kangavar attacking The United Cities and how there were multiple attacks which left all of Salleria in the dark.

Connor's mouth was half open. He didn't know what to say, so he didn't say anything. "Connor, here is a radio where you can keep in contact with me. It only has one channel and leads directly to me," Connor said. "It looks like Kayla was kidnapped and taken into that farm house," Brentley pointed about a mile into the distance. The property was huge and from where they were all parked, they were more than likely undetected. "The three of us, plus the big man walking up now," Brentley pointed to a large super hero looking man Aiden introduced to Connor as Derrick. "We are going to ambush this site, arrest who we can and rescue Kayla.

Jacob Smith was raised as a Shinobi, or ninja, to be the right hand of his brother, Finley. He was born into the membership of The Order of the Corrupted Leaf. Famed as Jacob, *The Performer*, Jacob would often make lavish performances come to life while in stealth operations. While a ninja is normally relegated to the shadows, Jacob kept his identity to the shadows, but played characters for each kill. By the time he was eight, he was the most deadly ninja alive in the West and one of the most talented ninjas in the world.

At an early age, Jacob emphasized the importance of both celebrity and teamwork; he believed for one to be great, the needed to be able to both overshadow people and to be able to make their teammates better. Jacob wold personify this idea and dedicated his entire life to making his brother, the leader of The Order of the Corrupted Leaf look good at all times. It was in Jacob's early years he would begin to call his older brother, *The Lord and The Master*.

Because his mother died at birth, Jacob, and his fraternal twin, Finley were raised by their evil father. Jacob in particular revered his father and followed him devoutly until his father, Declan ordered the assassination of his older brother Finley. Jacob was on one of his secret missions given to him by The Order's Ninja Academy - Jacob made the decision to end the lives of anyone standing in the way of his brother. From that day, Jacob never adopted another mission in life. He would protect his brother at all cost, and kill anyone who stood in the way.

Since his early childhood, Jacob was very independent and self-confident, at times even appearing arrogant and condescending. Despite that, Jacob was very perceptive and intuitive, a very critical thinker and a world class strategist. After his father's death, Jacob devoted himself more to his older brother, aloof and cold toward others, breaking every rule that did not serve his desires or wishes.

As it stands today, Jacob is one of the world's greatest martial artists and no none knows what he truly looks like today. He is known to have a thousand faces and a thousand voices. The rest of his story is coincided with that of his older brother's as it was Jacob, who is the hand of The Master.

UC

The front door to the farm house opened. The four mean were disguised well in the tall crops of the fields. It was dark and the mood showed twenty men coming out of the farm house. Kayla was tied up and gagged at them mouth. Before Connor could react, a bullet barely missed his face, tearing a hole into the ground about twenty feet behind him. "They know we are here," Connor yelled to the others. Ducking out of site and drawing his sidearm from his waist.

A shot came from behind Connor. Derrick, the man he just met took out one of the Rougarous and then all hell broke loose. There was no way to tell who was shooting at what, or who was dying, but Connor had his eyes on Kayla. She was in the last clothes Conner seen her and alive. Thank God she was alive, Connor thought. But he would have to save her later, the team was under attack. Connor lifted his hand an shot one of the men moving very quickly at him.

Another man left for Connor and then another. It was two against one. Connor shot off of the men in the chest, he dropped to the ground like a sack of potatoes. The second man got the jump on Connor and roared loudly and lunged at Connor's throat. Connor felt blood explode onto his neck and upper body, but he couldn't feel the pain. The man's body went rigid and Connor looked up. "Get up Connor. We have work to do," Brentley made fun of best friend after taking the half the man's head off who was trying to kill Connor. "Thanks man," Connor said to Brentley. "Don't mention it. Kill the enemy and save the girl," Brentley ordered.

Another shot rang out and another Rougarou was down. The bad guys were losing badly. This was too easy, Connor thought. The four men charged forward running towards the farm house and killing everything that tried to kill them. Some of the enemy threw their hands in the air and they were spared. Each member of the rescue squad was disciplined and only killed who was trying to kill them.

Connor took out another man shooting at him and finally made it to Kayla. She was bounded with ropes around her wrist. Connor tried to loosen the ropes but they wouldn't budge. "Do you have a knife," Kayla asked Connor. "No, I didn't," Connor stopped before he finished. He suddenly remembered his favorite belt had a unique belt buckle that had a hidden knife underneath. Connor never really had a use for it before until now. Reaching down and taking off his belt, he used the hidden knife to unbound Kayla. "I'm sure lucky you wore that belt today," Kayla said to Connor.

And, then it hit him. Papa Anthony mentioned the belt and kept reminding Connor to bring it. He even went so far as to tell him *Don't forget your belt, Son.* But how did he know? How did Papa Anthony know to send Brentley to Wakefield four hours in advance, and how did he know Kayla was in trouble? Connor was going to have a long talk with his dad when he got back to Lakota. Papa Anthony always knew something.

"Connor, I know you want to tell me to go to safety, but I watched them kill a person and hang them upside down and drink their blood and I was next." Kayla said these things to Connor. He got the impression he wasn't supposed to say anything but yes ma'am. Kayla kept going. "So, don't tell me to get to safety because this is payback and I want to bring this fuckers into justice." Kayla said. It was a one way conversation and Connor knew it. He wasn't supposed to say anything but he did any. "I have a feeling Papa Anthony knew you were going to say that. Here, take this." Connor handed Kayla his back up weapon. It was a Glock 30. Kayla took the gun with a puzzled look on her face. "Papa Anthony, what?" "I will tell you all about it after we catch these guys. It's a really long and strange story," Connor said. Together Connor and Kayla rain into the farm house.

There was nothing in the farm house but a few dead bodies. They looked like people were drained of all their blood. Connor couldn't say for sure because he was running so fast he was scanning the area instead of taking it all in. His focus was on living people trying to kill him. They dead could get his attention after the gunfire stopped.

Running through the farm house, there was a back entrance of sort sorts that lead to an even bigger opening. What was back here? Without caution, Connor ran into the room. It was pitch black and smelled of feces and urine. Was this an outhouse? No, this was way to big to be an outside. Why was it so dark in here. From what Connor could tell, where ever he was, it did not lead to the outside. There was no light anywhere. To say the room was pitch black would be an understatement. It was darker than that.

Connor got a really bad feeling in his stomach. He was a sitting duck, just standing here in the middle of... where was he? He didn't know. As his eyes adjusted, Connor see a large figure twenty feet away from here. Maybe it was another building. It was large and it wasn't moving. But how could another building be in a building. That didn't make any sense. Connor wondered what the figure was and as if he prayed for the answer as that exact moment, and loud and guttural growl broke through the darkness. Connor nearly passed out on the spot.

Oh. Jesus. It's the wolf! Connor knew instantly it was the wolf the killers haunted with and there was no time to think and no time to run. In an instance. The large figured ran towards Connor. He could heard the panting of breath and four legs pound on the ground. The growling was so loud. Connor couldn't see the wolf leap towards him but he knew it did.

He heard it. It was the unmistakable sound of one thousand pounds of brute force leaving the ground and going airborne.

Connor pulled out his other sidearm, jumped to his right and shot where he thought the wolf was in the air. It was a jump that Connor could not have pulled off in such a quick time without slipping because the ground was slippery like there was loose hay all over the ground. If it wasn't for the baseball cleats Connor wearing, he would be a dead man. Connor shot six shots while still in the air and then crashed to the ground out of the way of the wolf. The wolf cried out loud and Connor shot another four shots from where he heard the cries coming. The wolf cried more and then ran towards the entrance Connor had came and crashed to the floor in front of Kayla, Aiden, Derrick, and Brentley. It was dead. All ten rounds hit the wolf and all ten rounds did their job. "Holy Shit, Connor! You just killed a freaking wolf!" Only Kayla could string that sentence together and have it sound like comedy. Connor hurried and jump over the dead wolf and back into the moonlight just incase there was another large animal in that dark ass room.

Ashton decided he needed to change his plan one more time. After socking Kian in the nose, he could think more clearly now. Leaving the house was the best idea but they needed to be sure they could get in the Dodge and travel a mile before getting shot at by the enemy.

From the looks of it, Erynn had everything and everybody ready to go at at moment's nice. This was good. Real good. Ashton could always count on Erynn to handle the business that needed to be handled. Ashton knew there were miles of twists and turns between the crew and the hospital and he was connived the southern parts of Wakefield didn't know the North Kangavarians were on Sallerian soil. If he had to guess, they were attacking from the north, maybe even as far north as Yespax. This invasion wasn't complex at all. It was ingenious, but not complex. Disable Salleria, kill communications, destroy the government, cut off resources, and conquer the land. It's exactly what Ashton would do if he was in charge.

"Everybody gather around," Ashton said as he walked outside to where Erynn had taken care of everything. His resolve was firm. He was tired of being three steps behind the enemy. He knew enough from North Kangavar's recent attacks on them to make a few informed decisions. Ashton began, "Our brother, Officer Samuel Willis is dead. We cannot give him a proper funeral but we can remember him for his bravery." Ashton looked at every person in the eye who was left in his makeshift crew. He looked at Kian, first. He wanted to make sure he knew his place, and he wanted to make sure Kian understood Ashton would hit him if he persisted to hurt the team. Then he looked at Corporal Benjamin Hunter. "Hunter. You have done well. No, you have done excellent. You are a fine friend and I am very sorry for not protecting your brother, Willis." Hunter lifted his chin and gave Ashton a head nod of respect. Hunter understood. There was only so much a leader could control and The Rookie knew he was already dead and he faced it bravely. "Erynn, give these two kids pistols and teach them how to shoot immediately," Ashton said. Erynn looked at him like he was crazy. "I am not trying to turn them into soldiers, but the North Kangavarians have already proved they don't care who they kill. Erynn nodded her head and reluctantly agreed. Ashton was right. The North Kangavarians had already dropped plans from the sky, with babies on them. They had already killed babies on life support, too. So killing the two kids with Ashton and Erynn were just part of the equation.

Now that Ashton had everyone's attention, he finished what he wanted to say. "Our first objective is to protect his house. Although we can't stay in it, for now. It needs to be protected because getting ambushed in an open vehicle is certain death. We need to make sure for the next hour we kill anything approaching us, and that everyone in this crew, children including are armed." Ashton let his words sit in their hearts for a minute. Hunter hesitated but then nodded his head, yes.

"Good everyone," Ashton said to everyone. "No go back inside and reload your weapons and get ready to live or to die." That is all Ashton said to the crew. But he showed special attention to Erynn. "Do me a favor Erynn and park the Dodge behind the house so no one can see it. I have a feeling we have another battle or two coming up in the next few minutes."

Everything was messed up and it had been less than twenty four hours for the whole world to go to shit. Monique was lying on her back, too hurt and exhausted to move. She wasn't the President of the United Cities of Salleria, she was the President of Hell on Earth.

Fires raged in every direction, their flames were licking the sky. No one had any real answers and half of Salleria's governmental officials were confused. The other half was dead.

Monique tried to remain calm but intense terror ripped through her body. Monique suddenly realized she couldn't move her neck or feel her legs. She panicked but did her best to remain call. *Give it another shot Monique. You are not paralyzed.* She tried to move again, but nothing responded to her brain. Monique tried her arms, again nothing moved. A tear began swell in her eye and eventually rolled down cheek. Was she really paralyzed. Oh God, she thought. How would it be possible to save Chase if she was paralyzed.

A worse thought hit Monique like a ton of bricks— she couldn't feel any pain either. That had to be proof she was paralyzed. *You're dead Monique.* That is why you can't feel your pain. You have failed Chase. Just accept it, let it go, and go peacefully into the afterlife.

Slowly, very slowly, Monique's eyes began to make sense of the shapes she was seeing. They were hard to make out, at first, but they were a comfort to see. Hot wind began to whip at her body. Sounds began growing louder— too loud, in fact. She began to hear the thud of helicopter blades chopping the air. I'm in a chopper, she realized. How had she gotten here? All she could remember was burning pain and then darkness. And, then dying after pointing to the sounds of the Senator Anderson, her political enemy.

A gentle hand touched her shoulder, and she turned away from the burning world to see a handsome man looking down at her. "Madam President, can you hear me?" To the handsome's man right was a familiar face—a face that immediately brought peace into her soul. It was Weston. As soon as Monique and Weston's eyes locked, Weston nudged the soldier out of the way and cracked open his bloody lips. A single tear rolled down his face. It was the first time Monique had ever seen the big man cry. "You're going to be okay," Weston said to Monique. "We're going somewhere safe."

Monique tried to respond, but all that came out was something that sounded like someone gargling salt water for a soar throat. As her eyes gained more focused, she began to realize her hands were badly burned. When she tried to sit up, she used her hands as a brace, touched the floor of the helicopter, but her burnt hands stuck to the floor, leaving part of her hand stuck on the ground. Monique started to panic, but losing her beauty to burns paled in comparison to watching Washington, D.C. lose its beauty. It was burned to the ground. Pillars of ash were every where. Flames licked small buildings and everything was crumbled into pieces. The landscape looked like a scene out of a zombie movie five hundred years after the fall of civilization. Realistically, Washington D.C. was the new Chernobyl. It would be six to seven generations before any human being cold live there again. The radiation would be too high for that long.

Monique scanned the troop hold, trying to find her trusted ally Brayden. She could see Senator Anderson was on a stretcher with two soldiers working on him. Monique didn't know if he was going to make it. She didn't know if she was going to make it either. There was another person in the corner of the troop hold whose flesh was so badly burned she couldn't tell who it was.

"Where's Brayden?" Before Weston could reply, a loud and violent sound clappd in the sky. Monique's adrenaline shot to unhealthy levels for her current condition, as she twisted to look out the window. She was badly hurting and her hand was throbbing, since she left part of it on the floor of the chopper. That would be a part of her that would be missing from her body forever. After the sound of the clap that everyone heard, Monique was expecting to see the North Kangavarians air fighters tearing through the skies finishing what they had started, and leveling the rest of the United Cities of Salleria.

Instead, it was one of the largest buildings in D.C. falling into another large building, taking them both down and the same time. Monique made herself sit up to look out the window, she wanted to see how she had failed her nation. Monique didn't want to run from it. She wanted to get better because of it. Monique wanted to remember every single detail so she could make the North Kangavarians pay.

Her head felt loopy, maybe they gave her morphine because she couldn't feel the pain in her hand anymore. The view outside really was like looking down into hell. Fires burned across the horizon. Husks of buildings were all that remained in some areas, but ground zero was a flat, smoldering field. The Washington Monument was destroyed along with everything in the area. From what she could tell, the entire Washington D.C. was a dead, radiation zone. If anyone survived, she would be surprised. D.C., was the new Hiroshima. War had finally come to Sallerian soil.

D.C. was no more. From now on, Washington D.C. would only exist in history books, there would be no rebuild. Her once daily commute and favorite restaurants were now radioactive craters. Monique ran a hand over her head, and a clump of hair came out in her burned fingers. She figured she was exposed to so much radiation, that she was lucky to be alive. Just then, Monique realize she had asked about Brayden but didn't get an answer. "Al, where's Brayden?" Weston wiped his forehead and then slowly pointed toward the horribly burned body in the back of the troop hold. It was the body she had saw earlier that was burnt so badly it was unrecognizable. "He didn't make it ma'am."

Chapter Fifteen

Ashton leaned towards Erynn and rested his head on her shoulder. It had been a very long twenty-four hours, and Ashton realized neither he nor Erynn had been to sleep in over thirty-six hours. "I am sorry our house is getting destroyed," Ashton said to his best friend. Erynn didn't look too worried about the house. It didn't look that bad. Besides, they had plenty of money. But would money even be valuable in this new world?

To Ashton's surprise, Erynn wrapped her arms around Ashton and hugged him tightly. He needed it, too. It felt good. Tonight was going to be an even longer night. Through it all, Erynn was always by his side, and Ashton was always hers. There was nothing they wouldn't do for each other. For them to get through whatever was coming their way, they would need to depend on each other more than ever.

A loud blast clanged in the distance. A wave of adrenaline emptied into Ashton's system as the dark winter night stretched before his eyes and washed all over the house's interior. There was trouble on the way. The sky was wiped clean of clouds, and with all the power being out, a blanket of stars lit the heavens. Tonight would be beautiful if the North Kangavarians weren't trying to exterminate them at every waking turn.

Erynn gave Ashton a nudge. He knew what I meant. She told him to stop resting on her and take charge of the situation. Reluctantly, Ashton let go of Erynn and took control of the situation. "Let's secure the house and guard for any attacks," Ashton said to everyone. "The enemy has us outnumbered and cornered. But what we have is this house and a lot of weapons. Everyone is a soldier." Ashton made sure to look at both the kids when he said this. He didn't want to scare them, but he didn't want to give them any false sense of security. The enemy didn't care if they were only children. They were in danger. "Kids, only shoot when something is close to you, and don't shoot yourselves, and don't shoot one of us. Just think of it as a video game— shooting works that way.

Erynn and Ashton gave each other one more intimate stare-down, and then Ashton shouldered his rifle and commanded everyone to get behind something solid and get ready for more trouble.

Ernest drove the Dodge up Belledurn Pathway, following a map Aiden had drawn him. He hoped that the higher elevation would help him get a clear signal. Unfortunately, the pickup truck didn't seem like it would make it up the high climb. It strained and protested the higher Ernest drove. The Belledurn Pathway went between the mountains, and the elevation was too much for the old truck to handle.

The last twenty-four hours were terrible, Ernest thought to himself, but he was still alive, and that was good enough for him. His nephew Chase needed him, and he would rescue him, no matter what it took. As the truck kept climbing, Ernest couldn't help but notice the snow-kissed mountains and evergreen forests from this height. The sky was so clear he could see for hundreds of miles. Ernest began to wonder what it would feel like to give up his wings finally. Maybe it would feel something like this? It was hard for Ernest to imagine himself being anything else but a fighter pilot. It's all he ever wanted to be his entire life. He'd always known, ever since he was a kid. He laughed to himself at how quickly life had changed. He was now driving an old pickup truck, thinking about settling down with a woman for the first time in his life. The quiet night and the winding road provided him plenty of time to think about her.

Ernest suddenly realized how lucky he'd been to run into Alison in the woods. She certainly saved his life, but he was starting to think if she would become the rest of his life. Ernest thought Alison was so beautiful. Her mocha-brown face appeared in his mind's eye with her pride, champagne-brown eyes, and half-moon cheekbones. She reminded Ernest of his sister. She, too, was beautiful, fierce, and gentle. He wondered what it would be like to call her, *his Alison.* It had a nice ring to it. And he wanted to be *her Ernest.*

Ernest grew up with his sister Monique, but he was adopted into the family. Somewhere around when he was three, his parents were on a Christian mission trip somewhere in a Spanish-speaking country, and they died of some rare disease. His mom and Monique's mom were church members and good friends, so when Monique's mom found out what happened, she took Ernest into their home and adopted him a few years later when he turned eight.

Ernest was a scrawny white kid with black parents and a black sister. So he grew up with a different respective on many things— dating being one of them. Ernest dated black and white women because he didn't notice a difference. And he had a feeling Allison didn't mind that he was white; he had a feeling she liked him, too.

As his thoughts drifted with the winding road, Ernest prayed he would be able to see his sister Monique again. He didn't know if she was still alive, but she was the Vice President of the United Cities. He knew the government would do everything it took to keep the Presidential staff alive. Ernest thought about Chase, who he thought was the bravest kid he'd ever known. But he *was* just a kid. How could anyone expect him to survive a series of nuclear attacks without his parents being around? *I should have kept driving to Chesterfolk instead of turning around and going back into the base,* Ernest could not help but think. At least he had finally found a radio. The battery-powered analog shortwave radio was his best shot at reaching the outside world. He just hoped it worked. But that was wishful thinking because the damn thing wasn't getting a signal.

He planned to rig up the antennae he borrowed from the police station. The highest point of Belledurn Pathway was just over twelve thousand feet. If it still didn't work there, then he was shit out of luck. Then again, they were all out of luck if there was a radioactive cloud from the high-altitude nuclear blast. He didn't know much about how the radioactive particles were spread, but he knew it was hazardous in the short term. Wakefield might be okay if they blew east, but he wasn't sure about Chesterfolk. The small city was much closer to the blast zone. Luckily, the night sky was so clear he would have all of these questions answered pretty soon.

Ernest looked over the valley below as the road looped around the peaks. His heart stuttered when he saw all of the destruction. There were fires everywhere. Below, the burned skeletons of pine trees poked out of the ground. Everything was ruined. All of Wakefield didn't look like a city anymore. Instead, it looked more like ruins of some ancient civilization.

Ernest pressed down harder on the gas pedal. The truck jolted forward, the chassis protesting with a shriek. He was getting closer to the highest peak of the Belledurn Pathway. He was filled with the excitement of the possibility of hearing from anyone over the radio and the dread of being unable to get a signal and losing any chance of finding Chase forever. Nevertheless, Ernest was determined to make it to the peak.

Snow-capped mountains filled his view as the curved road past a large open meadow. A herd of elk raced away from the sound of the truck. In the distance, a storm was moving in, and it was huge. It had dark, bulging clouds that rolled over the mountains, and the temperature dipped suddenly. Neither Ernest nor the unsuspecting people of Wakefield were ready for a storm— no one even knew it was coming. There was no radio or television broadcast to let anyone know. Ernest prayed the storm didn't bring any nuclear fallout with it.

On the horizon, the stars and the moon lit the sky so well he could see total darkness as the clouds started to thicken and threatening lightning advanced and flashed in their swell. The wind came charging the frozen mountains at high speed, creating a cold chill that was near unbearable. The clouds seemed to cover every last part of the clear sky. It was eerie watching the sky change from clear and moonlit to dark and dangerous. Lightning and thunder snapped violently through the dense air, and snow began to drop furiously in the distance. Ernest was driving into serious trouble. It didn't take Ernest long to realize he only had one shot at getting a signal, and it would probably cost him his life. Still driving, Ernest had a real decision to make. Should he go back down the pathway and try again after the storm? If he did that, the whole city could die before the storm ended, which left his other option. Keep driving, find the highest peak, reach Command, and save the city, but he loses his own life. *Man, today sucks.*

It didn't take Ernest long to make his decision. He knew what had to be done. His life was worth hundreds of thousands of people's, plus the Chase. So Ernest decided to keep going. Besides, he was two minutes away from where he planned to stop. Two minutes.

After driving the longest two minutes of his life and reaching the highest peak of the Belledurn Pathway, the Major parked the truck on the side of the road and looked for a place to set up. After a quick scan, and he probably scanned too quickly, Ernest picked the slope to the east. He would make the easy trek across the snow and rig the antennae up there. Lugging his bag over his shoulders, he ran as fast as the storm grew violently in the distance. He was still wearing his rumpled, dirty flight suit, topped with a Wakefield Police Department sweatshirt. He looked terrible, and he was exhausted beyond what words could express. The good thing wasn't a Zoom Call, Ernest laughed to himself. He needed to laugh to focus better on the job at hand.

The snow was only shin-deep, but it quickly got deeper as he made his way across the meadow. It was halfway up his legs when he reached the top of the slope. A gust of wind bit into his side like a bullet from an automatic rifle, nearly throwing him off balance. It was cold, and he felt every bit of nature's fury. If he died out here, no one would ever find his body. Instead, he would be covered in snow, frozen to death, and eventually become part of the mountain peek. The cold crept through his layers and penetrated his soul. Ernest reached into his third layer of clothing and ripped off the right short sleeve of his t-shirt, where the arm's seam meets the shoulder's cuff.

In one motion, he put the ripped fabric over his head, starting with the ripped end first, and let the manufactured end of the ripped sleeve fall over his nose. Just that fast, Ernest created a makeshift face made to protect his face and lips from the hard-cold wind that was biting at his face and lips like a thousand mosquitoes. As a bonus, his hot breath warmed his face with every exhale, making his face warmer. Covering his ears with his new face mask, he raised his cupped hands to his mouth and blew in them before setting up the radio. The sharp peaks of the Wakefield Mountains lined the horizon. It was a beautiful sight, but the storm clouds grew in size and strength. Ernest bent down and unloaded his gear. After a few minutes of technical setup and troubleshooting, he set the radio on a rock and pulled the receiver. Then Ernest dialed all the even numbers to listen for chatter. There wasn't much, and what he did hear wasn't helpful. Just a lot of panicked-sounding civilians asking for information or begging for help. He was looking for a government channel and was confident he would recognize it as soon as he heard it.

"CQ, CQ. This is Sierra Tango Foxtrot Niner in Atlilaya. We've got refugees streaming in from I-80 with signs of radiation poisoning. Is anyone out there? We need help ASAP. FEMA, the military, anybody. Someone, please answer!" Ernest's mouth opens wide in his makeshift face mask. He decided to search for a clean frequency instead and see if someone from Wakefield would respond to him. After he found one, he checked to make sure it was open. Since he didn't have a ham call sign, he used his rank. "CQ, CQ, Major Maddox, United Cities of Salleria Airforce Special Operations Command, CQ, CQ. Is this an open frequency? This is Major Ernest Maddox calling CQ and listening." He waited a few minutes but didn't hear any chatter. He continued his call. "CQ, CQ, this is Major Ernest Maddox, United Cities of Salleria Airforce Special Operations Command. My Jumper was shot down over Wakefield. Anyone out there?" "That's affirmative. This is Hotel Hotel Charlie November One. Located at Sunderhill. Sorry about your Jumper, Major. Glad you made it out." The wind howled, and he covered the receiver to protect it from the gust. "Say again? I'm on top of a mountain, and a major storm is coming my way, making it hard to hear," Ernest said while yelling at the top of his lungs. "Major, you can't be outside right now! There's a radioactive storm heading your way. You have to get out of there now!" Ernest's eyes darted to the bulging dark void coming his way. "Come again, Hotel Hotel Charlie November One?" "Radioactive cloud heading your way, Major. I'm holed up at Hasly Mountain. We're tracing the radioactive patterns, and I've been tasked with relaying that information over analog."

Connor was feeling partially relieved. He had saved the girl. In this case, the girl was *his*. But was she? Is that what Kayla and Connor had become? Were they going to be an item? Sophia and Riley seemed to like her. Even Mama Linda seemed to like Kayla in her way. Papa Anthony was as strange as he had ever been, as per his usual. Connor didn't know what he and Kayla had become, but he had a sneaky suspicion they would be living together soon.

Kayla and Brentley stayed back to process the crime scene, and Aiden and Ashton had other things to do. Police Chief Aiden Jahmar mentioned he was on his way to a super soldier named The Ghost, and Connor had to return to his family.

The details of the case were still coming in through Connor's new radio, not the one Jacob had given him. The Rougarous in Wakefield was destroyed, but The Master, Jacob, and other high-ranking officials were not apprehended. They weren't at the farmhouse by the time the raid began. It was usually that way in a homicide case. Things rarely ended the way an investigator wanted them to end. Sometimes you won some, but most times you lost some. That's the most fundamental truth about being a homicide investigator, especially in high-profile cases. The public wanted answers, but answers didn't always show up in gift-wrapped boxes.

The Master's power had been weakened, and Police Chief Aiden now understood what was growing in the backwoods of his town. Supposedly, the one they called, The Master, had thousands of followers spread throughout Salleria, but Connor decided that would be a different case for a different day. For now, his family needed him. He was always gone, and it weighed on him and his family. His kids were growing up fast now. Sophia was ten, and

Riley was eight, and being an FBI Agent forced him to miss the most critical years of their lives. But he had a two-hour drive back to Lakota before he had to get back to that reality. So, for now, the case dominated his thoughts.

Something still bothered him, but he couldn't figure it out. All the murders didn't add up. Some of the murders were methodical and didn't draw attention, while some of the murders, the Anna's and the one at the Ogden theatre, demanded an audience and a huge spectacle. And then a different kind of motif confused him the most. These murders seemed to be revenge murders that almost certainly involved two people. Connor kept feeling they were all connected, but the evidence suggested all three different types of murders were connected to three different killers.

Connor didn't buy it. His gut couldn't prove it, but he was sure The Master was so much of a genius he orchestrated all of these killings. Connor couldn't shake the feeling all of these things were connected. Connor also couldn't shake the feeling that this war wasn't over. The more he thought, the more he connected the pieces that Kayla was in real trouble for escaping and causing many deaths. She was safe at the crime scene, but what would happen to her when she got home? And that was the problem. Connor didn't know where she lived. Everything between them had happened so fast that the *basics* never became conversation topics.

Connor knew he had no real reason to think Kayla was in danger, but he couldn't shake that feeling. Connor kept thinking Kayla would die a horrible death; if he didn't stop it, his thoughts would become a reality. There was no science behind it. He just had the feeling.

Papa Anthony would say it was God speaking to him, showing him the future. But Connor and Papa Anthony didn't share the same beliefs. Connor believed in his dad. Papa Anthony believed in his God. The Master was out here, wasn't he? It was the sense Connor had, and Connor couldn't let it go. Kayla was in trouble, and so was his family.

Ernest had a complete panic attack. He was a dead man if he stayed out here. The operator kept talking. "You all need to stay indoors for at least a couple of days just to be safe, and even after that, the radiation might be too high to leave shelter if it's as bad as we're predicting." Ernest pulled the mic away from his mouth and looked over the valley. Aiden was down there somewhere preparing a public talk. Everyone would die if he didn't get the word back to the Chief. "How long do we have?" Ernest asked. "Two and a half, maybe three hours." "That put's us at round eleven-thirty, midnight. Is Chesterfolk in that storm pattern?" "Afraid so, Major. Chesterfolk has been in the storm pattern for the past few hours." Ernest's bottom lip quivered. He held the mic away, hesitated, then brought it back to his lips.

"Hotel Hotel Charlie November One. I hate to ask, but I need a few favors, and they are both matters of life and death." "Why don't you call me Alex, sir? Staff Sergeant Alexander McDonald at your service." "Thanks, Alex. I appreciate this." Ernest said. "Right now, I have to get back to town to warn everyone in Wakefield about the nuclear storm headed their way, but please see if you can contact anyone listening in Chesterfolk and warn them. Tell them that kids and staff at the AAU Basketball camp need help. The AAU stands for Amateur Athletics Union. It is an extra league for most sports, such as basketball, baseball, and other sports, and is usually reserved for outstanding players trying to get looked at by scouts. AAU teams enter different tournaments for their sport, and at least for basketball, enter showcases. I also need you to reach Vice President Monique Maddox in D.C. She's my sister."

Ernest was doing his best to keep his spirit high and communicate understandably. "Sir, I have good news and bad news for you." There was a pause, and then the Staff Sergeant continued, "First, your sister is now the President of the United Cities of Salleria. President Andrew Shelton didn't make it. The bad news, sir," Staff Sergeant Alexander paused for a time that way was too uncomfortable for Ernest. "Washington was destroyed in the second wave of the attacks. It was hit by a nuclear bomb and has been destroyed. I'm very sorry, Major. We haven't heard of any survivors out of D.C. at all."

Ernest fell to his knees as all the hope oozed from his body. He cried tears, but the harsh winds froze them instantly before they could even form. Monique was gone. He missed the following messages as his mind filled with grief. Whatever Alex was saying was most certainly falling on dead ears. A beeping sound drew his attention back to the present. He glanced at the radio, but the noise wasn't coming from the device. Instead, the Geiger counter in his bag was chirping as the needle ticked higher toward the red zone. "Holy shit!"

Earnest said to himself and then pushed the radio receiver back to his mouth. "I have to get back to town. I'll transmit again as soon as I can." "Copy that, Major. Good luck." Ernest stuffed the radio in his bag and hurried back to the truck, his eyes on the growing storm. Getting back into town before this radioactive storm would be nothing short of a miracle for Ernest. If he did beat the storm back into town, it would be only by mere minutes. With his foot smashing the gas pedal, Ernest hoped he didn't fly off the mountain.

The gravel in the driveway came to life, bellowing under what sounded like dozens of horses galloping towards the house. Erynn put a finger over her mouth, telling everyone to keep quiet. Then, taking a look and immediately recognizing what was happening out, "Kian, take the kids upstairs and wait for the okay to come back down," Ashton motioned with his hands, and Kian did what he said without a sarcastic remark for a change. Everyone in the house was shocked. Ashton looked towards Hunter, "This is a different kind of problem. Please stay out of this one unless someone comes upstairs. Trust me. The less these people know you exist, the better for you. Erynn and I can handle this fight." Hunter opened his mouth to protest, but something stopped him. "Fine," Hunter said begrudgingly. "But if you need me, don't be a hero." "Roger that," Ashton replied while turning towards the front of the house.

"Shit," Ashton said under his breath. "Do we know how many he sent?" Ashton asked Erynn. She shook her head from side to side. Ashton tried to see how many men were outside himself, but it was too dark. And they were spread throughout the property. "Looks like I have to play weak," Ashton didn't mind looking like he was afraid of these guys. His niece was inside, two working cars were parked outside, and these assholes caught them by surprise. There was nothing else he could do but go outside unarmed and get an accurate count of how many were outside.

Erynn began to check her ammo. "Use your silencer, Erynn," Ashton said to Erynn while dropping all of his weapons on the living room floor. "I need you to kill as many as you can, as quickly as you can, until I get back to safety." Erynn didn't respond, but Ashton knew she didn't need to— these men were already dead. They didn't know it. Their best option was to shoot Ashton as soon as he walked out the door. Erynn would still kill them all, but at least they wouldn't die in vain.

Erynn twisted the suppressors on both her pistol and rifle. "Don't let them see you, Erynn, for as long as you can." Ashton pulled back the living room curtain. It was now tattered with a few bullet holes from their previous battle. There were two men on the front stoop, where The Rookie's body was about thirty minutes before. Ashton and crew took all the bodies around the back left side of the house. Everyone was a bit uncomfortable staring at The Rookie's torn-in-half body and the dead remains of the Artificials.

Both men wore stealth combat gear and bulletproof vests. Ashton turned to Erynn, pointed to his chest, mouthed the word, *vest,* and then pointed to the center of his forehead.

Erynn understood the message. There would be no chest shots tonight. Erynn took a firing position. She was out of sight, and her rifle barrel was aimed at the front door. "We know you're in there, Ghost!" one of the men shouted. Ashton knew he had to ensure he wasn't killed when he opened the door. Since he was unarmed, Ashton figured he would use a condescending attitude everyone told him he had to his advantage. He had to give the men outside the best trash talk of his life, which his life depended on it. His job was to get them so frustrated they all gave up their positions. Ashton also needed them to get close enough to him so that Erynn could shoot them in rapid succession.

"How do you know I am in here?" Ashton shouted. It was time to get under all of their skin. "Open up! I'm not going to ask again!" the military man shouted. Ashton opened the curtain wide enough so everyone could see him. He also wanted to see if he could get a quick count of the enemy— it didn't work. He still had to go outside. Ashton copied the telephone operator's voice, "I'm sorry. The number you have dialed is disconnected, or." Ashton couldn't remember how the rest of the message went, so he figured he would ask. "Hey, guys, at my door, how does the rest of that message go." "Shut the fuck up and come outside right now," the other man at the door shouted. "You know, you should watch how angry you get. I've heard anger makes you age faster." Ashton belted with extreme sarcasm. Erynn laughed, and Ashton could tell these guys were getting frustrated now. That's where he wanted them. It was better to have them want to punch him in the face for being an asshole instead of killing him the way they wanted. He knew they came to kill him, but if he could make them want to teach him a lesson first, it would give Erynn enough time to kill them before they killed him.

"Open the goddamn door. We kick it in," the original man shouted. Ashton had them both frustrated now. Good, he thought. "You wouldn't kick in this door if I am The Ghost, then you already know how dangerous I am, and the door could be wired with explosives that would detonate on impact. Then we'd all be dead." Ashton let those words linger in the air for a second or two. "Oh, also," Ashton's tone sounded like a class clown or a kid who never got corrected by his parents. He was downright irritating right now, and he knew it. "If I am The Ghost, how do you know the porch you are standing on is rigged to blow if I push the little button in my hand." Both men jumped back so quickly, it was like the porched had turned to lava, and they were trying to save themselves. Ashton laughed as loud as he could, apologizing to the men in between laughs. "I *laugh* am sorry. *laugh, laugh, laugh* I am playing too much. This is supposed to be a serious situation, isn't it?" Now angrier than ever, the two men drew their guns and stepped back onto the porch. "This is your last fucking warning, I swear to God." Ashton had no idea which one of them said something this time, but he knew it was time to open the door. Whoever had said that last sentence was very fucking serious.

"Okay, okay, gentleman. I am coming out. Is Ian Shaw with you?" Ian Shaw hated Ashton probably more than anyone on earth. Well, the hate-Ashton list was rather long. Ashton didn't have the best track record with people. Ian, Ian wanted Ashton dead. Ian was someone Ashton met on a Top Secret mission, and Ian was the fall guy. Ashton didn't know his mission was built around Ian taking the fall for everything, but it had. Ian was set up, and someone how miraculously got away. Unfortunately for Ashton, Ian was a government spy for Russia and was well-connected. Ashton had been on the run from Ian ever since, and it now looked like, at the end of the world, Ian finally caught up with Ashton. Ashton heard rumors that Ian was blackballed from his country, and now he was a professional hitman for hire.

Ian vowed to get his revenge on Ashton, and it looked like tonight was that night. First, Ashton was stabbed by a mechanical combat troop from North Kangavar, they had been fighting all day, and he still needed to get Paige back to the hospital. Wasn't there anyone going just to let things be easy for him, at least once? From what Ashton understood, Shaw started his own *Security Firm.* The word "Security" and "Firm" should be taken as a very loose translation because world leaders and bad guys both hired Shaw's firm to coordinate assassinations of the world's most influential people— and the Shaw Security Firm was the best in the business.

To make matters worse, the Shaw Security Firm only employed the most elite Special Forces, Black Ops, and covert government groups after their contracts were over. So if you wanted to keep doing covert ops but get paid ten times more than the government was paying you, The Shaw Security Firm was your ticket. Hundreds of people applied, but there was less than a one percent acceptance rate into the Shaw Security Firm. And all of this meant that the men standing outside Ashton and Erynn's house were far more dangerous than any North Kangavarian Artificials could dream of being.

The men outside were known as *ISSF*. They bore the Shaw's Security Firm logo embroidered on their top left chest. They were the world's deadliest covert operatives, so Ashton told Hunter to stay out of this one. Ashton didn't want to put Hunter on ISSF's radar. The less they knew about Hunter, the better. And from the looks of it, Shaw had no intentions of letting a little thing like the end of the world stop him from getting his revenge. Ashton was about to be a dead man if ISSF's orders were to shoot on sight. Ashton felt Shaw would want to kill Ashton himself unless Ashton created a reason to be killed.

"Why don't you come outside and see if Mr. Shaw is out here, Asshole," Ashton had almost forgotten he'd asked if Ian was outside. "Well, Gentlemen," Ashton said while opening the door. He grinned at the two killers standing on his front porch. The two men did not return Ashton's grin. The man on the left stared at Ashton coldly. The one on the right looked like he wanted to shoot Ashton but had orders contradicting his strong desire. "Where is your boss? Is he not here? How sad, I was hoping to get a bullet from him, not one of his minions," Ashton said as he opened the door as far as it would open. He was hoping the two men saw Ashton was alone. But, as the door was wide open, Ashton could see two more men standing in the distance. They looked to be about thirty feet behind the men on the porch. They were snipers, Ashton processed. It's the same thing he would do, and he often used Erynn that way. Pretending to put his hands on his hips and letting his left hand go further behind his back, Ashton singled to Erynn. The current count of tangos was now four.

Of the two dangerous men standing on the front porch in front of Ashton, Ashton figured these two men were either newbies or well-trained in close-quarter combat. There was only one way to find out how dangerous they were. One of the men is on the short side of humanity. Ashton figured the man would be sensitive about his height. "You're looking *short* winded," Ashton emphasized the word *short* so much that it was both comical and disrespectful. The short man threw a left uppercut to Ashton's stomach. With such skill and power, Ashton knew these two men were not newbies; they were close-combat specialists. Ashton fell to the ground. The short man was a skilled mixed martial artist and paid for that punch, but he did get the intel he wanted—two badasses on the porch and probably two of the world's best shooters thirty feet away. *How in the hell am I going to get out of this one,* Ashton thought to himself.

Grunting, Ashton picked himself back up onto his feet. "Good punch, *Shorty McFly.*" Besides, the punch angered Ashton. He didn't mind playing the fool, but he did see the punch coming, and he didn't like looking weak in front of these assholes. He didn't know why, but he didn't like it. Ashton said, after gaining his composure, "I'm sorry. I need to learn how to be perfect. God only lets things grow until they are perfect." Ashton paused for a few seconds. The taller man was confused but gave Ashton a severe death glare. Ashton knew he meant it, too. He knew he had to deliver his following line with venom. "You're so short. I guess God said you were perfect sooner than all of us, and now you a fucking midget." Ashton laughed at his joke, which proved to be a big mistake. This time the short man walked towards Ashton and hit him across the head with the butt of his rifle. Stars popped into Ashton's vision, and the familiar warmth of blood slowly crawled down his forehead. Ashton knew Erynn more than anyone in the world, and he could probably guess she was milliseconds away from pulling the trigger, but Ashton was outnumbered, and then men were too spread out. Ashton needed to get the men in a better position. And since Ashton didn't hear any shots, he knew Erynn, no matter how pissed she may have been, was trusting Ashton had a plan that would prove to be better than offensive short jokes.

Again, not pretending but seriously using more effort than he desired, Ashton struggling back to his feet, blurted out, "You're right. Midget is a very offensive term. I believe you all like to be called, *little people.* The smaller man growled and punched Ashton back in the stomach. Ashton curled over and barely kept his feet, but his pride wouldn't let him fall three times in a row. If they were going to kill Ashton, they would have to earn it. Finally, the taller man looked at Ashton and said, "I'm going to let my buddy here keep fucking you up. From what I hear, you need to be knocked down a pegged or two." Confusing everyone, Ashton didn't respond to the taller man, instead opting to dramatically look towards the sky as if he was dying and had something essential to say. "Keep looking up. That's motivational advice for most people, but necessary advice for *short people* like you, *little man.*" Ashton emphasized "short people" and "little man" so much it was like he punched those words out of his mouth. Undoubtedly, the punched words connected with Ashton's target because all at once, the taller man yelled out before Ashton could get hit again, "Cut the shit, Ghost. You know why were are here. We are getting paid a lot of money to knock that smirk off your face permanently." Ashton didn't realize it until the man pointed it out, but he had been smirking. He could see why these guys were getting angry. Ashton was enjoying this ass whooping. That had to be frustrating.

The short man who had taken all of Ashton's verbal abuse interrupted Ashton's thoughts, "We're here to collect what you owe, Mr. Shaw. And we're not leaving until we put a bullet or two in you." The short man had grown tired of Ashton's jokes at his expense because when he said bullet or two, he said those last words violently. Maybe it was time for Ashton to quit playing and do as they said. But he couldn't. Ashton didn't owe Shaw any money. These men were here to kill him, and Ian wasn't here. That made things a bit easier. Dealing with both Shaw and his men were have required a small army, and that was something Ashton did not have at the moment. "Yeah, I figured that much," Ashton said, looking at his feet and signaling to Erynn that the total count of tangos was now six. Ashton snuck a peak to his right as he looked down to his feet and saw two men flanked on the right side of the house. Ashton doubted any of these men would be able to take him in close-quarters combat, but he was about to find out in a few short minutes. There was no way of getting out of this without spilling blood.

I've got to get those two men thirty feet away, closer to the house, Ashton thought. And these to fuckers on the side of the house need to come up about six to seven feet. But even if they did, Erynn wouldn't be able to shoot them. So somehow, Ashton would have to disable one or both of the guys in front of him, get to his weapons, and then kill the two men on the right. As of right now, the two right-flanking men were his most significant threat. Any move Ashton made would get him shot before he could react to them.

It was now or never. The only way out of this was to take these guys out. Maybe he should have let Hunter help. But, no, Hunter didn't need to be involved with these guys. Shaw wanted Ashton and all his known associates dead, which included Erynn. Ashton would have to get this done without involving Hunter.

Ashton was ready. As loudly as he could and with dramatic flair to draw attention away from the hand signal he was about to give Erynn, The Ghost shouted, "Hey you. Number Three." Ashton was being clever at the moment. While he was shouting at the man, he was calling number Three. Ashton put his left hand over his left eye in a circle position, as if he was looking through a telescope or using one lens binoculars. While this gesture went unnoticed by the six men, it did not go unnoticed by Erynn. Ashton was telling Erynn to switch from the Glock to her HK416. Number three would need to be one of her first targets, and he would have to be a long-distance kill. Ashton identified the man as the lead sniper or the person who had the best chance to get the first shot. In Special Ops, the left hand circled over the left eye meant that a sniper had been identified in the battle space. While the other men should have noticed it, Ashton had been dramatic and irritating since he opened the door. It looked like he was being an asshole, so no one noticed the gesture except Erynn.

"Hey! Number Three." He was a hefty man, but The Ghost could tell he was in solid shape and no one to underestimate. He was too far away, so he had to do something to bring him closer. "Come here, you fuck. How's your mom and her weight loss coming? Do her panties still look like parachutes? "Number Three started walking towards The Ghost.

Erynn needed to take all three men out consecutively to give Ashton a chance to get back to his weapons so they could fight off the other three together. With just a few more steps, Erynn would know would shoot and get the party started. "Yeah. I miss your mom and her parachute panties. It's hard to find a woman whose panties can come off and give you a good time and help you skydive when you leave your parachute at home." Number Three was pissed and walking faster. It couldn't have been the mama jokes. Surely, the hardened assassin wasn't that sensitive? Ashton figured he probably just wanted to break Ashton's jaw to get him to shut up once and for all. Either way, Number three kept walking across the field and towards Ashton.

"Your mom is so fat that when she wears a yellow raincoat, people shout out *taxi*!" Ashton was on a roll now. "No, Yo Mama is so fat. I took a picture of her last Christmas, and it's still downloading to my computer" Ashton was laughing now. Before Number Three could say anything in response, and before the short man who just threw a punch to hit Ashton in the face could connect, the short man's head exploded, and less than a second later, Number Three, the man walking around the field to shut Ashton up was shot in the eye. He was dead before he could blink. There were only four tangos left. And Erynn had a hard decision to make. Did she shoot the man standing in front of Ashton, who was now making a move to draw his gun, or shoot the other sniper standing with Number Three?

Ashton's decision was already made for him. Catching the taller man's right hand at the wrist and grabbing his knife from the right sheath, Ashton stabbed the man between the part of the arm where the elbow meets. Ashton put the knife so deep into the soft, muscular skin of the man's arm he felt the tip of his knife touch the bottom of the man's elbow. The man would never use this arm again. It would matter because he was about to die in a few seconds. The stabbed man let out a howling scream, and the two men on the right side of the house began to fire and advance toward the living room door. But they were too late. Ashton had already secured the falling pistol from the man's stabbed arm and used the knife, still planted deep into the man's arm, and used the knife as a steering wheel to use the man as a meat shield. Bullets tore into the man's back as Ashton used his left hand to shoot at the closest flanking man. He hit him, but it was in the vest. Ashton removed his knife from the dying man's arm and shot him in the face with his left hand. The body fell to the ground with a hard thud. There was no time to shoot the last two men standing, so Ashton dove back into the living room to get his rifle.

Securing his rifle and getting to a kneed-prone position, Ashton heard a sound he wasn't expecting. Tires were crunching over the driveway. "Oh, for fuck's sake," Ashton shouted. It was a long night, and Ashton was tired of getting shot at. There was an old-school, classic pickup truck, and in the passenger seat was Ashton's least favorite police chief, looking like even more of a hard-ass than usual. Five tangos were down, and there was one left, and as if Ashton needed any more drama in his life, Aiden, the Police Chief of Wakefield, was directly in two highly trained assassins' line of fire.

Corporal Benjamin Hunter was guarding the upstairs, but he knew his time to join the find had come. Hunter watched as broken glass hit what looked to be Deputy Police Chief Derrick Mercer just below the eye and drew blood. Someone had just shot at them. Opening his passenger side door and pulling Derrick to safety, Aiden asked, "What the hell does Ashton have going on at his house now," Aiden said in frustration. He was sick of Ashton always causing trouble. Aiden and Derrick were on Ashton's property for twelve seconds, and now they were behind the pickup truck in a shootout. The sound of gunshots pelted the truck. Finally, the bullet hit something loud enough to catch everyone's attention. Whatever situation Ashton had gotten himself into, it was quickly escalating, and it was now all their situations. "That guy is going to pay for hitting my truck," Derrick growled. Aiden was driving to Ashton's house to ask him and Erynn for help, but trouble always followed this guy. Aiden should have known better—this was Ashton, after all.

"Put down your weapon!" Aiden shouted. He could see to shooters. As soon as Aiden shouted his order, he saw one of the gunmen had the drop on him. Before Aiden could react, the gunman's head exploded into a hot red mist. "Stop announcing yourself, Chief. These men don't care that you are a cop." Ashton said to Aiden right after saving his life. There was a gunman left. Hunter came running out of Ashton's house. "Corporal, is that you?" Aiden asked Hunter. "Yes, sir, you won't believe how many times Ashton and Erynn have saved our asses tonight!" Aiden made eye contact with Ashton.

Aiden looked toward where the shot came from and saw Ashton covering both of their backs as they hid behind the pickup. "There are two more Chief— well trained," Ashton said while scanning the terrain for the other two tangos. "Erynn, there are seven men, not six," Ashton added before running. Aiden considered trying to grab his Barrett M82 sniper rifle from the passenger seat, but he didn't want to risk moving. Instead, Aiden reached with his right hand and pulled out his Sig Sauer P22 with one motion of his thumb and took his weapon off safety. Hunter took to the right side of the house, opposite Erynn, and took a sniper position. Now both sides of the house were covered, leaving Ashton, Aiden, and Derrick the room to roam free to pursue the last two men. Hunter didn't bother to check his ammo. He knew it was fully loaded and ready to be used. He was itching to get in the fight when he was upstairs.

Another shot cracked through the woods outside Ashton's house, and the bullet kicked up the dirt by his left boot. It looked like Aiden resisted the urge to jump from his position and return fire. Hunter knew every move from here out was the difference between life and death. If he died here, he didn't have anyone he could think of who would mourn. His parents were dead, and Hunter didn't have a girlfriend. And if he left Aiden to die, then the whole city of Wakefield may die with Aiden. Also, with no power and no emergency services, anyone wounded out here could die later from infections.

Hunter could tell Aiden couldn't see where Erynn was, and Ashton was gone now, but there was no way to tell the Chief where she was without exposing him to gunfire. So, the Chief would have to get along with not knowing. After another long, tense moment, Aiden and Derrick exchanged a nod. Aiden held up three fingers, then two, then one. Derrick fired his shotgun into the woods and then immediately ducked back down. The shooter was momentarily focused on Derrick, giving Aiden his chance. He knew that with a pistol, he would be deadly accurate within seven-five feet, but he would have to get that close to the hostile to get a good shot.

Ahead, there was a massive tree about sixty feet to the North. As Aiden began to run for cover, Derrick became more suppressive. Hunter helped out and laid suppressive fire so the Chief could move freely. When he got to the tree, with his back facing North and his face to the South, where Ashton's house was, he could see Hunter and Erynn covering his back. Aiden raised his P22, aimed the sights at the shooter, and fired. The shot went wide. A well-hidden man roved his gun toward Aiden, and Aiden squeezed the trigger again. The shot clipped the man in the shoulder. He let out a screech of pain and ran in a hunch toward a cluster of trees. "After him!" Aiden ordered. Derrick was already on the move. Keeping low, Aiden bolted in the direction the shooter had run. He was followed by Erynn, Ashton, and Hunter, with Derrick leading the pack. Hunter still wasn't sure exactly what was going on, but he guessed that Ashton had pissed off some bad people.

All five moved side by side in combat intervals for several minutes, just like they were trained. Aiden flashed a hand signal, and Derrick took up position behind a rock a few hundred feet to the right. Hunter, The Ghost, and Erynn took flanking positions, with Erynn taking a sniper position. Silence washed over the woods. Aiden listened for the crunch of footfalls or the groans of their injured Chase, but nothing. They didn't know where he was, and Aiden didn't like it. He signaled for Derrick to take point. An instant later, Aiden saw a well-armored man moving toward Derrick. "Watch out!" Aiden shouted. There was an earsplitting crack, and Aiden knew the armored man had gotten off the first shot. Derrick's shotgun cracked in the open sky, and the well-armored man's body fell to the ground with a lifeless thud. Derrick had blown off his head. The shotgun didn't even leave a bloody mess. There was blood, but wherever most of the man's head went, Hunter couldn't see.

"Hey, Chief. Hey Derrick," Ashton shouted from his flanking position. "What's up, Ashton?" Derrick kindly responded. "Thanks, I owe you one," Aiden said to Ashton, hardly believing the words as they left his mouth. "Hunter, what the hell are you doing here?" Hunter briefly explained to Aiden and Derrick all the events that had happened until now. They all fell into a sad silence when he got to the part about The Rookie dying. Hunter explained to Derrick and Aiden about the Artificials as well. Aiden and Derrick took it all in. "We hadn't seen any machines yet," Aiden said with disbelief. We stored them around the side of Ashton's house Chief. The Artificial is next-level weird," Hunter responded on Ashton's behalf. He knew the Chief and The Ghost didn't have a good relationship, but after all, Ashton had done for everybody and the Town of Wakefield, Hunter wanted to help.

"I owe you one, as well, Chief," Ashton said after Hunter had explained everything. "I had no idea how I would get to those last two guys. I still don't know where the seventh one was hiding." "I'm glad we could get here in the nick of time," Aiden responded. "So what the hell is going on— Why were they trying to kill you?" Aiden asked. There was a bit of frustration and concern in his voice, but Ashton seemed to understand and ignored it. "A long time ago, I did a mission that left one of the most dangerous men in the world in a horrible position. He had been trying to kill me ever since," Ashton responded. Aiden looked at Ashton in utter disbelief. Derrick had a look of bewilderment on his face, too. Hunter couldn't help but wonder what kind of jobs Ashton did for the government. Finally, as if the Chief was reading his mind, Hunter got his answer. "Ashton, what the hell did you do for the military?" "A little bit of this, a little bit of that.

Most of the government's dirty secrets the government has, either Erynn or I had something to do with them," Ashton did his best to explain without giving out top-secret information, but it proved to be a more challenging job than he expected. Ashton kept talking, "To be honest, Chief, The CIA, well, a part of the CIA that doesn't exist, and if you knew about it, they would kill you," Ashton added to the conversation. Derrick laughed but then stopped when he saw Ashton wasn't kidding. "They are still recruiting Erynn and me. They want us to do special missions for a special team. That's about all I can say, or we all are dead. I'm serious." Everyone seemed to take Ashton's word. Hunter got the feeling if they didn't, a laser from the sky would beam down and kill them all just for having the conversation. "I think these gentlemen would have killed Paige, too, if they had seen her?" Aiden asked. "Yep. It's time for me to get her out of the house now," Ashton responded. He almost forgot about his niece and the Ankle Biter with everything happening. Derrick couldn't help himself. Smiling, he asked, "Why can't you stay out of trouble, Ashton?" "I'm working on it," Ashton responded. "It sure would make Erynn's life a lot easier. Erynn facepalmed, and everyone laughed.

"So, why are you here, Chief?" Ashton asked, holstering his weapons. Aiden sighed; he seemed exhausted. Hunter could relate. "I came for your help," Aiden said. "We found Rory

Cooper's body earlier today, hanging from a tree in his backyard with all his blood drained and two holes in his neck." "Oh shit," Ashton said. "We've only got two bodies so far, but I fear we might have a serial killer on the loose. Also, I just finished a raid with the FBI; apparently, Wakefield is a type of headquarters for something called Rougarou."

A Rouga-what?" Hunter interrupted. "A Rougarou," Aiden reiterated. Hunter noticed Erynn and Ashton share a troubled look at one another. "Frankly, Ashton and Erynn, I need your help Derrick agrees. You two are the best, and we are against some of the world's worst." Aiden finished talking. There was a long silence, and Ashton interrupted it. "We will help Chief, but I have to get Paige back to my sister first," "Understood," Aiden said while Ashton was talking. "And then we must check out Rory's house for ourselves. I can't tell you why, but you have to trust me. If I am right, you have much bigger problems than you think." Ashton said. Erynn nodded her head in agreement.

Alison was growing frustrated with her brother Ashton. He was supposed to pick her up from the hospital nearly ten hours ago. She was worried, sick, mad, and tired all at the same time. Ashton was careless, but he was always good with Paige. So him not showing up at one p.m. the way he said he was, was pissing her off. It was also making her worry. She could barely concentrate. Now that she thought about it, Alison hadn't seen or heard from Chief Aiden either. What the hell was going on? Where could they be, she wondered.

Ashton was always late. Sometimes she wondered if he only cared about himself. She quickly dismissed the thought. Ashton had Paige, and he was always a better man with her. Ashton was a terrible citizen, he didn't like to follow any rules, and ever since the Order of the Corrupted Leaf, Ashton proved to be an even worse subordinate. But he was a good family man. No matter what was happening, she could always count on Ashton to care for the family. Alison knew Ashton loved Paige; it had to be a good reason if he was late.

But dammit, today she needed her brother more than ever before. Everything about the work shift she had just finished was terrible. Her socks were wet from running to work in the rain over thirty-four hours ago. The hospital had no electricity, and there was no real way to feed the patients. And, to make matters worse, groves of new patients were coming to be seen every fifteen minutes, and more than a few patients were dying every hour. It was a terrible day to be a work, for sure. Some of the patients were delirious. They were talking about glowing red machines attacking houses. She didn't know what was going on, but glowing red machines were certainly not it. This wasn't a sci-fi movie. Alison decided she would go back inside to check on London. There was nothing else she could do right now, but wait on Ashton, so she figured she would make herself useful.

London was still on life support. She had just finished pumping air into his breathing tube as another nurse took over the life-saving duty. Alison's forearms were tired and burning from the constant manual labor. Everything that required power was dead: dialysis machines, ventilators, and feeding tubes. While the feeding tubes and saline drips could work by gravity, their pumps were offline. There were no easy ways to monitor vitals because the ECG monitors were dead. Drawing blood was useless because there was no way to test blood work in the labs, and if anyone needed an MRI or X-Ray, that would be impossible. The hospital might as well have time-traveled back to the early 1900s because that is precisely the shift she just left.

The entire hospital staff couldn't even be sure if they were saving anyone because there was no way to run tests to verify if their actions were working. The entire hospital was blind. Alison was tired. It was hot underneath her scrubs, but with no lights, there was also no heat or air conditioning, which allowed the cold air outside to turn the inside of the hospital into a refrigerator. Alison breathed in through her surgical mask and took an exhausted breath out. Her hot breath blowing back on her face was a hidden blessing, as It kept her face and upper body warm.

Doctor Kerry interrupted Alison's exhausted thoughts as he pulled back the privacy curtain, poked his head in, and asked, "How is he?" "The same," Alison said. Kerry examined London. He didn't like what he saw and was unsure if the kid would last through the day. And how would he survive in this new world if he did?

Alison was exhausted. She hadn't slept for over thirty hours for more than a few minutes. Her daughter was with her brother; God knows what. Her ex was a total asshole. They almost had to kill to get their daughter to safety. And London was about to die if she couldn't find a way to do something to extend his life. "Doctor Kerry, I know I just finished my shift, but I don't think any of us have shifts anymore. Can you get someone to cover me for just a little bit? I need some rest, maybe an hour." "Of course," Kerry replied. "Everyone is going to get—" The commotion in the lobby cut the doctor off. Several raised voices echoed into the ICU. One was Zara's, but Alison didn't recognize the others. "I better check this out," said Kerry.

"Hello, I'm looking for Alison Jace?" someone called. Alison nearly forgot to pump air into London's lungs. She carefully squeezed the bag, but her heart was beating rapidly. Who could be looking for me? Kerry politely walked closer to Alison and reached out for the bag. "Looks like you have visitors. Why don't you let me take over?" Coordinating the shift with the utmost care, Alison and Kerry changed places. Extremely nervous, she stepped onto the ER floor with her adrenaline pumping. She didn't know what to expect, and her heart dropped into her stomach.

"Mommy!" Paige let go of Police Chief Aiden Jahmar's hand and ran into the warm embrace of her mother. "Paige! What are you," Exhausted and confused, Alison looked to Aiden for an answer without finishing her sentence. "I got to shoot a gun, Mommy!" Allison looked at her brother in a fury. A man Alison didn't recognize introduced himself before she could kill her brother. "Hello, ma'am. I've heard a lot about you," Hunter said pleasantly. Allison did care of his niceness right now. What the fuck was her brother thinking, giving Paige a gun. "Without all due respect, sir," Alison rudely interrupted Hunter. Hunter pushed back kindly, "Just a minute, ma'am. Give me twenty seconds, and I can explain everything. Your brother is a hero. My name is Corporal Benjamin Hunter, and my partner," Hunter, and

I stared into space. His eyes began to burn, so he blinked, but it was too late. A tear had already fallen. He wasn't ready to talk about Officer Samuels again. Every time he did, it was like ripping his heart out. Alison saw the officer crying and holding back more tears. Whatever happened, Ashton had saved everyone. Corporate Hunter kept going.

"Your brother and Erynn saved us too many times today to count." Corporal Hunter explained this to Alison, who was explaining this same thing to the Chief thirty minutes ago. Hunter gave Allison a full recap of the events of the last twenty-four hours and how nothing that happened was Ashton's fault. He even went on to explain if he didn't do what he did, all of them would be dead, including the kids. Alison's mouth was wide open as she listened. She couldn't believe her ears. Artificials? And now there was another kid with them? Alison leaned into the new kid and asked, "What's your name, Sweetie?" The little boy smiled and answered, "Bryson Hess. Your brother saved us and then pushed that guy in the nose. He let me hold a gun, too." Bryson was pointing to another man she didn't recognize. "Fucking kids never know when to shut up," Ashton said. He looked like he was trying to say his comments under his breath, but he failed horribly. "Oh my sir, we need to get you fixed up. That's a broken nose," Alison said to the man. Kian took his opportunity, "That's right. I want to file charges, Chief. He assaulted me," Kian. "If you say another word, I will punch you in the nose and turn in my badge," Hunter said to Ashton's amusement. "Chief," Hunter pleaded, "This guy," Hunter honestly didn't know what to say.

While ignoring Hunter's last comment, Aiden politely said, "Ma'am," before Aiden could finish his sentence, everyone must have recognized Police Chief Aiden Jahmar was in the hospital because twenty-plus people, staff, and patients bombarded him with questions. "What can you tell us? Will the power be back on anytime soon? What the hell is going on, Chief?" Allison's eyes went wide. "Chief, are you okay? Your uniform is," her words trailed off, and she went silent. Aiden glanced down at his uniform, which was covered in blood. "There was an incident," he said with the politest tone before reassuring everyone that the blood wasn't his. Then, he looked toward Alison and said, "Ma'am, we need you to come outside." "What did my brother do now?" Aiden jerked his chin toward the exit. "You can ask him yourself." Alison grabbed Paige's hand and led her through the lobby and outside into the parking lot. Alison was tired of always having to deal with her brother's problems and clean up his messes. Even though this time wasn't his fault, she was still angry with him. He was a damn good brother, but Ashton was a magnet for perilous trouble.

Alison wasn't sure what to think, but she was relieved to see her brother was not in handcuffs. Instead, Erynn was in full battle gear. Even while exhausted in the middle of the apocalypse, Erynn was still gorgeous.

"Sis! Are you going to cut me some slack? Alison didn't answer. He jumped onto the pavement and walked over. Alison hoped she looked as furious as she felt. "Sorry for the trouble, ma'am, but I need both your brother and Erynn, or more people will die." Alison regarded Aiden with a scowl. "Help? Are you sure you aren't taking him off to jail again? Maybe he deserves it." Aiden looked around, seemingly checking to see who else was in earshot, and stepped closer to Alison to whisper, "Rory Cooper is dead, ma'am. Someone murdered him sometime this morning or last night. I think it's the same person that killed

Jared, which means we are looking at a serial killer. I trust you with this information because you are Ashton's sister. Plus, now that the lights are off, it will be good to have a nurse on our side if we need one. We might need some quick patchwork if things continue to get as bad as they have been. I need your brother and Erynn to help me find this killer." Alison wasn't ready to be friendly or forgiving. "Don't let him get you shot," she said. Aiden nodded as if this was good advice.

"Yes, ma'am. Is there someone else who can watch your daughter, the other kid, while you're at work? If not, my wife could." "That won't be necessary," Alison said. "I'd rather keep her with me. People will be looking for you at the rate you are going. However, you may want to let your wife know to be ready, just in case things worsen." Aiden nodded, smiled warmly at Paige, and said, "Good advice again, ma'am. She will be ready for anything that comes her way." As far as he could tell, Aiden politely turned away and then returned to probably the only two working vehicles in the world. He gestured for Ernest, Ashton, and Erynn to join him. "Good to see you again, Ms. Jace." "Don't let my fool of a brother get anyone shot." "From what I hear, ma'am, he has saved more lives in the last twenty-four than everyone in Wakefield combined," Aiden said defiantly. Allison didn't like it, but she heard him.

Ashton said. "I swear, I didn't do anything wrong this time." "You never do anything wrong, Ashton," Alison sighed. "You never take responsibility for anything either. What if those men had hurt Paige or Erynn?" Ashton stuck his hands in his pockets, his confidence left him, and his eyes flitted to the ground. He wore the same wounded look that Alison remembered from their childhood after their dad would yell at him. She hated seeing her brother hurt and knew she was the only person left alive that could make him react like this. Her heart hurt at the sight, but her brother would have to grow up sooner than later. Her brother had also saved Paige's life more than once today. "I'm being an asshole, aren't I?" "Just a little bit." Derrick said. He didn't have Aiden's smooth charm, so his words hit like a blunted object.

She joined the men at the trucks as Aiden gave them orders. "Ernest is in the mountains trying to get the ham radio working. There was an old truck the department had. I let him use it. Let's hope he returns with information we could use," Aiden told everyone. The Chief Borrowed Ashton's Dodge. Although it had a few bullet holes, Derrick still had his truck working. And Erynn and Ashton had the Humvee they acquired earlier that day. Ashton, is there anything you need to investigate Rory's crime scene? "I just need Erynn and a ride up to Cherry Hill. I think me and Erynn should go on foot, so we don't miss anything. We will try to pick up the trail at Rory Cooper's place." "I'll send an officer with you," Aiden said. Ashton nodded his head and looked at Alison. "Let me get Hunter, Chief. We killed many enemies, and he works well with Erynn and me." "Jump on it, Hunter," Aiden ordered. "Yes, sir," Hunter responded.

"Let's move out, everyone," Aiden commanded. Ashton hesitated and then put his arms around Paige. "I'm sorry, Paige. And give me a hi-five, Ankle Biter," instantly put a warm smile on Paige's face. Alison knew her brother always was the charmer because he could get out of anything he got himself into, which irritated her. He pulled away from Paige and reached out for Alison. The knuckles of his hand looked even more swollen, and a bruise was coming up on his cheek. Her heart filled with compassion for Ashton, remembering all the times she had to heal her brother from all the unfair beatings he would take as a kid. Their dad had thrown a lot of punches in that house. All of them were always aimed at Ashton. She honestly didn't know how he had ever survived it all. She instantly regretted how he treated him. "I'm so sorry," Ashton said again, turning to Alison. "Seriously. I'm sorry, Sis. I promise I'm going to change. I'll be a better man. I am trying, but no one believes me. It's not like I asked for any of this. I know what you all think of me, but only part is true." Alison wrapped her arms around her big brother, and her heart broke, and tears poured down her cheeks. "You're still the best man I have ever met. Don't die on me, please?"

Chapter Sixteen

Over a thousand people packed into the high school gymnasium waiting for Police Chief Aiden Jahmar to tell them everything that was going on and lay out his plan for the future. The walk to the gymnasium was cold, but the hundreds of conversations shortened the distance. The gymnasium was cold and dark; it was also thirty a.m. But desperate times they caused for desperate measure. Mayor Julia Harris and her staff demanded a town hall meeting, and Aiden agreed. The town had to be said something. It wasn't like people were in their houses sleeping. It seemed the whole town of Wakefield was outside looking for answers, so the logical thing to do was to have a town meeting as fast as possible.

The stars wrapped around the sky in a way Aiden had never seen before. The stars were nearly a hundred times more visible with the power out. Aiden almost forgot how many stars were in the sky because there were so many he could see. The moon almost seemed like a guest against billions of stars. The universe was such a beautiful place. It hurt when Aiden's mind snapped back to his current reality. The universe was beautiful, but humanity sure did know how to make it an ugly place.

Aiden looked over the crowd and wondered if the killer was in attendance. Was the killer that brave? Aiden also noticed people of all ages and health ranges packed into the gymnasium. It was the first time Aiden realized how bad their medical situation was. Everyone from infants to the elderly was packed into the gymnasium. Aiden couldn't help but wonder how these infants were getting their milk warmed at night. Even the mother's breastfeeding would be hampered by the power going out. It broke Aiden's heart to think how many babies across Salleria would die due to lack of nutrition because the electric grid wouldn't let their parents warm up the milk.

Another thing that bothered Aiden was the extra ten to fifteen thousand tourists in his part of Wakefield. If the power grid weren't restored, these tourists would become permanent fixtures of Wakefield. Was the killer a tourist? Aiden looked at everyone. He wanted to see if he could spot the killer. Were they in the crowd taunting or toying with him and trying to get his attention, and Aiden was missing it? Aiden could see the killer wearing a t-shirt that gave himself away. The shirt would say, *Hey, Chief. I Did It.* That would be something. Aiden learned from his friend Brayden a few hours ago that that was the kind of move the killer would make.

Aiden noticed something else while he was searching the faces of the audience. Everyone wore the same face of panic. Aiden knew what he said next would need to reassure everyone enough to prevent them from panicking, but he couldn't bring himself to lie to their faces, either. Aiden didn't want to tell the restless crowd everything was okay. It wasn't. It was far from okay, and Aiden didn't know when any hope of "okay" would ever show its face again.

A heavy burden began to weigh on Aiden. His role as Police Chief was a rewarding one, but right now, it felt like a punishment. The Mayor wanted Aiden to tell thousands of people who just wanted to be safe that they were not felt cruel. His heart began to ache as he walked toward the platform to face the crowd. It felt like the longest walk of his life; it was his most important. The short journey of no more than ten feet from his seat to the podium would incite a riot and panic, slowly killing thousands of people. Or, if he were lucky, he would inspire a few to turn the potential mob into teammates. Unfortunately, the odds were not on Aiden's side.

Sergeant Ewan Hawkins and a few others from Aiden's department were on the platform and Mayor Harris' entire staff. Aiden wasn't sure if it was a show of solidarity or a political display of power. For Aiden's sanity, he ensured Dawn and Lillian were on the platform. If he were seconds away from pushing the Mayor's staff in their noses, he planned to look at his family and remind himself why he was fighting the good fight. Instead, Aiden smiled at his wife and daughter, then nodded at the Mayor. The Mayor was convinced whatever needed to be said today should come from Aiden. Aiden was sure it was a setup, a chance for him to fail so the Mayor could correct him. It didn't matter. The time for worrying about the Mayor's motives had long passed.

Everyone grew quiet as Aiden approached the podium, waiting eagerly for what Aiden had to say. There was no microphone, so Aiden needed everyone quiet enough to hear me, but not this quiet. This type of silence was unnerving. The mixture of justified curiosity assumed chaos, and at length, a touchable breathless silence roared throughout the gymnasium. There wasn't a cough or a sniffle. Instead, Aiden could hear the wind howling outside the gym's open doors. Aiden understood he needed to be truthful, but he also understood he needed to give the most incredible speech of his life. The people needed to be inspired and informed. But how was he going to walk that line?

Gripping both sides of the podium, Aiden cleared his throat and began.

"The United Cities of Salleria is at war."

Aiden said these first words with blatant disregard for the plan the Mayor wanted him to follow. He was supposed to lullaby everyone into a fake sense of calm. But Aiden had other plans. He used his commanding voice and charisma to incite a minor panic and did it on purpose. And it worked. Thousands of unchecked whispers rattled the gymnasium. People were protesting, and everyone was hurling questions and curse words at Aiden. But it was okay. Aiden was expecting this type of outrage, which was all part of his plan.

Aiden needed their animal instincts to come out to have the speech he wanted. Instead, the audience came here to give a different one. Aiden was under no illusions. These people didn't want to be calm and helpful. They wanted answers and someone to blame for not giving them the answers they wanted to hear. Beginning with the hardest thing to say at the beginning of his speech was what he needed to get the hard part out of the way.

Aiden figured if he started this way, the worst would be out of the way, and his speech could only go up. Aiden could feel the angry eyes of the Mayor burning into the back of his head. Aiden didn't mind; he wasn't finished saying things that would make the crowd angry. Aiden had one more line to say that was worse than the one he'd just said. It was all or nothing now. Aiden went for it. He said his following line with such disregard for peace he lost the crowd.

"And all of us will starve to death, die from radiation poison, or get killed by the

North Kangavarian's troops, who are on Sallerian soil, if we do not work

together."

The crowd erupted into an inaudible roar. Aiden couldn't hear anything because everything was being said all at once. Aiden finished the first two sentences of his speech to the immediate disapproval of Mayor Harris and all of her staff. It felt like everyone was cursing him, even the Mayor's staff. Aiden thought he saw some of these officers reach for their holsters.

Aiden's plan had worked perfectly. Everyone was in a panic and asking questions Aiden couldn't answer. That's what they came here for, anyway. Aiden saw what Facebook did to the world. He saw how it gave everyone a platform to say something, and everyone chose to be negative. Aiden didn't expect anyone to behave any differently. The darkness and the number of people in the crowd allowed people to hide the same way they hid behind their keyboards.

The crowd was on the verge of uproar. No, the crowd was in an uproar. Mayor Harris protested loudly, and Aiden could hear the *"Hem, hem"* sounds she made with her throat. It also became clear that she wanted to remove him from the podium when she rose to her feet and looked as if she intended to speak. Nevertheless, Aiden never once rattled, ignoring the interruptions of Major Harris and her staff.

448

Aiden held his hand, signaling the crowd to calm down, so he could finish. However, he only made one hand movement and kept it in the air until the breathless silence returned. When everyone returned to their panicked silence, Aiden began his real speech.

"It is true what many of you have heard. A nuclear EMP attacked us, and the entire nation is dark. All of the North Sallerian Continent is without power, and it is the North Kangavarians who are responsible. As of an hour ago, I have accurate reports that ground troops armed with technology we have never seen before are on their way to us. I have seen this technology with my own eyes. The enemy has invented a new type of soldier.

Aiden could hear people grumble and whisper about a new type of soldier. They didn't know what that meant, but he didn't have time to explain. They would see the Artificials soon enough. Once again, he raised his hand until the moody silence returned. Aiden began talking again.

We are also in danger of nuclear fallout. The United Cities of Salleria is engaged in a war, and no one is coming to save Wakefield but us. Washington, D.C., was hit by a fourth nuclear attack, and from my understanding, D.C. has been destroyed. There have been no reports of survivors, and the radiation left behind in D.C. has left it uninhabitable for years. We are lucky!

We did not get this directly with a nuclear bomb, but it is believed nuclear fallout could head our way. Everything I have said so far is all that I know. I have told you everything, and now, as a favor to me, I ask all of you to work with us to secure our city— and our homes. We will need to work together to conserve our resources and save families. About thirty hours ago, North Kangavarians launched a series of nuclear weapons in the skies above the United Cities, triggering an electromagnetic pulse that knocked out our power grid and crippled our electronic devices."

Aiden could feel Julia glaring at him, and he didn't blame her. He wasn't following the narrative they had discussed just a few minutes ago, but part of being a leader was knowing when to improvise.

"Many of you remember the 2016 tornadoes. Unfortunately, this is much, much worse. Wakefield is a small but proud community. We will be one of the last cities in Wakefield to receive aid if help is available. You deserve to know what we face in the coming days, weeks, and months."

Everyone began to panic again, but Aiden stopped them.

"I know you are afraid. But I am telling you the truth because Major Harris and I will need your help to save our city. So if you are wondering how I feel or what plans I have made, I will tell you now.

Aiden paused for a long time. He wanted everyone's attention.

Honestly, I stand here before you now, truly unafraid! Why?! Because I have information, you do not? No! You now know the same thing that I know. Am I not afraid because I am trained to handle such situations, and you are not? Again, no! I stand here without fear because I remember. I remember that in 2016 when a series of the strongest tornadoes in recorded history nearly wiped our small town off the face of the map, we pulled together, saved our town, and defended our town with our lives.

I remember that none of us knew what we would do, but we came together, fed one another, and made Wakefield better than ever.

I remember!

I remember how we made sure there was no stoned left unturned and that no one went without.

I remember!

I remember how our Mayor, the longest-sitting Mayor Wakefield has ever had, led our city through the darkest times. I remember how as a woman, she showed more bravery than any man sent here to help us.

I remember!

I remember that for one hundred days, we went without power, and no one in our town missed a single meal.

I remember!"

As Aiden said that last, *I remember* someone shouted in admiration as if the Chief was giving a sermon. Then someone else began to shout in praise and admiration, as well. Soon there were hundreds of people chanted, *I remember.*

The energy in the gymnasium quickly shifted from panic to praise! Tourists who had no idea about the 2016 Tornadoes Aiden was talking about were moved to tears as they watched Aiden rally everyone, into inspiration. Tears began to swell in Mayor Harris's eyes, too. Then, to Aiden's surprise, the Mayor began to clap along with the already cheering crowd.

Aiden looked like a war chief giving his troops his final speech before his final battle. And maybe he was.

"I remember!

I remember how we fought together during those hot summer nights and ensured no one suffered alone. I remember nature did its very best to destroy us. Yet, I remember six years after the worse year in all of our lives that which matters most!"

"We are still here!"

Everyone broke into both cheers and tears. Aiden could see hospital staff shouting and clapping vigorously. Mayor Harris was standing on her feet with tears running down her cheeks. She looked grateful she let Aiden talk. The gymnasium was filled with blissful pandemonium. There was not an uninspired soul in the place, and suddenly, for the first time in almost two days, everyone felt like things would return to normal.

Aiden gestured for Mayor Harris to approach the center stage, finish the talk, and give out any special instructions she desired. He wanted to ensure he worked well with the Mayor during this time. Wakefield didn't need any additional problems. It already had enough.

As the Mayor began to speak, she said, "Our isolation isn't bad. We have plenty of clean water up here, and we can hunt, fish, and forage when our food supplies run out." The Mayor even told everyone how Aiden had already worked out a plan for food storage and to evacuate to shelters if needed.

As the Mayor kept talking, Aiden became lost in his thoughts. He wondered about his duty to save all of these cheering people. A speech would not save them— a plan and fortifying Wakefield was. Aiden knew he needed to perfect his plan and get as much food stored up in a secure place as fast as possible. He wanted to ensure everyone had enough to eat, but to do that, he knew he would have to ask everyone to chip in and donate what they had. It would be no small task to ask everyone to give up their goods to one central location when all they could see was the world's end. Aiden must have been thinking for a long time, or the Mayor didn't talk as long as she thought she would because before he knew it, she was gesturing for him to close the town meeting.

The crowd was now paying attention to him again. Aiden began, "We will need everyone's help, and all of us will have to make a few sacrifices." Bradley Holloway, a volunteer firefighter, stepped forward from the crowd. "I've got your back, Chief! Whatever you need me to do, whatever you need me to give, I am with you," he shouted. Within seconds, half of the gymnasium was offering their help and support. Even Colten Browning, the MSGA soldier Aiden had disarmed the night before, was pumping his fist in the air and bellowing *Hooah!* Hooah is an Army expression used for spirit and morale, generally meant to say anything and everything but "no." Aiden couldn't help but smile at that. Aiden was also glad he gave Browning back his gun and didn't humiliate him as much as he wanted. Unfortunately, he could not use Browning in the guaranteed fight against North Kangavar.

Ewan began clapping, and others soon joined. While Aiden was enjoying his smiling moment, a sea of bodies parted to make way for two men rushing to the platform. "Chief," Derrick said, gasping for air. He had Ernest next to him. "Chief, we need to talk to you right now." Aiden could tell something was wrong because Derrick was always the most composed officer and never demanded anything from Aiden. Aiden brought the Mayor back up to the podium and whispered in her ear that he would tell her first as soon as he saw what Derrick and Ernest wanted to tell him. The Mayor smiled and began talking to the crowd again.

"What is it?" Aiden asked, keeping his voice low. "I made contact with a Staff Sergeant out of Hasly Mountain," Ernest explained. "He said there's nuclear fallout and a ton of radiation coming in with that storm. We have to get everyone to the shelter; it will be days before they can leave. He even suggested when we could leave the shelter. But, unfortunately, the radiation may still be too high to survive." Aiden's heart hammered as he glanced back over the crowd. "How long do we have?" he asked. Ernest shook his head. "Two hours, max." "Shit," Aiden responded.

Aiden waved Mayor Harris over and relayed the news. "We have a shelter here at the high school, another at the hospital, and the third back at town hall," she said. "But what about people in the rural areas?" "Derrick, go get the bullhorn from the station and take your truck out to notify people they need to get indoors. They need to treat this as life and death, seal off their windows with plastic sheets, and get all their livestock indoors. Make sure they cover their water wells, too. Then, tell them to stay inside for at least three days and get on any ham radios they have to get further information. Derrick nodded. "I'm on it."

Aiden stepped back up to the podium. "Everyone, listen to what I say next very carefully." He felt the stares of a thousand people. "There's a major storm heading our way, which will contain deadly nuclear fallout. I say again. The storm will be deadly, and we have around ninety minutes to get to safety." Aiden said. Then he explained the basic steps to secure their homes for the people who wanted to return to their families. Everyone else would take shelter in the well-stocked basement of the high school. People began moving immediately, and he stepped away from the podium to give orders to his officers. Afterward, he told all the officers what to do and suggested that the Mayor head back to City Hall and seek shelter. Dawn and Lillian rushed to him, and Aiden reached for their hands.

As Aiden was getting ready to protect his family and ensure the town members were safe, he heard a voice. "Chief Aiden," said Ernest. "What about Ashton, Erynn, and your officer you sent with them?" "What about them?" Aiden cursed when he remembered that he had sent Ashton to Cherry Hill. They left all three of them on the mountain without a vehicle, and now they were all likely deep in the woods and out of range of the bullhorn. Aiden knew Ashton and Erynn were highly resourceful, and I am sure they would do whatever it took to keep Hunter alive. But they were all alone and had no idea that poisonous rain and snow would kill them all three an hour from now.

It was about ninety minutes after Ashton, Erynn, and Hunter left the Chief. Ashton looked down at his analog watch and saw it said two-thirty a.m. MST. They were hunting for a killer. Erynn had put every other concern out of her mind. Erynn was leading the way, and she moved like a panther stalking its prey. Erynn admired the view of the snow-capped Wakefield Mountains, but there was a dark mass in the sky with violent lighting exploding from within, completely messing up his view.

"This storm is enormous," Ashton said. "Ghost, I'd swear I saw green lightning more than once coming from inside it," Hunter responded. Ashton looks to Erynn. She was writing something in the snow. Ashton and Hunter walked to get closer to her. Erynn had written, FALLOUT in the snow. "Fuck" Ashton said. "Okay, Hunter. Rule number one. Erynn always knows what she is talking about," Ashton relayed to Hunter. Erynn grinned. It was true; she was always right. "Yeah, yeah, yeah, Erynn," Ashton mocked. He knew her well enough to know she agreed that she knew everything. Erynn always had great intuition, and since she hadn't talked in ten years, she had much more time to pay attention to others and her surroundings better than most people.

"If that is fallout, it is inside the biggest storm system I've ever seen," Hunter said. "Then I guess we better get a move on it." Aiden looked down at the valley. She could see Wakefield looked to be directly in its path. Everyone was about to be cold and wet, she thought to herself. Oh well, they can handle it.

With Ashton and Hunter walking in stride with Erynn, Ashton muttered, "Great." His socks were wet, and he hated wet socks. They were about to get wetter and radiated with this colossal storm system. "Just great! Now, we have to find this guy in a monsoon." Ashton was in a foul mood, and Erynn couldn't blame him. They needed a long nap.

It was already cold, and the temperature was dropping by the second. "Erynn, we may want to be prepared to suffer more than we expected. That storm looks like it could be snow or rain. It's pretty cold out here," Aiden said while pulling out the laminated map Aiden had given him. Erynn remembered Jared was last seen getting off his bus near this area before he vanished, and Rory Cooper's place wasn't far. She was starting to think the killer had a base camp around here somewhere, but there were too many possibilities. Erynn hated when there were too many possibilities. Too many possibilities were worse than procrastination. She preferred to eliminate all the possibilities and go in one direction in one-hundred percent *Ghost* mode. That's what Erynn called it when Ashton became so focused on something that he couldn't see anything else. When he was like that, he was a dangerous man. Ashton didn't like being stopped and was the bravest person Erynn had ever seen.

For all Erynn knew, the killer could be watching them now, squatting in someone's summer vacation home, or walking them right into an ambush. Erynn knew the killers were clever and thought of every single scenario. She also thought there were more than two killers, as well. Erynn didn't like the idea of being outsmarted or hunted, but she knew they were not the superior mind in this hunt.

Ashton and Erynn were ten steps behind the killer. And the worse part about all of it, the part Erynn hated the most, is that the killer seemed to know how to cover their tracks and plant fake tracks they would follow. Erynn couldn't help but think whoever they were following was a highly trained killer and an expert tracker. But that wasn't a long list of people. Everyone left traces of where they had been unless— Erynn put that thought out of her mind. That was crazy and nearly impossible. The odds of what she thought to be true were less than one in a billion.

So far, Erynn still needed to come up with something. No sign of any vehicles or a camp. No sign of any recent activity either. Without any other clues, she was at a loss. But she knew they had to go back to Aiden with something. The storm was approaching them fast, and they ran out of time. Her mind was racing. She had to figure out their next move, but would it be enough to keep all three of them safe?

Thunder boomed in the distance, and lightning flashed and danced within the black fortress of clouds. As they rolled over the mountains, a yellow mist seemed to lead the clouds. Erynn thought the yellow cloud looked like the dust storms in Bakghanistan. Erynn stopped and gave the hand single for everyone else to stop. She could swear she heard something like a bullhorn squawking in the distance. Bending over, Erynn wrote in the snow, BULLHORN.

"Yeah, I think I hear something, too," Hunter offered first. "Me, too," Ashton said. "But I can't make out what is being said." The noise continued for another minute, but it was so faint neither of the three could make out any of the words. "That's strange. Who would be using a bullhorn out here, in the mountains," Ashton asked. Erynn had a troubled look as she kept looking at the storm. She didn't say anything for a long while. Then, without saying a word, Erynn took off in a paced jog, and the others followed.

The crew ran for nearly twenty minutes, keeping low and quiet along the side of the road. Erynn never stopped looking for the killer, and she kept looking for potential ambush spots. But she knew it was time to get to safety, and she had a plan. First, they should be able to hold up at Rory's house. It wasn't the best plan, but it was the closest four doors and a wall she could think of entering without getting shot at. Erynn also knew they needed to search for clues at Rory's house before the storm washed everything away or covered it with snow.

The distant clap of thunder and the black void of storm clouds followed them as they ran down the road leading to Rory's house. With their weapons at the ready, all three team members crouched by the fence and scanned the area. Nothing. There was no movement besides some small wildlife. Finally, Erynn gave a hand signal that said she was taking point and ran towards the house. Ashton shouldered his HK416, suppressor attached, and ran across the front yard. When Erynn got to the porch, she slowly turned the knob of the door and breached the cabin. Hunter followed behind her, with Ashton taking the rear. The cabin was clear.

Erynn hurried back outside, checking the sky. Sheets of rain were coming down on the mountains now. Erynn started to point to the windows and doors and looked through Rory's dressers to find the duct tape. As soon as she found a roll, she tossed it to Hunter. He got the idea. Erynn wanted all of them to seal the cabin with duct tape. Radiation was coming. Erynn wasn't ready for the killers right now. They didn't want to get radiation poison either.

It turns out staying in the cabin wasn't a bad idea. Rory had everything they needed, much more. While Rory was sealing the cabin, Erynn called for Ashton to investigate. Unfortunately, they only had a short time and had to make every moment count. Erynn and Ashton split up to cover more ground quickly. There had to be something left behind.

After a few minutes of searching, Erynn whistled to get Ashton's attention. She found something that nearly stopped her heart. There was something on the ground where she was standing, and Ashton needed to see it ASAP. She couldn't believe what she saw, and it had to be the last thing she expected. Truthfully, she had let it cross her mind earlier, but she thought it just couldn't be true. Erynn picked up a square piece of paper, grimy at the edges. It was hidden by the barrels and other debris Rory had in his backyard. The clue was easy to miss. You couldn't have found it if you didn't know about the legends.

Her eyes widened, and her face went pale with shock. She got Ashton's attention. She handed him the paper. On it was a drawing of a large wolf that looked more like a man. It had blood-red eyes and fangs sticking out its mouth. Ashton dropped the paper in disbelief. "Erynn, whoever we are looking for isn't just a killer. They are *Rougarou.* It was the very last thing Erynn wanted to hear. Ashton and Erynn left that life behind years ago, and now it had followed them to Wakefield. "Fuck," Ashton said. So, now we are facing killers with superhuman strength, faster than normal people, and fucking shapeshifters." Ashton said. Erynn looked at him, shaking her head. Ashton understood. Erynn and Ashton would be chasing people as strong as them. Erynn hoped it wouldn't be anyone from their past. If that were the case, making it out of this situation would be impossible. There weren't too many people alive who could defeat Erynn or Ashton. But there were a few people from their past, from Clemenceau, from The Order of the Broken Leaf, who had a fighting chance.

Connor was supposed to be back in his office at 758 Fillmore Street. Instead, he'd taken Kayla back to her car, which, non-surprisingly, was unharmed. There weren't any people driving the highways and the busy streets. Connor made sure to follow Kayla all the way home. He wanted to ensure she was safe and walked her to the door of her house, then he left. But Connor didn't go home; he couldn't. Something didn't feel right.

He was feeling partially relieved, better anyway. He found Kayla, and the team helped save her before she met a gruesome death. There were about two dozen of The Master's Rougarou on the way to the morgue and another couple dozen on the way to the Wakefield prison. But, The Master Mind and the two men who kidnapped Kayla were not present. After the raid, Brentley, Connor, and more than enough of Chief Aiden's officers searched the grounds from top to bottom, but no one else was found. As far as Connor could tell, everyone they arrested or killed was just low-level henchmen.

Connor now had two radios on him, one for Jacob and one for Brentley. Brentley's radio kept details coming in, but Connor feared most of what they wanted to know would never be discovered. That was the single most fundamental truth about police work, and you would never see it on TV or read it in the books. Most of the time, cases were never solved to the investigator's satisfaction.

But something was still bothering Connor. Why kidnap Kayla and put her last on the list to kill? Connor had a gut feeling The Master was never at the farmhouse and had no intentions of coming, which made things make even less sense. So why? Why go through all the effort? Why spare the most crucial victim they had? Did The Master order Jacob and his partner not to kill Kayla? Or was it something different? If so, what was it? Connor hated not knowing, but he couldn't shake the feeling that if he drove away, Kayla would not make it alive in the morning.

Instead of leaving, Connor asked Kayla if he could borrow her keys, pretend that he left, and then sneak back in on the backside of the property. He was sure he could do all of this without being seen, but he was sure Kayla was their next target, and kidnapping was not on the agenda.

Connor had a powerful gut feeling that one of the Killers was targeting Kayla, and the top Generals of The Master's Rougarou army would show up at any time.

Connor was read in a book by Mark Henwick, "My paranoia wasn't always right, but just to be on the safe side, I never went to sleep with a clown in the room." Connor could relate right now. He was probably paranoid, but he wasn't going to invite the enemy into Kayla's house to prove him wrong.

Connor wasn't sure about a few things involving the case, so he whispered a few thoughts he had brewing to Kayla. "Here's what I've been thinking." Connor said to Kayla. "I think you are overreacting a bit, but considering I followed my instincts and was kidnapped and almost murdered, let's put my thoughts to the side for now. I'm listening." Kayla said conversationally. Connor couldn't imagine what she was going through and didn't give her any time to process or deal with what had happened to her. But there was simply no time. He was convinced someone was coming to kill Kayla.

"Okay," Connor said to Kayla. He didn't bother easing her into the conversation. Instead, he began laying it all out. "We have multiple killers. Sometimes they work alone, and sometimes they work with a team." "This matches with the evidence so far," Kayla responded. "Exactly, and that is the problem. Killers don't normally have multiple ways of working. So, we either have a group of multiple killers, or we have a leader that can become all things when he desires," Connor put out there for pushback. "I'm not sure I understand exactly where you are going, Connor," Kayla said. "Look at it this way," Connor added. "Killers find a way to be successful and stick to that way. When the steaks are high, most humans perfect a certain method to reduce their chances of getting caught. So far," Connor paused here because he had a bad habit of going too fast when he was excited, "But our killers are working with a team, and they are working without a team. To add to that, when one of our killers, and I believe this one to be Jacob," Connor explained to Kayla about the radio call he got from Jacob on the way to get her. "When Jacob does his performance kills, he always seems to do it for The Master." "Okay, I get it," Kayla interrupted Connor. "You think there are only two people actually in charge. The one called The Master and the one called Jacob." "Exactly." "Okay, so if I am hearing you correctly, The Master gives orders, but so does Jacob." "Right." "Got it. But I don't see what your problem is right now. That doesn't give me a reason to think I am in danger," Kayla said.

"Your confusion is exactly my point, as well," Connor said to Kayla. I haven't figured out this part, but I have a theory. "So we are both confused at the same part of the evidence, which means we are both missing something, or there is nothing to be missed," Kayla said. Before Connor could jump back into the conversation, something in Kayla's mind must have snapped into place because her face twisted into an expression of joy and triumph. "I think I just grabbed hold of something important," Kayla said to Connor.

"Hear me out just for a second," Kayla paused. Her eyes rolled, and she looked at her brain; then Kayla shared something she was piecing together. Connor could tell she had just figured out what had bothered him so much. "Up until now, Connor. Their pattern was smoothed, and anything they executed was well thought out." "That's right," Connor added to the conversation. "Even my kidnapping was well thought out. It was genius how they were following me," When Kayla said, following me, her eyes met Connor's. "Now you see what I am seeing," Connor said. "Tell me what you have," Connor said quickly, trying not to interrupt her thoughts.

"My kidnapping was perfect. It was as perfect as anything the killers had ever done, but when they took me to the farmhouse. There was no plan. It was just forty-something people waiting around as if they were waiting on instructions." "Exactamundo," Conner nearly burst into a scream. Connor took over the conversation now that Kayla had figured it out. "Since your kidnapping was perfect, you were being followed. I think the killers have been following me, you, and Brentley for a long time. That is why your kidnapping was so smooth. But at the farmhouse, they couldn't contact The Master, so they didn't kill you immediately. The Master hadn't permitted them to kill you. So if I were them," Kayla interrupted Connor's sentence and finished it for him. "I would let me leave the farmhouse, follow me back home and wait until The Master permitted to kill me," Kayla said. She finally figured out what was bothering Connor, and it all made sense. The killers had watched them both come into Kayla's house, and just like they did Connor, they followed him until they knew where he lived.

Kayla's mind clicked to something as she was reaching for her sidearm. "Connor, if they are on the way to kill me, they are also on the way to kill your family." From the look on Connor's face, Kayla figured he thought about that possibility as well. But Connor was calm and unbothered by the thought. "After I killed the Wolf," "And that was some next-level shit there," Kayla said to Connor. "Yeah, I owe Papa Anthony a lot for that one. He did the spooky psychic shit that he does," Connor said.

Kayla must have looked puzzled because Connor told her he would tell her about it after they caught whoever was about to break into her house. Kayla noticed something odd about Papa Anthony when she and Connor were talking. He seemed to have a prophetic gift; he knew what to do before anyone else did. Kayla knew it was a rare gift. "Isn't that called clairvoyancy," Kayla asked Connor. "It is," Connor responded. "With your Quantum Physics background, is that hard for you to accept," Kayla asked Connor. She wanted to know. She felt a bit guilty for asking because she was sure that question was coming from the *girlfriend* side of her and not the detective. "As a Quantum Physicist, no. I have no problem with clairvoyancy. I could explain his "prophetic gift," as you called it, by understanding the Quantum Entanglement. Quantum Entanglement occurs when two particles are inextricably linked together no matter their separation. Although these entangled particles are not physically connected, they still can share information instantaneously— *seemingly breaking one of the most hard-and-fast rules of physics: No information can be transmitted faster than the speed of light,*" Connor explained to Kayla. Since all of us came from the stars and connected in the big bang, we are all still connected. Therefore, it would be no problem to accept that some of us humans have allowed in your conscious observation of this life to remain connected to the whole of *energy* more than others."

Connor paused, making sure Kayla understood what he said. She understood most of it but told herself she would let Connor teach her later if he played his cards right. Connor concluded. "It's the FBI Agent in me that hates every part of what Papa Anthony does. As you know, all investigators hate things we can't explain, especially gut feelings. But here I am, trapping you in your house, because of my gut feelings. I guess me and Papa Anthony aren't so different, after all."

Kayla didn't say anything; she laughed a bit but told herself she would return to this conversation a few days from now, after all of this murder, murder, kill, kill stuff was over.

After a bit more conversation, Kayla discovered Connor had been thinking about his theory that Kayla was being followed before he left the farmhouse and had Brentley send some agents to Connor's house as protection until he returned home. It was a smart move, and Kayla was glad Connor came to protect her, even though she didn't need it. She was fully capable of protecting herself, but nothing wrong with a man doing it for her.

For a moment, Kayla wondered what her old-school black family would think when she brought a white man home for the holidays. Damn, it was going to be some fun holidays, if they lived to see the

Kayla wanted to tell Connor to calm down, which was all just a theory, but whenever she considered pushing him away, she had her gut feelings. Kayla thought long and hard about why she wanted to push Connor away. Was it because she could take care of herself? Or was it something closer to she had been running from love all of her life for reasons she didn't even know herself? When she met Connor, she felt this unexplainable pull; or maybe it was an irritating pull. It was probably both.

Kayla asked her to take the first shift and let her get about fifteen minutes of sleep. Fifteen minutes turned into two hours, but she never worried about her safety. Kayla knew Connor was her protector. That was two hats she had given him now. The first was *teacher* and the second was *protector*. Both titles she would never give to anyone, but Connor was earning them freely. Part of her hated the power he had over her. Part of her prayed he would break her trust.

Kayla was tired of taking care of herself and taking care of men. A big part of her felt a great shame. Black women didn't need a white savior. Kayla loved all people and didn't have a single problem with interracial dating, but, and this was a big but, the white savior trope was killing the black community, and Kayla knew it.

You can see it in books and movies. *Why do so many stories about racism revolve around the White Savior?* The thought made her want to throw up in her mouth. Black people didn't need white people to save their lives. So, the more she thought about giving Connor the titles of "protector" and "teacher," the more Kayla felt like she needed to ensure she was doing the right thing and not being programmed by White Supremacy.

White saviors often speak passionately about their desire to *"do the right thing."* Yet their actions usually involve little input from the people they're attempting to help. Their intentions may be noble— many white saviors believe their actions challenge the white supremacy and racism so profoundly threaded into Sallerian society. But, in reality, White Saviorism tends to emphasize inequality because it continues to center the actions of white people while ignoring, or even invalidating, the experiences of those they claim to help.

Kayla was so conflicted with Connor. Her open-mindedness saw a beautiful and caring man who deserved everything coming to him for treating a woman well. But it also echoed the idea that the white savior echoes imperialist and colonialist beliefs by putting white people in the role of guiding responsibility figures. White colonialists considered people of color "primitive," ignorant, or childlike. White savior syndrome reinforces these false beliefs, implying that people of color need strong, capable white leaders and educators to create change — guides who light the way and rescue them from their helplessness.

Kayla understood that White people who perpetuate white saviorism tended to show support for marginalized groups outwardly but did not exhibit any real support, substance, or action behind their displays. But Connor wasn't doing that. Instead, Connor was putting his life on the line to ensure he was okay— even though he didn't need to.

The white savior problem was so challenging to move around that it was not affecting her desire for this beautiful man who had done nothing to exhibit any of these toxic traits.

Before Kayla could go any deeper into her subconscious dream state, she was relieved to be awakened by the pressure of a killer coming after her. It was far better than falling for a white man as a black woman, conscious woman in Salleria. In her mind's eye, she laughed at herself. It was easier to be killed than to navigate racism in Salleria. *Sheesh.*

"Kayla, Kayla, are you awake?" Connor said to Kayla in a low voice. It took a few seconds, but Kayla finally snapped out of her toxic dream and back into her present situation. "I can see the killer. He is sneaking through the front of your house now. I have no doubt it is one of them. He is extremely fit, and for some reason, he elected not to wear a shirt," Connor told Kayla. "That is one of them," Kayla said to Connor. She didn't want to disclose how even though she was being kidnapped, the two men who took her were some of the most beautiful men she had ever seen— and the most seductive. She couldn't explain it, but they had a power about them. It was like in the movies when the vampire is so seductive the person can't help but get bit by them. So Kayla figured she would leave that part out of it.

Kayla wasn't frightened. If anything, she was pissed. She was ready to do significant damage to anyone trying to kill her. Kayla was thirty-seven and had a lot of years ahead of her. She wasn't about to die because some asshole had a plan.

This time, Kayla and Connor were ready for the bastard. And, this time, it was two against one— advantage, Kayla.

UC

Harrison had been tasked with following Kayla for Jacob. They had been waiting for the word to kill her, and it had finally come through. It was four-thirty a.m. MST and Harrison wanted to kill Kayla before the sun came up. Connor was with her. He had tried to pretend he was leaving, but Harrison watched as Connor drove the four blocks around the loop of Salton Way and then another two blocks North West on East Alameda Ave. Harrison supposed Connor planned to park six blocks away and hoped he would be out of sight. But Harrison was trained by The Master.

Harrison was used to hunting killers, and Connor and Kayla made no difference. His only disappointment was neither The Master nor Jacob would get to witness his work as he killed both the cops.

Harrison moved with such ease and snuck into the building with no problem. There was no one even outside, making it much easier than expected. Harrison had been an elusive killer since Jacob, and his Master took him under their wing. He didn't want power, he just wanted their admiration and respect, and he had it. Killing Connor and Kayla on the same night would give him more.

Now the game with Connor and Kayla had to end. Part of him felt the need to taunt Connor and rape Kayla, but he didn't want to get cocky. This was his moment for glory. Until now, The Master, for the most part, was only killing people who had something to do with his trial ten years ago, and Connor and Kayla had nothing to do with it. But they wouldn't stop meddling, so now they had to die. When Jacob and Harrison kidnapped Kayla, The Master tells Jacob to let Kayla live. She was not part of his plan, and her involvement didn't bother him; it drew the Ghost closer. So, they didn't kill her. But The Master didn't take kindly to so many of his followers getting killed, and someone had killed The Master's wolf. So, Kayla and her family, Connor and his family, had to die, but The Master wanted them tortured first.

Since Harrison knew both Connor and Kayla were in the house, he had the edge on them. So he made his next best move. But, unfortunately, there was only one safe way into the house through the front door, and Harrison had just picked the lock so quietly he even surprised himself.

Connor was waiting behind the door, and as soon as it swung open, he was going to rush Harrison the way he assumed Jacob rushed his Anna. Instead, Connor heard soft footsteps outside the door. The killer must have been barefoot because he barely made a sound. Connor watched as the killer picked the lock within three seconds. It was less than that. Connor was shocked. They didn't even teach agents down at the Bureau how to pick locks that fast.

The door knob made a soft click as if a ghost was pushing from the other side; the door opened without a sound. To Connor, it felt like the door took an eternity to open, but Connor held his patience. He needed to attack at the right moment. He knew his opponent was fast and agile, but Connor was a boxer, and he wasn't slow. Connor knew his best punch was a left hook, so he knew if he stayed close to the acrobatic enemy, his left hook would eventually connect. If it did, it would be lights out for the killer.

The killer took a step inside the door. He *was* barefoot. Connor rushed and speared him into the wall as soon as he cleared the door. So Connor struck the killer into a wall that he forgot to protect his head and Connor crashed his head into the wall. For a split second, Connor knocked himself unconscious. But the killer was down. Too. Connor had broken at least two of the killer's ribs.

Both men were slowly getting up. The killer snarled and showed his fangs. Connor didn't give it shit about the killer's fangs, and he threw a right jab that hit the killer in the nose. He didn't break it tho. *Next time Connor. Break his nose—next time.* The killer moved so fast that before Connor knew it, he was clipped in the chin with some karate kick Connor didn't see coming or understand. Connor regained his footing and clipped the killer's chin with a straight right jab to the face. It hit the killer in his left eye. This time, Connor felt a satisfying crush. Connor was sure he had broken the killer's orbital socket. The killer winced in pain and dropped his guard. Connor seized his opportunity.

Because it connects perfectly with the right side of the jaw or temple, the effects of the left hook make it one of the most brutal punches in boxing and the most powerful. The resulting head snaps from connecting with the jaw or temple cause a knockout, and the bigger the fighter, the more knockouts that tend to occur. Connor was six foot three inches, weighed two hundred and twenty-five pounds, and was solid muscle. If Connor were a professional boxer, he would be a heavyweight boxer. Connor sized up Kayla's would-be killer and connected with a left hook that nearly took the killer's head off. The killer crashed into the wall, putting a hole in it, and he was either out cold or dead. Connor didn't care. Kayla was safe, and sure he had stopped the killer from making the acrobatic moves Connor kept hearing about because he broke a few of his ribs first.

The killer was down. Kayla tied him in and had her gun trained on his head, just in case. Connor closed and locked the door so no one else could get inside.

Erynn Justice was the Queen of The Order of the Sacred Branch, the second most powerful Rougarou clan in Salleria. She was arranged to be married by the time she was fourteen but escaped the clan on her eighth birthday. Erynn was the love interest of many men from many clans but wanted to be a warrior. It is believed Erynn has Dissociative Identity Disorder, having at least three personalities. It is also rumored that all three of her personalities are deadly killers. This disorder began in her childhood when Erynn faced trauma that no man could ever survive.

Her original personality Erynn was that of the loving ninja assassin dedicated to only one person. If Erynn's, *Erynn* personality should ever fall for anyone, that person would have to be honorable and a champion of good. While Erynn is her most dominant personality, it will only ever show for one person, who must be worthy of protecting the world among all other men.

As a child, Erynn was distrustful, withdrawn, and frustrated. Others discriminated against her because of her natural beauty, which made her peers believe she could not become a ninja assassin. However, Erynn proved everyone wrong and became the best ninja in the world for many years.

Erynn's parents never returned to The Order of the Sacred Branch after she turned three, and thinking that her parents abandoned her, she was also ostracized by The Order of the Sacred Branch. Erynn was bullied and treated contemptuously by other children, all because of her parents abusing her. A few years later, it turned out that Declan Ward, the father of Finley and Jacob Smith, who was also the Chairman of The Order of the Corrupted Leaf, the most powerful of the Rougarou clans, killed her parents in cold blood after a disagreement. Erynn didn't understand why she suffered so much discrimination, so she trained harder than anyone else at firing weapons, wielding a sword, and hand-to-hand combat. No one trained harder than Erynn; to this day, anyone who knows anyone knows Erynn is one of the greatest hand-to-hand combat fighters of all time.

When Erynn met Ashton, he took her under his wing, and they became as thick as thieves. Erynn and Ashton made a sacred vow when Erynn was eight never to leave one another's side and always to protect one another until death. Eventually, Erynn and Ashton went to work for the Order of the Corrupted Leaf, under the new leadership of Finley Smith, the new Chairman, as deadly assassins that defended innocent people.

Chapter Seventeen

Twenty-One Years Ago — Ashton's Story.

Ashton was born to an unknown mother. He was found in front of the tire of a car, where he was left to die alone and be crushed as soon as the driver started their car and drove. A mercenary group led by a man named Renaud Doisneau eventually happened upon the grisly site, presuming Ashton was dead. However, when the baby began wailing, to the surprise of the mercenaries, Renaud Doisneau immediately took to the child and came to his aid. Renaud Doisneau kept Ashton for his consolation. Renaud Doisneau felt finding the child to be a good sign from God.

Under Doisneau's tutelage, Ashton began honing his swordsmanship and knifemanship at six years of age and joined the mercenary's band three years later, looking up to his leader as a father figure of sorts. However, on the night following Ashton's first victory as an elite warrior, a high-ranking mercenary in Renaud Doisneau's army named Basile Mossé put a powerful sleeping aide in Ashton's drink and ambushed and raped Ashton in his tent, revealing he bought Ashton for a night from Renaud Doisneau. When Ashton regained consciousness, he isolated Basile Mossé and eliminated him, refusing to believe the man's claim that he was sold for a night by the man who saved his life.

Ashton is forced to kill Renaud Doisneau, the closest thing to a father he had ever known, when Renaud Doisneau revealed he hated Ashton and wished he never saved him because a year earlier, Renaud Doisneau had a dream Ashton would cause his downfall and take his mercenary group from him. Unbeknownst to Ashton, Renaud Doisneau's

relationship with Ashton deteriorated, and things went from verbal to physical abuse.

Ashton was subjected to various forms of degradation before Renaud Doisneau eventually

attempted Ashton's life because he was convinced Ashton was the reason for his

misfortune; Renaud Doisneau revealed he did indeed sell Ashton out to Basile Mossé, voicing

his disgust for the boy's existence. Heavily disheartened by this revelation, Ashton

retaliated and killed Renaud Doisneau when he attacked him a final time. When Renaud

Doisneau's men saw Ashton defend himself, Doisneau's small mercenaries branded Ashton a

Father Killer, and they all attacked the nine years old Ashton. Against his wishes, Ashton

killed all of Doisneau's mercenaries except one. Ashton also spared Renaud's daughter,

Alison, and her mother. To the mercenary Ashton left alive, Ashton told the mercenary to

flee and tell the story of everything that happened; and to warn everyone that Ashton would

kill anyone who dared to kill him, Alison, or Alison's mother. After the mercenary escaped

with his life, Ashton told Alison and her mother that he was dropping his last name Doisneau

and would make his middle name, Jace, his new last name. In gratitude for saving their lives,

as Renaud Doisneau mistreated both Alison and her mother, they took Jace as their last

name. Ashton would go on to provide for both Alison and her mother. Some years later,

Alison's mother died of natural causes.

When Ashton was ten, for reasons Ashton did not understand, he was attacked by The

Order of the Corrupted Leaf's mercenaries seeking to claim a reward. Ashton quickly

dispatches most of them until Finley meets him. Ashton is allowed to join The Order of the

Corrupted Leaf, though he promptly refuses, instead opting to challenge Finley to a duel. Ashton tells Finley he can lay claim to Ashton in defeating him in combat. Harboring a vested interest in Ashton, Finley agrees, and the two engage in a sensational battle, with Finley ultimately defeating the swordsman and enlisting him as a member of The Order of the Corrupted Leaf.

Ashton began as a mercenary in The Order, and over the next year, Ashton quickly becomes the most deadly and strongest of everyone in The Order, including Finley, which pushes his reputation far beyond the two brothers in charge, Finley and Jacob Smith. Then, during a battle with another Rougarou clan fighting for dominance, Ashton joins the fray alongside a mercenary band and narrowly defeats the enemy leader, Auguste Courtial, lowering the enemy clan's morale and allowing Ashton to take control over the entire clan. Without question, Ashton gives control over Finley, who is impressed Ashton never tries to fight for power.

Due to Ashton's numerous victories for Finley, he is promoted to The Order of the Corrupted Leaf's Rougarou Captain at eleven years old and given men to follow under his command. Unfortunately, during a raid to take over another Rougarou clan, The Order of the Corrupted Leaf finds itself at a standstill while making its final push into a well-guarded city, roughly fifty of Ashton's soldiers being slaughtered by a single enemy burrowed deep within the city walls in a narrow corridor. Fed up with these results, Ashton goes in to finish the job himself and meets a ten-year-old girl. Shocked that she is the one who killed fifty of

Ashton's men, he battles the girl, and Ashton learns she is the greatest fighter he'd ever seen outside himself. Her name is Erynn.

Initially taken aback by his opponent's overwhelming aura and Erynn's bone-rattling strikes, Ashton ultimately gambles his life on one swing, and with it, he disarms Erynn. Accepting defeat, Erynn smiles and admits to Ashton that it was her destiny to find him, and she would give up her clan freely to him if he let her serve by his side. Ashton agrees but feels strongly connected to Erynn. They both agree to stay by one another's side until death. Ashton also reveals to Erynn that he must give her clan to Finley, as Ashton was not the leader of The Order of The Corrupted Leaf. He was just the strongest. Erynn agrees to Ashton's terms. When exiting the narrow corridor, Ashton and Erynn walk out into the open, holding hands, and Ashton announces the battle is over and hands Finley Erynn's clan.

Ashton was now with The Order of the Corrupted Leaf for the next two years. Finley, Jacob, and Ashton had become close friends and allies. Ashton would do anything they asked, always open and honest with them. One night Finley confides to Ashton and his brother Jacob about his dream to be the head of all the Rougarou's in Salleria and then much more. Finley explains how they have faced death many times and how Jacob and Ashton were his most valuable comrades. Finley told Ashton he appreciated how Ashton devoted himself to Finley's dream of coming into power.

Finley then tells Ashton that a friend is someone who would never depend upon another's dream, and if Ashton were Finley's friend, then Ashton wouldn't follow Finley the way he does because a friend is someone who wouldn't be compelled by anyone but would determine and pursue their reason to live. Finley tells Ashton that if anyone were to stop him from rising to power, he would hate that person with his mind, body, and soul and kill them. Finley believes a friend would be his equal. Therefore, Ashton cannot be his friend because Ashton is not his equal. Ashton is his closet asset. Ashton is puzzled by what Finley has said, and this becomes the first splinter in the Ashton and Finley relationship.

A month later, Finley and Ashton would battle again as Finley grew suspicious of Ashton and his loyalty. Believing that Ashton wants to ruin Finley's dream, Finley seizes Erynn and rapes her while Ashton is out to battle. When Ashton returns, he discovers what Finley has done, and in his rage, he kills every person protecting Finley and allows all others to flee.

After defeating hundreds of men, Ashton wounds Jacob and brutally defeats Finley, and beats him into an inch of his life. Ashton decides not to kill Finley because he wants him to stay alive so he can witness his dreams of ruling all the Rougarou clans destroyed. Ashton wants Finley to know that as long as he lives, he will kill anyone claiming to be a Rougarou or claiming to know Finley or Jacob. Ashton turns his back on Finley and picks up Erynn. As Ashton walks away, Finley vows to get his revenge, and The Order of the Corrupted Leaf crumbles and becomes no more. From that moment on, Clemenceau was no longer the headquarters of the Rougarou clans, and all Rougarous spread across Salleria, fleeing from the wrath of Ashton. Erynn never talked again after her rape. She vowed to never speak again, until she regained her honor Finley took from her.

Aiden was driving at top speed and having a hard time looking through Ashton's rearview mirror of his Dodge because it was packed full. Julia, the town's Mayor, sat in the passenger seat beside him while his wife and daughter huddled in the back seat with Ernest. All of them tried not to get hit in the head by falling boxes as Aiden drove the Dodge at NASCAR speeds.

Christian Barrett had gallantly volunteered to ride back in the cargo area, but he seemed to regret the decision. He was being tossed around every which way, and Barrett was lucky Ashton's Dodge had an enclosed cargo area. If not, Barrett, the town's administrator, would have fallen to the road miles ago. Instead, he crashed against the glass and fiberglass with every bump. Aiden didn't mind. Mr. Christian Barrett could use a bit of humbling.

Lillian, Aiden's sixteen-year-old daughter, was complaining that she was smushed, but Dawn looked as if she was more worried about her husband and his mental health than anything else. "You've got this, Aiden," Dawn said to her husband, wishing her words made him drive a bit slower. "Everything's going to be fine, baby." Aiden's wife felt like a lie, but he hoped he was wrong and everything would be alright. Wakefield was descending into chaos, and Aiden was sworn to protect it. Unfortunately, Aiden couldn't remember the last time he had been to sleep, and now he had to work a miracle and keep food, water, and shelter for God knows how long. Oh well, Aiden thought. Just another day on the job.

Aiden could see many people running towards the shelter at the town hall building. In all the confusion, an older man fell, but no one stopped to help. It was every man for himself now. Aiden pulled the Dodge over and handed a pistol to Julia. "If anyone jumps in the driver seat, shoot them in the leg." Aiden wasn't trying to scare Julia, but he needed her to know that people would try to steal their working car, and her city was no longer a political haven. She lived in the apocalypse now. People wouldn't care about politics for much longer. The incredible speech Aiden had just given minutes ago was no more an extended matter.

Aiden helped the older man and helped him in the back cargo area with Barrett. To the west, the storm was growing. It was a dark and ghastly sight to behold, and it had a strange yellowish tint that seemed to be leading it. Aiden wondered if that is what nuclear fallout looked like. "This is madness," Barrett said as Aiden was helping the old man in the cargo area. "We'll be okay," Aiden said, trying to sound like he believed his own words. He didn't. He wasn't sure what would happen, but he was smart enough to know that being *okay* was not an option. "The shelters are well stocked. They can take care of the whole town for a few days," Aiden added, hoping it would make him more confident about their situation. "And if we have to stay longer than that?" Barrett asked. "Then we go out and hunt for food," Julia said from the passenger seat. Aiden caught her gaze in the rearview mirror. The Mayor was handling all of this surprisingly well. They'd clashed often, but he was beginning to think that she might be a capable leader. "Okay fine, but what about when we come out? What if everything is poisoned?" Barrett asked.

Aiden genuinely didn't have a clue how to answer this question. He was just as clueless as the next person. He'd thought living in a post-nuclear-fallout world was so far-fetched that he never thought about what would happen after they'd left the shelter. "That's a possibility, but we will figure it out. We have to," Aiden said to Garret while walking back to the driver's seat. Julia handed Aiden back his gun. Aiden nodded as to say thanks. Then, Aiden decided to share something he was thinking about with the group but hadn't said it out loud. "I am also worried about babies. Babies crawl on the ground, and if we have nuclear fallout everywhere, every baby in Wakefield is dead. So we won't have a future. Plus, I haven't figured out what we will do with the soil to make it farmable again." Suddenly, Julia screamed. Aiden whipped his head around to find her pointing at the storefronts lined the main street. A dozen people were looting her grocery store, running in and out of the main entrance, which was now only broken glass and metal door frames. Her store was ruined and now looted. "I'm sorry, Julia. I will come back and stop them as soon as I drop you off," Aiden said, returning his focus to the road.

Aiden drove around the throng of citizens toward the rear of the town hall. The back door to the station opened as soon as he pulled up to it, and Detective Skylar Schwartz rushed out to meet them. As everyone got out of the Dodge, Aiden couldn't help but think that the worse was yet to come. Even if they survived a nuclear winter, how would they recover from everything? How long could they survive eating poisonous fruits and vegetables? Would the wildlife even make it? "We're headed to the shelter," Julia said, glancing backward at her store. "I will return to your store immediately and stop the damage, Julia. I give you my word," Aiden offered to Julia. Julia's eyes swelled with tears. She was finally getting what Aiden had been saying all along. Political wars had no place in this new world. People were going to get crazy, and they needed to work together to stay in front of them.

Julia took off with Barrett, leaving Aiden with his family and the Major. Skylar brushed a lock of midnight-black hair away from her face as she approached the Dodge. Her eyes were paradise-green, and she opened her full berry-red lips to speak. "We have a situation at the grocery store, Chief. People are trying to stock up on food before the storm, and apparently, things are out of control." "Yeah, Julia just saw it, and I promised I would go back to help. Who do we have stationed there?" "Just Michael," she said. "We don't have much workforce, Chief. We might need to deputize people later down the road if you see fit. We have many officers who have not shown up since the EMP strike. They could be dead or just abandoned their post."

"Yeah. Probably." Aiden replied to Skylar. He didn't have much time to think about awol officers, and he could only think of the rookie officer guarding Julia's store. He had a wife and a newborn at home. Then he looked at his own family. "Babe, I need you to get in the shelter and wait for me to return. Michael has a young wife and kid, and I need to ensure he gets to them, too." Aiden said. "Make sure everyone gets to the shelter safely, Skylar. Leave no one behind." The detective nodded and motioned for Dawn and Lillian.

Aiden climbed in the Dodge and had his mind made up. He was going to put an end to this looting and get those idiots into the shelter before they got themselves killed over canned meat and peanut butter crackers. But, before the Chief could drive off, the Major was waiting in the passenger seat for Aiden. The Chief smiled. "Thanks, Major." "My pleasure, Chief." Aiden was starting to like Ernest; he was proving to be very valuable. "Major," Aiden called out to Ernest before driving off. "I promise I will give you everything you need to get to your nephew after the fallout passes us."

Aiden looked out into the driver's side of the windshield. He knew he should probably look at Ernest, but he probably would have teared up if he did. So instead, he needed to keep it together for everyone. "You won't have to ask me. I will come to you first," Aiden assured Ernest. "I don't," Ernest seemed to be struggling for words. Aiden wasn't sure if it was the thought of his nephew being all alone or the heartfelt moment they had just shared, but Aiden knew that he understood. "You don't have to say anything, Ernest," Aiden said while putting the Dodge in drive, "We've got your back."

Ernest smiled, and that seemed to make him feel better about everything. Aiden couldn't imagine what Ernest was going through, but he knew it couldn't be easy. Aiden liked Ernest. He sure hoped he would stay around a while. Wakefield needed a few more men like Ernest. Squealing out of the parking lot, the two men raced down the street to Julia's store.

Aiden took a left toward Julia's grocery store and noticed Ernest seemed more upset than usual. Ernest was staring out the window, his hand gripping his chest like he was in pain. "You good, Major?" It took Ernest a long moment to reply. "Not really. I was thinking about our conversation," Ernest replied to Aiden. His words came out forced as if he was trying to hold them back but couldn't. "My nephew is in the middle of the radiation zone, and apparently, my sister became the President of the United Cities and then got killed in the nuke that destroyed D.C." "Holy shit!" So you've been walking around with all of this since you got back?" Aiden asked. Ernest didn't respond. Aiden didn't think he could.

Aiden had no idea how the Major was still standing. Not to mention watching his back after he found out his entire family was dead, or at least one was dead and the other was irradiated. All he could think about was if it were his family, he would have lost his mind and his will to live. "If we make it through this storm, I'll find you a working vehicle and give you enough food, gear, and ammo to make it to Chesterfolk. I give you my word," Aiden said. "I've got a few CBRN suits at the station. You are welcome to take one. After the 2016 Tornados, we applied for a grant and bought all disaster equipment." Ernest pulled his hand away from his chest and patted Aiden. "Thanks, brother." "You are a good man Ernest."

As they pulled into the parking lot of Julia's grocery store, both men saw Officer Peyton Michael standing with his shotgun shouldered. He jerked the muzzle back and forth at three suspicious-looking men. Aiden didn't recognize any of them. Nevertheless, he assessed the situation quickly as he drove toward the crowd. There was more than one person armed with makeshift weapons and baseball bats. They looked to be threatening Michael. Behind the three suspicious men stood a group twenty- or thirty-strong; more people filed in and out of the front doors. This place was a complete mess. Ernest immediately felt bad for Julia. "Dammit," Aiden said. "It took all but thirty mins for people to start looting."

"I've got your back, Chief," Ernest said. He un-holstered his M9 and pulled the slide back to chamber a round. Aiden parked the Dodge and pulled his Sig Sauer P22. The three civilians surrounding Michael all looked at Ernest and Aiden. "Drop the weapons and the bags." Aiden said. "They raided the pharmacy," Michael said, his voice surprisingly calm for a rookie cop. He kept his shotgun aimed at the man with the bat. He was twirling the bat and making threatening gestures toward a police officer. Aiden was instantly pissed. "We took our fair share," the man said while twirling his bat in one hand. The other man smirked, revealing blackened teeth. Fucking Meth-heads, Aiden thought to himself. Who in the hell had a meth lab in Wakefield. These three assholes did. Ernest moved into a flanking position. Aiden was grateful Ernest was a soldier with advanced military training. They were two seconds away from needing every bit of it. Mr.*Meth Batman* centered a crazed gaze on Aiden. There was no mistaking the wide eyes and sweat pouring down the man's forehead. These three were all meth heads, and they were here to still opioids.

Suddenly, Aiden realized people like this were going to be a problem as their supplies of prescription drugs dwindled. "We are not going to ask you again," Michael said. The guy with the bat stepped toward the officer. Both of his friends followed, but Michael held his ground. With the storm approaching, they had less than an hour to get these people to safety. Unfortunately, the looters were making everything worse. The sealed doors and glass would have more than likely preserved all the food and medicine in Julia's store, but now everything left would be contaminated. "Drop your bat and your bags, last warning. The next word from me will be with my gun, and I will shoot everyone in the legs and leave you handicapped and bleeding in nuclear fallout," Aiden said. He directed his Sig Sauer P22 at the man's kneecaps, and the bat clattered on the ground, and Aiden nodded at Michael, who lowered his shotgun. "Give Officer Michael everything you stole so it can be saved from radiation, and be glad I am not locking you up in jail," Aiden said with irritation. "This way

Ernest." Side by side, they approached the entrance, weapons angled at the ground. "Unless you want to get shot in the knees and left to fend for yourself during a radioactive storm, drop everything you are holding and get your asses into the shelter in the town hall right now!" Aiden yelled.

Aiden didn't bother giving any further explanation. He said what he said, and there was no time for debating. As far as Aiden was concerned, it was kneecaps or shelter. The choice was theirs. He didn't know most of these people, but they all got the message. Everyone dropped their bags, stopped pushing their shopping carts, and ran toward the shelter. A few people kept cookies and chips in their hands as they fed, but Aiden didn't make much of it. The problem, for the most part, had been solved. How in the hell would he secure this store before the storm arrived? Just as Aiden pondered how to save all the merchandise in Julia's store, the glass front door shattered. People in the parking lot were shouting, and then a woman screamed. A shotgun blast rang out. Aiden and Ernest ran outside to find them pointing at two previous men trying to steal opioids.

Aiden hated himself for not securing the situation better than he had, but there was just so much going on. And, with the imminent threat of radioactive rain coming their way, he couldn't make all the best decisions. There were no *best decisions* to be made. Beneath Officer Michael laid the twitching body of *Batman*. With blood pooling around his chest area and the same evil Aiden saw on him earlier lying next to his body, Aiden understood what had happened. The man thought he could regain his advantage since Officer Michael was by himself, picked up his bat, and tried to overpower or disable Michael. There was no need for medical attention. The man's chest was gone. It looked more like orange juice pulp, which told Aiden it was a close-range shot his officer had taken. His two buddies had already taken off running in opposite directions. He hoped they would go to the shelter but doubted they would risk getting arrested. Aiden knew they were as good as dead. Arresting these men would be unnecessary.

"I'm sorry, Chief, but the bastards got away." Aiden nodded because he had more significant problems on his hands. The storm was almost overhead. It wouldn't be long before the skies opened up, and deadly rain began to fall. Michael, Major, our time is up. It's time to get back to the shelter, or we are all as good as dead. The three men entered the Dodge and drove away silently, leaving *Batman's* body twitching on the ground. There was nothing they could do for him now.

Chase had been playing basketball since he was seven years old. The love he has for the game is indescribable. If he could never play again by chance, his soul would leave his body and die a thousand times. Chase glanced up at the scoreboard. The clock read 15 seconds left in the fourth quarter and his team was down by four, making it a two-possession game. With twelve seconds left on the clock, Chase received the inbound pass and swished a three-pointer with the quick release he had practiced millions of times in the gym. The opposing team passed the ball on the court, and Chase applied full-court pressure. There were no time-outs, and Chase knocked the ball loose around the half-court line with six seconds left to play. Everything goes silent, and the world seems to slow down—one dribble. Chase palms the ball with his right hand and takes four steps between dribbles. The ball pounded the wooden court again for a second dribble. Chase plants both of his feet behind the three-point line without thinking and operating on pure muscle memory. His feet are shoulder-width apart. His right arm is tucked parallel and close to his body. His elbow is bent at a ninety-degree angle, forming the letter "L." He jumps slightly and snaps his right wrist quickly as if he was stealing cookies from a cookie. Two seconds are left on the clock as the ball rotates in the air. One-second. *Swish!* The net pops with that beautiful sound Chase loves to hear so much when he practices alone. The buzzer sounds in the arena, and the crowd goes wild as Chase hits the final bucket and his team wins the State Championship by two points with his miraculous buzzard-beating shot.

A wave of blistering heat pressed Monique's body to the ground as she cheered for Chase. Someone rushed to her unconscious body with an unfamiliar voice and screamed, "Ma'am, can you open your eyes?" The man's voice sounded both far away and closed at the same time. Monique forced her burned eyelids open, squinting at several blurred figures standing above her. "Where...where am I?" she asked. The words came out as a whisper. "You're safe, Madam President," said the voice. It was familiar. Chase? No, Weston! Her fingers quested over the blanket covering her body, and they found her bodyguard's vast, warm hand. "Where's Brayden?" she asked. Monique had a strong sense of Déjà vu. She could have sworn she had been through this already and asked the same question. Was she in a time loop? Or, losing her mind? She struggled to sit up. She had to find her Chief of staff. They had to get that bill filed before the next session of Congress, and she needed him to set up the next round of fundraising events. "Don't try to move," a woman's voice said. "Madam President, you were severely injured. We need you to take it easy. The whole nation needs you to stay alive." Her vision finally cleared enough to make out the faces of the people looking down on her. Weston was wrapped from head to toe in so much medical gauze he looked like he was wearing a Halloween costume, but he was smiling at her. He was smiling his usual comforting smile that always made her feel safe. The other two people were strangers. Both men and women wore scrubs and lab coats, which instantly spiked her adrenaline levels in her body.

"Wait a minute. Where am I? How badly am I hurt? What is going on?" Monique repeated. "And who are you?" The woman answered. "You're aboard the USS George H.W. Bush," she explained. "I'm Dr. Callen Russell. This is Dr. Ava Marsh." "Where's Brayden?" she asked. Weston's smile faded away. "He didn't make it, ma'am." Monique took in a long breath and winced. "No," she whispered. "I'm sorry," Weston said. "They did everything they could for him, but he was too badly burned." Monique knew she would have to grieve Brayden later, but now she had to focus on saving the United Cities. "Damn! Why am I in so much pain?" Monique asked as stars moved across her vision. She felt like she was going to be sick. "Where are we?" she managed to say. "Three hundred miles east of Stonewick, sailing south to avoid the fallout from the ground detonation," Russell said. "My son, he's in Chesterfolk. I have to get to him." She palmed the bed and attempted to sit up again, but she was hit by agonizing pain. Russell raised a hand. "Ma'am, I don't think you understand. You're not going anywhere. You are lucky to be alive. You have first-degree burns on over twenty percent of your body, second-degree burns on your face, and third-degree burns to your right hand. You're also being treated for radiation sickness. If we didn't evacuate you when we did, you would be glowing green and turning into a radiated ghoul-like in the movies or a video game." Monique smiled at the joke but kept insisting on saving Chase. She forced herself up as far as she could with all her might, ripping flesh from her charred hand. Multiple hands forced her back down into a resting position. Why didn't they understand?

She had to get to her baby. "Madam, President. We will help you find your son, of course. But right now, you cannot move." Russell said. "I'm going to sedate you now for your safety." "My baby," Monique mumbled. "I have to," A heavy numbness began to spread through her body. She fought to hold her eyes open for a few minutes before giving in to the darkness.

The rain flew in sideways and battered the cabin. It sounded like an ocean of water dumped onto the roof every five minutes, and mustard yellowish tint crawled down the windows. Ashton sat on Rory's couch with Erynn, and Hunter sat in the reclining chair, neither saying a word. They knew they were lucky, but there was no way to tell when their luck would run out. Outside, the yellow tint of nuclear fallout was after them.

Hours earlier, the first drops had begun to fall on Cherry Hill. Erynn had decided to return to Rory Cooper's cabin to search for clues, which saved both of their lives. Ashton had discovered an old, home-built radio sitting on the kitchen table and fired it up. The radio also looked like it could send messages, too. It also picked up a station playing an emergency message: *Seek shelter immediately. Put plastic and tape over the windows and doors. Don't go outside until the storm has passed. The storm is radioactive. This message will repeat.* It had taken an entire roll of Duct tape and all the tarps and plastic sheeting he could find in Rory's well-stocked cabin, but in the end, Ashton and Erynn had sealed the place tight.

"Thank God Rory was a nut-case Prepper. It seemed like we would be dead right now if he were normal." Ashton said to Erynn. They both laughed. Erynn laughed silently, of course. Rory had water and food for months. And, now that the cabin was sealed up from radiation, Ashton made a mental not to come back to Rory's place for any emergencies that would come shortly. Rory was so paranoid he created a Faraday cage, which he kept in his office area for safe-keeping. From what Ashton could remember, A Faraday cage is an enclosure made of conductive material that protects against electromagnetic fields. The most common type of Faraday cage is a metal mesh, but any conductive material will work. In Rory's case, he used his Faraday cage to protect a pair of walkie-talkies, and man-oh-man, did they work?

Erynn was happy about the walkie-talkies but wanted a cold beer. She was hoping Rory prepped for a beer-filled apocalypse, too. So she walked to the fridge and saw a few six packs, popped open a bottle, and drank an apocalyptic two-day-warm beer, which tasted like heaven in a bottle. Today was a good day, she thought. I accidentally saved my life from toxic rain and found some of the last beer on earth.

Lightning cut through the darkness as Ashton was lost in his thoughts and playing around with the walkie-talkies. Erynn sat next to Ashton and handed him two beers. Even though they were trapped helping out a Police Chief they didn't even like, they were alive, safe, and together. All they ever needed was each other— and a few beers and Ashton and Erynn could make the best out of any situation. They drank their beers and relaxed, but the beers couldn't take either of their minds off the Rougarous. As kids, Ashton and Erynn were the things that went bump in the night. They had seen the worst of man and became the worst of man. But, there was a reason Ashton and Erynn were some of the best soldiers in the world; they were trained to be. Ashton and Erynn had been trained assassins for as long as they could remember, and they both were the best.

"Hey, Ashton," Hunter shouted across the room. "What's up, Hunter?" That picture you and Erynn found out back? I wasn't going to ask, and I was trying hard to act like I don't see you both spazzing out about it, but I guess I want to know now," Hunter said. Ashton was shocked at his boldness, but he was a cop, it was his job to know, and Ashton liked the guy. "It's a lot, man. It would take a long time to explain." "Well, If I got outside in the rain, I am going to die, so I guess it's story time," Hunter said while getting out of the chair and dragging it closer to Ashton and Erynn. Ashton looked at Erynn. She shrugged her shoulders, kicked her feet on Rory's table, and leaned against Ashton. It was his story to tell now. Erynn had left the choice up to him.

Ashton began to tell about the legend of the Rougarous and *The Curse Of Julia Brown, The Manchac Swamp's Voodoo Priestess.*

The mysteries and legends surrounding Clemenceau's infamous Manchac Swamp are deeply rooted in its past, making the dense forest one of the city's most famous haunts. Not only does Manchac Swamp have direct ties to the Rougarou, Creole werewolves of legend, but it's also said to be haunted by the ghost of voodoo priestess Julia Brown, who used her powers to destroy an entire town.

Julia Brown was a well-respected magic practitioner in Clemenceau. If someone got sick, they had two options— they could make the journey into southern Clemenceau or turn to Julia for supernatural healing. It wasn't uncommon for Julia to travel around the city performing rituals to help with childbirth, fight off infections, and cure illnesses, and more often than not, the afflicted would recover quickly. By all accounts, whatever strange powers Julia was harnessing, they worked.

Though the townsfolk respected Julia, they also began to take her for granted. When she started to feel like her neighbors were using her, Julia began predicting when terrible things would happen to them. Whether foretelling future events or placing a curse, Julia was always right about what would happen to someone and how they would die.

On September 28, 1915, Julia made her final terrifying prediction and died a few moments later. In the final weeks leading up to her death, she was often heard singing, "One day I'm gonna die, and I'm gonna take all of you with me." Every day, she could be heard singing this song, over and over again. Finally, when the entire town gathered at Julia's funeral, hoping that the show of attention would help her soul rest easy, true to her word, Julia's prediction came to pass. As the nails were hammered into her coffin, a devastating hurricane ripped through the entire area and killed everyone, and turned any survivors into Rougarous. Thousands of people died during the storm. Legend says it is common for skeletons to surface today if you sail down the muggy swamp long enough.

In the Creole legends, the Rougarous are said to prowl the swamps around Clemenceau and the region's sugar cane fields and woodlands. Rigorous are mortals cursed with lycanthropy, giving them an appearance similar to a werewolf. A Rougarou shares a trait with vampires; that is, they suck the blood of mortals. Furthermore, some believe only a witch can make a Rougarou by turning themselves into wolves or cursing others with lycanthropy. This way, three horrific folk monsters are combined into one horrible beast in their monstrous Rougarou form. The cursed individual has incredible strength, razor-

sharp claws, heightened senses, and tremendous speed. They can easily knock a

door off its hinges, kill other apex predators, and show no fear of firearms.

Hunter stared at Ashton and Erynn. "That sounds like one of those old stories that come out of history," Hunter said. "That's because it is, but that doesn't make it untrue." "Yeah, but it doesn't make it true, either." "Oh, it is very true, and if Rougarous are in Wakefield, everyone who gets in their way is going to die," Ashton responded.

"Okay, fair enough. But It sounds like I am missing some key details to all of this," Hunter said. "Oh, you are. But, as I said, it would take years to tell you everything. But I will see if I can give you many details during the next few hours," Ashton said.

Erynn drank the last of her beer, got up, and brought her and Ashton new bottles of beer. Ashton popped the top of his and told Corporal Hunter all about the Rougarou.

Chapter Eighteen

It had been eight hours since the rain started, and it finally stopped. Erynn stared out the window, her eyes fixed on a treelike to the east. She could see the outlines of dozens of animals lying sideways in the dirt of what had been a farm. Now, it was an irradiated graveyard for cows. The sight disappeared as she looked back to check on Aiden. He was his usual self, with unchecked bravery and the overwhelming desire to be good to people. Erynn could relate. Ashton and Erynn were raised to be cruel, so they both wanted to reverse all the negative things they had done.

"Where are all the Artificials?" Hunter asked. "I was just wondering the same thing. I don't think they are human-piloted, so I guess Rory's place is so secluded it's not high on North Kangavar's radar," Ashton responded. Erynn agreed. In high elevations, there were in the middle of nowhere, and Rory lived off the grid. But she knew they would run into the Artificials soon. Machines didn't die from radiation poisoning.

Erynn knew thousands of defenseless people were probably littered across the highways and streets and suspected they would see a lot of bodies since it was morning again. North Kangavar didn't seem to want war, and they wanted extermination. From what Erynn could tell, the North Kangavarians were killing all Sallerians. This attack felt more like an invasion than a war.

Erynn led the three-person screw away from Rory's house. First, they had to get to the town hall shelter and tell the Chief everything they had discovered. He needed to know about the Rougarous and what was coming. Erynn didn't know what radiation smelled like, but the air smelled funny. Then, a deafening boom echoed throughout the morning sky. Erynn froze, both petrified and angry. They weren't even one hundred feet away from Rory's house. Were the Artificials waiting on them to leave? Did they come on top of the roof or something?

Hesitant to turn around, Erynn did anyway, and sure enough, the outline of a drone was racing toward them. "I thought the coast was clear," Ashton said in anger. Erynn shrugged her shoulders. "It was clear, and I think these drones detect movement," Hunter guessed. It made sense, Erynn thought. There was no movement until they all walked outside, and she checked the area as best as possible from inside the cabin. There were no immediate threats present. Then, without giving in another thought, Erynn stopped walking and stood very still. Ashton and Hunter followed her lead.

"Quiet," Ashton whispered. The drone hovered over Rory's house and seemed to be searching. Hunter was right. The drones did react to movement, which would certainly explain a lot. The bright red glow of the drones moving mechanical parts sent a surge of fear through her body. Erynn told her body to relax, and she held her breath. The drone was scanning for them. She hoped they would look like trees to the drone. Erynn couldn't help but wonder who was piloting the drone. If it was a human pilot, they should be able to see all three of them standing here, making their best impression of mall mannequins. Or, maybe the image relayed to the human observers wasn't as straightforward as she thought it would be, which is why they needed movement. Of course, the third option was even scarier.

The North Kangavarians made drones and Artificials that didn't need any copiloting. They were one hundred percent autonomous and hunted without aid. The thought of that got of technology existing scared Erynn.

Just when Erynn thought she couldn't hold her breath longer, the electrical red light vanished, and another explosion echoed in the distance, far away from them. Erynn gripped her rifle and began to hug the tree lines, and barrels Rory had lining his drive.

"That was close," Hunter blurted out. "Damn good thinking, Hunter. You saved our lives," Ashton said. Erynn could tell Ashton was glad Hunter turned out to be as helpful as he was. It wasn't that often Erynn or Ashton could get good help. Chief Aiden was an exception. They always worked well with him. He had some issues with Ashton he needed to get over before Erynn would have to kill the Chief one day. She shook that thought out of her head. The Chief was a good man, and Erynn and Ashton were in the business of protecting good people. But Erynn did want Aiden to ease up. Maybe she could break one of his fingers so that he could learn his lesson. Erynn thought that option over in her mind for a few seconds. Maybe she should break both of Aiden's thumbs if he wasn't nicer to Ashton, she wondered.

Erynn had the team well hidden within the tree lines now. They were still quite a bit away from town, and the enemy was still looking for anyone to kill. Now and then, Erynn could hear the *Thump. Crash. Thump. Crash,* but she kept the crew out of the Artificials' lines of sight. Erynn knew there was no real way to escape from the Artificials. One day, they would soon have to go to war and kill them all. But, for now, it had only been forty-eight hours since the EMP strike, and she doubted everyone in Salleria knew about the North Kangavarian invasion.

The emptiness was eerie, and there should have been more foot traffic and noise at nine a.m. As Erynn kept moving the team forward, she kept putting the puzzle pieces together about the North Kangavarian attack. She knew the North Kangavarians knew they would get nuked as soon as Salleria discovered they were behind the attack, which would leave North Kangavar inhabitable. And, the way the North Kangavarians were in Salleria killing everyone, she became more and more convinced of her theory. But it was crazy! Erynn figured she would keep it to herself until she had more evidence for the insane theory she was working on in her mind.

In the distance, the city buildings began to emerge. The team would lose tree cover, but the city building would be able to disguise their movements. Of course, Erynn expected hundreds of Artificials to be patrolling the city streets. Erynn had to think of the safest route to the town hall shelter and the quickest route. "How are we going to get inside the shelter?" Ashton asked. Erynn hadn't thought about that yet. The shelter would be locked and have blast doors that couldn't be kicked down. Plus, everyone inside it would be afraid. As if Ashton were reading her mind, he said, "More than likely, the Chief had all politicians with him. Once we knock on the shelter door, assuming they even hear our knocks, there may be a power struggle to open it." Erynn thought about that for a good moment. Ashton was right. Getting into the shelter may prove to be complicated. "Fucking politics," Hunter whispered in disgust. Erynn agreed.

66

"That building to the right," Ashton whispered loud enough for Erynn and Hunter to hear him. He was in the rear, and they needed to hide quickly. Erynn raced past a bullet-riddled man with his chest blown apart. He was dead, right in front of the Mayor's grocery store. Something terrible went down here. As soon as they got to cover, four Artificials walked by. They must have been patrolling the area. Hunter asked, "How did you know when they were gone?" "Because I'm a soldier, and I know how others soldiers think," Ashton responded. It didn't matter if the Artificials weren't humans, they were soldiers, and soldiers did things a certain way.

"Okay, we have to get through all of these buildings and somehow downhill while staying alive," Ashton said to Erynn and Hunter. "Oh, and if we run into trouble, we must kill everything before we get to the town hall shelter because we can't let the enemy know where hundreds of innocent people are hiding." "So, we need to be invisible but superheroes, too," Hunter offered to the conversation. Erynn smiled and threw her hands up in the air in defeat. "Pretty much," Ashton said.

The team was deep into downtown Wakefield now. There were hundreds of buildings and kill zones. Ashton knew what to do if he was in charge of the invasion. First, he would have enough streets open to funnel anyone trying to escape into kill zones.

Erynn was doing an expert job of dodging as many Artificials as possible. So far, everything has been good. The morning sun was moving on top of them, but another glow stopped Ashton's heart. The incandescent glow of markings over black leather or some material. Three hundred feet down the road they were on, a dozen Artificials surrounded the only pathway to freedom.

"Artificials," Hunter whispered loudly as a dozen heads tilted to look at the team simultaneously. Twenty-four eyes stared at them— studying them. Erynn stayed in front, and her rifle pointed at any Artificial that dared to move. A loud spectacle of gunfire and gore was about to ensue. It was three against twelve, and Hunter, Erynn, and Ashton were about to fight for their lives.

Thump. Crash. Thump. Crash.

The Artificials broke out into a slow run towards them. They scattered in each direction, and Ashton could have seen one of the Artificials scales a wall. "These motherfuckers can climb now?" Ashton asked out loud. But it wasn't a question but more of a declaration. Erynn took the first shot; she got one of the Artificials in the eye and then put another round in the throat area. Ashton wasn't sure if it was dead, but he made a mental picture of wear it fell so he could shoot it in the head later to be sure. Hunter sent a volley of rounds into the Artificial that climbed over the one Erynn shot, and it fell to the ground with a hard thud.

Rounds were flying everywhere, and it seemed none missed a shot. The Artificial were well coordinated, but they moved in predictable paths. Ashton had a thought enter his mind in between kills. He hadn't seen an Artificial use of a gun yet. Who needs an army of machine soldiers who can open doors and shoot guns? Salleria didn't need those types of problems.

Ashton ran to the right and switched from his rifle to his knives. He was a swordsman and made a mental note to get his sword from the hidden compartment in his Dodge. Ashton darted to a fallen Artificial to make sure it was dead. Before he could check, he barely missed the ravenous red glow of a hand that nearly took his head off. The Artificials punch was so powerful it left a hole in the brick where Ashton's head was a few moments before. Before the Artificial could get its hand back into a fighting position, Ashton cut volcanic red liquid and wires out the Artificials throat, and it fell to the ground. Its lifeless body crashed like a kid's toy.

"We have to kill them all," Ashton shouted. Erynn had already taken down six by herself, and Hunter grunted, firing another volley of rounds through one of the surviving Artificial openings. A mechanical shriek of metal and electrical sparks broke through the air.

The last Artificial was headed towards Ashton. The click of a dry magazine sounded somehow louder than Ashton's racing heart. *Why do I keep forgetting to count my rounds?* Ashton thought to himself. Ashton threw his rifle over his back and took one knee aiming his pistol. Before he knew it, a three-round burst left his pistol clustered in a tight shot group where a person's nose should have been. "Bullets over machines, motherfucker," Ashton screamed.

Paige stood next to Bryson while Paige asked Alison questions that were too hard to answer. Alison welcomed the complicated conversation, though she was tired of Kian's complaint for the last eight hours. She completely understood why her brother punched him in the nose. "Why did that nice man have to die, Mommy?' Paige kept asking questions about the young officer's body she saw torn in half. Part of her wanted to be mad at Ashton, but what could he have done? From all the questions she asked Paige, Ashton kept her perfectly safe and saved her life over a dozen times. And, then, Erynn saved Paige's life a dozen more. Paige also told her how Aiden and Erynn went out to look for survivors and returned with Bryson. She was fighting her war in the hospital, but it wasn't nearly as bad as being outside.

"Sometimes people die, Hunny," Alison said to Paige. "It's a sad thing, but it does happen." Both of the kids looked to Alison for more answers. But she didn't have them. "No one would have died if we had left a long time ago like I told the Dick-Ta," Kian stopped in the middle of his sentence. Alison told him hours ago that if he said another bad word about her brother, she would stab him with a Herpes infected needle. Of course, she wasn't going to do it, but she was so mad at Kian. All he did was complain, and she would not let him keep talking about her brother. He saved his life more than once, and the least he could do was stop being so privileged and show some freaking gratitude.

Kian changed his words mid-sentence while Alison was staring at him coldly. "If we had left sooner, as I said, everyone would still be alive," Kian redacted his statement. His tone was considerably less offensive. "If my brother had left earlier, as you suggested, he never would have found you in your Humvee, running for your life, right?" Kian didn't have a reply. How could he?

"The monsters outside are big and scary," Bryson added to the conversation. He was standing next to Paige, rocking from side to side. "I heard," Alison responded gently to the kid. But unfortunately, Paige kept calling him Ankle Biter, and Alison had to tell her to stop because it wasn't pleasant. "But Uncle Ashton calls him that, Mommy." Suppressing a laugh, which she didn't do well at all, Alison told both Paige and Bryson that Ashton wasn't being mean, he just meant that kids are short, and he didn't know what to call Bryson yet. But she knew he was lying. She knew Ashton hated kids, but he was so good with them.

Ashton had a hard time as a kid and saved Alison long ago. He was the only brother she'd ever known, and then Ashton became a father figure to Alison as well. But he never got to enjoy his childhood. So, seeing kids reminded him of a life he never enjoyed.

Alison finished her response to Bryson. "They are just machines, Hunny. They can be killed, and we will protect you from them," Bryson smiled. He didn't frown, either. "I'm hungry," was his response. "Me, too, Mommy." "We have a vending machine with cookies and candy in it." Alison responded to both the kids. "Yay," Paige and Bryson cheered in unison.

And just like that, all the depression and trauma these two kids experienced in the last forty-eight hours was gone. The mere mention of cookies and candy replaces forty years of therapy. The kids were so resilient.

The volcanic red ooze of the Artificials was slowly crawling down Erynn's knife hand. She was tired of shooting these damned things without having any answers. She wanted to know what they were dealing with once and for all. A few minutes earlier, when the last Artificial dropped to the ground, Erynn, still leading the crew, ordered everyone to stop. She was angry. She didn't like being ambushed, and she wanted answers, and she wanted them now.

Erynn used her knife to gut many animals before in the wild. When you spent years of your life in combat, you got used to not having the delivery pizza guy drive through a combat zone and ask the enemy what foxhole he should take your pizza. Since that wasn't an option, Erynn learned to skin animals and cooked them for survival.

Erynn peeled back a layer of the Artificial skin. She had no idea was this black skin was. It was like leather, but it was stronger than leather. It could be a thicker type of leather. It wasn't bulletproof, but shooting the Artificials in most of their bodies didn't do much because there was no machinery where organs should have been. Erynn had the Artificial's skin pulled down from the neck to its pubic area— not the Artificial had gentiles, but she didn't get the chance to dissect advanced technology every day.

Where there should have been a heart, there wasn't. It was as if the designers knew to keep vital power supplies away from commonly known areas of the human body. For example, the neck area seemed to connect the brain functions to the torso. So any severe neck trauma, like the kind Ashton loved to do on the Artificials, would sever the power supply, and it would fall dead.

Erynn poked out one of the Artificial's eyes with her knife. It came out pretty quickly. The eyes seemed to have motion sensors attached to them and were cameras more than they were eyes. Erynn followed the sophisticated wiring system back from the eyes to the brain. She had to crack open the Artificials skull with great effort. Ashton had to hold one half of the skull while Hunter held the other. Following the writing from the brain, she recognized a bit of the tech, but most passed her skill level. But there was something she noticed more than anything else. A sophisticated electrical relay system was set up to send and receive signals.

"Is that what I think it is, Erynn?" Ashton asked. Erynn nodded, wiping the sinister read glowing ooze away from her face as much of it got all over her. "Guys, I play video games. I don't build them. Tell me what the fuck I am looking at," Hunter said. His face showed all of his confusion. "What you are looking at is evidence that these Artificials are a part of a bigger piece of North Kangavar's army. Its eyes and brain are set up to send and receive signals which means someone has been watching us, and when they are not, these

Artificials can make sure they know to start." Ashton answered. Hunter swallowed hard. "So, someone is piloting these things?" Hunter asked, and Erynn shook her head no. Ashton answered for her, "Not necessarily. More likely, these Artificials are self-sufficient but are getting smarter with every fight they have because someone can reprogram them in real time since signals can be sent back and forth."

Erynn was impressed Ashton explained it so well, but there was something she was worried about now. If the Artificials could receive programming in real-time, it also meant every time they fought one, it would become faster and wiser. Someone was learning from the Artificials and updating their programming. That would explain why one of them scaled a wall like a spider earlier. They were getting more intelligent. Erynn feared soon the would-be facing Artificials that knew karate, then after that, Artificials that knew how to open doors, and then, Artificials that knew how to fire guns.

This revelation made Erynn's heart flutter. She would have to communicate with Ashton in sign language when she could. If her theory was correct, then she had just found the Artificial's greatest strength.

A strange, metallic drum-like sound rang out from all around them. It took a lot of work to tell from which direction it was coming. Erynn saw Ashton reload the magazines in both weapons, and Hunter did the same. Erynn understood now. She kicked the Artificial's body out of the way and sheathed her knife. It was time to fight again, and it sounded like tangos were coming from all sides and closing them into a tight circle.

Erynn shouldered her rifle as she recognized the sound.

Kian forced himself to be quiet for now. But he didn't like the Dick-Tator's sister either. His nose throbbed, and he had a black eye. The painkillers his stupid sister gave him had worn off. It would take a week before his black eye disappeared, but he was already plotting revenge.

Men like Ashton made Kian vote for Capitol Punishment. He hated them. Bullies like The Ghost had tortured Kian his entire life, and he was sick of it. He wasn't going to sit around and be weak anymore. If Ashton made it back, he would get his revenge. He might even start with his sister. Yeah, Kian thought to himself. That bitch is going to pay. I am going to get her real good.

For now, he pushed his anger to the side. He was very important, and they still hadn't found out who he was, which worked fine for him. All of them could rot in hell as far as he was concerned. Kian hated when the working class didn't know their place. He wasn't racist, but this world had a natural order, and these people had better respect it.

Kian grabbed a paper cup and filled it with water from one of the coolers that weren't electrically operated. He couldn't even taste the damn water because his nose was broken, but it still satisfied him. Later he would break the glass on one of the vending machines and get some good, and then kick in the plastic glass on one of the soda machines and get him something to drink. It was the hospital's job to take care of people, and he deserved to be at the top of the list.

Kian needed to get back to Hasly Mountain. That's where he was headed back to when the North Kangavarians attacked him. He wasn't as careful as he thought and got caught. But the drive that should have taken him three hours to complete took him twelve, but it was worth it. Finally, he got what he was looking for, a matter of life and death. Kian would die before he let these sons of bitches know what he was hiding and who he was. He would teach them all a lesson just like he did the three hundred and fifty-plus assholes in Hasly Mountain. He hoped all of them were dead. NORAD couldn't run without him because he was NORAD!

Somewhere behind him, a faint, metallic thud kept echoing softly in the distance. What was that? Kian thought he had heard it before. But then, everything rushed to him, and Kian dropped his water cup on the floor. Its clear liquid contents spilled out in every direction.

Kian saw the two kids talk to the Dick-Tator bitch of a sister. He could tell the dark-skinned woman wasn't listening to the kids, but he saw precisely what was happening. At once, the woman who threatened him opened her mouth wide and unleashed a bloodcurdling scream.

Kian froze. *Thump. Crash. Thump. Crash.* Everyone screamed, and more people from the back of the hospital rushed to see what the screams were about. In front of the Emergency Room doors were two Artificials. Their vibrant red eyes glowed gloriously with the morning sun. Kian wasn't sure, but the Artificials seemed to be analyzing. It was like they were calculating their best option of attack. Stepping back slowly, Kian had already figured out the Artificials reacted to motion; Kian stepped behind a gathering crowd of idiots in hospital attire. There were a few officers on guard as well. He wondered if they were trained to shoot well because they were about to be tested. Kian closed his eyes as the screaming began.

UC

The block was brightly lit, and Ashton, Erynn, And Hunter were exposed. Hunter knew he was an experienced fighter, but The Ghost and Erynn were killing machines. He'd never seen anything like it. The noises came from all around them. *Thump. Crash. Thump. Crash.*

Hunter ignored his mind and body, telling him to run and save himself. If he were going to die, he would die as well as his friend Officer Samuel Willis did. The Rookie knew he was going to bleed out, so he chose his way to go. Hunter decided he was going to do the same. He would take as many red glowing machines with him as possible.

Erynn took off and led them into a building. It was a grocery store that had already been looted. The front doors were broken. Hunter followed behind Erynn, and Ashton followed behind him. Hunter didn't get the impression Erynn sent them in here to hide, and she could have picked a more secure building than that. It was like she picked this building because it was already broken, and she didn't want to cause damage to any other businesses if she didn't have to do so. Before he could ask why Erynn chose this building, Ashton answered, "Hunter. This is our last stance," Ashton said to Hunter. But there was not a hint of fear in his voice. He sounded excited. Hunter could see why this guy was called The Ghost. He was fearless. "There are only so many tangos that can get through that broken doorway. When they come for us, concentrate all your fire on that choke point. Their numbers won't mean anything in here."

The Ghost made it all make sense. It was brilliant. Without communicating with each other, The Ghost knew what Erynn was thinking, and Erynn knew how to lead them. It was beautiful to watch. Their relationship was so pure there was no clear leader between them. It was like they were both in charge and were subordinate to one another.

Hunter had heard the rumors about how these two were married, or together, or something like that. Whatever the truth was, Hunter decided they were together. They knew each other too well.

Thump. Crash. Thump. Crash. It sounded like there were hundreds of them. "It was nice fighting with you two," Hunter said to The Ghost and Erynn. Erynn sat her rifle on the counter and walked to Hunter. She had no regard for the impending attack. She didn't sneak-walk or anything. Instead, she stood with her shoulders high, and this gorgeous woman walked directly to Hunter. He looked away towards Ashton, he didn't want to be disrespectful, but Erynn was the most beautiful woman he'd ever seen. And she was walking towards him. Even covered in the Artificial's blood she had just dissected, she looked like a runway model, but she had a track sprinter's body.

Erynn kneeled and turned Hunter's face away from Ashton and onto her. She stared at Hunter with those beautiful eyes. She was so close to Hunter he could see that she wasn't nervous. Her breathing was relaxed. She took her pointer finger and gently pushed it into Hunter's forehead. Then she pointed the same finger at Ashton and herself, and Erynn did the unexpected. Erynn ripped off her skull bandana and tied it around Hunter's neck. She went into her pocket and grabbed another skull bandana. It was the same color as the one she just gave Hunter and the same as Ashton's. Erynn tied it around Hunter's face; it smelled like sweat and perfume and was still wet from rain and Erynn's perspiration. Erynn pointed back to Ashton and then to herself. And then, unexpectedly, Erynn pointed outside, slashed a finger across her neck, walked away, and picked up her rifle.

Hunter didn't understand what she said, so he looked to Ashton for answers. Ashton was already smiling. "She said you are one of us now, and there are only three— and you are the third. That skull bandana is not only a mark of who we are, but no one can wear it unless you are one of us." Hunter didn't know what to say. So he didn't say anything. He was honored. And he wanted to be one of them. They were his best friends, and he didn't even know them. Ashton said one more thing that nearly made Hunter cry. "She also said the enemies die today, not us." Hunter looked toward Erynn, and she smiled back.

The moment was perfect. Hunter felt he had finally found a family. He felt honored, and he wouldn't let them down. He wanted to tell them thank, but he was interrupted by that very familiar sound. But this time, it was at the front door of the grocery store.

Thump. Crash. Thump. Crash.

One of the officers had taken down one of the Artificials. Kian didn't bother getting his name. He didn't want to know anyone here. The remaining Artificial had killed a dozen people already, and it was coming after Kian. There were a few moments of serenity Kain experienced while the Artificial was in the air. Its red eyes were a beautiful red.

Ever since Kian was a child, he wondered how an Alien invasion would look. He guessed this would be as close as he got to an Alien invasion. Kian would have to settle for a tech invasion instead. That figures. Nothing ever went well in his life.

The moment before his death, he didn't worry much. He closed his eyes and waited for the Artificial to take off his head. His head must have exploded because he felt warm blood all over his face. Kian opened his eyes and saw the bitch who threatened him with herpes standing over him. She had a gun in her hand. Kian looked down at the floor and saw the body of one of the Artificials. It was lying lifeless, and its warm red glow slowly dimmed into black. Kian started to thank Alison, but she didn't deserve it. He was supposed to save her. That was her job. This world had a natural order, and saving him was her fucking job. She is lucky to even be in this country.

He decided to fake a smile, and the Dick-Tator's stupid sister bought his fake gratitude and became a hero— just like her fucking brother. God, he hated people like them. People like her, Erynn, and Ashton not knowing their place in society is what was wrong with Salleria. He would teach them all.

∪∁

The battle at the grocery store took everything out of Erynn, but they all survived. He must have been a hundred Artificial soldiers. Erynn searched her memory, but she had no recollection of seeing a single human soldier. So what the fuck was going on, and how many of these things did North Kangavar make? Erynn wondered to herself.

They needed to return to the Dodge quickly because all of their ammo was getting low. Everything was going to shit, and getting to the town hall shelter seemed impossible. Why was it so hard for them to move without being attacked?

It hit her all of a sudden. How didn't she see it before? The Artificials were targeting them. Between the three, they killed almost two hundred of them and were now on North Kangavar's radar. "Oh my God," Hunter screamed. Erynn turned her head. As they walked out of the store, another wave of Artificials was coming their way. *Thump. Crash. Thump. Crash.*

The sound was so plentiful it sounded like thousands of Artificials. From the looks of it, it was about two hundred more. The stupid machines just kept coming. Erynn started shooting. If she went back into the store, they would send wave after wave until all three ran out of ammo. The only way out of this was to fight forward.

It was so many Artificials conserving ammo that it was no longer a concern. Instead, it was another kill-or-be-killed situation. Angered, Erynn took out three Artificials before they could even get close enough to do any damage. "Erynn, any suggestions on how to get the fuck out of here?" Hunter asked. Erynn used her left hand to signal *follow me.* She took off running to the left, between buildings. She needed to get to the town hall shelter, but she needed to lose the Artificials before they made their move. Over her shoulder, she could hear Ashton taking out a few Artificials.

Erynn risked a glance over her shoulder a watched what appeared to be hundreds of Artificials coming their way. Erynn stopped running. She didn't feel like hiding anymore. She had six grenades, and she was fucking over playing with North Kangavar. Between the buildings, Erynn unleashed a fury she didn't know she had. To her right was her best friend, Ashton. And Hunter took up the left position. "Frag out," Ashton threw a grenade into a crowd of Artificials. It destroyed the businesses he was trying to protect but disabled twenty or so Artificials.

Farther down the road they created for themselves between the buildings, Erynn saw hunter shooting long-distance shots. He was taking out quite a few. Ashton and Erynn threw grenade after grenade until the enemies' numbers were less than fifty. Again, there were mechanical bodies everywhere. This time, both Erynn and Ashton took off running toward the Artificials.

Erynn ran and executed a flying knee and knocked an Artificial back. Then, drawing her pistol, she put two rounds into its forehead. Then, spinning to her left, Erynn stabbed another Artificial into the neck and shot it in the face. Now, in a kneeling firing position, Erynn emptied her remaining bullets into six more Artificials. While she reached for another magazine, Erynn saw Ashton slicing the throats of more than a dozen Artificials.

Once all the Artificials were dead, Erynn took off running. She wanted to get out of sight and lead the men to a temporary hiding place, and as soon as the Artificials left the area, they would knock on the shelter door. After all, she had been through for the last three hours, Erynn was hot and hungry, and she had to pee. Somebody was going to open the shelter door, or she would kill someone.

Chapter Nineteen

Mayor Julia Harris had difficulty going back to sleep when she noticed Major Ernest Maddox following Detective Skylar Schwartz through the shelter under the town hall. Sleeping civilians lined the walls and were scattered everywhere. With the power off and the body heat of hundreds of civilians cooking in the air, everyone in the shelter was hot and sticky.

"There is no way we can stay in a shelter forever," Skylar grunted. The Detective seemed uncomfortable, but she wasn't making a big fuss about things.

As Julia thought about the probability of everyone running out of oxygen, she wondered if Aiden was thinking the same thing. The Chief and Julia always had their fair share of dislike for one another, but Julia was impressed with how he handled everything. Men often hated women in positions of power, which made Julia never try to befriend Aiden. It was always hard to tell which men would be easy to work with and which men would not. Aiden always proved easy to work with, but Julia never made it easy. Why would she? Everyone wanted him to run for Mayor while she did a great job. The man was likable, far more than her, but replacing Wakefield's most successful Mayor of all time because a man was likable, was just the sort of thing that made it difficult to work with men. Julia was convinced if she was a man and Aiden was a woman, no one would be trying to replace him as Mayor.

As Julia breathed another air, she worried about everyone around her. She had to get them out of there soon, and working with Aiden would be the best option, or the shelter would eventually run out of fresh oxygen, and everyone would suffocate to death.

Julia could see Ernest and Skylar were investigating a loud noise that made them both stop tinkering with the shortwave radio moments earlier. Julia had heard it, too. She had also seen Aiden respond to the loud noise first. Any second now, Ernest and Skylar would walk into Aiden. Julia decided to see how things played out. Eventually, a decision would have to be made involving the lives of all these people, and she wanted to see if Aiden would come and consult with her before he made the decision. Julia wasn't sure if he would; she had never proved to be a friend to him. But she felt Aiden would do the right thing, no matter what. Aiden never played politics. If it was the right thing to do, that is what he did.

As they approached, Aiden was already at the bottom of the stairs. Someone was pounding on the door outside. They were in the shelter for over nine hours, and it had finally stopped raining, but no one knew what the conditions were like outside. Julia began to worry about the other two shelters.

"Someone else was knocking a few hours ago while it was still raining." Aiden whispered to Ernest and Skylar as they approached. "Whoever this is, has been knocking for an hour. I don't think it was raining when they began knocking." Aiden continued. He had a mixture of calmness and uncertainty on his face. "We better check it out," Skylar said.

Ernest, Aiden, And Skylar walked up the narrow staircase toward the blast door. It wasn't easy for all three of them to fit comfortably; Julia could see Ernest squeezing himself next to Aiden. The two men pressed their ears to the blast's door, but it was a failed assignment. The cold and hard, reinforced steel of the blast doors made it impossible to hear well. On the other side of the blast doors was the main entrance to the shelter, but there was a long hallway between the blast doors and the door leading to the outside entrance of the town hall. Skylar wanted to help them, but the corridor was only wide enough to fit two people, and shouting would only scare everyone inside the shelter.

Knowing what was happening outside these doors was challenging, but it didn't seem like Aiden didn't want to risk the radiation getting inside the shelter. "Chief," Skylar whispered, "If someone is outside and it has been this long, maybe the radiation isn't as bad as we think it is." Aiden seemed to think about what Skylar had said for a long moment before responding. "Excellent point, Skylar. Very good point," Aiden responded. Julia agreed. "I'll go get the Geiger counter Chief," Ernest said hesitantly. A few minutes later, he returned with a Geiger counter and wearing a Chemical, Biological, Radiation, and Nuclear suit. The Major looked like a six-foot-tall dill pickle in a space mask. No, Julia corrected herself. He looked like a *wrinkled* dill pickle in a space mask.

"I figured you wouldn't sacrifice any one of us to go outside and check on the radiation levels Chief, so I am volunteering myself," The Major said to Aiden. "Stubborn ass," Aiden snorted with a bit of laughter. "I will take the next suicide mission." Julia noticed the two men seemed to like each other.

Julia was sure Ernest was right. Aiden would have done it himself to keep everyone safe. "Nope. You can't have the next one either," Skylar added herself to the heroic conversation. I will be taking the suicide mission after, The Major. Wakefield needs your leadership too much." Skylar was right, Julia thought. Aiden was a valuable resource to Wakefield, and Julia was starting to see him as irreplaceable.

Julia got the feeling Aiden knew they were serious because he didn't put up much of a fight. The three shared some ideas they had to make sure everything was safe. Julia didn't know what to think, but she understood that hiding in a shelter was not a plan.

"Keep that suit, Ernest. You are going to need it on your way to Chesterfolk to find your nephew." Aiden was talking to the Major. Julia thought giving away a CBRN suit wasn't in Aiden's authority but was it in hers? Did authority even matter anymore? "I have not forgotten the promise I made to you." Julia felt guilty for listening without helping, but she wanted to see the character of everyone she would be working with during these challenging times. From the looks of it, Aiden made the Major some promise, which involved him needing a CBRN suit. It must have been a dangerous promise Aiden was keeping.

Thanks, Chief." Julia could hear Ernest responding. "Now, how do we check who is knocking and the conditions outside without compromising the safety of this shelter?" The Major asked. That was the question Julia was trying to work out in her head. But, unfortunately, she didn't have an answer, and it seemed neither did the three of them.

Out of nowhere, Julia heard a voice that was way too loud and equally rude. "Do not open that door," Julia recognized the voice. Aiden didn't need to look to see who it was. He recognized the voice, too. It was the Town's Administrator, Christian Barrett. But why was he being so loud? He could easily cause panic if he kept that up. Julia could see Aiden taking a deep breath to control his anger. Aiden's response was kind, considering Barrett was way out of line. But Aiden was also firm. "Keep your fucking voice down, Barrett." So much for controlling his anger, Julia thought to herself. She didn't like what Aiden said, but she put herself in his shoes for a change. After all, Aiden had done to save Wakefield and Barrett's life, she thought her colleague could show Aiden a little more respect. The realization hit her like a ton of bricks. She was the reason Barrett didn't respect Aiden. She set the tone. She talked to Barrett about how she didn't like things Aiden did behind his back. Guilt roared through Julia's veins.

Julia could understand Barrett's outcry, but by her calculations, the shelter had about twenty-four more hours of fresh air. And under the circumstances, each hour of fresh air was precious. At some point, the door would have to be opened. Julia reviewed the facts. She was an objective woman and preferred to make no emotional decisions. The knocks came after the rain stopped, and the shelter ran out of air. The food and water would also be gone in two days.

"Do not open that door, dammit!" Barrett was much louder this time. "Whoever is out there is contaminated!" Julia was about to intervene when she saw Aiden straighten his back, broaden his shoulders, and Aiden walked over to Barrett. Aiden was always a professional, but he wasn't walking to Barrett like a cop. Instead, he looked like an angry man. Aiden leaned in so close to Barrett that his long locs dangled in Barrett's face. "You are scaring people and making our Mayor, your friend, look bad," Julia was taken aback by Aiden's demeanor and what he was saying.

But he was right; Barrett was scaring people and making her look bad. She didn't think she would care about Aiden taking up for her, but Julia felt warmth spread throughout her body. "I'm going to say this once, and only once. You are not in charge," Julia was sure Aiden was about to disrespect her and her office. And she started feeling sick to her stomach with the embarrassment of hoping for the best of someone and then hearing them talk behind her back.

Aiden kept talking. "I am not in charge, and Julia is not in charge," Aiden let his words sink in for a moment. He wanted Barrett to know he was earnest. "Do you know who is in charge, Christian?" Aiden said Barrett's first name with malice. Barrett either didn't have an answer or didn't want to answer. "No one is in charge but fear. That is what will tear us apart. That is what will make me go against the Mayor, and that is what will cause a fucking riot. Do you want to cause a fucking riot in here, asshole?"

Julia could tell Barrett was angry and embarrassed, but what would he do? He couldn't punch the Chief of Police in the face. Besides, Aiden was right. Julia couldn't move. She wanted to say something but her words wouldn't leave her mouth. She was fixated on everything Aiden was saying as if he had her in a spell. She couldn't take her eyes off what was happening. Aiden wanted Barrett to know he was not in charge and that no one was in charge.

Nose to nose, Aiden was now close enough to smell Barrett's breath. Barrett didn't say a single word. Instead, Aiden kept staring into Barrett's eyes with a stare she had never seen from the Chief. Everyone was still asleep, but Barrett was causing a commotion and waking people up in a panic. Aiden said something else to Barrett, but Julia couldn't hear, but whatever Aiden communicated, the Town Administrator got the message. He turned away without even mumbling something under his breath.

Julia was shocked. She didn't know what to say or what to think. Then, the knocks became more consistent. It was beginning to sound like more than one person was knocking. Finally, Julia decided to watch Aiden walk back over to Skylar and Ernest. "Guys, this is not my situation to call. I need to wake up the Mayor. She deserves to know what's going on and decide if we open the doors."

Julia was shocked. She pretended to be asleep. She was embarrassed for eavesdropping, but Aiden had defended her and was now submitting to her authority. I've been a bit of an asshole to this man, Julia thought. Julia could hear Aiden walking over towards her. She was pretty close to Barrett.

"Come with me, Barrett. We are going to get the Mayor," Aiden said, firmness still in his tone. A few moments later, Julia heard, "Excuse me, Mayor," Aiden was lightly shaking Julia's shoulder. She pretended to wake up. His tone was gentle, and his eyes were kind. The firmness he showed to Barrett seconds earlier was absent from his face and tone. He wasn't pretending to be kind, and he was kind. His outburst with Barrett was for the shelter's safety, not his ego. Julia saw that now.

Julia opened her eyes, and he said, "Ma'am, the rain has stopped, and someone is knocking on the door." Julia pretended to be shocked. "What's the situation?" Julia asked politely.

Aiden began to run down the whole story to Julia. He didn't leave out a single detail, but when he got to the part of Barrett disagreeing, Aiden said, "There are some who want to worried about contamination, ma'am, and they are right. Whoever is outside could be contaminated. This should be strongly considered."

Julia noticed that Aiden had left out Barrett's name, and that he was rude and panicking. "That is the full situation as of now, Mayor," Aiden finished. "Thank you, Chief. What do you want to do? You are the one that got us this far," Julia said to Aiden. She could tell it was, to everyone's surprise. They all wore shocked faces, no one more shocked than Barrett. Julia decided to start mending their relationship on the spot. "I want to hear your thoughts. There is no sense in me letting our history cloud my judgment. From what I can tell, we are all only alive because of you. If you didn't send the Major to get intel, we would all be dying of radiation poison."

Julia meant every word, and she wanted Barrett to hear her same them. It was true. Aiden was the only reason they were alive. The government didn't save them, but this under-appreciated Police Chief did. "Thank you, ma'am," Aiden responded. Julia could have sworn she saw a hint of a smile form on his face. But Aiden hid it quickly. He went back to business. "I can't help but think about a few things. First, the knocks came two hours after the rain stopped, and we let them knock for an hour. Second, it rained for eight hours. That would poison whoever is knocking exposed to radiation for at least eleven hours."

Julia could see a question forming in Aiden's head. The question was bothering him. "My fear of being wrong and exposing everyone to radiation poison wants me to keep the door closed, but we are running out of air," Aiden said. Julia could tell he was thinking things over with his best effort and removing his emotions from the equation. She liked that. Julia liked a leader who could be objective.

Aiden kept saying, "But something is nagging at me, no matter how much I try to dismiss it." "Speak freely, Aiden; I honestly want to know what you are thinking." "Yes, ma'am," Aiden said. He was still showing Julia the respect she never gave him. "The knocks, ma'am. Whoever is outside," Aiden paused. Julia could tell he didn't want to share what he was thinking out loud. "The knocks are getting louder and stronger." Julia didn't understand. "Why does this bother you, Chief?" "Because of the radiation. If they died of radiation poison, the knocks should be getting weaker."

Julia understood now. Aiden was starting to think there wasn't much radiation poison outside, which didn't make sense. Because they all saw the nuclear fallout. "One more thing, ma'am," Julia nodded for Aiden to continue. "We have three shelters. Everyone knows where they are. If I were dying of radiation poisoning, I wouldn't knock hopelessly for an hour. But, unfortunately, we have not given our knockers any sign of life or proof that we will open the doors." To this, even Julia became puzzled. "Does anyone have any thoughts on this before Aiden finishes?" Julia asked. But no one answered.

Taking the silence as his clue to continue, Aiden concluded, "I think the people knocking on this shelter want to get in *this shelter*," Aiden put a strong emphasis on the phrase *this shelter*. "I have a haunch, but with your permission, I don't want to say it out loud. But If I am right, we would be better off opening the door."

Julia thought about everything Aiden said. She wanted to know what his haunch was, but she respected he didn't want to expose his unproven thoughts to a judgmental public. After a short pause, Julia looked at Aiden and said, "It's your call, Chief. Everything you said makes sense, and our friend here is already in a space suit." Julia gestured at Ernest jokingly. Everyone but Barrett laughed. Can't hurt to check it out, right?" "No, ma'am. It can't hurt to check," Aiden responded.

Aiden looked at Julia. She wasn't sure what he was thinking. "Thank you, ma'am," Aiden said to Julia and then turned to Ernest. "Ernest, let's go check it out, but you aren't going alone. Give me five minutes, and we will go out there together. If someone tries to break in, I want you to have a gun over your shoulder." Aiden turned to Skylar, "Grab a suit, youngin', and you are covering the hallway just in case they get passed up. Oh, and Skylar, give Ernest an AR-15. He will need more than his sidearm when he heads out to Chesterfolk." Aiden began walking away to get changed.

"One more thing Skylar." Aiden turned back to Skylar. "Yes, Chief," Skylar responded. "Find the Major a working vehicle too. I don't want him walking to Chesterfolk." "Roger that, Chief!" Ernest looked at the Chief, grateful he was a man who kept his word. Five minutes later, Aiden and Skylar returned, matching Ernest looking like a wrinkled dill pickle in a space mask. Together, both men walked up the stairs and approached the blast doors.

There was a thick mist rolling over the parking lot. The sky was an angry grey, like the color of an ugly sweater or the print of an old fashion newspaper. "About time someone opened the damn door!" Ernest lowered his weapon. It was Ashton, Erynn, and Hunter. Ashton stood in a relaxed pose, and Erynn and Hunter leaned against the wall. "We would keep knocking until you decided to open up, Chief." "How the heck did all three of you survive? We sent Derrick with a bullhorn to try to warn you all." "Oh, is that what that sound was?" Hunter asked. 'I thought I heard a bullhorn, but we were too far away to hear what it said," Hunter finished. "We are okay, Chief. No hair falling out or anything.

Hunter looked at Aiden and Ernest, "Walk around the side of the building. You want to see what's over there," Hunter said. Suspiciously, Aiden, Ernest, and Skylar walked down the street and froze. In front of them were in the streets were hundreds of Artificials. They were all dead. "What the hell happened out here?" Aiden asked. Hunter told the Chief everything that happened in the last two hours and their fights with the Artificials. It was the first time Ernest or Skylar had seen the Artificials. They were left speechless.

Let's get back inside quickly before your hair does start falling out. The six of them began to walk back towards the blast door. Ernest grabbed the Geiger counter from the top step and then closed the doors behind them. "Careful where you put that thing, Major," Ashton protested. Laughing, Ernest *accidentally-on-purpose* put the Geiger counter in every unnecessary body placement he could find. Fortunately for his own health and safety, he didn't give Erynn the same treatment.

To the Chief's surprise, neither of them had high radiation levels. It didn't make any sense. Their radiation levels should have been reading off the charts. So Ernest, Aiden, and Skylar went outside to test the radiation levels. Everything was normal. The radiation was slightly higher than expected, but nothing that would make anybody sick. With Hunter, Erynn, And Ashton's radiation levels testing at normal levels, they could go into the shelter without any issues. And everyone could go outside. But Aiden needed to understand how any of this was possible.

Aiden, Skylar, and Ernest also noticed the Geiger counters on their CBRN suits didn't go beyond the dangerous levels when they were outside, either. The radiation was just under the danger line. Everything was safe, and so was everyone. Was it a miracle? Aiden couldn't believe it, so he asked them, "How in the hell are you three not radiated zombies right now?"

"The storm dumped most radiation on Cherry Hill Mountain where we were," Ashton said. Hunter and Erynn nodded their heads in agreement. "How could you three possibly know that?" Ernest responded with apparent skepticism. Ashton reached into his pocket and pulled out a two-way walkie-talkie, and Erynn did the same. Ashton tossed his walkie-talkie to Aiden, and Erynn tossed hers to Ernest.

"We found these two walkie-talkies inside a Faraday cage inside Rory's cabin. "A Faraday cage?" Skylar asked. "That is where we took shelter from the radiation storm," Ernest asked, showing his skepticism again. "Rory had a Faraday cage with walkie-talkies inside?" Aiden asked the bigger question. Ashton took the time to answer all three of their questions. "He sure did, Chief. The paranoid bastard probably saved our lives, too. We found a channel on which the government is giving information, and they told us about the attacks and the nuclear fallout." Ashton turned to Skylar. "Skylar, a Faraday cage is essentially a container, or a shield, that blocks out electromagnetic radiation, which means these radios were completely unharmed by the EMP."

Turning towards Ernest, "Yes. Erynn was smart enough to see something was wrong with that storm, and we didn't feel like being cold and wet, so we took shelter in Rory's cabin," Ashton addressed Ernest's earlier question. "I saw his place Chief, and even went inside; Rory's cabin was very prepared for an EMP attack," Ernest said to Aiden.

"We also found a missing clue your guys missed at the cabin, as well," Ashton said with a smirk. "That's because we haven't had time to search his place or follow proper protocol. Hell, we have barely had time to breathe as of lately." Ashton looked towards Ernest and lowered his voice. "I have bad news, Major. According to the government, most radiation was dumped mostly in Chesterfolk. But, unfortunately, it sounds like it hit them pretty badly, too." Ernest's heart sank to the floor, and his knees buckled. He couldn't take any more bad news.

Mr. Smith was hiding in plain sight and thinking about killing someone. It had been too long since his last kill. But a smile came across his face whenever he thought about planes falling from the sky. The United Cities was in total darkness, and he loved it. He killed his father and all of his elders. He was once the undisputed leader of The Order of the Corrupted Leaf until The Ghost destroyed it. And, now, he was looking at him.

Fate was kind. Ashton and Erynn had just entered the shelter, and no one even knew Smith was out of prison. But, of course, Smith was wearing one of his prosthetic masks. He was an unarmed tourist in the shelter, and his brother Jacob was next to him. He didn't know who Jacob was playing today, but he was sure it was an elaborate character of his choosing. As for Mr. Smith, his character didn't need a name. He was a scared tourist trying to get home as soon as the rain stopped.

Smith was probably going to kill someone in this shelter. It would be so risky, he thought to himself. But that is what made it so fun. As they entered the shelter, no one checked for weapons, and Smith had his knife and pistol with him. But the shelter was so packed that Smith decided his knife would be the best option. But when was he going to kill someone? He was excited with anticipation.

Smith thought about telling the Police Chief he was the one who killed Jared. He thought about telling the Chief all the gory details about Jared's last breaths on earth, but he decided against it. Smith thought about telling the Chief why he killed Rory. The paranoid idiot kept staring at one of Smith's prosthetic faces waiting for Finley to blink. The damn mask was perfect until you tried to blink, and Rory caught on to this, so he had to die.

There were locked in a shelter, and no one was coming to save them. *He* was God. *He* was The Lord. *And vengeance was The Lord's.* And apparently, fate wanted Mr. Smith to kill Ashton and Erynn. Everyone celebrated when the Chief told them it was safe to go outside. Now was his chance. Ashton was about to die, and so was Erynn. Just twenty more steps and his greatest enemy would be dead, and his little girlfriend. Mr. Smith still remembered how she felt all those years ago. He took her virginity.

Ten more steps. Ashton was right there. This was going to be an easy kill. No one saw him coming. He would disappear before they knew he was dying on the ground; the face they would have seen was not even his own. Three more steps. Two more. One.

"Okay, everyone," the fucking Chief stepped in front of Ashton. Smith almost screamed in anger. He should stab the fucking cop right now for getting in his way. "Step back just a little bit, sir,' Aiden said to Mr. Smith. The idiot didn't know how close he came to death. "I'm sorry, sir," Smith got into character. He played his part well. "We are all leaving the shelter now, and it's about two p.m., that's two p.m. Mountain Standard Time, for any of you who aren't from here. So that means we are two hours behind D.C. and New York."

A shelter evacuation saved Ashton. The lucky bastard. Everyone cheered, and Smith wanted to kill them all. But instead, he pretended to cheer with them as they all packed up and started walking out of the hot and sticking shelter.

"What are you looking at, little brother?" Mr. Smith turned his head slightly to address his younger brother Jacob. His brother Jacob was as ambitious as he was beautiful and was Mr. Smith's second in charge. Jacob was a lover of intellect, so he always found The Ghost to be boring, but Jacob had found interest in Connor Mason and his family and friends.

Together, Smith and Jacob ran The Bitterfang Pack. It wasn't quite The Order of the Corrupted Leaf, but it was something to marvel at. Mr. Smith loved watching these people fight amongst themselves. It was as though the world had given him a gift. They weren't out of the shelter for twenty minutes and already bickering about food and water. Neither Smith nor Jacob gave a damn about cell phones and wifi connections. Instead, they enjoyed the finer things of life, like killing sprees and disposing of bodies. Both men knew how to live off the land; they needed a knife and an excellent target to hunt. The rest of the world could go to hell as far as they could care.

Smith needed to kill, and his eyes had settled on a tall, slim, dark-haired woman. Her hair fell over her shoulder, and she walked as if she was the last beautiful woman on earth. He'd spotted her in the shelter. He didn't know why but she deserved to die. At first, Smith thought she was Ashton's sister Alison. She looked just like her. The mocha-brown skin aroused him instantly. She was voluptuous and supple but younger than *his* Alison. As his arousal for this woman grew, so did his rage.

He imagined killing her for taking away his baby and then letting another man raise his child while he was in prison. The bitch had to die! He might kill his daughter since Alison and Ashton took her from him. Yeah, it was all feeling good to him now. He would kill them all.

Jacob followed closely behind Smith. The two moved like wolves waiting for the right moment to attack. Then, strolling and blending into the crowd, the two brothers crossed the park. The woman's sneakers left a distinctive square pattern on the soft, wet earth. She was so easy to follow. She could die at any moment and behaved as if she didn't have a care in the world. But she was already dead; Jacob only needed to grab her so she could find out for herself.

Ms. Mocha-Brown stopped to tie her shoe, waving for the others to go on without her. She was confident. Mr. Smith liked that. "I will catch up with you guys soon," She called out to her friends. No, you won't, Missy, Smith thought to himself. Your next stop is heaven, if there is such a thing.

The attractive woman propped her foot up on a park bench, and Smith imagined how pretty her toes were. He liked women with pretty feet. It didn't matter; he would find out in a few minutes when he strung her upside down and drank her empty. Smith gave Jacob the order to grab her. He missed working with his brother. Smith often had Jacob working important missions because he was just so good.

Jacob moved swiftly, and without making a sound, he approached her from the side. It took only a moment for Jacob to grab her and move her away from the crowd without them ever noticing. The unsuspecting women didn't realize what was happening until it was too late. Jacob clamped his massive hand over her mouth, his palm quickly covering the lower half of her face. She kicked and struggled, trying to scream. "Hold still, or I will snap your fucking neck right here, little lady. I will do it. I love the sound it makes," Jacob said. His voice was both sinister and seductive. Jacob twisted her neck so far that it almost broke to show he was serious. The woman stopped fighting, and Mr. Smith almost laughed. "That's right. Do as you are told, and I won't kill you," Jacob lied to her. Of course, he was going to kill her. Or, Mr. Smith would. Either way, she was as good as dead.

Once they were far enough from the crowds to risk moving his hand, he gagged the girl and hung her upside down with zip ties. The zip ties cut into her ankles, and blood began to pour from her legs. She must have realized then what her fate would be. Salty tears streamed down her cheek. Jacob licked them softly as her body trembled in his arms. "We are going to drink you dry. Consider yourself lucky. When they find your body, you will be remembered forever." As her eyes widened with fear, Jacob raised his hand and knocked her unconscious with a near-deadly blow to the side of her head, nearly crushing her temple in the process. He carried her through the woods for the next hour until they reached the Bitterfang Pack lair. There was no debate when Jacob dropped her body on the ground. With one look from Mr. Smith, Jacob understood. It was time to feed. With a menacing look, Jacob turned towards the mocha-brown woman he had just met, and without ever knowing her name, he bit into the side of her neck and drank.

Soon—too soon— she died. Mr. Smith watched as his little brother fed and grew stronger. Alison was next, Smith thought. He was going to kill her because she broke his heart.

Alison peeled off her gloves and tossed them in a trashcan overflowing with other medical supplies. It was afternoon. It had been three days since the attack on the United Cities, and the hospital was working with the skeleton screw of a skeleton crew. Besides a nap here and there, Alison worked the entire time. So did everyone else in the hospital.

Some strange machines attack the hospital, and Alison barely makes it out alive. She saved Kian, which she now regretted because he had been complaining to everyone who would listen ever since. Equally as irritating, only one cleaning person returned to the hospital, and the place was a mess. She grabbed another pair of gloves and walked to the E.R. Dr. Kerry had been working on someone with a gunshot wound for the past ten hours, but she didn't recognize who it was. "Who the hell has been shooting people in the middle of a radioactive storm and complete power outage," Alison said to an already overworked emergency room. "The hell if I know," someone answered, but it was so busy and so loud she couldn't tell who responded.

"Check his vitals," Kelly said without looking at Alison. "Then check the drainage." Alison did as she was told with expert speed. Kelly was thankful Alison was there. Next, Alison took the man with the gunshot wounds wrist. First, she took his heart rate by placing her index and middle finger over the radial artery. Then she counted for fifteen seconds and multiple by four. "Heart rate is ninety-two," she announced. Next, she took his blood pressure. "Blood pressure is now ninety-six over fifty." "Shit," Kerry replied. "His breathing is getting worse, too!" Finally, Alison opened the patient's eyes. She raked a light back and forth, hoping for any signs of pupil dilation, but there was minimal movement.

Alison examined the four small holes in the patient's skull. Three were left open for pressure relief, but the fourth had a tube draining a mixture of blood and clear fluid into a sterile bag. "Everything looks good, Doctor Kerry. As good as it can be, considering." Everything they seemed to be doing simply wasn't working. Second, by the second, they were losing this guy, and the entire E.R. was feeling the pressure of saving his life. Standing next to Kelly, the doctor ordered Alison, "Go check on London. We have to save at least one damn person this morning." Alison sucked in a long, deep breath. She needed a vacation and a strong drink, but there was no time for relaxation. The world was dying, and all the people in it.

She approached London's bed, where a transportation worker was pumping the bag that allowed him to breathe. Everyone had to be a nurse, and everyone had to be a janitor. Even the transportation worker stepped in and learned how to be a nurse. "I could have sworn London was trying to open his eyes earlier, but I'm not a nurse, so I'm not sure if you should trust what I saw," the transportation worker said humbly. It was a self-deprecating remark, but Alison understood that he wasn't trying to do anything else but help as best as he could.

Alison was grateful the transportation worker was willing to step up. Most people didn't even return to the hospital, but he did. She wasn't about to make him feel stupid for his thoughts. Instead, Alison responded kindly, "I will keep an eye out for it. I am sure you saw exactly what you saw. Whether it was involuntary or not, that doesn't matter." The transportation worker didn't respond audibly, but the warm look on his face of both confidence and relief let her know that he was happy to be heard and heard with medical respect. For all she knew, he wanted to be a doctor, and she wasn't going to be the one to discourage him from becoming one. Alison was so happy for his help, she told him, "I'll take over now. You can take a break."

London's parents have been sitting in the lobby since their son was admitted. They were volunteering around the hospital in any way that they could since the lights went out. They even watched Paige for a spell while Alison worked on other patients. Then, Alison passed off the manual breathing duties to another nurse so she could report back to Doctor Kelly. Just then, she saw her brother Ashton in the hospital lobby playing with Paige. He couldn't have been here more than five minutes because she had just looked in Paige's direction, and she was playing with a puzzle or something at the feet of London's parents.

Walking towards her brother, she could see a mischievous grin on his face. Seeing him made her heart smile; she had been way too mean to him earlier. Alison was glad he was okay and felt terrible about their last encounter with one. "Ashton Jace, what the heck are you doing here? And where is Erynn?" "She is over there." He pointed to the other side of the hospital lobby. Erynn was leaning against a vending machine with a relaxed posture. "We have Corporal Hunter with us now. I will explain that later," Ashton said. However, there was something wrong with his face. Alison could tell. Something was bothering Ashton. "What's wrong, Ashton? Tell me." Ashton took a few seconds and then came out with it. Ashton's mischievous grin went away and was replaced by a serious look. "The Rougarou is back."

Alison nearly fainted. She remembered their childhood. She also remembered Erynn and Ashton were the best Rougarou and the deadliest when they were kids. If the Rougarou were back, then every one was dead. "I know what you are thinking, Alison, but you need to know I am not playing. That's who killed Jared and Rory." Alison had her own secrets she didn't tell anyone about and she felt guilty now more than ever. In the midst of this guilt, she replied, "That explains the bodies being drained of blood." "We found a clue only a Rougarou would have left behind and Rory's house. But it gets worse," Ashton said.

He had Alison's full attention now. "The Rougarou from Clemenceau is back," Ashton said to his sister. Alison did faint this time. Erynn rushed over, picked her up, and sat her in a chair. "I didn't do anything, Erynn. She fainted from the news you told me to tell her," Ashton said defensively. It was a short spell, and Alison opened her eyes.

Alison looked at Erynn and Ashton and said, "The Order—" Ashton interrupted her. We don't know if Finley is involved yet. Remember, he is locked up in a Supermax Correctional Facility," Ashton said to his sister. But she knew he didn't believe it. She knew Ashton would look for Finley and kill him before Finley could kill Alison. And it was all her fault.

"Have you told Chief Aiden everything?" Alison asked. "He has been fully briefed and knows everything I know. I don't know how much he knows about the legend, but he knows everything else."

Just then, Aiden and Derrick both walked into the lobby. "Ma'am," Aiden was talking to Alison. "We need to speak with your brother and his," Aiden trailed off. Alison could tell, just like the rest of us, no one knew what to call Erynn and Ashton. Alison responded, that's fine, but I am not going anywhere. Trust me; whatever he has done or is going on, I have more information than you do now." Aiden thought for a moment and then continued, "Ashton, we need you to tell us everything about the Rougarou."

"Chief, we need to go somewhere privately. And I want Hunter to come, too," Ashton said to Aiden. Alison took everyone to an empty back hospital room, and Erynn sat by Ashton. She made her presence known. Before Ashton began talking, he said, "Before I get started, I need permission from Erynn and Alison on how much I can discuss." Alison gave Erynn permission to discuss one hundred percent, and Erynn nodded in agreement.

"One more thing, Chief?" Ashton was asking. Aiden didn't respond, so Ashton asked anyway. There was nothing the Chief could do to stop him. "I need my sword out of the Dodge." "You have a sword?" Aiden asked. Before Ashton could respond, Alison jumped into the conversation. "Listen up, everyone. You do not have the authority here. If you want the answers, stop being cops and start listening to what you do not know."

Aiden didn't know what to say. He didn't like ambiguity in his city, so he did the only thing he could. "I agree with everything you are saying. Go get your sword, man." Ashton left and came back within a few minutes. He now had a real sword strapped to his back. He looked like a Samurai with guns.

By the time Ashton came back, Ernest was in the room now. Ashton said the room consisted of Erynn, Ashton, Alison, and Hunter. Along with Aiden, Derrick, and Ernest. Ashton proceeded to tell the Chief and Derrick everything. Ashton told them how Erynn and Ashton were raised as assassins in a secret order since they were young. Ashton also told them how they were members of The Order of the Corrupted Leaf and how all three of them, Ashton, Erynn, And Alison, were raised to be Rougarou.

Ashton gave everybody Erynn's backstory, his own, and Alison's. "Gentleman, I know you must all think this is fake, but there is a hidden world you know nothing about, and this world is now killing people in Wakefield," Ashton said. He had to explain three times what a Rougarou was, but he was patient with everyone. "Make no mistake about it, and your military training is not enough for those like Erynn, my sister, and myself. Anyone who is newly recruited is debatable. But I can assure you, gentle. Even your government at its highest levels knows about this. Why do you think me and Erynn were both Special Forces? We have been trained assassins since the day we were born." Ashton said to everyone.

"I don't care if you believe me. But, if you want proof, attack Erynn and me and see for yourselves," Ashton didn't care if they believed. He was finally getting this burden off his chest.

"And I am afraid we have an even bigger problem," Ashton said. "How can there be a bigger problem?" Ernest asked skeptically. "First of all, Ernest, I don't like you much, and you have made your opinions about me. So do us all a favor and stop being perfect and open your little brain before I show you personally what you doubt," Ashton said with venom. Ernest rose to challenge Ashton, but Erynn beat him, disarmed the Major, dropped him to the floor, and was back by Ashton's side before he realized what had happened.

"As you can see from what Erynn just did to our well-trained Major, your military and police training mean nothing to people like us." Ashton continued. "Let me say again that we have been trained to be the world's best assassins since birth. You cannot defeat us."

Ashton let his words sit in for a moment. Ernest wanted to retaliate, but Alison gave him a look that told him to stop.

"We are on your side," Ashton explained to the group again. "Chief, I let you arrest me every time you arrested me. No disrespect to you, but I am not that weak." Aiden didn't say anything. Instead, he seemed to be listening intently.

"Now, back to the worse news," Ashton said. This time, everyone seemed to drop their doubts and listen. So rigorous are shapeshifters, at least the real ones are. They have superhuman strength, and bullets barely work on them." Ashton paused again. Aiden took advantage of this pause and said his first words. "Gentleman," Aiden said to everyone. "Ernest," Aiden looked at his new friend. "I believe every word Ashton is saying." Ernest gasped. Hunter didn't, however; maybe the battle he fought with Erynn and Ashton made him believe in their abilities before he got to this conversation.

"About twenty-four hours ago, on my way to Ashton, Derrick and I were with Special Agent Brentley Miller, the head of the FBI on this entire side of Salleria. We raided a farmhouse of about forty-give Rougarous, and they were as Ashton has described. Even a big wolf was killed by one of the agents." Aiden was interrupted.

"Did you say a big wolf?" Ashton asked. "Yes, a huge one. Why are you asking?" Aiden asked. Alison burst into tears, and Erynn put her hand on her knives. "Then the leader of the Rougarous, who used to be all of our best friends," Ashton was talking about Erynn, Alison, and himself. "He has broken out of prison and is now the most dangerous man you know. It's no longer Erynn or myself."

The room fell silent, and no one knew one to say. But Ashton did. He didn't want to say what needed to be said, but he said it anyway. "He will be looking for me. All the murders in Wakefield have been my fault. We can say the same thing about Salleria, too."

The room fell silent.

UC

A magnificent sunrise peeked through the cloud and slowly jumped over the horizon of the Atlantic Ocean. Monique sat impatiently in her wheelchair, and it didn't take long to realize she hated wheelchairs. Still, aboard the USS George H.W. Bush, her trusted bodyguard Weston sat by her side. Big Wes and Monique were both injured, bandaged, and exhausted, but they were alive. Unfortunately, their good friend Brayden was not. The breeze blew salt water into Monique's face. "Salty air is better than poisonous air, ma'am," West said as if he was reading her thoughts. With a nod of her head in agreement, she ignored, telling Weston how the back of her neck burned with pain as the saltwater midst was blown on her open burns. The person who suffered the worse burns inside the PEOC was Brayden. He didn't make it. The second worst burned person was Monique, the newest President of the United Cities of Salleria.

So many top officials had died. Secretary of State Hallie Barrera was one of them. She was grateful to Weston for always being there to protect her. Even now, injured and burned, he was by her side. "How are you feeling, ma'am," Weston said gently. Monique considered Weston to be her closest friend. He always had a way of making things better. He was making things better, even now. "I feel pretty good, Wes. I could be better, but I am grateful to be alive." Weston was a gentleman in all circumstances. He had a smooth way about him— even under fire. Monique looked up to Weston with a tear forming in her right eye and asked, "Wes... your family? You are here with me and," her words trailed off as the once-forming tear rolled down her cheek. They both knew his family was most likely dead. They lived in D.C. and West sent them with a family member when the lights went off but that was no guarantee they evacuated in time. Monique wanted to say something reassuring, but she couldn't. She suddenly realized that she had only been trying to save Chase. Monique never mentioned his wife Tracy, his daughters Sasha and Tera, or his brother Thomas. She felt guilty and ashamed.

Instead of words, she reached up and touched his arm with her left hand. The other lay curled up in her lap, still swaddled in bandages. She hadn't been brave enough to look at her burns yet.

Her attention was caught by a Black Hawk loading six men from Special Forces and Special Ops teams from all the armed forces to various places all morning. These men were the best of the best. Some men were from the United Cities of Salleria Marine Corps (USMC) Fleet Anti-Terrorism Security Team, also known as *FAST*, an elite unit ready for rapid deployment when UCS Government installations worldwide require additional security. They are stationed at different naval command posts across the globe. This unit of close to 500 Marines is specially trained using state-of-the-art weapons.

Another elite unit that has been in and out of missions all morning is UCS Army 75th Ranger Regiment. This elite infantry unit, also known simply as *Rangers*, is a Special Operations unit composed of a single Special Troops Battalion and three special operations battalions, specially trained with various skills needed for several different specialized missions. These three light infantry battalions can be rapidly deployed and take turns rotating into the "Ranger Ready Forces," where they are in constant readiness with the ability to respond to any crisis, anywhere in the world, in less than 18 hours.

Also included were the MARSOC Raiders. Activated in February of 2006, this specially trained Marine Corps group is a module command of the UCS Special Operations Command encompassing the UCSMCs contribution to SOCOM. The primary capabilities of MARSOC include direct action, special reconnaissance, and also foreign internal defense. They are also in charge of counter-terrorism, information operations, and unconventional warfare. These highly specialized and trained individuals must be functionally capable of operating in fast-paced, often remote and complex, environments.

The UCS Army Intelligence Support Activity was also in rotation. This top-secret UCS Army intelligence unit's primary function is to gather intelligence information to pave the way for a plan of action. Some sources for their information include (but are not limited to) local operatives working undercover and monitoring and tracking radio communications.

The USMC Force Reconnaissance team was also available. Force Recon has been active since June 1957. The USMC Force Reconnaissance is capable of performing both deep reconnaissances as well as direct action operations. This specialized task force is trained to operate independently behind enemy lines while unconventional special ops while supporting conventional warfare. Their primary focus is to support Marine expeditionary and amphibious operations.

The last four specialized units in rotation were The Army's Green Berets, UCS Navy Seals (Regular teams), UCS Army Delta Force, and SEAL Team 6. The Army's Special Forces soldiers, known as "Green Berets," are military legends for service members and civilians alike. They take on terrorists through quiet, guerrilla war-style missions in foreign countries. The UCS Navy Seals are probably one of (if not) the most well-known Special Ops groups in the world. They are highly specialized and trained in the air, land, and sea. The UCS Army Delta Force unit generally consists of versatile, quiet professionals involved in unconventional warfare, special reconnaissance, counter-terrorism, information operations, and various other roles. SEAL Team 6, The UCS Naval Special Warfare Development Group has a classified number of teams deployed worldwide. The original Team 6 was dissolved in 1987 but then re-established by the U.S. Navy as the Special Warfare Development Group – DEVGRU. Most information about DEVGRU remains highly classified, and neither the White House nor the Department of Defense will comment on the details of its activities.

The United Cities of Salleria was on the prowl to defend its nation. All the Armed Forces of the UCS were working in tandem like never before. Yet, many civilians were homeless, poisoned from nuclear fallout, and living in the dark. It was amazing how quickly civilization collapsed without the infrastructure to support it. Finally, the hatch to the command center opened, and Captain Andres Espinoza stepped onto the platform. "Madam President," he said with a reverent nod. "How are you feeling?" "I am feeling much better. The pain meds are working, and my mind is getting clearer by the second. The radiation treatment seems to work too, but I still feel like I want to throw up every time I breathe in or out." Espinoza nodded with great understanding. He had seen his fair share of war and saw more than most men could handle. "Where are the Black Hawks headed now?" Monique asked. "Evac ops and recon missions, ma'am," Espinoza replied. "We are bringing the government's top brass back together, ma'am so that you can run the nation properly. Also, we have a thousand other high-ranking individuals."

Monique immediately thought about the Senators she left behind who were not high enough up the flag pole to be considered high-ranking personnel. She remembered they begged to get in the car with her and wondered if they had survived. She knew the likelihood of them surviving was near zero. Monique was still struggling to accept the massive damage that had been done to her body. She couldn't believe it. "Madam President," Espinoza said with concern. "We need you healthy. The entire world is depending on you to put it back together." Monique thought about that for a second. How many other countries did the North Kangavarians attack? Was it just the UCS? If so, which one of their enemies would try to take advantage of a wounded United Cities?

Monique looked back to the deck as a third Black Hawk took to the sky. The deck of the supercarrier was a hectic place. It was alive with organized chaos, and there was not an inch of it that did not include some hyperactivity. All Monique could do for now was sit in her chair and watch. But she knew that was about to change. She was *not* about to run the United Cities of Salleria from a seated position. The hatch opened again, and Natasha Clark walked toward the President, Weston, and Espinoza and greeted everyone graciously. She gave President Monique extra attention. "Ma'am," Clark said as she came to the position of attention.

"At ease, my friend. Thank you for being part of the crew who saved our lives." Monique replied with heartfelt empathy and gratitude. "It is an honor to meet you, Madam President. You are the first woman ever to lead the United Cities of Salleria. That is both amazing and long overdue." Monique smiled at the X.O. In one motion, Clark turned towards Espinoza. "Captain Admiral Pittman made contact and requested we send F-18s for close air support while civilians are evacuated from the East Coast. They are worried about more attacks and want to be on the safe side." "How many more times have the North Kangavarians attacked us recently?" Monique asked. "

"Plenty more times Madam President." Monique's heart dropped to her stomach in crippling fear. "The North Kangavarians are attacking us with more than nuclear warfare, ma'am. From our latest reports, they have stolen more than one billion dollars of Bitcoin from Sallerian investors and more than ten billion from the Federal Reserve, Madam President," the X.O. said with regret. "My God," Monique replied with shock. "They are financing World War III by crippling The United Cities and stealing all of our money." "Those fucking bastards are brilliant," Captain Espinoza said with the most disgust he could produce from his throat. "Agreed." Monique reluctantly replied. Monique knew that her job as President of the United Cities had become much harder than she wished. With very little power and no way to defend themselves from any military attack, the North Kangavarians were also defeating Salleria in a cyber war.

"Clark, get Admiral Pittman whatever he needs. Clark saluted Espinoza and returned to the bridge. A few minutes later, a dozen pilots ran across the flight deck toward their birds. Everyone sensed that the North Kangavarians were waiting in silence for the right time to attack again. "Captain," Monique took her eyes off the dozen pilots and fixed them on Captain Espinoza. "Yes, Madam President?" "Before North Kangavar nuked The White House, I saw dozens of nukes leaving our bunkers and headed towards North Kangavar. Would you happen to know the results of our attack on them?" "North Kangavar is destroyed, ma'am. It was hit with so many nukes that the entire country is now a series of radioactive craters. Any forces or government they have left are already in Sallerian borders— at least, that would be my best guess," Captain Espinoza replied. Monique didn't know what to say or what to ask. She knew Secretary of State Hallie Barrera, who died in the PEOC explosion just a day ago. She was a nice person, and he ordered the nuclear execution of an entire country. She wondered how many innocent civilians were now dead. She wondered how much it hurt her to give the order. She, then, wondered if *she* could give that order herself.

"How many people live in North Kangavar, again?" Monique asked. "A little over twenty-five million, ma'am," Weston replied quickly. Monique wanted to cry but couldn't show weakness in front of people like that anymore. She was the leader of the free world right now. So instead, she opted to stare in silence for twenty seconds before she said another word. "Did Krasnovia help the North Kangavarians?" Monique asked. "As of right now, ma'am. There is no evidence that North Kangavar collaborated with any other nation," Captain Espinoza replied.

The last pilot closed the canopy over his cockpit and gave a thumbs-up sign. Monique, a fire pilot herself, gripped the arms of her wheelchair tightly and began to stand up. Weston took a few steps closer and helped her to her feet. He knew what she wanted and what was in her fighter pilot's heart. With the burning pain of fire shooting through every nerve in her body, Monique forced her body to stand in the position of attention, and with every bit of her energy, she saluted the pilot as he took off. For a long split second, the pilot and the President of the United Cities of Salleria held eye contact with the most powerful mutual respect they could send. They both knew that they might not live to see tomorrow.

After her salute, Captain Espinoza caught Monique staring at a Black Hawk and positioning her body as if she was about to walk toward it. Quickly responding, Espinoza said, "Ma'am. I understand your son is trapped in one of the radioactive zones. We will do everything we can to find him, but try not to steal one of my birds and go, rogue. Your reputation as fighter proceeds, you ma'am." Monique smiled because she was just about to get into one of these birds and get her son. "Guilty," she said outlaid to Espinoza. "Guilty, guilty, guilty."

Ashton looked at Alison rubbing her eyes like never before. Every five minutes, she yawned and then rubbed her eyes. He had never seen his sister this tired before. I didn't realize how rough it would be working in a hospital but during an EMP strike. Everyone was screwed, especially hospital workers. He could only compare it to her being in combat; the hospital was now her battlefield.

It was almost three in the afternoon, Mountain Standard Time, and the United Cities were almost seventy-two hours into this EMP strike, and for the first time in days, the sky was clear. Everyone was walking into town, and the sun was working overtime, bringing in unnecessary heat. No air conditioning units were working, so the inside of the building became musty, muggy, and hot. As they got into town, Ashton could see his Dodge next to Derrick's pickup. Everyone was salvaging food or working on cars, trying to get them back working. Erynn nudged Ashton on the shoulder, indicating it was time for them to go. Ashton said his goodbyes to Paige. "Uncle Ashton, why do you have to go?" Paige said with a broken heart. Ashton kneeled, promised her he would be back soon, and told her some people needed his help. Alison hugged Erynn, and Paige followed with her hug, as well.

Aiden was standing in front of a few more working cars. Erynn assumed this was the new version of the Wakefield Police Department fleet of vehicles. It was about six vehicles. Five, if you didn't count Ashton's Dodge. Ernest and Derrick were standing next to each other with a map spread over the hood of Ashton's Dodge. Every police officer was armed to the teeth with semi-automatic rifles and handguns. Erynn sized each man up and down, giving each a nod of approval. Hunter was with Erynn and Ashton now, his skull mask affixed to his face.

Before Aiden could begin giving orders, Alison spoke up. "Chief, I expect you to keep my brother safe since you keep pulling him into dangerous situations." "Yes, ma'am. I will, but now that I know your bother, I think he will keep me safe, ma'am." Aiden responded with his usually calming charisma. "Ernest, how is your shoulder... and don't lie," Alison now directed her anger towards the Major. Feeling like a kid being chastised by his mother, the Major promptly responded, "It's doing great, Alison. I promise." There was something about the way Ernest looked her Ashton's sister that pissed him off. He was almost certain Alison looked at him with the same energy, which only made him angry. Ashton looked like he wanted to throw up in his mouth, listening to Ernest and his sister flirt.

Erynn followed Ashton to his Dodge. Aiden had a severe and stern look on his battle-scarred face. "This ends today, people. I want this killer found and brought to justice." "We have another lead, as well," Aiden told everyone. Detective Schwartz found the signs of a camp at the top of Cherry Hill. It is well hidden. Erynn looked at Ashton to say, *How in the hell did we miss an entire camp?* Aiden answered the question they both were wondering.

"Schwartz was checking on the folks with homes up on the mountain, and she found this." Aiden handed Erynn a green mitten.

Erynn didn't need to ask to whom it belonged. She recognized it immediately because Ashton still had Jared's other mitten somewhere in his Dodge. "And there is another thing," Aiden said. He was full of heavy news today. "We know our killer, so we now have the advantage. So stay sharp, people."

"Chief, is it true the killer is acting out some Creole urban legend about werewolves?" One of the officers asked. "It's a bit more complicated than that, but what you have heard is true. And according to Erynn and Ashton, we are looking at two killers with a team of killers in their corner." Aiden turned to Ashton, Erynn, and Alison. "Do you want to add anything right here, Ashton? Maybe something we need to know or something you may have left out? You, Erynn, and Alison are all Creole, so all of you will know much more than us."

Ashton responded. "We are hunting predators. The main two will be just as fast as your bullets. They will kill on-site, and they can track your movements and cover their tracks. Finley and Jacob are two of the best killers in the world." Ashton was finished. He didn't have anything else to say.

"Damn. Is it that bad, Ashton?" Detective Schwartz asked. "Yes. Yes, it is," Ashton said as Erynn nodded. Everyone pushed the magazines to their weapons and added ammunition to their jacket and vest pockets. Derrick chambered a round, pushed the scope to his eye, and scanned the tree line on Cherry Hill. Ernest loaded the Barrett M95 sniper rifle that Aiden had given him. As an officer, he was more used to his sidearm, which was a Browning

Hi-Power pistol. Technically, Browning discontinued the classic Hi-Power handgun in 2017, but enough of these classics have been made to go around. Ashton had his sword.

Aiden turned on one of the walkie-talkies Ashton had brought him. There were four in total, and Erynn and Ashton had a pair. Aiden and the police station had the other pair. "Janice, do you copy?" Aiden asked into his radio. "I'm here, Chief," Janice replied. "We're moving out. Stay by the radio." Aiden clipped the radio to his belt, checked his weapons, and motioned for everyone to move out.

Ernest stole a look at Alison and smiled in her direction. She returned the gesture. She ran over to Ernest before he got too far away and kissed him. Ernest returned the kiss, and Ashton rolled his eyes. Erynn smiled. "I hope I get to see you again, Ernest," Alison said in a flirtatious tone. "I'd like that very much, Ms. Jace." "Didn't I tell you to call me Alison?" "I'd like that very much, sexy Alison," Ernest responded playfully. Alison's eyes lit up, and she smiled a huge smile. "You be careful, too, big brother. And you too, Erynn. And both of you need to get married and stop acting like y'all are not in love," Alison said, not knowing when to mind her business.

"We will be safe, Sis. We are the best in the world, remember. And We both know we are in love." Ashton responded. "Well, what the hell are you two waiting for; it's the end of the world," Alison couldn't help herself.

Chapter Twenty

Connor had to say goodbye to Kayla Lowe again, and it got a little harder each time he said goodbye. But she was safe, and now it was time to return to his neck of the woods and make sure his family was safe. Connor and Kayla made both made a promise to see each other soon. Secretly, Connor hoped it would be very soon, but time would tell. Relationships had a way of falling apart around him.

Connor tried, but he couldn't stop thinking about the mysterious radio call he got from Jacob. How did he know when he got to Wakefield, and how long was he watching Connor? These were the questions that raced through Connor's mind. Who the hell was this Jacob guy, and what did Connor do to piss him off; Connor had no clue?

The kids enjoyed playing board games with Mama Linda and Papa Anthony when Connor returned to his house. Papa Anthony mentioned he had an idea to get the electricity working in the house. "That would be great, Dad, but it would also make us the only house in Lakota with lights," Connor told Papa Anthony. "You let me worry about that, Son."

Connor laughed and played games for another two hours, and life was good. He had his family back, and everyone was safe. However, Connor is still worried about the case. It was dark times in Salleria, and Connor needed a break. The more he thought about it, the more he inched towards leaving the FBI and going back into Quantum Physics full-time. Then, he could discover the following mathematical equation that would change the world.

Around four p.m. MST, Connor decided to go upstairs into the second den. He didn't like working tonight. He just wanted to rest. But, before he reached the stairs, Papa Anthony came to Connor. "Where is your blanket, son?" "Huh?" Connor responded. It was a weird question. "Don't worry, Son. I will go to your room and get it." "Okay, Dad." Before Connor could finish the short sentence, Papa Anthony was already gone.

Connor dreamt he was drinking an ice-cold beer. Just that fast, Connor nodded off and took a five-minute nap. Closing his eyes again, Connor was interrupted by the crackling of white noise on the radio. "Brentley, let me get some rest, bro," Connor said to no one. Instead, he was talking out loud to himself. *As long as you don't answer yourself, Connor.* Isn't that what the shrinks say? Connor thought to himself.

Tired and ready to kick his feet up and unwind for the night, Connor picked up the radio. "I killed them, Connor, and I did it because of you. You are the reason they are dead," the familiar voice over the radio violated Connor's ears. It was Jacob. "It was all your fault, Dr. Quantum. I didn't want to kill them, which wasn't part of the plan, but The Master told me I could do what I wanted, and you are my new favorite person, Connor."

The horrifying confession came as a taunt. "Who the hell was this? Are you Jacob?" Connor wanted to scream into the microphone but used a controlled explosive volume instead. His family was downstairs, and he didn't want them to hear anything. Connor's adrenaline dumped into his bloodstream. "I am your new best friend, Connor. You are my intellectual equal. Isn't this so fun?" "Fun? How in the world could any of this be fun?" "Oh, Connor, You're hurting my feelings. Do you not find me fun?" Jacob said on the other end of the receiver.

"What is fun about a serial killer having some sort of man crush on me?"

"Oh, Connor, there you go again, hurting my little feelings. Don't you like me?"

"No."

"Then that is why I had to kill the. Because you don't like me."

Connor was outraged— and sleepy, and he had forgotten the call began with a confession of murder. Get it together, Connor. Connor stood up so the blood and flow back into his brain. "Who did you kill, Jacob?" "I killed your friend, silly? What kind of question was that? Who else would I kill?" Connor's heart nearly jumped out of his chest! Who did Jacob kill? Which friends? Connor had a lot of friends. Maybe the Son of a bitch was bluffing.

Connor calmed his voice and asked, "Which of my friends did you kill Jacob?" There was a long silence on the other end of the radio. Connor hated it. What was taking so long for Jacob to answer? "Sorry for the delay, The Master and I finished feeding about an hour ago, and we are as full as a tick." Connor laughed at his joke. The bastard was enjoying himself.

"You didn't answer my question, Jacob," Connor said. He was getting frustrated. "Look, stop jerking my chain. Pretending to kill one of my friends is not nice, Jacob. I am turning this radio off." As Connor was reaching for the power button to turn it to the off position, Jacob's playful voice turned as cold as Connor had ever heard a killer to be. "Turn it off, and I will kill Mama Linda, you arrogant son of a bitch," Jacob was nearly growling. His change was so rapid Connor was taken back. "Besides, I never said I killed one of your friends. I said I killed *them*. As in, *I killed them all, motherfucker*. Don't ever don't me again, asshole."

Connor's throat closed. He didn't know what to do at this point. So he did the only thing he could. He asked more questions. Jacob was in charge now; this was his game. "Okay, Jacob. I give up. Who did you kill? I am asking nicely."

"Before I tell you who I killed, let me tell you why I killed them," Jacob responded.

"Okay, I'm listening."

"See, I knew you could be obedient, Dr. Quantum. I killed them because I like you. The more I like you, the more people I will kill because of you. And, the better you do your job as an FBI Agent, the more I will kill people."

"That doesn't make any sense," Connor was getting irritated all over again. "It's downright fucking stupid."

"Either way, that is why I killed them," Jacob said.

"Okay, so who did you kill Jacob?"

"Well, I killed them before it started raining. That was hours ago."

"But who did you kill, Jacob?" Connor asked, forcing himself to remain calm.

"Silly, Willy. I killed Maxine, John, and Terrance."

Connor dropped the indestructible two-way radio left behind for him at Anna's house, jumped down the stairs, and nearly knocked the screen door off its hinges.

No, no, no! Connor was sick to his stomach. He hadn't expected to come home to such a violent crime scene. His next-door neighbors were dead. Maxine baked cookies for Mama Linda every Christmas, her husband John, who played dominoes with Papa Anthony, and their sixteen-year-old Son Terrance. They were all stabbed to death, and their throats were cut open.

Connor stood silent and transfixed in their living room. His eyes blurred with tears and Connor broke down. Finally, he couldn't take it anymore. He had been bottling up so much death and so much pain. He was so tired. How could anyone do this to innocent people? And why did Jacob say to tell Connor they all died because of him? Connor would never forgive himself.

Logically, Connor knew he was not responsible for the gruesome murders, but emotionally, Connor felt guilty. He felt fully responsible. His job with the FBI was becoming too much. He was tired of seeing bloody murder scenes— maybe it was time for a change.

There was nothing Connor could do for them now. They were dead, and finding their killer was his only option. Connor heard a noise at the front door, rolled over to his back, and pulled out his Glock 19. "Dad, I almost shot you in the face," Connor yelled to his father. "Don't let anyone else come over here, Dad," Connor asked. "I already handled that, Son. Here's your radio. It's not over yet." "Thanks." "I will have your blanket ready. Two pillows, too." "Dad, what are you," Connor asked his dad, but Papa Anthony was already walking away. The radio roared to life before Connor could process the weirdness of his father.

"There you are, Connor," It was Jacob again. Connor was starting to hate this guy. "I left more for you upstairs," Connor kept his gun in his hand and marched upstairs carefully. He was going to nail this Son of a bitch. "There you go, keep climbing those stairs." The killer was in here. Jacob was still in the house, and Connor would nail him to the cross.

"You know, you had me concerned there for a little bit, Connor. I thought you had died or something," Jacob was messing with Connor. He wanted Connor to lose his cool again, but Connor refused to let him win. "No, I didn't die. But one of us will. It's a beautiful day to die, wouldn't you say," Connor asked. He was tired of taking Jacob's shit. He was about to dish it back to Jacob.

"You want to tell me where you are, Jacob? Why don't you come out and play."

"You want to play with me, Connor? That sounds like so much fun." Jacob was up the stairs and in the hallway. He checked both rooms, and there was no one there. He checked the bathrooms, too— still, no none.

"I don't see you, Jacob. I thought you wanted to play with me," Connor said into the radio. Then, he was back in the hallways.

"Unfortunately, Connor, you can't play with me right now, I am about to kill someone else, but you can play with my friend."

The radio went silent. "Hello, hello," Connor tried. Where are you, Jacob? I am—"

Connor heard a terrifying growl coming from above. He looked up, and there was a massive beast of a man falling from the attic. He crashed into Connor with such force he was sure he broke a rib.

You forgot to check the attic, Connor. You are better than this. Get up before he kills you. He has the advantage now. Connor was coaching himself in his head. It was all he could do to stay alive. He had to return to his family and stop this guy before he went next door and killed his family. It was now or never.

The man was fast, and Connor couldn't keep up. He was growling like a madman and using both walls in the hallways to jump side to side on all four limbs. How do you fight a man who is acting like an animal? The man growled and launched toward Connor. Connor didn't see the knife until it was too late; all he could do was jump to the side. Connor's attacker missed his chest, but his second knife slash ripped through his left leg. Razor-sharp pain soared through Connor's leg.

Connor jumped to his feet at about the same time the man did. He stood on his legs now. Connor didn't know where his gun had gone. Connor tried to shield his face, but he wasn't fast enough. The man slashed Connor's left forearm with the knife, too. Pain seared through Connor's body again.

The man raised his fist to strike with the knife again; this time, Connor was ready. Connor parried to the right and hit the man with a left hook. The man fell to the ground, and the knife crashed somewhere. "You're in my world now, motherfucker," Connor said to the fallen man. "Get up. Get back to your feet," Connor taunted the man. He and Connor were about the same size, which made it a fair fight in Connor's mind. Forgetting all about his pain, when the man rose to his feet, Connor threw a straight right jab. After it connected, Connor threw a three-punch combination to the body. The man screamed in pain.

"Come on! You wanted to fight me! Here I am," Connor was so angry. He wanted to cause the man excruciating pain. Connor thought about subduing the man, but he wanted to fuck him up. He was so angry. He was tired of people growling and creeping through the city, trying to kill him and his friends. The man had come here to kill Connor. He wouldn't kill him, but he would kick his ass.

Connor threw a right-hand jab to the head and then a left cross to the head. He dodged the man's wild swing, and Connor went in for the kill shots. First, Connor hit the man with a two-punch combination to the face and a three-punch combination to the body. Then, as soon as the man folded from the body punches, Connor threw a right uppercut so beautiful he felt like Muhammad Ali. The man's head nearly fell, and Connor ended the fight with his favorite punch. It was his knockout shot. Connor's combinations served one purpose; to weaken his opponent so Connor could finish them with his devastating left hook. And that is precisely what Connor did. Connor walloped the man with his second left hook. *SPLAT!* The man crashed into the wall and didn't move again.

Connor screamed; he was so angry. Connor stood over the man's body. He wanted to kill him, but instead, he said, "You're under arrest, you unconscious Motherfucker. You have the right to remain silent— and sleeping."

Ten Years Ago — The Forbidden Fruit.

Alison's hands were shaking. She knew she was wrong but couldn't help herself. Seeing him again brought back so many memories. Sure, many of them were terrible, and he was dangerous, but he had this power over her she couldn't tame. He made her body ache, and she wanted him inside her now.

Knock. Knock. Knock.

Alison answered the door. God, this man looked so good, but this was so wrong. If they were caught, she would be in so much trouble— they both would be. But no one understood what they shared; Alison didn't even understand it. So the second he entered the door, and it shut behind him, she pressed her body against his. He forced her against the front door and brought his mouth down on hers.

Alison dropped everything. She didn't even remember what it was at this point. Her arms flew around his neck, and she arched her body against his. She wanted him now.

She knew his touch so well, but it had been so long. The feel of his lips felt new against hers. The way he kissed her, he was different. He changed. There were safe; no none was going to find out. His body was rigid, and his muscles flexed through his shirt; Alison pulled it over his head.

When his young slid against her lips, she opened for him with a moan. *Finally,* after all these years. Alison's tongue glided on top of his, and she loved his taste. They've been sneaking around all year, but this was the best time. They were both single, and people shouldn't have a problem with what she did with her life. She was a grown woman.

"Touch me. Please"

He did. He didn't have to take off her clothes; she only wore a towel. It was damp from the shower she had just taken. She wanted to be fresh for him. She wanted him to know she was ready for him to enter her.

He cupped Alison's bare breasts in his hands, and all she could do was sigh and say, "Take me."

He dipped his head and pressed his open mouth to her nipple. The warmth of his tongue brought Alison's to a peak. She released in pleasure— only he could make her do that.

Alison took off his pants, and he was bare. She looked down, and he stood proudly. His cocky demeanor drove her crazy. He knew he was sexy, and he knew he was endowed. He picked Alison up and took her to the bedroom. This was so *bad*. She shouldn't— but it was too late. She was fully committed.

He laid her on the bed, and she looked into his eyes, and then she looked back down to her favorite part of him. He was rigid, and she could see veins throbbing in it. He slid into her with something like a growl, and she released again. That's two, she thought. God! Yes!

She loved every bit of it, and she loved every bit of him. Alison took everything he had to offer, and she pushed back as he gave it. Their hands roamed, and she let her hands do the looking as she closed her eyes and released them repeatedly. She lost count of how many times he pleased her.

"Harder," she whined, arching her hips impatiently. She wanted more, and he did not disappoint. He never did. A second later, her release seized her, and he held her through it, kissing her and rubbing her, and before she could come down from her release, she released again, and he came with her.

Alison wrapped her legs around his body and wanted to receive all of him. When he was finished, she snuggled her face into his right shoulder, leaving just enough room to breathe. Alison wanted him to stay inside of her. It had been so long since she'd fallen asleep with a man. A warm, relaxed feeling spread over her, and she whispered into his ear, "I love you, Mr. Finley Smith." A tear fell from her face as he whispered it back. "I love you, too, Alison Smith."

They had eloped, and now they were consummated.

Finley was a brand new person now. His name was Neil Stevens; Jacob cooked this character up himself. Finley's younger brother was a genius at disguises. Neil wasn't too hard to pull off for Finley. Neil was from Clemenceau, just like him. Like him, he was settling down in Wakefield to start a new business. And he moved out to Wakefield to be closer to his daughter, just like him.

He put on an extra Cajun accent, just in case anyone wanted to have any small talk. Finley was going to let people talk to him this time. He wanted to be seen, and he wanted to be heard.

The hospital was a shit show, so blending in wasn't going to be much of a problem. Finley was already inside and sitting in the lobby, looking at his daughter, playing with another kid. A couple was watching little Paige. Finley pretended not to notice them. But he would have to talk to them soon, and they were a big part of his game, so he studied them.

Everyone in the hospital acted like this was the world's end. It wasn't. It was the end of Paige's world. By the time Ashton, Erynn, and Hunter arrived, it would be too late. They would be in Neil Steven's final game. Alison would recognize the name immediately.

Don't worry, Alison, my wife. You have a significant role in Neil Steven's story; your role is the best one.

"Did you see the machines earlier?" Some chatty guy with a broken nose. asked Neil. "Yeah, I sure did," Neil responded with a heavy Cajun accent. He didn't know what the fuck man was talking about, but he assumed it was the red walking things that had been attacking people. "Yeah, man, they came in here and attacked us; I almost died." The chatty guy just kept talking. Neil wanted to kill him, but he reminded himself that talking was all part of the plan. No killing right now, Neil.

"My name is Kian, by the way." The chatty man said." I'm Neil. Neil Stevens," Mr. Smith responded. "I was thinking about causing some trouble," Neil said to the chatty man. He didn't need to lie. No one would believe him anyway. He knew he could say I am here to kill and woman and her daughter and no one would believe him or pay attention to him because everyone was so preoccupied with the end of the world being near. "Trouble? What kind of trouble," Kian asked. "Because if you aren't trying to kill someone for me, or turn the lights back on, then I can't help you with any trouble."

"Sure, I could kill someone for you." "Hey man, keep your fucking voice down. I was playing," Kian said, hushing the Cajun man quickly. "You can't just go around saying shit like that so loudly."

"Yes, I can."

There was a long silence, and Neil didn't interrupt it. He liked silence. "What did you say your name was again?" Kian asked.

"Neil."

"Neil, where are you from? You sound like some people I know. However, your accent isn't from around here."

"Nope. I guess it's not."

Another silence interrupted the conversation. Neil could tell Kian was building the courage to do something. Maybe he wanted to ask him a question. Neil knew, of course. Neil always knew.

"What kind of trouble are you looking for, Neil?"

"Any kind," Neil said with his strong Cajun accent. His natural accent was Cajun, but it wasn't this thick. It was just part of the game Neil was playing. Mr. Smith spent hours watching Kian and his dynamic with The Ghost. He knew Kian didn't like The Ghost, so Smith was reeling Kian in; Kian was the most significant piece to the plan. He needed Kian to talk to the couple watching Paige.

Kian was spending too much time building up his courage, and Mr. Smith decided he would help him a little. Smith broke the silence first, "I like helping out people. You know, from bullies. So I'm a fan of helping the little guy." Neil purposely used the phrase *the little guy*, because he knew his size was domineering. Neil looked like a tree with legs. He figured Kian was sizing him up so he could see if he could take on The Ghost.

Kian still didn't say anything. There was only one thing to do now, Kian was afraid to ask, so Neil had to show Kian he would miss his opportunity. "Well, partner," Neil said in his heavy Cajun accent, "See you later; I've got some things to do." Neil stood up without drawing any attention to himself. His prosthetic mask is still working like a charm. Before he could take two steps, Kian finally found his courage.

"Hey, hey. Neil," Kian called out to him. "Wait a minute, and I know someone who needs a lesson taught to them." "Do you really, now?" Neil was working his Cajun accent well. "I do." "Well, point him out? Is it the fellow that did that to your nose?" Neil asked.

"Yes. Well, no. He isn't here."

"So, who needs to be taught a lesson?"

"His Sister."

Rage filled Neil's body instantly. Kian was talking about Finley's wife. But he wasn't a hothead. He knew what to do. "I can help you there, partner," Neil said. "All you have to do is tell that couple over there that her Uncle Neil will pick her up for Uncle Ashton and then meet me around the back of the hospital when it is done. I will have your problem solved in the next five minutes." Kian hesitated for a moment. "Don't worry, partner, we are just using the couple as a distraction. They will go to the back and get the lady for you." "She needs to be taught a stronger lesson than that." "Okay, I can do that, too."

Neil got up and walked out of the hospital and around the back. He didn't give Kian a chance to change his mind. Five minutes later, Kian came around the back and told Neil it was done. "What exactly did you tell the couple?" "Exactly what you told me to tell them." *Crack!* Neil moved so fast that Kian never saw it coming. His body hit the ground, and his head was facing the wrong way. Neil twisted it all around to the other side of his body. His neck was broken.

Neil walked away and went back into the hospital. It was his time to do his second performance of the hour.

Alison was falling asleep while pumping air into London's lungs. The crew was away tracking a ruthless killer, and Alison's place was at the hospital. She was raised to take lives, and now she saved them. She must have nodded off between pumps of air because she felt London softly touch the back of her elbow. Then, opening her eyes, staring at the wall, lost in her thoughts, she nodded again. Alison dreamed of London's small hands trying to get her attention. Then, shaking the exhaustion from her head, she turned to see London staring at her. She almost forgot to pump the next breath in excitement.

"London, can you hear me?" She asked. His eyes darted across the room and landed on her as if he were answering them. She smiled the kind of smile only a mother could accomplish. "You will be out of here in no time, London. Your parents can't wait to see you. They are right outside." London smiled with his eyes.

Alison looked at the bandages on London's amputated arm; everything looked good. His vitals looked normal; if he awake, it was time to call Dr. Kerry to check him out. Sandra flagged down the first staff member she could see and asked them to get Dr. Kerry immediately. Alison continued to observe London. His chest rose up and down slowly and weakly, but it was unassisted. He was breathing on his own. It was indeed a miracle he was still alive. The last seventy-two hours did everything possible to end his life, but London's will to live was far stronger.

Dr. Kerry rushed into the room and assessed the situation. He checked London's breathing, listened to his lungs with a stethoscope, and removed the endotracheal tube. London coughed, groaned a bit, then flashed the best smile he could produce. Alison, being a mother, asked Dr. Kerry if he could bring in London's parents quickly. It wasn't the standard operating procedure for this ordeal, but Dr. Kerry went to the lobby to get them. After all, the end of the world was near, no one knew when the power was coming back on, and at this point, the *new* goal was to get people out of the hospital as fast as possible and back into farmlands or something that could help the community.

As London began to gain more control over his body, the E.R. doors suddenly swung open voices filled with the happy tears of Clara and Brandon Brewer, London's parents, filled the room. Finally, with London able to breathe on his own and his vital signs looking great, she left the room to give the three of them some much-needed privacy and room to celebrate. Wanting to reunite with her child, Alison walked into the lobby but couldn't find Paige. Instantly, her heart dropped into her stomach.

"Where is Paige?" Alison asked the hospital staff. "Your brother came to pick her up," said one of the hospital staff. "How is that possible? My brother is miles away from here hunting a killer with Chief Aiden!" "What do you mean? We got a message from your friend with a broken nose. He came over and told us your brother was coming to get her, and your brother came and got her."

Alison's heart stopped beating. She just saved London, and now they have lost Paige! Alison ran up and down the hospital lobby, calling for Kian. "Kian! Kian!" Alison screamed at the top of her lungs. "He went outside. That way." London's parents pointed to the back side of the hospital.

It took Alison thirty seconds to find Kian; he was dead. Someone had broken his neck. Alison ran into the hospital and yelled at the on-duty police officer, there was just one of them now, and Aiden took the other officer with him. "Kian is dead. Someone broke his neck." Pandemonium ensued. The hospital lobby began a circus, and Alison narrowed her eyes on London's parents. Rage filled her body. "Clara," Alison was talking to London's mother, "Tell me exactly who picked up my daughter." Before Clara could answer, Bryson spoke," He told me to tell you his name was Neil Stevens, Ms. Alison." "Yeah, that's what his name was. Neil, right Baby," Clara looked over to her husband for backup. "Right," her husband answered.

It was too much. Alison only knew one Neil Stevens, and it was the name her ex-husband Finley used whenever he didn't want to know his name. He had emails with it and everything. They used to joke about meeting the real Neil Stevens one day. Alison fell to the floor. She cried in a way only a mother who had just lost her child could. Paige was gone, and she was with the worse person possible.

"Alison! Alison, tell us what's happening." Dr. Kerry was trying to break through Alison's tears. By this time, the on-duty police officer had returned to the building with a note in his hand. He handed it to Dr. Kerry. "That man who said he was Paige's uncle left this note at the desk before he left," the officer said to Dr. Kerry. Alison was crying too loud to hear anything.

With every passing second, Alison wanted to kill Finley. She wanted to kill London's parents, Brandon and Clara. Finally, Dr. Kerry's mouth fell open, and he dropped the paper the officer just gave him. It fell in front of Alison. The paper was neatly folded. Alison tried to open it, but her hands were shaking too badly. The young officer bent to his knees to help her open the letter.

It was Finley's handwriting. The psycho wasn't even trying to hide. She knew he was crazy and realized all at once that the strange messages she'd been getting were from him. She didn't want to believe it, but the scary pictures she kept receiving on her phone were of Rougarou. All the signs were there. So how didn't she notice them? And why didn't she tell her brother what she saw when he asked as they picked Paige up from Nathan? How was she supposed to know Finley broke out of super-max prison?

Alison swallowed tears and read the letter, and she nearly had a heart attack.

THERE IS A MOUNTAIN WITH A MOUTH AS WIDE AS A WHALE AND A HEART AS DEEP AS HELL. JUMP INTO THE MOUTH OF THE MOUNTAIN AND WALK ALL OVER ITS HEART LIKE YOU DID MINE. COME ALONE OR I WILL DRINK YOUR BASTARD DAUGHTER'S BLOOD, AND SHE WILL DIE SCREAMING YOUR NAME.

P.S. I'm your Serial Killer.

Captain Finley Smith, Alison's Husband, Ashton's Brother, and Erynn's First

Aiden swerved around a deer, his tires and the wake of dust in the air signaling the convoy to do the same. It didn't make sense to kill Erynn, Ashton, and Hunter, who had to kill many Artificials today and then die by driving off a cliff because of a deer. So all three of them, Ghost Hunters, which Aiden was calling them now, were in the pickup truck with Aiden.

"That storm system seems to be headed our way, and it looks nasty," Aiden said to his best friend, Derrick. They were riding in the car with Ashton. "Then we will catch our killer in the rain, my friend," Derrick replied to Ashton without missing a beat. Ernest and Hunter were in the back seat, and Ashton, Erynn, and Hunter were in the pickup bed. If anyone were going to get wet, it would be all three of them. He was grateful for their company. Derrick had to be here; he was a police officer, but those three getting Ernest, Erynn, And Ashton didn't have to be here. Each of them was with Aiden for their reasons, and Aiden respected each reason.

Aiden's radio roared to life. Aiden unclipped his radio, "Janice do you copy?" After a few seconds of back and forth between Aiden and Janice, the convoy was on its way to Cherry Hill. One of the largest mountains part of the world's famous Wakefield Mountain range.

"Over there, brother," Derrick said while pointing to a fort of cars positioned strategically on the highway. That was no accident. That is a barrier meant to keep people out. After further investigation, the team discovered the blockade was not an enemy threat but the work of Bradley Holloway, keeping his word to keep Wakefield safe. Bradley had marksmen strategically set up in sniper positions. This place was completely secure. Anyone who was coming this way was checked and checked thoroughly. Bradley informed the Chief that everyone coming this way was searched and questioned for legitimate reasons to enter Wakefield. Any suspicious answers didn't make the cut, and those people were denied entry and turned away.

Aiden was conflicted about barricading the city. He knew it wasn't the most excellent thing to do, and everyone deserved help, but he also knew that people would try to take advantage of the town being weak and defenseless. "How are things?" Aiden asked. "Any problems?" "No, not really," Bradley responded. "It's been a pretty quiet night. We had a few refugees this morning. We turned away a family but let a man through because he said he was a plumber. So we can use all the technical help we can get." Aiden nodded in agreement. "Great. Let's be on the lookout for mechanics and farmers, too. Oh, and electricians. We need to get some lights back on ASAP," Aiden said to Bradley.

"That makes plenty of sense to me, Chief. So will do.", Bradley responded. "Bradley, you are doing a damn fine job. We are close to catching this killer, but you should know. The same person who killed Jared is the same person who killed Rory. So be careful, okay?" Aiden said with concern. He had a way of making people feel better about themselves and their work. Aiden could make a man fixing a peanut butter and jelly sandwich feels like he was saving the world one slice of bread at a time. "You got it, sir," Bradley said with more excitement than he began.

Aiden signaled for the crew to get ready to move again. They drove around the roadblock, and in the rearview mirror, Aiden watched with pride as the roadblock receded. "We could use a few more like him, Chief," Derrick said. Aiden nodded. He was thinking the same thing. For a long time, they drove in silence until they got closer to Cherry Hill. They were driving about half a mile west of Rory Cooper's place. That is where Detective Schwartz found the hidden camp.

"Chief, do you copy?" The radio on Aiden's right hip crackled to life. Aiden slowly pulled the radio to his mouth. Aiden responded, "I copy. Go ahead." "Chief, I have terrible news. The killer kidnapped Alison, Jace's daughter, and left a note where to find him." Aiden, Ernest, And Derrick all stopped breathing.

"Say that again, Janice," Aiden said. He couldn't believe his ears. The white noise from the radio made it hard to hear sometimes. Between the sound of the engine roaring in his ear and the white noise of the radio, Aiden pulled over to hear. "Janice. Say again. I'm in front of Ashton, Erynn, and Hunter. Over." "I am so sorry, Ashton. Your sister reported that Paige is missing, and the killer has taken your niece hostage. He left a message as to where you can find him. Alison is safe but hysterical, to say the least." Ashton didn't say a single word. He pulled up his skull bandana, and his eyes hardened. Erynn and Hunter lifted their bandanas, too.

"Chief, I have more bad news," Janice's voice crackled over the white noise of the radio. "Give me all the bad news at one time, Janice, over," Aiden barked into his radio. He had already lost too many people, and Paige would not become another.

Aiden couldn't take the death of another child. He couldn't take it. He was supposed to keep everyone safe. "Alison is already gone, Chief. She went after the killer. The letter told her to come alone," Janice said as concisely and quickly as she could. "Well, what the hell did the letter say?" Aiden snapped, trying to keep his cool. "*There is a mountain with a mouth as wide as a white and a heart as deep as hell. Jump into the mouth of the mountain and walk all over its heart as you did mine. Come alone, or I will drink your bastard daughter's blood, and she will die screaming your name.*

P.S. I'm your Serial Killer.

Captain Finley Smith, Alison's Husband, Ashton's Brother, and Erynn's First

Ashton knew where that cave was. Finley was going to die today.

Monique was saddened by the thought of her new life on the USS George H.W. Bush. There was no land in sight, and she wasn't healthy enough to fly a fighter jet or a helicopter. But she was doing everything she could to be grateful. So, good people died for her to live and run the country.

Monique was severely burnt, but her body was healing faster than she expected, and she was about to give a Presidential Address to all present. And also to anyone with a Ham Radio tuned into what they were now calling the *Presidential Frequency*.

Of course, they changed this frequency every hour to keep the North Kangavarians working hard to spy on them. It was time. Everyone was waiting for her to be the leader they needed her to be, and Monique did not disappoint. There was one microphone and one speaker belting out her voice. She needed to figure out how they got the audio equipment set up, but she needed to put more thought into it. She approached the podium.

" Even though large land masses of the United Cities have fallen, and our entire nation's electrical grid is corrupted and inoperable, the people of the United Cities of Salleria will not fail. We shall go on to the end and defend our soil. We will avenge the souls we cherished who now rest in the great unknown; we shall fight with growing confidence and strength, knowing that everything has been taken from us, which makes us very dangerous. We will defend what is left of our precious resources, whatever the cost. We shall fight on the beaches, and we shall fight in the fields and the streets. Because we are the United States of Salleria, and we shall never surrender."

Everyone cheered, and after a long round of applause, President Monique Maddox continued with a Martin Luther King flair to her voice,

"I will not lie to you, my brother and sisters. We are in for a very rough next four weeks. I call you brothers and sisters, which is a bit strange coming from the Presidential podium but to survive what comes next, we will all need to be brothers and sisters as we help bury our real brothers and sisters. Right now, we estimate that over a quarter of the United Cities population will die in the next two weeks as a result of the radioactive fission products from the air detonations and the nuclear fallout that is happening as we speak. To be clear as to what a quarter of the United Cities population means mathematically, we are expected at least seventy million of our brothers and sisters to die in the next fourteen days. Dark times are coming."

Monique could hear people crying. She wanted to cry, but she was the President now. The people need her to be a leader with a clear head.

"Nationwide recovery efforts have already begun. Working closely with the military and FEMA, we are setting up safe zones and Survivor Centers around the nation. These Survivor Centers are placed outside radioactive zones and offer food and shelter. Everyone must pull their weight, as it is time for us to learn how to live off the land. I must ask you for the hard part now. There is no real way to say what I am about to say politically, so that I will say it. Our new problem is that we have plenty of surviving equipment, but we will have to prioritize it and send it to places and people who need it the most. Lastly, we recalled most of our troops from overseas to help with our defense and recovery efforts.

Even with all the bad news delivered, Monique's speech was well received:

1 Monique told everyone to learn how to farm, band together, and share resources because the government expected fifty-million Sallerians to die from starvation and dehydration before winter's end.

2 She explained how medical care was crippled, and those dependent on medications in nursing homes or hospice were at significant risk.

3 And she told the nation they were expecting another twenty-five million elderly and sick Sallerians to die in the coming months.

Monique clarified that more than one hundred million Sallerians would die from causes after the attack within the next six months. This number did not include the people who died due to the EMP attack on Salleria. Just as everyone was gripped with silence over the nationwide wide address President Maddox had given, before anyone could panic even more or steady themselves back to a sense of calm, the hatch to the room opened quickly. Lieutenant Natasha Clark, the ship's X.O., was honored to meet Monique earlier that day. She had a look of urgency on her face. "I am sorry, Madam President. But, Sir, we have a problem." Clark's gaze was aimed in the direction of Rear Admiral Zander Woodard. "What is it, Lieutenant?" Woodard asked calmly and quickly. "We are picking up faint sonar hits that could be enemy subs, sir!" "Do we have their location, Lieutenant?" "No, Sir. We can't lock on to them long enough to get an accurate track." "Then get ready for a battle on the ocean, Lieutenant. No one on this ship will die today," Woodard said.

Alison couldn't feel her legs, but she knew they were in pain and moving fast. She didn't care. Alison would find her daughter and deal with her ex-husband once and for all. Her mind was a complete mess, and she was tired of Finley Smith always taking everything from her. It is all he ever did. But all of this was her fault because she married him when Ashton was out of the country. Alison allowed him to get her pregnant, and when she was the one who turned him in to the police. She hid her pregnancy from Finley. Maybe she deserved everything that was happening to her.

Three miles into her run, she noticed a car speeding behind her, and it was Detective Skylar Schwartz. Skylar sped to a stop next to Alison. "Get in!" Skylar said. Without thinking about the letter saying to come alone, Alison jumped in the vehicle, "I'll drive." Skylar looked into Alison's eyes and immediately gave up without a fight. She crawled over the armrest and adjusted herself in the passenger seat. Before Skylar could say anything, Alison was already gunning the engine through the rugged terrain. The oversized off-road tires ripped through the earth like a hot knife going through butter. She recited the note from memory.

THERE IS A MOUNTAIN WITH A MOUTH AS WIDE AS A WHALE AND A HEART AS DEEP AS HELL. JUMP INTO THE MOUTH OF THE MOUNTAIN AND WALK ALL OVER ITS HEART LIKE YOU DID MINE. COME ALONE OR I WILL DRINK YOUR BASTARD DAUGHTER'S BLOOD AND SHE WILL DIE SCREAMING YOUR NAME.

P.S. I'm your Serial Killer.

Captain Finley Smith, Alison's Husband, Ashton's Brother, and Erynn's First

There were so many places to check and so little time. She figured the *mouth of the mountain* was a cave entrance. That was easy to guess. She scanned her brain frantically, trying to see if she could remember anything location that sounded like that which was described in the letter. It all made sense now. The picture of a Rougarou she received the day before the lights went out. It was all Finley. He had found out where they lived and had been watching them for God knows how long. She was so angry with herself for not putting all the pieces together. Only Finley and his overgrown little brother could have pulled all this off. They were the only two people outside her, Ashton and Erynn, who were from Clemenceau's swamp lands. The legend of the Rougarou was rare knowledge. You had to be from Clemenceau to even know about the tales.

Think Alison think. She sped up the road and dangerous, breakneck speeds. Detective Skylar Schwartz never complained. Alison figured she understood what she was going through mentally right now. "I got it!" Alison said to herself but loud enough for Skylar to hear her. There is a huge cave near the top of Cherry Hill. It has a restricted access sign on it, and the roads and trails that lead to it are blocked off with government trespassing signs that say *Do NOT Enter! A $2,000 trespassing penalty will be enforced.*

The cave entry was massive, and many people died trying to see the heart of the cave. This is where *JUMP INTO THE MOUTH OF THE MOUNTAIN AND WALK ALL OVER ITS HEART LIKE YOU DID MINE.* "This line had a double meaning," Alison said to Skylar. This is a message about how I broke my ex-husband's heart and how everyone died trying to get to the heart of the cave. She drove so fast towards the restricted cave entrance that she lost track of time and had to slow down violently as she arrived at the restricted board signs.

Wiping tears from her face, she stared at the trail that led to the restricted cave entrance. She was pissed. Skylar unholstered her pistol, and without another thought, Alison sprinted onto the trail that led to the forest. Skylar figured she would let Alison go first and get far in front of her to keep the illusion that Alison was alone— as instructed. "Be strong, Alison," Skylar said to herself. "You've got this."

Gasping for air, Alison was now running at full speed. She was pushing her lungs and legs harder than she ever had before. Sweat dripped down her face; her calves felt like lava had jumped up and bit her. She would find her daughter no matter what it took, and she would tear her ex-husband apart. In her panic, she realized she had forgotten to bring a weapon. It didn't matter to her; she was ready to strangle Finley with her bare hands. He thoroughly deserved it. She ran, and she ran until something she heard took the air right out of her lungs. "Mommy!" Paige yelled out. Two figures were standing at a distance, overlooking her baby girl.

"It's been a long time, disloyal one," Mr. Smith said with a scary-calm voice. Alison immediately recognized the voice; It was Finely. He was cold and calculating. In his voice, Alison could hear both pleasure and apathy. She assumed she got pleasure from torturing his victims and their loved ones and didn't care about anything about them simultaneously. She knew Finley was capable of. She had seen him kill before, which is why she left in the first place — at least, that was a major reason amongst major reasons. Alison accepted her and her daughter's fate and knew there was no way either of them was coming out of this alive.

Derrick, Ernest, and Aiden silently approached Ashton, Erynn, and Hunter, and there were other officers with them. No one said a word. Everyone knew what was at stake. It was time to enter the cave, and everyone knew they were walking into an ambush.

Aiden broke the silence, "It's an ambush." "And a deadly one, at that," Ashton responded. "Then what's the plan?" Ernest asked. "I don't know yet," Ashton responded. He was still thinking. He needed to find out how many men were inside or what they were up against. "The cave will be dark, but when we enter, we will be sitting ducks," Aiden started. "You can expect snipers, and I would assume some or all the men will use NVGs."

A tense silence fell over the men. Erynn looked at Ashton and pointed to him and Hunter, then she pointed her finger to the right and then moved her hand in a circular motion over her head. She did the same thing to the left but pointed to Ernest, Aiden, And Derrick. All the men were ex-military; they knew what they meant. Erynn was taking the lead and setting their rally points. Erynn, Hunter, and Ashton would take flanking positions to the right of the cave, while Ernest, Aiden, and Derrick would flank the left side of the cave.

Erynn pointed to each of the remaining officers, split them into teams, and pointed to their rally points. No one questioned her, and they knew who she was. "Chief, I could use one of those motivational speeches you give so well," Ashton said. Aiden turned to all the men and asked them to gather around.

"Men, there will be blood. I won't lie to you. But this is who we are— the people

who risk their lives when others won't. I don't have the right words to tell you today, and I wish I did. But how do you ask a friend, a brother, a sister to give their lives for another— you don't. So I won't ask you. I want you to live.

But if someone must die, it will be me, and I don't plan on dying today. The people inside this cave have complicated our lives and murdered our children. They are about to murder another one of our children, and we cannot allow this to continue.

So, I said fight. Fight for your city. Fight for your values. Fight for your families.

Aiden finished, but there were no cheers. Instead, everyone moved into position and began to enter the cave. The hunt was on, and this was the end of the chase. Erynn ran into the cave; first, she was fearless, and Ashton followed behind her. Soon after their entry, they were swallowed by darkness, dodging rocks and springing over obstacles.

Pop, pop. Two shots were fired; Ashton couldn't see who fired the shots. Everything was happening quickly. Ashton turned around, and to his shock, he saw two officers down. Ashton forced himself to look away, and there was nothing he could do for them now. He had to finish the mission and defeat Finley, or the officers' deaths would be in vain.

"I'm okay, brother," Aiden said quietly to his best friend, Derrick. Aiden took a nasty fall over something hard in the cave. He didn't break anything or accidentally discharge his firearm, but he scared Derrick half to death. Aiden couldn't shake the feeling he was leading his team into a death trap, but what was his other option? Wait until the killers decided to become preachers? That wasn't going to happen. But he was tired of losing people, and now two more officers were down.

He needed to go back and check on his men. An overwhelming wave of anxiety hit him harder than he expected. Aiden felt the death of his two men deep in his heart, and he was so tired of being ten steps behind this serial killer.

Aiden didn't try to do it. He didn't even know he had turned around and was headed back to check on his man. It just happened. It was like someone had taken over his body because, before he knew it, he was kneeling before his men. They both were down, but one of them gargled in blood. Aiden held the man until he passed. It took a few seconds, but he didn't want the kid to die alone. "It's okay," Aiden said to his young officer, "We will take care of your baby," Aiden whispered to Officer Peyton Michael, the young officer who helped him at Julia's Grocery Store. He died in Aiden's arms and welcome death like an old friend.

Aiden was so angry. Officer Michael survived the meth heads a day before, a nuclear rain storm, and now he was dead. Aiden wanted to scream or beg for help, but nothing came out. His mouth wouldn't move, and Aiden couldn't move. He'd finally given up. The losses were too hard.

Aiden closed his eyes. He wasn't ready to die, but he knew the sniper would shoot him at any moment. He wanted to move, but he couldn't. A noise burst into Aiden's left ear. It sounded as if rocks jumped from the ground. Aiden opened his eyes to see, at the very last second, a copper-skinned man with a dark, scraggly beard leaped into the clearing with a knife. His teeth were filed into fangs, and he was a foot away from Aiden. Aiden turned, but it was too late; the man had the drop on him. Dropping his rifle and reaching for his pistol, Aiden barely moved his neck in time to dodge the knife. He raised his hand as high as he could before he was tackled hard by the airborne man, but Aiden managed to get a shot off in time. The man groaned in pain, and Aiden shot him in the stomach. One second later, Aiden tossed the man off him and put a few rounds in the man's chest— he wasn't wearing a vest. The airborne man died on the ground.

Aiden shook the stars out of his vision, picked up his rifle, and ran back to the left side of the cave. "Chief," Aiden heard a woman's voice. "Over here, Skylar, behind me. Stay low." Derrick ran towards Aiden. "Stay alive, Chief. Let's go." That's all the big man said, and that's all Aiden needed to hear. People depended on him to be strong. He didn't have the opportunity to give up.

Another man jumped in front of Derrick and another one behind Skylar. Derrick shot the first man in the chest with his shotgun. He was dead before he hit the ground; his chest was missing. Skylar shot the man advancing on her, but he had a gun. He shot Skylar in the chest, and Aiden screamed in agony! "Noooo!" Aiden shot the man in the forehead before he could get off a second round. He, too, was dead.

"Skylar!" Derrick cried out. She was coughing and struggling to breathe. "I'm okay," Skylar said. Her voice was strained and sounded like she couldn't breathe. "I'm wearing my vest." "Oh, you smart, smart lady," Aiden joyfully said as he helped Skylar to her feet. "Can you move?" Aiden asked. "I'm good, Chief. I just wanted to see what getting shot felt like," Skylar said with her usual dark humor. "Well, don't do it again," Aiden ordered. "Roger that, Chief."

Before they could catch their breath, Ernest shot an incoming attacker in the chest. Unfortunately, he wasn't wearing a shirt, which meant no vest. "Thanks, Major," Derrick said gratefully. Unfortunately, the attacker was ten feet behind Derrick, who didn't notice him. "Eyes open, everybody. Get as close to the cave wall as possible so they can only attack us from three directions," Ashton ordered everyone on his team and all the other teams in earshot.

Ernest was in the rear, Skylar was in front of him, and Derrick was now behind Aiden. At least thirty shots were fired back and forth for the next two minutes, and Aiden's four-person team was forced to scatter and take cover behind rock formations. Bullets pinged against every hard surface available. But, between all the teams, they dispatched the enemy threats pretty quickly.

One of the men played dead and waited for Aiden to walk by him, and then he leaped to his feet and hit Aiden so hard in the side of his head that he almost knocked the Police Chief unconscious. More shots were fired toward the team, and they were forced back into safety. Aiden collapsed onto his back. Stars filled his vision, and the fanged man mounted Aiden and went for the kill. But, unfortunately, the volley of rounds kept coming, and there was nothing anyone could do.

Suddenly, gunshots from the right side of the cave erupted and shot back at the enemy. With all his teeth showing and Aiden's neck exposed, the killer lurched for Aiden's exposed throat, and Aiden's vision went black. The man's total weight was crushing Aiden's chest as Aiden slowly slipped into darkness. Out of know where Ashton leaped through the air and pushed the muscular copper-skinned man off the Chief. Erynn dragged the Chief to safety as Ashton ended the man's life with a quick draw of his sword. It entered the man's body and back into Ashton's sheath as quickly as it exited. The man crashed to the ground, and Ashton and Erynn ran back to the right side of the cave. Aiden had never seen this side of them. He knew they were highly trained, but those weren't movies you learn in Special Forces. Darkness swallowed Erynn And Ashton, and the Chief could tell they were using it to their advantage.

Still on the ground, Aiden rolled over to his left side and saw one of the knives The Ghost and Erynn always carried with them sticking out of the fanged man's right temple; all that could be seen as the handle of Duane Dieter's Close Quarters Combat knife. The blade was in his brain. He removed the knife for them. Aiden knew they loved their knives and would want them back.

"You good, Chief?" Skylar asked. "I think so," Aiden replied. Did all of you see how they moved? Aiden was talking about Erynn and Ashton. "I've never seen anything like it," Ernest admitted. Derrick asked what everyone was thinking, "So Ashton and Erynn are fucking ninjas?"

Chapter Twenty-One

The shadow knelt over the dead body and pulled a knife out of the corpse's head. It took a bit of twisting, but with one more wrench, the knife was free. The shadow wiped off the brain matter and returned the knife to its proper place.

Ashton stood up, he was the shadow, and Finley made him return to a life he left. This man was dead, and he would kill everyone in the way of him and his family. With barely any discernible motion or effort, Ashton launched the corps out into the middle of the cave. Erynn was with him, and she was the shadow's shadow. Within seconds, both shadow's disappeared, having become one with the darkness and leaving no trace of their existence except the trail of dead bodies in their wake.

Raising his Barrett M95, Ernest moved the crosshairs across the dark parts of the cave. There was no movement and no muzzle flashes. So where the hell were the shooters? Ernest continued walking towards the heart of the mountain. His back was against the West wall, and Derrick was directly behind him; Skylar was behind them.

All four of them moved in by an inch. There were still no signs of Alison and Paige. Now and then, they would see a glimpse of Erynn and Ashton, but there was no way to tell it was them. Those two were ninjas. How could there be ninjas in Salleria?

Ernest heard a noise, it sounded like Paige, and it sounded like she was crying. Ernest looks up at the darkness. The cries were coming from the center of the cave. Ernest understood the letter now.

JUMP INTO THE MOUTH OF THE MOUNTAIN AND WALK ALL OVER ITS HEART LIKE YOU DID MINE.

Paige was being kept at the heart of the cage— the center of it.

The Rougarou leaped, and Ashton sidestepped; for a second, Erynn thought Aiden wasn't moving slowly, but when the leaping body fell to the ground in two halves, Erynn realized Ashton moved so fast he withdrew his sword, sliced the man in half, and then returned his sword. It had been long since Erynn and Ashton used swords, but Ashton was still the best.

Ashton turned away from the dead body and approached Erynn. "Erynn, take my NVGs and bring them to Aiden's team. Then, come back to the spot and cover me," Ashton told Erynn. His tone was soft and gentle with her. "Keep your NVGs," Ashton turned quickly, withdrew his sword, and cut the head off an attacking Rougarou. When he returned to Erynn, he was as calm as ever. "What was I saying? Oh, yeah. Keep your NVGs because I will need you to cover me since you are a better shot." Erynn took Ashton's NVGs and disappeared into the darkness.

Ashton took three steps backward. "You can't sneak up on me," Ashton said to the darkness. "I was born into this life, and you were simply recruited." Then, without warning, Ashton ran forward and slashed his sword download. He barely felt the man's skull split open. His body fell to the ground with ease. Ashton turned one hundred and eighty degrees. His four remaining attackers wore NGVs, but Ashton didn't need them. He learned the ways of the ninja in the dark— his Father trained him well. First, Ashton was blindfolded, and then ear plugs were put into his ears, and every day and night, he had to train to see with his mind and his body.

Soon, his nose became eyes, and his arms became ears. When you are deprived of your two primary senses, your body finds other ways to see and hear. Ashton could hear the faint noise of the NVGs, where the average person couldn't. The cave only made this easier for Ashton because it stopped the wind from blowing and the hundreds of other sounds that happened in nature.

Slash. Crouch stance and Sword thrust, and then there were three. Ashton could hear their labored breathing. None of these men were Finley. Finley wouldn't be afraid, Ashton thought to himself. All three men rush Ashton at once, and now all three men are dead. Their stories will never be told, and they will be forgotten forever.

Erynn disappeared into the shadow, leaving Ernest a gift— a pair of Night Vision Goggles. Ernest put them on, and after a one-second delay, the familiar green hue of NVGs took over. However, Ernest could still hear the cries coming from somewhere a bit further in the direction they were walking.

Ernest was separated from Aiden and his crew in the darkness, but he was okay. He could see now. Stepping forward methodically, Ernest could hear Alison talking. "Don't do this. I'm begging you, please just let Paige go."

Ernest looked around. He didn't know how he did it, but he was the first to get to Paige, and now he could see Alison was a hostage, too. Terror ripped through his body. Ernest didn't want anything to happen to Alison or her daughter, and he was falling for Alison.

Immediately, Ernest lost it and ran towards Alison; a large hand yanked him to the ground. It was Derrick. Ernest was back with the crew again. "Calm down, Major, before you get killed." Ernest didn't respond. Derrick was right. "Erynn found me and gave me these NVGs," Ernest confessed. "Good. Tell us what you see," Ernest said. After some investigating, Ernest reported he saw three people. One was the killer, and the other two were Paige and Alison.

"One of you take the NVGs; I think I can sneak closer and get off a good shot," Ernest said to the crew. But he wasn't asking. He had already taken off the goggles and was handing them to Derrick. "We will wait for your shot to move in, Major," Aiden responded to him while retrieving the goggles from Derrick. Ernest disappeared into the darkness.

From this vantage point, Hunter could see the sniper waiting for them. It was supposed to be an ambush for the three of them, Ashton, Erynn, and himself. It didn't work. Hunter let the bullet fly, his breath returning to him in his skull bandana. There was a quiet moment and then a soft *thunk*. The glint of the sniper's rifle barrel was long more. And then it happened. It was like watching a movie. Erynn shot anything moving too close to Ashton, and Ashton, well, he was a ninja. He moved as if gravity didn't apply to him. His sword slashed and raked across the enemies' bodies. Hunter could not believe what he was seeing.

Erynn and Ashton were not a duo to be antagonized. Hunter was beginning to believe the Chief was lucky he was so hard on Ashton and lived to tell about it. Chunks of flesh flew across the cave. Hunter still couldn't believe Ashton had a sword and he was a ninja. Erynn moved like a ninja, but it was hard to tell how much of a ninja she was, but Hunter could tell she didn't miss a single shot. She was deadly accurate.

Hunter watched as someone thought they had the drop on Ashton. The man whirled and went for Ashton as if he had a fighting chance, and he did not. In mid-air, Ashton did a three-sword combination that ended with the attacking man's head falling from his body in the air. On the way down, Ashton ran his sword through the top of another man's skull. Everyone was dead, for now. When Erynn and Ashton said they were raised as assassins, Hunter didn't fully believe them. That was then. Now, Hunter understood how much of an honor it was when Erynn told him he was one of them.

Meanwhile, Ernest's eyes were adjusting to the darkness. Pushing his scope to his eye, Ernest finally saw the bastard that kidnapped Ashton's family. The man was tall, muscular, and built like a truck. He ran his hand over his short, thick hair but moved out of sight before Ernest could get a clear shot. Ernest used his scope to locate Alison and her daughter. They were tied up and hanging upside down, and there was a barrel beneath each of them as if someone wanted to collect whatever fell from their bodies.

Ernest roved his Barrett M95 back to the hulking kidnapper. This Motherfucker was huge. The lack of visibility extremely limited his options, and if he were to try to get a shot from this angle and miss, he was confident the kidnapper would kill Alison and Paige out of retaliation. He had to find a different vantage point and do it quickly because the kidnapper was losing his cool and about to explode on Alison and Paige.

Alison's head was about to explode. Finley hit her pretty hard, and her blood rushed to her brain. She was upside down and helpless. She couldn't help but throw up from being hung upside down for so long. Paige cried at the sight of her Mother being so weak. She didn't want to imagine what Paige was going through, but she couldn't avoid it— it was staring Alison in the face.

"Calm down, Baby, we are going to get out of this," Paige consoled her daughter. "No, you aren't," Finley said to Alison. "Both of you are going to die in front of your Ashton," Finely said. He was signing his words but in a taunting way.

Paige cried so much. Alison tried so hard to calm Paige down, but she was scared to death, and rightfully so. "Tell her who I am right now, or I will kill her," Finley demanded of Alison. Now, Alison was the one crying. She knew Finley was telling the truth. He would kill his daughter because Alison took her from him. "Baby," Alison called out to Paige. "Stop crying, Baby. Mommy has something very important to tell you," Alison said to her daughter. Paige did as she was told, and after a minute, she stopped crying. "That man right there, that is your real Father, Baby," Alison cried as she had never cried before. "In between her sobs, Alison told Paige Nathan was not her real Father."

Alison wanted to die. "Uncle Ashton already told me, Mommy." Alison didn't know what to think about what she was feeling. How could he? Why? Alison did the only thing she knew how to do. She asked Paige when did Ashton tell her. "Earlier today, Mommy," Paige told Alison. "He told me not to be scared, and I would know what to do when the time came." Alison was perplexed. "Uncle Ashton told me to be strong, and if anything was to happen to me, to let you know that if my Daddy kidnapped me, to let you know, he was on the way," Paige utterly shocked Alison.

"Oh, big brother Ghost is on the way, is he?" Finley said to his daughter. "Good, then my plan is working perfectly." Alison was still unable to speak and didn't know what to say.

She wasn't sure if she should be mad at Ashton or something else. The anger felt like the best option, though.

Alison knew she had to be strong so her daughter wouldn't die or need years of therapy to forget this ordeal. So Alison decided to take matters into her own hands. She struggled against her restraints and looked for ways out of their situation. She wasn't sure how Finley tied them up. It looked like her ex-husband built a makeshift platform and used that to restrain them because the cave ceiling was too high for anyone to reach.

Without warning, Finley slapped Alison and threatened to kill Paige. "My Uncle says I don't have to be afraid of you, and just because you are my Daddy, I don't have to listen to you, either." Finley walked over to Paige and slapped her, too. Paige yelled out in pain, and said more curse words than her was aware she knew.

Still reeling from her pain, Paige told her Father, "My Uncle to me, you wouldn't like it if I wasn't afraid of you." "Oh, did he?" Finley asked. "Yep, and he told me he could beat you up."

"Well, did your uncle tell you I beat him up before?"

"Yes, he did, and he told me he killed all of your men and let you live because he felt sorry for you," Paige was getting under her Father's skin, and she knew it. Alison was mad at Ashton for telling her daughter all these things.

"My Uncle also told me we would get out of this alive because you were too arrogant to do what he would have done," Paige screamed at her Father. "Shut up, dammit!" Alison saw Finley was losing his cool. She had never seen Finley lose his cool. "My Uncle also told me to tell you that if I see you, to ask you how your dream of being the leader of the Rougarous was going. He said he took that from you." Finley walked to Paige and started choking her. "Stop! Stop! Leave my baby alone!" Alison screamed. Finley finally stopped before Paige passed out.

Paige couldn't breathe. She did everything Ashton told her to do, and so far, it was working. Paige didn't like her Father; he was a poo-poo face. But she knew her Uncle was coming soon. He told her he was coming and always kept his promises to her. Uncle Ashton also told her not to say these things unless necessary because Mommy wouldn't understand.

But Uncle Ashton always saw that I was different. I didn't understand, but he explained everything to me before we left his house. Uncle Ashton told me I acted more like my Father than I did my Mother, and that wasn't a bad thing. It meant I was strong. He told me it meant I could take a lot of pain, and when the time came, I would have to save Mommy if he couldn't get here fast enough.

Before we left his house, Uncle Ashton gave me a present and taught me how to play with it. Paige watched her Mother pull on her restraints, trying her best to twist her feet through the ropes. Her Mommy kept trying to break free and was met with a loud, *smack*. Paige screamed at her Father. She even said a few curse words she learned from WeTube.

"I told you to stay still, Alison. You never did know how to submit to your husband," her Father said with the calmest voice possible. Paige's Father stared at her Mommy through his long twisted hair and let out a menacing laugh. Sweat poured down his leathery skin.

With the same sinister, sing-song cadence, Paige's Father spoke. "You told me you would never leave me, Hunny. You promised it would be you and me forever. Do you remember your promise, Baby?" Paige watched her Mommy swallow and nodded, trying to fake a smile. Uncle Ashton had told her to wait until the right moment.

"It was supposed to be me and you forever. You promised we would start a family. You promised you wouldn't leave me. But," There was a very long pause, "You lied just like you always do. And you took my daughter away from me and made her hate me." "You aren't my Daddy," Paige yelled out. The words left her mouth before she knew it. "You see." Her Father hit her Mommy again.

Paige hated her Father. He didn't love her; Uncle Ashton loved her. "You made her think her Daddy was crazy. And you took her from me." "You don't love me. You love to hurt my Mommy." Paige was angry. She wanted her Father to know she hated him. Finley walked over to Paige and hit her in the face again. Paige thought Uncle Ashton said I could take more pain than most people.

Alison responded, "I left because you controlled me, beat me all the time, and killed a man just for complimenting me. You made me watch you kill him. You made me watch him bleed out and drown in his blood as you slit his throat. Who would stay after that, Finley?" Paige's Mom said

"See, why would you say that in front of our daughter?" "I am not your daughter," Paige screamed at her Father. "Yes, the hell you are, little girl." "Well, you suck,' Paige responded. It was the only thing she could think of saying.

"Since you put Paige before me, Alison. And since she doesn't want to be my daughter, how about I kill you both?" "You have it all wrong, baby; I still want to be with you forever," Mommy said to the Poo-Poo face. "No, she doesn't," Paige screamed. "Yes, I do, baby," Mommy corrected Paige, but it was too late.

Slap! A loud pop hit the same cheek that was wounded earlier by her Father.

There was nothing Alison could do. If she tried to escape, he would kill Paige. If she said anything he didn't like, he would kill Paige. And now, he was blaming her for hurting Paige. Alison cried. "Okay, baby. If you still want me, I am yours. I will submit it. You can still have me if you still think I am worthy. Please take me back."

Finley blinked; he seemed to consider it for a moment and then shook his head. Smith stabbed Paige in the neck and drew blood. "Nooooooooo!" Alison screamed in horror. She couldn't tell if Paige was dead. Finley laughed, and his eyes turned flat and predatory, but

Paige refused to scream in pain. "I told you to play nice, dear. Don't try to trick me," Finley said to Alison. "Please, I'll do anything; just don't hurt my baby again." "Our baby," Finley corrected Alison. "I am not your baby. You will never be my Father," Paige yelled to Finley. Paige was acting like Ashton. Where did she get all of this? Alison thought to herself.

"It's good to see you being submissive, darling. I guess you do know your place, after all." Finley taunted Alison. "We could have been a good family, Alison, but you betrayed me. This is your fault, Hunny. Why didn't you tell me I had a baby before you sent me to prison?" Finley asked.

Alison noticed a motion behind Finley. She did her best not to draw attention to it. An athletic man had scaled the side of the cave wall and jumped down quietly. He then climbed the makeshift deck and aimed. Alison went to work on her performance. "Please, baby. I love you so much, and I know we can get back what we had." To be convincing, Alison figured she would have to adopt her old mindset and feelings for this sadistic, asshole ex-husband of hers. "I will be all yours. I will do everything right this time. I promise. Look, I am submitting now, baby. Look how good I am being. I can do this all the time for you," Alison performed her life.

"You had your chance, Hunny. Now, I am going to kill your daughter, "Oh, now I'm her daughter, Paige corrected her Father. Finley was so angry at Paige that he lunged for her. His teeth, sharpened into large fangs, went for his daughter's neck. *Crack!*

A bullet caught Mr. Smith in the right side of his chest, but he was wearing a bulletproof vest. Smith reacted mid-air and violently crashed into Paige, taking them down with her and the makeshift platform. Alison screamed as the platform began to crash to the ground in the direction where Mr. Smith had crashed into Paige. Mr. Smith stood up and roared. There was no way to tell if Alison or Paige were still alive. *Crack!* The kneeling shooter was Ernest, aiming center mass and connecting with the kidnapper again. Ernest shot Mr. Smith in mid-roar, but he did not go down. Ernest couldn't believe it. He hit him twice, and he was still alive.

Mr. Smith was stronger and much faster than Ernest anticipated. Smith took two swift strides towards Ernest, and before he could get off another shot, he barred into Ernest so hard that it felt like he cracked a few ribs. The Major's Barrett M95 went flying. It was probably too late, but Ernest wished he had used a weapon with a much faster fire rate which would have kept him out of his current position. Mr. Smith was huge, and the Major felt like a truck was sitting on his chest, crushing him to death. Mr. Smith punched Ernest across the jar a few times and completely disabled him. Smith saw Derrick and jumped on Derrick before he could get a shot. Derrick did not go down as quickly as Ernest. Derrick was almost as big as Mr. Smith.

While all this was happening, Paige took off her Uncle's necklace. It was the present he gave her. She put the bullet charm in her mouth and pulled off the cap with her tied-up hands. It was a Bullet Necklace Knife. "Mommy, Uncle Ashton told me the bad man likes to tie people up, and he gave me this and told me to use it when it was time," Paige said to her daughter while cutting her Mother free. Paige cut her free, as well.

Derrick threw a right hook that connected with the left side of Mr. Smith's jaw. A satisfying crunch followed, but there was no time to celebrate. Instead, Smith countered with a clean right kick to Derrick's mid-section, a straight left jab to Derrick's throat that connected and stole the air from Derrick's body, and then finished the big man off with a right-handed superman punch that sent Derrick's face flying to the cave floor at Mach Speed. Next, Mr. Smith went in for the kill stomp that would sever Derrick's spinal cord from his neck, but before she could execute the stomp, Aiden shot a round that missed the tank-built werewolf of a man by centimeters. Then, with one quick backward leap, Smith regrouped, picked up Ernest's body as a human shield, and hid in darkness.

Smith was an excellent rock climber, and the cave had plenty to grab. Before he disappeared, Mr. Smith tossed Ernest's lifeless body toward Alison. Alison screamed in anger. She felt her insides sink. Finley had just killed one of the only good men she had ever met. She closed her eyes, but no tears came out. She had cried them all out. Aiden rushed to Derrick to check on him, who was still alive and catching his breath from the throat punch; his pride hurt more than his body. Derrick hadn't lost a fight since... well, ever. He never lost a fight.

While everyone was distracted, Mr. Smith used his expert climbing skills to scale one of the cave walls and sneak his way back to Alison and Paige. He was standing over Alison and now using Paige as a human shield. He was back to his sing-song cadence. "I told you nothing would ever keep us apart, baby. It will take much more than them to get rid of me." Mr. Smith shouldered his rifle.

"Don't fucking move, asshole." With a shotgun shoulder, Derrick was back on his feet and pointed at Mr. Smith. "That's a shotgun, big man. If you shoot me, you shoot the little girl," Smith said. Derrick and Aiden were both walking toward the giant kidnapper. To everyone's surprise, Alison and Paige both kicked free and escaped.

Derrick ripped the kidnapper's sniper rifle from him and stripped him of his knife. Derrick didn't have to, but he kicked him in the solar plexus. "Crazy piece of shit," Derrick said after his kick forced Smith down to one knee. "Are you okay, Alison," Aiden asked. "Yes, but he killed Ernest." "Cover him, Derrick," Aiden said while never taking his eyes off the kidnapper. He kneeled to check the Major for a pulse. "His pulse is strong," Aiden said in Alison's direction.

Alison was relieved to hear Ernest was still alive. Derrick turned his head for a split second to check on Ernest, and Mr. Smith jolted up with a pistol Derrick had overlooked. Paige screamed, and Derrick turned his head just in time to return fire. *Crack! Crack! Crack!* Each round shook the cave like a house of cards. Derrick was hit in the chest, but he was wearing his vest.

A second round, however, caught Derrick in his unprotected thigh. The third shot was Derrick returning fire, but he missed. Mr. Smith ran deeper into the cave, fleeing from the crowd and getting lost in the darkness. Derrick staggered and took a seat. He extended his leg to apply pressure to the wound.

Alison scanned her daughter, seeing the cut marks on her neck were only superficial and wouldn't require any stitches. Somehow, everyone was okay. Derrick tried to stand to his feet. "Stay down, Derrick," Aiden said to his best friend. "Not a chance Chief. We have to get everyone to safety and catch this asshole—" his head exploded before Derrick couldn't finish the final words in his sentence. Blood and brain matter flew into the faces of Aiden, Alison, and Paige. The top of Derrick's head was missing.

"Get down!" Aiden screamed and dove into Alison and Paige, shielding their body with his own. Skylar returned fire, aiming where she saw the muzzle flash. Aiden told her to stay back, keep a sniper firing position, and cover them. She saved everyone's life except for Derrick. Her friend.

Derrick's lifeless body crumpled to the ground. Through a blur of tears, Aiden checked what was left of his best friend. He looked out into the darkness of the cave where Mr. Smith had fled. He was gone.

Ashton's heart lurched when he saw Derrick's headless body. He felt awful for the Chief. That was his best friend, and Ashton couldn't imagine losing Erynn that way. "You three are alive?" Aiden asked. "We had a whole army on our side, Chief," Hunter responded. "That explains a lot," Aiden responded.

Ashton's heart was broken for Derrick's family, but he didn't have time to grieve. Grieving would come later. For now, there were still dangerous killers on the loose. Derrick's body proved that.

"The son of a bitch ran deep into the heart of the cave," Aiden said furiously. "We'll get him, Chief," Hunter said. So Ashton and Erynn ran down the heart of the cave, following Mr. Smith. Hunter stayed behind to help his Police Chief with everything.

Mr. Smith was milliseconds away from squeezing the trigger on The Ghost. But if he did pull the trigger, Erynn would see his location and take Smith out. That was okay, Smith thought to himself. He planned for this contingency, just in case. Smith had one more trick up his sleeve, and this was the best trick of them all.

Ashton's minutes were numbered. Smith just needed them to keep walking into his trap, and the two unsuspecting imbeciles were doing a great job walking into it. Smith put his sniper rifle away. He was going to kill Ashton in hand-to-hand combat. Smith was tired of everyone saying The Ghost was the best, and he'd beaten him before. He was going to beat him again.

Smith always hated how Allison looked to her brother to protect her; he was all she ever needed. Smith was supposed to be her everything. Alison's disordered love was precisely the reason he wanted to kill Paige. She loved the little girl too much. She looked at their daughter as if she was a blessing. *He was the blessing, goddammit!*

There could be no child with him. If Alison knew her place, she would worship the tree and not the fruit that came from the tree. Smith was the tree. The bitch lied to him and convinced him to have a family, only to hide the fact that they had a child. Smith was going to kill The Ghost, and he was going to taunt him while he was killing him. Every minute of Ashton's death would be special. He thought about slitting Erynn's throat right in front of him. The Ghost would suffer the most pain he ever endured in four more seconds. One. Two. Three.

Halting in his tracks, Ashton signaled for Erynn to get behind him. They were back outside after finding a side exit to the cave. Finley was a very dangerous foe, but Ashton felt their decades-old feud was ending today. The Sun was beginning to set over the Wakefield Mountains.

Ashton thought back to when he saw Finley stab a man in his brain with both thumbs. He pushed his thumbs into his eye sockets until the man died. Finley hated the man so much that he asked, "Are you stupid?" And before the man could respond, Finley jumped on the man and said, "Let me see." A few moments later, Finley was scooping the man's brains out of his eye socket's looking to see if he could see if the man was *stupid.* This is who was after him, Ashton thought to himself. The evil force who once took a man's brains out of his eyes to see if he could find evidence of stupidity.

Ashton signaled Erynn to take the open area to the right, which curved around the front of the cave, about 900 feet away from a secret entrance to the cave. Fresh air smelled much better than cave air, Ashton admitted to himself. But, on the other hand, it was good to be back outside. He could see better, anyway.

The air stopped blowing. It smelled better than the cave air, and the visibility outside was much better than inside. The cave entrance area was massive, but the idea was to flank Finley and box him in. That way, if things did turn into a gunfight, Finley wouldn't be able to shoot both of them. They were too good to be taken out that way. If Finley shot one of them, he would give up his position and die.

The blood trail continued around the corner of the cave entrance. Raising his Glock 19, The Ghost followed the blood trail. Erynn kept her HK416 at the ready to even out the firepower of the two-manned team. Ashton listened for any sign of noise. He listened for breathing and the crunch of footsteps, but Ashton didn't hear anything.

Bursting around the corner of the cave entrance, The Ghost aimed his Glock 19 while Erynn covered the flank. There was no sign of Finley. Something felt very wrong. He followed the trail accurately and ended here, but there was no sign of their Finley. Swinging his head around, Ashton checked the trial of blood, but it ended in the dirt right where he was standing.

Bending down, he examined the last drop of blood. His heart dropped to his stomach as his brain processed what was happening. *It was a trap.* Ashton rose to his feet and spun around, but it was already too late. Finley rushed him. He was hiding behind Ashton in the tree line. It was an ambush, and Ashton walked right into it. A well-trained left cross crashed into the right side of bones under Ashton's right eye. Ashton screamed in agony as he lost sight of Finley.

Two the size of Finley, with sharpened teeth, tackled Erynn from behind and pinned her down. Another man, the most arrogant of them all, sat on Erynn's chest and choked her. Erynn almost had a shot on Finley and was milliseconds away from pulling the trigger until she was clobbered by a big truck of a man. Her rifle flew so far that she didn't know where it was. It didn't matter. Between the three men, there were six hundred-plus pounds of solid muscle pinning her down.

To make matters worse, as Erynn fell forward from the impact of being tackled, she fell on a rock the size of a baseball, which knocked the air out of her lungs. Erynn felt the familiar crack of one of her ribs. When they rolled Erynn onto her back, one of the men kicked her so hard in the head that she lost consciousness. By the time she woke back up, someone was restraining her lower body, another restrained her upper body, and the strongest of them had the total weight of his knee in her chest. He mounted her, and with each of his legs bent at the knee, he fully mounted her. Her arms were stretched above her head, and the asshole holding them was stopping her from defending herself. Someone must have told them not to let her fight them. Lucky bastards.

Erynn was utterly defenseless. The men stripped her of all her weapons, knives included. How had Finley had another three men hiding? Erynn thought to herself. They killed everyone. How many men did this asshole bring? Pinned down, Erynn began to think. Finley had these men waiting on here as a failsafe, just in case everything went sour.

"We're going to drink you dry, pretty lady," one of the assholes said. Erynn couldn't tell who was who. She couldn't lift her head high enough to see. "Maybe we should have fun with her first?" One of them asked. "No," The man mounting her chest said. He was the alpha. "She's too dangerous. We kill her. Then we drink her."

No one argued with him. The man on top of her didn't even rush. He knew he had the advantage. He leaned in slowly and sank his teeth into the right side of Erynn's neck. Fighting for her life, Erynn gave her best effort to fight off her attackers, but a burning pain shot through her neck. She could smell his rancid breath. The man drank from her blood, and there was nothing Erynn could do. Darkness covered her vision, and the mounted man kept drinking.

Mr. Smith knocked the Glock 19 away from The Ghost, grabbed him by the face, and pushed him outside the cave wall. The back of Ashton's skull hit it with a crack. Ashton didn't see stars this time, and he didn't see anything at all. Instead, he lost his ability to stand. There wasn't much pain, mainly pressure and a weird smell in his nose, followed by temporary blindness and the loss of dexterity in his hands.

"Get up, Ghost. You're the best. Fucking show me," Finley taunted Ashton. Ashton struggled to his feet, and Finley kicked him in his already woozy head. Ashton could not control his hands. His legs felt like someone else was controlling them. Focus Ashton. Focus. Ashton willed his body to follow his mind.

"Hey Ghosty-Woasty," Mr.Smith returned to his taunting sing-song voice. "Been a while, brother. So how the heck are you," Finley asked. "I'm doing pretty good," Ashton said. "Just entertaining some asshole." Finley laughed. "Yes! That's what I miss about you. I miss the way you mock death," Finley celebrated. Ashton could tell he was enjoying himself. "Did you bring your sword?" Ashton asked.

"You know, I couldn't find it when I returned to my house a week ago," Finley responded.

"So, you've been out a week and didn't bring me a beer?" Ashton still couldn't see. But he knew he didn't need to see, yet his body still wasn't responding to his brain.

"I gave up beer. Haven't you heard I've been locked up for ten years?"

"That's one hell of an Alcohol Anymonous Program you joined?"

Finley laughed again. He knew he was in control. "Let's say you put your sword away, and I put these guns away, and we finished this like real Rougarou?" Ashton took off his sword, rifles, and knives.

Dazed but determined, Ashton stood balanced on his feet. Finley threw a right punch, and Ashton dodged. Then Ashton threw a straight right jab. Smith dodged it with ease. Ashton was still weak and moving slowly; his head had regained its normal faculties. Ashton ducked in the nick of time, narrowly dodging a counter punch that was perfectly thrown with Smith's right hand. It was a perfect right cross aimed directly at Ashton's left eye socket. The punch was thrown with so much force that it would have detached Ashton's retina if it had connected.

Ashton was in the fight of his life. Besides his Father and Erynn, no one had ever beaten Ashton hand-to-hand combat. If he had his sword, it would be over for Finley, even if he had a gun. Unfortunately, Ashton's mind still wouldn't clear enough for him to be at full strength, so he mixed things up a bit.

Finley and Ashton were just as quick and agile as one another, but Finley was much stronger. With two deliberate steps toward Finley, Ashton closed the distance between him and Finley. If he couldn't see him, he would stay so close that he didn't need to see Finley.

Ashton knew Finely was a master at close-quarters combat, but so was he. Any strike at this distance could be deadly for either of them; Ashton knew he had to be careful. *Strike through your target, Ashton. A ninja strikes through his opponent. A ninja doesn't hit their opponent. A ninja incapacitates him— while protecting himself.*

Ashton took his left hand and pushed Finley's right shoulder, and turned him just enough to expose him to an overhead right cross that connected. Ashton punched through Finley, and Finley screamed in pain. Ashton took another three steps closer to Finley; his face was in his chest. *Crack!* Finley hit Ashton with a brutal head butt. Pain shot through Ashton's face like hot needles, and blood began to fall from Ashton's nose.

Ashton ate the head butt and used the momentum of his backward fall to roll his chest back, creating enough rotating and twisting force, which allowed him to land a violent one, two punch to Finley's face. Smith countered with a straight right hook that hit Ashton between the eyes. Ashton was dazed.

Now, it was Finley who took three steps forward and closed the gap between him and Ashton. A right elbow with perfect form hit The Ghost across the face, and Finley followed that elbow strike with a left front kick to the midsection. The Ghost was unable to block either. Smith continued his assault on The Ghost with a right knee to the midsection, which was blocked, but the overhead right elbow that followed the blocked kick was perfectly timed and executed. Ashton was thrown back into the cave wall.

Finley closed the gap between him and an Ashton like Mike Tyson looking to close the first-round bout. Smith through a knee to Ashton's midsection, causing The Ghost to fold forward, and Smith rushed him with his left arm extended outwardly at throat level. Smith's massive left bicep closed the gap under Ashton's neck and executed a picture-perfect rear naked choke hold. After that, there was no escape for Ashton. The rear naked choke is such a crucial attack that there is almost no defense technique to get out of it. Especially if your opponent is bigger and stronger than you and has executed a perfect rear naked choke hold, Finley checked all three boxes. Ashton was a dead man. The rear naked choke hold is known as the "choke of all chokes," and Smith was a choke artist.

Ashton gave up his back, and now he was going to die. Ashton had only one choice now: he had to fight Smith's "top hand," which was placed on the top of Ashton's head. Ashton tried, and he tried, but the more he did, the more he lost vital energy. Finally, there were no more options. I'm sorry, Alison. I'm sorry, Erynn. I lost.

Ashton decided to try one more thing. It had to work because he had only given more seconds before he was about to pass out. *Crack!* Finley lost hold of his grip. Holy Shit! It worked. Ashton returned to the cave wall as hard as possible and returned the favor by smashing Smith's head against the cave wall. Now they had matching concussions. Dazed, Ashton unleashed a six-hit combination hitting Smith's head and body. Ashton dropped his right hip and turned to Finely's left side of his body. He was wobbling on his feet.

The Ghost threw two crisp elbows to Smith's rib cage, then threw his body downward, connected with a right elbow of his own that was thrown upwards to Smith's right jaw. Then, face to face, The Ghost threw a straight right jab, and after it connected, Aston threw a right elbow to Finley's upper chest, followed by a straight left jab to Finley's throat.

Desperate for air and his pride wounded because he was losing, Smith pulled his combat knife from his right hip. The sharpened blade shimmered in the setting sun. After a two-second standoff, Smith sliced the knife downwardly through the air missing The Ghost boy inches. Smith sliced the blade through the air in a four-hit combination, each attempting missing Ashton. Finally, a proper kick from The Ghost threw Smith back into the cave wall with force— this was the last place Finley wanted to be again.

Ashton grabbed his knife off the ground and put it back on his hip. Finley stabbed his knife threw the air with his right hand, and The Ghost countered with a straight right punch. Each time Finley swung his knife, The Ghost countered with one punch, then a two punch, and then a three-punch combination that ended with a punch to the back of Finley's head.

The Ghost let Mr. Smith get back to his feet. "You ready to die, brother-in-law," Smith snarled. Saliva webbed across Smith's lips like a wild animal frothing at the mouth. Ashton reached for his knife, and the other was missing. Smith darted forward, telegraphically swinging both his knives in long arcs. Ashton could see the attack coming miles away. The blades whooshed through the air in front of Ashton's face, The Ghost sidestepped to the left, and the edge of his blade slid along Finley's rib. "You should have kept this a fistfight, brother," Ashton said to Finley, who forgot this was Ashton's God role— knives or swords.

The wind stopped blowing for Ashton. The pain in his head stopped, too. Finley was all that existed, and it was time for him to die. The Ghost strode forward and swung his knife at Finley's knife-hand. The cut was deep, and Finley dropped his knife. Ashton picked it up. "You let me get two knives?" Ashton asked. Ashton attacked Finley again, and his right blade found the soft flesh deep in the back of Smith's right leg as he turned away. Smith dropped to his knee in pain.

For the first time, Ashton saw Erynn was pinned down, and someone was drinking her blood. Smith seized the distracted moment as an opportunity to strike. He charged The

Ghost and speared him in the gut. The Ghost fell backward, and more stars danced before his eyes. He blinked and tried to clear his vision, but it didn't work. Smith walked towards The Ghost. As Finley got closer, Ashton lifted his knee into Smith's stomach. The bigger man fell on top of Ashton.

The Ghost bent his right knee, lifted his hip, and rolled Smith over onto his back. The Ghost, now on top, blocked an incoming right knee from Smith and countered with a right elbow to the face. Blood poured from Finley's face. Ashton threw two elbows to the left side of Smith's face. Then, with a series of left elbows to the right side of Smith's face, The Ghost rolled all of his weight to the right and rolled Smith on top of him. With his back to the ground and the larger man on top of him, stomach to stomach, in one quick move, The Ghost twisted the bigger man to his back while using both of his legs to keep his attacker in place; The Ghost put Smith into a rear naked choke hold.

Finley was pointlessly swinging for Ashton's face, to no avail. Smith began gargling for air. The Ghost felt the satisfying crush of his esophagus give in under the pressure of his bicep right bicep. Smith was already dead— he just didn't accept it. The Ghost squeezed harder and harder. There was nothing Smith could do. His neck was entirely in Ashton's arm, and in a matter of seconds, Smith stopped moving— he was dead. Panting for air— The Ghost was not.

Erynn pushed back with all of her strength. She couldn't fail, and she couldn't let down her family. Alison, Paige, And Ashton were not just friends who took her in; they were her only family. So she had to fight and kill this demon on top of her and then kill the other two men restraining her. But no matter how hard she pushed, it wasn't good enough. Pain flared as the man on top of her teeth punctured the muscle in her neck. Finally, she closed her eyes and apologized to Ashton for failing him when he needed her the most.

All of a sudden, Erynn could breathe again. She had no idea what was happening. Was she in heaven? She didn't feel her body in a lake of fire. She didn't see any flames. How was she breathing? The guy restraining her upper body seemed to be fighting a blurry figure. And the guy holding her lower body seemed to be fighting two blurry people. As her vision cleared, Erynn recognized Ernest fighting, fighting one of the men. She thought Ernest was dead. The pilot looked like shit, but he was winning. Aiden and Alison were fighting the man restraining her lower body— they were winning, too.

Erynn sprang to her feet and found the disgusting asshole that drank her blood; she would kill him. The bloodsucker leaped for Erynn with rage in his eyes. Sidestepping the blow, Erynn grabbed the Rougarou by his arm and twisted it into an unnatural position. But she didn't break it yet. That would come later.

Someone got the best of Alison and Aiden put two rounds into his chest. The agile man died when he hit the ground. Aiden turned to Ernest, but as soon as he turned his way, Ernest twisted his attacker's neck unnaturally. The attacker's body collapsed to the ground. He, too, was dead.

Now surrounded, the largest of the three men was the last man standing. Erynn waived off Ernest and Aiden. The Blood Sucker was going to die by her hand. "I guess we are sitting this one out," Aiden said jokingly. "I could use the rest," Ernest said. "Guys, you are in for a treat. Erynn is the best. She knows just about every martial art known to man," Alison told everyone.

Erynn threw a front right kick so powerful she threw her attacker backward a few feet. Then, she let the man regroup. "This isn't going to end for you well, big fella," Alison taunted the last man standing. "Do you know who you are fighting, asshole?" The man said something back to Alison, but Erynn didn't pay attention. She didn't care. He was going to pay slowly for drinking her blood.

The man, through a perfectly executed, ducked under his wold right cross. Erynn blocked it, and the right jab he threw after and the left hook he also threw. "She's not even winded, bro," Alison taunted again. The wannabe wolfman was blazing fast, but Erynn was faster and more agile. She moved with grace and struck with surgical precision. She never attacked until she needed to, and she never lost control.

"You are getting beat up by a girl, buddy," Alison kept going. Without warning, Erynn delivered two left kicks, one mid and one high. They both connected. She followed the left kick that cracked her attacker's head with a spinning back kick. Aiden was shocked at her power, and he had no idea how Erynn put together that kick combo. "She just went from Wing Chun to Taekwondo, buddy. You should have let her shoot you," Alison taunted the man. "Holy Shit. Is this how Erynn fights?" Ernest asked. "Even I've never seen this side of her,

Ernest," Aiden commented. "And how do you know all these fighting styles, Alison?" Aiden asked. "I was raised in a ninja cult, remember? I thought we went over this?" Alison said sarcastically. "So, can you fight, too?" Ernest asked. "I grew up in a ninja cult, remember?" Ernest didn't respond.

Meanwhile, Erynn closed the gap on her Blood Sucker. She delivered another two-kick combination with her left leg again. This time she followed that combination with a sweeping right leg kick, nearly taking the Blood Sucker off his feet. He didn't fall, but his leg was useless now. He wasn't going to be moving quickly anymore.

Erynn blocked a sloppy left cross and stayed inside his chest, and with her attacker's left leg severely injured, there was no way any of his left-handed attacks could generate enough power to hurt Erynn. Erynn punched the man in his chest, then dropped her hand and returned the punches in a loop. The second punch started just before the first punch landed, and the cycle repeated. Her first punch combination was like a chainsaw eating away at the man's life who thought he could restrain Erynn until she died. With each chain punch loop, her punches grew stronger and faster.

"How many punches did she just throw?" Aiden asked. "Looked like over fifty to me," Ernest responded. Alison didn't bother to guess, but she taunted the man. "That was Wing Chun, by the way, asshole. After that, she switched techniques again."

Her attacker, filled with rage through a ten-punch combination at Erynn, all of them missed. Erynn wanted him to know he could never touch her. She wanted him to suffer. Erynn began to taunt the man herself when she put both hands behind her back and dodged every punch. The man threw another punch combination, and Erynn dodged with her hands behind her back. Bringing her hands forward, Erynn returned the volley of punches and threw a three-hit combination that ended with a right front kick that knocked her opponent backward. Erynn closed the gap. "That was Judo, that time, asshole."

The man threw a right kick to her midsection, which was his fatal mistake. Erynn used her ribs to block the kick while catching his foot with her left hand. Then, Erynn superman punched the defenseless man and knocked him to the ground.

It was time for the man to die now. Controlling her weight correctly, Erynn mounted the main, just as he mounted her. With every attack her opponent made, Erynn used the *action-reaction principle,* to force her opponent to utilize his hands. The man threw a right punch from his back at Erynn; she caught it and broke his arm in two places. The man threw a punch with his good arm, and Erynn caught it, and she finished the man off with a triangle choke hold. The Blood Sucker died a minute later. "And that was Brazilian Jiu-Jitsu," Alison said. She wasn't talking to the dead man. She wanted Ernest and Aiden to know.

Aiden and Ernest were shocked. Skylar arrived with the surviving officers. "Was that Erynn kicking that guy's ass like that?" Skylar asked. "Yep," Alison answered. "Never mess with Erynn. No one is better at hand-to-hand combat. The only person who can beat her is Ashton." Alison was all in shock. "I knew she could shoot, but," Aiden's word's trailed off. Ashton walked over to Erynn, "I never did understand why people try to fight you." Erynn shrugged at her best friend's comment.

Aiden reached down and put Paige on his shoulders. She smiled big. "Thanks, Chief. Thanks for watching my family for me," Ashton said. Aiden nodded his head as a sign of respect. "You okay over there, Major?" Aiden asked. "Not really," Ernest grunted. He was hurting all over but was surprised he didn't have anyone broken bones. "It's been one long ass day," Ashton snorted.

Ashton wondered how the Chief was still standing. He lost his best friend today. That kind of pain doesn't go away, ever. "I'm sorry about Derrick, Chief," Ashton said. "He was my friend. He died protecting all of us. That's the way I would have wanted to go. That's the way I want to go," Aiden said. No one said a word in response. What could they say?

Instead of talking, Aiden walked directly to Ashton, met his gaze, and shook his hand like a man on even ground with him. No words were exchanged, but you got the feeling that whatever problems they had between them were dead now. As dead as the Rougarous who tried to murder the town of Wakefield.

Epilogue

Monique executed the most dramatic fist pump humanity had ever seen. Her arm cut the ocean air with a flare. She was finally walking again. It had been three days after the initial attacks on the United Cities of Salleria, and millions of Sallerians were dead, and from what Monique could tell from the intel she received. The total death count in the world could have reached a billion. Monique shuttered at the thought.

Monique counted her blessings, even if it was just as simple as walking without assistance. The doctors wanted her to use a cane, but she kept forgetting the damn thing everywhere, so she decided to go without it. Her most trusted confidant, Weston Levy, smiled in her direction. "Need any help, Ma'am?" "Not this time, Big Wes, but I know you will help me when I need it. Like always," Monique meant what she said. She knew he always had her back. Each step she took was agonizing, but she never let anyone but Weston see her as weak.

As she walked through the ship, soldiers snapped to the position of attention to salute their Commander and Chief. Sometimes Monique forgot she was President of the United Cities of Salleria. After all, she had only been president for the last seventy-two hours and was unconscious for most of it. Walking towards the Presidential Command Center, Monique felt the weight of all her future decisions resting on her shoulder blades. She was already tired from making life-saving decisions and hadn't even made them yet. Monique didn't sleep last night. She was going through everything she wanted to do today in her mind. All of her decisions would determine the fate of her son and the lives of all the citizens of the United Cities.

Entering the PCC, she saw her peers and many sailors she did not know. Monique didn't waste any time with small talk. As soon as everyone was seated, she began.

"I am grateful for everything everyone did to keep this battleship working and for what you all did for us down in that bunker. There is no way that we could ever repay you. There is no way Salleria could ever repay you. I will not forget all of your bravery. It will all be rewarded at the right time. There are two things I want to talk about immediately," Monique said firmly. She talked more in great detail, and after a long pause, she said, "There are two things I want to accomplish as fast as possible. The first is rescuing my son and any other survivors that may be with him. The second is to set up Safe Zones in every strategic area across the United Cities. These two things have no particular order but are first on my agenda." Monique paused to allow what she had said to sink in.

Monique grabbed a glass of water from the table and took a slip. She drank slowly and deliberately. She wanted the silence to linger and the tension to thicken because there would be no politics about these two things.

"Madam President," Captain Andres Espinoza said gently. "Your right-hand man Weston already came to us about your son. He gave us the specifics, and I sent a team of Marines to get him about two hours ago, ma'am." Shocked, Monique smiled and stole a look at Weston. "We will talk about this later," She said jokingly. Everyone in the room laughed, and the tension in the room eased. "Thank you, Captain Espinoza," Monique directed at the head of the battleship. "My pleasure, ma'am."

"There is one more thing, ma'am," Espinoza said with caution. "We just received a transmission over the shortwave radio from Hasly Mountain. The message came from Wakefield, one of the impact zones of the EMP strikes, Ma'am. A senior officer has been trying to reach you, ma'am. Your brother Major Ernest Maddox is alive," Monique's world stopped. She was mixed with both fear and gratitude. She was afraid to hear about everything he had been through because she understood it would make her imagine what Chase was going through. Yet, she was also afraid of the hope she felt.

Captain Espinoza said something to Monique that she didn't hear. "Madam President," the Captain broke into Monique's attention. "Yes. Sorry, Captain. That is amazing news," she replied. "Well, your day is about to get even better, ma'am. Your brother is on the comms, asking to speak to you."

The sun had set, and the moon took its rightful place as Aiden looked towards the seven-thirty p.m. MST sky. Aiden turned towards Ernest and patted him on the back in celebration. "Sis! Oh my God. It is so good to hear your voice," Ernest said. The shortwave radio filled with white noise. "How in the hell did you survive? I thought you were dead!" In less than sixty seconds, Aiden heard Ernest ask his sister about a hundred questions. Monique responded. "Not a chance. The grim reaper can come for me long after I bring your son back safely back to you," Monique wanted to cry, but she was in a room full of subordinates. "I am delighted I was wrong, brother," Monique said with a calm voice that couldn't hide her excitement.

Aiden walked away from the Major's family reunion. He turned toward Derrick. He had to tell Derrick's family and his own what had happened. Derrick's wife and daughter were going to be a crush, rightfully so. Aiden had failed to keep another man alive, which was starting to weigh heavily on him.

Ashton and Erynn were smiling at the Major's joy while Alison and Paige played a kid's game that Paige had made up just a few moments ago. Aiden caught Ashton's attention and walked towards him and Erynn. "You two okay?" Aiden asked. "Yea, we are good, Chief," Ashton replied. Ashton wanted to say something but didn't know what to say. "Derrick was a legend, Chief. We will be here for you— whenever you call.

Ernest and his talked for a long time catching each other up on what neither of them knew. Finally, the conversation ended with Ernest explaining to his sister that he was going to Chesterfolk no matter what. However, she knew better to try to stop him. "I've got more bad news, Ernest," Monique said. "Tell the Police Chief you were telling me about and the Ghost-guy and his lady friend to get close to the radio so everyone can hear me simultaneously.

Ernest did what she asked. Alison, Skylar, and all the officers gathered around the radio. Once Monique got the word that everyone was listening, she continued, "We are getting reports from reliable sources that the North Kangavrians are no longer our only threat. Gangs are forming all over the United Cities, and they are killing any and everyone who crossed their paths." No one said a word. They were all too shocked.

After a long pause, Monique said, "Well, there's good news, too." "Oh yea, I was told you are the President of the United Cities," Ernest said, teasing his sister and congratulating him simultaneously. Monique briefed everyone for a few more minutes, and the conversation ended,

Aiden couldn't even worry about gangs forming right now. He had to bury his best friend. "Major!" Aiden shouted in Ernest's direction. "Catch!" Aiden threw Ernest a set of keys to a working vehicle, keeping his promise that he would help him get to his nephew, no matter what. "You are a good man, Chief," Ernest said. "And so are you, Major. I sure wish you could stay, but I know you have to go," Aiden said. "I would rescue my nephew, too, Ernest. I don't blame you one bit. "Stay out of trouble and come back and tell me about it," Aiden said. "Now, that I can do, Chief. We can talk all about it over some beers," Ernest responded.

"Chief," Ashton said while walking over to Aiden and Ernest. "Erynn and I will stick around and give you a hand. I owe you one." Aiden looked at Ashton for a long time, never breaking eye contact. "Are you going to let me arrest you again," Aiden joked? "Not a chance, Chief. I don't think Erynn would like that too much, and ya'llyou'll just saw how well she fights." "Yeah, that's the understatement of the year. From how she took down that big guy, she can beat everyone out here up and never miss breakfast," Aiden responded. Erynn looked up and shrugged her shoulders. She agreed.

"Before we get too, buddy-buddy. I have to confess something to all of you. I understand if you don't want me around after that," Ashton said. Ashton didn't know how to tell everyone this was his fault.

"I didn't tell anyone because it is top secret information, but I don't think that matters anymore now. Twenty-four months ago, I was sent on a mission to North Kangavar. I was part of the team that started this whole mess, and we broke into the prison. We set the place on fire and didn't leave any witnesses. We didn't even know what we were getting into until it was already happening. I am surprised they didn't kill us, too. All of this is my fault. I am why we don't have any power and millions of people died."

Whispers spread throughout the crowd, and Alison hugged Ashton, "This is not your fault, Ashton. Your job is to follow orders and don't ask questions. "Your sister is right," Ernest said. If you didn't follow orders under those conditions in the field, you would have been executed on the spot. Court Marshall would not have been an option," Ernest finished in support.

Aiden never asked about Ashton's military service. Of course, he had suspicions and heard rumors, but everything made sense. Ashton wasn't the troublemaker Aiden thought he was; he was burning alive with all the things he had done in the military. War could break the strongest of men— no one was exempt.

"Ashton, I have to apologize to you. I've spent the last twenty-four months not trusting you because of your actions instead of trying to figure out what caused your actions. So again, I am very sorry." Aiden shook Ashton's hand. "Something tells me I will need you and Erynn more than I know. We will have to save Wakefield together. Or die trying."

38

Now, this was glorious. Truly. The last place Jacob Smith ever thought he would be was here— The Connor Mason house. Or, Dr. Quantum, as they called him. Jacob liked that name for Connor. Dr. Quantum. This was so much fun.

758 Fillmore Street was a beautiful place. The Master told Jacob about Connor's House and all its beauty, but The Master was dead now. It wasn't hard to enter Connor's house, and no one, but Connor's little whore knew how he looked. He was the greatest actor alive, and today he was Special Agent Brandon Palmer, sent by Special Agent In Charge Brentley to investigate the gruesome murders next door.

Jacob pretended to be concerned. He even faked, wanting to throw up at the site of the bodies, lying twisted, cold, and stiff. This was so much fun. From next door, Special Agent Palmer snuck peeks at the children, Sophia and Riley; Jacob thought about killing them, but today was just research.

632

Mama Linda was feisty; Special Agent Palmer made a note to kill the children in front of her so that he could knock her down a peg. Palmer would kill Papa Anthony first to scare off everyone, then the children and Mama Linda, and after Connor couldn't take any more pain, Palmer would torture Dr. Quantum for a few hours.

The thought of being so close to them was exhilarating, but Agent Palmer had to get closer and hurry before everyone started going to sleep. It was getting late.

Knock. Knock. Knock. Special Agent Palmer knocked on the front door of the Mason house. He wanted them to see his face. He wanted to see them. Mama Linda came to the door. "Yes, how can I help you?" She was being nice. After all, Special Agent Brandon Palmer did work for the FBI. "Yes, Ma'am, I'm Special Agent Palmer," Jacob said in a low voice. He wanted it to look like he cared about the kids not hearing his conversation with their grandmother. Jacob didn't care about those little brats. They could both die right now.

"I just wanted to come over and tell you, Ma'am," Special Agent Brandon Palmer's eyes began to tear, "Your son is the reason I am alive today, and I just wanted to personally tell his mother that, her son, Dr. Quantum is a hero." Jacob wasn't lying. Connor was the reason he was living. Thirty minutes before everyone arrived at the cave, The Master told Jacob to watch everything and not to get involved. And if anything should go wrong, it was up to Jacob to finish The Master's story.

"You are such a sweetheart, dear," Mama Linda said happily. "He's not here right now, but I will tell him when he gets back."

"Thank you so much, ma'am. I won't take any more of your time." Special Agent Brandon Palmer dipped his head in a respectful bow, turned around, and walked down the stairs. He stayed next door for about another hour and then took a deep bow in Maxine's living room. It was Jacob who killed Maxine and her family nearly twenty-four hours ago. And now, he bowed in her living room.

He'd just performed the role of a lifetime. He cheered for himself. He was more significant than his Master now.

Connor finally got the chance to rest; of course, he couldn't walk up the stairs with a fresh knife wound to his thigh, so Papa Anthony had Connor's blanket and pillow on the living room couch. How does he see these things? Connor asked himself. And why doesn't he tell me how to avoid them?

Connor received word from Brentley over his radio that the Master and most, if not all, of his Rougarou clan, was dead in a cave. Police Chief Aiden surrounded them, and they didn't want to give up without a fight.

It was seven a.m., and Mama Linda had everyone doing something. "Just because the lights are off doesn't mean y'all are going just to lay down all day," she screamed through the house. Connor didn't mind it at all. He'd almost died last night and couldn't hear his bossy mother again.

Papa Anthony was still working on his plan to restore electricity to the house, but it seemed to be a more challenging task than he thought. Connor kept his first radio, the one from Jacob. He didn't know why because Jacob was dead. But he had a feeling he had a nagging feeling everyone wasn't over yet.

But it would be over for Connor because he would resign from the FBI when his leg got better. And something good for a change: Connor thought he was falling in love with Kayla. Maybe he would get her to move into 758 Fillmore Street one day. But that's another story for another day.

UC

The seven a.m. sunshine danced in the clear sky above the Wakefield Mountains Range. The cloudless sky brought brilliant colors and hope into Ashton and Erynn's house.

The Artificials had not attacked them yet, but Ashton knew it was coming. It was just a matter of time, but he wasn't going to run or worry. Instead, he planned to kill them all and protect the innocent.

The handle of Ashton's sword glimmered in the sunlight as he sucked in a breath of the dry, chilled air. Winter was coming. Ashton turned to see Hunter tossing a football to Bryson;

Ashton knew the kid's name now. Bryson would have to stay with Erynn and Ashton now, and his parents were more than likely dead.

"Oh, what a great catch, Alison called out to Bryson." "Great catch!" Paige echoed her mom. Ashton went from a two-person home with no children to having Erynn, Alison, Hunter, and the two kids living with them now. A lot of things sure changed quickly in the last seventy-two hours.

Hunter's apartment complex was destroyed. The Artificials must have been there, and police officers, or at the army, there was no way to know for sure, had shot the place to hell. It was okay, though; Erynn and Ashton's house had plenty of room. They didn't have any issues with money, so they bought a beautiful multimillion-dollar house isolated in the woods. Ashton and Erynn had it built to their specifications.

Alison didn't want to be home anymore. She told Ashton she realized how much Paige consistently needed him, so she decided to move in, too.

Erynn was strolling across the perimeter of the house, pretending to watch everyone play football, but Ashton knew what she was doing. Erynn was doing the same thing he was: thinking and protecting. Someone had to make sure the house was safe.

"Here you go," Paige handed Bryson something. Ashton couldn't see what it was. "Bet you can't catch me," Bryson yelled in laughter. The two kids ran towards Erynn, and she bent over and played with them. Ashton never could understand how Erynn was able to be great at everything. She was an assassin, a soldier, a best friend, the most beautiful woman on earth, and now, from the looks of it, *she was also a great mother.*

A smile broke across Ashton's face. It was then it finally hit him. He was looking at his future. He was looking at all their futures. All this time, he wanted to prove he was a good person, but he wasn't. Or, maybe he was. He wasn't sure. He killed people. It's not what he wanted to do, but what other choice did he have?

Ashton began to realize him proving to people he was a good person wasn't the most important thing to him anymore. There was no way he would prove it anyway, and they were in the middle of World War III. Watching his best friend play with kids while she was armed and dangerous taught him one thing. *It wasn't about being a good person right now; it was about being good to everyone in his life.* That is all he could control. His job was to protect everyone at his house.

He'd killed over three hundred people in seventy-two hours— that probably wasn't going to get him into heaven, nor was it what good people did. But, watching Erynn, Ashton accepted his fate. He would let other people be good, but he would be good at protecting his new family.

It was like some higher power coordinated it. Then, when everything was perfect, the radios Ashton and Erynn got from Rory's house crackled to life. Static filled the channel for several seconds, and everyone froze. Everyone looked toward Ashton, and he waved to everyone next to him on the front porch. Whatever was happening, Ashton knew it wasn't going to be good.

A voice broke through the white noise before everyone could reach the porch. "This is Lucas Young with Hasley Mountain Air Force Base. Over" Ashton froze. Approaching the porch, Alison asked Ashton, "What do we do?"

Erynn walked and stood next to Ashton. Her eyes were as soft as clouds in the sky. She put her hand on this hand, gave him her radio, and nodded her head up and down.

"Tell them we know how to kill the Artificial's Ashton. And if they need help, we are on the way," Hunter said. Ashton laughed. "You are one of us, Hunter." Everyone else joined in the laughter.

In the distance, faint explosions could be heard in the sky. Ashton looked at Erynn and touched her forehead with his own. Ashton took in a deep breath and let it out slowly. Then, he brought the radio to his mouth and pressed the button to speak. "Lucas Young, this is Staff Sergeant Ashton Jace, Leader of the *Ghost Hunters*. You are clear to go with your SitRep?" Erynn lifted her black skull bandana and checked her ammo.

—End of Book 1—

Get ready for the next thrilling chapter in the Salleria Cities Universe! As we close the book on the epic adventure of Book 1, we invite you to stay tuned for the next pulse-pounding tale, where you'll join

Kofi Sai and The Anansi Guardians

on his mission to protect The Wizarding World from the forces of darkness. The excitement is just getting started, so buckle up for an adventure you won't forget!

Kofi Sai And the Anansi Guardians

Chapter One: The Phoenix Prince

Two Years Ago, Which Is Also Two Years After The EMP Events Recorded In Ch 2 of The United Cities of Salleria, Burn Together.

Mr. And Mrs. Sai, stepped out of the Kumasi Airport, their bags in tow, their hearts nearly beating out of their chests. Something was wrong and they both felt they were walking into a trap. Their only son, eight-year-old Kofi ran closely behind his father. Kwame Sai, made sure he not to run ahead of his son, so he did the only thing that made sense. Kwame put Kofi between him and his wife Adwoa. They were in the last place they'd ever thought they would be in again, Kumasi, Ghana.

The hot and murky rain beat against the left side of Kwame's face, as he and his family left the covering of the Sallerian Arrivals terminal. The rain had already taken over the city. The storm was in full force, with lightning striking the sky at regular intervals, illuminating the hot and dreadful dark night.

The Shadow Council had cars waiting for them in a nondescript location in the parking garage of the airport. With each panicked stepped forward, Kwame knew none of them should have been in Ghana. It wasn't safe for them anymore.

Kwame's heart raced as he and his wife, Adwoa, made their way towards the waiting car. It was his job to make sure his family was safe after everything happened. It had been seven years since they were last in Ghana, and under the orders of the Supreme Commander, Kwame and Adwoa hid their son Kofi in Salleria. There time in Salleria was peaceful, even with the invasion of North Kangavar two years earlier, the Sai's managed to keep their heads down and stay out of trouble.

The Sai family went unnoticed, which Kwame considered to be a miracle, since they were... well, different. Kwame took his eyes off his surrounds for a split second and stole a nervous look at his son. The little kid was special and seven years ago he became a target. Today, on the twentieth day of July, Kofi was the biggest target in the world.

Kwame couldn't shake the feeling this whole meeting was a trap set by the Shadow Master. Twenty-four hours ago, the Sai family received a letter from the Supreme Commander specifically telling them to not apparate, but to take a commercial flight back to Ghana as not to be detected by the enemy. Ordinarily, Kwame would have questioned the authenticity of the letter but it passed all magical inspections and The Supreme Commander was the only person in the world to know where the Sai family was hiding. Yet, Kwame was certain they were being pursued by The Shadow Master and his minions, The Shadow Walkers, and his minions.

Kwame was a level three wizard, one of the most powerful in the world and so was his wife. Today was Kofi's birthday, but Onyame hadn't given Kofi is legacy yet. "There are the cars," Adwoa, yelled over the rain hoping her husband could hear her. "Onyame should have given Kofi his legacy by now," Kwame said loudly in response to his wife. It wasn't an actual response to what she said to him, but the words slipped from his mouth before he knew he said them. He should have had his legacy by now, Kwame thought to himself. Kwame was angry now. Rage coursed through his veins and was replacing his fear by the second. "How is he going to be able to protect himself if he doesn't have his legacy, Adwoa?" "Onyame knows all, M'ade Pa." Kwame recognized the Twi phrase his wife called him that mean, *My good thing.* She always had a way of making him feel better even in the worse of times.

As they approached the car, Kwame's fears were only compounded by the dark and stormy night. The winds howled, and lightning illuminated the surroundings, revealing familiar landmarks that only added to Kwame's anxiety. He clutched his wand tightly in his right hand, ready to defend himself and his family if necessary. His left hand tingled with the pressure of his legacy ready to release from it. Kwame was a Fire Thrower. His legacy was the fireball. The more angry he got, the more his left had glowed off the red-orange fire that flew from his hand whenever he needed. It was a rare legacy and very few people had it. He was a level three and his fireballs were powerful, destructive, and fast-moving.

"Kwame, are you alright?" his wife whispered to him, her voice filled with concern and her eyes looking at the water evaporate as it collided with his left hand.

Kwame nodded, but he could tell his wife could see the fear and anger in his eyes. He was scared for her and for their son. Kofi looked up at them both, and then he stared at his father's glowing hand. His eyes went wide in shock. This was the first time Kofi saw magic. Kwame and his wife kept this life from him. The Supreme Commander gave them the option to tell their son the truth, but the opted to wait until he was eight. They found other ways to train their son, but for all that Kofi knew, those were just games played in the back yard. The thought of his wife and son in harm's way made Kwame's heart ache, and he couldn't help but wonder if they had made a mistake by coming back to Ghana.

"Wow, it's really coming down out here, isn't it?" Before the young woman who asked the question could introduce herself, Kwame sent a fireball in the direction of her voice and a fiery explosion erupted into a hundred smaller explosions. "Hey, Calm down. I'm a friendly," the woman shouted in Kwame's direction, but after she used the biggest electric legacy Kwame had ever seen to shatter his fireball in midair.

The crash of the two legacies was like nothing Kwame had ever seen before. The two opposing forces of magic, one a vibrant orange ball of fire and the other a pulsing blue-white electric current, collided in midair with a deafening boom. The explosion was blinding, with orange flames and blue sparks flying in all directions.

As the electric force reached out from the mysterious woman's hand, it was like a serpent of lightning, crackling and spitting with intense energy. The electric legacy was unlike anything Kwame had ever encountered. It was thick, like a physical entity, writhing and pulsing with raw power. The bright blue-white light cast stark shadows across the woman's face, making her appear almost otherworldly. The sound of the electric current was like a freight train, the roar of the energy dominating everything else in the rain.

"The only way you have stopped my fireball is if," Kwame was interrupted and the woman finished his sentence for him. "If I am a level four." "Exactly." "I guess you don't see many female level four wizards?" The mysterious woman wizard asked.

She was a force of a woman and her presence filled the Sai family's eyes. She stood tall and regal, her long, dark hair cascading down her back like a waterfall of midnight. Her skin was the color of rich, creamy chocolate and her eyes were a deep, piercing blue. They seemed to glow and spark with an inner light, reflecting the energy of the electric legacy she wielded so effortlessly.

She was dressed in a simple, yet elegant, gown that hugged her curves, the fabric a deep shade of midnight blue. The dress was adorned with intricate gold embroidery that shimmered in the light of her electric charge. The woman wore a crown of gold on her head, studded with diamonds and other precious gems that sparkled like stars in the night sky. She was a picture of power and mystery, her very presence commanding attention and awe.

With his fire still pulsating in his left hand, Kwame pocketed his wand and responded. "No one is use to seeing any kind of level four. Male or female." "You'll be a level four soon, your fireball almost broke my hand. Impressive." "Thank you," Kwame responded. He still let her legacy flicker in the night's rain. He wasn't ready to let down his guard just yet. He still didn't know this woman.

"And who is this beautiful young lady?" "You first," Kwame demanded. He wasn't being rude, but he wasn't in the mood to play nice with strangers either. Especially a stranger blocking their get away car. "Fair enough. Mystique. Ama Mystique. He was too angry to be impressed right now. There weren't to many level fours in the world and Kwame almost had his fireball to level four power, but he was standing in the presence of a real live level four.

"These cars are just decoys," Ama said. "We just had to be sure the right people were coming our way. Can't ever be to safe, right?" Finally feeling better, Kwame let the fire in his palm go out. "Ever." Kwame responded. "We are headed this way," Mystique said as she jerked her head over her left shoulder pointing into more darkness with her chin.

As they began to walk, Mystique began to small talk, "It's been too long since you have been home, yes?" Her tone was pleasant and empathetic. "Absolutely, but we had to keep our son safe," Adwoa replied. "He is all that matters."

"That's very sweet of you," Mystique offered as a gentle replay. "Just a little bit further ahead," she gestured into the darkness. Everyone continued to walk, the rain soaking through their clothes, as they made their way towards the get away car. Despite the harsh weather, they couldn't help but feel a sense of excitement and anticipation for what was to come. They were finally back in Kumasi, and they were ready to explore their hometown once again.

Kwame, Adwoa, and Kofi followed the level four wizard down a dark corridor, her electric legacy crackling and pulsing with raw power. The sound was like a constant hum, a low growl that filled the air and made their hair stand on end. The crackling was intense, with blue-white sparks of energy snapping and jumping along the lengths of her body. The sound echoed off the walls of the corridor, amplifying the power of Mystique's legacy, making it feel like a living, breathing entity.

Kwame couldn't help but feel intimidated by the sheer power and raw energy of the legacy. They felt uneasy, unsure of what was going to happen next. But despite their fears, they continued to follow the wizard, staying close and alert, ready for anything that might come their way.Kwame and Adwoa whispered back and forth, their voices filled with unease. They had no idea where they were going, and the eerie feeling in the air made them both nervous. Kofi followed in step, his eyes darting around, taking in the unfamiliar surroundings.

Just as they reached the getaway car, four figures appeared from the shadows, blocking their path. They seemed like ominous apparitions, emerging from the darkness like specters. He could sense the danger radiating from them, and a cold feeling of fear settled in the pit of his stomach. Despite his fear, he was determined to protect his family, and he stood protectively in front of Adwoa and Kofi, his hand radiant with the burn of his legacy's fire.

The figures were imposing, their broad shoulders and imposing postures giving them an air of authority. Their eyes were cold and unyielding, their expressions unreadable. The flickering light from Mystique's electrical glow cast harsh shadows across their faces, making them appear even more menacing. Kwame could feel the pressure of their gaze, as if they were sizing him up, trying to decide if he was worth the effort of killing. He could feel the weight of their power, and he knew that he and his family were in serious trouble.

Despite the fear coursing through his veins, he was ready to do whatever it took to protect his family.

The four men were wielding strange legacies of their own: one had the power of stone projection, another earth manipulation, the third acid spraying, and the fourth plant manipulation.

Kwame's was quick to respond and he unleashed a powerful burst of orange flames, aiming straight for the first attacker. The man countered with his slow but precise stone projection, causing the room to shake and rubble to fall from the ceiling. Kwame's second fireball didn't miss. The man was too slow and he went down.

The man writhed and thrashed on the ground as the orange flames licked at his skin, engulfing him in a scorching inferno. The heat was intense and palpable, singeing the hairs on Kwame's arms as he watched the man burn. He was no longer recognizable.

Adwoa activated her Level Three Time Manipulation, slowing time to a crawl, providing her family a tactical advantage. She quickly analyzed her opponent's movements and was able to dodge their attacks with ease.

Kofi stood frozen, watching in awe as his parents battled for their lives. This was the first time he'd seen magic. This was the first time he'd seen his parents fight. He had no powers of his own yet, and was completely helpless.

The three new attackers were relentless, their legacies providing both offense and defense. Mystique was the first to pull her wand. The acid sprayer was fast-moving, and the plant manipulator had the ability to control the surrounding foliage, using it to their advantage. With a flick of her wrist, bolts of blue-white electricity raced from her wand, arcing towards Kofi like deadly snakes. The sound was deafening, like a million thunderclaps all at once, as the electricity crackled and danced across the stone floor. Adwoa slows down time just long enough to step in front of her son. She dies in an instant. Kwame's screams fill the concrete corridor with his agony.

Kwame and Kofi are outnumbered and outmatched, Kwame is ready to give up when he catches a glimpse of his son. He is beginning to glow. His legacy is coming. Onyame did not forget him. Kwame was forced to run and try to outsmart their enemies, or stay and fight to the death. Grabbing his son by the shirt and lifting him off his feet, Kwame and Kofi run, dashing down the corridor, hoping to escape the deadly ambush.

The battle was intense and chaotic, with legacies flying and crashing into each other with explosive force. The sound of the electric currents, the stone projections, the acid sprays, and the plant manipulations filled the air, Kwame's ears felt like they were going to explode. This fight was about keeping Kofi alive. He was humanity's last hope. He was the Wizarding World's last chance.

Kwame and Kofi ran as fast as they could, dodging the explosive magic of their pursuers. The sound of the electric currents, stone projections, and melting acid sprays filled the air as they ran, with Kofi clinging onto Kwame's chest for dear life. Kwame could see Kofi's glow was growing. It was taking over his body, but it would be another hour before it would be become a useable legacy. And even then, there would be no way to know if it could help them. That's if they were alive an hour from now.

Kwame's kept his mind focused on keeping Kofi safe, his heart pounded in his chest. As they reached a bend in the corridor, Kwame saw a figure standing in their way. The figure was shrouded in darkness and reality seemed to bend around him. Kwame could feel the immense power radiating from him. At once, Kwame knew it was the Shadow Master, the Dark Lord of the Wizarding World coming to kill Kofi. The last remaining— a shadow began to move violently at Kwame and Kofi.

Kwame skidded to a stop, holding Kofi tightly in his arms. He could hear the footsteps of their pursuers closing in behind him. Kwame was trapped, but he stood his ground, facing the Shadow Master.

Kwame's heart sank as he faced the Shadow Master, a towering figure of darkness and power. Time and space seemed to bend around him, as if his very presence was distorting reality. The Shadow Master's eyes glowed a florescent color, illuminating his face with an eerie light. His nose was sharp and hooked, giving him a sinister appearance, while his muscles were well-defined, rippling with raw power.

His dark robes flowed behind him like a cloak of shadows, each movement of his body causing the fabric to ripple and swirl as if it were alive. The Shadow Master radiated an aura of fear, a feeling that was compounded by the knowledge of his terrifying powers. Possession, memory modification, shapeshifting, mastery of death magic, animal control, flight, and immortality were just a few of the many gifts he had acquired through his dark arts.

The Shadow Master's skin was a dark, ashen gray, with spikes jutting out along his forearms and across his back. His skin was covered in scales, giving him a reptilian appearance. With his enhanced strength, his muscles bulged, looking like they were made of solid stone. He stood tall and imposing, a true embodiment of darkness and terror. His mutations only added to his already intimidating presence, making him a force to be reckoned with. Despite his monstrous appearance, his movements were graceful and fluid, displaying a preternatural grace that was both mesmerizing and terrifying.

The Shadow Master's face was surprisingly attractive. He had chiseled cheekbones, a strong jawline, and piercing, florescent, emerald green eyes that sparkled with intelligence and cunning. His ashen grey skin was a warm, with golden brown veins glowing on the outside of his skin like golden armor, and his entire body seemed to glow softly with an inner light. He had a charismatic smile that could charm even the most stubborn of opponents, and his deep, smooth voice was like music to the ears. Darkness lingered in his eyes, a hint of the evil that lurked beneath the surface. He was the epitome of a charismatic and brilliant mind, using his charm and cunning to manipulate those around him to further his own ambitions.

His enhanced strength is visible in the corded muscles that run along his arms and legs, and the veins that bulge from his skin as he uses his strength. This makes him a formidable opponent in hand-to-hand combat.

His ashen gray skin was now a deep shade of black, covered in scales that gleam in the light, providing him with an additional layer of protection. His gift of Invisibility is achieved through the manipulation of light, causing him to fade in and out of sight at will.

His regenerative powers are a result of his control over death magic. Wounds heal quickly, leaving behind scar tissue that adds to the fearsome appearance of his body.

His telekinetic abilities are reflected in the glowing aura that surrounds his body, crackling with energy as he uses his power. His control over the elements is demonstrated in the way his skin reacts to the elements, taking on the properties of the element he is manipulating.

Finally, his mastery over the minds of others is shown through his piercing gaze, which can freeze a person in their tracks, leaving them at his mercy. The Shadow Master's mutations are a testament to his mastery over the dark arts and a reflection of his insatiable thirst for power.

The Shadow Master stepped forward, his dark robes billowing behind him. "You cannot escape," he said in a deep, menacing voice that threatened to crack the concrete. "The end of the Wizarding World is at hand, Kofi is the last of his kind, and he dies tonight."

"You will have to kill me first!" Kwame yelled while raising his hand as the strongest fireball he ever produced jetted from it. The orange flame that blazed from his hand was like a miniature sun, growing in size and intensity as it roared from his outstretched hand. The heat was palpable, crackling and sizzling as it consumed everything in its path. Kwame was shock he didn't burn Kofi. His son must have been gaining the fire resistance Kwame had, because what flew from Kwame was every bit of a level four fireball. Kwame had finally reached level 4 to protect his son. The brightness of the flame was almost too much to bear, bathing the surrounding area in a warm, radiant glow. Concrete melted, but Kwame and Kofi remained unharmed. The intense heat and light seemed to reach out and touch everything, leaving a trail of destruction in its wake. The fireball was a symbol of Kwame's power and determination and the love he had for his son.

As the smoke cleared and the bright light dimmed, there was The Shadow Master. Laughing and unharmed. It was a dark and evil sound. "Your legacy is no match for mine," he said, raising his wand hand and screaming, *"Ignis Eternus!"* A blast of dark magic hit Kwame and engulfed him and Kofi in flames. Kwame knew at once the Shadow Master used the most powerful of the unforgivable curses, the Infernus Curse. It was the most powerful and evil of all curses. Kwame and Kofi were consumed in an eternal flame, and Kwame's body was reduced to ashes in mere moments. The magic words echoed through the corridor, sending shivers down Kwame and Kofi's spines. They could feel the intense heat radiating from the spell, their skin prickling with the energy of the dark magic. The light from the curse was so bright, it was as if the sun had descended upon the earth. And yet, in the midst of the light, there was an aura of darkness, a shadow that seemed to be moving and shifting within the flame.

Kwame and Kofi were trapped, surrounded by the blazing inferno of the Infernus Curse. The heat was intense, the roar of the flames deafening. They could feel their skin beginning to blister, their clothes starting to smolder. They could feel the heat of the flames closing in on them, the crackling roar of the fire growing louder.

All of the Shadow's Master's Shadow Walker's witnessed came from the shadows and witnessed the death of Kofi, the weakest of the prophetic twelve.

The Shadow Walker's cheered and the scene was one of chaos and horror. As the roar of celebration echoed through the concrete garage, the strangest thing began to happened. The shadow-clad figures watched in disbelief as Kofi's eight-year-old head emerged from the ashes, his body still aglow but now unmistakably changed. His skin was ashen grey, like the Shadow Master himself and his skin looked as if it was mutating at that very moment. As the Shadow Walker's gasped in shock and, some in fear, a loud crack echoed through the concrete corridor, causing some to jump.

Suddenly, the Head Master of the Anansi Tower of Enchantment and School of Wizardry appeared out of nowhere and swiftly grabbed Kofi from the ashes. The Head Master's eyes glimmered with an unspoken determination, as if he had a plan for Kofi's new found powers. The Shadow Walker's stepped back, recognizing the raw power radiating from the Head Master, and watched in awe as he disappeared into the shadows with Kofi in tow, leaving the scene in stunned silence. There was only one person in the world stronger than the Shadow Master, and that was the man who just saved Kofi from his father's ashes. But now, it seemed, there was someone who would become stronger than them both, and he was now an eight-year old orphan.

United Cities of Salleria, Fight Together

Prologue

Three And A Half Days After The EMP Events of Chapter 2 of Book I.

Victoria Reid looked like a crazy person walking east on Interstate Highway 70 in Chesterfolk. She was somewhere near the Arapaho National Forest in a makeshift radiation suit she made out of garbage bags. She insulated the garbage with newspaper to help keep the radiation out and keep her warm on the cold Wakefield nights. She wasn't a soldier and didn't know how to survive an EMP attack. Victoria was just a chemistry teacher.

A nuclear blast had almost killed her three nights ago, and half the Arapaho National Forest was on fire, and she was pretty confident the other half wasn't going to make it, either. All around her were the views of the end of the world. Everything had gone to shit, and it got there quickly. She hadn't had a drop of water in three days and was dying of thirst. Flames engulfed the forest, and houses were burning to the ground. Everywhere she turned was filled with black smoke.

By her best guess, it was eight or nine in the morning on the third day after the nuclear strike. Her car stalled on the road three days ago, and the police and the National Guard told everyone to stay put and wait for help. But help never came. After three days of waiting, Victoria decided to take matters into her own hands. If she were going to die, she would die walking.

She had no children, and her husband died a few hours ago. He was an avid smoker, so the radiation killed him faster than it was killing her. Unfortunately, her cloth mask over her face wasn't enough to stop the radiation from getting into her lungs. Victoria flashed to her husband dying in her arms a few hours ago. She felt so much regret and sadness.

As a chemistry teacher, Victoria knew she was dying, and while she did an excellent job protecting her skin from the radiation, the damage to her lungs couldn't be reversed. But she knew if she got to safety and out of the radiated areas, she would be damaged but not dead.

The deep rattle of a cough rose in her throat, but she kept moving forward, hoping to find supplies, food, and water. She hadn't seen another living person for a few hours, and the last person she saw was screaming about black and red aliens killing people. He was experiencing radiation poisoning and experiencing hallucinations.

There were abandoned cars everywhere, and dead bodies were littered everywhere. Victoria didn't have any weapons and didn't even know where she was going. Her only plan: keep walking east. Interstate Highway 70 would eventually get you to Lakota, Victoria. That is where the National Guard said they were taking everyone. But she was so far away from

Lakota. The highway sign she just passed read: *LAKOTA 42 MILES.* Victoria had no idea how long it would take to walk forty-two miles, but she was going to make it.

She scanned the road again. There was a motion coming toward her. Victoria wondered if she was hallucinating, like the man who saw black and red aliens. Because what was coming her way didn't make any sense. It looked like a bunch of cars.

Victoria blinked her eyes, but the cars kept coming. Finally, cautious and doubting she could even trust her eyes, Victoria hid and ran to the side of the road. People were going crazy, and they were starting to fight each other. She didn't want to risk being seen. But if they looked friendly, she decided she would ask one of them to give her a lift to Lakota. It was a long shot because they were going in the opposite direction.

A few seconds later, Victoria could hear a motor's roar. A bunch of them. She wasn't hallucinating. Without thinking, Victoria jumped from her hiding spot and tried to wave at the convoy headed toward her. It was hard to see how many cars there were because the black smoke was thick.

Victoria could see several men wearing green CBRN suits. Several vans held women and children of all ages. These men were rescuing people and taking them to safety.

Victoria's excitement grew, and hope flooded into her bloodstream. She was saved. "There!" Shouted a voice. Victoria put her hands in the air, as she didn't want to seem like a threat to the soldiers. Instead, she imagined what she looked like to them. A grown woman was walking the highway covered from neck to toe in garbage backs. She must have looked like a crazy person. But Victoria didn't care. She was just happy to see that help finally did come.

And then, sadness hit her like a ton of bricks. Her husband died waiting on help. Maybe her husband would still be alive if they had come just one day sooner.

"Stay where you are, Ma'am," one of the soldiers with a rifle in his hand said. "I'm friendly," Victoria shouted. The soldier didn't have his weapon pointed at her, so she figured he believed her. The soldier in the van's passenger side jumped out and swept his rifle back and forth, looking for enemies. Victoria could see the man's eyes looking at her through his visor as he talked to her. His eyes were crystal blue.

"Where are you headed to, Ma'am." The soldier asked Victoria, "Lakota, or anywhere but here," Victoria said with relief. "I'm just trying not to die." "You can put your hands down, Ma'am." Victoria forgot she still had both her hands in the air.

"I see you, Ma'am; you built yourself a fancy suit," the soldier chuckled. Victoria didn't answer because she was beginning to see something was wrong. She looked at all the vehicles and saw strange markings on the side of the vehicles.

"What unit are you with, Sir?" Victoria asked. "Unit. You think I'm military?" The soldier asked.

"You have on a military," Victoria stopped talking. She finally looked at the man's CBRN suit. It was military, but it had blood over the front. Victoria then looked at the cars; none of them was military-issued. Instead, there were old model cars and vans.

"I'm not military, Ma'am," the man said to Victoria. His voice was muffled as it came from the CBRN mask. Victoria's mind began to race. What were they doing out here if they weren't military? "So, what are you then, Sir?" Victoria asked, wishing that she didn't want she hear the answer.

"We are with the *Saviors of Salleria,*" the man answered her. Victoria didn't know what to say. A chill spiked through her sweaty body. "What do the Saviors of Salleria do, if I may ask?" "We are taking back Salleria and returning it to its former glory. Back to the way our Forefather's intended it."

"And what does that look like?" Victoria asked while taking a step back. She looked over the soldier's shoulder and saw one of the vans had a kid's basketball team inside of it. There was a tall, handsome black kid mouthing the word "Run" and waving his hands at her.

"Well," the soldier was thinking about his answer. "The media would call us an alt-right group, and they would lump us in the pot with white supremacists," the soldier said. "Stop walking backward, Ma'am. I am trying to answer your question. Now, why would you be rude like that?" Victoria stopped.

"Where was I? Oh, yes. The media would lump us with white supremacist groups, but we are much more than that." The soldier stopped talking and looked at Victoria. "You're supposed to ask a question right here, Ma'am." "But I don't know what to ask."

"That's okay; I'll just keep going," The soldier said. "The Guardians of Salleria represent an unconventional strain of Sallerian right-wing extremism. We even have people of color in leadership. And our job is to purify Salleria of anyone who doesn't belong in our country."

Victoria took a few fearful steps backward. "Now, didn't I tell you to move back, Ma'am? And where are your manners? We were having a decent conversation." Victoria didn't say anything. She didn't know what to say. "Are you not talking to me anymore?" "Don't hurt me, please," Victoria accused the soldier.

"Is that what you think of me? Someone who would hurt a defenseless woman?" The soldier asked. His voice was cold now, and two of his men came to his side. There were three of them in front of her now.

"I was thinking about giving you a lift out of here, but you weren't much fun talking to, and you were rude." Victoria's eyes widen with fear. "When you get to heaven, tell God I got more on the way to him. You can tell him *The General* sent you."

The General raised his rifle and blew Victoria's skull away from her face. His men cheered, and the General walked back to the lead van of the Guardians of Salleria convoy.

Lucas Young cleared his visor of grime, wishing he could wipe away the beads of sweat forming inside his helmet. Lucas was on a top-secret mission for the United Cities of Salleria, but black and red demons were everywhere.

Lucas adjusted his lean, athletic body. His CBRN suite was too small, but he didn't need it as much as he thought he would. The radiation in Lakota and Sunderhill wasn't harmful.

Between the black and red machines and the treachery, Kian Price did to their mission, Lucas Young was now six miles away from the Safety of Hasly Mountain and was on foot.

A blur of images entered his mind, and the solidified picture of huge black and red fighting machines killed everyone in sight. Lucas was being hunted and only had six more miles to go.

A gust of whine whistled past his suit, peppering his visor with dirt. Lucas threw his head into the air looking for the flying machines. But, unfortunately, he didn't see any. He was almost out of ammo, but his rifle saved him more than once in the last twenty-four hours.

Lucas couldn't grasp why he was alive and should have been dead a while ago. The six-man team left on the mission with him, and he was the only person left alive. Lucas could remember when he promised to defend his country from within and without harm. He failed at both. Kian sabotaged the crew at Hasly Mountain and the Artificials; that's what he heard them called over his radio by Staff Sargeant Ashton Jace had killed all his men.

Lucas stumbled over a rock as he returned to the underground fortress inside the mountain. He hadn't seen any Artificials for a while now. Three days earlier, he was planning a vacation out of the country, and now, there was little of a country left to leave. Lucas and his buddies were in the safety of Hasly Mountain, and then he heard that terrible sound.

Thump. Crash. Thump. Crash.

The glowing red lights invaded the Hasly Mountain facility, and a few got past the blast doors all because Kian purposely let them enter. Lucas promised he would kill Kian if he ever saw him again.

Lucas shook his head as another beat of sweat burnt his yes. He grimaced and waited for the pain to subside. Lucas knew he was going to die one way or another. He was going to die in battle or die some other way.

Crossing the road cautiously, Lucas walked towards a part west of Interstate Highway 25, and hundreds of Artificials were just ahead. Lucas ran towards the first house he could find and asked if anyone was home. There was no answer, so he tried the front door. It was locked, but he found an unlocked window and climbed inside. Lucas prayed he made it in time before he was seen. From what he could tell, the Artificials were getting more intelligent, and now they were communicating.

Lucas froze in place once he was inside for several minutes. He didn't want to make a move. His heart jumped in his chest as Lucas suddenly heard the familiar sound, *Thump. Crash. Thump. Crash.*

He felt an uncomfortable feeling he was being watched. With trepidation, he glanced up at the window he had just crawled into, and looking down at him were the volcanic red eyes of an Artificial. It was looking at him. Lucas could have a sword for a second, and it was... thinking.

Lucas stood up, wanting to face death head-on. He was so afraid to be he wanted to die fighting. When he reached eye level to the window, Lucas looked out and saw one hundred or more Artificials coming towards the house. His ears nearly exploded for all the sounds of *Thump. Crash. Thump. Crash.* Lucas was an enemy target that needed to be destroyed.

Jacob Smith was staring at the Mason house again. He was here a few hours ago but wanted to see it again. First, however, there was more research that needed to be done.

Jacob's eyes moved slowly from window to window, taking in everything from the peanut butter brown brick to the neon green swing hanging from the tree in the front yard.

On two occasions, Jacob caught Papa Anthony working on a generator or the house's electrical wiring. Jacob figured he was determined to get the power working again. Papa Anthony's long and tedious life would end very soon. That made Jacob feel a warm feeling of joy inside. Jacob felt joy whenever he thought of killing one of Connor's family members, but none brought him as much joy as killing Papa Anthony. He wanted Connor to know that he'd been robbed of everything. To kill a man's father would do that.

He fantasized about going inside the Mason house. He wondered if the house had a cellar. He wanted to know how Connor's office looked and smelled. Jacob even thought about going into the kitchen after he killed everyone and making himself a ham sandwich with extra cheese.

Jacob was infatuated with Dr. Quantum. He was his perfect match: Connor, the protagonist, and Jacob, the antagonist. Jacob wanted to rush to the house and kill them all, but that would be boring. He had yet to create a new character. He needed to be someone amazing when he entered the Mason house. Which mask would he wear? What would be his name? He had so many ideas.

Finally, Connor lifted himself from his hiding spot and stood up straight. Then, he slowly turned and walked away, looking for a crowd to blend into because soon, Dr. Connor Mason would be dead, and so would everyone he loved.

Thank you for buying this book.

Are you an Antonio T Smith Jr fan? Join him on social media. He would love to hear from you!

Official Facebook Page: https://www.facebook.com/theatsjr

Facebook Fan Club:

https://www.facebook.com/groups/theofficialantoniotsmithjrfanclub

Author Website: AntonioTSmithJr.com

Catch Me On Tour: https://antoniotsmithjr.com/

Instagram: instagram.com/theatsjr

Email: books@antoniotsmithjr.com